ISBN Hardback 978-1-80424-009-0
ISBN Paperback 978-1-80424-010-6
AUK ePub ISBN 978-1-80424-011-3
AUK PDF ISBN 978-1-80424-012-0

Published in the UK by
MX Publishing
335 Princess Park Manor, Royal Drive,
London, N11 3GX
www.mxpublishing.co.uk

David Marcum can be reached at:
thepapersofsherlockholmes@gmail.com

Cover design by Brian Belanger
www.belangerbooks.com and *www.redbubble.com/people/zhahadun*

Internal Illustrations by Sidney Paget

THE MX BOOK OF NEW SHERLOCK HOLMES STORIES

PART XXXII
2022 ANNUAL
(1888-1895)

SOUTHAMPTON STREET

359

EDITED
By
David
Marcum

OFFICES

TRADITIONAL HOLMES
ADVENTURES
COMPILED FOR THE
BENEFIT OF THE
RESTORATION OF
UNDERSHAW

The
MX Book
of
New
Sherlock
Holmes
Stories
Part XXXII – 2022 Annual
(1888-1895)

CONTENTS

Forewords

Adventures

(Continued on the next page . . . .)

(Continued on the next page . . . .)

(Continued on the next page . . . .)

PART III: 1896-1929

PART IV – 2016 Annual

(Continued on the next page . . . .)

PART V – Christmas Adventures

(Continued on the next page . . . .)

PART VI – 2017 Annual

(Continued on the next page . . . .)

PART VII – Eliminate the Impossible: 1880-1891

PART VIII – Eliminate the Impossible: 1892-1905

(Continued on the next page . . . .)

Part IX – 2018 Annual (1879-1895)

(Continued on the next page . . . .)

(Continued on the next page . . . .)

Part XII: Some Untold Cases (1894-1902)

PART XIII: 2019 Annual (1881-1890)

(Continued on the next page . . . .)

PART XIV: 2019 Annual (1891 -1897)

(Continued on the next page . . . .)

(Continued on the next page . . . .)

Part XVII – Whatever Remains . . . Must Be the Truth (1891-1898)

Part XVIII – Whatever Remains . . . Must Be the Truth (1899-1925)

(Continued on the next page . . . .)

Part XIX: 2020 Annual (1882-1890)

(Continued on the next page . . . .)

The Adventure of the Matched Set – Peter Coe Verbica
When the Prince First Dined at the Diogenes Club – Sean M. Wright
The Sweetenbury Safe Affair – Tim Gambrell

Part XX: 2020 Annual (1891-1897)
Foreword – John Lescroart
Foreword – Roger Johnson
Foreword – Lizzy Butler
Foreword – Steve Emecz
Foreword – David Marcum
The Sibling (*A Poem*) – Jacquelynn Morris
Blood and Gunpowder – Thomas A. Burns, Jr.
The Atelier of Death – Harry DeMaio
The Adventure of the Beauty Trap – Tracy Revels
A Case of Unfinished Business – Steven Philip Jones
The Case of the S.S. Bokhara – Mark Mower
The Adventure of the American Opera Singer – Deanna Baran
The Keadby Cross – David Marcum
The Adventure at Dead Man's Hole – Stephen Herczeg
The Elusive Mr. Chester – Arthur Hall
The Adventure of Old Black Duffel – Will Murray
The Blood-Spattered Bridge – Gayle Lange Puhl
The Tomorrow Man – S.F. Bennett
The Sweet Science of Bruising – Kevin P. Thornton
The Mystery of Sherlock Holmes – Christopher Todd
The Elusive Mr. Phillimore – Matthew J. Elliott
The Murders in the Maharajah's Railway Carriage – Charles Veley and Anna Elliott
The Ransomed Miracle – I.A. Watson
The Adventure of the Unkind Turn – Robert Perret
The Perplexing X'ing – Sonia Fetherston
The Case of the Short-Sighted Clown – Susan Knight

Part XXI: 2020 Annual (1898-1923)
Foreword – John Lescroart
Foreword – Roger Johnson
Foreword – Lizzy Butler
Foreword – Steve Emecz
Foreword – David Marcum
The Case of the Missing Rhyme (*A Poem*) – Joseph W. Svec III
The Problem of the St. Francis Parish Robbery – R.K. Radek
The Adventure of the Grand Vizier – Arthur Hall
The Mummy's Curse – DJ Tyrer
The Fractured Freemason of Fitzrovia – David L. Leal
The Bleeding Heart – Paula Hammond
The Secret Admirer – Jayantika Ganguly

(Continued on the next page . . . .)

Part XXII: Some More Untold Cases (1877-1887)

(Continued on the next page . . . .)

The Dundas Separation Case – Kevin P. Thornton
The Broken Glass – Denis O. Smith

Part XXIII: Some More Untold Cases (1888-1894)
Foreword – Otto Penzler
Foreword – Roger Johnson
Foreword – Steve Emecz
Foreword – Jacqueline Silver
Foreword – David Marcum
The Housekeeper (*A Poem*) – John Linwood Grant
The Uncanny Adventure of the Hammersmith Wonder – Will Murray
Mrs. Forrester's Domestic Complication– Tim Gambrell
The Adventure of the Abducted Bard – I.A. Watson
The Adventure of the Loring Riddle – Craig Janacek
To the Manor Bound – Jane Rubino
The Crimes of John Clay – Paul Hiscock
The Adventure of the Nonpareil Club – Hugh Ashton
The Adventure of the Singular Worm – Mike Chinn
The Adventure of the Forgotten Brolly – Shane Simmons
The Adventure of the Tired Captain – Dacre Stoker and Leverett Butts
The Rhayader Legacy – David Marcum
The Adventure of the Tired Captain – Matthew J. Elliott
The Secret of Colonel Warburton's Insanity – Paul D. Gilbert
The Adventure of Merridew of Abominable Memory – Tracy J. Revels
The Affair of the Hellingstone Rubies – Margaret Walsh
The Adventure of the Drewhampton Poisoner – Arthur Hall
The Incident of the Dual Intrusions – Barry Clay
The Case of the Un-Paralleled Adventures – Steven Philip Jones
The Affair of the Friesland – Jan van Koningsveld
The Forgetful Detective – Marcia Wilson
The Smith-Mortimer Succession – Tim Gambrell
The Repulsive Matter of the Bloodless Banker – Will Murray

Part XXIV: Some More Untold Cases (1895-1903)
Foreword – Otto Penzler
Foreword – Roger Johnson
Foreword – Steve Emecz
Foreword – Jacqueline Silver
Foreword – David Marcum
Sherlock Holmes and the Return of the Missing Rhyme (*A Poem*) – Joseph W. Svec III
The Comet Wine's Funeral – Marcia Wilson
The Case of the Accused Cook – Brenda Seabrooke
The Case of Vanderbilt and the Yeggman – Stephen Herczeg

(Continued on the next page . . . .)

Part XXV: 2021 Annual (1881-1888)

(Continued on the next page . . . .)

(Continued on the next page . . . .)

Part XXVIII: More Christmas Adventures (1869-1888)

(Continued on the next page . . . .)

Part XXIX: More Christmas Adventures (1889-1896)

Part XXX: More Christmas Adventures (1897-1928)

(Continued on the next page . . . .)

The following contributions appear in this volume:
The MX Book of New Sherlock Holmes Stories
Part XXXII – 2022 Annual (1888-1895)

The following contributions appear in the companion volumes:
Part XXXI – 2022 Annual (1875-1887)
Part XXXIII – 2022 Annual (1896-1919)

Editor's Foreword:
"We can but try."
by David Marcum

Some approach the Sherlockian Canon, that small batch of just five-dozen original Holmes adventures, as if that number – *Only sixty stories!* – is unalterable. They're quite firm: *Verily, verily, the Canon shall be sixty stories – No more, no less!* But then the exceptions creep in . . . .

Sixty may be absolute – *No more, no less!* – but then there's *The Apocrypha*, that extra-Canonical material that maybe ought to be included too. "How Watson Learned the Trick" and "The Field Bazaar", though not full-length adventures, are important slices-of-life from the famed Baker Street sitting room. And if one accepts those, then there are the Canonical plays – all by way of the First Literary Agent: *The Crown Diamond* and *The Speckled Band*. Then onward to the lesser-known (and most confusing) play *Angels of Darkness*. And don't forget the two stories which clearly feature Holmes in an off-stage setting, "The Man with the Watches" and "The Lost Special". So already the pure Sixty-story Barrier has been breached.

And then there are those absolute purists who make other exceptions. "*Sixty adventures – No more, no less!*" they cry, prepared to defend that idea to the death. But then, a moment later, they follow with, "Well, except for these two or three pastiches written by a friend of mine, or by the person whose attention I'm seeking or whose celebrity favor I want to curry with my praise." Thus, their conviction of The Immaculacy of The Canonical Sixty is already cracked and compromised.

Along the same lines, some insist that The Canon be insulated from the bigger picture, keeping Holmes's world a cozy little place solely defined by only what is found recorded in the "official" sixty tales. If it isn't recorded there, they insist, then it didn't happen. But there's a loophole for that: The Canon mentions over one-hundred-forty "Untold Cases" in addition to the Told Sixty, and the details of these are often so vague that they are very much open to infinite interpretation. It's a bold concept, and too much for some to assimilate: Holmes and Watson are doing things off-stage that we don't get to witness in the Canonical Sixty.

I haven't done the math, but it would be a good project for someone to make a solid estimate of just how much time accrues in just the events of The Canon that we actually see recorded and presented. For instance, the bulk of "The Five Orange Pips" – around 82% – consists of just an

1

hour or so in the Baker Street sitting room on a late September 1887 night, either hearing the client's story, or discussing it after he leaves to go be murdered. The rest occurs in a short breakfast scene the next day, followed by another concluding conversation that evening.

It would be interesting if someone were to calculate the amount of time that is actually recorded in The Canon – either passing from the beginning of a case to the end, or simply what's shown "on screen", against how much total time that passes within the forty years between Holmes's first *recorded* Canonical case, "The Gloria Scott" (in Summer 1874) and the last, "His Last Bow" (in August 1914). I'm certain that it would be stunning for some just how much unrecorded time there is, wherein Holmes and Watson live all those other parts of their lives beyond the lens of the pure Canon that so many defend.

And in that recorded time, there are historical events occurring all around them. Many don't want to acknowledge those either. They like the idea that Holmes and Watson interact with anonymous folk like Jabez Wilson or Hall Pycroft, or others that no one has never heard of before or since. They don't want to hear about Holmes actually functioning in *The World*. But he does. In some of those Canonical Untold Cases, there are references to Holmes's interactions with historical figures, so it isn't a total impossibility, even for the Defenders of the Sixty, that he had contact with others. Holmes assisted the Pope (Leo XIII, whose Papacy ran from 1878 to 1903) in two Untold Cases, that of the Vatican Cameos, and also the death of Cardinal Tosca. He assisted the Royal Family of Scandinavia (as mentioned in "The Noble Bachelor" and "The Final Problem"). He was hired by the King of Bohemia (although such title was rather flimsily moribund by the late 1880's), and he assisted the British Prime Minister (whose name was changed for security's sake.)

So when Canonical purists dislike those post-Canonical stories wherein Holmes is involved with recognizable historical figures, they really don't have a Canonical leg to stand upon. The door for this was thrown open with the publication of Nicholas Meyer's Game-changing 1974 work, *The Seven-Per-Cent Solution*, wherein Holmes and Watson meet Sigmund Freud. Before that, in Canonical adventures which had been prepared for publication in *The Strand*, Watson and the First Literary Agent had pointedly changed names to protect identities. But not so in the document that Meyer uncovered. And when it was understood that Watsonian manuscripts could be published without the need to cross the First Literary Agent's desk, such editorial protections were no longer honored – or necessary.

The list of historical figures that Holmes and Watson have encountered who appear under their own names in latter-day post-

Canonical adventures is staggering, and many show up multiple times: The Queen of England and the Prince of Wales (and later the King). Gladstone and Disraeli and Lord Salisbury (and other Prime Ministers). Actors like Ellen Terry, Henry Irving, Lillie Langtry, and Basil Rathbone. Writers such as Bram Stoker, Henry James, Charles Dickens, H.P. Lovecraft, H.G. Wells, and F. Scott Fitzgerald. Inspector Abberline and Montague Druitt. The Dalai Lama and Henry Ward Beecher. Dr. Joseph Bell and Dr. Cream and Dr. Joseph Lister and Dr. Crippen. Both of my grandfathers, William Marcum and Ray Rathbone. Bismarck and Kaiser Wilhelm and Winston Churchill. Theodore Roosevelt and Franklin Roosevelt. J. Edgar Hoover and Adolf Hitler.

The list is overwhelming – although the *School and Holmes* website has made a good start at cataloging various figures encountered by our heroes in post-Canonical adventures. Here's the link for the letter *"A"* – Dive in, and like Jabez Wilson in "The Red-Headed League", you can progress through that letter, and *"with diligence [you] might get on to the B's before very long. . . ."*

https://www.schoolandholmes.com/charactersa.html

Many who try to limit Holmes to the Canonical Sixty are unwittingly limiting what makes him the greatest detective. If we only accept what's presented in The Canon, then we find that a good many of Holmes's cases are small affairs indeed, giving the impression that Holmes is a very skilled *but very small-time* problem solver. Of course, he loved the problem for the problem's sake, no matter its size or seriousness, and to him it didn't matter if a client was a pawn-broker or a king, a stockbroker or a banker or baronet. Yet many of the recorded Canonical cases are rather insignificant in the great scheme of things. If not for being memorialized in The Canon, for example, no one would have ever known or cared about the existence of Jabez Wilson or Hall Pycroft.

Holmes was involved with so many people over the course of his career, and his reputation grew and grew through the decades. Therefore, it's certain that even though a sizeable percentage of his clients were those who lived *small* lives, there were also just as many who lived *big* lives. And if Holmes was interacting with these historical *figures*, then he was interacting with *history* as well.

Many Canonical limiters don't want that. They *want* Holmes to be a shabby small-timer who mopes around the sitting room in brown studies, getting in the dumps at times and not opening his mouth for days on end, until he's consulted by an otherwise unimportant figure who has a curious vexation – five orange pips, for instance, or a blue jewel in a bonny goose container. Granted, there are the occasional cases of greater importance – stolen naval treaties and that irksome Napoleon of Crime – but many stories presented in The Canon are much smaller in scale. Yet just because that's what's on the "accepted" Canonical stage doesn't mean that it's the whole story.

In 1989, one of my few heroes, Billy Joel, released "We Didn't Start the Fire", a nearly-five-minute long song detailing the events from 1949 (the year of his birth) to 1989. He wrote it after speaking to a twenty-one-year old who told him that things were much rougher in 1989 than it had been when Joel was in his twenties. Joel responded by pointing out all of the historical events – some quite grim, like the Korean War – which occurred in those bygone days, all just as rough as what the young man was facing in the present. The chorus states, *"We didn't start the fire – It was always burning since the world's been turning. We didn't start the fire, No, we didn't light it, but we tried to fight it."* The implication of this is that these historical challenges have always been with us, but that one can meet them as they appear and do one's best to succeed.

And this, believe it or not, is rather like Sherlock Holmes's own creed.

In both "The Problem of Thor Bridge" and "The Creeping Man", Holmes makes a statement that's easy to slide over too quickly, but which, in fact, is something well-worth remembering:

"We can but try."

In context, Holmes first makes the statement in "Thor Bridge" when explaining that he has a theory, but it might be wrong:

> *[Y]ou have seen me miss my mark before, Watson. I have an instinct for such things, and yet it has sometimes played me false. It seemed a certainty when first it flashed across my mind in the cell at Winchester, but one drawback of an active mind is that one can always conceive alternative explanations which would make our scent a false one. And yet – and yet – Well, Watson, we can but try.*

"Thor Bridge" was first published in February and March 1927. The next Canonical tale to be published was "The Creeping Man", a full year later (in March 1928, just a little over a year before Watson's passing). In that, Holmes is suggesting that he and Watson bluff their way into seeing an antagonist, to which Watson replies:

"We can but try."

"Excellent, Watson! Compound of the Busy Bee and Excelsior. We can but try – the motto of the firm."

The motto of the firm indeed! Even though this statement only appeared in the fifty-fifth and fifty-sixty published Canonical adventures, it was certainly Holmes's philosophy long before that. It served him well as he carried out his investigations, and also as he lived his life – for besides encountering many historical figures, Holmes encountered a great deal of challenging history as well.

Holmes was born in 1854. Watson's birth was two years earlier. We can look at the world around us now and bemoan all that is legitimately wrong – and it truly is wrong in so many ways! – but the challenges people faced in those days, while different, were also quite grim indeed. Disease and genocide – different forms then and now, but still the same human suffering under different guises. Wars and starvation on all levels – they had it, and we have it. Societal unfairness, foul corruption, and evil injustice and from top to bottom, with the haves always greedily clutching at theirs while the have-nots scramble – some surviving and others not.

Google, that amazing tool undoubtedly brought back from the future to this time by some as-yet unborn time-traveling Prometheus, provides an instantaneous way to find out this or that fact. It is truly an amazing thing. A quick check shows that between 1854 and 1900, there were nearly *three-hundred wars* around the world! Eight of those were in the year of Holmes's birth. And while that seems like a long time ago, and they might have been small compared to the World Wars and possible Nuclear Wars and Cold Wars that we've been conditioned to in our lifetimes, they were very real and devastating and disruptive and deadly for those who were involved. Lives were ruined or lost.

During that same period, there were several dozen pandemics and endemics and plagues – fevers and cholera, influenza and bubonic plague, malaria and smallpox.

The world was a dangerous place. It *is* a dangerous place. It always has been. It isn't just bad now. This – the history we're living in right now – is just a different kind of bad.

We didn't start the fire. It was always burning since the world's been turning.

But we can be strong and face it.

Like Sherlock Holmes . . . .

We can but try.

5

I had the idea for *The MX Book of New Sherlock Holmes Stories* in early 2015 as a way to have more stories about the *True Canonical Holmes* – a hero, and not a modernized broken sociopathic murderer who had stolen Holmes's name, a version that was insidiously creeping into the world's perceptions of him. The idea for volumes of stories about the True Holmes was more popular than I could have ever imagined, as so many people still need *Heroic Holmes*. My 2015 hope for possibly a dozen or so new stories grew and grew over that year to become the first MX three-volume set with over sixty new adventures – the largest Holmes anthology collection of its kind ever produced. (We've since regularly surpassed that.)

It quickly became obvious that both authors and readers wanted more, so the series was established as an ongoing venture. From nearly the beginning, it was decided to direct the royalties from the books to a school for special needs children that was located at Undershaw, one of Sir Arthur Conan Doyle's former homes in Hindhead, England. The school was originally called *Stepping Stones*, but it has since been renamed to match the building where it resides, *Undershaw*. As of this writing, this series, by way of the incredible contributions from over 200 authors and the amazing support of countless fans around the world, has produced nearly 700 new traditional Holmes adventures and has raised nearly *$100,000* for the school. That's nearly *One-Hundred-Thousand Dollars!* That number will almost certainly be exceeded by mid-2022. (And I'm told that even more important than the money has been the spread awareness of the school around the world and its valuable work.)

When COVID-19 came upon us in early 2020, I was worried about this series, and how everyone's suddenly upside-down lives might be affected in terms of contributing new Sherlock Holmes stories. While some people found it more difficult to write when conditions became unfavorable, most rose to the challenge, and the books continued as before, with multiple volumes of high-quality traditional Holmes adventures. There were six volumes in 2020, and six more in 2021. Now as I write this, the world watches as a vile Beast has invaded Ukraine, and still the contributors have done an amazing job, and I continue to receive stories for the next set of books, *However Improbable . . . .* planned for Fall 2022.

I cannot express my admiration and gratefulness enough for those who have provided stories under ongoing challenging conditions.

Each and every contributor who has added to this series with stories, poems, forewords, and artwork are the finest kind of people, and they are heroes of the first order, and should all be incredibly proud of what we've accomplished. And as conditions still prove to be challenging . . . .

We can but try.

* * * * *

"Of course, I could only stammer out my thanks."
– *The unhappy John Hector McFarlane,* "The Norwood Builder"

As always when one of these sets is finished, I want to first thank with all my heart my incredible, patient, brilliant, kind, and beautiful wife of nearly thirty-four years, Rebecca – every day I'm luckier than the day before! – and our amazing, funny, brilliant, creative, and wonderful son, and my friend, Dan. I love you both, and you are everything to me!

In late 2020, I was fortunate to obtain my dream job, working as a municipal civil engineer for the city whose specific infrastructure had inspired me to go back to school in my thirties to be an engineer. It's the best job I've ever had with an amazing group of people – and the learning curve has been amazing in its own way as well. I knew the engineering, but learning things from the municipal side is a new challenge. On top of that was family time – most important – and also the various Sherlockian efforts that I've pursued.

In 2021, through the new job, I found time to write a number of new Holmes pastiches and essays, and also to edit and get published twenty-two different books. (These included six of my own books, six MX anthologies, five Holmes anthology volumes for Belanger Books, the remaining four volumes in *The Complete Dr. Thorndyke* collection, and a book of Holmes stories by Nick Dunn-Meynell.) Then, in late 2021, the boss I was hired to replace retired, so my work responsibilities increased exponentially.

Thus, the editing of the *2022 Annual* took on new challenges as it fit in around my real life. Thankfully, the various contributors were wonderful as usual, and I can't thank them enough for their patience, and for the stories that they sent, even as they worked around their own ever-more-complicated lives.

For the *2022 Annual*, some contributors simply couldn't join the party this time, due to all sorts of reasons – too busy or too stressed. Perhaps there were health- or job-related issues, or burnout. Several experienced tragic deaths of their loved ones over the past few months. I completely understand, and cannot express my gratitude enough for their past participation, and I hope that they'll be back in the future.

Other authors found that Watson was whispering to them much more urgently than before, and they ended up with more than one story to submit. Some had two or three, and in a couple of cases, a full half-dozen

7

tales. In these trying times, I was incredibly grateful to receive them, and they are invaluable additions to the latest set.

Back in 2015, when the MX anthologies began, I limited each contribution to one item per author, in order to spread the space around more fairly. But some authors are more prolific than that, and rather than be forced to choose between two excellent stories, I began to allow multiple contributions. (This also helped the authors, as their stories, if separated enough from each other chronologically, could appear in different simultaneously published volumes, thereby increasing their own bibliographies.)

Hal Glatzer and David MacGregor each contributed two stories this time. Dan Rowley, Tim Symonds, Arthur Hall, and me (your editor) provided three, and the indomitable Tracy Revels wrote an amazing six of them.

Also of note are the six stories contributed by the late Terry Golledge. In early 2022, I received an email from Niel Golledge, Terry's son, with a sample story, "The Addleton Tragedy". Terry had written it, along with nine others, in the 1980's, but they were never published. Niel had recently approached another editor about them, but that chap felt that it would be too much work to prepare the original typewritten manuscripts for modern publication. That was his big mistake, for it was absolutely worth the extra editorial work, as Terry Golledge's stories are wonderful and Watsonian. Niel graciously agreed to let me edit and include six of them for this collection, and later in 2022 they, along with the remaining four stories, will be published in their own separate volume, to the delight of Sherlockians like me who can *never* have enough tales about the *True Sherlock Holmes*. (An interesting side-note: Terry Golledge's mother worked as a governess for Sir Arthur Conan Doyle for several years in the early Nineteenth Century, so these tales have a bit of extra associational history.)

I can never express enough gratitude for all of the contributors who have donated their time and royalties to this ongoing project. I'm constantly amazed at the incredible stories that you send, and I'm so glad to have gotten to know so many of you through this process. It's an undeniable fact that Sherlock Holmes authors are the *best* people!

There is a fine group of people that exchanges emails with me when we have the time – and time is far too rare for all of us these days! I don't get to write back and forth with these fine people as often as I'd like, but I really enjoy catching up when we do get the chance: Derrick Belanger, Brian Belanger, Mark Mower, Denis Smith, Tom Turley, Dan Victor, and Marcia Wilson.

There is a group of special people who have stepped up and supported this and a number of other projects over and over again with a lot of contributions. They are the best and I can't express how valued they are: Ian Ableson, Hugh Ashton, Derrick Belanger, Deanna Baran, Andrew Bryant, Thomas Burns, Nick Cardillo, Chris Chan, Craig Stephen Copland, Matthew Elliott, Tim Gambrell, Jayantika Ganguly, Paul Gilbert, Dick Gillman, Arthur Hall, Steve Herczeg, Paul Hiscock, Mike Hogan, Craig Janacek, Susan Knight, Mark Mower, Will Murray, Tracy Revels, Roger Riccard, Jane Rubino, Geri Schear, Brenda Seabrooke, Shane Simmons, Robert Stapleton, Tim Symonds, Kevin Thornton, Tom Turley, DJ Tyrer, Dan Victor, I.A. Watson, and Marcia Wilson.

Next, I wish to send several huge *Thank You's* to the following:

- *Jeffrey Hatcher* – I missed my chance to meet Jeff in person at *From Gillette to Brett V* in October 2018, although I very much enjoyed his presentation. I was already aware of him for the incredible work that he had done in bringing a rather grim Holmes novel with a remarkable lack of hope, Mitch Cullin's *A Slight Trick of the Mind* (2005) to the screen in the form of *Mr. Holmes* (2015). My deerstalker and I were at the theatre on the film's opening day, having just re-read the book in preparation, and I wasn't sure what to expect. An elderly Holmes's life in the book is very bad, and it only get gets worse, with more bad piling high with each new chapter. Still, I normally defer to the printed version of things as the "true" version – especially when changes are made for a film. In this case, I happily made an exception to my rule.

  My own father had passed away in 2011 after struggling for several years with both Parkinson's and Alzheimer's, and to see Holmes's decline on screen was almost too vivid to bear – but Jeff's deft handling of the script, and the wise changes he made to the original plot in order to give Holmes a happier better future than shown in the book, were exactly what was needed.

  When Steve Emecz interviewed Jeff for the MX Publishing Audio Collection and then put me in touch with him, I was very pleased, and this was exceeded when Jeff agreed to write a foreword for this collection.

  Jeff, thanks very much for all your work, and the contribution of your time to these books. It's very much appreciated!

9

- *Steve Emecz* – As I've explained elsewhere, Steve works a way-more-than-full-time job related to his career in e-finance. MX Publishing isn't his full-time job – it's a labor of love. He, along with his wife, Sharon Emecz, and cousin, Timi Emecz, *are* MX Publishing. In addition to their very busy real everyday lives, these three sole employees take care of the management, marketing, editing, production, and shipping, and they absolutely cannot receive enough credit for what they accomplish.

Some people have a picture in their minds of a publishing company with several floors on some skyscraper, hundreds of employees running around like ants, with vast departments devoted to management, marketing, editing, production, shipping, etc. That is not always the case. Those old giant dinosaur publishers are still around, and they might squeeze out a Sherlockian title or two every year for those readers who foolishly think that there are only one or two Sherlockian titles every year (thus cheating themselves of some really incredible stories), but those publishers don't represent the modern way of doing things. MX has become the premiere Sherlockian publisher by following a new paradigm: Avoid the sucking whirlpool of traditional publishing and get books to readers as soon as possible. And they manage to get all of this done with a truly skeleton staff.

From my first association with MX in 2013, I saw that MX (under Steve's leadership) was *the* fast-rising superstar of the Sherlockian publishing world. Connecting with MX and Steve Emecz was personally an amazing life-changing event for me, as it has been for countless other Sherlockian authors. It has led me to write many more stories, and then to edit books, along with unexpected additional Holmes Pilgrimages to England – none of which might have happened otherwise. By way of my first email with Steve I've had the chance to make some incredible Sherlockian friends and play in the Holmesian Sandbox in ways that I would have never dreamed possible.

Through it all, Steve has been one of the most positive and supportive people that I've ever known.

With his and Sharon's and Timi's incredible hard work, they have made MX into a world-wide Sherlockian publishing phenomenon, providing opportunities for authors who would never have had them otherwise. There are some like me who return more than once to Watson's Tin Dispatch Box, and there are others who only find one or two stories there – but they also get the chance to publish their books, and then they can point with pride at this accomplishment, and how they too have added to The Great Holmes Tapestry.

From the beginning, Steve has let me explore various Sherlockian projects and open up my own personal possibilities in ways that otherwise would have never happened. Thank you, Steve, for every opportunity!

- *Brian Belanger* – Over the last few years, my amazement at Brian Belanger's ever-increasing talent has only grown. I initially became acquainted with him when he took over the duties of creating the covers for MX Books following the untimely death of their previous graphic artist. I found Brian to be a great collaborator, very easy-going and stress-free in his approach and willingness to work with authors, and wonderfully creative too.

  Brian and his brother, Derrick Belanger, are two great friends, and several years ago they founded *Belanger Books* which, along with MX Publishing, has absolutely locked up the Sherlockian publishing field with a vast amount of amazing material. The dinosaurs must be trembling to see every new Sherlockian project, one after another after another. Luckily MX and Belanger Books work closely with one another, and I'm thrilled to be associated with both of them. Many thanks to Brian for all he does for both publishers, and for all he's done for me personally.

- *Roger Johnson* – I'm more grateful than I can say that I know Roger. I was aware of him for years before I timidly sent him a copy of my first book for review, and then on my first Holmes Pilgrimage to England and Scotland in 2013, I was able to meet both him and his wonderful wife, Jean Upton, in person. When I returned on Holmes Pilgrimage No. 2 in 2015, I was so fortunate that they graciously invited me to stay with them for several days in their home, where we had many wonderful discussions, while occasionally venturing forth so that they could show me parts of England that I wouldn't have seen otherwise. It was an experience I wouldn't trade for anything.

11

Roger's Sherlockian knowledge is exceptional, as is the work that he does to further the cause of The Master. But even more than that, both Roger and Jean are simply the finest and best of people, and I'm very lucky to know both of them – even though I don't get to see them nearly as often as I'd like, and especially in these crazy days! (The last time was in 2016, at the Grand Opening party for the Stepping Stones School (now called Undershaw) at Undershaw in Hindhead.

In so many ways, Roger, I can't thank you enough, and I can't imagine these books without you.

And finally, last but certainly *not* least, thanks to **Sir Arthur Conan Doyle**: Author, doctor, adventurer, and the Founder of the Sherlockian Feast. Honored, and present in spirit.

As I always note when putting together an anthology of Holmes stories, the effort has been a labor of love. These adventures are just more tiny threads woven into the ongoing Great Holmes Tapestry, continuing to grow and grow, for there can *never* be enough stories about the man whom Watson described as *"the best and wisest . . . whom I have ever known."*

David Marcum
April 5ᵗʰ, 2022
128ᵗʰ Anniversary of
"The Empty House"

Questions, comments, or story submissions
may be addressed to David Marcum at

thepapersofsherlockholmes@gmail.com

Foreword
by Jeffrey Hatcher

I've never written a Sherlock Holmes pastiche. At least not in prose. I've written the plays *Sherlock Holmes and the Adventure of the Suicide Club*, *Sherlock Holmes and the Ice Palace Murders*, and *Holmes and Watson*. I also wrote the screenplay for the film *Mr. Holmes*, based on Mitch Cullin's novel *A Slight Trick of the Mind*. But I've never attempted a classic short story or novel of the sort Arthur Conan Doyle excelled at. The reasons are two-fold:

I've never had the stamina to write prose fiction, be it the short story or a long form narrative. There's something about the density of the words and the requirement to depict a complete world with both exterior action and interior thought that defeats me. When I was in junior high, I started writing a shorty story – maybe it was going to be a novel, I can't remember – and around that time I'd read Dashiell Hammett's *The Maltese Falcon*. Its opening is devoted entirely to a description of what Hammett's private eye hero Sam Spade looks like:

> *Samuel Spade's jaw was long and bony, his chin a jutting v under the more flexible V of his mouth. His nostrils curved back to make another, smaller, V. His yellow-grey eyes were horizontal. The V motif was picked up again by thickish brows rising outward from twin creases above a hooked nose, and his pale brown hair grew down – from high flat temples--in a point on his forehead. He looked rather pleasantly like a blonde Satan."*

So, I figured that's what a writer's supposed to do. Start with your main character and describe him in laborious, infinitesimal detail. So that's what I did. I can't remember who my main character was or if he even had a name, but I was onto my third page and hadn't gotten below his upper lip. And he wasn't going to be the only character in the story. I was going to have to do this with all the characters. Then I'd have to describe the rooms they inhabited, their homes and offices, their cars. Not to mention the outdoors. It came down to this: I don't like having to describe what the tree looks like. I never finished that story or novel or whatever it was supposed to be. It was properly abandoned. Instead, I turned my interest to dramatic story telling: Plays and screenplays, the first fully executed

13

one being a one-hundred-forty page film adaptation of Ian Fleming's *Moonraker*, five years before the Roger Moore movie. (Mine was better.)

The second reason I've never attempted a Sherlock Holmes story is that although the form seems simple enough, schematic even, the content, tone, and style that Conan Doyle mastered with such apparent ease is actually very hard to impersonate. The joy in a familiar form such as the Holmes stories lies in the reader experiencing the changes the writer rings within the form.

I wrote a few *Columbo's* in the 1990's and each classic *Columbo* episode had the following structure:

Act One: *Meet the polished, sophisticated murderer and watch him or her commit the ostensibly perfect crime.*
Act Two: *Columbo investigates, discovers a clue that tells him the perfect crime isn't so perfect.*
Act Three: *Columbo and the murderer play cat and mouse as more mistakes are uncovered and more chess moves take place.*
Act Four: *The murderer finds the means to save himself.*
Act Five: *Columbo tricks the murderer into incriminating himself or reveals the final damning clue that closes the case.*

The fun was in watching the form reenacted in different settings with different characters, clues, twists, and surprises.

Similarly with Holmes, we start a story expecting a scene in Baker Street, the arrival of a client, a mystery posed. "Will you help me, Mr. Holmes?" Then Holmes and Watson set forth into the streets of London or the Great Grimpen Mire to investigate the case. They meet increasingly desperate and malevolent characters. Another crime is committed or foiled. Finally, the culprit is captured. Throughout the story Holmes will reveal his deductive powers, his psychological perceptions, his wit, his courage, his humanity – along with those of Dr. Watson's. Yes, there are occasional departures from the form, but, with rare exceptions, the departures are not what we crack the spine for.

Enjoy the stories you're about to read. Think of them as an old and dear friend who's come to visit you – and he's got something terribly new and exciting to tell you.

Jeffrey Hatcher
March 2021

"These little narratives"
by Roger Johnson

Younger readers – and writers, for that matter – may not be aware that it's not so very long since the choice of new Sherlock Holmes stories was very limited indeed. If you were lucky, you might find a copy of *The Misadventures of Sherlock Holmes*, edited by Ellery Queen and published in 1944. There were two printings before the Conan Doyle family's lawyers spotted a copyright infringement in another Ellery Queen anthology and used it as a reason to have *The Misadventures* withdrawn. Sir Arthur's sons could never be persuaded that the non-canonical stories might encourage readers to seek out and read the great originals.

The occasional new story did get published. In 1945 J.C. Masterman, a distinguished Oxford University academic and wartime intelligence chief, contributed "The Case of the Gifted Amateur" to *McKill's Mystery Magazine*, and S.C. Roberts, the no less distinguished Cambridge University academic who became the first President of the Sherlock Holmes Society of London, included a short story, "The Adventure of the Megatherium Thefts", in his classic 1953 book *Holmes and Watson: A Miscellany*. The specialist Holmesian journals occasionally published good new stories, but until 1974 the only book of consequence was *The Exploits of Sherlock Holmes*, comprising twelve tales written by Adrian Conan Doyle and John Dickson Carr, and published in 1954. (Adrian had made himself so intensely disliked among American Sherlockians that Edgar W Smith, head of the Baker Street Irregulars, dismissed the book as "Sherlock Holmes Exploited". In fact, the stories are never less than good, and several are excellent.)

1974 was the year of wonders, beginning with the Royal Shakespeare Company's hugely successful new production of William Gillette's play *Sherlock Holmes*. Adrian Conan Doyle had died in 1970, predeceased by his brother Denis, and, despite some subsequently dubious handling of Sir Arthur's estate, the attitude towards sincere fictional tributes to his most celebrated creations was now more relaxed. The first novel-length pastiches had only recently appeared, derived from the scripts of successful movies: *A Study in Terror* and *The Private Life of Sherlock Holmes*. More would come, but the real breakthrough was Nicholas Meyer's *The Seven-per-Cent Solution*, which would itself become a notable film.

The floodgates were not yet breached. That would come with the expiry of Sir Arthur's British copyright in 1980 – and would be followed by problems when copyright in all countries of the European Union was extended to seventy years after the author's death. Freedom was finally declared in 2000 – except in the U.S.A., whose copyright laws are unlike any other nation's. Nevertheless, it was now legal to write and publish new Holmes stories almost everywhere, and, as long as publication was a matter for the professionals, we could be pretty confident that the result would be of at least reasonable quality. But fashions in the book world change, and even Sherlock Holmes doesn't always appeal to the professional publishers.

What actually destroyed the floodgates was the rapid development of the home computer and the world-wide web. Self-publishing became much easier and cheaper, and in time the authors didn't even have to produce a printed version of their works, as the internet made it possible to post them online for anyone to read. One result is easy access to stories created with admiration and affection. Another, alas, is that the good stuff is vastly outnumbered by the less good – often poorly constructed and badly written, sometimes actually offensive.

Fortunately, it isn't hard to find new Sherlock Holmes stories of genuine quality. The book you're reading now is evidence of that. This series began in 2015, with the publication of three volumes, whose editor, authors, and publisher generously donated all their royalties to the restoration and maintenance of Undershaw, the house that Arthur Conan Doyle had built in the Surrey Hills for himself and his family. The fact that *The MX Book of New Sherlock Holmes Stories* continues, six years on, is heartening. That it now exceeds *thirty* volumes is amazing!

The apparently indefatigable David Marcum ensures that the standard remains high, and the proceeds still go to the upkeep of Undershaw, which since 2016 has been home to the Undershaw School, providing care and education for children aged 8 to 19 with Autistic Spectrum Disorder and associated learning needs.

Could there be a better recommendation?

Roger Johnson, BSI, ASH
Commissioning Editor: *The Sherlock Holmes Journal*
December 2021

An Ongoing Legacy
for Sherlock Holmes
by Steve Emecz

Undershaw
Circa 1900

*T*he *MX Book of New Sherlock Holmes Stories* has grown beyond any expectations we could have imagined. We're very close to having raised $100,000 for Undershaw, a school for children with learning disabilities. The collection has become not only the largest Sherlock Holmes collection in the world, but one of the most respected.

We have received over twenty very positive reviews from *Publishers Weekly*, and in a recent review for someone else's book, *Publishers Weekly* referred to the MX Book in that review which demonstrates how far the collection's influence has grown.

In 2022, we launched *The MX Audio Collection*, an app which includes some of these stories, alongside exclusive interviews with leading writers and Sherlockians including Lee Child, Jeffrey Hatcher, Nicholas

Meyer, Nancy Springer, Bonnie MacBird, and Otto Penzler. A share of the proceeds also goes to Undershaw. You can find out all about the app here:

https://mxpublishing.com/pages/mx-app

In addition to Undershaw, we also support Happy Life Mission (a baby rescue project in Kenya), The World Food Programme (which won the Nobel Peace Prize in 2020), and iHeart (who support mental health in young people).

Our support for our projects is possible through the publishing of Sherlock Holmes books, which we have now been doing for over a decade.

You can find links to all our projects on our website:

https://mxpublishing.com/pages/about-us

I'm sure you will enjoy the fantastic stories in the latest volumes and look forward to many more in the future.

Steve Emecz
March 2022
Twitter: *@mxpublishing*

The Doyle Room at Undershaw
Partially funded through royalties from
The MX Book of New Sherlock Holmes Stories

19

A Word from Undershaw
by Emma West

Undershaw
September 9, 2016
Grand Opening of the Stepping Stones School
(Now *Undershaw*)
(Photograph courtesy of Roger Johnson)

I am delighted to bring you news of Undershaw . . . from Undershaw. Since September 2021, under our new name, vision, and values, our wonderful school has been focussing on Undershaw community pride. To that end, we have focussed on recruiting, retaining, and upskilling a talented staff cadre, each one a specialist in their field, experienced with SEND education, and each one an innovator of new teaching and learning practices.

We have fortified our school life with robust qualifications and have strengthened our relationships with exam boards to ensure our students leave us with the qualifications they deserve, and of which they are eminently capable. Our school is awash with academic, artistic, and musical talent, and we feel privileged in our role of unleashing that potential in a way that works for our learners.

Our traditional classroom learning is complemented by a variety of other techniques. For example: Our outdoor learning area, for which we are currently fundraising. A Fire Pit shelter will double as an outdoor classroom, and will enable us to continue our learning in nature all year round and in all weathers. We know that learning outdoors amidst nature does wonders for well-being and contentment. We have such a beautiful and inspirational campus and, as much as it is our *raison d'etre* to equip our provision for all our learners, it is also our role as caretakers of Undershaw to nurture and improve the campus for the generations to come.

It is only through our relationships with benefactors such as MX Publishing, and the wonderful authors who support its charitable giving, that we are able to thrive through 2022 and beyond. The culture at Undershaw is an extremely positive one, and we're delighted that you are joining us on our journey. For up-to-date news about our school and our work within the Special Educational Needs sector, please see our website at www.undershaw.education. Our newsletters carry a vast array of student activities and daily goings on, while our news articles take a deep dive into some of the ways Undershaw is redefining opportunities for our young people.

As ever, my heartfelt thanks to you all for your unrelenting support. Our students, staff, and families are full of pride at belonging to #teamundershaw, and I look forward to writing to you again soon with more tales from the Surrey Hills.

Emma West
Acting Headteacher
March 2022

"Undershaw," Hindhead. Conan Doyle's House.

Editor's *Caveats*

When these anthologies first began back in 2015, I noted that the authors were from all over the world – and thus, there would be British spelling and American spelling. As I explained then, I didn't want to take the responsibility of changing American spelling to British and vice-versa. I would undoubtedly miss something, leading to inconsinstencies, or I'd change something incorrectly.

Some readers are bothered by this, made nervous and irate when encountering American spelling as written by Watson, and in stories set in England. However, here in America, the versions of The Canon that we read have long-ago has their spelling Americanized, so it isn't quite as shocking for us.

Additionally, I offer my apologies up front for any typographical errors that have slipped through. As a print-on-demand publisher, MX does not have squadrons of editors as some readers believe. The business consists of three part-time people who also have busy lives elsewhere – Steve Emecz, Sharon Emecz, and Timi Emecz – so the editing effort largely falls on the contributors. Some readers and consumers out there in the world are unhappy with this – apparently forgetting about all of those self-produced Holmes stories and volumes from decades ago (typed and Xeroxed) with awkward self-published formatting and loads of errors that are now prized as very expensive collector's items.

I'm personally mortified when errors slip through – ironically, there will probably be errors in these *caveats* – and I apologize now, but without a regiment of professional full-time editors looking over my shoulder, this is as good as it gets. Real life is more important than writing and editing – even in such a good cause as promoting the True and Traditional Canonical Holmes – and only so much time can be spent preparing these books before they're released into the wild. I hope that you can look past any errors, small or huge, and simply enjoy these stories, and appreciate the efforts of everyone involved, and the sincere desire to add to The Great Holmes Tapestry.

And in spite of any errors here, there are more Sherlock Holmes stories in the world than there were before, and that's a good thing.

David Marcum
Editor

Sherlock Holmes (1854-1957) was born in Yorkshire, England, on 6 January, 1854. In the mid-1870's, he moved to 24 Montague Street, London, where he established himself as the world's first Consulting Detective. After meeting Dr. John H. Watson in early 1881, he and Watson moved to rooms at 221b Baker Street, where his reputation as the world's greatest detective grew for several decades. He was presumed to have died battling noted criminal Professor James Moriarty on 4 May, 1891, but he returned to London on 5 April, 1894, resuming his consulting practice in Baker Street. Retiring to the Sussex coast near Beachy Head in October 1903, he continued to be associated in various private and government investigations while giving the impression of being a reclusive apiarist. He was very involved in the events encompassing World War I, and to a lesser degree those of World War II. He passed away peacefully upon the cliffs above his Sussex home on his 103rd birthday, 6 January, 1957.

Dr. John Hamish Watson (1852-1929) was born in Stranraer, Scotland on 7 August, 1852. In 1878, he took his Doctor of Medicine Degree from the University of London, and later joined the army as a surgeon. Wounded at the Battle of Maiwand in Afghanistan (27 July, 1880), he returned to London late that same year. On New Year's Day, 1881, he was introduced to Sherlock Holmes in the chemical laboratory at Barts. Agreeing to share rooms with Holmes in Baker Street, Watson became invaluable to Holmes's consulting detective practice. Watson was married and widowed three times, and from the late 1880's onward, in addition to his participation in Holmes's investigations and his medical practice, he chronicled Holmes's adventures, with the assistance of his literary agent, Sir Arthur Conan Doyle, in a series of popular narratives, most of which were first published in *The Strand* magazine. Watson's later years were spent preparing a vast number of his notes of Holmes's cases for future publication. Following a final important investigation with Holmes, Watson contracted pneumonia and passed away on 24 July, 1929.

Photos of Sherlock Holmes and Dr. John H. Watson courtesy of Roger Johnson

The MX Book
of
New Sherlock Holmes Stories
Part XXXII – 2022 Annual (1888-1895)

The Hound
by Kevin Patrick McCann

Down the yew tree alley
Baskerville fled his bane,
Heart bursting like ripened fruit
Felled by Autumn rain.

Within this gargling quagmire
A pony thrashes in vain
As into ancient granite
Howling seeps like a stain.

Above each tor and fog bank
The moon shines clear and bright
Bathing gigantic paw prints
In cold deductive light.

The Adventure of the Merryman and His Maid
by Hal Glatzer

Chapter I

"Sabotage!" declared Helen Lenoir Carte. "A malefactor is at work, Mr. Holmes. And before you ask: No. We have not informed the police."

"We are hoping that will not be necessary," said Richard D'Oyly Carte. "Our new production opens in just a few weeks, but rehearsals are being interfered with, and some of our more . . . *sensitive* actors and actresses are becoming agitated."

"We wish to retain you, Mr. Holmes, to make an examination – to determine who is responsible for these outrages, and put a stop to them."

"Quickly!"

While it is commonplace nowadays for middle-class husbands and wives to keep a shop or run a small business together, it is rare among couples in the wealthier classes. But this husband and wife were the most successful impresarios in London's theatrical *milieu*. It was they who had brought together the playwright William S. Gilbert and the composer Arthur Sullivan to create modern English comic operas.

In 1881, as a showcase for these works, the Cartes had built the Savoy Theatre, the first in the world to be entirely lit by electricity. Coincidentally that was the year Sherlock Holmes and I met and took our lodgings in Baker Street. One of our first evenings together was spent in that new theatre, and over the following years we have attended every new "Savoy Opera", some of them more than once.

But our paths and that of the Cartes had never crossed until September of 1888, when they requested an appointment with Holmes. They arrived on the eighteenth at four in the afternoon and accepted our offer of tea. But they sat bolt upright on our sofa, clearly unable to recline or relax.

They were on the small side: He a bit less than average in height, and Mrs. Carte decidedly petite. But they radiated the kind of authority that comes from being influential in society. Through a close-trimmed beard and moustache, Carte's voice was soft. Newspapers had said of him that he was a "quiet" man in negotiations, but always ended up getting his way. Mrs. Carte had appropriately delicate facial features, but a rather more strident tone of voice than his, likely from having to work extra hard as a woman in what has always been a man's profession.

Holmes leaned toward them from his chair. "What is the nature of these 'outrages'?"

"Properties – stage props – have gone missing," said Carte. "Most have never been found, and the few that have turned up are broken, and must be repaired or replaced. The blade of an axe was loosened from its handle, and slipped off while being carried onstage. The *marotte* – the stick a jester carries – was decapitated, and we had to commission a new little head for it. Several 'flats' of scenery have crumpled while being shifted into place, because saw-cuts had been made in their wooden frames. Yesterday, a counter-weight fell onto the stage. Its rope had been cut. Luckily, no one was injured."

"We fear that someone *will* be injured, or worse, if the perpetrator is not swiftly apprehended."

After a moment, Holmes said, "Why have you not informed the police?"

They glanced at one another before Mrs. Carte spoke. "We are in the final weeks of rehearsal. The opera must open on the third of October. We simply can't have uniformed constables patrolling backstage."

Carte said, "You come highly recommended by a friend in the . . . highest circles of London society. He asserts that you are exceptional in your abilities, Mr. Holmes. We are satisfied that you are just the man we need to seize the malefactor and put an end to his scheme, without . . . raising a fuss. Everyone in the company must be interrogated. Cast. Crew. *All*. But this must be done in the most subtle way, without disrupting the progress of rehearsals."

"Be assured, I am intrigued by your problem," said my friend. "But you must give me leave to resolve this matter in my own way. Else I cannot accept your commission."

Another shared glance. Then: "All right."

"I must also insist upon a full disclosure of what this new production is all about. Everyone connected with it is surely familiar with the opera: The action, the characters, and so on. Before I can begin, I must know everything that all the members of the company know. And you must let me attend the rehearsals."

"Outsiders are not admitted."

"Nevertheless, I must see for myself where opportunities for malicious mischief might arise. If this new opera is anything like its predecessors, there is likely to be a lot of activity on stage, and a great deal of movement, before and behind the scenery."

I couldn't suppress a grin. "We do enjoy your productions! All those funny people with their ridiculous predicaments! Everyone in confusion over who is who!"

"'Topsy-turvydom'."

"I beg your pardon?"

She smiled. "That is what Sir Arthur calls the way Mr. Gilbert's characters get all twisted up in their own folly, only to be miraculously unwound. Of course, he is a master of comedic confusion. But this new production breaks precedent."

"We are confiding in you, gentlemen, something to which no one outside of the Savoy Company is privy, and which must not be disclosed until the *première*." Carte glanced at me.

"Dr. Watson is a master of secret-keeping," Holmes declared. "Pray continue."

"Let me put this in its proper context." Mrs. Carte took a moment to frame her next words. "The contractual partnership of Mr. Gilbert, Sir Arthur, and ourselves very nearly came to an end last year, over an intractable dispute. Mr. Gilbert proposed a plot – and not for the first time – in which a character swallows a magic lozenge and turns into a different person altogether. Their first full-length opera, *The Sorcerer*, employed a device like that."

I nodded. "A love-potion, as I recall."

"Yes, Dr. Watson. Subsequently, Gilbert has given us faeries in *Iolanthe*, imaginary Japanese – really, Englishmen in kimonos – in *The Mikado*, and ghosts in *Ruddigore*. Sir Arthur felt he'd had enough of such fantastical inventions. He announced to Mr. Gilbert and to us, in our office, that he would not – will not – ever again set to music any of Gilbert's plots that hinge upon nonsense or the supernatural. He was especially adamant against setting what he derided as 'a lozenge plot'."

"That was a terrifically fraught meeting, as you may imagine," said Carte. "Gilbert was incensed. He declared that he would write no other plot but one with his magic lozenges and stormed out."

"We had no idea," said I, "that there was such a breach in their collaboration."

"Of course not. We kept word of it out of the newspapers, in hopes of a reconciliation. And we immediately scheduled revivals of some of their previous works, so the theatre wouldn't go dark. But that would not do for the long haul. Audiences want new operas. We let it be known, quietly, that we would consider *libretti* from other playwrights. Sir Arthur told us that he now felt free to write a grand, romantic opera."

"The very prolific and, may I say, profitable collaboration of Sullivan, Gilbert, and ourselves had apparently come to a full stop," said

Carte, "and there the matter stood for months – until last Christmas Day." They both gave out with a chuckle. "Mr. Gilbert and Sir Arthur came to our home on the twenty-fifth of December – together! – to tell us that Mr. Gilbert had written a fresh script, with an entirely different kind of plot, and that Sir Arthur had agreed to set it."

"This new plot was the perfect Christmas present!"

"No 'lozenges'?"

"None, Doctor. In a departure from all of his previous work, Gilbert's new play is almost 'natural' in its setting. It is equal parts drama and comedy, blended into a more 'human' story than any they have ever brought to our stage. The characters in it are not caricatures, but people for whom one might actually feel sympathy."

"It was as if Mr. Gilbert had swallowed his own lozenge!"

I said, "Excuse me?" and Holmes said, "How's that?" simultaneously.

"As though Mr. Gilbert had suddenly turned into a more nuanced and serious playwright."

"That being so, Mr. Carte, it will certainly be necessary for me to read the script, ahead of my investigation into your problem."

Carte nodded. "We anticipated that, Mr. Holmes." He opened the leather folder that he'd kept beside him on the sofa and withdrew a thick sheaf of pages tied with a blue ribbon. "Mr. Gilbert always has his latest manuscript drafts set in type and printed, so no one in the cast has to squint through handwritten notes and changes."

"It is an extra expense," said his wife, "but well worth it. This is the script he delivered to the company yesterday, and therefore it is what the cast will be rehearsing from now on."

I accepted the bundle and set it on a side-table.

"You shall hear from me tomorrow morning," said Holmes, and stood up – by which he meant that the interview was concluded. The Cartes expressed their thanks, shook our hands, and took their leave.

Chapter II

Holmes lit a cigarette and, sprawled on the sofa with the script, passed each page to me as soon as he'd read it.

He and I have always enjoyed the Savoy's broad, comic farces, especially those in which pompous officials are held up to ridicule, and young lovers miraculously overcome adversity. My personal favorite is *The Mikado, or The Town of Titipu*. Holmes, perhaps because he is a better detective than those of the police, is fondest of *The Pirates of Penzance, or The Slave of Duty*, in which constables are silly, sentimental buffoons.

Since our investigation on behalf of the Cartes was to bring us into the theatre, face-to-face with the actors and the rest of the company during critical weeks of rehearsal, I must digress here, and give a synopsis of this new opera. It was called *The Yeomen of the Guard, or The Merryman and His Maid*. And as the Cartes had implied, it was well-endowed with antic comedy, but it wasn't entirely funny.

In The Tower of London, during the reign of Henry VIII, young Colonel Fairfax has been unjustly imprisoned, and is soon to be beheaded. But his fortune will go to his accuser if he dies unmarried. So for spite, he gets wedded to a blindfolded stranger: Elsie Maynard, a strolling minstrel girl who has come, with a jester called Jack Point, to entertain the crowd.

Sergeant Meryll, Chief Warder of the Yeomen – the Tower Guard – is devoted to the Colonel and convinced of his innocence. Hoping to delay the execution until exculpatory proof can arrive, Meryll spirits Fairfax out of his cell and passes him off, in disguise, as his son, Leonard Meryll. But Wilfred Shadbolt, the chief jailor, is blamed for letting Fairfax escape.

Of course, there are also romantic plots and plotters. Shadbolt is in love with Meryll's flirty daughter Phoebe, but she detests him. The Tower's veteran housekeeper, Dame Carruthers, loves Meryll, but he has no eyes for her. And the jester, Jack Point, is in love with his ward, Elsie, but cannot marry her while her husband, the fugitive Fairfax, still lives. So Shadbolt and Point contrive to announce that they have killed the missing man, although they somehow cannot agree on how it was done. At last, a reprieve comes, enabling Fairfax to resume his true identity. All is resolved, happily or grudgingly, for everyone – except the brokenhearted Jack Point who, Gilbert writes, *"falls insensible"* at the final curtain.

Mrs. Hudson brought up a platter of cold veal, tomatoes, and porter ale, and over luncheon, we reflected on Gilbert's atypical story.

"I hear echoes of Shakespeare, Holmes. It is the Sixteenth Century, and the dialog is very much a pastiche of that old style. But it is really neither a comedy nor a tragedy."

Holmes nodded. "Recall: Shakespeare himself wrote some problematic comedies with unsettled endings. Here, the comic bits are very funny, but the pathos . . . well, I wonder if audiences will be disappointed by this sudden departure from the usual Savoy fare."

"We'll never know, if the opera does not open."

"Then we must ensure that it does."

"How do you intend to proceed?"

Holmes swallowed the last of his ale, grinned as he set down the stein, and said, "Topsy-turvy."

I snickered. "That's what this play has gotten away from!"

37

"Not the play, Watson. Ourselves. Let us partake of Mr. Gilbert's magical lozenge."

Chapter III

At noon the following day, I was admitted to the Cartes' office in the theatre. Above the wainscot of polished mahogany, the walls were adorned with posters from their productions. The sconces and chandeliers held electric globes which illuminated the room, but also gas lamps with modern mantles, which weren't lit. Electricity, I could tell, produced at least as much light as the gas would have, but it gave off no heat, keeping the office much cooler than I'd expected it to be on such a warm September day.

The partners rose to greet me from their matching desks. Carte's was piled somewhat higher with paperwork than his wife's, but both were exceptionally tidy. A large oaken box, on its own table between the desks, held a telephone instrument. Their smiles disintegrated, however, when they saw I was alone.

"We thought – "

"Yes. I know. But here is the plan: You shall introduce me to the company as Ormond Sacker, a private enquiry agent."

"Where is Mr. Holmes?"

I looked at my pocket-watch. "We shall hear from him momentarily."

Sure enough, there was a knock at the door, and a middle-aged man with a bald head entered, holding an envelope. Mrs. Carte turned to me, saying, "This is our stage manager, Jabez Darnell." Then, to him, she said, "As we discussed yesterday, we have decided to engage a detective. May I present – "

I put out my hand, saying, "Ormond Sacker." We shook and exchanged how-do-you-do's.

"An actor," said Darnell, "has just come to the stage door, wishing to join the production. I informed him that it is too late, that we are so far into rehearsal that we cannot expand the cast. But he claims to have wide experience in regional productions of the Savoy operas, and has given me what he says is a letter of recommendation, addressed to you, Mrs. Carte, from the director of his last appearance."

She slit it open with a paper-knife, and when she had read the letter, she passed it to her husband, who said merely, "Ah."

Darnell added, "I would have sent him packing, but he said he is so keen for the chance to work here at the Savoy that he will accept half-wages."

Carte smiled and, with a glance at his wife, said, "All right, Mr. Darnell. Give him a job."

"I am concerned that it may be difficult to bring in a new actor at such short notice."

"And you are right to be concerned," said Mrs. Carte. "But you know how worried we have all been that some members of our cast might quit if there were any more . . . accidents." She pointed to the letter. "This fellow comes highly recommended. I think it would be good to have an additional actor for, let us say, 'insurance'. Assign him to a supernumerary position in the chorus, have him fitted for costumes, and . . . oh, it doesn't say in the letter whether he can sing."

"No matter," said Carte. "Let him take one of the speaking but non-singing 'Citizen' roles. That will free up a chorister to understudy a singer. Let us have this Mr. – " He glanced down at the letter. " – Sherrinford Hope join the company."

Darnell squinted. "You are satisfied with his credentials?"

Carte folded the letter and returned it to his wife's hand. "Quite."

Darnell led me to the hydraulic lift, and we descended to the stage level, emerging backstage on the left-hand side as one faced the auditorium, and hence called "Stage Left".

"I notice that there are gas lamps as well as electric lamps," I said. "Isn't the building entirely lit by electricity?"

"Oh, yes, Mr. Sacker. But for safety's sake it is also fully piped for gas illumination. We did this to ensure against plunging the audience into total darkness, should our steam engine outside suddenly fail to generate electricity. A single pilot light, which the pipe-fitters call a 'sunburner', is kept alight at all times. The apparatus is just inside there – " He pointed to a heavy iron door nestled below some narrow stairs leading to a catwalk overhead. "If necessary, all the gas lamps can be lit at a moment's notice, simultaneously. But we have never needed to – Oh. Here is the man you must interview. Mr. Craven is the designer of our scenery." Darnell introduced us and told him my purpose.

Hawes Craven was gray-haired and slight of stature. He carried a fistful of artists' brushes with which he was touching up the paint on a piece of scenery, dipping into a can labeled *Amberley's Fine Colours*.

"Thank goodness you've come," said he, setting down his brushes. "I was sure the Cartes would engage a detective of the highest caliber. So I assume they told you: Someone has been damaging my sets, and causing several of the larger pieces to nearly collapse."

Craven walked me over to one such piece, and showed me how repairs had to be made by screwing in strips of wood like splints, bridging both sides of each cut.

"Do you suspect anyone in particular?" I asked.

"I have my eye on someone."

"Whom?"

"Mr. Richards."

"He sings in the chorus," said Darnell, "and has one of the small but highly visible supporting roles, as the Tower's Headsman. He's quite competent. Been with the company a few years, now. But in his off-hours, away from the theatre, he . . . well, he fancies himself a great orator. He has prepared a number of set-speeches, which he declaims to passers-by on Sundays, in the northeast corner of Hyde Park."

"Mr. Richards believes," Craven said, "that the future of Great Britain lies in Socialism. When you interview him, Mr. Sacker, pray do not get him started on that subject. You will be forced to listen to – "

"I understand. I'll be careful. Thank you."

"Now you must excuse me," said Craven. "I have more touching-up to do. And I need to check, once again, all of the set frames and flats. I dare not delegate the task to anyone until I know I can trust them completely. Thank you, Mr. Sacker. Your help will be greatly appreciated."

Darnell also excused himself to prepare for that day's rehearsals. I was left alone at the edge of the stage, planning whom I should next approach. But I found myself chuckling, and covered my mouth with my hand, lest anyone see me and wonder why.

I had passed my first test: I was accepted as a real detective!

It must be remembered that Holmes was by no means the only practitioner of detection in London. There were private enquiry agents who were engaged by insurance underwriters to establish or disprove the validity of claims. Others specialized in locating missing persons or long-lost heirs. And a few scurrilous fellows made their pound-notes by obtaining proof of marital infidelities in support of actions for divorce. Holmes's clientele, by contrast, fit into no pattern. He was sought after by rich and poor alike, to solve *outré* puzzles, or to rationally explain a confounding sequence of events. But among all the private investigators who were active here in the 'Eighties, Holmes was unsurpassed in his knowledge of crime and criminals, and therefore it was to Holmes alone that senior police detectives turned when they needed help.

I was glad that no one would be likely to compare my skills of detection against his, because for most of the first decade of our acquaintance, Holmes was not famous. He had successfully concluded many cases, and had gained a reputation among highly influential people (through whom he had, obviously, come to the Cartes' attention). But he always preferred to let policemen or public figures be celebrated as the heroes of those adventures.

In 1888, practically nothing of Holmes's work was known to the public at large. My account of the Lauriston Garden mystery, entitled *A Study in Scarlet*, had appeared in the 1887 Christmas edition of *Beeton's* magazine, but few critics took notice. And although a pamphlet of the story had just been published, there were no calls for extra runs of the press. I had already chronicled several more of Holmes's adventures, but none saw print until early 1890, when my account of the tragedy at Pondicherry Lodge appeared in *Lippincott's Monthly* magazine as *The Sign of the Four*. And the first of my shorter stories wasn't published until 1891 in *The Strand* magazine.

So I felt sure no one would discover that "Ormond Sacker" was a demobilized Army doctor with literary ambitions. And since I knew Holmes to be a master of makeup and disguise, it was unlikely in the extreme that "Sherrinford Hope" would be unmasked.

Chapter IV

I am affable by nature, and generally find it easy to introduce myself to strangers. But I hesitated to do so when I came around a blind corner and nearly collided with a veritable giant.

Well over six feet in height and broad of frame, he had bushy eyebrows, thick but tousled brown hair, and muttonchops that middle-age was graying. Beneath an unruly moustache, his mouth turned down in a scowl, giving the distinct impression that a scowl might be its most natural expression, even in repose. Before me stood the living model for all the caricaturists, including himself. And the first words that William Schwenk Gilbert spoke to me were: "Who in blazes are you?"

His voice was much higher in pitch than one might expect from a big man, but I kept myself from smiling at the incongruity, and said, "My name is Sacker, Mr. Gilbert. I'm a private enquiry agent whom the Cartes have hired to find the person or persons responsible for acts of sabotage here in the theatre."

"Finally, something is being done!" He regarded me with a squint. "Are you any good at your work?"

I wasn't prepared for that. But I replied, "Obviously!" to seize as much of the upper hand as I could get away with. "And to do my work, I need to intrude upon your time for a moment."

"Very well."

I had been coached by Holmes to pose my questions in the simplest, most direct fashion, with few if any prefatory remarks. "What are the most serious offenses?"

He nodded. "Mr. Craven discovered the first saw-cuts, and showed them to me before telling anyone else. We went over all the scenery together, and were able to spot four additional places where they had been made. Regarding the missing stage props, you will need to ask Mr. Phillips, the property master. He will know which – if any – have been recovered, and which must now be replaced. For me, however, the most serious incident was the dislodging of a counterweight from the set-fly." He pointed up at the ropes and pulleys above the stage that raise and lower the largest pieces of scenery. "It was a heavy sand-bag that fell, nearly striking our *soubrette*, Jessie Bond. A stage-hand later discovered that someone must have climbed up the ladder to the catwalk and cut through the rope."

"I must ask a delicate question, Mr. Gilbert: Do you suspect anyone in particular of causing these untoward incidents?"

"I do."

"Who would that be?"

"Sullivan."

I think I may have gasped. "You can't mean that."

He shrugged. "It is only a suspicion. But Sullivan wants to dissolve our partnership with the Cartes. He feels that these little entertainments we have constructed are beneath his dignity."

"I wish to understand you correctly, Mr. Gilbert. Are you saying that you believe Sir Arthur himself is sabotaging this opera?"

"No. He would hire someone."

"And do you believe he is doing this to force the opera to close, before it opens, in order to terminate his involvement with the theatre?"

"No. His involvement with *me*! I'm the one standing in his way, don't y' know! I'm holding him back, says he. Have you met him?"

"Not yet."

"The man is a sycophant. He swans about among the royalty. Prince Alfred fancies himself a poet, so Sullivan composes music to his verses. In '83, the Queen made him a knight of the realm. And last year, she asked him, personally, to write a grand opera, based on – uh, something by Scott. *Ivanhoe*, I think. If there were such a thing as 'Composer-Laureate of England', she would confer the title upon him in a trice. Do you wonder that he wishes to be done with all *this*?" He opened his arms wide and shook his head.

I waited a moment to let his choler subside. "If you don't mind, Mr. Gilbert, I would prefer to assume that Sir Arthur is *not* the saboteur, and that he is not employing someone to commit these acts on his behalf."

"You are probably right."

"So is there anyone else on whom your suspicions fall?"

"Well, there is one supporting actor: Charles Richards. He is portraying the Headsman."

This was the same man whom Craven and Darnell had named. "Why does he arouse your suspicion?"

"He is a malcontent and a bad influence. He asserts that actors should form a trade union, to bargain for higher wages. 'Richards' is a stage name, by the way. He is not English, but a native of some village in the Carpathian mountains of Austria-Hungary."

"Is it not common, among actors, to take a stage name?"

"Of course. But I believe he styles himself an Englishman to conceal his profession of Communism and labor-agitation. I am concerned that he may be threatening the production with all this mischief."

"If he is such a threat, why has he not been terminated?"

"Ah. Well, Carte alone has the power to summarily discharge someone. And though it pains me to admit it, Richards is a strong and reliable actor who gave a good account of himself in our last two operas. Moreover, like all of our actors, he is signatory to a contract that would require Carte to produce real proof of malfeasance before he could be discharged. And there's the crux of it, Mr. Sacker: We have no such proof. In my youth I was called to the bar, and served as a barrister. So while I am certain we would prevail, I do not fancy being on the receiving end of an action for breach-of-contract. Besides, Richards has a following among his fellow supporting actors and, to some degree, among the leading actors as well. Bring us proof of his cupidity, Mr. Sacker, and we shall act swiftly indeed. Good day to you."

He turned aside and took a seat at a small table nearby, on which stood a miniature model of the stage, with wooden blocks of various sizes. These, I surmised, represented actors, and the model enabled Gilbert to move them about in their scenes. He consulted a sheaf of handwritten notes, shifted a few blocks, crossed out something he'd written, shifted the blocks again, wrote a few words anew, and then sat back in reflection.

"One more question, please," I called. "Where in the theatre will I find Sir Arthur?"

"In the theatre?" He gave a snort. "Hardly. Sullivan never comes 'round unless he has business with the musicians. Then, he might pop in with a handful of orchestrations or arrangements. But the musicians are

43

not engaged today, so he likely won't come, either. You'll have to go to his house. Good day, Mr. Sacker."

Chapter V

Sir Arthur Seymour Sullivan occupied a large suite of rooms at Number One Queen's Mansions, in Victoria Street. The porter showed me inside, where I found a young man at a desk – evidently the composer's *amanuensis* – copying sheets of musical notation. He continued to hold several pages in one hand while he stood, opened an inner door, and announced me.

"I have been expecting you. Won't you sit?" Sir Arthur raised a hand just enough to indicate a wing chair, but without rising from the sofa upon which he reclined.

I had expected to find him at the piano. (Is that not where all composers do their work?) But this room was furnished as a parlor, with comfortable chairs in the modern style. There were no musical instruments, but piles of paper, large and small, crowded with handwritten staves of musical notes, littered the floor all around his sofa.

He was a small man – plump of face, and thick in the neck, with very dark eyes. His hair, too, was dark, though I couldn't tell its color, for the lamp stood behind him as it would behind a writing desk. A monocle was crimped in his right eye, and the hand that had greeted me wielded a cigarette at the end of a long ivory holder.

"You are, I presume, the enquiry agent about whom Carte informed me by telephone this morning?"

"Yes, sir. I am Ormond Sacker."

He didn't proffer a hand, so I refrained from extending mine.

"Well, you will find little to enquire about here. I have not been inside the theatre these past three days. And I did not stay beyond half-an-hour – only long enough to disburse my newest instrumental scores and parts among the musicians. I have not seen, with my own eyes, any of the damage that Carte tells me has been discovered backstage, so there is nothing I am likely to add to the sum of knowledge or evidence which you have been hired to accumulate and interpret."

"Let me assure you, Sir Arthur, that I will not make any hasty judgements or accusations. For a detective, it is a mistake to theorize in the absence of all the facts. So may I ask, based on what you have heard from Mr. Gilbert – "

"I hear nothing from Gilbert."

"I beg your pardon?"

"We are not on speaking terms. All I know about the matter has come from Carte or Mrs. Carte. They relay to me whatever Gilbert may wish to tell me, and vice versa."

"Oh. Has something happened to cause – ?"

"'Happened?' Twelve years of association is what has 'happened'." He had leaned forward while saying that. But then he lay back again and grimaced before drawing deeply on his cigarette. I didn't need to be a doctor to see that Sullivan was in great pain. Unfortunately, under the circumstances, I could neither ask about it nor offer medical advice. I did notice some healed-over puncture marks just above his wrists, suggesting that he might be obtaining relief by injection of morphine.

"Mr. Sacker," he continued, after a moment's rest with his eyes closed, "I am assured by Helen Carte that I can rely on your discretion. So let me be plainspoken. All the world believes that Gilbert and I are in a divine partnership, that we gad about all day, singing his bump-ditty rhymes to my tinkling little tunes. But in fact, although we are colleagues, we are not collegial. We have never been friends. We move in different social circles. And in all the years of our association, the only occasions on which he has visited me here at home were those at which he would propose that I set music to another of his fantastic topsy-turvy plots."

"I have read the script for *The Yeomen of the Guard*, and it is certainly quite a change from . . . from the other operas."

"That is so. And I admit I was amazed when Gilbert first read it to me, last year. No lozenges. No faeries. No ghosts. Characters as near to real people as one may ever find in a light opera. Gilbert told me it took him five months to write it – the longest time he'd ever needed. The only problem for me was the title. He called it '*The Beefeaters.*' How atrocious is that!"

"It is what most people call the Tower Warders."

"Yes, but it's an awkward word. It gave me no musical inspiration. I'm pleased to say Gilbert eventually agreed to change it. *The Yeomen of the Guard* is quite mellifluous. But I did see the operatic potential immediately. For that reason – and to preserve my good standing with the Cartes – I agreed to work with Gilbert on this one production. But it may well be the last I shall ever to do with that insufferable man."

I let a moment go by in silence. "Are you acquainted with a member of the cast called Richards?"

"Oh, yes. Fine fellow. Irritating on the subject of labor and capital, but I have no cause to complain. He has a fine singing voice. He leads the baritone section in the Chorus when he is not portraying the Headsman. Why do you ask? Is he under suspicion?"

"By three members of the company. Yes."

45

"Who?"

"I'd rather not say."

"Has it to do with his agitation among the cast for higher wages?"

"That has been mentioned."

"He is not alone in doing so. Miss Bond, our *mezzo-soprano*, has implored – no, that is too weak a word. With each new production, she has *demanded* that we raise her salary. And Mr. Richards has lent his voice to hers in that regard, though he does so on behalf of the entire cast – not just Miss Bond or the other principal actors."

"Could he and she be conspiring to – "

"Oh, no. I cannot imagine that Richards or any of the others would risk their futures in the Savoy company with vandalism and theft. I suggest you look . . . elsewhere."

"Whom do you have in mind?"

"It galls me to point a finger."

"I understand."

"And you must be very diplomatic when you meet him."

"Of course.

"Approach him with great subtlety."

"Approach whom?"

"Mr. Grossmith."

"No!"

If anyone personified the essence of the Savoy operas, it was the comedian George Grossmith. He'd created all of their funniest roles: The titular *Sorcerer*. Ko-Ko in *The Mikado*. The Major-General in *The Pirates of Penzance*, and so on. That he might sabotage the theatre was unthinkable.

"Understand me, Mr. Sacker," said Sir Arthur, quietly, "I do not believe or assert that he is responsible. Not at all. But he could benefit."

"In what way?"

"There is a popular anecdote – perhaps you have heard it? I am sure it is apocryphal, but it contains a germ of truth. The story goes that a pale, middle-aged man comes to a doctor's consulting room one day, asking for help. 'I suffer gravely from melancholia,' says he. 'I take no pleasure in anything. There is no joy in my life. And I fear that, if I cannot ever laugh again, I must surely commit suicide.'

"The doctor is well-educated but unable, of course, to cure disorders of the mind. And as there is no drug he could prescribe that can reliably generate mirth, he counsels: 'Go to the Savoy Theatre this evening, and see an opera by Gilbert and Sullivan. There is a hilariously comic actor called George Grossmith. He is the funniest man alive. He will make you laugh out loud.'

"'Alas, Doctor,' the fellow replies. 'I am George Grossmith.'"

I nodded and smiled. One of my friends had told me that anecdote, and wondered what I might have said, had I been that physician.

"What," I asked, "is the 'germ of truth'?"

"Grossmith has a nervous disposition and a rather delicate constitution, yet he forces himself to perform. He indulges in . . . stimulants, for temporary strength of body. But after the last-act curtain, he repairs to his dressing room where – I have this on good authority – he slips into near-total collapse, and must summon stage-hands to help him out the door and into a cab."

"I had no idea."

"No one does. But as you so rightly said, you must have all the facts before you theorize."

A smile came upon me, but I shut it down by asking, "Is that why you think he may benefit? So he wouldn't continue to risk his health at work?"

"He would get out from under his contractual obligation to the company. Which is why I believe that if anyone knows the name of the perpetrator, it will be he."

Chapter VI

"Sullivan is rigorous with the musicians in the pit," said George Grossmith, "but he does not interfere with us actors. The stage is Gilbert's bailiwick, and there he is a perfect autocrat!"

I stood behind him as he sat before his make-up mirror, around which small electric globes exaggerated a complexion so sallow it nearly resembled jaundice. He was a small man, wiry of frame, squinting at his reflection through spectacles he evidently needed, offstage, for close-work. Contrary to what Sullivan had told me about Grossmith's torpor and lethargy, he was in perpetual motion, wriggling like a marionette, nodding as I posed my questions, and waving his hands when he replied. Perhaps he was under the influence of "stimulants", but the object of my enquiry lay in a different direction.

"If not Sir Arthur, are you having difficulty with Mr. Gilbert?"

"'Difficulty?'" he mocked. "That's an understatement. This role of Jack Point is the most difficult he has ever written for me."

"But you are a professional funny-man, and Jack Point is a jester."

"I am expected to be funny all the time. Yet Gilbert requires that I drop dead at the final curtain."

"I have read the script. Is that what 'falls insensible' means?"

"To him, yes. To me, that is an insult. I simply cannot play a doomed man. I am a comedian, not a tragedian. My public expects me to make them laugh, not weep. They would be appalled if I were to die on stage."

"Have you no recourse?"

"None. Though not for lack of trying. Yesterday Gilbert was, as always, directing the rehearsal from a seat in the stalls. Well, I improvised a little gag. When I fell 'insensible', I rolled over and opened my eyes, to suggest that I had merely fainted. Gilbert warned me never to do that in performance. I protested, saying I would get an enormous laugh by it. To which he had the temerity to say, 'So too you would, if you sat on a pork pie!'"

I couldn't suppress a chuckle.

"So! You hold with Gilbert against me!"

"No, no. I'm sorry."

"That's all right." He resumed applying rouge to his cheeks.

"I am more interested in the accidents and incidents that are plaguing the stage.'

"We are all concerned."

"Have you given thought to who might be responsible."

"No one in the company, I'm sure."

"Then who?"

"Someone with a grudge against Mr. Gilbert."

"Anyone in particular?"

Grossmith swung around to face me. "There is a rivalry of long standing between Gilbert and the editor of *Punch*, Frank Burnand. Gilbert began his career writing those 'Bab Ballads' for the rival humour magazine *Fun*, and in the ensuing years he has contributed practically everything to *Fun* and nothing to *Punch*. This would be of no consequence, except that Burnand is also a playwright who collaborated with Sullivan before Gilbert did. Back in the 'Sixties, they created the little one-act farce called *Cox and Box*."

"Oh! I've seen that! It's charming."

"Well, as it happened, Gilbert reviewed it in the pages of *Fun*. He praised Sullivan's music, but he called Burnand's libretto 'grotesquely absurd'. That's ironic, is it not, given Gilbert's penchant for the absurd, for topsy-turvydom?

"Isn't twenty-some-odd years rather a long time to hold a grudge?"

"It would be, had their feud not taken a new and nastier turn in '81, when they both wrote satires on the Aesthetic Movement. Burnand's is a three-act play called *The Colonel*, and Gilbert's comic opera is – "

"*Patience, or Bunthorne's Bride*. Yes. I know."

"Well. Burnand made sure that *his* production opened a few months before *Patience*. I was speaking with Oscar Wilde shortly after he saw *The Colonel*. He said it was 'a dull farce', and that he was certain Gilbert and Sullivan would make something better. Perhaps Burnand got wind of that. I don't know. But *Patience* was far more successful – it ran for many more performances than *The Colonel* did. Don't misunderstand me, Mr. Sacker. I think Frank Burnand is a most amusing man, and brimful of good humour, whereas Gilbert, in person, is not. Burnand will chaff you out of your life if he gets a chance, but his chaff is always good-tempered. No one minds being chaffed by Burnand. Except Gilbert."

"Do you think his 'chaffs' may conceal a darker purpose? Could he be wreaking new revenge against Gilbert by interfering with the rehearsals for *The Yeomen of the Guard*? Could he even gain entry backstage?"

"The Theatre is not The Tower. A determined intruder . . . I don't know. But of course, Burnand would not do these things himself. He would have a confederate in the company."

"Who might that be? One of the actors?"

"An outsider among the insiders."

"I don't understand."

Grossmith fixed me with a stare, his small eyes magnified by the spectacle lenses. "I think it's the American."

"There's an American in the cast? Who?"

"Geraldine Ulmar. A soprano from Massachusetts. She has played much of the Gilbert-and-Sullivan repertoire over in the States, but this is her debut at the Savoy. She's playing Elsie Maynard, the strolling singer who comes to the Tower with Jack Point. Which is to say: She arrives on stage with *me*."

I knocked on the door of her dressing room and called, "Miss Ulmar? May I speak with you about the unpleasant events backstage?"

"Do I know you?"

"My name is Sacker. I'm a private enquiry agent, hired by Mr. and Mrs. Carte."

"Wait a moment, please."

After half-a-minute, the door opened. Geraldine Ulmar was in her mid-twenties, tall and exceedingly slender, with a cream-white face. She left me at the jamb and took a chair before a dressing-table mirror to have her thick raven hair brushed by another woman in the room.

"What do you want to know, Mr. Sacker?"

"Do you have any idea who might be causing these . . . problems?"

She shrugged. "None. I just don't want any sandbags to come crashing down on me. This is the most important role of my life. I have

49

just joined the Savoy company, and I must make a good impression on the critics."

"Of course you will!" said the woman with the hair-brush.

"Oh," Miss Ulmar glanced back at her. "This is Jane Hervey, my understudy."

(I had, of course, assumed that she was merely a dresser.) I smiled and nodded. "How do you do, Miss Hervey?"

"Very well, sir." She was stockier than Miss Ulmar, though far from plump – peony-pink in complexion, with a mouth bracketed by conspicuous dimples.

"Have you – have either of you any thoughts concerning the problems backstage?"

Miss Hervey gave a little shrug. "I'd rather not speculate."

"But you may be in an admirable position to notice things. I assume you must be present for every rehearsal and every performance, waiting here or backstage, in case Miss Ulmar is unable to perform."

"Not at all! I have a role of my own!"

"I'm sorry. I didn't realize. Whom do you portray?"

"Kate – the niece of Dame Carruthers."

"Jane is Sir Arthur's cousin. So he really should – "

"Gerrie! You're not supposed to tell!" Then she sighed and said to me, "My father is his uncle, John Thomas Sullivan. But my sisters and I perform under the name of 'Hervey' so we will not be asked all the time if we are – "

"You'd think he would give you a bigger part, Jane!"

"No, Gerrie. He doesn't want anyone to complain of nepotism."

"What's wrong with 'cousin-ism'?" They both giggled.

I closed my eyes for a moment, trying to visualize the script. "I'm sorry. I don't recall . . . Please tell me: Who is 'Kate' in the opera?"

"Do you promise not to laugh?"

"Of course."

"Kate," said Miss Hervey, "has the smallest 'name' role, with a very short speech in Act Two. She has heard Elsie – "

"That's me!"

" – talking in her sleep, and tells Dame Carruthers, '*I wrote it all down on my tablets.*' That's my big line! It is significant at that moment, but makes only a tiny contribution to the drama."

"Kate *is* important in the opera," Miss Ulmar chided. "She sings the soprano line in the madrigal."

"The madrigal?"

"The quartette in the second act," said Miss Hervey. She cleared her throat in a grotesquely theatrical manner, and commenced singing in a

50

voice that was risibly well below her natural range. On top of this, Miss Ulmar gave out with a "harmony" in outrageously high falsetto: "'*Strange adventure, maiden wedded to a groom she'd never seen.*'"

Then they burst out laughing and embraced each other.

"I don't know if I shall recognize the real thing when it happens."

"You can't do a madrigal with only two voices."

"You see," said Miss Hervey, "we have Colonel Fairfax the tenor, Sergeant Meryll the bass-baritone, and Dame Carruthers the contralto. All harmony parts. They need a soprano on top, to sing the melody. And other than being that one thing at that one time, 'Kate' is a woman of no consequence in the opera."

"Mr. Sacker," said Miss Ulmar, "you really should interview Miss Bond – Jessie Bond. She plays Phoebe Meryll, the *soubrette*."

"Excuse me. I have heard that word, lately, but I don't know what it means."

"The *soubrette* is the 'other' girl in an opera." Miss Hervey's smile exaggerated her dimples. "*Not* the romantic heroine."

Miss Ulmar nodded. "The heroine in 'Yeomen' is Elsie – *my* role."

"The *soubrette* typically does a lot of comedy, but it's always a role for a *mezzo-soprano*. Gerrie and I are *sopranos*, whereas Jessie is a *mezzo*. Hence, in the Savoy operas, she is always the *soubrette*. Now, would you excuse me? I have to speak with the property-master about my 'tablets'."

"Good day, Miss Hervey."

"See you on stage!" She closed the door behind her.

Miss Ulmar said, "Jessie is the 'leading lady.' So you really must interview her. She would be terribly unhappy to learn that a great detective has asked everyone about our backstage troubles except her."

Jessie Bond was petite, smaller in person than she seemed to be on stage, with all the lively charm of the girlish characters whom she portrayed. Yet she admitted me to her dressing room in a surprisingly masculine way, extending her hand for a shake and firmly gripping mine. I couldn't help noticing that she walked with a slight limp when she turned, crossed the room, and settled onto a *chaise longue* with a sigh, as though from exhaustion.

"I am sorry," I said, "if this is an inconvenient time."

"It's all right, Mr. Sacker. But please be brief. Rehearsal will begin presently."

"Are you aware of these backstage accidents – "

"I am all *too* aware! When that counterweight sandbag fell, it landed less than a yard from me. I could not finish the scene."

"Which scene was that?"

51

"The very *first* scene in the opera. *My* big scene!"

Before I could think of how it looked on the script page, she said, "The curtain rises and there's Phoebe Meryll, sitting alone at a spinning-wheel. No chorus in full voice – no prancing dancers. Just me and my solo. Everything the audience needs to know about my character is contained in that song, and from the dialogue that follows immediately, with the entry of Shadbolt, the jailor. In all my years with the company I have never been given such an opportunity to shine on my own."

"I see."

"It is not false modesty to tell you, sir, that Mr. Gilbert created the character of Phoebe, and the lyrics of that solo, just for me. At the first reading, when the scripts were first handed out and we all read our parts aloud, Mr. Gilbert handed me my copy and said – " She mimicked his voice. " – 'Here you are, Jessie. You needn't *act* this. It's *you*.'"

"He obviously values your work."

"Yes. But not enough to pay me what I'm worth – until now! May I trust in your professional discretion, Mr. Sacker?"

"Of course."

"After such an encomium from Mr. Gilbert, in front of the entire company, I was emboldened to ask for a rise in wages. I told him I would decline to appear unless my salary were increased from twenty pounds to thirty pounds a week."

I suppressed my shock with a tiny cough. I am not accustomed to hearing a woman speak with such frankness about money.

"I was the only one who asked for a rise," she went on, "although Mr. Richards – one of the supporting actors – has long advocated that we should – all of us – enjoy higher wages. Mr. Gilbert was furious. He bitterly resisted my request for a rise. But Mrs. Carte felt I deserved it, and persuaded Mr. Carte and Sir Arthur to agree. Three against one. But Gilbert found his own way of expressing displeasure. During the initial rehearsals, earlier this month, whenever I made an entrance, he would call out, 'Make way for the high-salaried *artiste!*'"

"In the end, you did prevail."

"Yes. But Mr. Richards did not. Neither he nor anyone else in the company has gotten higher wages for this production. And he was nearly sacked for being so assertive. You know, now that I think on it . . . ."

"Yes?"

"I wonder if he could be the vandal."

I nodded. "Is that whom you – ?"

"Places!" someone yelled from the corridor, and rapped hard on the door.

"We must continue this later, Mr. Sacker," said she. "We are called to rehearse."

Chapter VII

A platform with two levels had been erected over the stage floor, covering a little more than half of it. A few actors, some in costume as Yeomen, others in costume as sixteenth-century commoners, were huddled stage left. I could see another knot of actors in the wings, stage right, talking amongst themselves.

To watch the rehearsal, I stepped down off the stage on a little step-ladder and took a seat close behind the orchestra pit, in the second row of the stalls. Reviewing the notes I had recorded after each of my interviews, I made a tick-mark against what seemed to be the most relevant comments and circled three names: Richards, Burnand, and Ulmar.

Gilbert strode out from the wings stage left and nodded to the cast. "Good afternoon to you all. A few announcements before we begin." He consulted a paper in his hand. "The costumer informs me that the final batch of Yeomen's uniforms is promised for delivery by the end of the day. So tomorrow, we shall have all our Yeomen properly attired. The replacement for Jack Point's *marotte*, however, is delayed. Again."

Someone pointed toward the stalls, and said, "Look! Here's Mrs. Carte."

She came down the aisle, stopped near to where I sat, and addressed the company: "Mr. Carte and I would like to remind you that the gas lamps in your dressing rooms mustn't be used at any time. We are all so accustomed to turning up the gas upon entering a room. But with so many electric lamps, it isn't necessary to use gas at all. And escaping gas could pose a hazard, should it encounter a flame or spark. Which it should not, because –" She shot glances at a few members of the cast. " – *smoking backstage is forbidden!*" She let that sink in. "Anyway, please use *only* the electric lamps for illumination. And when departing from your dressing areas, please extinguish them." She looked around in case there were questions. "That's all I came to say. Have a good rehearsal!" Whereupon she departed.

"Now," said Gilbert, "I would like to run the finale of the first act, as I have made some changes." A murmur arose from the cast, but he held up a hand. "Not to any of your lyrics – "

Two voices called out, "Thank you!" and the others laughed.

"I meant to say: Changes to the *tableau vivant*."

This may well have been the scene for which I'd watched Gilbert, earlier, manipulating his little wooden blocks.

"Citizens! You are now the first to enter." He gestured with his right hand. "Array yourselves downstage, in a loose group. Tomorrow I will specify a position for each of you." The men and women portraying the non-singing Citizens gathered themselves together near the front of the stage.

"Yeomen! You enter next. Remember not to tread heavily, but do keep in step." A dozen men came forward. Gilbert took two by the elbows and led them up onto the first of the platforms. The others followed until they had formed a semi-circle just above the Citizens.

"Mr. Richards!"

"Yes, Mr. Gilbert." He was a broad-shouldered youth with a full head of curly brown hair. In both hands he carried an antique-looking wide-bladed axe.

"Is that the replacement for the broken one?"

"Yes, Mr. Gilbert. And it is intact. I checked it myself."

"Good. See the block on the topmost riser? It has been set there, clamped into place, for you to strike."

"I see it."

"So when you enter, stage right, you will move upstage, ascend the risers, and stand on the topmost, center-stage, just to the right of the block. While the rest of the cast makes their entrances, you shall do as headsmen have always done: You shall *practice*."

A few chuckles arose from among the cast.

"This will remind the audience that they are not in the make-believe 'Town of Titipu', but London in the sixteenth century. Henry the Eighth is their king, and they are in the Tower Green, surrounded by the stone walls that are, in fact, only a short way down the river from here. In that time and place, a beheading is no joke! A public spectacle, yes. But not a laughing matter. In this play, you must all believe – and make the audience believe – that an innocent man's life is really at stake."

Murmurs arose among the cast, and I was compelled to wonder how audiences would react upon seeing this opera, which differed so strongly from Gilbert's previous lighthearted caprices.

"Now, Richards – As you lift the axe over your head to strike the block, I want all the Citizens to be watching. Citizens, you will give out with a hearty cheer when he strikes the block, just as common people would have done in real life. Is that understood?"

Several called 'Yes,' or 'Yes Mr. Gilbert.' Others made wordless noises of assent.

"Excellent. Let us run that much of the scene. Please go out now, and prepare to enter and take your new positions."

54

While everyone was leaving the stage, Gilbert stepped down the little ladder, took a seat in the stalls, and called, "Enter Citizens!"

They strolled in, pretending to talk among themselves, look about, and point toward the Tower scenery.

"Enter Yeomen!"

They marched onstage in ranks of two at a time, and formed up into their assigned semi-circle.

"Enter Headsman!"

Richards emerged holding the axe and mounted the first riser. As the Citizens began to pay attention to him, he stepped up onto the highest level and addressed the big black block.

Wielding the axe with both hands, he raised it up over his head, and brought it down in a swift arc. But the blade glanced off one corner of the block, sending it careening away, and embedded itself in the wooden riser.

As directed, the Citizens cheered, but stopped short when Richards screeched and hopped about on one foot, clutching the other in his hands. From my seat, I could see that it had cleaved away part of his boot. In my Army days, I had dressed many wounds. If his foot had been severed, there would have been an enormous outpouring of blood. Fortunately, there was none.

While Gilbert trotted up the stepladder, Richards sat down on the riser. Several people huddled around him, offering words of sympathy.

The nearest Citizen examined the damaged shoe. I heard him say, "You're all right, Richards. It's only the leather that's cut." Then the fellow climbed down to where the block had landed, took it up, and squinted at all of its sides. Then he set it back down and, separating himself from the other actors, he ambled off stage right and disappeared into the wings.

Chapter VIII

Gilbert gave everyone half-an-hour's time to recover their composure. The urge for a smoke came upon me. I'd had no tobacco since before coming to the theatre. Prohibited by Mrs. Carte from smoking within, I took my way outside through the stage door which gave onto the Strand, about fifty feet from the daytime entrance to the box office. I filled my pipe, set it alight with a safety match, and leaned back against the red brick-and-Portland stone of the Savoy's façade.

"You there! I saw you leave by the stage door. How did you get let in? Are you a journalist? A critic?"

I turned, saw the fellow hailing me, and said, "Neither."

55

He was older than I, a trifle taller, barrel-chested, and sported an impressive full beard and moustache. There was a pugnacious stance to his posture that made me wonder if he had ever been a pugilist. But like me, he carried a small notebook, and was therefore more likely to follow journalistic or intellectual pursuits.

He looked me in the eye. "Are you in the company?"

"Not exactly." I drew on my pipe to gain time, and decide how to conceal not only my real identity but my *nom de guerre* as well. "My name's Amberley. I supply paint to Mr. Craven. His sets for the Tower are all decorated with my colours. Here – Oh. Sorry." I patted my waistcoat pocket. "I have given away the last of my calling cards today. But if *you* are a journalist, perhaps you could slip a mention of Amberley's Fine Colours into your column?"

"Some day, perhaps." He consulted a pocket-watch, leaned against the wall beside me and lit a cigarette. "I've got a little time before the actors break for supper. Were you just backstage?"

"Yes."

"Did anything . . . exciting happen?"

"I don't know. I was busy with the painters."

"Ever meet Gilbert?"

"On occasion."

"Formed an opinion of him, have you?"

"Excuse me. Who are you?"

He smiled broadly and put out a beefy hand. "Francis Cowley Burnand. They call me '*F.C.*' at *Punch*."

I was flabbergasted, but concealed it. Here was the very man whom Grossmith thought might be responsible for the sabotage. As we shook hands, I said, "Oh! *Punch*! Well, I'm pleased to meet you." Then I smoked for a quiet moment, watched the traffic in the Strand, and waited for him to fill the conversational void.

At length, he said, "Do you enjoy the Savoy operas?"

"Yes. Doesn't everyone?"

"Bet I could tell you something about Gilbert that you don't know."

"I'm not a betting man."

"Care to know what it is, anyway?"

"If you wish to tell me."

"And you're *not* a journalist?"

"Amberley's Fine Colours."

"All right. Gilbert is a plagiarist. He stole the plot for this *Yeomen* opera from not less than *three* sources. And I intend to expose him for doing so."

56

Now I needed to segue from the disinterested colourman to the enquiring detective, but without revealing my purpose. I looked away from the street and into his face. "That is a serious charge."

"Have I piqued your curiosity?"

"Of course. Paint is not my only connection to the stage. I am a regular theatre-goer. I see all the new productions – nearly always on their *première* nights. Naturally, I intend to see this one. So if you don't mind telling me, Mr. Burnand: On what evidence do you accuse Mr. Gilbert of plagiary?"

"Have you read a novel called *The Tower of London*, by William Harrison Ainsworth? It was published in 1840, and what Gilbert has written bears a striking similarity."

"I've read a couple of Ainsworth's historical romances: *Windsor Castle*, for one. They were in my father's library. But *The Tower of London* . . . ? No. I'm sure I never read it."

"But you do attend the theatre frequently."

"Indeed, I do."

"I don't suppose you have seen the opera *Maritana*."

"No. Is it playing currently?"

"Not just now. *Maritana* is based on a play called *Don Cesar de Bazan*, and had its London *première* at the Drury Lane Theatre in 1845. It was revived there in 1862, and again in 1879."

I chuckled. "I was a child in '62. And in '79 I was in Her Majesty's service, posted to Afghanistan."

"Have you read Gilbert's script?"

I deflected the question by squinting at him. "Has Mr. Gilbert copied the *Maritana* libretto and passed it off as his own?"

"Not exactly. He has, however, appropriated important elements of the plot, with quite a lot of Ainsworth's novel thrown in. It's the sixteenth century. A man unjustly imprisoned marries a veiled gypsy girl. The jailor is a clumsy oaf. An arquebus is discharged, but kills no one. There is also a – "

"Enough, Mr. Burnand. I understand what you're saying. Do you mind my asking how you come to be so familiar with *The Yeomen of the Guard*? No one from the outside is allowed to observe rehearsals. And Mr. Gilbert is said to keep a close watch on all the copies of the scripts which he gets printed."

"I have . . . a connection with the company. Let that suffice."

"Assuming you are correct, are there not many playwrights who base their works upon older sources? Did not Shakespeare draw his historical plays from Hollinshed's *Chronicles*? And some of his comedies from the *commedia dell'arte* of Italy?"

"Shakespeare did not live in the modern age, Mr. Amberley. No periodical was in a position to challenge him over his sources. Hardly anyone could read!"

"Point taken, sir." I drew on my pipe for a long moment. "Why have you not published your accusation in *Punch*? Made known these connections to *Maritana* and Ainsworth's novel?"

"There is a rule, laid down by Richard D'Oyly Carte himself, which I must not break. The London periodicals that review theatrical presentations . . . we are all, even the sporting papers, enjoined from printing news of the latest Savoy production in advance of its *première*. The penalty for breaking this rule is to be excluded from attendance during the entire first month of performances. Failing to give our readers a timely account of the new opera would fatally damage our credibility. So the facts of Gilbert's plagiary will necessarily have to appear in *Punch* a week *after* the opening night."

"Given that late date, do you still believe it will ruin Mr. Gilbert's reputation, or force him to pay compensation of some kind for *Maritana*?"

"Oh, Gilbert will not be defenestrated! And there is no legal recourse. The lyricist and the composer are both deceased. Ainsworth too."

"Then what do you hope to achieve with this . . . excuse me, this rather trivial information which does not rise anywhere close to the level of scandal?"

"All I intend to do is show that he is somewhat less of a genius than he is reputed to be. He will not face ruin. But on the cribbage-board of reputation, I would dearly like to see him taken down a peg or two."

Chapter IX

"Mr. Hope, I presume!"

Holmes was in his chair when I returned to Baker Street. "Right you are, Mister Sacker."

"Mr. Hope, I accuse *you* . . . of examining the shoe and the executioner's block."

"Very good, Watson! Now, tell me all you have learned."

I took whisky with carbonated water from the gasogene, sat at my desk, and read aloud from the notes I had taken, adding my subsequent impressions, and whatever snatches of the interviews I could recall verbatim.

Holmes nodded. "I, too, heard disparaging remarks about Richards," said he. "But I'm certain, now, that he is not the miscreant. No man would risk amputating his own foot to conceal culpability for vandalism."

"What happened?"

"The block was supposed to have been clamped to the riser – that's what they call the platform on which it stood. It's possible that the clamp was not properly tightened. But more likely, someone loosened it shortly before the rehearsal began."

"I do have two more suspects: The American soprano Geraldine Ulmar, and the editor of *Punch*, F. C. Burnand, who seems to be an enemy of Mr. Gilbert."

"'Seems to be' or 'is'? I will endeavor to find out tomorrow. But there are rivalries in every profession. One of these days, I may grow jealous of Ormand Sacker!" (That prompted a toast.) "But speaking of Miss Ulmar, I also conversed with her understudy Miss Hervey. She introduced me to the choristers and the other understudies. In fact, by dint of a few stories I told them, I am now accepted in their ranks."

"Might you be required to serve as Headsman?"

"I hope not. By the way, the understudies, men and women together, have their own little *clique* backstage. They pass along announcements of casting-calls, and their impressions of directors and producers. Some producers, I have learned, are not to be trusted. A woman finding herself alone with certain of these men may not be safe from . . . interference."

"Holmes! Has someone accused Carte or Gilbert of – ?"

"No. The hierarchy of the Savoy appears to be free of that taint – else someone backstage would surely have alluded to it. Now, if you please, tell me about this fellow Burnand."

When I had finished, Holmes called down to Mrs. Hudson for our supper.

"Can we take Sir Arthur seriously?" I asked as we finished our coffee. "Could Gilbert or Grossmith actually be undermining their own opera?"

"You said Miss Bond has a limp."

(I have long accepted Holmes's tendency to tack away from the course of a conversation.) "Right leg. Not congenital – both lower limbs are normal."

"You saw her ankles! That's life upon the wicked stage, eh, Watson?" He let a moment pass. "A recent injury, would you say?"

"No. In Afghanistan, a limp like that would suggest a wound that failed to heal and left an abscess."

"Would it prevent her from sneaking about, backstage, and damaging the scenery?"

"She certainly couldn't climb up onto a catwalk, dislodge a sandbag, hurry back down, and wait almost directly underneath for it to fall!"

"Indeed."

"And she is the 'leading lady'. Even if she were in great pain, would she really try to stop rehearsals, or even postpone them?"

"I doubt it. Neither would Gilbert. Nor Sullivan. Nor Grossmith. We must look elsewhere."

Chapter X

Next day, at Holmes's suggestion, I sought out Eric Lewis, the chorister who understudied the role of Jack Point. Where Grossmith was slender, Lewis was scrawny, and his head was slightly upturned to the left, which made me wonder if he had a touch of scoliosis in his back. Costumed as a jester in motley, he might bring to mind Poe's pyromaniacal "Hop-frog".

He snarled when he saw me, "What do *you* want? Can't a man get some peace around here?"

I introduced myself and explained my purpose, which had the effect of lowering his temperature.

"My apologies, Mr. Sacker."

He led me into the empty dressing room, but by the number of lighted mirrors, he shared it with five other choristers.

"You will pardon me for saying so, Mr. Lewis, but it seems incongruous for someone like yourself, who is rather choleric, to portray a funnyman on stage?"

"I am an actor! I earn my living by being funny, but I do not have to be funny offstage. To be frank, I resent it that people expect me to be jolly all the time in public."

"There is something about that very thing in one of Jack Point's songs."

"You mean this?" He struck it up, in a very mellifluous baritone: "'*It adds to the task of a merryman's place, when your principal asks with a scowl on his face, if you know that you're* paid *to be funny?*'"

"I hope you will have a chance to sing it on stage."

"Doubtful. Grossmith never misses a performance. Well, hardly ever. He was ill for one week in January of last year, when we were doing *Ruddigore*. But I wasn't his understudy for that opera. It was Henry Lytton. He made a great success of it. Gilbert was very fond of Lytton's performance. Another opportunity lost!"

"I'm sorry."

"Few understudies ever go on, really. But I'm luckier than most, what with being grotesque. No. Don't shake your head, Mr. Sacker. I know what I look like. If we revive *H.M.S. Pinafore*, I can play the nasty sailor Dick

Deadeye, but no one's going to cast me as Ralph Rackstraw, the romantic lead. Still, I'm lucky. There'll always be roles for odd-looking fellows."

"This could well be one of them."

"No, Mr. Sacker. I won't get to shine in this new Savoy opera. As long as Grossmith's alive, he – "

Someone knocked at his door and called from the corridor – it was a woman's voice. "May I speak with you, Mr. Lewis? It's about your motley garb."

"Which I may never actually need! This interview is concluded, Mr. Sacker."

He opened the door, letting the costumer in and showing me out.

A man who plays comic roles has a great advantage in the casting if his appearance itself provokes amusement. Walter Denny's head was round, and his face so broad that, in any other man, the eyes would be too far apart. He seemed, therefore, to be preternaturally suited to portray the buffoonish jailor Wilfred Shadbolt.

I introduced myself and followed him into his dressing room. By the hand-lettered sign on the door, he shared it with Courtice Pounds, who portrayed Colonel Fairfax.

"If you're asking about yesterday – that business with the headsman's axe – I've nothing to do with it," declared Denny. "I actually go offstage before that scene begins, and I don't come on again until after everyone else is in place, and two songs are performed. So all the time that Mr. Gilbert was staging the scene, I was in the wings, stage left, along with Whitsun Brownlow, who plays Cholmondeley, the Lieutenant of The Tower.

While Denny talked, his hands were busy arranging all the components of his makeup kit on the dressing table, lining up the tubes of greasepaint in a straight row, making equilateral triangles with sticks of pigment for black shadows around the eye, and rolling up freshly laundered washcloths into tight cylinders. It seemed incongruous that someone so compulsively tidy would portray the slovenly unkempt Jailor. But the theatre is a world of make-believe, is it not?

Courtice Pounds burst through the door, exclaiming, "Richards has quit!"

Denny spun around. "Who's in line for Headsman?"

"You'll never guess!"

"I don't know too many people in the chorus, but you're new here, too, Pounds. Have you been eavesdropping again? What have you heard?"

Although he'd closed the door, and we could hear that no one walking in the corridor, Pounds leaned down and whispered. "Phillips."

61

"The property-master? He isn't even an actor."

Pounds was tall and strikingly handsome, with a thin, sharp nose and chin, bright blue eyes, and brown hair long enough to pass, unaided by a dresser, for that of a sixteenth-century man.

I asked, "Is it often done – replacing an actor with someone who isn't?"

"Rare, but not unheard-of."

"It's only a walk-on role, and he appears in that one scene only." Denny added. "No singing required. No lines to speak."

"As Mr. Gilbert said yesterday, the Headsman makes the audience keep Fairfax's dire situation in mind."

"Although sometimes," said Pounds, "I find myself laughing at how easily Fairfax – that's my character, Mr. . . . uh – "

"Sacker. I am retained by the Cartes to enquire into what happened at yesterday's rehearsal."

"The axe and block."

"Yes."

"Nothing to do with me! Or Denny!"

I nodded to Denny, but said, "Where were you stationed, Mr. Pounds?"

"Just off stage left, ready to enter." He turned a chair around and straddled it, folding his arms on the backrest. "Fairfax is disguised as Sergeant Meryll's son – one of the Yeomen. So I enter with two of them who have singing roles called 'First Yeoman' and 'Second Yeomen'. They are the second-tenor, and the baritone in our trio. We announce that the prisoner – that is to say, that *I* have escaped." He broke into song: "*The man we sought with anxious care had vanished into empty air.*'"

"So you were not behind the riser where the block was clamped?"

"Certainly not. Anyone can tell you I was nowhere near it."

"Mister Pounds, I hope you will not take offense, but Mr. Denny let slip that you are inclined to eavesdrop."

He shrugged. "I am a 'noticing' sort of fellow. If my curiosity is piqued, I may occasionally linger out of sight and . . . overhear what is being said."

"Were you doing so yesterday?"

"I may have done."

"What did you hear? Understand me, Mr. Pounds: I am not interested in backstage tittle-tattle."

"Too bad. There's quite a lot of it going around. Don't you care to know who might be, shall we say, 'amorously involved'?"

"Not my business."

"What *is* your business?"

"To discover who has been sabotaging the scenery and properties. These are dangerous acts of vandalism which, if they continue, will surely prevent the opera from being performed at all."

Denny leaned toward me from his chair. "We'd all like to keep safe from danger. If I knew – if any of us knew – surely we would inform Mr. Gilbert directly."

A *Yeoman of the Guard* Poster

"I have no idea who's doing these things," said Pounds. "But Denny and I are most *un*-likely suspects. We are making our Savoy debuts. If we are well-received and well-reviewed here, we will stand closer to the front of the line when producers are casting about for actors to play leading roles. None of us – no actor and no crewman – would want to keep the opera from opening. Besides, if we aren't working, the Cartes have no need to pay our wages."

Properties were kept in a small room on the far side of the stage from the dressing rooms. The door was open, but no one was there. I stepped inside, where I was surrounded by the various artifacts called for in the opera: Yeomen's halberds, the Headsman's axe, Jack Point's (still headless) *marotte*, Elsie's tambourine, the Jailor's ring of keys, Kate's writing tablets, and an extraordinary firearm.

During my Army service I'd known armorers who still maintained a handful of weapons from the last century. But this piece was even older: A gun from the Tudor era, with a stock and flintlock like a musket, but a much wider barrel for shooting lead pellets. In the script, an "arquebus" is heard to fire in the second act, and then is carried onstage by Shadbolt, claiming to have killed Fairfax with it. So this must be that arquebus. I picked it up to examine it closely when I heard someone behind me.

"May I help you? I'm Trelawny Phillips, property-master."

I set the gun down, strolled back to the doorway and shook his hand. "Ormond Sacker, Mr. Phillips. I assume Mr. Darnell or Mr. Carte has informed you of my presence here, and my purpose."

"Yes."

"How did the executioner's block come to be dislodged?"

"I don't know. I secured it firmly to the riser. There is a groove in one face, to which I crimped one end of a clamp. The other end went under the tread of the riser itself. I ensured that it was tightly affixed before I returned here, to my property room. Between that time and the time Mr. Richards struck it, someone must have loosened the clamp."

"Can you think of anyone who might have done so?"

He looked about, not as if to locate something but to pause while composing his answer. "It's not my place to say."

"It is very much your responsibility to say, if you know."

"I do not 'know', but I do suspect. I saw – "

"Who?"

"I was rather far away. I'm not entirely certain, but . . . it was a woman."

"Miss Hervey? Miss Ulmar? Miss Bond?"

"Of course, I may be mistaken. But I had the impression of someone . . . larger. Our Dame Carruthers: Rosina Brandram."

Chapter XI

I introduced myself at her dressing room door. She was, indeed, a large woman, as tall as me, but with such a pleasant combination of rosy cheeks, warm brown eyes, and a gentle smile, Rosina Brandram's natural face was in stark contrast to the fierce, even tyrannical visages that she typically projected when playing a character.

Towering over the diminutive Grossmith, with whom Gilbert often paired her for comic effect, she typically played elderly maiden-ladies yearning for the love of a man who doesn't return her affection. She had been Katisha in *The Mikado*, opposite Grossmith as Ko-Ko.

But as Dame Carruthers in *The Yeomen of the Guard* – as in so many aspects of Gilbert's sudden turn toward the dramatic – the object of her character's adoration was not Jack Point, Grossmith's titular Merryman, but stolid Sergeant Meryll, played by Richard Temple.

I introduced myself and my mission, and inquired if she had seen anyone tampering with the executioner's block.

"Possibly," said she. "While Mrs. Carte was warning about the gas, two members of the company were behind the riser where the block was clamped. I was nearby, but Mr. Gilbert would not have been able to see them."

"Who were they?"

"Wait, Mr. Sacker. Please do not misconstrue what I said: I did not see either of these people actually loosen the clamp. They were slouching against the riser – one had his hand . . . you know, I'm really not certain. It may have been on the block, or it may have been merely *near* to the block."

"Not actually touching it?"

"I can't say definitely that he touched the block. And he did not stay long, behind the riser. He went around it, and climbed up onto the first level."

"Who did you see?"

"Jane Hervey and Richard Temple."

Temple had been with the Savoy company from its earliest days and was most famous for playing the Mikado himself. Here, he'd be the Sergeant of the Beefeaters. He wasn't what anyone would describe as beefy, but he was tall and just a trifle paunchy. So his Sergeant Meryll would be well matched, physically, against Rosina Brandram's Dame Carruthers.

He was reading his script pages when I approached, introduced myself, and asked, "Did you see anything untoward at yesterday's rehearsal?"

"'I really couldn't tell from where I stood. I enter along with the Yeomen under my command."

"Were you in the wings all the time?"

"No. Not at first. Miss Hervey waved to me, wishing to talk in private. We stepped behind the riser, where she told me she was unsure of how she should sing certain lines in our second-act madrigal."

"Had you not rehearsed it?"

"Sir Arthur hasn't given us his final arrangement. So for instance, in the line, '*Pretty maid of seventeen. Seven, seven, seventeen*', she asked my opinion: Ought she to emphasize the '*seven*' or the '*teen*'? Well, I would not presume to give a definite answer without guidance from Sir Arthur. But I did suggest that, since we are a quartette, we might work up an arrangement together, before we rehearse it today, and ask Sir Arthur if it might be acceptable. I promised to ask Mr. Pounds and Miss Brandram to join us in one of the alcoves, stage right, before we are called on stage again. And that will be today. I saw the notice that our scene would be rehearsed, posted on the board beside the stage entrance."

"When you were behind the riser, were you near the executioner's block?"

"We were . . . three yards away, perhaps a little more."

"Rehearsal!" someone called from the corridor. "Mr. Gilbert wishes to have Miss Brandram, Miss Hervey, Mr. Pounds, and Mr. Temple on stage!"

"As I expected," said Temple, "we are called for."

Chapter XII

I followed him down the corridor and stood to one side as he and the others gathered on stage. "Oh!" he turned back to me. "I'm still holding these. Would you take them?" He handed me his copy of the script. "Gilbert might think I hadn't already committed my lines to memory."

I sat in the stalls, near to where I'd been yesterday.

Gilbert mounted the stepladder and strode onto the stage, beckoning the four actors to approach him. "I would like to start with the dialog that comes just after Fairfax sings '*Free from his fetters grim*'."

"Excuse me, Mr. Gilbert," said Temple. "Will you be wanting us to go into the madrigal afterward?"

"No. We have no musicians today."

"We can sing it *a cappella*!" Miss Brandram said – in character – haughtily.

"That is Sullivan's domain! For me, today, you three will exit stage right, leaving Fairfax on stage, whereupon Elsie enters from . . . ." He looked up and shouted: "Elsie? Elsie!"

Miss Ulmar emerged from the wings, half-skipping in haste. "I'm here, Mr. Gilbert."

"All right. Elsie, you will come in from where you just were, when you see the others exit. You and Fairfax will play your scene, which culminates when we hear the arquebus discharged. Today, however, it will not be discharged. I will simply give the cue. Sergeant Meryll and Dame Carruthers, you will then rush back in, followed by members of the Chorus. But we will get to that point in the script after you have concluded the present scene." He shouted toward the wings, "Mr. Darnell!"

"Yes, Mr. Gilbert."

"Call 'places' for the Chorus. They'll be coming on in fifteen minutes." Turning back to his actors, he asked, "Is everything understood?" and waited for their nods and yes-es. "Very well."

He descended the stepladder and took a seat near mine. "Places!" He let them get into position. "And now, if you please . . . enter Sergeant Meryll."

I read along in Temple's script as the scene unfolded. It was the one in which Kate – Miss Hervey – speaks her only lines. She says that Elsie had talked in her sleep, revealing that she was the blindfolded bride. And that causes Fairfax, still disguised as Sergeant Meryll's son Leonard, to realize that it was she whom he had married.

The scene would end with the quartette's madrigal, but when that moment came, Gilbert waved for them to stop, and pretended to sing a few bars of the madrigal's wordless syllables. "'*Bim-a-boom! Bim-a-boom! Bim-a-boooom!*' And we are through with that! Exit Meryll, Carruthers, and Kate." The three of them departed.

"Fairfax, you give your speech. Elsie, you enter after Fairfax says, '*Tis not every husband who has a chance of wooing his own wife.*' All right? Places!"

She walked on and they began talking. Fairfax couldn't yet reveal his true identity, so he attempted to woo her as Leonard Meryll. She chided him and rejected his advances, insisting that she was already married. As they neared the last lines, I could hear a clatter and a shout coming from backstage.

Gilbert yelled, "A little less noise there!"

Just as Fairfax tried to apologize to Elsie, saying, "I did but jest. I spake but to try thee!" the arquebus was fired backstage, its report a terrific *bang*.

Miss Ulmar jerked up stiffly, clutched her side, spun around moaning and sobbing, and fell to the floor.

Pounds dropped to his knees beside her. Gilbert, Temple, and Miss Brandram rushed over. I leapt up from my seat and mounted the stepladder, calling out, "I was a medical orderly in the Army!" and motioning the others to part and let me through.

The left side of her dress was bloodstained. The antique arquebus hadn't merely been primed with powder, but loaded with a lead ball and discharged directly at Miss Ulmar. Fortunately, the thick cotton fabric of her costume, though perforated, had kept the ball from penetrating more than a quarter-inch into her skin. I felt secure enough of my diagnosis to look up and say, "Miss Ulmar is not in mortal danger, but she will need a surgeon. Miss Brandram, please take her hand and tell her she'll be all right."

She knelt down and said so, stroking Miss Ulmar's forehead as well.

Gilbert shouted, "Temple! Run up and tell Mr. Carte. He can use the telephone to summon a physician."

I stood up and ran backstage toward where someone was yelling, "Let go of me! *Uh!*" and other people were shouting.

From somewhere came the clatter of heavy objects tumbling onto the floor, and the *clang* of metal striking metal. I looked toward that sound and saw that the great iron door below the staircase to the catwalk had been flung open.

Another voice yelled, "Watch out for the gas!"

The open door revealed the heart of the theatre's illuminating gas system: A huge iron vessel from which pipes radiated like spiders' legs. The pilot-light "sunburner" was lit, silhouetting the figure inside the enclosure, brandishing the arquebus, and swinging it widely left and right."

Craven and Darnell were cowering beside the iron staircase. "Look out!" Craven called to me.

"If one of those pipes should rupture, and the gas escape," Darnell cried, "it would ignite a terrible explosion!"

Gilbert came up alongside me. And so did Holmes, who was still garbed as a Citizen. I clapped him on the back.

"We have cornered the malefactor," said he.

"My revolver – "

"No! The arquebus has not been reloaded. And we don't want to puncture a gas pipe. I alerted Inspector Bradstreet first thing this morning. He's been ready, outside. . . . Ah! Here he is!"

I turned to see the young policeman come from outside, through the stage door, with two constables behind him.

"Bradstreet!" cried Holmes, "Have one of your men go with Darnell and Craven around to the left of the apparatus. Send the other man with Gilbert and me around it to the right. Mr. Sacker, you stay here, just in case."

Gilbert demanded, "You there – Sherrinford Hope. Who do you think you are, ordering us about?"

"Your fox has gone to ground, and Bradstreet is the Huntsman. Will you not join the hounds?"

Gilbert lips curled up – the first time I ever saw him smile. "Tally-ho!"

Employing Holmes's pincer manœuver, the six of them blocked any escape from behind the apparatus. The vandal drew back, but was no longer backlit. The sunburner – the pilot-light – illuminated the far interior of the ironbound room. And suddenly, this malicious creature who had caused an actor to nearly lose his foot, and two actresses to nearly lose their lives. . . . We could see who it was!

Chapter XIII

It is rare, I suppose, for actors and stage-hands to ever sit in the stalls of their own theatre. But there they were, all of them, in the first two rows.

On stage, Gilbert, the Cartes, and I sat in folding chairs, and just as I stood to address the company, their attention shifted toward stage left. Sir Arthur had arrived. I gestured toward the empty chair. He hesitated momentarily when he saw it was next to Gilbert's, but he sat upon it and gave an acknowledging nod to his collaborator. Bradstreet stood at stage right, arms folded across his chest.

"For those who did not meet me before now," I told the assembly, "my name is Ormond Sacker. I am a private enquiry agent. And this gentleman – " I extended my arm. " – is Inspector Bradstreet, of London's police. Inspector?"

He strode to the center of the stage, and stood just behind the prompter's box. "Thank you, Mr. Sacker, Mr. Carte. The information which you supplied was of great importance to our investigation. I had posted a constable this morning to watch the theatre from across the Strand. And when the alarum was raised, an additional constable was called from nearby to effect the arrest.

"Your bobbies were spying on us!" someone shouted.

"Would you not agree, sir," Bradstreet replied, "that the end justified the means? Perhaps you thought this backstage mischief was nothing to worry about. Just a nuisance. But it got out of hand. A couple of you got scared, and one of you got shot! If anybody'd been killed, the theatre'd be closed, and you'd all be out of work right now. You're lucky my men and I were here!"

Mrs. Carte rose, shook Bradstreet's hand, and said "You've done a fine job, Inspector. Thank you." Then she turned to the company. "Fortunately, Miss Bond was not struck by the falling sandbag, and Mr. Richards was not crippled by the axe when the block was dislodged. It cut only into the leather upper of his boot. As for Miss Ulmar, she was not seriously injured by the lead shot from the arquebus, and will rejoin the rehearsals tomorrow. Miss Jane Hervey, however, will not be returning. She – "

"She'll be arraigned on Tuesday next!" announced Bradstreet.

"Yes. And she will be replaced by her sister, Miss Rose Hervey."

Someone muttered, "Another cousin!" But several people went, "Shhh!"

"Also, Mr. Lewis has resigned, citing nervous distress. He will be replaced by Mr. Henry Lytton, who was understudy to Mr. Grossmith in *Ruddigore*."

Mr. Carte stood up and joined his wife. "To the Inspector who has rung down the curtain on this melodrama, let us give three cheers, and one cheer more!"

Chapter XIV

I was anxious to hear what Holmes had learned backstage that led him to single out Jane Hervey as the guilty party.

That evening, over whisky and soda water, he started – as he often did – by saying, "You know my methods, Watson."

"Not this time!"

He smiled, put his feet up on the sofa and leaned back against the armrest. "It was quite refreshing to assume the *persona* of an actor. Did you feel it likewise stimulating to be a detective?"

"Often. But I found far too many suspects and motives to be able to sort through them. No one accused Miss Hervey, though. How did you conclude it was she?"

"Through the process of elimination. It was apparent from the beginning that the composer, the playwright, and the Cartes themselves could not possibly be the perpetrators. They had the most to lose if the opera were forced to close. However, it was instructive to learn from your interviews that all is not sunshine and roses in the partnership. Mr. Gilbert and Sir Arthur cannot tolerate one another, yet they are able to create these operas together. How that can be is a mystery I may never be in a position to solve.

"But from those interviews – and you showed great powers of *investigation*, Watson! – you gave me news of tension and anger in the company, which might have motivated our vandal. You found, did you not, a kind of roundelay, with each person pointing the finger at another in turn?"

"Indeed. Gilbert blamed Sullivan. Sullivan blamed Grossmith. He blamed Miss Ulmar. Darnell and Craven blamed Richards. Accusations were tossed out against Miss Brandram, Mr. Temple, Mr. Burnand . . . . Had I pursued it further, perhaps it would have come full circle."

"Quite likely, and that would have been another dead end. But you also reported to me some facts that may have seemed trivial, but which confirmed what I had already heard from the understudies. These were most instructive. Mr. Lewis complained that Mr. Grossmith never misses a performance. How frustrating that must be! And Miss Hervey must have felt she deserved a larger role."

"I didn't get that impression when I talked with her. Miss Ulmar actually suggested that, but Miss Hervey made light of it."

"A smoke-screen, Watson, to conceal her true intention. I had spoken with Mr. Temple and Miss Brandram. When they were practicing the madrigal with Miss Hervey, they noticed that she had an unrealistically high opinion of herself, and considered her talent under-utilized there. Also, she harbored a great resentment toward her sisters, who already enjoy greater success on the stage. I'm told that the eldest, Lucy, is a leading actress in another comic-opera company, and that the youngest, Rose, who will now replace Jane, has sung grand opera.

"All understudies come to their theatres in hopes that, one evening, they shall be called upon to fill a leading role and receive the adulation to which they feel entitled. A few may be content to remain in the chorus for their entire careers, but most, even those with ambitions, understand that great success is likely to be out of reach. They will go to, or return to, the regional theatre companies of the nation or the empire where they can be celebrated."

"Greater fish in lesser ponds."

"Exactly. Mr. Lewis will likely take that path. Miss Hervey, however, chose to leap ahead of her place in the Savoy company by disabling the woman whose role she coveted."

"But if that were her object, why commit petty theft? Why damage the scenery?"

"She did those things not to close the opera but to set the stage, if I may put it that way, for her more serious crime. By engendering suspicion against everyone, she would not be singled out for greater suspicion than anyone else. Tampering with the Headsman's axe and block, of course, was her great mistake.'

"How so?"

"First, she damaged the axe, causing it to be replaced."

"Yes."

"So when the new, sturdier axe was brought onstage, all eyes were on the axe, and not on the block. She was seen standing near to the block, was she not?"

"Yes. Miss Brandram saw her and Mr. Temple. But he said she'd waved him over, to discuss their song, and that they stood a few yards away from the block."

"Surely she got his attention just *after* she'd loosened the clamp. Drawing Mr. Temple alongside her further distracted anyone who might have seen her there, behind the riser."

"All right."

"You must have noticed that the properties room is often left unattended."

"Indeed. And the door was open when I came by."

"Phillips kept the arquebus primed with powder, well in advance of the cue for its discharge. But he always has a lot to do backstage and leaves the door ajar. Hervey seized the opportunity to slip in and load the gun with lead shot.

"As to her motive, I gave considerable thought to the accusations that you reported to me, and heard one or two more backstage. So I began to think that an understudy with a fierce, unhealthy drive to prove his or her mettle could well be the perpetrator. The question, of course, was how far such a person might go to remove the actor or actress who stood in their way. I had my eye on Lewis at first. You interviewed him. What was your impression?"

"An insecure man by nature, but quick-tempered and easily roused to anger."

"I concur. But our villain would not have an angry nature. To perpetrate thefts, and increasingly dangerous acts of vandalism, one must be cool, unruffled, and not call attention to one's self. Jane Hervey had the right sort of demeanor."

"You must have been very near to her backstage when she fired the arquebus."

Holmes sighed. "I hadn't deduced that it was she until I realized that she would exit the stage just before Miss Ulmar and Mr. Pounds have their scene together as Elsie and Fairfax. That scene ends with the arquebus discharged. But Gilbert said it wouldn't actually be discharged in today's rehearsal, so logically, it would still be in the properties room. I was standing by the properties room, glanced inside, and saw that the arquebus was missing. Someone had already gone there, brought out the gun, and concealed themselves. I raced about backstage, knocked over some chairs in my haste – to Gilbert's displeasure – and caught sight of Miss Hervey behind one of the scenery flats at stage right. There she had a view of the stage and was lifting the arquebus up to put Miss Ulmar in her sights. I have to admit, I reached her only just in time to bump against the barrel, deflecting the ball away from Miss Ulmar's heart."

"Well done." I refilled my whisky glass. "Has anyone backstage learned who you really are?"

"No. After the constables took Miss Hervey away, I was cornered by the men who'd helped to apprehend her: Darnell, Craven, and Gilbert. They demanded to know why it was I who'd been leading the chase."

"What did you tell them?"

He smiled. "That I was an operative in your employ, 'Mr. Sacker'! I said that you insist on keeping secret the true identity of your undercover assistants, and that you always prefer to let the police take the credit for apprehending criminals.'"

"He's a first-rate detective, that Sacker!"

Holmes raised his glass. "I give you Ormand Sacker!"

"Ormond Sacker!"

"I guess it was Jane Hervey who gave a copy of the script to Burnand at *Punch*?"

"I think not, Watson. And a first-rate detective does not guess."

"Mr. Sacker is humbled."

"More likely, the script came to Burnand from high up in the organization. Recall: He had an early success as a librettist, collaborating with Sullivan on *Cox and Box*. Recall, too: The Cartes told us that, during all of last year, they were worried that Sullivan might never again set one of Gilbert's plays to music. They were relieved, of course, last Christmas Day, when Gilbert told them the plot of *The Yeomen of the Guard*, and Sullivan said he would compose the score for it.

"But when they read the script, they must have grown anxious. Audiences would have every reason to expect a Savoy opera to be full of topsy-turvy comedy. What would they do when they saw how serious this one was? Would they accept having the funniest man on the London stage drop dead? Would public opinion turn against Gilbert?"

"They might have screamed, 'You're paid to be funny!'"

"Exactly. So I deduce that Richard and Helen Carte got word of all this to Sullivan's erstwhile colleague, Burnand, as a kind of insurance. For the Savoy company, Burnand would be Gilbert's . . . well . . . understudy."

The Four Door-Handles
by Arianna Fox
Illustration by Mike Fox

My Dear Lord Mayor and Lord Mayor's Consort,

Due to the recent events which relate to Mr. John McCarthy's new acquirement of Birmingham Construction Company, I have found myself compelled to share with you the precise and singular details of the case which was presented to my friend and colleague, Mr. Sherlock Holmes, and was thoroughly investigated. These are the facts in as concise a manner as I could compile for your viewing.

It all began with a familiar knock at the door. It is no uncommon thing for Inspector Lestrade of Scotland Yard to look in upon us now and again and bring news of the police headquarters. Thus, when upon one gloomy October evening, the lean and ferret-like fellow with dark and perceptive eyes stepped into our sitting room, we weren't surprised in the slightest that he should come to visit us.

"Good evening, Inspector," said Holmes as Lestrade removed his hat and sat upon the sofa in our sitting room. "I trust that all is well with you."

"Good evening, Mr. Holmes. Dr. Watson. Indeed, we at Scotland Yard have been quite occupied of late."

"I perceive so."

"You must have heard of our recent cases in the newspapers?"

"Not at all."

"You have had a visit from one of my colleagues then?"

"No. My last visitors were clients."

"Then how on earth do you know that we've been occupied?"

"Your exhaustion was quite evident. The weary circles beneath your eyes give away the mental. The rest of your attire gives away the physical. I cannot help noticing the state of your attire, which has clearly been drenched in today's rain before drying out over time – it certainly wouldn't be as wet if you hadn't been so occupied with whatever is on your mind that you forgot to open your umbrella until after the rain soaked your clothes. I also observe the many stains of mud upon the soles of your leather shoes which tell me that you walked a good deal today, even after the rain stopped. Indeed, your entire person seems to carry the look of one who has exhausted himself and has come to our abode looking for something of a respite."

Lestrade smiled. "All which you have said is true. I admit that I have come for a respite, though I did also come to inquire as to . . . ."

His eyes drifted away to the mantelpiece, his face taking on a perplexed expression, and he sat for some seconds, absorbed in his thoughts.

"I take it that there is something on your mind?" Holmes remarked at last.

"Well, yes, Mr. Holmes, there is indeed a case which weighs upon my mind. It is so queer, and yet no one at Scotland Yard has been able to make anything of it. It isn't the usual lot, you see."

Sherlock Holmes leaned forward in his chair.

"Pray tell me about it."

"There was a series of events in which four houses of illustrious businessmen have been broken into. However, in each house, nothing has been identified as stolen. The only things which have been altered were the luxurious knob-shaped bedroom door-handles. In each occurrence, they were removed from the door and set outside upon the front steps. No further alteration has been made to the houses, nor to the belongings of the owners."

"And there was no crime apart from the burglary?"

"Nothing at all, as far as we have concluded. That's what makes it so peculiar. I truly don't know what makes these four houses so singular, other than the fact that they were villas belonging to well-to-do gentlemen. The streets were, I believe, Tottenham Court Road, Gray's Inn Road, Gower Street, and Farringdon Road. Nothing rather special at all. Anyhow, I know that such trivialities interest you, so I thought to present it to you and see if you should like to accompany me tomorrow and assist in the investigation."

Holmes leaned back in his chair, thinking the matter over before he responded at last.

"Well, Lestrade, this has been fascinating. It is indeed quite a pretty little problem. However, I have various cases at hand, all of which require my full attention at present. I wish you luck with the investigation, and do tell us the results when you have reached your conclusions. I have no doubt that with your usual happy mixture of cunning and audacity, you will find the man or men for whom you are searching."

"Why, I must confess that I am rather taken aback. You always tell me of your interest in the trivial aspects of the criminal world. Why on earth would you be anything but interested in solving such a singular case as this?"

"Oh, this certainly does interest me. However, I believe that your fellow inspectors at Scotland Yard ought to figure it out with your own

76

methods in this case. I should, however, like to have the addresses of these burgled houses. Perhaps I will look them over further when I have more time."

"Fine, then," said Lestrade, with some annoyance. "Here you are."

He scribbled something in his note-book, tore off a page, and handed it to Holmes.

"Good day, Mr. Holmes. Doctor."

"And to you, Inspector."

Lestrade took his hat and departed.

"It surprises me that you shouldn't want to investigate the case," I remarked, sometime after we heard the clattering of hoofs and wheels upon the streets of London.

"There is little to investigate. Lestrade has already stated that there was no crime. Thus, there really is no case."

"There is no case?"

"None at all. At present, I don't see any reason why I should spend my time to look into it. I know you might protest by alluding to the many affairs we've solved in which there was no real crime involved. However, I have been a very busy man of late, Watson, and I cannot waste my time with trivial affairs such as this at present. I do, however, hope that Lestrade finds the answer to this peculiar riddle. It will certainly be another joyous triumph for Scotland Yard. And now I must continue my studies, as Monsieur Leroux of the French Government is waiting very patiently for an answer to his little problem."

For the remainder of the evening, Holmes buzzed about the sitting like a bee, often oscillating between the use of his chemical instruments and the use of his large round magnifying glass as he inspected a piece of parchment which appeared to be burnt and torn.

As for myself, I thought it best to leave him to his work. Thus, I plunged into a grand novel which was filled with mystery and intrigue. It didn't take me long, however, to toss it aside in disgust – for although I once found myself enamoured with the mysterious novels and brilliant detectives of fiction, I now found myself observing all the little erroneous details of which I had never before taken notice. After witnessing the incredible powers of deduction and reasoning with which my friend Sherlock Holmes has been endowed, it became more frequent to replace a novel of fiction with a document of fact, and I would oftentimes find more interest in the Agony Column of *The Times* than an intricately written detective tale of Edgar Allan Poe.

I retired to my bedroom as night approached, and in the last moments of consciousness before drifting off to sleep, I remember that I couldn't help thinking of that strange case which Lestrade placed before us, and of the great anticipation of hearing its conclusion from the inspector's point of view. Surely a simple matter such as this would have a very simple answer.

The next morning, I awoke to the strong smell of coffee and the harsh blowing of autumnal wind. When I came down to our study, I found the breakfast already laid on the table. Holmes finished pouring out the coffee as I sat down.

"Have you any plans for the afternoon?" he inquired.

"I intend to write," replied I. "I plan on chronicling the case of that poor woman in Croydon with the missing dog."

"Pshaw, my dear fellow, that really is too ordinary a thing to record. It was simplicity itself. However, if you haven't yet read the morning paper, it may perhaps give you something much better and indefinitely more interesting to recount."

Holmes made a gesture towards the newspaper lying upon the table, one of the flashier but more lurid rags, the headline of which concisely read:

Construction Accident Causes Death of Famous Chairman of Birmingham Construction Company

"Why, that's terrible!" I said.

"What, the accident? Oh, yes. But I wasn't referring to that. It gets more interesting as you read on. If you would have the kindness to read it aloud, I should be most obliged."

It ran as follows:

> *Yesterday morning, on Saturday at half-past-eight, a terrible accident occurred at a charming villa on 534 Farringdon Road, which was still in construction. The well-known chairman of Birmingham Construction Company, Mr. Vincent Birmingham, was inspecting the attic when he stepped on unsteady wooden planks and fell through the second floor and down to the first. The house in itself, when it finishes construction, shall be a luxurious two-story villa. However, construction has been halted due to recent events. The house and corpse are still being investigated.*
>
> *Fifteen small, vividly blue diamonds were scattered over Birmingham's body. Thirteen of them weighed two carats, and the remaining two weighed three carats. It is probable that they were in his pocket when he fell.*

In other news, many wish to know who shall take his place as new chairman of the company. Birmingham Construction Company, formerly Birmingham and Morris Construction Company, has been considered by many as the most highly recognised firm of its type in London, one whose houses reflect the illustrious clients whom the company frequently serves.

As for Mr. Birmingham, he was a true gentleman, regularly giving to the poor and generously donating to local and county charities. There is no doubt that a great shadow shall fall over London with the loss of Mr. Vincent Birmingham.

I looked at the unexpectedly graphic photograph of the dead man's body which was printed upon the paper. It had been circled with a pencil, which must have been Holmes's doing. I was immediately struck with the terrible sight of the chairman lying upon a pile of broken, wooden planks. Though the photograph was sufficiently wide to capture all of the details which could fit in the picture, I could clearly see the diamonds scattered about and upon his person, and even through the printed image I couldn't help feeling that there was something rather unsettling about the thing: To find such pretty items of wealth, scintillating in the light of the sun which shone through the open spaces betwixt the beams of the roof, and, indeed, to find them spread over such a sight of horrible death – the sheer contradiction of it struck a nauseous contrast in an almost ethereal manner.

As for the gentleman himself, Birmingham looked to be a rather robust man with a broad, clean-shaven face, his skin pale as death, and an expression of absolute terror fixed upon his countenance. His clothes were quite fine, suiting well his character and wealth. He wore a dark frock-coat, a white satin cravat, and luxurious spatted shoes, all of which told of the great fame which he had acquired.

"What a dreadful accident!" I remarked as I set down the paper.

"An accident? Oh, yes, indeed. What a dreadful accident."

There was something in his words which made me turn to look at him. There was that expression of amusement upon his features which led me to think that there was more to this event than that which the press would have us believe.

"You don't think it was an accident?"

Holmes chuckled to himself.

"My dear fellow, you do possess a perception for which I seldom give you credit. No, I do not. It is either deliberate or a coincidence. No – it *cannot* be a coincidence. See here!"

He pulled from his pocket a little slip of paper.

"Look at this. This, if you recall, is the paper of addresses which was given to us by friend Lestrade regarding the case of the four knob-shaped door-handles. Do any of them stand out to you, Doctor?"

I examined the paper. It read, in the familiar handwriting of the inspector:

467 Tottenham Court Road
62 Gray's Inn Road
17 Gower Street
536 Farringdon Road

"Yes," said I, pointing at the fourth address on the list. "That last house is on the same street as the house in which Vincent Birmingham met his death."

"Precisely. Do you notice anything else?"

I took a few moments to closely examine the paper for any additional clues, but all that it was to me was a mere collection of numbers and street names strung together in a senseless list. I have often in my life endeavoured to use the methods of my companion and piece things together using as much reasoning and deduction as I could, but never could I quite see the thing at which Holmes was driving. How he observed minute details and used them to arrange other facts in their proper places to transform an insoluble mystery into the fully revealed truth was completely past my comprehension.

With a certain amount of disappointment, I put down the letter.

"No, I don't see what it is that you see."

A slight look of annoyance passed over the face of my companion.

"How often have I said to you that you can see everything, but you fail to reason from what you see? Well, now, let us see what we can deduce from this. We take into account the fact that it is most common for one construction company to build houses on the same street. We already know that 534 Farringdon Road is the house in which the poor Mr. Birmingham met his death, and that this house was one of the many luxurious villas constructed by his company. Just two houses down, a doorknob was removed from the bedroom and placed so singularly on the steps of the house. We can either accept this as a coincidence that proves nothing, or as two threads that both lead to the same point."

"Birmingham Construction Company," I answered.

"Now, my dear Watson, you begin to form hypotheses from reason, instead of guesswork from mere sight. There is something singular about that case which Lestrade presented to us, and I must say I was foolish to ignore it. I believe this door-handle business may be a trifle more interesting than we first thought."

"You think it is somehow related to the accident?"

"Ah, yes, the 'accident'. Did you know that thirteen of the cases I have solved in my time – mostly before you began to assist me – involved a death that was, although truly deliberate, originally covered up as an accident? Hmm! It is just food for thought. *Nous verrons.*"

I had opened my mouth to reply when there was a knock at the door. In stepped Mrs. Hudson, with a telegram upon her salver which Holmes promptly took.

"It's a wire from Inspector Lestrade, sir," she reported.

"Thank you, Mrs. Hudson. It will not surprise me if his message has something to do with the death of Mr. Birmingham about which we read in the paper."

He read it aloud as our landlady left the room:

> *Suspicions about construction accident at 534 Farringdon Road. Shall give additional details. Come at once.*
>
> *Lestrade*

"Come along, Watson," said Holmes as he put down the message. "I think it's high time we pay a visit to Farringdon Road."

Within the next few minutes we were in a hansom, dashing through the London streets as the sun began to pierce through the perpetual fog. We passed by people of all sorts, from the well-dressed gentleman to the unkempt urchin, all of whom briefly glanced at us through the side windows of the cab before we continued plunging away at a rapid pace through the damp streets.

Holmes, who was sitting with his head sunk upon his breast, said nothing. As it was customary for him to act in such a manner when he was buried in the deepest thought, I remained silent also. However, though I was quiet, I couldn't but wonder what marvellous and intriguing notions had formed in that singular and keen mind.

It didn't take us long to arrive at the house of interest. Though it was still in construction, one could easily notice that, by the composition and size of it, it was to be a lovely residence. There was a certain grandeur about it which commanded the attention of all passers-by. Indeed, even as I gazed up at it and the other neighbouring houses, I felt a certain smallness compared to these villas of extraordinary luxury. They seemed to loom above our heads like castle towers, opulent compared to the little apartment on Baker Street in which we lived.

Holmes's face, however, wasn't turned upward to the top of the villa. He was instead surveying the lawn, where a small number of constables bustled about, some going in and others coming out through the open space where a door would be had construction finished. A lone, tall man with a shabby hat and get-up stood near a corner of the house, almost sulky in his demeanour.

The cab door opened, and as we made our way to the front of the building, we were approached by a smiling Lestrade.

"Ah, Mr. Holmes, I see that you received my telegram."

"Indeed. It surprises me, Lestrade, that you are investigating Mr. Birmingham's death, and that you should want my assistance in the matter. It was, after all, distinctly described in the newspaper as an accident."

"Why, yes, that is correct. I see that you have read up on the affair. I visited yesterday when the body was still here and the blood still fresh – and yes, it is most probable that the thing was simply a terrible construction accident, but I couldn't help coming back here today to see if I missed anything. I asked you here, Mr. Holmes, because I have a suspicion or two in my mind that all isn't as it appears to be. I should be most obliged if you would inspect the house and tell me what you think of it. There is also a man here – one of Birmingham's employees – with whom I spoke yesterday who had a very strange narrative. He has come back today at my request to relate the facts."

Lestrade had just finished his explanation when Holmes responded with a very brusque acknowledgment of thanks and entered the house. The inspector and I followed behind.

"The body was removed yesterday," Lestrade explained once we entered, pointing at the barren wooden floor below us. "It lay right here."

"Yes, I observed what I could from his photograph in the newspaper. There is nothing to see here."

We three climbed the wooden staircase, cautiously watching for stray beams and ascertaining whether it was safe to step on the next plank. Once we finished ascending, we stood looking at the very large hole through which Birmingham had fallen. The remaining adjacent planks were quite frayed, clearly broken by his body.

Holmes rounded the gap, studying it intensely. He flitted about the room, occasionally pulling out his magnifying glass and studying the splintering on the edges of the boards. It didn't take him long, however, before he stood and announced that he was ready to view the original point from which Birmingham fell. We advanced upstairs. The attic was barren and, like the rest of the house, carried the unique smell of freshly cut wood.

The planks above seemed to me to be no different from those below. However, Holmes must have noticed something which I did not, for his eyes gleamed with the satisfaction of a lawyer who found some piece of telling evidence to support his case.

"Hmm!" he remarked. "That is suggestive."

Neither I nor Lestrade said anything in reply. We simply watched as Holmes noiselessly moved about the room with the swift and furtive motions which were characteristic of him.

At last, he stood and addressed us.

"Thank you, Lestrade. I believe I have seen all I wish."

The three of us made our exit, stepping out onto the lawn once more. The sun was now shining brightly, casting a dreamy effect on the emerald grass as we walked by, and the wind seemed to have lessened a bit, as if summer and autumn were still struggling for the mastery.

"Now, Mr. Holmes," said Lestrade, "there is a man whom you may perhaps desire to meet."

He led us to the tall, poorly dressed man who stood sulking near the corner of the house.

"What is your name?" asked Holmes.

"Sam Perkins, sir."

"I am Sherlock Holmes, and this is my friend and colleague, Dr. Watson."

"Aye, sir, the inspector 'ere told me you'd be comin'."

"Indeed. We are here to make a few inquiries about the terrible occurrence which befell Mr. Birmingham, your employer."

"Well, all right, then," replied the man. "What d'ye want to know, sir?"

"The facts, Mr. Perkins. I want to know the facts. Where were you and what did you see from the moment in which Birmingham arrived to the moment in which he fell?"

"I was workin' away in the 'all, sir, until Mr. Birming'am came towards the 'ouse from the open window. I went to greet him, see to his wishes, answer his questions, an' all that. After all, it isn't every day the 'ouse that you're building gets inspected by Mr. Vincent Birming'am."

"And what then?"

"'E made his examinations an' all, then 'e went up to the attic. A few moments later, I 'eard somethin' a-crackin', and then I saw Mr. Birming'am fall down to the floor. There was a worker who came a-rushin' down the stairs – I didn't recognise 'im. I saw 'im whisper somethin' to the man and put those diamonds over his body before 'urryin' away. An' Mr. Birming'am's face, sir – Oh, his face! It was filled with absolute terror. Then 'e pointed up at the attic, and, well – "

"Go on, man – what then?"

"I heard Mr. Birming'am sayin' something. On 'is dyin' breaths, sir, I 'eard 'im say the word 'more'."

Holmes stood in deep thought for a moment before responding.

"That's most fascinating. Is there anything else?"

"No, sir. That was it."

"That's all I wished to know. Thank you, Mr. Perkins. Lestrade," continued Holmes as we walked across the lawn, "I trust that you will alert me of any fresh developments."

"Certainly, Mr. Holmes. Ever since I heard this strange account yesterday, I began to organise a search for the person who poured out the diamonds. I say – I do wonder what Mr. Birmingham meant by uttering the word 'more'. More time, perhaps? More money? Perhaps a name – a man by the name of *Moore*! Countless theories already begin to form just from one word. Remarkable! What do you make of it, Mr. Holmes?"

"Well, now, you mustn't let me influence you in your course of action. I am sure you'll find a suitable answer soon enough. Good morning! Come along now, Watson – this really is turning into a remarkable case."

With those few parting words, Holmes and I started off for the cab to return to our comfortable rooms in Baker Street.

Throughout the afternoon, Holmes spent his time languidly smoking his pipe, buried in the deepest thought. As for myself, I too sat smoking in my armchair, my imagination attempting to conjure up possible solutions and, indeed, reasons for the various actions which Holmes performed during his morning investigation.

At last, at approximately four o'clock, it was time to take action. Holmes stood in an instant, setting aside his pipe and putting on his hat.

"I think I had best investigate some matters," he remarked. "I shall return in a few hours."

Though his last statement seemed to indicate that his return would be somewhat soon, he was absent for much longer. It wasn't until nine o'clock that he finally returned, and when he did, I knew already from his expression of slight disappointment that his outing hadn't been a very successful one.

"You haven't had much luck?"

"While there were a few triumphs, it wasn't ideal. No one could provide any further light upon the matter."

"The 'matter'? Surely you mean the death of Mr. Birmingham?"

At last he glanced up at me with a smile.

"Do you truly believe that I spent so many long hours investigating the death of Vincent Birmingham?"

"Why, yes – Is that not the most pressing matter at hand?"

"My dear Watson, you know my methods. The matters which are truly the most pressing are often those which are the least obvious. No, I wasn't investigating Birmingham's death. I was instead inquiring as to the four illustrious residents whose door-handles were so singularly removed."

"I confess that I still don't see a connection between the two events."

"The deadliest crimes are often connected to some little occurrence with nearly invisible thread. Only the trained reasoner who looks for such a thread can find the missing link in the chain of events. Anyhow, I'm now quite certain that Mr. Birmingham's unfortunate death wasn't an accident. Here is one piece of good news for you: I've recalled from where I recognised the diamonds which were over the body of Mr. Birmingham. Now, from the description of the diamonds which the paper gave, do they strike you as familiar?"

"I can't say that it does."

"Those diamonds were of a distinctly vivid blue colour, which is a rare and expensive variant which can be found in only a few mines in the world. Now remember the number of diamonds. According to the paper, there were fifteen diamonds exactly, weighing two carats each – save two of them which were instead three carats. That is the precise amount, colour, and weight of diamonds which, when connected on a string, made up the necklace worn by Lady Marie Cavendish, *née* Devereaux, the late widowed Countess of Devonshire – a charming French woman indeed, who had the honour of marrying the Earl of Devonshire before his untimely death. She married once again, years later. I recall her stately figure and jewelled necklace only because I've seen her photograph so many times in the news."

"Lady Cavendish!" I said. "Was she not murdered three years ago by her own husband?"

"Murdered, yes. The identity of the murderer, however, is a trifle more obscure. I was even called to investigate the case, but it presented no features of interest to me at the time."

"Does she, then, have something to do with Birmingham's murder?"

Holmes chuckled. "Ah, Watson – I can always depend upon you to be the most practical man in the room. Yes, I fancy that she does – or, rather, *did* – have something to do with it. I'm to visit the library's newspaper archives tomorrow, and when I return, I shall inform you of what I find. Now, it is rather late. I recommend that you get some rest, as tomorrow shall hold many more adventures. Good night!"

I took his advice and headed up to my bedroom and, as I began to fall asleep, I could hear the wailings of Holmes's violin as he droned away into the night.

When morning came, there was no sign of him. When Mrs. Hudson brought breakfast, I was compelled to eat without him. After all, it was no unusual thing for Holmes to miss meals if he was actively pursuing a case.

He stood again and opened the paper, his features filled with excitement.

I spent the whole of the morning in the deepest thought until, two hours later, Holmes returned to Baker Street, a small valise in his hand and a delighted twinkle in his eye.

"One must never underestimate the power of the press, Watson," he said as he sat in his armchair. "Indeed, what we learn of current affairs is often controlled by the distribution of news. Simply from a long visit to the archives, I've found nearly all of the missing links to this singular chain."

"I should be most obliged to hear about it."

"Well, well, there is still much which I would prefer not to disclose until the time is appropriate. However, one thing which I can tell you is that Lady Cavendish most certainly had a part to play in all this. You remarked last night that this woman was murdered by her own husband – according to the press, that is. He was never charged, let alone convicted. Do you recall the husband's identity?"

"No."

"Well then, I shall read you the article which was published three years ago."

He opened his valise, which was entirely filled with newspapers, and rummaged it until he found the one for which he was searching.

"Ah! Here it is."

He stood again and opened the paper, his features filled with excitement.

"Allow me to read it to you."

I gladly acquiesced.

> *Countess of Devonshire Murdered by Husband! Only a week after the grand marriage between the illustrious Lady Marie Cavendish and Mr. Cyril Morris, the whole of London has been in a state of confusion and incredulity regarding the unexpected murder of the bride, allegedly committed by none other than Morris himself. Such is the allegation of Morris's former business partner, Mr. Vincent Birmingham.*

"Business partner!" cried I.

"Indeed. The article continues.

> *"It's truly a horrid travesty," said Birmingham. "I don't know what it is that has changed Morris in such a way, but I hope he is ashamed for what he's done." In addition to Birmingham's allegations, there was evidence found that a man of Morris's build and description entered the house of Lady Cavendish and committed the murder.*

"There is more, but I shall not read more than is necessary. I've discovered from my quite eventful trip to the archives that the lady's husband, Cyril Morris, was the connection between Lady Cavendish and Mr. Birmingham."

"But why would he murder his own wife?"

"Indeed! That is the question. However, I have reason to believe that Morris wasn't guilty of such a thing at all. Look here. This was published three weeks before Morris's marriage. I apologise for the rather incoherent order of all this, but when you ask such questions, I am compelled to dig further into the past."

He reached into the valise and pulled out another paper:

> *Cyril Morris and Vincent Birmingham End Partnership After Four Years,* [read the headline]. *After four years of working*

together, Birmingham and Morris Construction Company has now simply become Birmingham Construction Company for reasons unknown. Neither of the two gentlemen wish to expound upon this strange and sudden decision. However, as shown from a photograph taken by one of our reporters, Lady Cavendish was seen walking and conversing with Mr. Morris, and there is much local gossip that perhaps the reason for the partners going their own ways is much more personal that it first appeared.

"Of course, the press never can resist a good matter of gossip," said Sherlock Holmes with a smile. "However, there does appear to be a ring of truth in what the article said. I suspect that there was some sort of feud between the two partners, and that it revolved in one way or another around Lady Cavendish."

"But what about Morris? You said you didn't suspect him of murdering his wife."

"I do not. I believe he was falsely incriminated, though I have a few things I should like to clear up regarding that."

"Then according to what you're implying, it was actually Birmingham who killed Lady Cavendish."

"I suspect it wasn't Birmingham himself who did it, but rather a hired man. Vincent Birmingham was powerful, and powerful people have strong connections."

"I say – if he was truly in love with Lady Cavendish, why would he hire someone to kill her?"

"Men go to great lengths to exact revenge. All the same, I think there is more to the story than that which I can explain in simple and precise terms at present."

"I understand. What of the door-handles then?"

Sherlock Holmes had opened his mouth to reply when we heard a loud ring at the bell, the dismayed voice of Mrs. Hudson, and a pattering of naked feet upon the stairs with which I was now quite familiar. The door opened and in dashed a dozen filthy street Arabs, their faces all alight.

"Ah," I remarked, "I see you have called upon the Baker Street Irregulars to assist with the case."

It appeared that they had learned a trifle more respect after the last time in which they invaded our apartment, as they assembled themselves in a line and stood still for the most part. The boy in the middle was significantly taller than the rest, and he stood forward with an air of authority.

"As I have frequently mentioned," Holmes responded to me, "they go everywhere and hear everything that we cannot. Now, Wiggins, what have you to report?"

"I found this in the refuse bin, sir. It's the same work-apron which the construction workers wear, and there was an 'otel bill inside."

"Excellent. Here you are, then," said Holmes as he produced some silver and handed them a shilling each. "I think that shall be all. Off you go!"

"Thank you, sir!" said Wiggins, and dashed with the rest of the boys down the stairs and out of the apartment.

"This is most remarkable," said Holmes, taking the hotel bill from the pocket of the work-apron. "And now, let us see what this has to tell us."

He examined the paper, muttering some of the contents aloud as he read them.

"Date . . . rooms . . . breakfast . . . lunch . . . A-ha! Here we are. The Langham."

He handed me the bill, and I saw the name of the hotel written at the bottom of the paper.

"It is a lucky thing, I suppose," said he, "that I happen to know the manager of the Langham quite well. I solved one of his simple problems some time ago, and I believe he would be more than willing to inform me of the room number of our evasive friend."

"Then we should go at once."

"Indeed. We must learn what we can from the state of his hotel room, for I don't believe he is out of our reach just yet. Come along, Watson. We haven't much time."

In an instant, Holmes and I were out the door and dashing through the London streets in a brougham at a most furious pace. A light rain was beginning to fall, and I could hear the water-drops tapping against the glass as we rattled away. It was a curious thing indeed to see the gloomy dispositions upon the faces of the passers-by, all of whom seemed to be employed on some monotonous business while we were embarking upon a thrilling adventure.

It didn't take long – though it must have seemed like an infinity of time to Holmes, for he drummed his long, thin fingers on his knee throughout the entire trip – before we arrived at the Langham Hotel. Once we were back outside, Holmes said in a low voice, "I shall have to trouble you to wait here for a few moments before I return."

I assented gladly.

He walked into the hotel and, as I stood there and waited, I couldn't but wonder what strange yet effective method Holmes planned to employ in order to investigate the hotel room.

Within some minutes, a man came through the door in the attire of a hotel attendant with a thick black moustache, holding in one hand a large mop, and the customary hat of his trade with the other. He gave me a courteous smile.

"Right this way, sir," said the attendant.

"Thank you, but I am waiting for someone."

"There is no need, sir."

The man stared at me with a slightly enigmatic smile, and for a moment, I was rather perplexed as to his behaviour until something upon his face arrested my attention. Upon closer inspection, the grey eyes sparkled in a steadfast manner with which I was quite familiar.

"Holmes?" I whispered.

"Yes, yes, it is I. We must move quickly before we arouse suspicion. Wear this."

He handed me the attendant's hat which he was holding, and I put it on.

"That shall have to do," said he. "Come!"

I nodded and, following him, entered the hotel and walked towards the hall, Holmes having completely plunged into his rôle like a master performer. He easily assumed the nonchalant air of a man who worked in the same hotel and performed the very same duties every day. I have said it once before in a previous account of my companion, and I shall say it again, that the stage lost a fine actor when Sherlock Holmes became a specialist in crime.

Upon arriving at the correct door, Holmes took out a leather bundle from his apron and unravelled it, revealing many fascinating metal objects.

He had once, long ago, observed my curious expression when first seeing it, and explained, "It is a first-class burgling set." Now, his voice was low but eager as he worked with precision and meticulous care. "I always enjoy the opportunity to use it."

A slight smile played over his face as the clicking of the door revealed his success.

"You know, Watson, I have always fancied the idea that I would have made an efficient criminal."

The idea of a criminal with a mind like that of Sherlock Holmes was undoubtedly a startling thought.

Holmes walked inside the room before me, and I shut the door behind us.

"The manager proved to be quite helpful," explained Holmes as soon as we had entered. "Just as I thought, he was able to provide the proper room number and confirm that Mr. Cyril Morris was indeed a guest."

He turned and began to investigate the room as I glanced round at it. It appeared as though our man had left in haste, for waste-paper baskets were turned over and a few drawers were left open. Crumpled papers were scattered about the room in an untidy fashion, and it was those untidy papers which Holmes was examining at present.

"Ah!" cried Holmes, triumphantly, as he held up one in his hand which had evidently been much folded due to the creases. "I believe we have found the location of our evasive friend."

I glanced at the paper. It had a list of locations written in the spluttered grey hotel ink which was always of a poorer quality:

Liverpool
Bristol
Brighton
Manchester

The topmost three were subsequently crossed out in the spluttered ink, but the fourth was not.

"Manchester, certainly," I answered.

"Indeed. I have reason to believe it almost would have been Brighton. You observe, of course, the manner in which the ink of the line through the word '*Brighton*' is quite fresh, while the word itself is more grey. The locations themselves have evidently been written some time ago. It appears that our man made his final choice almost immediately before he left the hotel."

He lifted his thumb, which was stained by ink, to further prove the freshness of it.

"I have many times tested the visibility of the stain of ink upon one's finger at various intervals in order to deduce how much time has passed between the writing of a note and the discovering of a note. I see that my studies have not been in vain. By the clarity of the ink upon my finger, he must have left only ten minutes ago."

"He appears to be quite out of our reach now that he is off to Manchester."

"Nonsense! It is the very opposite. The net which we have crafted already begins to close upon him. If he is *en route* to Manchester, he is clearly planning to depart by train. Thus, it all falls back upon the art of deduction and its practical uses. As for which station he shall go to, the closest – and, indeed, the most efficient way to get to Manchester – is Euston Station."

Holmes checked his watch.

"By Jove! It's already ten-thirty, and the next train to Manchester leaves at eleven o'clock. We haven't much time, but if we get to the telegraph office promptly enough, we shall get to Euston before the train is gone."

"The telegraph office?" I cried. "What use have we for going there?"

"To send a wire to the head of the police forces at Euston Station to not let Cyril Morris out of their sight until we arrive, and to Lestrade to come at once. Now, we must be off, or we will be too late."

Within minutes, we were racing to Euston in a hansom at a furious pace. I could not but feel my heart bubbling over with the thrill of the chase. The hands of time seemed to be turned against us, and as we raced onward through the streets of London, I was reminded of how much more exhilarating an adventure was this compared to the fiction of great authors. How captivating it was, and so much more it all seems when one lives a life of intrigue in the stead of simply reading about it.

We arrived at the telegraph office, where I stayed in the cab while Holmes, who had already removed his moustache and apron and had donned a proper waistcoat which he had rolled up and brought with him, despatched the wires. In only five minutes, we were on our way to the Euston Station. Holmes checked his watch every minute, and by the expression which he wore, I could see that his nerves, like mine, were tense with emotion and anticipation. We were nearing the climax of this strange chase. It was so tense, in fact, that neither of us said a word to one another as we rattled away into the streets.

The trip lasted no longer than a duration of five minutes. We entered the station, and upon hearing that the eleven o'clock train was to be departing in five minutes, we made our way through the crowd which seemed to be mostly comprised of two sorts of people: Weary Londoners who wished to get away from the characteristic vapour, and delighted travellers who were glad to arrive in the heart of the metropolis. All of them, however, glanced at Holmes and me with questioning looks as we ran alongside the train which was to go to Manchester.

At the very moment in which we arrived at the platform, we saw a bearded man sitting on a bench about three yards away, wearing a broad-brimmed hat, and looking warily round at the other men and women who were waiting for the train. Upon turning his head and spotting the both of us, he gave a dreadful start, his face turning pale, and his lips parting.

"You!" cried he in a fearful voice as he rose. "I know you!"

"It is a nice thing to be recognised," said Sherlock Holmes calmly.

The man gasped for words, but none came. Instead, he rose and took a few steps backward. Then, with a sudden look of resolution, he turned round and began to sprint down the platform.

Within an instant, Holmes was bounding after him like a hound towards his prey. I too began to chase the criminal, but the sudden pressure on my leg, which was wounded by a Jezail bullet some time before, was rather taxing upon me. Nonetheless, I felt a thrill in my heart as I raced after my companion.

It indeed resembled two blood hounds after some wild animal. The man whom we were pursuing was erratic in his movements, weaving in and out of the crowd with the quick agility of a mouse. He pushed past the people which were in his way, and, in his haste, he upset a hat of alms which was held by a beggar. Holmes was consistently gaining, even as the man attempted to shake us off his trail. Soon he reached the end of the platform, and so out onto the tracks, crossing them and winding up in the middle, rendering it a dangerous place indeed to run. However, instead of deterring us – as was most likely expected – Holmes was gaining speed as the man began to stumble along. He turned and retreated to a safer platform further along the station, with Holmes and me close at his heels. There was a very tall and wide pillar near the exit, which he rounded as he glanced back with a look of terror in his eyes, evidently to gauge how far away we were. However, it wasn't in his best interest. After rounding the pillar, he ran directly into a lean little man who had been walking down the platform with a companion.

Holmes and I pulled up, breathless and panting. It quite surprised me to see the strength of the man who was run into, as he immediately held our prey in his place in a sort of embrace, with the criminal struggling to get out.

"The handcuffs, Gregson – quickly!" cried Holmes.

The lean man's companion – a rather tall, white-faced, flaxen-haired man – instantly acted, though he bore a look of confusion. A pair of glittering handcuffs was immediately clapped round his wrists.

For a moment, the criminal tried to break away from us and run, but when he saw the four of us blocking each direction, he gave it up with a moan of defeat.

"That is better," said Holmes.

"Now that we have just handcuffed this man, would you do us the great kindness of telling us who he is?" the lean man – Lestrade – asked with some perplexity.

"Gentlemen," said Holmes with a twinkle in his eye, "let me introduce to you Mr. Cyril Morris, formerly of Birmingham and Morris Construction Company, our mysterious door-handle burglar, and the murderer of Mr. Vincent Birmingham. Thus, I congratulate you, Inspectors Lestrade and Gregson of Scotland Yard. With your swift tactics and admirable tenacity, you have once again got your man."

93

He clapped his hands in appreciation and encouragement, giving me a glance with a knowing smile.

Indeed, I hadn't initially realised the identities of the two men who apprehended Morris, as every detail seemed to be blurred into one dream-like recollection. My mind was, in fact, still comprehending the rapidity of the thing. However, now that I stared in awe at the two of them, there was no mistaking that they were the Scotland Yarders to whom Holmes had wired some time ago.

"I received your telegram," replied Lestrade, "and the directions to bring a colleague. However, I had no idea of who it was that we were to apprehend. I see now that this is the very man – but the criminal behind *two* crimes? I should be most obliged if you explained it."

"And explain it I shall. I must say, you have followed my directions to the letter and have laid hands upon the very man for whom we've been looking."

"To be clear about things," added Gregson, "*I* was the one who laid hands upon him."

"Oh, that's neither here nor there," said Holmes with some impatience. "The facts are that we have all succeeded in hunting down our man,"

"I ask again, how did you find it out?" Lestrade asked. "We've been investigating the case for a couple of days."

"And I am certain that you did a marvellous job in doing so. However, I have my methods, and you have yours. Inspectors, pray sit down on this bench. That will do. You also, Watson. Mr. Morris, I am about to explain what I know of the situation. If you've anything to add, or any details to fill in, I should be most obliged."

Morris, whose face was quite full of shame, nodded once.

"Then let us begin. Lestrade had originally informed me of the case of the four door-handles which were removed from their respective bedrooms and placed upon the front steps of the houses. I confess that I thought little of it, for I had many cases on hand, but it did leave an impression of fascination upon my mind, trivial as it seemed.

"My interest and suspicions, however, were aroused considerably when I heard of the death of Mr. Vincent Birmingham, which was committed only one day later, and in a house on the same street as one of the burglaries. As I studied the newspaper's photograph of Birmingham's corpse, I took notice of the description of the diamonds which were scattered about him and upon his person. Now, here was something interesting. It was suggested that perhaps the diamonds came from his pocket or some other unknown source, but such a theory was highly unreasonable, for the diamonds wouldn't have been spread out in such a way if they had simply escaped his pocket. From such a fall, if one took into account the gravity and the posture of Birmingham, it wouldn't make any sense in the slightest.

"When Watson and I visited the location of the crime, the body had already been removed, but there was still much to learn from the house. When I examined the second floor, I confess that I wasn't impressed with the results of what I found. There was nothing which could have guided me in my investigation. Everything was as it should have been, were it an accident: The wooden boards were frayed by Birmingham's fall, and there was no trace of footprints. However, there was much more interest to be found in the attic. The boards, as you may well have observed, Lestrade, weren't at all splintered or broken in erratic places. Instead, one could feel the smoothness upon the insides. It was quite evident that they had been cut. This was no accident.

"Upon returning to the lawn where many of your constables were walking – and destroying any possibility of identifying footmarks, I might add – I spoke with the worker, Sam Perkins, who was nearby when Birmingham fell to his death. He recounted shortly the things which he saw – particularly the man who rushed down to Birmingham, whispered in his ear, and placed the diamonds before scrambling off. According to the workman, Birmingham pointed up at the attic and uttered the word 'More'."

"Yes, yes," interrupted Lestrade rather impatiently. "I already know all this. It was I who brought Perkins back so that you could hear his account of it all. Shall we move on, then?"

"I'm simply relating these facts to Gregson, who wasn't present at the time. We shall, as you wish, move on.

"It was after this when I began to fully contemplate the connections between the death of Mr. Birmingham and the singular incident of the removed door-handles. By the colour, size, and weight of the diamonds which were found on the body – and the irregularity of two out of thirteen gems – they are, as I have already explained to Watson, none other than those which were once worn by the illustrious Lady Marie Cavendish, Countess of Devonshire, the late wife of Mr. Vincent Birmingham. When we have these connections, we can begin to weave it all into one web. Gentlemen, you are likely familiar with the singular details of the death of the Countess of Devonshire and the suspected murder by her own husband – Mr. Cyril Morris here – three years ago. However, all wasn't as it appeared to be.

"Morris and Birmingham were business partners for years until there was argument which became more personal than professional. Gossip circulated quickly, and talk of the state of affairs between Morris,

95

Birmingham, and Lady Cavendish was quite widespread. Then came the infamous parting of ways between the two businessmen. Most said it was strictly professional, but after the countless cases I've studied in which some bond of brotherhood was broken when in the presence of a woman, I can easily tell you that this matter wasn't related to the company at all, but instead to Lady Cavendish. Indeed, they both were warring for her love. When Morris and Birmingham parted ways and Morris started his own small company, Lady Cavendish chose him. They were reportedly very happy.

"Many were therefore incredulous when it was reported that, just one week after their marriage, Lady Cavendish was murdered – with all indications that the crime was committed by her own husband. However, that explanation didn't satisfy me. I examined the results of the inquest, and it certainly didn't prove Morris's guilt. From the evidence gathered by your colleagues at Scotland Yard, there were indications that the culprit was a rather lean man – quite unlike the description of Birmingham, I must admit, and very much like the description of Morris. However, there are many things which appeared to my eye that the public failed to observe.

"For example, Lady Cavendish was murdered with a long and exquisite Indian dagger, and only one newspaper thought to mention that Mr. Vincent Birmingham had recently been to India for some time not long before and was an avid collector of weapons, even if only to hang them in an ornamental display. I don't believe Birmingham possessed the nerve or the skill to murder Lady Cavendish himself. Thus, he would hire one of his most trusted and loyal workers to do it for him, using the dagger in order for Morris to know who was behind the murder. If you recall, however, Birmingham didn't hesitate to immediately accuse Morris of the crime of murdering his own wife."

"And why would Birmingham do such a thing?" Lestrade interrupted suspiciously.

"Revenge, of course! Birmingham was still furious with Morris for his actions, particularly for taking the only woman about whom he cared, and marrying her. Birmingham had nothing left in his heart for Morris save revenge, and thus he decided to strike in the most painful way possible. And here we also arrive at his financial tactics – yet another way to turn Morris and his life into a disaster.

"I was remarking to Watson that most of the ways where we learn about current affairs are controlled by the press, and thus, when one is in a position of power and can control the paper, one can then control the public. Mr. Birmingham did just that. After accusing Morris of the crime, he then led everyone to believe his words by way of his statements to the press, and in doing so, he plunged Morris into financial ruin.

"The object of all this was to return fire upon Morris as an act of vengeance. However, Birmingham would not – no, he *could* not – stop there. After all, he had lost his only love, and he was already furious with Morris. Thus, he performed one last action to rid Morris of all hope and meaning in life. The diamonds from the *rivière* which Morris presented Lady Cavendish as a wedding gift were missing at the time of the inquest – this was noted at the time. If Birmingham hired one of his workers to assassinate Lady Cavendish, then the worker clearly didn't take the diamond necklace for himself – it would have been too dangerous if he was caught trying to sell it. If he took the necklace, it would only have been done in order to follow his superior's instructions. But why would Birmingham want the jewels?

"We can eliminate that he would want them for their worth, as Birmingham was quite wealthy. The only reason for possessing the jewels would be for sentimental value – or, more likely, due to the remaining bitterness in his heart about the whole affair, and for one last display of vengeance against Morris. And now, gentlemen, you understand my meaning when I repeat the old axiom of mine that when one eliminates the impossible, whatever remains, however improbable, must be the truth. We have already eliminated two courses of action, and now we are left with one.

"What did Birmingham do with the diamonds? Let us see: Birmingham Construction Company constructs every aspect of a house that one can imagine. They, with their extensive departments, build walls, windows, doors, and yes – even the door-handles."

"Upon my word," interjected Gregson, "I believe I know what it is you are implying."

"Indeed. The knob-shaped, luxurious handles which were sent off and distributed to even more luxurious houses were the perfect capsules in which he could enclose the diamonds, ensuring that Morris would never see the gems again – which were, from what I gather, the last remaining token of his dear love. Isn't that so, Mr. Morris?"

Cyril Morris nodded sullenly.

"Yes, you've got it all right. I still recall vividly the letter which that fiend Birmingham sent to me at the time of the distribution of the diamonds – anonymously, so I had nothing useful to show to the police. '*I have enclosed your precious diamonds in four luxurious bedroom door-handles, and I intend to spread them all over villas in London. Now every one of these noble house-owners shall have a little piece of Marie – every one but you.*' I felt as if my heart had been shattered into pieces, quite like the necklace which I treasured nearly as much as my wife treasured it. I kept an eye on the news for the next four villas to be constructed, but it

97

took two or three years before all of them were built, considering the company's many other projects. However, with each new villa, I docketed the addresses and was greatly anticipating the execution of a plan to retrieve them.

"However, by the time all the houses were finished, I decided upon giving up the idea of gaining the diamonds back – not because of an inability to locate them, as I had already done so, but because of the fact that I had secured a job as a carpenter under the name of Howard Carver, and at last I escaped the terrible spell of poverty in which I was trapped for so long. The idea of revenge was still in my heart, but suppressed by the meagre amount of money which I earned each week.

"Just over a week ago, I saw something in the newspaper which disgusted and enraged me beyond measure and inspired me to act: Vincent Birmingham had attended an event where he received public recognition and congratulations for his most recent accomplishments. I declare, that was all I needed to see before the fire once again lit up in my heart, and I couldn't put out – the passionate fire of love, which inevitably turned into a terrible fire of revenge."

"A fascinating account indeed," muttered Holmes. "Thank you for your additional information. It is most interesting, and it shines a little light in the dark gaps which I left unresolved in my narrative. Now, we continue to the last point upon which I would like to touch – the crime itself. Due to this sudden public recognition of your foe, you were, as you said, inspired to act. You researched it well, finding the four villas which were built by the same company, and you then burgled them on various days for their bedroom door-handles – or, rather, for what was *inside* them. After having collected all the remaining diamonds, you plotted your grand finale: The murder of Vincent Birmingham."

Morris nodded with a clear expression of guilt upon his features.

"Yes, Mr. Holmes, that is correct. I saw in the newspaper that Birmingham was to inspect the largest and most grand villa under construction, thus I came up with a plan to pose as a workman on the day before this inspection and cut the wooden boards of the attic so that when Birmingham would take a step, he would plunge to his death. When the day arrived, I went up to the attic, and at the very moment in which Birmingham stepped on the faulty boards, I saw him staring directly at me with utter terror in his eyes. He knew that it was me who had murdered him and avenged my wife. When he fell, I spread the diamonds over him in a feverish haste – I now found it easier to part with the jewels. I then ran away and discarded my work-apron so that no one could draw any suspicion or would recognise me."

"Yes, although that harmed you more than it aided you," Holmes replied. "The hotel bill which you left in the pocket of your work-apron led me to the fact that you stayed at the Langham Hotel, and from there, I asked the manager of your whereabouts. He told me with all eagerness, as I had helped him in the past, and he was more than willing to repay me. We found the list of locations to which you desired to flee and, calculating the quickest route to Manchester by train, we hurried to this very train station.

"Now we move on to the last point. One of the workers who saw you at the site reported that Birmingham pointed up at the attic and whispered the word '*More*'. While I'm sure Inspector Lestrade here spent time searching for a man by the name of Moore, it only took a bit of research before the answer was quite apparent to me: Mr. Birmingham was attempting to whisper your name – *Morris* – but died before he could finish the word. Now, sir, have you anything to add?"

"I've nothing, save the fact that if I were given the chance to reverse time and spare Birmingham, I would not change a thing. It was for my dear wife, and I would do it again a hundred times if I could."

We all sat in silence for a long moment, each of us considering the man's story. Inspector Gregson at last broke the silence.

"Incredible!" said he. "It all seems so absurdly simple now that it's explained – and yet, it truly was a remarkable line of reasoning."

"Thank you. And now, I think it's high time you were off to the police station, and Watson and I to our humble abode. I think we shall just be in time for dinner."

And thus, My Lord Mayor, I conclude this letter by summarising the current state of affairs. Cyril Morris was arrested upon the charge of murdering one Vincent Birmingham and invading the property of others, and Inspectors Gregson and Lestrade of Scotland Yard, as Holmes and I anticipated, received the credit for tracking down Morris. A friend of Vincent Birmingham, a lively Irish fellow by the name of John McCarthy, now takes Birmingham's place as chairman of Birmingham Construction Company.

As for Sherlock Holmes, I am happy to have the pleasure of continuing to work as his colleague and biographer, and thus I can report that he is always glad to solve any little problem with which you may be concerned.

Dr. John H. Watson, M.D.
Late of the Army Medical Department

Sherlock Holmes put down the letter with an expression of absolute disgust.

"Rubbish! It is complete rubbish."

I could not but be incredulous at my friend's immediate and rather frank response.

I was sitting across from him in my armchair in our rooms in Baker Street, only an hour after I finished writing this extensive letter to the Lord Mayor. I had been working at it for an entire day, and I confess that I was rather proud of this narrative which I'd carefully crafted, attempting to keep in mind all of the important pieces of evidence and fact about which my friend was so passionate.

"It makes pretty poetry, Watson. I shall give you credit for that," he continued. "Indeed, it reads as a most captivating tale for one who wants nothing more than to sit before the fire and read a fabricated novel of mystery. However, I really cannot commend you for these embellishments of the case which took place only some weeks ago. It is all so saturated with romanticism that fact has become inferior, and sentiment superior. I have often told you that detection ought to be an exact science and should be treated as such. I doubt the Lord Mayor has time enough to read these poetic ramblings."

I confess that, at the first several times in which Holmes stated such a thing, I was rather offended and hurt at these callous remarks, but as Holmes has levelled this very string of criticisms regarding my work countless times, I've become rather accustomed to this response and wasn't very much surprised by it. At the very least, I thought it was written quite well. Thus, I folded up the paper, put it in an envelope, and then placed the envelope in my coat pocket.

"I shall take my chance of that. Perhaps you should write it yourself on the next occasion in which the Lord Mayor requires a detailed explanation of a case."

Holmes smiled languidly.

"Perhaps I should."

I donned my hat and overcoat.

"I'm off to the post office. Who knows? Perhaps the Lord Mayor takes a fancy to poetry."

The Merton Friends
by Terry Golledge

As the reputation of my friend and colleague, Mr. Sherlock Holmes, grew, so did the number of cases in which he was consulted. Many were so mundane that he either provided the solution without stirring from his favourite chair, or the applicant was dismissed with the icy contempt he reserved for obvious time-wasters. Nevertheless, his work-load was prodigious, and as one case followed on the heels of the last I found little opportunity to flesh out the skeletons from my notes and diaries.

However, there is one case that will forever remain vividly in my memory – not so much for its complexity as for the sheer callousness and inhumanity displayed by the perpetrators, and also for the sense of remorse engendered in my companion.

"If only I had foreseen the course of events and taken up the case at once," he said later, and no words of mine could lift his burden of guilt.

It was a fine morning in early summer, and we hadn't long returned from Hampshire where we had extricated Miss Violet Hunter from the peril of the Copper Beeches, The lady was both courageous and beautiful, and her sweet face lingers yet in my memory. Mrs. Hudson had removed the remains of our breakfast, casting an exasperated eye on the tangle of newspapers at my friend's feet. I could never fathom how a mind so orderly as his was incapable of keeping a newspaper together. We had filled and lit our post-breakfast pipes when the muted jangle of the doorbell was shortly followed by the reappearance of our good landlady to announce that a Mr. Marcus Perry waited below.

"Will you see him, sir?"

"Why not?" replied Holmes carelessly. "Nothing else presses."

The caller, somewhat less than thirty years of age, was of medium height and build, with a frank, open face. His brown, curly hair was unruly above eyes of the same hue, and a fine moustache adorned his upper lip. His expression would have been pleasant but for the lines of worry and anxiety that now shadowed it, and his whole bearing had the signs of suppressed agitation. "Come in, sir!" cried Holmes, unfolding his long limbs to greet our visitor with a vigorous handshake. "You are most welcome. Be seated, I beg you."

Perry lowered himself into the chair so placed that the light from the window fell directly on to his face. "Thank you, Mr. Holmes. It is very good of you to see me so promptly, for I know you must be a busy man."

"Nonsense, Anything you have to say may be said in the presence of my friend and confidant, Dr. Watson. Pray feel free to fill your pipe with the Fantail Mixture which you favour, and then tell me what brings you from Bromley so urgently."

Our caller's jaw fell in amazement, "I have read of your powers of deduction, sir, but it is beyond belief that you could have read so much within minutes of my entry."

My companion shrugged. "It was no great feat. The distinctive aroma of your tobacco clings to your garments. That particular blend of burley, latakia, and fire-cured leaf is peculiar to John Myers, who has a small shop in the Market Square of Bromley, and isn't widely known farther afield." He smiled. "I venture to suggest that while your eyesight is reasonably good, you occasionally wear *pince-nez*, denoting an acquaintance with books. You are a bachelor, and your hurried breakfast included a soft-boiled egg. Beyond that I know nothing of you."

"You are correct in every detail, but how – ?"

"Merely logical observation. The faint but definite marks on the bridge of your nose, and the black ribbon leading from your lapel to your breast pocket suggest the *pince-nez*. A trace of egg on your moustache points to a hastily eaten breakfast, and no caring spouse would allow you to leave home thus adorned." He raised a hand to stop further comment. "Now, sir, to the purpose of your visit, if you please. You have my full attention."

Perry began to charge his pipe from a soft leather pouch. "I own a small bookshop in Bromley, but my concern is for my sister Charlotte," he began. "Some two-and-a-half years ago, at the age of twenty-four, she formed an attachment for a Mr. Julius Swan, much against the wishes of my mother and myself. On her twenty-fifth birthday, she announced her intention of marrying him, and as she was of age we were helpless."

"You disapproved of her choice?"

Our visitor shifted uncomfortably in his chair. "We didn't like the man, and we found him most unpleasant in an oily way. Also he was reticent regarding his antecedents. But then we had never envisaged marriage for her at all."

"Come, sir, I don't think you are being completely frank with us," said my companion sharply. "What are you concealing?"

Marcus Perry showed signs of agitation as my colleague eyed him severely, then he went on in a low voice. "Charlotte is a good, sweet girl, and I love her dearly, but she isn't as other women. She has never matured, and although it pains me to say so, she is physically unattractive and of limited mental capacity." He leaned forward and spoke with a fierce intensity. "Do not mistake me, Mr. Holmes. She isn't an imbecile, but she needs constant care and supervision in the most simple of tasks. And," he added, "a great deal of love and affection."

"Which no ordinary husband could be expected to provide?"

"Least of all Julius Swan!"

"Yet he took her as his wife. Was there an ulterior motive? Did she take a sum of money to the marriage?"

"A tolerable amount. When our grandfather died soon after Charlotte was born, she and I had eight-hundred pounds apiece placed in trust until we were of age. That appreciated over the years, but I have never touched mine." His face saddened. "As I grew older I came to believe that my poor sister would always need caring for."

"And she took her portion to her marriage?" said Holmes keenly. "But what is your problem?"

"I am her only living relative. Father has been dead several years, and Mother died soon after Charlotte left us. I am convinced that it contributed to her death. After she married Julius Swan, she went to live at Morris Drive, Dulwich, in a household that included Julius Swan's brother Patrick and his wife Caroline. Since then I have been barred from any contact with her, even by letter, and she wasn't even at Mother's funeral! I have called at the house on several occasions, but have always been rebuffed in the rudest fashion – in most cases by Patrick Swan, who went so far as to offer me physical violence. I was told that my opposition to her marriage had embittered her, and she wasn't in a fit state to see me. Two weeks ago I made one last effort to see her, but I found The Walnuts closed and empty, and no one could tell me to where they had moved."

"So you wish me to trace her for you." My colleague shook his head. "No, Mr. Perry, I need more than that to tangle in a family dispute. Have you evidence to suggest your sister may be in danger?"

The other shook his head. "Not directly, but since I last spoke to Patrick Swan, almost a month ago, I am convinced that I am being watched and followed. I know he trailed me from Dulwich on my last encounter with him, and this very morning I saw him in the crowd at Charing Cross."

"Has he followed you here?" Holmes sounded dubious. "What would be his object in acting thus?"

"If I knew that, Mr. Sherlock Holmes, I wouldn't need your advice," Perry said with some asperity.

At a sign from my companion, I got to my feet and looked down on the busy street, but saw no furtive figure lurking below, I gave an imperceptible shake of my head and returned to my seat.

"Listen, Mr. Perry," said Holmes. "I believe you are overwrought and seeing danger where none exists."

"You don't believe me?" He seemed on the verge of tears. "You refuse to help me?"

"I did not say that. Let me have twenty-four hours to consider the matter, and I promise you shall have my answer by this time tomorrow. More than that I cannot say."

Perry stood up to leave. "Very well, sir. I cannot force you to take my worries on yourself, but you will give it due thought?"

"I have promised to do so. Good day to you, sir. Watson," he said with a lift of his eyebrows, "be so good as to see Mr. Perry to the street door and summon a cab for him." When I returned Holmes was turning from where he had been looking down from the window, his brow furrowed with thought. He raised an interrogative eyebrow at me.

"No obvious followers. I watched the cab out of sight, so perhaps the gentleman has an overactive imagination."

"And the bicyclist on the corner who pedalled off so energetically in the same direction?" he asked drily.

"I saw no cyclist," I protested.

"Perhaps I had a better vantage point at this window." He lowered himself into his chair and for more than an hour-and-a-half he remained lost in reverie, sucking furiously on the unsavoury old pipe which accompanied his deepest meditations. It wasn't until the shrill cry of a paperboy drifted up from the street that he sprang to life.

"'Orrible accident at Charing Cross! Man falls under train! All the latest!"

"What was that?" he cried. Then he was on his feet and clattering down the stairs. He came back with the paper clutched in his fist, and a grim look on his face.

"Confound it!" he said savagely, "I have been a fool! A blind, culpable fool!"

He thrust the paper at me, a bony forefinger jabbing at the smudged print of the stop press. I read it through in stunned silence:

> *A terrible accident occurred at Charing Cross Station when a man fell in front of an incoming train and was killed instantly. The platform was crowded at the time, but no one could tell the cause of the man's fall. The contents of his pockets showed him to be a Mr. Marcus Perry, a bookseller from Bromley in Kent.*

"Good Heavens above!" I gasped as I looked up at his set features. "Do you think – ?

104

"What am I to think?" he replied bitterly. "How far can coincidence stretch? That man came to me for help and left to meet his death. I owe Marcus Perry a life, a debt which I shall repay."

Seldom had I seen my friend so consumed by angry remorse, and twenty minutes later we had brushed by an outraged Mrs. Hudson, who was about to convey a succulent steak-and-kidney pudding up to our rooms. A cab took us to London Bridge Station, and not until we were on our way to Dulwich did he utter a word.

"I misread the urgency of this matter," he said glumly as we passed through Bermondsey. "Had I but heeded Mr. Perry, I may have saved his life, and perhaps delayed the peril to his unfortunate sister."

"His sister? She too is in danger?"

"Of course she is!" he said impatiently. "You took notes this morning. Marcus Perry told us he and his sister each inherited eight-hundred pounds. The lady's naturally went with her on her marriage, while his was invested against the time when he was unable to care for her, and must have appreciated considerably over the years."

"And she being his next of kin, that sum will now go to her," I said as I followed his reasoning. "You believe that her brother was murdered, and Mrs. Swan is now in considerable danger of meeting a like fate?" I shook my head. "Two deaths for less than two-thousand pounds?"

"Murders have been committed for as few pence, and it is an assumption I dare not ignore. If I err, nothing is lost."

Two other passengers alighted at East Dulwich, and the short journey to Morris Drive took less than ten minutes in the ancient station fly. The Walnuts was a square, yellow-brick pile with its windows shuttered and bearing obvious signs of neglect. It was screened from view by a high wall, with the nearest dwelling set fifty yards away.

"What now?" I asked. "Shall you enter?"

He shook his head. "No, I think not. If these people are as cunning as I think, they will have left no clue behind them." He looked along the road. "Perhaps this honest fellow can give us some information."

He pointed with his stick to the figure of a postman heading towards us.

"Good day to you, Postman," he said as the man drew near. "I wonder if you can help me." He jingled some coins in his pocket.

"What's your problem, sir?" The postman seemed prepared to talk.

"It's Mr. Swan at The Walnuts. He seems to have left in some haste."

"Them?" The man laughed scornfully. "The Lord alone knows where they went. D'ye know, in two whole years I never took above a dozen letters up there."

"Did you ever see the people?"

"I've seen them come out when I've been passing, Two blokes and a young woman – nice looker, too."

"No one else?"

"Not to say seen, but a couple of times I caught sight of a woman's face at that attic window." He nodded towards the house. "Kind of scary, it was, with a dead white face sand her hair all tangled."

"Do you know when they left?"

The postman tugged at his beard. "Now, today's Tuesday, and it wasn't last week. That's it!" he cried. "Two weeks last Saturday. I always walk through here on my way in, and I was on early turn so it must've been about five in the morning. There was a plain black van at the door, and the two blokes were loading up. They were gone by the time I'd sorted and started my walk, and that's all I know."

"No name on the van?" Holmes asked sharply. "No driver with it?"

"No, sir. Like I said, that's all I saw."

My colleague pressed a florin into the postman's hand. "What do we do now?" he said when the man was out of earshot. "It is evident they intended to slip away leaving no easy trail. Think, man, think."

I thought, but no bright flash of inspiration came. "I have only one idea," I said tentatively. "What about the cabbie at the station? Could he have picked up anything?"

"A forlorn hope, but it is more than I have come up with, so I suppose it's worth a try." He lengthened his stride, his lips set in a thin line, and we were back at the station almost as quickly as the hackney had brought us away.

The driver of the decrepit old cab was dozing in his seat, opening his eyes reluctantly when Holmes called to attract his attention.

"The house in Morris Drive you took us to. Do you remember it?" The man nodded. "Have you been there before?" Holmes flipped him a coin.

"Time or two," the driver said taciturnly.

"Do you know the folk who lived there?"

"Not to say 'know'. There was two gents and a young lady I took out there now and then, but they've been gone a couple of weeks or more, I reckon. Old Tom in the booking office might know a bit more."

We entered, and my companion put his question to the booking clerk, who scratched his head thoughtfully.

"Queer lot, them," he ruminated. "One gent used to go up to town regular, but later it was the other. Could be brothers." He frowned.

"Funny thing is he had a return ticket until he started buying a single just before they stopped coming a couple of weeks back. Charlie out there – " He jerked his thumb. "He reckons they just upped and went."

"Were there ever any women with them?"

"One young'un, but I don't know which one she was with. Tell you what, though. The taller one did ask me to look up the best way to get to Merton. About a month ago, that'd be."

"Not much to go on, but it's all we have," Holmes mused when we were on the train back to London.

"I fail to see that we have anything," I objected.

"Merton, my dear chap, Merton. A small village just beyond Wimbledon, best known for its association with Lord Nelson. It could be where the Swans have gone to ground. Have you a better idea?" he said snappishly.

I had to admit I hadn't. "But it is a long shot," I added huffily. Conversation languished. From London Bridge, we took a hansom straight to Scotland Yard where we found Inspector Lestrade in his shabby office.

Ignoring the latter's less-than-enthusiastic greeting, Holmes came straight to the point. "A man was killed this morning at Charing Cross Station," he said abruptly. "For how long can you delay the inquest?"

"Why on earth should I want to do that?" Lestrade asked with a scowl.

"Because I suspect foul play, and because a woman's life may be at risk if a verdict of accidental death is recorded now. I can say no more yet, Inspector, but trust me as you have done in the past."

"I must have more than that to interfere, Mr. Holmes."

"Say that you haven't yet notified the victim's next of kin. That should suffice, and also bring my suspects into the open."

Lestrade shook his head, then capitulated with a sigh. "Very well, Mr. Holmes. You've never let me down in the past. But," he added grimly, "I want to know the facts sooner or later,"

"And so you shall, along with such credit that accrues. When will the inquest open?"

"Thursday. I shall need a word with the constable who was at the scene, but there will be no difficulty there."

We left the gloomy building and, to my relief, took the first cab that appeared to return to Baker Street, and the prospect of food."

"What now?" I asked.

"We wait. Before long those we seek must reveal themselves, or the whole business would be pointless."

At my colleagues behest, I attended the inquest, seating myself as unobtrusively as possible. The first witness, a P.C. Parsons, affirmed that he had been on duty in the precincts of the station at the time of the incident, and was drawn to the scene by the screams and shouts of the horrified crowd. "No, sir," he answered in reply to a question from the coroner, "nobody I spoke to could say how the man came to fall."

Next, the police surgeon confirmed that he pronounced Marcus Perry dead at the scene, and he was followed by a man whom I recognized as one of Lestrade's sergeants. Due to the multiple injuries to the victim, the identification had only been possible by the contents of the victim's pockets, and in view of that, an adjournment was requested until the next of kin could be traced and informed.

At this point a surprise development occurred. A youngish, fair-haired man rose and, with great respect, asked that he might be heard.

"You have some relevant information, sir?" asked the coroner.

"Indeed I do, sir. My name is Hector Moscrop, and I am the Perry family solicitor. At this moment I am endeavouring to trace a Mrs. Julius Swan, the deceased's sister, and his only living relative. I would welcome an adjournment until such time as she can be told of this unhappy occurrence."

"Then so it shall be, Mr. Moscrop. I shall adjourn this inquiry for seven days, and I suggest you liaise with the police in the matter."

We all rose, and on leaving the room I found Moscrop closely engaged in talk with the plain-clothes sergeant.

"Why, Dr. Watson," he grinned as I approached. "I thought there was something in the wind when Inspector Lestrade spoke to me. Perhaps you would like to join Mr. Moscrop and me at the Yard."

I thought rapidly. "Why not come to Baker Street, Sergeant Groves?" I suggested. "I'm sure the good Lestrade can spare you for an hour, and you may glean something of interest from Mr. Sherlock Holmes."

Hector Moscrop's eyes widened. "You are *that* Dr. Watson?" he gasped. "The great detective's friend?"

"I have the honour of his trust and confidence, sir," I said modestly. "He is most concerned over the manner of your client's death."

Both men acquiesced eagerly, and a little later a four-wheeler dropped us at 221b Baker Street, where I found my colleague pasting cuttings into his commonplace book.

"Sergeant Groves! You are quite a stranger these days. And this gentleman – no, don't tell me. He is a lawyer representing the late and unfortunate Mr. Marcus Perry."

"That is so, Mr. Holmes. Hector Moscrop, Solicitor, of Bromley. In what manner may I assist you – or you me?" His manner was brisk and business like.

Holmes considered the attorney for some seconds. Then, liking the man's approach, he waved him and the sergeant to chairs. "Tell me, sir, without betraying confidences, how well did you know Mr. Marcus Perry?"

"Barely at all, Mr. Holmes. Of course, I knew of him as the family had long been clients of my late father, who passed on five years since, but it wasn't until the death of Mrs. Perry that I had any dealings with young Mr. Perry." He hesitated before going on. "Do I gather that you suspect an irregularity in the manner of my client's death?"

"I think we must be frank with each other, Mr. Moscrop," Holmes said. "It is my firm conviction that Marcus Perry's death was no accident, but a deliberate act of murder."

Moscrop gasped, but Holmes pressed on.

"My problem is to trace the miscreants quickly before another crime is perpetrated. Oh, I am pretty sure of their identity, but not their present whereabouts. That is why I need your help. Be assured anything you say will be treated with the utmost circumspection, and I speak for Dr. Watson and Sergeant Groves."

"Ask away. I have absolute faith in your discretion, Mr. Holmes,"

"Thank you, sir. I believe Marcus Perry's sole surviving relative is his sister Charlotte, who is now Mrs. Julius Swan. Unless he made other provisions, his whole estate goes to her. Is that correct?"

"It is. He rewrote his will at the time of his mother's death, and that is the only time I net the poor fellow. It came as something of a surprise to learn that Miss Perry had married. Let me elucidate. When I went into partnership with my father with a view to eventually taking the practice, we discussed the clients, among them the Perrys. I learned that Miss Perry was somewhat – to be blunt – less than bright."

"If we are to be blunt, I would say closer to feeble-minded," said my companion brutally. "However, she did marry, and that started a chain of events that led to her brother's death. She now inherits a considerable sum of money that Marcus had invested for the future when he thought his sister would need the care and attention he couldn't give."

Moscrop nodded. "The total sum when all is settled is likely to be well in excess of three-thousand pounds. That is taking into account the fact that he owns the freehold of his shop and living quarters at Bromley, and anything his stock may realize."

"As much as that," murmured Holmes. "A tempting sum indeed."

"What do you require of me? Anything I can do that is within the law I shall consider, if you can convince me of the necessity."

"Let me say this, sir: The longer the settlement of the estate takes, the longer Charlotte Swan may live. Can you see your way to delaying probate for as long as possible?"

"That will need little help from me." The attorney smiled thinly. "I am sure you are familiar with the leisurely processes of the law."

"I'm not so sure I should be listening to this," Sergeant Groves put in uneasily.

"Then close your ears," Holmes said dismissively. "In any case, Inspector Lestrade has been acquainted with my fears, although I have no evidence to present." He turned back to the young lawyer. "When the result of the inquest is made public, you may expect a visit from those whom I wish to trace. I need to know precisely where they are hiding out. Keep me informed of all that transpires – every little detail as far as you think is proper to your integrity as a man of law. Much depends on it."

"If a crime is contemplated, it is my duty to take all practical steps to prevent it." Hector Moscrop spoke earnestly. "I am honoured to be of assistance to you, Mr. Holmes, and you, Doctor."

In the days that ensued my colleague was restless and jumpy. When I suggested that we might hasten events by going out to Merton to make our own inquiries, he gave me short shrift. "Use your head, do," he snapped. "If these people had so much as a hint that I'm involved, the whole business could run out of control. No, we must wait." It was early forenoon on Tuesday that a telegram came from Moscrop.

Holmes threw it across to me and sprang to his feet. "Stir yourself!" he cried. "The game's afoot!"

The telegram was terse and to the point. "*Developments. Must see you here. Moscrop.*" By the time I had read it, Holmes was on his way downstairs and, grabbing my hat and stick, I hastened after him.

A train for Bromley was about to leave, and we managed to tumble into a carriage even as it began to move. Holmes uttered not a word until we alighted more staidly at our destination and had secured a four-wheeler to convey us up the hill to the town centre where Hector Moscrop had his office. We mounted the stairs to be greeted excitedly by the solicitor.

Immediately we entered he took us to his inner sanctum, telling his clerk and office boy that under no circumstances was he to be disturbed.

"You have news for us?" said Holmes as soon as the door closed.

"Indeed I have." Moscrop had an air of satisfaction about him. "It was as you surmised, but I confess to some perplexity."

"Pray continue, sir. Perhaps I can explain.

"I arrived at the office to find I had been preceded by callers whom my clerk had admitted to wait in the outer office. They announced themselves as Mr. and Mrs. Julius Swan, brother-in-law and sister of the late Marcus Perry."

"Naturally," said my companion drily. "No doubt they were eager to hear when they could expect to get their hands on your late client's money, and how much to expect."

"Indecently so, and when I explained that It could be some weeks, the man became agitated. What puzzled me though, was the lady's appearance. I had been led to expect a very different woman from the one before me."

"You interest me, sir." Holmes leant forward intently. "Describe them to me, please."

"As one would expect from a woman in mourning, she was dressed in black and heavily veiled. Nevertheless, beneath her outer garments I could discern a slim and graceful form." Moscrop blushed and hurried on.

"Although she spoke in a low voice, she was lucid, and with an instant grasp of what I said – not at all as I had been led to believe. Naturally, I asked if she had the necessary proof if her identity, and from her capacious bag she produced a birth certificate and marriage licence, together with such other documents that, had you not aroused my suspicions, would have left me in little doubt that she was who she claimed to be." He paused to sip from a glass of water at his elbow.

"What followed then?" my colleague prompted.

"The man asked what would happen now, and I explained that Mrs. Swan would have to attend the resumed inquest, and give evidence of her relationship to the deceased. At this he appeared uneasy, and the lady asked nervously if she would be required to view the body of her brother. When I said that the injuries were so extensive that identification was only possible by the possessions found on him, and also the fact of his absence from his business, both seemed most relieved." Here the lawyer gave us a self-satisfied smirk. "What I did next was to have her swear on oath an affidavit of all she had told me, which she did with same reluctance, but when she raised her veil to affix her signature I saw her to be an attractive, almost beautiful young woman."

"She actually signed the affidavit? It was properly witnessed in your presence?" Holmes's eyes gleamed.

"Of course." Moscrop sounded offended. "She signed fluently as 'C. Swan, née Perry' in the presence of my clerk and office boy."

"Capital!" Holmes rubbed his hands together almost gleefully. "If my theories are correct, we have them for misrepresentation and perjury to start with. You have done well. Now, sir, did you get an address where they might be contacted?"

"I fear that was more difficult," Moscrop confessed. "They inquired as to the amount that might be expected from the will. I was deliberately vague, and also warned them to expect some delay in obtaining probate. That was when they showed agitation. I said I would get in touch with Mrs. Swan when I had more information, but they demurred on the grounds that their movements were uncertain. They proposed that they

111

called on me at regular intervals, but I replied I didn't conduct business like a tradesman awaiting casual callers." He drummed his fingers on his desk. "Finally the man – with marked reluctance – agreed that I should contact them by writing to Wimbledon *poste restante*. Beyond that he wouldn't go. I'm sorry, Mr. Holmes, but it was all I could do."

"So be it. They will be at the resumed inquest on Thursday, of course. Describe the man to me, Mr. Moscrop."

"Tall, almost your height, with fleshy features and eyes that were cold, and never still for a minute. When he spoke his voice was harsh."

My friend pondered for a few seconds before coming to a decision. "I think the matter gathers pace. I assume that once the inquest has passed a verdict of accidental death, and accepted Mrs. Swan as Perry's next of kin, she is his sole legatee. If she dies even before the will is proved, her husband will inherit." The lawyer nodded, and Holmes went on. "This is what you must do: Write to Mrs. Swan at Wimbledon on some pretext or other, but don't post it until after the last post tomorrow. Then tell her a letter is on its way to Wimbledon. Do you follow?"

"I don't pretend to understand, but it shall be as you say. Shall I see you on Thursday?"

"We shall be there, but on no account must you acknowledge us. You will hear from me in due course. Come, Watson. There is nothing more to do immediately, so we can call on the tobacconist, John Myers, to see if his reputation is justified."

We emerged from the cramped shop some half-an-hour later, each with a new pipe and half-a-pound of tobacco apiece blended to our own taste. I had some inkling of the manner in which Holmes meant to proceed, but it came as a surprise when, on Wednesday morning, he disappeared without a word, leaving me to my own devices. It was tea-time before he returned, flopping loose-limbed into a chair to gulp thirstily at a cup of tea.

"Old friend," he said, placing his cup on the floor, "I fear there are some members of your profession unfit to called doctors."

I bristled. "That is a sweeping generalisation, Holmes! Pray explain yourself."

"I said some," he replied urbanely. "Surely you wouldn't defend Palmer, Pritchard, and their like? Of course not, but I speak of those who by reason of age or infirmity are no longer competent to continue to practise their art."

"You have a point there," I admitted. "Why did you make it?"

"Let me start at the beginning. My first call was on our old friend Lestrade, and I think I have persuaded him that a particularly callous crime is in the offing, and also that Marcus Perry's death was part of the plan. Next I went to Merton." He smiled at my raised eyebrows. "I was careful

112

not to advertise myself, but my inquiries showed that there were but two practising medical men in the area. One, a Dr. Stevens, is young and energetic. The other, Dr. Drury, is an octogenarian, almost blind and frequently the worse for drink."

"That is indeed disgraceful," I said. "But what does it signify?"

"Suppose you needed a death certificate properly issued without too many questions being posed? Would you send for a young, alert doctor to issue it when an old and senile practitioner is at hand?"

I thought for a few seconds. "I see your point, but if the doctor was new to the case, a second signature would be needed."

My companion looked nonplussed, then dismissed the objection with an impatient gesture. "If the stakes were high enough, a cunning and ruthless man could find a way around that – more so if the doctor had paid several visits to the deceased. We must proceed on that assumption."

The next morning, Thursday, we were at the venue of the inquest early, remaining outside in a convenient doorway to watch the trickle of arrivals. Hector Moscrop was among the first, followed some ten minutes later by a couple who we recognized from the lawyer's account as the pair who had visited him on Tuesday. It was easy to see why Moscrop had been surprised by the woman's appearance, for under her shapeless mourning apparel and heavy veil I could discern a woman in no way resembling the picture Perry had drawn of his unfortunate sister. The only others to enter were P. C. Parsons and Sergeant Groves – the latter, Holmes told me, sent at his insistence by Lestrade.

My colleague consulted his watch. "Now," he said, "our birds are caged for at least an hour, and for as long as Mr. Moscrop can delay them afterwards." He hailed a passing hansom which took us to Waterloo where we boarded the first train to Wimbledon. Once there, we ensconced ourselves in a pleasant tea room that commanded a view of the post office and settled down to wait. I had a fair inkling of what we were about, but it proved a long wait, and by the time our quarry appeared, I was awash with tea.

"At last," breathed Holmes, his elbow digging me sharply in the ribs. Peering through the lace curtains at the window, I saw our quarry alight from a four-wheeler. The man paused to speak to the driver, and the woman had raised her veil to reveal her as being even more lovely than Moscrop's description, although even at this distance her face showed lines of strain.

I became aware that Holmes was speaking. "As soon as they enter the post office, secure a conveyance as quickly as may be. We dare not lose them at this stage. Now!" he said urgently.

I was already on my way, and luckily secured a four-wheeler that had dropped its fare at an adjacent bank. Even so, the pair we meant to follow had already emerged from the post office and re-entered the cab that had waited for them. As it drove off, my colleague came out and said a few words to our jarvey before climbing in beside me.

We drove through the busiest part of the town, and eventually came to more open country when our cab slowed perceptibly. Holmes ducked his head out of the window and called to the driver before casting a quick look behind us. He sat down with a faint smile curving his thin lips.

"I may have maligned Lestrade in the past," he murmured, "but this time he must be commended."

"Lestrade?" I frowned. "Where does he fit in?"

"Oh, he took me at my word, and even now he is close on our heels."

"Good grief!" I exploded. "You said nothing of this! I swear there are times when you don't trust even me."

"I am sorry, old friend. With the best will in the world, I cannot think of everything, and I wasn't even sure that the good Inspector would appreciate the urgency of the matter." He looked so abject that I couldn't hold my wounded dignity, and contented myself with a snort.

After some twenty minutes, during which Holmes took frequent glances out of the window, our cab stopped, and the driver got down to speak to us.

"What now, Mister?" he asked. "They've turned off down a lane that don't lead nowhere except for one old house that was empty last I heard. They'll spot us for sure if I carry on after them." He grinned knowingly. "What's the caper, Guv – a bit of hanky-panky?"

"More serious than that," Holmes said as we got down. "This gentleman will tell you as much as you need know." Lestrade had also alighted from his following vehicle and was approaching in the company of two uniformed constables and a solidly built middle-aged woman whom I guessed to be a police matron.

"Trouble, Mr. Holmes?" asked the inspector. My companion explained the situation as Lestrade looked sharply at our driver, who appeared to be an intelligent young man.

"I am Inspector Lestrade of Scotland Yard," announced he. "These gentlemen are Mr. Sherlock Holmes and Dr. Watson." The driver caught his breath as Lestrade went on. "We are engaged in official business of the utmost importance, and you, my man, will do exactly as you are told."

"Always ready to help the law, Mister. Stand on me – Bert Scroggins won't let you down."

114

Holmes took charge smoothly. "Good man! Wait here, but be ready to come to our assistance if you are needed." He drew Lestrade to one side. "Who is your driver, Inspector?"

"Got him and the others with the wagon from the local police station. Mrs. Russell, the matron, came down from the Yard with me. What next, Mr. Holmes?"

"Better you remain in ignorance until Watson and I have the lie of the land, but be within calling distance. If I'm right, you will have the pleasure of arresting three of the most heartless and callous people it has been my misfortune to encounter in many a year."

"And if you're wrong?"

"Then you may have to arrest Watson and myself for breaking and entering, but I don't anticipate that."

Before Lestrade could remonstrate, Holmes had seized my arm to propel me quickly out of sight down the narrow lane, but we had gone less than fifty yards when we were alerted by the crunch of wheels on the pot-holed surface. I found myself dragged willy-nilly into the cover of a hedge just as the cab we had followed from Wimbledon hove into view.

"Lestrade will deal with him," my colleague said as it passed. "Hurry, time is of the essence."

We pressed on. A few minutes later we saw the house, an old, decaying two-storied place with small attic windows set in the slate roof, one of which was closely shuttered. Through the uncurtained ground floor window to the left of the front door, we could see shadowy figures moving to-and-fro, apparently engaged in an animated discussion.

"I would give a lot to hear what they are saying," Holmes muttered fractiously. "We must gain entrance to the house somehow."

"What about the rear?" I suggested. "There appears to be a path on the far side that might lead in that direction."

"Well observed, Watson. Let us explore."

The path showed little evidence of recent use, overgrown with hawthorn bushes that tore at our clothing as we made our stealthy way along it until we came to the end of the rotting fence where the track ended. A loose board came away easily in my hand, and we crept silently up the neglected garden until we reached the wall of the house, with a locked and unpainted door set in. My companion pressed his ear to it, then took out the set of lock picks he had acquired by his own mysterious methods. The door yielded in seconds, and we were in a dirty stone-floored outhouse or scullery. Now we heard voices, and although the words were muffled, I decided that they belonged to two men and a woman. With infinite care we crept closer towards the point from where the sounds came and found ourselves facing another door which appeared to lead into the house.

"They aren't in there," Holmes breathed in my ear. He opened the door a fraction to peer through the gap before easing it wider. Looking over his shoulder I glimpsed a sparsely-furnished hallway that had a flight of stairs ascending to our left, while on the other side there was a half-open door through which the voices came, raised in contentious argument.

"I did what I thought best, Julius," a man said pettishly. "We need the old fool to visit a time or two more before she gets worse. She is in a bad way."

"I'm sure Patrick was right," a woman said nervously. "He couldn't let things slide."

"And what if that confounded letter was a plot to discover where we are?" said the man called Julius in harsh, grating tones. "There was no need for Moscrop to write vague nonsense when he knew Caroline and I would be at the inquest."

"Were you followed?" asked Patrick anxiously.

"I think not, but I don't like it. Caroline, go up and put her in the next room before Drury gets here."

Holmes pulled back swiftly, leaving the merest slit through which to observe the hallway beyond. There was the sound of a door shutting, then footsteps on uncarpeted stairs.

"Our chance to see what devilry is in train," he said. "Quickly, not a sound."

He was through the door as he spoke, leaving me to follow as he tiptoed lightly along the hallway and up the stairs. He paused on the first landing, then carried on up another steeper flight that could only lead to the attic rooms before coming to a sudden halt. My view was blocked by Holmes's body, but I heard the scrape of a vesta being struck, then a metallic clink as of a key being inserted in a lock. My companion continued up, testing each tread carefully before allowing it to take his weight. We reached the top where the yellow glow of a guttering candle came from a doorway which I guessed to be the attic with the shuttered window we had seen from the front of the house. Holmes extended an arm to hold me back. Then came a stifled cry from the attic.

"Charlotte!" The woman's voice rose. "Charlotte! Wake up!" Footsteps hurried over the bare floor, succeeded by a low whimper as of an animal in distress.

"Quick!" Holmes leapt forward as if propelled by a spring, I close on his heels, all caution thrown to the winds. As we exploded into the room the woman turned, her mouth opening in a silent scream.

"Quiet," my colleague almost snarled. "Quiet, if you wish for any mercy. Doctor, there is work for you."

In the brief second that followed I saw it was the woman we had followed from Wimbledon. She had discarded her veil and outer clothes to reveal a shapely form and features that would have been almost classically beautiful in other circumstances. Now her face was chalk white, her large luminous eyes wide with fear. I took this in at a glance, but my attention was drawn to the far corner of the room to a scene the like of which I wish never to see again.

The light from single candle hardly reached the corner, but I could just discern a low truckle bed with the vague outline of a body covered by a ragged blanket. The stench in the room was well-nigh unbearable, and I hurried to open the window, throwing back the shutters to admit light and the sweet summer air before turning again to the bed. As daylight flooded in, I saw it was a woman lying there, though barely recognizable as such. The matted grey hair hung about her gaunt face like tendrils of weed, and her eyes were sunk deep in their sockets. A thin dribble of saliva ran down her chin, but apart from the faint fluttering of her eyelids there was almost no sign of life in the wasted form.

Drawing back the filthy verminous covering, I found her clad in a once-white nightgown even more soiled than the blanket. Taking her wrist to feel for a pulse, I was shocked by the fragile bones and the blue veins that stood out starkly against the paper-thin skin. Behind me, Holmes was speaking to the woman in a low, intense voice, but the words passed over me as I concentrated on my search for a flicker of life. The seconds ticked away until I looked over my shoulder to where my companion held the woman's arms in a steel grip.

"She's barely alive," I said, hoarsely, "She needs more attention than I can give – urgently,"

He dragged the woman over to the fouled bed, his face a mask of anger.

"If you have a spark of humanity in you, Mrs. Patrick Swan, you will obey my every word. It is your only hope of escaping the gallows. Do you understand what I am saying?" She nodded fearfully and he went on. "You will control yourself and summon your husband and brother-in-law. They must be together. Can you do that?"

Again she nodded, and Holmes led her to the door, still maintaining his grip on her arm. She was near to swooning, but he looked at her implacably until she took a deep breath and called out in shrill tones.

"Patrick! Julius! You must come! Patrick! Julius!"

Almost at once a harsh voice came up the stairs. "What the deuce is it, Caroline? Drury should be here any minute."

"Please, you must come!" she cried in response to a shake from Holmes. There were some muttered words from below, then footsteps pounded on the stairs. Holmes thrust the woman away and shot me a meaningful look.

I rose and retrieved my stick as two figures appeared in the doorway. On seeing me they halted their headlong rush, but my colleague shot out an arm to seize the first man and flung him across the room for me to deal with. Even as I raised my stick, Holmes was leaping at the second man.

For the next half-minute I was fully occupied. My opponent was strong, and his momentum sent me reeling backwards. He grabbed at me instinctively, partly to keep his balance, partly to ward me off. It was his undoing. His arms flailed wildly as he ran full tilt into my half-raised stick which caught him squarely in the mid-riff. The breath was driven from him, and before he could recover I felled him with an upper-cut that snapped his teeth together with a satisfyingly loud click. As he dropped to the floor, I snatched a quick look to see how Holmes was faring, but he had his man in a vicious arm-lock which forced the cursing man to his knees. The whole affair was over in less than a minute.

"Nicely done, old chap." My friend grinned wolfishly as he dragged his opponent roughly to where my victim lay with eyes glazed over. With his free hand he took a pair of handcuffs from his pocket. "Just slip these in to our two beauties, then do what you can for that poor creature." It was soon done. Then Holmes went to the open window to blow a shrill blast on a police whistle. I turned back to the pitiful object on the bed, but as I bent over her I saw now she was beyond any aid that I or anyone else could give. The pale lips fluttered in a last expiring breath, and I knew it was over for her.

I stood up and looked with loathing at the manacled figures, one still unconscious, the other mouthing a stream of obscenities. A red mist swam before my eyes and, losing all control, I drove my fist into his evil face.

While this had been going on, the woman had cowered in a corner, her face buried in her hands, and now Holmes turned to her.

"The police will be here within seconds," he said in clipped tones. "Your husband and his brother are sure to hang, but you may save yourself by turning Queen's Evidence. Are you prepared to do so?"

She raised her tear-stained face to him. "Yes, I never wanted this," she sobbed. Then she smiled slyly. "They wouldn't hang me in any case."

Before any more could be said, the front door crashed open, and a babble of voices came from the hallway below.

Holmes went to the top of the attic stairs. "Up here, Lestrade!" he called. "Bring all your men and the matron."

Soon the room was filled to overflowing, for not only had the inspector brought his own team, but had included our cabbie to add to the numbers.

While Holmes spoke to Lestrade, I took the police matron to view the poor dead woman who at last lay at peace. Death had softened her features, but even before the terrible suffering she had endured, she could never have been at all attractive.

"What killed her, Doctor Watson?" asked the matron shakily. "I've never seen a sight such as this."

"I think starvation along with general neglect, but the *post mortem* will tell us for sure." I felt revulsion and rage at the thought of so-called human beings acting thus towards this helpless woman.

"Leave it to me, sir. I'll do what is necessary." Mrs. Russell, the matron, sensed my anger and eyed me sympathetically. "She'll be avenged, have no fear."

By now the unconscious man, whom I learned was Patrick Swan, had opened his eyes. Finding himself manacled to his brother, he glared balefully at the woman, Caroline, who returned his look defiantly before turning her head away. Holmes and Inspector Lestrade concluded their brief conference, and the latter went over to the two men.

"Patrick Swan," he intoned, "I arrest you for the murder of Marcus Perry." He went on to recite the usual caution, ending with: "Other charges may follow. Julius Swan, you will be charged with being an accessory before and after the fact. Other charges may follow."

"What about her?" spat Julius.

"Mrs. Swan will be charged in due course," Lestrade said coldly. "Take them away, Constable."

Some months later, we were visited by Inspector Lestrade, who had come hot-foot from the trial of the Swan brothers.

"They'll swing, Mr. Holmes," he announced, taking a pull from the tankard of beer I had placed before him. "The woman got off, though."

My colleague nodded. "Naturally. I never believed she thought matters would turn out as they did. She was happy for Julius to marry Charlotte Perry to gain her money to share among them, but that was all. In any case, she had no idea at the start that murder was planned, and when it became obvious to her, she was afraid of them both. Besides, she did give you a lot of help, did she not?"

The inspector shrugged. "We had a case anyway, but two things tipped it her way: First, she has a pretty face, but mainly because she is in an interesting condition. What first alerted you, Mr. Holmes?"

"Elementary, Inspector. Why would any man marry an unattractive, feeble-minded woman, and then cut her off from her family other than for mercenary reasons? It was obvious from the start, but I was slow off the mark. Marcus Perry's visit to me precipitated matters and made the Swans

119

move faster than they intended. If I had grasped the urgency of the case at once, both Perry and his sister may have survived."

"Maybe." Lestrade wiped his lip and rose to his feet. "Well, I have work to do. This will make interesting reading when I retire to pen my memoirs. Good afternoon, gentlemen."

As the slam of the door was followed by his footsteps on our stairs, my companion raised a mocking eyebrow towards me. "Another triumph for the great Inspector Lestrade, eh, Watson?"

I contented myself with a snort of disgust.

The Distasteful Affair
of the Minatory Messages
by David Marcum

CAVEAT: A bit of familiarity with the events of The Hound of the
Baskervilles *would not go amiss when reading this narrative. Watson,
having recorded these events in his journals several months after* The
Hound *occurred in September and October 1888, likely had no idea then
that he'd later be publishing the Baskerville narrative, or that he might
be spoiling some details of that initial investigation's solution . . . .*

It had been less than a year since I stood before Baskerville Hall, and
while I'd always supposed that I'd return someday, being there that
afternoon was a complete surprise. When I'd arisen that morning, in an inn
a hundred miles north, I'd had no expectation of traveling later that day to
that ancient pile of weathered black stones, mullioned windows, and
centuries of dark history. But it had seemed like the best course of
treatment to prevent Sherlock Holmes from dropping into one of his black
moods.

Throughout my life, with travels and experiences across three
continents, Holmes has been the best and wisest man whom I have known,
but he has his limits. Early in our association, when I had nothing better to
do than heal from certain devastating war wounds and try to learn more
about my new flatmate, I had constructed a list, attempting to catalog what
I knew of him, but it mostly consisted of tallying what technical and
learned subjects he did or did not know. I had thrown it into the fire in
frustration before moving on to those questions of his character and
personality.

Even in those early days, I had found that he was contradictorily quite
proud of his abilities – he'd once cried, "What is the use of having brains
– I know well that I have it in me to make my name famous!" – while
curiously willing to let the police take credit for his successes.

Holmes has little patience for willing and intentional ignorance, but
if someone is curious and interested in learning or bettering themselves,
no one will make more of an effort to help than he. His sense of justice is
second to none, and those who have been victimized by the strong earn his
special attention. And yet, for every instance where I am aware of him
making an effort to aid and assist someone, there are certainly a dozen
others which I never know about. He tends toward secrecy, for a number

of reasons. He is discreet when dealing with the affairs of others, and withholds information when necessary, even from me. Additionally, he likes to keep back some of his cards until such a moment when he can make a dramatic revelation. But mostly he tends to keep a tight grip on all the threads that he's gathered, refusing to make any final declarations until he is certain he has all the facts in his possession, as well as a complete understanding of their importance and relation to one another.

Another more unfortunate aspect of his personality is his occasional tendency to fall into extended brown studies – although that has lessened markedly as the years have passed. I well remember how he'd warned me of it within minutes of our introduction to each other in one of the old laboratories in Barts on that long-ago New Year's afternoon. "I get in the dumps at times," he'd explained, causing me to smile at his forthright explanation – which was hard to credit seeing how enthusiastic he was at that moment – "and don't open my mouth for days on end. You must not think I am sulky when I do that. Just let me alone, and I'll soon be right."

We had shared rooms for a number of months before I ever saw the first signs of this aspect. Even before I knew of his profession, I was aware that he was always moving about – seeing his mysterious clients in the mornings in our shared sitting room (after I'd excused myself and retreated upstairs to my own bedroom), and then departing on various errands – sometimes returning quickly, or occasionally vanishing for several days in a row. It was only in the late spring of that first year that I first saw a sign of these "dumps" as he'd called them.

I knew he'd been burning himself rather freely. For the most part in those early days I didn't join him, as my own health was still fragile – although even then I realized that assisting Holmes on his investigations, which required me to rouse myself from the tempting womb of our comfortable sitting room, was the best rehabilitation that I could have. I came down that morning to find him very unexpectedly on the settee, wrapped in a blanket, still in his sleeping clothes. It took him quite a bit to convince me that he wasn't ill, and I finally recalled his initial warning that these moods occasionally came over him, and that eventually all would be well. And it was – within a day, a new case had captured his attention, and we were departing for Morcott, in the East Midlands.

Over the years, I had seen the same symptoms occasionally present themselves, only to depart again quickly enough, and I'd learned that some sort of distraction was usually the best way to get things back on track quickly. On the morning of which I intend to write, the ninth of June, 1889, we were in a small sitting room in a nondescript hotel, where we had just spoken with a most remarkable visitor, now departed. I glanced from the just-closed door and back to Holmes, where I could see the incipient signs of one of his dark moods stirring.

We'd just heard the confession of an elderly man in relation to a recent killing. His future son-in-law was being held for the crime of murdering his own father, and now we knew truth. But what to do with it? Both Holmes and I felt that the affair was unpremeditated and long justified. The old man had told us of the years wherein he'd been blackmailed by the dead man, and how the situation had finally become intolerable.

We were in a delicate position: We had knowledge of a killer's identity, but we were choosing not to reveal it for what we'd determined was the greater good. Did we have that right? I knew that Holmes's sense of justice confirmed the decision in his own mind, and I agreed, but that gave us no legal standing whatsoever. We'd had the killer – I hesitate to elevate the designation to "murderer" – sign a statement confessing his guilt before he walked from our door as a free man. And now we were withholding evidence.

"Well, it is not for me to judge you," Holmes had told the old man just before he left. "I pray that we may never be exposed to such a temptation." Then, when the man had gone, Holmes had murmured after a long silence, "God help us! Why does fate play such tricks with poor, helpless worms? I never hear of such a case as this that I do not think of Baxter's words, and say, 'There, but for the grace of God, goes Sherlock Holmes.'" And his voice faded away, his gaze locked on something far from that sitting room in a small hotel located near the Boscombe Valley.

When Holmes had first sent me a wire the previous morning, asking if I'd like to join him for a couple of days in the west of England, I had initially expressed reluctance, as my practice's list was rather full at that time, but my wife Mary had said, "Oh, Anstruther would do your work for you. You have been looking a little pale lately. I think that the change would do you good, and you are always so interested in Mr. Sherlock Holmes's cases."

As I went upstairs to grab my case – as I'm always a prompt and ready traveler – she had joined me, stating that she'd been worried about my state overwork in recent weeks, and that the trip would do me the world of good. She'd gone on to say that after the investigation was complete, I should extend it for a couple more days, making it a proper holiday. It was with that in mind that I suggested something of the sort to Holmes, hoping to deflect his grim ponderings from our recent visitor before they had chance to take root.

His gaze returned from wherever he'd been focused, almost looking surprised to find himself back in that small sitting room. He seemed to

123

understand the reason for my effort, as he didn't ignore my idea completely, or reply with a sigh and some snide comment that he wasn't interested. "Where do you suggest?" he asked instead. He waved a hand dismissively. "Here? Somehow I think we've already exhausted the charms of Rye."

I was at a loss, as I had considered this to be an excellent base of operations from which to explore the countryside, particularly the beauties of the nearby Wye Valley, of which I'd heard much throughout the years. Seeing that I was losing his interest, I had another thought.

"I had a letter," I said, surprised that I'd forgotten to mention it already. "Just the other day – an invitation, really. Sir Henry has returned to the Hall, and asked if we might visit him. At the time I ignored it – for how often do we find ourselves in this direction with nothing to do? But now it seems rather like a perfect idea."

In fact, I wasn't so sure. The previous fall, Holmes and I had spent an extensive amount of time in Dartmoor, over a hundred miles to the south, assisting a young Canadian who was the victim of a long-standing plot to cheat him of his inheritance. Holmes's solution, to which I admit some regret because of the danger in which our client was placed, had involved allowing the young baronet to walk unknowing across the foggy moor as bait, luring his scheming enemy into making an attack. Holmes had felt that there was no other way to conclusively catch the villain except to force him to act. Sadly, before we could reach the young man, Sir Henry Baskerville, the attack had begun, and he was somewhat physically injured in the process. Worse, however, was the mental breakdown that followed as the terror of the incident, following weeks of stress while accustoming himself to a completely new life.

It was recommended that Sir Henry get away – and he had done so, travelling extensively throughout the past winter. He'd been joined on his journey by a fellow Dartmoor resident and recent friend, Dr. James Mortimer, who left both his patients and his patient wife for the duration of the journey. I knew that however friendly Mortimer's motives had been, he was also being practical: Sir Henry's continued well-being, and his willingness to reside on the bleak moor in the ancient family home, would mean the world to the local community. Should Sir Henry move away – into London, or even back to Canada – the financial resources and support that he would provide by his presence and stewardship of Baskerville Hall would vanish, as would whatever other advantages might have benefited the nearby residents.

Now Sir Henry was home and wished to see us, and this seemed to be a perfect opportunity. Rather than give Holmes the chance to raise objections or change his mind, I set about efficiently arranging our departure. Within the hour, we were packed and on the train, first to Gloucester, where we passed the impressive cathedral on our right within a few hundred feet of the station, and then on to St. David's Station in Exeter, bypassing Bristol entirely on the way, and pausing for only a moment in Taunton. In Exeter, we weren't far from their cathedral, where Holmes and I had previously had some grim business a few years earlier, but as it wasn't directly on our way, I was unable to see it on that day.

The further we removed ourselves from the morning's earlier conversation, the better Holmes's mood seemed to be, and I was glad of it. I could see that I'd made the correct decision, and felt fortunate that the option of returning to Dartmoor had been available. Holmes had bought a stack of newspapers when we left Gloucester, and he spent most of the longer leg of the trip reading them, occasionally making comments as we headed south. He told me a bit of his brother's involvement in the passage of the recent Naval Defence Act, which led to questions whose answers revealed a bit more than I'd known about Mycroft Holmes's unique position within the government. Then, as we left Exeter for the shorter trip to Coombe Tracey, Holmes mentioned that one of the newspapers had noted that the previous day was the Feast Day of Ephrem the Syrian, and he just had time before we reached the station to relate the story of a short investigation he'd carried out for the Orthodox Church in relation to the Saint a decade earlier, in those years before I knew him when his practice was in Montague Street, alongside the Museum.

Before we'd departed Ross, I'd sent a wire to Baskerville Hall, and there was a reply from Sir Henry waiting for me at the station in Exeter, announcing that we were more than welcome and would be expected. I'd also sent one to Dr. Mortimer, but there had been no response. However, we found him waiting for us when we left the small wayside station at Coombe Tracey, with a wagonette parked outside the low white fence. He greeted us with great warmth and ushered us aboard his vehicle. Then, gigging the pair of cobs hitched to it, we lurched into motion for the final piece of our journey, leaving me impressed, yet again, with how easily it was in that modern age to journey between various regions of the country as compared to the difficulties one had faced when I was a lad.

We spent the first part of our reunion reacquainting ourselves, and Mortimer told us some details of their international journey – initially back to Sir Henry's original home in Canada, where his health had improved, even if his spirits had not. "It was the betrayal, you see, that broke his heart," the doctor explained. "He had truly loved that woman, Beryl, and he believes that she loves him – he still believes it – and he has struggled to understand how she could have allowed him to remain in danger."

125

"And your opinion, Doctor?" asked Holmes "How do you assess the lady?"

Mortimer was silent for a while. Then, "I think that she did – does – love Sir Henry as well. Any secrets she kept from him were due to fear of her husband and what he would do if she betrayed him." He shrugged. "You saw her condition when we found her – what had been done to her when she did try to warn Sir Henry."

"Where did she go after her husband died?" I asked, recalling those grim events from the previous October, and the terrible damage that he been left upon the unfortunate woman.

"Go? Why, she never left. She remained at Merripit House. I don't know the state of her funds, but I can't imagine she has much left. My wife and a few of the local women have done for her what they could, but the lady is proud, and will only accept so much charity – although she has been wise enough to at least accept some, or she would have been much worse off than she is, and much sooner too. I believe," he added as we lurched around a corner and the grade steepened, "that she has been waiting. For Sir Henry to return."

"And have they reunited?" asked Holmes.

"Not to my knowledge – and I think that I'd hear. My wife seems to know everything that happens on the moor."

As we'd progressed, the sun was lowering into the sky, although full dark would still take several hours to arrive, so close as we were to the summer solstice. We climbed gradually higher, and our gaze was constantly drawn this way and that by the jagged rocks pushing from deep inside the earth, some no more than scattered discolorations, while other great tors towered so high that they could be seen long before we reached them.

The early evening was clear, with none of the rolling fogs or sudden rains which so often swept across the area. We constantly trundled past free-roaming sheep and the moorland ponies, most ignoring us completely, while a few raised their heads to note our passing with otherwise no reaction. We went by patches of darker green contrasting with ploughed earth alongside lonely stone moorland cottages, and overhead the evening birds flew here and there, catching insects and dipping and diving to impress one another with their energy, and simply full of the joy of living in that beautiful spring setting. For it *was* beautiful, despite the grim history and mysteries of the place, and the sometimes-terrible lonely feeling that would occasionally sweep across when one is there long enough.

We had fallen into silence after Dr. Mortimer finished speaking, each with our own thoughts, and I idly watched as we reached and then passed the great tor where Holmes had stood on that night, just three-quarters-of-a-year ago, silhouetted briefly against the moon while Sir Henry and I foolishly wandered about below, searching for an escaped convict as the terrible cries of a hound echoed across the dark and ancient moor. The night had been so dark, and neither of us had been able to see much beyond our own hands, for even in the stark light of the October moon, the shadows had been absolutely black. But in spite of our limited physical vision, that search had been one of the most vivid experiences of my life, with my senses sharpened in a way that has rarely ever occurred. I doubted that I should ever forget it.

I saw that Holmes was glancing toward the tor as well, and I felt like pulling his typical trick of seeming to read my thoughts based on where he'd looked. But the mood wasn't right just then for such a glib conversational gambit, and in any case, Dr. Mortimer chose that moment to speak once more.

"He still isn't well, you know," he said. "Sir Henry. After Canada, and then traipsing around the Continent, he said that he was ready to come back here. 'Back home,' he said. I had my doubts, but I was also selfish. I missed my wife and my practice, and my studies. It's longest I've ever been away, and in spite of seeing parts of the world where I would have never been able to travel otherwise, I wanted to come home, too. So I let him talk me into it – in spite of hearing from my wife that conditions here might not be best for Sir Henry's recovery."

"Conditions?" I asked, as Holmes turned his gaze from the distance toward the doctor. "Do you mean Beryl Stapleton?" I feared some new *faux*-supernatural threat.

Mortimer nodded. "As I said, the lady of his affections is still here. Perhaps she had nowhere else to go, but my wife seems to think she's waiting for Sir Henry." His lips pursed. "As if she hasn't caused him enough pain."

I withheld comment. I understood Dr. Mortimer's protective stance, and I knew full well the lady's complicity in the previous year's crimes, but I also had been with her on several occasions, and had seen she and Sir Henry together. True, she'd been a married woman when they met, though in secret, but she couldn't have truly loved such a brute as her husband, scoundrel that he was, and if she wanted to await the baronet's return, I would not judge her.

Our day's journey was drawing to a close. The land before us dropped into a small cuplike valley, ringed 'round with bent timeworn trees that had stood for ages before the sometimes-terrible Dartmoor storms and ever-steady winds. They served to both protect the manor which we approached and to mark the boundaries of its immediate grounds. A pair of high towers rose into view, and the rest of the building became visible as we rounded a turn to find ourselves before the aged and weathered lodge gates. Each was surmounted by a large carved boar's head, curiously representing the Baskerville family. I'd always wondered why these were chosen, as the story of the legendary hound was so much more associated with them. However, I also instinctively understood that such a reminder and connection would not be something that they would wish to be reminded of, or to promote to their visitors. I wondered how many hundreds of years it had been since the last boar had traversed these lands. The fact that such was chosen as their symbol was another indication of how deep were the Baskerville's roots in this primitive and curious place.

We clattered down the avenue toward the front door. When last I'd passed this way, it had been fall and the passage was like a dark tunnel, muffled by countless fallen leaves along our path. Now the evening was still bright enough that the building itself looked interesting rather than grim, with its lichen-blotched stonework and countless mullioned windows arranged haphazardly at different levels across the face of the structure. To our right was a newer, half-constructed building which had been started by Sir Henry's predecessor, his uncle Charles Baskerville, before the man's death just over a year before, in May of '88. I could see that no work had progressed since Sir Henry had departed – not a surprise. Neither was the fact that there was no sign of the Swan and Edison electric lamps that Sir Henry had declared would be up within six months of his initial arrival.

As we waited at the door to be admitted, Dr. Mortimer whispered that the Barrymores, the servants we'd met on our first trip, had left the region for Penzance, where they used their savings and a legacy from Sir Charles to purchase a small pub. Currently the Hall's needs were being seen to by Mrs. Hayes, a local widow, who lived there with her young son. It was the former who answered the door. She was a gruff woman of middle years, her countenance dour and weathered, but she was welcoming enough as we entered the old building, and she seemed to hold no resentment about extra visitors showing up nearly unannounced. We set our bags down in the entryway, telling her that we would take them up ourselves when the time came, both being familiar with the place after our visit the previous year. That little bit of consideration seemed to thaw her just a bit.

We were led into the great room where Sir Henry was rising from a deep chair to meet us. He was the same man that I'd known before, but changed nonetheless. He moved as if he was recovering from an illness – a slowness to his movements as if he were conditioned to expect pain from every motion. And there was a gauntness to him now, with an expression that looked as if he were constantly expecting to flinch from a blow. Dr.

Mortimer saw it as well, and while I wasn't surprised, based on what I'd heard, apparently it was worse than our friend had expected.

"What has happened, Sir Henry?" Mortimer asked, taking a step forward before we could even exchange greetings. Clearly some sort of set-back had occurred.

"Nothing, nothing," the man replied nervously. Then his glance cut toward a nearby table, with an opened letter upon it. One didn't need to be Sherlock Holmes to observe such an obvious reaction.

"It's those notes!" explained Mrs. Hayes, still standing behind us in the doorway. "Fourth one since he's been home. And now those scratchings on the moor wall . . . ."

Sir Henry frowned. "That's enough!" he snapped, his voice shrill. Then, in a slightly more controlled tone, he added, "It's nothing. It's my problem. It's time I stood on my own two feet again."

"May I?" asked Holmes, stepping forward without acknowledgement or permission and retrieving the sheet.

"I've found them propped by the front door, every time," said Mrs. Hayes. "Maybe I shouldn't have delivered the others after I saw how the first one upset him. And I never would have told him about the scratchings – but Davey opened his mouth."

Sir Henry seemed as if he were trapped in some sort of electric current, jittering as if he wished to storm from the room in anger, while also paralyzed into place. Finally he dropped into his chair and sagged back, covered his eyes with a shaking hand. Dr. Mortimer knelt beside him, offering him soft words of comfort. I stepped over to Holmes's side and read the letter over his shoulder.

It was a typed note, simply stating: *You will pay. Vengeance is mine.*

Holmes looked up toward the housekeeper. "The other notes?"

She shook her head as Sir Henry replied, "I destroyed them."

Holmes handed the sheet to me for closer examination. It was on plain cheap paper, with matching envelope. I noted that the typing was uneven and, having been around Holmes enough to pick up a bit of information, I could see that it seemed to have been composed by an amateur typist who was using two fingers instead a more learned and practiced method wherein all the fingers labor equally. The envelope was similarly typed, and addressed simply as *"Sir Henry"*.

"Were the other notes of a similar nature?" my friend asked.

Sir Henry lowered his hand and looked up. Somehow having Holmes taking charge seemed to give him strength. "Not exactly. One – the first – had a Bible verse – I cannot remember which. The second something about a ghost who walks. The third . . . the third said that blood – *my blood* – will be spilled to pay the debt."

129

Holmes pursed his lips. "And you didn't keep the others."

The baronet shook his head, his eyes locked on Holmes's features. "I burned them."

"Why didn't you tell me?" asked Dr. Mortimer, rising to his feet. "I could have helped!"

"How?" cried Sir Henry, his control cracking as he sat upright. "What could you do? Is this place cursed to me even now – after what I went through? Is there no safe haven to be found here? And besides," he said, his voice lowering, "how could I ask even more of you, my friend, after you traveled with me, and worked so hard toward my recovery over these last months? I have no claim upon even more of your time."

"You have every claim!" snapped the doctor. "For the very reason that you *are* my friend!" Then he clapped his mouth shut, as if afraid to say more.

"These 'scratchings'," said Holmes, turning back toward Mrs. Hayes. "You said they're on the moor wall. Can you show us?"

She nodded, and then seemed to wait, as if to determine whether Holmes meant right then. He did, and he started toward her. From the corner of my eye, I saw Sir Henry pull himself to his feet. Dr. Mortimer took a step forward and grasped his arm.

"Is this wise?"

Sir Henry nodded, his mouth a tight line. "When – when the first message arrived, I suppose that I thought of you, Mr. Holmes – of whether you could help me. But it was too much to ask. Even with the other messages, I couldn't presume . . . But finally I – I finally couldn't wait. I wrote to you, Doctor Watson, without specifically defining the problem. Doing so at least made me feel as if I'd made some effort to fight back, little enough though it was. I had no hope that it would actually result in your visiting here. To receive your wire this morning – that you were in the area and wished to stop by – It seemed like a miracle. I was suddenly hopeful again. But then Mrs. Hayes found the latest letter, just an hour ago, and Davey told me right after what was marked on the wall, and it felt as if I'd had my feet kicked out from underneath me all over again. Now, however – having you both here – I feel as if there might be an explanation for this after all – that you will find it."

I nodded, not wishing to mention that it was only by the merest chance that we'd ended our day in Dartmoor. If not for Holmes's dark mood, and the need for a change and a distraction, with the realization that we couldn't find it in the area of Rye, we might never have even thought to journey in this direction. And then what further suffering and persecution would Sir Henry have faced?

The five of us walked through the house and out the back, toward the Yew Alley and the gate that opened onto the Moor. As we passed I looked for indications of the housekeeper's son, Davey, but saw no signs.

We reached the gate, which was at the end of the long row of ancient yews. As had been the case every time before that I'd passed this way, I glanced at the ground, fruitlessly trying to locate in just which spot Dr. Mortimer had seen the footprints of a giant hound when Sir Charles Baskerville's body had been discovered there. I glanced toward Sir Henry and saw him doing something similar. Perhaps he would never be able to walk that path without considering what had occurred there, and the evil intent that had caused it.

The old gate wasn't very high, and it squealed with disuse when we opened it and passed through. Instead of heading onto the moor, which rose before is in a distant dreamlike vision, Mrs. Hayes turned sharply to the right and led us back along the yews until they ended at a six-foot stone wall that continued on around the back of the grounds. She then pointed toward one of the wider wall stones, about five feet above the ground, which had several curious markings upon it. "Found that this morning," she explained.

Holmes thanked her and then indicated we should all stay back. Before looking at the wall itself, he bent to examine the ground before it. I could see the indications of where someone had stood, but I didn't know if they were the prints of the housekeeper or the person who had defaced the stone. Holmes glanced toward Mrs. Hayes, whose shoes were visible beneath the hem of her plain skirt.

Satisfied with what he'd seen, Holmes then took a step closer to the wall. Even from where I stood, I could see what the markings represented. They were scratched into the lichens adhering to the face of the rock – a wide triangular shape at the bottom, forming a base for four smaller elongated ovals arranged across the top of it. They could only be meant to imply the footprints of a hound – a giant one, based on the unusually large size.

The markings were clearly fresh. The newly exposed stone was white, almost gleaming in the fading light. Around the marks, the lichens had been uprooted, peeled away and hanging limp, further highlighting the stylized footprint.

Holmes had pulled out his glass and was leaning in to examine the stone further when a curious thing happened. A chip of stone suddenly exploded from one of the stones just a foot or so higher than his head. It was so unexpected that none of us save Holmes had any reaction for a second or two. He however immediately jumped back and turned, dragging Sir Henry to the ground. His action set me into motion, and I pulled the housekeeper down as well, even as we heard the echoing sound of a distant rifle shot. Dr. Mortimer remained upright, looking like a confused long-legged bird, until I hissed for him to drop like the rest of us.

I myself wanted to rise and look around – it was instinctive curiosity – but I knew that the service revolver in my coat pocket would be a useless defense from someone shooting our way with a rifle. The revolver was only accurate at a very limited range, and based on the time between the shot hitting the stone and the following sound of the gun's discharge, the unknown sniper was quite some distance from us. The good news was that whomever it was that had fired the shot was probably far enough away that he couldn't approach very quickly now that we were pinned down – assuming that this person was working alone and didn't have a nearby confederate. The bad news was that we had to find a way to get back inside the house without being exposed to further shots.

Sir Henry was surprisingly calm. I had expected more of an emotional reaction after this attempt on his life, but he seemed to have snapped out of what was plaguing him. Perhaps the idea of an actual physical enemy with a very prosaic firearm versus anonymous threats with the weight of supernatural associations gave him something to focus upon. In any case, he was calmer than Dr. Mortimer, who was muttering to himself and becoming more agitated as the seconds passed.

Holmes had crawled over to the bushes that shielded us, and he returned to report that he could see nothing on the distant moor. "I suppose that it could be a coincidence – a stray hunter's bullet hitting just where we'd paused along the wall – but I'm inclined to think that this was intentional." He turned his head to Mrs. Hayes. "As I recall, we can continue along this wall to the turn at that corner, and there's another back entrance on around."

She nodded, and I was impressed that she appeared to be more irritated than frightened. Without being asked to lead, she took that job on her own, rose to a half-crouch, grabbed her skirts, and then started along in a curious scurrying that might have been comical in another setting. We followed in a hurry, and I had the terrible sense the entire time that I was in someone's cross-hairs, but we made the corner and then the turn without further incident.

Inside, Holmes set us to making sure that the doors and windows were closed and locked, and then we gathered in one of the central ground-floor rooms. In the meantime, Mrs. Hayes had wasted no time in gathering her son, Davey, and he stood watching us silently, a boy of about eight with dark curious eyes and sandy hair.

"We cannot just hide here!" snapped Dr. Mortimer. "This attacker can't simply lay siege to the Hall until we step out to be shot."

"I suspect that all of us but one are safe," said Holmes, "unless we were to be accidentally shot if the real target is missed."

Sir Henry sighed at that. "I don't understand. I'd never planned on coming here to this place, to Dartmoor – not in my entire life – but then the inheritance was thrust upon me. Since then, it's seemed as if I'm suddenly in a boat, and the river is rushing faster and faster toward a dark destination that I can't see, and I have no way to stop or steer to the shore – I can only go forward. Since I've arrived here, it's been nothing but danger and fear and . . . and heartbreak." He closed his eyes.

"We will put an end to this, Sir Henry," said Holmes firmly, taking a step forward and gripping the young baronet's shoulder. "And I suspect before nightfall."

"But what can you do?" asked Dr. Mortimer, his skepticism threatening to undo whatever confidence that Holmes had hoped to impart. "The moor is vast. The shooter might have already vanished – or he could be creeping closer even as we speak to invade the house!"

"Calm yourself, Doctor," said Holmes. "I believe that, with a few verifications and conversations, this affair will be soon be at an end."

I already had a sense what he suspected, although he probably had a dozen reasons more than my one vague notion. He turned to me. "I'll need to slip out and move around a bit. Can you maintain calm here?"

I nodded. He didn't need to ask if I could keep things safe as well until his return. I would do my best, in spite of wishing to join him. I knew that he could move quicker alone, and that he would find the answers he needed with the quick precision of a skilled surgeon. In any case, the occupants of the Hall didn't need to be left unprotected.

"I'll be back when I can – or I'll send word. Watson, I'll have my messenger knock in the same pattern as Fleming did in the Elford affair. Do you recall it?"

I did, although it had been five years at least. I wasn't likely to forget such a grotesque and tragic murder.

Without further comment, he turned to go, but I followed him into the hallway.

"The typed messages?" I asked softly.

He nodded. "I suspect so. It fits with what we already know. As you recall, I continued to ask a few questions when the matter last fall was concluded – to satisfy my own curiosity." He gripped my shoulder as he had Sir Henry's. "Stay alert. And see what weapons you can find. Who knows what this deranged villain may try next."

Then he slipped open the front door and was gone. I saw him vanish around the corner of the unfinished building, and could only imagine what he would be forced to do in order to get away unseen from the estate.

I closed and locked the door and returned to the inner room – something of an unfurnished windowless passage between the rear of the building and those large front rooms where the Baskervilles had spent their idle hours over the centuries. I queried Sir Henry about our defenses, should it be necessary, and he led me deeper into the house to a mostly disused gun room. There were a few rifles, apparently stocked by Sir Charles before his death, that were in reasonable condition. We brought all of them back to where the others waited, along with several boxes of ammunition, and spent a quarter-hour getting them cleaned and loaded. Mrs. Hayes took a rifle, and clearly she knew what to do with it. Then we brought in some chairs from the dining room – carefully, as there were tall undraped windows there – and settled in to wait for word from Holmes. It would prove to be a long evening.

Occasionally soft conversation would begin, but it would fade away just as quickly, as if people preferred their own thoughts – or perhaps they didn't want to miss the sound of stealthy approaching steps. A few times early on, Dr. Mortimer alternately expressed outrage that we were in such a position, and then he would ask who could be responsible, but no one offered any answers. He had set his rifle aside early on, but he would reach out and touch it regularly, finding comfort in the cold steel.

Sir Henry was a curious study, and I watched him closely. He had also set his rifle down on the floor, and then folded his arms tightly, as if he were very cold. He didn't move from that position, or loosen his grip upon himself, throughout the long vigil. It appeared as if he were trying to hold himself together, and if he relaxed, even once, he would separate into pieces and slide to the floor.

I had been listening as closely as I could to the sounds which made their way into the inner room. Such a place, even one as old as that which had been settling for centuries, still had creaks and ticks as the sun set and the air cooled. It was difficult to know which sounds were natural, but I heard nothing that indicated someone was trying to enter the building – and certainly nothing as dramatic as a broken window or forced door.

It was in one of the long periods of silence in which we'd settled that Mrs. Hayes abruptly stood. "I'm getting food and drink," she whispered. "Davey, stay here," she added in a tone that didn't allow debate. Then, before I could respond, she had slipped into the darkened hallway that ran from that room to the back of the great house, leaving her rifle behind.

I stood up, rocking with uncertainty for a few seconds. Sir Henry still held himself, and Dr. Mortimer looked to me as if seeking some kind of explanation. I finally muttered, "Stay alert," and followed the housekeeper.

She was in the kitchen, efficiently setting meat and bread and a couple of jugs of something on a tray that already held a small stack of plates. She glanced up when I came in, but said nothing as she then reached for five glasses. I looked past her, toward the windows that were lit with the last of the dying June sunlight. Without approaching the windows, I tried to be aware of any threats that might be lurking there, half-expecting something to suddenly appear before me, suddenly silhouetted. Should such a one appear, would I have time to react? Forcing myself to breathe deeply, I resisted the urge to raise my service revolver and hold it ready to fire. At the same time, I cursed to myself regarding Mrs. Hayes's thoughtless impulse to seek food. "Please hurry," I whispered, my voice tight.

She spared me a glance of the sort that is recognized by men instantly, wherein the woman makes it clearly known that she will do what she wants, and in her own good time. Fortunately, she was nearly finished, with only utensils and napkins left to complete her efficiently loaded tray. Then, without comment and ignoring my offer to assist, she lifted the whole thing, pivoted, and headed back to our refuge.

After she stepped away, I moved forward once more to look carefully from the window. The view was limited across the back of the house, a distance of fifty feet or so before a series of closely planted trees separated the grounds from the moor. The kitchen being darker than the outside, there was still enough light to illuminate the portion of the grounds that I could see, and all looked well. But I knew that this was just a fraction of the entire perimeter, and our enemy – should there actually be one, and this not just the result of an errant hunter's bullet – could be approaching from an entirely different direction, even as I tarried at these unapproached windows. I hurried back to join the others.

They were already sharing out the food, humble though it was, and Dr. Mortimer's mood in particular was markedly improved, to the point that he started softly relating some tale or another of a Cavalier who had hidden on the moor in days of old in a cave otherwise reputed to have sheltered a witch. Barely had he begun, however, than I reminded him of the need for silence. He stopped speaking abruptly, and there was something of a wounded surliness in his manner after that, until I caught his attention and directed him toward Sir Henry, who was eating nothing. After that, he resumed his normal solicitous manner.

Although it was already dim in the room, we'd had some residual light by way of the adjacent rooms with their tall windows. We were near the longest day of the year, and the sun set late, but even so, it was getting darker with every minute. I dreaded when the night fully arrived, and we had nothing to do but sit in the black room, listening for every noise and adjudicating whether it indicated a threat. It was while I was pondering such thoughts that a loud knock came from the front door.

Mrs. Hayes gasped, and Sir Henry sat up straight for the first time since we'd retreated there. Dr. Mortimer half-rose with a jerk, and Davey, who had made no sound since I'd met him, gave a small whimper and leaned toward his mother.

I listened – three knocks, followed by a long silence. Then five more, with the second and fourth considerably softer. Then four more in quick succession, much faster than the deliberate effort of the others. It was the same pattern used by Clifford Fleming when he'd arrived with a surgeon during the affair of Lionel Elford's abominable inheritance.

Holmes had returned – or someone representing him who had been taught the secret signal.

Motioning for Dr. Mortimer to say where he was, I slipped through the shadowy house to the front door. Unfastening the great lock, I stood to one side, gun in hand, and pulled it open to find Holmes before me, along with a constable that I vaguely recognized from our previous visit.

"Doctor," the man nodded.

"Officer Claiborne," I responded, remembering his name just in time. Meanwhile, Holmes walked past me, into the house. The constable and I followed.

Back in the darkened room, I could just make out the faces of the others as they circled Holmes, questioning looks upon their faces.

"There is nothing to fear here," said my friend without preamble. "All is known, and there's nothing left but to confront your persecutor, Sir Henry. If you'll join us, we'll have the matter settled before another hour has passed."

The young baronet looked confused, as if he didn't understand the language. Meanwhile, Dr. Mortimer said, "I shall join you."

"There was never a doubt," said Holmes. "We have a carriage outside large enough to carry all of us." He glanced toward Mrs. Hayes. "We shall return in a few hours – might you have something hot waiting for us?"

The woman, in spite of her grim features, seemed to have a look of relief about her, and she brushed a hand across her son's head. "I will." She waited and watched without moving, however, as we all left the room, heading toward the front door.

In spite of Holmes's assurances that all was now safe, I still kept my hand resting on my service revolver, and glanced here and there around the courtyard as we all found seats within the carriage. Then, with two sizeable horses pulling us, we set out through the gate and away, back on the same track we'd driven only a few hours before.

"After the events of last fall," Holmes began without further preamble, "I continued to investigate, as there were a few unanswered questions. At the time, I felt sure that, based on what I'd learned, the matter was at an end. But your return, Sir Henry, shows that there was still a grievance against you that someone wanted settled."

"It's Stapleton," muttered Sir Henry. "You were wrong – he didn't die on the moor as you said. As you *promised*!" His voice cracked a bit then, and Constable Claiborne gave him an appraising stare, as if thinking *Is this the rich man who is supposed to do so much?* I could see that he was not too impressed by our young Canadian.

"No," said Holmes, raising his hand. "All indications are that Stapleton did indeed perish while trying to cross the mire. His carelessness – and his hubris – destroyed him. No, this was someone else who also has a grievance."

"Who, then? Who is this person?"

"All in good time. Soon, all will be known."

I looked at Holmes with a bit of irritation. As was typical, he wished to reveal the truth in his own way – as if he couldn't help doing so in a dramatic fashion. In this case, if I were him, I would have shown Sir Henry a bit more mercy and simply revealed the name then and there. I thought that I knew it myself, and was tempted to go and say it – but then I realized that I wasn't entirely certain, and this carriage was no place to debate the matter.

It was no surprise – to me at least – when I perceived that our route was terminating at a centrally located and well-appointed set of rooms in Coombe Tracey. I had been right, and the typewritten notes had been the clue. I had been working with Holmes long enough by then to recognize certain aspects of the message – the manufacturer of the typewriter, as based on the type, and various indicators by way of the two-fingered typing style. While I was unclear of motivations, I had expected that this person was involved in some way. I glanced at Holmes and saw that he recognized that I wasn't surprised, and he smiled.

When I had first visited Mrs. Laura Lyons the previous fall, I had initially been struck by her extreme beauty. The rich hazel color of both her eyes and hair were uniquely attractive, and her freckled cheeks had been flushed with rose over a complexion that one typically found on a brunette. Altogether, it was most striking, but my second impression had almost immediately been that there was something subtly wrong with her face, a coarseness and looseness which otherwise spoiled her near-perfect features.

When she'd first greeted me the previous year, it had been with a pleasant smile of welcome. Now there was no such expression upon her face. With a snarl upon seeing us, she tried to slam the door, and then leaned into it, but it was useless. The solid figure of Constable Claiborne was immovable, and with a quiet tone, he informed her that we were inviting ourselves inside "for a little talk".

I looked at Sir Henry, who appeared to be baffled. I realized that he likely had never even met the lady, although he might have heard about her. She was the estranged daughter of one of his neighbors, old Frankland of Lafter Hall, an amateur litigator who would rather fight with his neighbors than get along. In typical fashion of one of his type, he had disowned his daughter when she'd married against his wishes, and then provided no help when her scoundrel husband had abandoned her. It had been up to many in the local community to provide what aid they could, and Sir Charles Baskerville had been helped to set her up in a small typewriting business to make ends meet.

Stapleton, the man who had made Sir Henry's life such a living hell the previous year, had wooed Laura Lyons, making use of her help in his own plot. She hadn't known that he was already married, and whatever hopes she'd had for improving her own future had been dashed with Stapleton's death. I could understand that she might seek some sort of retribution.

We settled ourselves in her small parlor and I glanced over to the nearby desk, where her Remington typewriter sat, the same as it had the previous fall.

"It's late," said Holmes, "and there's no need to beat around the bush, Mrs. Lyons. Of course you know of the letters that Sir Henry has recently received – you wrote them on that typewriter. Both Watson and I recognized the typeface of machine that wrote the messages – a Remington. From our visit here last fall, I had observed that you owned a Remington and, while there may be one or two others in the surrounding area, it's unlikely that any of the other owners have a connection to Sir Henry's affairs.

"Additionally, it was obvious that today's message was typed with two fingers, but the uneven strength used for the different letters was indicative in that an effort had been made to give the impression that the message was prepared by an unskilled typist – when exactly the opposite was apparent. You would have been better off to write the messages by hand.

"Regarding the scratching of a hound's footprint on the stone wall – that was simply a lure to get Sir Henry outside so that you could take a shot at him, after having unnerved him for several days with the anonymous letters. You clearly placed scratchings there early this morning. Alongside those of the housekeeper and her son who discovered the markings, there were footprints still on the ground that match the unusual shoes you're wearing now – and were wearing last fall too. I noted them at the time Watson and I visited you on the morning of Stapleton's death, and after examining the typed notes which implied your involvement in the matter, I wasn't surprised to see the same footmarks along the wall by the stone wall. Those same footprints were also in the mud near the tor where you'd climbed this evening with your rifle, lying in wait for Sir Henry to come out and look at the markings. No doubt you learned to shoot from your father, old Frankland, when you were young.

"I suspect that you've had vengeance in your heart for months after the death of your lover, Stapleton, and when Sir Henry returned, you set out to carry it through. It's only fortunate that Watson and I happened to be on hand."

Through Holmes's recitation of the facts, as one link in the chain followed by another, the woman had expressed a gamut of expressions, from feigned shock to indifference to anger. But as Holmes finished his last statement, her expression turned to amused contempt. Then she laughed – a jarring sound in the small room.

"Mr. Sherlock Holmes – the high-and-mighty detective who understands everything. You understand *nothing!* I wasn't trying to kill Sir Henry. I was trying to kill *you!*"

It isn't often that I see Sherlock Holmes taken aback, but this was one of those occasions. He sat back, his eyes wide, as if this was a solution that he had never predicted. I imagine that the same expression was on my face as well.

"You thought you were so *smart!*" Laura Lyons snarled, rising to her feet. "You both came here that day to ask me about Jack, and then you let me know that he was married, as if it would turn me against him. You fool! Of course I knew that he was married! I was helping him with his plan! When he couldn't care for that beast out on the moors, I offered my assistance. I grew up here – I knew the moor better than he did. When he was able to kill this one – " She tossed her head toward Sir Henry. " – his wife would have been next. He and I would then be together, free to leave this cursed place and go wherever we wanted. And you ruined *everything!*"

Her voice rose, and I considered what she had revealed. I had wondered at the time about the wisdom of telling the woman that Stapleton was married. I had feared that her wrath would be overwhelming, and that she would in turn try to contact the man immediately before our trap was ready and somehow warn him. But I had underestimated Holmes, who had made additional arrangements of his own.

"You were unable to warn Stapleton that day, weren't you?" he asked. "After we revealed that we were on to him."

She nodded but didn't speak.

"Do you recall why?"

She frowned, and then her eyes widened. "Because before I could get word to Merripit House, I received a wire to meet him in Exeter, as fast as I could get there. But I went . . . ." Her voice faded, and then she swallowed and continued. "But I went there immediately, and he was nowhere to be found. There was just another wire, where he told me to stay there, in the restaurant of the Great Western Hotel until he called for me. I waited and waited, but he never arrived. I finally sent a wire back to him – "

"A wire that I intercepted," interrupted Holmes. "It was I who arranged for you to be falsely summoned to Exeter to prevent you from letting him know that he was discovered, and I also arranged to have a watch kept on you while you tarried in Exeter. When you sent the wire back to Stapleton, its delivery was prevented. I suspected that you would try and warn him – it was a perfectly reasonable response from someone who thought that she loved him and had learned she was cruelly wronged, but we couldn't allow you to disrupt our plans. Unfortunately, your message of warning was vague enough that you gave me no indication that night of your own involvement or guilt – it simply informed him that he was under suspicion. If you'd been more specific, and described your complicity in the affair, we would have arrested you then and there, and avoided today's little skirmish."

Even as the woman considered that Holmes had outmaneuvered her from the beginning, he continued.

"As I mentioned, the typewritten messages immediately alerted us to your possible involvement. After slipping out of the Hall following the rifle shot, I worked my way around to see if I could locate the shooter on the moor. You were gone by then, but indications of your unique footwear were easily located. From there, it was only a matter of making my way into Grimpen and getting a message to Constable Claiborne, and then trying to locate you while making sure this house was watched. You made it easy for use by simply returning home. Once you were trapped and corked in this bottle, we fetched Sir Henry and the two doctors, and here we are.

"I only have one question," he added. "If I was your target, why make your attempt in such a convoluted manner? You could have simply come up to London and shot me through my front window from the house across the way while I looked down upon the street."

At that, tears rimmed her eyes. "I would have done so, were I able to afford the trip. I barely get by – the purchase of a train ticket to London is far beyond my means. My father won't – He still won't help me, now more than before. I . . . I could only hope that you might return here someday – to walk into my trap. Then, I learned that Sir Henry was returning, and it seemed likely that you might visit him. From there, it was no great leap to decide that possibly I could manipulate events so that he would have to summon you, sooner rather than later. I started sending him the warnings. I have my own agent – a lad who is in my pay. He runs errands for the telegraph office. He saw your wire this morning that you were coming down later today, so I put the rest of my plan into motion. I hurried out to the manor and left another message, along with scratching the dog's paw on the wall.

"I knew that Sir Henry was bound to mention it to you. I got into position and I had you in my sites. And then . . . then you leaned over, and the rest of you dropped to the ground after my shot missed, and I realized that I'd lost my chance. There was nothing to do but make my roundabout way back here." She looked around the room, looking at the bleak four walls that must have already seemed to her like the cell she'd soon occupy, and repeated, "Here – " but that time with a grinding combination of sadness and contempt, as if her meagre existence had finally overwhelmed her. It wasn't worth pointing out that her problem was technically solved – she would soon be leaving this place and wouldn't be coming back anytime soon.

There wasn't anything left to discuss. The woman's guilt was confirmed, and her motivations explained. The constable stood, took her arm, led her to the door, and it seemed as if she had no fight left in her. Then she yanked free and spun to face my friend.

"You killed him! *You* did it! After you shot the dog, you couldn't let it drop – No, you had to pursue him into the mire! It would have been over then, and he and I could have still been together, but you had the follow him – "

Constable Claiborne had retaken her arm or I think she would have jumped forward to claw at Holmes's eyes. By then he'd risen too, watching her as if he were an alienist clinically observing the symptoms of madness.

"It would never have been over for Stapleton," he replied gravely. "Such a one as he is a cancer, and as such, his removal was the best possible treatment. It's unfortunate that your life had to be bound up with his."

"I won't forget," she countered. "He wouldn't want me to forget. They won't hang me for this. I'll survive – and I'll remember, Mr. Holmes. I'll remember that excellent suggestion of yours – to watch you from the street. When you someday look out from your window . . . ."

141

They departed, leaving the four of us in the woman's sitting room, and it suddenly felt very close and oppressive.

Sir Henry took in a deep breath and then let it out with a long shudder. He looked up from one to the other of us, as if waking from a long illness.

"I am ashamed," he said softly. "I had thought my recovery was more settled. It certainly didn't take much to knock me off the tracks."

Dr. Mortimer opened his mouth as if to reply, by Holmes spoke first.

"Nonsense. You have no reason to be feel that way. You were the victim of a terrible plot – one that was already long in motion when you were drawn into it. There is no way that a man can prepare himself for such a thing. If anyone should be ashamed, it is I. After your injuries last fall, I never had the chance to properly apologize to you – for placing you in such danger. I had a plan in place, but I never took any account of the fog. I – "

Sir Henry raised a hand. "You owe me no apology, Mr. Holmes. Without your intervention, I would have likely been murdered not long after I came to the moor. I understood that even as I recovered from my injuries. And it sounds as if you even suspected the possible danger posed by this woman here today, for you took steps to keep her from warning Stapleton on the day I was attacked."

"Apparently I suspected less than I should have," was Holmes's reply, "for I certainly never thought that I would be her target."

"Then possibly this has been useful for both of us," countered Sir Henry. "I hope that this roots out the last of my enemies, and you will have learned to be more careful yourself, as she has vowed further vengeance."

"Perhaps. In any case, you can now return home in peace."

"Home," Sir Henry murmured. 'Home. Is it, though?"

"You have the chance to find out," I offered. "No more threats await you, and you have several months of beautiful summertime to explore the moor properly – possibly, dare I add, with a certain lady who still resides here?"

Sir Henry's gaze sharpened, but he suddenly saw nothing there in the room. He wasn't looking at any of us. Rather, I knew that he pictured the woman he had loved half-a-year before, and who had loved him as well – I was sure of that. Beryl Garcia – that had been her name had been before her husband, also a Baskerville, had taken the false names of Vandeleur and then Stapleton. Originally from Costa Rica, she was now left alone in this strange land. Seeing Sir Henry's features soften as he thought of her, I was confident that she would not be alone forever.

And I was right. Holmes and I would return that fall for their wedding.

But for now, Sir Henry still needed some settling. We returned to Baskerville Hall and informed Mrs. Hayes and Davey of the details of what had happened in Coombe Tracey. The latter's eyes were wide, while the housekeeper, who knew of Laura Lyons, declared that she was not surprised at all.

Holmes's mood improved markedly from when he'd apologized to Sir Henry, and when I considered how I'd feared the approach of one of his brown studies just that morning, I was quite grateful for this unexpected trip – for more reasons than one. As I sat and sipped whisky and listened to the others talk, I pondered if there was an overall plan that had led to today's events, a higher view – something greater than all of us. In London I would scoff at such thoughts, but here, with the moor just on the other side of the walls and yew hedges and gates, where an ancientness brooded beyond our understanding, the idea didn't seem so ludicrous.

I took another sip and settled deeper into my comfortable chair.

The Adventure of the
Tired Captain
by Craig Janacek

As I have previously noted, the July which immediately succeeded my marriage was made memorable by three cases of interest in which I had the privilege of being associated with Sherlock Holmes and of studying his methods. I find them recorded in my notes under the headings of "The Adventure of the Second Stain", "The Adventure of the Naval Treaty", and "The Adventure of the Tired Captain".

The first of these, however, was of such importance that I shall likely never be able to make the details public. [1] The second on my list was also marked by an incident of national significance, and I have already put this case down upon a stack of foolscap and intend to send it round to my literary agent forthwith. The final case was quite unique, and while I anticipate substantial official opposition to it being told, I feel that I must at the very least record it for the sake of posterity. The case was both a matter of some grave concern to the powers of the land, and a comedy of sorts – for the daring rogue at its heart was an amiable sort of scoundrel.

It was a blazing Sunday afternoon towards the end of the month, the hottest day the city had seen in over eleven months. My house at Crawford Place was akin to an oven, for my wife insisted on keeping the curtains up during the day despite the uncomfortable temperature said custom would produce. Conversely, at my former suite of rooms, I knew that Holmes would likely be curled upon his sofa, the blinds fully drawn, his unsavoury pipe lit, and engaged in some deep meditation upon the criminal element of London. Consequently, I resolved to pay him a visit forthwith.

Few people were about in the middle of the day, for the glare of the sunlight upon the bricks of the pavement was almost painful to the eye. It was a far cry from the gloomy fogs and drizzling rain of winter! While the thermometer upon my wall read ninety, this seemed little hardship owing to the preparation that I had received during my term of service in India. I therefore spared the poor cabman and his horse and took my feet to Baker Street in order to call upon my former suite-mate.

To my surprise, I caught Holmes just as he was going out. Placing a broad-brimmed straw hat upon his head, he clasped my hand warmly. Although the hat served to keep the sun from his grey eyes, in these I could detect a gleam of excitement.

"Do you have a case?" I asked.

"So it seems," said he, with a smile. "It is not every day that Lestrade urgently summons me to Scotland Yard."

"Really!" I exclaimed. "That is most unusual. Lestrade typically comes round here for advice."

"Of course," said Holmes. "He does not like to admit in front of his fellows when he is out of his depth – which is most of the time. Something remarkable must have occurred in order to induce him to alter his habit. What say you, Watson – Do you fancy a trip round to Whitehall?"

"Of course. I was longing for something to do."

"You shall have it then. Whistle for a cab, will you?"

The heat had kept most traffic from the roads, so the trip progressed faster than the usual third of an hour. Holmes explained that he knew little of what we were to expect upon our arrival, for Lestrade's summoning telegram was rather terse.

"I expect, Watson, that a shower of rain will soon cool off this heat," said my friend, changing the subject.

I frowned and peered out of the cab window at the cloudless sky. "While relief from this oppressive weather would be welcome, I fail to see any chance of rain in the near future."

Holmes smiled. "Since your last visit, Mrs. Hudson installed a barometer in the hall. As I stepped out, I noted that the mercury had fallen. Even now, I feel a bit of wind picking up. You shall see. Before too long, I expect that we will have a nice little deluge. Ah, here we are at the Yard."

Inspector Lestrade was waiting for us at the entrance of the old building at Whitehall Place. Contrary to his usual dapper appearance, the wiry-framed policeman appeared flustered, and this made his ferret-like features seem even more prominent.

"It is a disaster, Mr. Holmes!" cried Lestrade. "We shall be the laughingstock of Europe if this gets out. You must find him before the press hears of this, or it will be the talk of papers around the world."

"I can hardly do so, Lestrade, unless you tell me what has transpired," said Holmes, cheerfully.

The inspector shook his head. "Mr. Holmes, the Borough of Camberwell has been robbed! It is just too incredible for words. Come with me. You too, Dr. Watson. Better you hear it straight from Corporal Miller."

Lestrade led us into one of the Yard's interrogation rooms, where a young soldier of some twenty years awaited us behind a table. He sprang up at our entrance and I could see that he was on the short side, barely four inches above five feet, with sandy hair and dull blue eyes. The uniform of the Royal North Surrey Regiment hung on his frame a bit untidily, and all-in-all, he seemed the opposite of the typical smart army corporal. [2]

"Corporal Ezra Miller," barked Lestrade, "this is Mr. Sherlock Holmes and Dr. Watson. You have orders from your commanding officer to answer all questions to their fullest, do you not?"

"I do, sir!"

"Then you will treat Mr. Holmes as if he were the C-in-C himself. [3] Do you understand?"

"Yes, sir!"

"Very good, Corporal," said Holmes. "Pray start at the beginning."

"Well, sir, earlier today, round noon, my squad – led by Sergeant Burns, and composed of myself and four privates – was marching down the Palace Road when we were challenged by a Coldstream Guards captain who was coming from the direction of the Mews." [4]

"Can you describe him?" asked Holmes.

"He was about fifty," said Corporal Miller.

"Rather old for a captain," remarked Holmes. "But there was no doubt of his uniform?"

The corporal nodded. "None, sir. Coldstream Guards for certain."

"What else?"

"Well, sir, he was a slim fellow with sunken cheeks, and tall – an inch or two above six feet. The outline of his skull was prominent about a white moustache. In his left hand, he held an attaché case. Truth be told, sir, he perhaps lacked some of the neatness typical in an officer and looked strangely exhausted."

"But you did not find that unusual?"

"No, sir. He explained why later on."

"Very well, we will get to that," said Holmes. "Proceed."

"'Where are you taking these men?' the captain asked, his gloved white hand resting casually upon the hilt of his sword. 'To the barracks, sir,' said Sergeant Burns. You see, Mr. Holmes, we were on our way back to the St. George's Barracks after a long march to the Royal Hospital Chelsea." [5]

"Yes, yes, this is clear," said Holmes. "What happened next?"

"The captain said to Sergeant Burns, 'Sergeant. You will report back to RHQ. [6] This message is for General Sir Thomas only. [7] If he is not present, you are to await his return. Tell him that Captain Black has commandeered your men and is engaged on orders from on high. Furthermore, you may say that I will follow you within the span of three hours and should be able to report a successful conclusion to my mission. Your men will be returned to your command at that time. And you,

Sergeant, may be dismissed once the General has heard your message.' Sergeant Burns nodded his understanding and saluted. Captain Black then turned to me and said, 'Turn them around, Corporal, and follow me. I have an urgent mission from the Queen Herself.'"

Holmes's eyebrows rose in interest. "The Queen you say?"

"That's right, sir. So said Captain Black. Therefore, we followed him as he marched towards Victoria Station. Outside, the captain spotted another squad – from the 117th Foot – on their way back to Aldershot. 'You men,' said he, to their corporal – whose name I learned was Knox. 'Yes, Captain?' answered Corporal Knox. 'Fall in behind,' said the captain. 'The Palace has commanded it,' he continued. Corporal Knox saluted. 'Yes, Captain,' said he. All ten of us then joined Captain Black aboard the next train to Camberwell. Although it was only a twenty-five minute ride, the captain pulled the busby down over his eyes. He said, 'I am tired, lads. I have not slept in over three days while working upon this case. Wake me when we reach Camberwell.' Well, sir, we did as he requested, and when we disembarked at Denmark Hill, Captain Black led us down the Peckham Road. He stopped in the little green area in front of the town hall. [8] There he said, 'Corporal, line these men up for inspection.' When I had done so to his satisfaction, Captain Black then ordered us to fix bayonets. 'I have an important arrest to make,' said he. 'Follow me, men!' We then ran across the street and burst into the town hall, heading straight for the office of the Mayor."

"George Langevin is the mayor of Camberwell," interjected Lestrade. "He and his wife – along with Mr. Herbert Wilton, the borough's treasurer – are waiting in the room next door. They are quite agitated."

"All in good time, Lestrade," said Holmes. He waved to Corporal Miller to proceed.

"'You are under arrest!' cried the captain at the Mayor," continued Miller. "'The Queen has declared that you are a wanted man.' Well, the mayor was not too happy about that news, sir. 'What is the meaning of this?' the mayor exclaimed. 'This is illegal!" he stammered in astonishment. 'Where is your warrant?' The captain scoffed at him. 'My warrant?' said he. 'It is in the case – and signed by the Queen herself – should anyone need to see it. My warrant is also the men I command. You!' he cried, pointing at Mr. Wilton. 'Sir?' the man replied. 'What is your role here?' asked Captain Black. 'I am the town treasurer,' said Wilton. 'Then open the safe,' commanded the captain. 'The cash reserve is to be confiscated for safe-keeping, and we shall be examining the accounts for evidence of treason.'"

"Fascinating," said Holmes. "Go on."

"Well, sir, the treasurer cried, 'Treason!' and the captain said, 'That is correct. We have uncovered indications that the mayor has been accepting bribes from German businessmen in exchange for copies of the blueprints to the local factories. The Queen has determined that such actions are tantamount to treason.' Although the mayor strenuously denied such an accusation, the treasurer rapidly complied with the captain's orders and opened the municipal safe. Meanwhile, the captain had turned to two of the privates from the 117th Foot. 'You two,' said he. 'Find Mrs. Langevin and arrest her. She will be interrogated alongside her husband. But treat her with respect.'"

"And what was in the safe?" asked Holmes.

"The Camberwell municipal exchequer," explained Lestrade, "was flush with taxes recently collected from the local residents, as well as businesses and music halls. It contained £1,557 in a mixture of notes and coins, in addition to forty-five pence." [9]

"That is a rather precise amount," remarked Holmes.

"Oh, yes," interjected Corporal Miller. "Captain Black was most meticulous about the count. He then ordered me to pack all of the money into the mayor's attaché case. When this task was complete, the captain turned to the treasurer. 'Here is your receipt,' said he. 'Stamp it and keep it safe.'"

"May I see the receipt?" asked Holmes. "Ah, this is most enlightening! It seems, Lestrade, that a Mr. James Hannen is your culprit," said he, with a small chuckle.

Lestrade shook his head. "We suspect that Hannen is an alias. He would have hardly signed his own name."

"Yes, of course," said Holmes, mildly. "What happened next, Corporal?"

"Well, sir, Captain Black searched the town hall office for some papers, while we kept the town hall officials under arrest. By the time the captain was done, the mayor's wife had arrived, as had some of the local constables. 'Very good,' said Captain Black, upon seeing them. He then ordered the constables to guard the town hall and generally care for law and order. 'In case the Mayor has any accomplices in his scheme, you are to prevent calls from the post office to London for one hour. We do not want the guards ambushed while they drive the mayor and treasurer to Scotland Yard.' He turned to the Mayor. 'There you will be detained and interrogated.' He then turned to the Mayor's wife and spoke to her in a gentler tone. 'Mrs. Langevin, I pray that you will agree to accompany them?' When she nodded her astonished agreement, he again addressed the troops. 'Two men will accompany me back to the railway station. You, Corporal,' said he, pointing at me, 'and one of your privates.' I motioned for Dick Toomey to join me. Captain Black took up the case containing the money – which balanced out the one holding his warrant. After the captain commandeered two local carriages to take the other men and their prisoners to London, Dick and I followed him back to the railway station.

"We had gotten as far as the entrance when the captain needed to sit down on one of the benches. His face was drawn, and he explained that he was still exhausted from his many sleepless nights. Captain Black pulled a watch from his pocket and glanced at the time. 'Corporal,' said he, 'I do not have the energy, but if you two men run, you have just enough time to make the 1:20 train back to Victoria. Take this.' He slid the mayor's case over to me. 'Report immediately to Scotland Yard. Tell them that Captain Black will be on the next train and will join you presently.' I began to reach for the case, when he paused and looked at me and Dick significantly. 'This is a great deal of money, men. You understand that we have counted it precisely, and if a penny were to go missing, it would be noticed. You seem like bright lads and I would hate to see a court-martial in your future.' I stiffened at this insinuation and guaranteed that the money would be delivered safely. Captain Black smiled and said, 'Good man. Now go. And hurry!' So Dick and I ran off to catch the train. We then came straight up the Mall and presented our charge to the inspector here."

"Corporal Miller and Private Toomey reported in at a few minutes after two o'clock," said Lestrade. "I was rather baffled, for no one had notified the C.I.D. about any of this. Corporal Knox and the remaining men appeared fifteen minutes later, with their prisoners in tow. I sent a constable 'round to the Barracks to inquire about what they would have me do, but he returned with a puzzled note that no one had heard anything about the Queen demanding the interrogation of the Mayor of Camberwell or his wife, and they had no Captain Black in their ranks. I sent another message over, and presently, the head of the Guards himself arrived in order to resolve the situation. The general explained that no one at RHQ had received any such orders, and he had sent a colonel over to the Palace for an explanation. When the colonel returned saying that neither the Queen nor any member of her staff had issued orders to that effect, General Sir Thomas decided to see for himself what was going on."

"Therefore, you opened the attaché case," said Holmes. "Wherein you found a considerable supply of lead ingots."

"That is correct, Mr. Holmes!" responded Lestrade. "How did you know?"

Holmes shrugged. "It is what I would have done in his stead." He turned to Corporal Miller. "I presume, Corporal, that the case carried by

Captain Black when you first encountered him was exceedingly similar to the one confiscated from the mayor's office?"

"That is accurate, sir," said Miller, his face red and his voice tinged with chagrin. "Almost identical."

"Do not blame yourself, Corporal," said Holmes, kindly. "You were passed a heavy case by your superior officer. You were told that the other case that he carried only held papers. Plainly, a case containing papers alone would not weigh as much as the one you were given. Hence, why would you have any reason to doubt that the case that you received contained anything other than the contents of the Camberwell borough safe?"

"Thank you, sir," said Miller, gratefully. "But I am not sure that the general sees it that way. I think the lot of us are going to be drummed out."

"Well, once matters are resolved, I shall see if I may possibly persuade him otherwise." Holmes turned back to the inspector. "Now then, Lestrade, I would like to see Captain Black's former prisoners.

The room next door contained two men and a woman. We were first introduced to Mr. George Langevin. The Mayor of Camberwell was a mild-looking fellow in his late thirties, with *pince-nez* spectacles over blue eyes, a pointed goatee, and a large well-groomed moustache.

Holmes asked Langevin to tell his version of the tale, which precisely matched what Corporal Miller had reported.

"I presume, Mayor Langevin," said Holmes, "that you have not had any recent dealings with German businessmen, as insinuated by the supposed Captain Black?"

"Certainly not!" said the man, hotly. "However, I could hardly protest when an armed band storms my office. I figured it was safer to comply and allow it to be sorted out in due time by the proper authorities."

"That was a wise choice, and as far as I am aware, you may be absolved of any blame in this matter. However, there is the unfortunate problem of your empty safe."

The mayor shook his head and turned to the other man. "I don't know why you gave over the money so readily, Herbert," said he, in an accusing tone.

Mr. Wilton was a man of about fifty, short and rather portly, with a fleshy face upon which resided a look that I interpreted as extreme mortification at being embroiled in such a scandal. "The man had a warrant – or he said he did, at least – and how else could he have come by the services of the soldiers?" said Wilton. "Furthermore, he gave me a proper receipt. I saw no reason to not expect the return of every penny."

"Quite so," said Holmes. He then turned to the mayor's wife. She was a handsome woman, a little short and thin for symmetry, but with a fine marble complexion and a wealth of flaxen hair. "I understand, Mrs. Langevin, that you too were swept up by Captain Black's spate of arrests."

"That is correct," said she, stiffly.

"And were you not rather surprised by this sudden detention?"

"Of course I was surprised!" she exclaimed. "But I knew it was simply a mistake. George is as honest as a mirror."

"Did you ever doubt that Captain Black was anything other than what he claimed to be?"

She shook her head. "He was so gruff towards my husband, but he was extremely polite to me. That convinced me that he was a real officer and a gentleman."

Holmes nodded. "Yes, it certainly seems that Captain Black looked and acted the part. Is there anything else that has been omitted?"

The treasurer's eyebrows rose, as an idea suddenly occurred to him. "There is one thing, Mr. Holmes." Then he paused. "On second thought, it is probably nothing."

"The smallest trifle may be of use, Mr. Wilton," said Holmes. "Pray continue."

"You heard that the captain searched the office for some papers?"

"Yes," said Holmes. "What of it?"

"Well, at the time, I thought he was looking for evidence of George's treason – I mean, *supposed* treason. Sorry, George."

Holmes appeared intrigued by this. "But now you believe that he was after something else?"

"Now that I think about it, he seemed less interested in the ledgers. And I believe that he took a paper from the blank documents that we use to issue records of identity for the registry office."

"He is planning to create a new identity for himself!" exclaimed Lestrade.

"Yes, perhaps," said Holmes, musingly. "Very good, Mr. Wilton. Here is my card. Pray send a telegram if you think of anything else."

After taking our leave, Holmes paused in the hall. Lestrade and I waited for him to say something. From the look upon the inspector's face, I believe he was as surprised as me when Holmes began to chuckle with delight.

"Is something amusing, Mr. Holmes?" said Lestrade, irritably.

"Your Captain Black is a rather bold rogue."

"He is a thief!" cried the inspector. "Over one-and-a-half-thousand pounds are missing!"

"A fair sum to be sure, but hardly something that will bring down the national economy."

"We cannot allow this man to get away with such a thing!" protested Lestrade. "It would embolden other bandits to attempt the same."

"Very well, Lestrade. I must admit that the case of the tired captain interests me very much. I expect that I should have some results for you within the next day or two."

"You believe that you can catch him?" asked Lestrade, eagerly.

Holmes shook his head. "I did not say that. At the moment, without any further data, I would estimate there is a fifty-fifty chance."

"How so?" said Lestrade, with a frown.

"Captain Black is currently either on a ferry to the Continent – in which case he is likely beyond our reach – or he has another shenanigan up his sleeve. We must hope for the latter."

"It seems impossible, Holmes," said I. "How can we possibly track down this man?"

We were seated in a second-class carriage on the Camberwell train from Victoria, apparently retracing the footsteps of the captain and his commandeered troops. Holmes had been quiet for the entire hansom cab ride from Scotland Yard to the station. His oily pipe was clasped between his teeth, and from the rapid bursts of smoke that billowed forth, I could tell that he was deep in thought. I knew better than to interrupt such ratiocinations, and that silence would be appreciated, but could restrain myself no longer.

My friend plucked the pipe from his lips and smiled. "Well, Watson, the Captain of Camberwell has left us a few meagre clues."

"Which are?"

"First, he is a man who is exceptionally familiar with the ways of the Army."

"Not an officer surely!" said I.

Holmes shook his head. "An officer can go bad as easily as a common soldier. Do not forget the case of Major Nelson. [10] But I do not insist upon Black being an officer. He may simply be a soldier who has carefully observed to the behaviours of his officers to the point where he is able to mimic them convincingly. We may imagine a man who committed some offense – theft, perhaps – that led to a dishonourable discharge."

"Surely the Army must have a list of all such men?"

He nodded. "True, though it is, sadly, a rather long list. Especially as we must go back over quite a few years. Still, let us imagine our Captain Black: Discharged from the army without a penny to his name, and no pension. What does such a man do next?"

"Try to find a job?"

152

"Yes, perhaps, if he is an honest man. Who knows, he may have even done so. However, he eventually turned to crime."

"How do you know that?"

"Because of the receipt, Watson. Did you note the name?"

"James Hannen, was it not?"

"That is correct. This was a crucial mistake on the part of Captain Black – though I suspect that the temptation proved to be too great for him to resist such a bit of panache."

I shook my head. "I do not understand."

"Sir James Hannen is a rather strict magistrate of the Queen's Bench. Clearly, the Captain of Camberwell once stood before Sir James – and the ruling was not to his liking. Now we begin to get a picture of our man – and should all other leads falter, we may always attempt to cross-tabulate the lists of men who were both dishonourably discharged from the Army and for whom Sir James stood in judgement."

"I still do not understand it. How could a man get away with such a thing?"

"Well, our tired captain has nerve, that much is true. But he also played his part well. Like any man in uniform, the captain would have looked even taller, due to his boots, smart red overcoat, and towering busby. Such an imposing stature immediately places him at an advantage over the rather short Corporal Miller."

"It seems to me that Burns and Miller are to blame for the whole mess. They should have asked the captain for identification."

"And would you have done so, Watson?" asked Holmes, his tone reasonable. "For the first thing the captain did was merely ask Sergeant Burns where his squad was going. Burns would hardly wish to risk a reprimand over such a simple question."

"But then Miller followed the captain!" I protested.

"Ah, yes! Such was his stroke of genius. You see, Watson, after the first question, the die was cast. Sergeant Burns has already addressed this stranger in a uniform as 'Sir'. The sergeant has now established in his mind that the man is precisely what he purports to be. And how unreasonable a request was it? These men march down the street upon the orders of a superior officer every day. Furthermore, the captain planned it well. He chose the hottest day of the year, when Sergeant Burns, Corporal Miller, and the privates would all be exhausted and hungry from a long march across the city. Can you truly blame them for not thinking clearly in such a situation?"

"Well then, what about the second squad – the one led by Corporal Knox? Surely they should have protested."

"And why would they? The second squad sees that the Captain is already at the head of a half-dozen men. That is all the evidence that they need that he is precisely who he claims to be. The pattern then repeats itself, one small step at a time. From the simple request for information, to the slightly larger one to follow him to the station, to the slightly stranger – but not that unusual, at the end of the day – request to board a train with him. Even the order for the fixing of bayonets was not too unusual – surely, they do it all of the time when drilling. By the time it came to arrest the Mayor, it is possible that the doubts may have begun to set in for some of them. However, by then, Miller and the other men had been following the captain for over an hour. It would have been quite difficult for Miller to suddenly ask for identification at that point – to admit that he should have done so way back at the very beginning. No, Watson, it was far too late in the day for any man to have the presence of mind to stop and challenge the supposed captain. This is the trick. Present an individual with a man who looks the part, and make your requests so smoothly and so gradually – from the reasonable to the incredible – that he will not stop to think. Poor Corporal Miller was in far too deep – he was committed and could not turn back. There is little doubt that Captain Black is a confidence man of exceptional skill."

By the time Holmes had finishing explaining his theory how the supposed Captain Black had managed to fool so many people, we had arrived at Denmark Hill. After we stepped off the train, to my surprise, Holmes did not head for the town hall. Instead, he sat down upon one of the benches at the entrance to the station and looked about him. After a minute or two, he rose and strode over to where a grizzled one-legged news-vendor displayed his evening papers. A queue had formed of people heading into London for the evening, and it was a matter of some time before Holmes could sequester the man's attention.

"Did you see," asked Holmes, "an Army captain and two soldiers come through here around quarter-past-one o'clock today?"

The man paused his hawking endeavours and peered at Holmes. "You want a paper, Guv'nor?"

Holmes handed over threepence and received in exchange a black-upon-yellow news-sheet. "The captain would have been sitting upon that bench over there," said he, motioning with the folded paper.

The news-vendor rubbed his stubbly beard and considered this. "What time did you say?"

"Quarter-past-one o'clock."

"Sorry, Guv'nor. That's the lull, it is. All the passengers have already read the morning edition, and it is too early for the evening. I usually take an hour off round then to rest my leg and take some tiffin."

154

"The Mutiny?" asked Holmes.

"That's right, Guv'nor. Not all of me made it out of Cawnpore," said he, gesturing to his missing leg, "but I am lucky compared to those poor souls who surrendered to Nana Sahib." [11]

Holmes thanked the man and turned away, disappointment plain upon his face. "There is one more possibility, Watson. Follow me."

He made his way through the crowds to a locale on the opposite side of the bench where he had earlier been sitting. There we found a young boy engaged in the task of polishing shoes. After learning the bootblack was called Sutter, Holmes repeated his question.

"Mayhaps," said the bootblack, noncommittally. "Your shoes look like they are in need of a shine, Guv'nor."

Holmes smiled and put his foot upon the boy's box. "How much?"

"A halfpenny for the shoes. And two sovereigns for the information."

"You drive a hard bargain, lad. I hope your information is worth such a princely sum."

Sutter shrugged and tipped the brim of his cap. "Times are tight. A soul must eat."

"Very well," said Holmes, handing over a pound-and-halfpenny. "Half now, and half if it proves useful. Now what did you see?"

"Just as you said – 'round quarter-past-one o'clock, an old officer and two young soldiers came through here. The officer sat down on the bench over yonder and, after talking to the soldiers for a minute, he passed them one of the two cases he was carrying. The two of them then ran off."

"And what did the captain do after the soldiers left?" asked Holmes, eagerly.

"He stood up from the bench and went over to the left luggage office," said the bootblack, waving his cloth in the direction of said locale. "I saw him collect a tattered cardboard case, and then step into the lavatory across the way."

"Very good," said Holmes. "And did you see him come out?"

"No, indeed. You see, the officer never came out."

"Never?" I cried.

"That's right, Guv'nor," said the boy, glancing at me. "But another man did a few minutes later. He was wearing a shabby suit and did not have a moustache any longer. Still, I knew it was the same man."

Holmes's eyebrows rose. "How so?" he asked.

"By the way he walked," said the bootblack, with a shrug. "He had the same curious bandy-legged gait as the officer. You spend enough time looking at shoes, you get to know how people walk." He looked over at me. "Like you, Guv. You once took a wound to your left leg, and still have a slight hitch in your step from it."

155

"You have a rare eye for detail, Mr. Sutter," exclaimed Holmes, with a smile. "What did the man do next?"

"He set down his cases, took his handkerchief from his pocket, and blew his nose, while looking about the station. After a moment, apparently satisfied by what he saw, he picked up his cases and went over to Platform One."

"Platform One," asked Holmes, intently. "You are certain?"

"As the sun will rise," replied Sutter.

"Capital!" said Holmes. "Here is your other sovereign, and a half-crown for good measure."

The bootblack beamed with pleasure over this unexpected largesse, while Holmes turned and – rather than heading into town, as I expected – walked back into the depths of the station.

"I don't understand," said I, after catching up to him. "What have we learned?"

"Several things. First," said he, beginning to count his points upon his long fingers, "as I already suspected, our Captain Black planned his escapade rather well. It was no coincidence that he happened to carry an attaché case identical to the one belonging to Mr. Langevin. He must have spent some time watching the Mayor. He also left a case holding a change of clothes here at the station. Second, he carried his handkerchief in his pocket rather than his sleeve. This confirms that the man was not an officer. Third, the captain took the train from Platform One, rather than its counterpart. Platform Two is where trains on their way to Dover and Folkestone stop. Therefore, our man returned to Victoria."

"Given what you told Lestrade earlier, that seems like good news, I suppose," said I, "but how are we to trace him? There are some five-millions souls in London."

"I wager, Watson," said Holmes, an enigmatic smile upon his lips, "that the answer lies at Baker Street."

In his usual fashion, Holmes would say no more about the case on the trip back to his suite of rooms. Instead, he declaimed widely about the flight of Boulanger from Paris, the railway disaster in Ireland, and the attempted assassination of the emperor of the Brazils. [12] When we arrived, he vanished into one of the lumber rooms, which I knew to be packed with piles of old daily papers. For my part, I sat in my old armchair and considered the facts of the case until a heaviness briefly came over my eyes.

When at last Holmes descended, it was with triumph in his eyes and a copy of *The Times* in his hand.

"What do you make of this, Watson?" he asked, dropping the paper in my lap. I picked it up and glanced over the various items on the page in question. Beside the agony column, I read through the announcements of various births, marriages, and other miscellaneous bits of news. The only entry that seemed pertinent was found at the top of the list of people who had sadly passed unto that undiscovered country. It read:

Deaths

On the first of July, at Brighton Pier: Captain James Barnard Nichols, late Coldstream Guards, of drowning, while on vacation, age 39.

"I perceive," said I, handing the paper back to Holmes, "that Nichols was a captain in the Coldstream Guards, which is an interesting coincidence."

"It is no coincidence. It is the *primum movens* of today's farce."

"How so?"

"Tell me, where is your service uniform?"

"In my closet, of course."

"Where it comes out whenever you attend a reunion of your fellows from the Berkshires, correct?"

"Yes."

"Therefore, while the uniform of a retired corporal down on his luck may potentially find its way into the hands of a civilian, we may conclude that it requires a very peculiar circumstance for the uniform of an officer to do so."

"Perhaps after his death?"

"Come now, Watson, surely you have attended enough funerals of your fallen comrades to know what happens to their uniforms?"

I frowned. "They are buried in them."

"Precisely. Therefore, it takes a most unusual situation for the uniform of a decreased army officer to find its way anywhere other than six feet under the earth."

"By Jove!" I cried. "His body must have been lost at sea!"

Holmes smiled and nodded. "That is how I read this pitiable epitaph."

"But how did Black – or whatever his name is – come by it? Surely, the grieving widow would not wish to part with such a poignant memento of her lost husband?"

"That is just the question I intend to put to Captain Nichols' surviving family." He glanced at the clock upon the mantelpiece. "It is too late to do so tonight. You should return to your home, Watson. However, if you

157

should like to see this through to the end, I would be happy call upon you in the morning."

"Certainly!" I exclaimed. "I will ask Jackson to take my practice for a day."

The following morn, which had thankfully dawned a far cry cooler than the day prior, Holmes appeared at my door promptly at nine o'clock sharp. A hansom cab waited behind us, but he stopped to first pay his compliments to my wife. This task complete, the two of us bundled into the cab and Holmes instructed the cabman to take us to an address in Fitzrovia. As we rattled our way, I asked whether he had made any additional progress on the case during the night.

"A little. I learned that Captain Nichols' wife preceded him to the grave last year after a brief illness. His sole heir is his son, Stephen, who resides at Mortimer Street."

We were soon standing at the door of the man in question, who proved to be a pale, taper-faced individual of some twenty years. He had sandy hair with a thin moustache and wisps of reedy whiskers. I did not require Holmes's powers of observations in order to deduce his occupation, which was evident from his paint-smattered stock coat and the brush that he held in his hand.

Holmes introduced us. "I am sorry for your loss, Mr. Nichols."

"Thank you," said the man, his manner somewhat stiff and uncomfortable.

"I wonder if I might ask after your father's uniform. Do you know what happened to it after his passing?"

"Of course," said Nichols with a shrug. "I sold it to a broker on Tottenham Court Road, along with the rest of the lot of his things."

"I am surprised that you did not wish to keep it," I interjected.

"And why would I? My father cared only for his precious army. He did not take kindly to the fact that I would have nothing of such violent pursuits and instead wished to fill the world with beauty. I saw no reason to keep the trinkets of his warrior ways lying about."

"Just so," said Holmes. "Do you recall to which broker you took it?"

"The one across from Morton and Waylight's."

Holmes thanked Mr. Nichols for his time, and the two of us stepped back out onto the pavement.

"Where to now?" I asked.

"Why, the broker, of course."

"Surely he must sell dozens of items every day," I protested. "You cannot possibly expect him to recall each and every customer."

Holmes smiled. "No, but I have something else in mind."

As I predicted, Mr. Rosenberg had little memory of selling an army coat, though his books confirmed such a sale for five shillings on the night of 20 July. I thought the trip around here rather a waste, though Holmes appeared rather enamoured of a sterling-handled walking stick, which he purchased for the sum of ten shillings. This transaction completed, He stepped down the road to a corner public-house called the Bedford Arms. Sitting down in the tap room, he proceeded to order two glasses from the white-aproned landlord.

While the man left to fill our glasses, I looked at my friend in puzzlement. "Are you thirsty?"

"Tell me, Watson: When you still resided at Baker Street and found yourself desiring some convivial company, where did you go?"

"The Green Man," said I.

"Why? Is their beer particularly excellent?"

"It is fair enough, I suppose, but no better than the next place."

"Then why did you habituate that particular establishment?"

I shrugged. "It was the closest."

"Precisely. *Quod erat demonstrandum.*"

"You believe that Captain Black frequents Rosenberg's shop because he lives nearby," said I, following his line of reasoning.

"I think it likely. But here is the landlord with our drinks. Let us test my theory." He turned to the barman, and asked his name.

"Rutledge," the man offered, tersely.

"I am looking, Mr. Rutledge," said Holmes, "for a man of about fifty years who I believe frequents your house. He is a slim fellow, with sunken cheeks and a prominent skull. He may or may not wear a moustache, but if he did, it would be white."

The landlord shrugged. "Lots of men come through this place, and quite a few would fit that description."

"What if I told you that he was a consummate actor, and had a remarkable ability to persuade people to do his bidding?"

"Ah, yes, that sounds like old Willie White."

"And who, pray tell, is Willie White?" asked Holmes.

"He's a common loafer round these parts."

"Do you know where Mr. White typically resides?"

"I think he sleeps rough most nights," said Rutledge, with a shake of his head. "I let him do odd jobs around here from time to time in exchange for a square meal and a few pence."

"And has he done any recently?"

The man considered this. "Now that you mention it, he came around here about three days back, asking if I had any work. I had him clean out the gutters. He wanted five shillings for the job – and would not take no for an answer. I finally gave him what he needed, just to make the poor beggar go away."

"Five shillings, you say?" said Holmes, significantly. "Very good." He reached into his pocket and pulled out a few coins. "Here are your five shillings back, Mr. Rutledge, for your information has been invaluable."

After finishing our drinks and stepping back to the pavement, I glanced over at Holmes. "What now?" I asked.

"Now comes a period of tediousness, Watson. It cannot be helped, for I find that most cases require just such a thing, though it will be of little interest to you. I suggest that you return home and catch up on what you missed regarding your patients during our merry jaunts about town. I will call upon you as soon as I have something in hand upon which we may take firm action."

I followed Holmes's suggestion and did not hear from him again that evening. However, the following morn, I was surprised by the maid gently knocking upon my door before the first rays of the sun could rise above St. Paul's.

"Begging your pardon, sir," said she, after I pulled on my dressing-gown, "but Mr. Holmes is downstairs, asking for you."

I blinked in surprise and looked at the wall clock, which showed me that it was only a quarter-past-five. Since Holmes was – as a rule – a late riser unless he was engaged upon a case, I deduced that he must have located White and decided that he couldn't wait any longer to lay hands upon the scoundrel. My resentment at the early hour vanished in an instant, for I would hardly wish to miss such a meeting.

Therefore, ten minutes later, I was dressed and ensconced in a cab rattling its way to Mayfair. Although I had not time to take either tea or coffee prior to my hasty departure, the excitement itself was sufficient to clear my brain.

"What have you learned?" I asked.

"I spent the evening attempting to learn about the antecedents of Mr. William White. I found records of his date in court with Judge Sir James Hannen, but was unsuccessful in locating the details of his military service and discharge."

"But I trust that you have found the man himself?" I cried.

"Of course," said Holmes. "I would not trundle you out of bed at such an hour unless there was some positive development. Do you recall the lad Cartwright, who works in Wilson's district messenger office?"

"How could I possibly forget how you employed him last year to keep your provisions fresh upon the Black Tor," said I, dryly.

"Well, I decided to make use of his services again. Armed with the Hotel Directory, I sent him round to the top fourteen hotels in London. He

160

visited each in turn armed with a supply of shillings, and upon his fifth stop, he was successful in learning from the outside porter that a Mr. William White took residence there two nights ago."

I shook my head. "Surely he would not check into a hotel under his real name?" I protested.

"And why not?" said Holmes, throwing open his hands. "In his mind, what link could anyone possibly make between Mr. William White and the *faux* Coldstream Guards captain who robbed the Camberwell town hall?"

We soon turned on Albemarle Street and pulled up in front of the elegant Brown's Family Hotel. Stepping inside, Holmes handed his card to the head attendant.

"I wish to have a word with Mr. White," said Holmes.

"Certainly, sir. I will have your card sent up."

"Ah, I think that Mr. White would rather not announce my visit to the entire hotel."

"But why not, sir?" said the attendant, his face puzzled. "The inspector from Scotland Yard was already round here last night."

Holmes appeared startled by this news. "An inspector from the Yard? Lestrade?"

"No, his name was Forbes, I believe."

"And why did Inspector Forbes call upon Mr. White?"

"The highway robbery."

"Mr. White was robbed?" asked Holmes, with a frown.

"That's right, sir. In broad daylight too, if you can believe the audacity of those roughs. A little knot of them accosted him in the labyrinth of small streets that lie at the back of Percy Street. They took his wallet and papers. Fortunately, he was able to hold on to his case."

"His wallet and papers," repeated Holmes, with a small smile.

"Yes, sir. Mr. White went right round to the registry to get a blank form, and Inspector Forbes himself signed it."

After getting the number of the room occupied by Mr. White, Holmes thanked the attendant and turned us away from the desk. As we climbed the stairs, he burst out with a hearty chuckle. "By Jove!" cried Holmes. "I fear, Watson, that I am in danger of developing a fondness for Mr. White's audacity. Imagine having Scotland Yard sign off on replacements for his purportedly stolen identity papers!"

Holmes knocked upon the door and a voice bade us enter. We found a man – whose visage perfectly matched the description of the Captain of Camberwell – sitting at the table, a napkin tucked into his throat, thoroughly enjoying his breakfast.

"I wonder if I might have a word, Mr. White?" asked Holmes.

161

"I am afraid that the timing is a little inconvenient, gentlemen," said he. "I should like a moment to finish my meal."

We watched as White broke open a crusty roll, spread on a thick layer of butter, and washed it down with his coffee. When he was finished, he turned to us. "Excellent. I am ready now, gentlemen. I suppose that you have come about the money?"

"Indeed," said Holmes, dryly. "My name is Sherlock Holmes."

"I have heard of you, Mr. Holmes," said White. "They say that you caught the man who killed poor Jenkins, and it was you who recently took Hugh Boone off the streets."

"I assure you that Mr. Boone removed himself of his own accord. He found a more prosperous situation."

"As have I," said White, with a smile and a wave of his hand. "What is your interest in this matter?"

"I am acting on behalf of Scotland Yard."

The man smiled. "That's a good thing, for otherwise I might not have ever been caught. In fact, one of their men was around here last night and did me a good turn."

"Unfortunately," said Holmes, with a shake of his head, "Inspector Forbes is the worst of a bad lot. Evidence would need to hit him over the head before it registered in his pea-brain."

White snorted in amusement. "You can say that again."

"I, on the other hand, can accurately describe the majority of your movements over the last the last few days."

"Is that so?"

"Indeed," said Holmes, before proceeding to relate all that we had learned thus far regarding his purchase of Captain Nichols' coat and the robbery. "After you changed your outfit at the station, you took the next train to Victoria. You then proceeded to Bond Street – or somewhere thereabouts – in order to purchase a new suit and case. The tailor was likely a bit surprised by your down-on-your-luck appearance. However, I imagine that the sum of cash that you proffered was sufficient to assuage any such misgivings. So attired, you then proceeded here to the hotel, where you concocted your absurd little tale of being robbed for the benefit of the attendant and, later, Inspector Forbes. Surely, it would be against their standard policy for Brown's to let a room to a man who appeared with no papers. However, your fine suit and your ready cash again opened doors that would normally have been closed to you."

"You forget, Mr. Holmes, that I also had a reservation."

"Of course," said Holmes, with an appreciative smile. "You planned the whole thing perfectly."

"Thank you, sir. Your account is entirely correct. Now, if you have the receipt that I gave to Mr. Wilton, I will be happy to return the money to you."

Holmes's eyebrows rose in astonishment. "You have the money?"

"Of course. It is sitting in the case, right over there," said White, with a wave to the side-table, where rested an attaché case identical to the one described by Corporal Miller.

"All of it?" asked Holmes, dubiously.

"Down to the last shilling."

"What of the sum that you have already spent?"

"That has been replenished."

"How?"

"I will give you a free tip, Mr. Holmes. *C.P.R.*"

Holmes shook his head. "I am afraid that you will have to elaborate, Mr. White."

"Very well," said White, with a smile. "You will be amazed at what you might hear if you keep your ears open, Mr. Holmes. I was sitting in the Bedford Arms not four nights past, when I heard two gents speaking about how the Canadian Pacific Railway had just won the contract to bring supplies up to the Yukon territory, and that there were rumours of gold in Klondike. [13] I knew immediately that I might be able to make a tidy sum if this news had not yet made its way round the Exchange – and since it was a Saturday evening, it was possible that it would not. The only issue was that I needed a sum that might allow me to purchase a satisfactory number of shares to set me up for good. I was mulling over these thoughts later that evening when I passed the broker's shop and spotted the army coat through the window. The plan immediately leapt into my brain. If you are as sharp as they say – and since you are standing in my room, I would guess the stories are true – then you know the rest."

"The borough of Camberwell is not in the business of providing loans, Mr. White," said Holmes, sternly. "And certainly not at the tip of a bayonet."

"All a good bit of fun, Mr. Holmes. Look," said he, pulling ten guineas from his pocket, "I will even throw this in for good measure. You can call it interest on the loan. Not bad for two days of missing funds, eh?"

"What happened to the price of the C.P.R.?" I asked.

Mr. White smiled at me. "It went up by fifty percent. Just last night, my broker divested me of sufficient shares to ensure that I could pay back the principal of my loan. I figure the C.P.R. still has a bit of a run in them before the wheel turns against then, and then I will let another man have his go. If all goes according to plan, I should have realized satisfactory gains to set me up for a good while."

"Little good it will do you in prison," said Holmes.

White shook his head. "I am not, perhaps, an honest man, Mr. Holmes. But I will be honest with you now. I have no desire to once again stand in the dock."

"Ah, yes, I know of your run-in with Sir James Hannen, back when he was sitting for the Bow Street Magistrates' Court." Holmes turned to me. "You see, Watson, in 1880, Mr. White was found guilty of robbery."

"I won't deny it," said While. "But you cannot disagree, Mr. Holmes, that the system treated me rather harshly. If you look, you will find that I filed a legitimate appeal, only to have it lost in some cabinet or another. After I served my time, I was run out of town after town, for I had no papers. And without papers I could get no job. Without a job, I could get no address. Without an address, I could get no papers. If that ain't a vicious circle, then I don't know what is. When I robbed the Camberwell Town Hall, I was mainly looking for the paperwork that I required to get a job. The money was an afterthought."

"You could argue that you were persecuted by an uncaring bureaucracy," said Holmes. "One never knows, it may go differently this time."

"Indeed?" said White, the sarcasm plain in his voice. "I can just see it now. The judge may even take off his wig, step down, and clasp me by the hand, wishing me good health and prosperity."

"Perhaps not, after all," chuckled Holmes, at this thought.

"Then mayhaps you will see to letting me go?"

"You broke the law, Mr. White."

"So what if I did?" said he, with a mighty shrug. "In the end, who was harmed?"

"The soldiers who followed you may be punished."

White shook his head. "I would hope not. They were merely following commands, like any good soldier should do. If they begin to question the actions of their superior officers, all order would break down. It would not be an army, but a mob."

"Yes, well, we must hope that the general staff sees things in a similar light," said Holmes. "Moreover, I believe that the innocent officials of Camberwell were rather traumatized by their sudden incarceration."

"Give them a little while, Mr. Holmes. I have often found that near-run calamity plus time becomes amusement. I guarantee you that the Mayor and his treasurer will be eating out for years on the great tale of the day they were robbed. And Mrs. Langevin will be invited to tea at every house from Mayfair to Belgravia to tell of how she faced down the terrible Captain of Camberwell."

I saw Holmes's lip curl up in a smile at this ostentatious braggadocio. "I must say that I sympathize with how you have been treated by the system, Mr. White. I have only one remaining question: I spent last night poring over the army's records and cannot find any record of the crime which led to your discharge."

"That's because I never served in the army," said White, with a smile.

"Never served!" I exclaimed. "Then how did you feign the actions of a captain with such precision?"

"You can thank Colonel Parrish for that."

"Parrish," said Holmes, his eyes narrowing. "The warden of Headlands Prison?" [14]

"That's right. The man is half-mad. He is obsessed with military history. He used to have his prisoners re-enact famous battles. I decided that if I played along, I might get on the man's good side, so I volunteered for every battle that I could. From Worcester to Sedgemoor, and from Quarte Bras to Alma, I have been to war time and time again – if only in spirit. [15] Still, these manoeuvres served me well when I got out. For thanks to Colonel Parrish, I now have a rather deep knowledge of military ranks and how the men talk."

Holmes stared at White for a long minute, and then began to chuckle. "Very well, Mr. White – or shall I say, 'Captain Black'? Due to a series of implausible events – from the unique training that you received under Colonel Parrish, to the loose lips of the Canadian railway men, to the tragic death of Captain Nichols – you have seized the rare opportunity to make your fortune. I trust that the funds that you know possess shall be adequate from hereon. Therefore, I suppose that there is little harm in letting you off this time. However, please note that I too have ears, and if I hear that you have returned to your larcenous ways, I assure you that I am capable of locating you once more. And I shall not be so lenient a second time."

Lestrade and the Camberwell officials were immensely grateful at the prompt return of the missing money, but the inspector was rather put out by Holmes's steadfast refusal to provide any additional details regarding the identity or location of the thief. For his part, General Sir Thomas was initially reluctant to absolve of blame Sergeant Burns, Corporal Miller, and the rest of the men for their willingness to go along with White's audacious robbery. However, after a few minutes of discussion with Holmes, the general saw the wisdom of sweeping the whole incident under the proverbial rug.

"Lestrade is correct, Watson," said Holmes, as we strode along the crowds in front of the National Gallery. "I'm afraid that we cannot allow news of this absurd fraud to reach the ears of Fleet Street. I suspect that

165

they would consider Mr. White to be the most humorous figure of the century. They would gleefully lampoon the poor soldiers who, during the task of carrying out their orders, were taken in by the supposed Captain of Camberwell. Such a story would bring widespread shame upon the brave lads of our armed forces. No, this case must remain locked in your dispatch box until such long-anticipated times have come when we have no further need for their stout protection." [16]

> *The July which immediately succeeded my marriage was made memorable by three cases of interest, in which I had the privilege of being associated with Sherlock Holmes and of studying his methods. I find them recorded in my notes under the headings of "The Adventure of the Second Stain", "The Adventure of the Naval Treaty", and "The Adventure of the Tired Captain.*
>
> – "The Adventure of the Naval Treaty

NOTES

1. Historians are divided about whether the case eventually published as "The Adventure of the Second Stain" – released in 1904 as part of *The Return of Sherlock Holmes* – is at all related to the one mentioned here. Most arguments centre on the identification of the actual Lord Bellinger, which – they contend – situates the case in the autumn of 1894. The most common explanation for the confusion is that there were, in fact, at least two adventures dealing with "second stains". Although Watson never published it, the second such case was mentioned in "The Adventure of the Naval Treaty" as involving Monsieur Dubuque and Fritz von Waldbaum. That tale appears to be set in 1889, the year succeeding Watson's marriage to Mary Morstan.

2. No such regiment exists in the British Army. Watson apparently changed the name to protect the actual regiment's reputation.

3. The Commander-in-Chief of the Forces at the time was Prince George (1850-1904), Duke of Cambridge and cousin of the Queen. He was stoutly opposed to any reforms and therefore, in the eyes of historians, has taken much of the blame for the failures of the Second Boer War.

4. The Coldstream Guards are the oldest continuously serving regular regiment in the British Army. As part of the Household Division, one of its principal roles is the protection of the monarch.

5. The St. George's Barracks was located in Orange Street on the site of the National Portrait Gallery. It was the main recruiting depot for London and troops were kept on hand in case of disturbances in Trafalgar Square. The building was erected in 1826 and demolished eighty-five years later.

6. Regimental Headquarters was situated at the Wellington Barracks, located close by Buckingham Palace.

7. General Sir Thomas Montague Steele (1820-1890) was the Regimental Colonel of the Coldstream Guards from 1884-1890.

8. The Camberwell Town Hall was located in an old vestry hall, which was later demolished in 1934 in order to make way for the current neoclassical building.

9. Roughly £4,210,000 (or $281,000 in 2021 terms).

10. See "The Adventure of the Queen's Pendant" in *The Treasury of Sherlock Holmes*

11. The news-vendor likely served in the Second Battle of Cawnpore (19 November – 6 December 1857), when British troops under Sir Colin Campbell thwarted the rebels' last chance to recapture Cawnpore and Lucknow. Most of the British survivors of the Siege of Cawnpore were massacred by troops under the command of Nana Sahib, a Peshwa of the Maratha Empire, thereby setting off a series of brutal reprisals.

12. In April of 1889, the French Defence Minister, General Georges Boulanger fled Paris ahead of charges of conspiracy to lead a *coup d'état* against the legally elected government of Sadi Carnot.

On 12 June, a steam train carrying school children and others failed to complete a steep incline near Armagh, Ireland. The resulting crash killed eighty people, and injured another two-hundred-sixty people. It was the worst rail disaster in the United Kingdom during the nineteenth century.

On 15 July, Pedro II of Brazil (1825-1891) survived an assassination attempt by a young republican named Adriano do Valle. Pedro magnanimously refused to prosecute do Valle, perhaps to avoid making him a martyr for the republican cause.

13. White's report is a bit muddled, for the Klondike Gold Rush did not get fully going until August 1896. However, some prospectors had discovered gold deposits there as early as 1883.

14. There is no such prison in the United Kingdom. Watson must have changed the name in order to obscure the identity of the idiosyncratic Colonel Parrish.

15. The Battle of Worcester (3 September, 1651) was the final battle of the English Civil War, after which Charles II escaped to France. The Battle of Sedgemoor (6 July, 1685) was the last engagement of the Monmouth Rebellion. The Battle of Quarte Bras (16 June, 1815) was a preliminary engagement that took place two days prior to Waterloo. The Battle of the Alma (20 September, 1854) was a victory of allied British, French, and Ottoman forces over Russian troops in the lead-up to Balaclava.

16. Unless it was a monstrous coincidence, it appears, however, that news of the fraud at Camberwell did eventually slip out and made its way over to the Continent, where seemingly it inspired Friedrich Wilhelm Voight (1849-1922) to carry out a nearly identical escapade on 16 October, 1906. The so-called "Captain of Köpenick" was eventually captured and served a brief sentence. He later capitalized upon his fame, appearing in plays and publishing a book about his feat. In the ultimate happenstance of fate, Voight's likeness was even displayed at Madame Tussaud's wax museum at 58 Baker Street, London. Given his connections upon the Continent, one wonders if Watson's first literary agent, Sir Arthur Conan Doyle, was perhaps responsible for spreading the story to Berlin?

The Grey Man
by James Gelter

It was late one night in October, and I had just laid down to bed when there was a ring at the bell. I rose with a groan, believing it could only be a patient who would call at so late an hour. I was taken aback, therefore, when I opened my front door and saw Sherlock Holmes standing in the rain. More surprising still, he was not alone, but was accompanied by a woman wearing a man's overcoat.

"Good evening, Watson," said Holmes. "Would you mind letting us in? It is rather damp out."

"Not at all!" I answered, stepping aside in welcome.

It was in the second year of my marriage, and I hadn't encountered Holmes for several days. I was delighted to see him, regardless of the hour.

"Thank you," said Holmes as he entered. "Allow me to introduce you to Mrs. Josephine Hoftshot of Northmoor, in Yorkshire."

She was a beautiful woman, tall and graceful, though her sharp features spoke of the hard country living that our northern region provides. Deep wrinkles branched off of her brown eyes. Her dark, curling hair was broken up by an occasional strand of brilliant white. Though the overcoat she wore was quite heavy, she was shivering.

"Sorry to bother you so late," said Holmes, "but Mrs. Hoftshot has brought a case before my attention that I suspect will require your assistance in clearing up."

My wife, Mary, appeared at the top of the stairs. She had heard Holmes's recognizable voice and came down to see what was the matter. She immediately offered Mrs. Hoftshot the sofa beside the fireplace. As the maid had already gone to bed, my wife prepared a pot of tea for our late visitors while I threw some coal upon the dwindling fire.

"Thank you," said Mrs. Hoftshot as she took the tea. "It's an honor to meet you, Dr. Watson, though I wish to God it was under different circumstances. My housekeeper simply adores that story you've written about Mr. Holmes. Many an evening she has read it aloud to me and her son, Michael."

"Mrs. Hoftshot has just finished telling me a remarkable tale of her own in Baker Street,' said Holmes. "Now, my dear lady, if you would, please repeat your story just as you told it to me, or with more detail, to Dr. Watson. It would be most helpful for me to hear it again."

169

The lady nodded but seemed unable to begin. My wife sat down beside her on the sofa. Mrs. Hoftshot stared at her tea with bloodshot eyes.

"I am sorry," she began at last, "I have had such little sleep these last few nights. I cannot close my eyes, but I see the Grey Man hobbling before me."

"It's quite all right," replied Holmes in his most soothing tone. "Take what time you need."

The lady let out a long sigh.

"I am a widow," she began, "and have been these five years. I live in Lapwing House in Northmoor, not far from the Yorkshire coast. I moved there after my marriage to Mr. John Hoftshot eight years ago. It's a small house, and I have only the one housekeeper, Annie, and her young son to keep me company. We live a quiet life and are comfortable enough. But the moor is a sparse, empty place, and I have often dreamed of returning to my family's home in Leeds.

"After my husband passed, I rented out our fields to a farmer, Mr. Guy Morton. There he built a sort-of rough bungalow for himself. Every year after he slaughters his pigs, it has become a tradition for him to join us in celebratory pork dinner. This year's dinner was ten days ago, and it was wonderful as always. Mr. Morton is delightful company and entertained Annie and me with his amusing stories well into the night. It wasn't my custom to stay up late, and I was exhausted by the time he left for home, sometime past one o'clock.

"As I was about to climb into bed, I looked out my bedroom window and was surprised to see a man walking along the road. The moon was full, but the road is a good hundred yards from the house, so I could only just make him out. But even at that distance, I could tell there was something dreadfully wrong about the man. His skin and garments were all so pale he seemed to glow in the moonlight. He moved slowly and with an uneven gate. As I watched, he made his way up the road and disappeared from my sight.

"He was so strange and spectral in appearance that I couldn't get the image of him out of my mind. I slept horribly that night, and I couldn't escape thoughts of him all the next day.

"The following night, I found myself unable to sleep. The image of this haunting figure had so unnerved me that I feared his return. I felt compelled to sit by the window and look out for him, but he didn't appear. This did little to allay my unease. I sat up the next night as well, but again, he didn't appear.

"On the fourth night, I went straight to my bed and tried to sleep. I found it impossible, however, and as one o'clock neared, I arose and sat by the window once more to watch for him.

170

"I want to say that I was surprised when he appeared, just as he had three nights before, but really I wasn't. It was as though I knew it was going to happen. He made his way up the road and passed out of sight, just as before. But this time, I stayed by the window and continued to look out. Half-an-hour later, he appeared again, heading back the way he came. I stared out across the moor for another hour, but he didn't return.

"The next night, I asked dear Annie to stay up with me and witness the man for herself. He never came. I could see the doubt in Annie's face, but she agreed to join me the following night. Once more, one o'clock came and went, and the man was nowhere to be seen. Annie fell asleep in her chair, but I kept my eyes on the road. Close to two in the morning, the man appeared. I woke Annie. She gasped when she saw him. As before, he travelled north up the path, and an hour later, made his way back south.

"Annie found his presence as unnerving as I did, perhaps more so. She would talk to me about him every day. 'The Grey Man' she began to call him. Some sort of spirit he was, of that she was sure. She had me half-believing it too. But then, yesterday morning, she suggested that I bring the matter to Mr. Morton. I did so. He was sure it was nothing to be alarmed by but, seeing how frightened I was, agreed to wait down by the road that evening to see if he might talk to the stranger. I insisted on accompanying him, and though he tried to argue me out of it, I stood firm upon the point. I wanted to know who this man was and why he crossed the moor at night.

"We waited behind a clump of junipers that stand near the road. The night was freezing and, even clad in my late husband's heaviest coat, I was shivering within minutes of us taking our post. One o'clock came, then two. I had just concluded that our man wouldn't appear when Mr. Morton grabbed my arm. I looked down the path and saw the man coming. As unnerving as he had been at a distance, I wasn't prepared for what I saw up close. The man was terribly emaciated, with a gaunt face and bulging eyes. His skin was pale and thin as paper. His old-fashioned suit was so faded the colour matched his long grey hair and beard, which hung limply from his head. He shambled forward as though each step was an immense undertaking. In one of his long, bony hands, he held a short stick that had been sharpened to a fine point.

"So frightening was the figure that I decided it was best not to confront him but to let him pass without seeing us. Before I could whisper my thoughts to Mr. Morton, however, he stepped out onto the road and confronted the stranger.

"'You there – ' said he, but before he could say more, the Grey Man charged at him, his stick raised high above his head, his eyes wide. With a shriek, he brought the point of his weapon down on Mr. Morton, who had

171

thrown his hands up in self-defense. He struck Mr. Morton on the arm. The Grey Man then turned and dashed wildly back the way he came. I ran to Mr. Morton. His arm was bleeding, but the blow had been a glancing one, and the wound wasn't deep. I looked down the road and saw his attacker stumble and fall. It seemed to take all of his effort to get back to his feet, and he limped slowly away. Mr. Morton wanted to pursue him, but I held him back. The man was too dangerous, I argued, and we must tend to his wound.

"Early in the morning, Mr. Morton and I made for Saxdale, the nearest village, to inform the police that this mad man was on the loose. Confound them! Old Joe Caulsby came out to investigate. He is a joke of an officer. He walked up and down the road, asked the same questions of us again and again, and, after all that, could offer nothing to help us save that he would keep an eye out and suggested we do the same. Then I remembered Mr. Holmes. I haven't been all the way to London since I was a wee girl, but I made up my mind to travel down here and see him. My travels took longer than I had hoped, and I wasn't able to call upon him until quite late, I am afraid."

"You did exactly right," said my wife, taking the lady by the hand.

"I agree," said Holmes, "The events of last night may have scared this unfortunate man from going through with whatever plans he may have. Therefore we must act swiftly before we lose any chance of learning what those plans were."

"John will come with you," my wife said to Mrs. Hoftshot, "You will never be safer than with the two of them looking after you."

"Would it be possible for Mrs. Hoftshot to get a few hours rest here?" asked Holmes.

"Of course."

Mary led the exhausted woman upstairs to the guest quarters. Holmes stood and warmed himself by the fire.

"Well, Watson, what do you make of it?"

"I don't like the sound of it – not in the slightest. Who could this man possibly be? And what on earth would cause him to behave in such a manner?"

"Yes, it is rather enticing, is it not?" said Holmes, his eyes shining. "But we can talk more on the train. We must prepare for Yorkshire."

"Will you stay here tonight?"

"No. I have a few matters I would like to attend to before we leave. I place our client into your capable hands. See that both of you are at King's Cross for the 8:30 to York. I'll meet you on the platform. Thank Mrs. Watson for her assistance. Goodnight!"

172

Mrs. Hoftshot was quiet and demure all through breakfast and on our way to the station. Though when Holmes met us on the platform, I did glance a small, short-lived smile come across her face.

For the first hour of our journey, we sat in silence. Holmes was poring over a map, smoking cigarette after cigarette. At last, he tossed the map aside and sat back.

"When faced with such little evidence," he began, "there is only so much that one can deduce with a surety. And yet, I believe that there are some conclusions that can be reached before we make it to Northmoor. What, for example, can we deduce from this spectral man's actions?"

"Beyond the fact that he is a seemingly desperate fellow, I'm not sure that there is anything that we can," I replied.

"No? There are two facts that I would say are absurdly obvious. If this man was travelling up a road, I think we can safely deduce that he was travelling *to* somewhere and that he was travelling *from* somewhere."

"Well, that is obvious."

"Too obvious to mention, apparently," Holmes said with a smile, "and these facts lead us then to the obvious question: Where was he going, and from whence?"

"A difficult thing to determine, given the expansiveness of the moor."

"Really, Watson, I fear I should never have interrupted your rest last night. Your mind is evidently too weary for this business. The expansiveness of the moor greatly limits our options, as there are very few places where one can find anything other than heather and brambles. I visited Stamford's early this morning to procure this ordinance map of the area. Look here." He retrieved that map and spread it over his lap. "Just there is Lapwing House. Mrs. Hoftshot said our man was travelling north. But look, there is no structure north of Lapwing House for dozens of miles except this." He pointed to a marking indicating a large structure. "Raventree Hall."

"That is the home of the Baronet Sir Willem Darvish and his wife, Lady Clara," said Mrs. Hoftshot.

"What do you know of them?" asked Holmes.

"Why, Sir Willem is a fine man. I see him ride by on occasion. He owns a vast amount of the moor. My own property is bordered by his on three sides. He has been very generous to the community. When the terrible snows hit three years ago, and our barn roof collapsed, Sir Willem sent his men down to help. Rather than simply repair the roof, he ordered them to build an entirely new barn! He wouldn't accept a single gesture of gratitude in return. And Lady Clara is a darling, though she can be quite distant at first and rarely leaves the Hall."

Holmes pulled a pencil from his pocket. He held it and the map out to the lady.

"Could you roughly outline the borders of his property?"

"I think I could, roughly."

"But surely, Holmes," said I, "Our man couldn't have made it all the way to the Hall and back to Lapwing House in half-an-hour. An hour, perhaps, but he wouldn't have much time to do anything when he got there."

"Which would lead to the conclusion that although it was his intention to reach Raventree Hall, he was compelled to turn back before he could."

"But what is it that would so compel him?" I asked.

Holmes turned to the lady.

"This map indicates a rather abrupt change in elevation between your home and the Hall. Is that so?"

"Aye, Mr. Holmes, it is quite the climb. Raventree Hill, it is called. The road becomes almost impassable when the rains are heavy."

"You say this man was terribly feeble?"

"I had never seen feebler, not even when my father wasted away before his death."

"There we have it," said Holmes. "He turned back because the effort was too much for him in his state, and he must save his strength to journey home and try again another night. Which draws us, inevitably, to our next question: From whence does his nightly journey commence? I think we can safely assume that he begins his travels after dark, as someone would have certainly noticed his appearance during the day. If he left just after dark but had to return before sunrise, he could only come from one of the half-dozen houses scattered on the moor to the south of Lapwing House. The village is too far. Do you know the residents of all six of these houses, Mrs. Hoftshot?"

The lady looked over the area of the map Holmes had indicated.

"Certainly, Mr. Holmes. And I am sure that the man couldn't possibly have come from any of them."

"Still, if you would be so kind as to name the residents that you do know . . . ."

"There are the McCreadys at Brownstone, a kindly couple with two young boys. Dr. Emmit Paul, a retired botanist, lives there. That's the Holbrook family farm. This here is Old Jack Peck's place. He was once gamekeeper at Raventree Hall – keeps to himself mostly. The Henderson's farm is there. And this cottage belongs to the Widow Spiglett."

"We will have to visit them all in turn," said Holmes.

"Why should we not just wait for the man to come up the road again tonight?" I asked. "Surely his sharpened stick would mean nothing against my revolver and your riding crop."

"There is no guarantee he will appear tonight. Besides, it's doubtful he will ever travel that way again now that he knows the road is being watched. No, I think our answer lies somewhere in these six houses."

Holmes spent the next hour asking our client to detail each of the households we were to call upon.

The train carried us to York, where we caught a smaller engine to take us on to Pickering. There we met Mr. Morton, waiting for us with his horse and hay cart.

"You have good timing, Mrs. Hoftshot," he said with a smile as we approached. "Just missed the rains."

In dress, he presented himself plainly as a gentleman farmer, with a collarless shirt, tweed jacket, and trousers, knee-high brown leather boots, and a waxed canvas cape. He wasn't a handsome fellow in the traditional sense, but there was something about the kindness of his blue-grey eyes and the strength of his solid, square build that put one instantly at ease in his presence.

"Awfully kind of you to come all this way, Mr. Holmes," he said, "I thought you would probably be too tied up in important cases to even grant Mrs. Hoftshot an appointment."

"The importance of a case is entirely subjective," Holmes replied. "I take on those cases that I believe I'm uniquely qualified to solve. I have no other criteria than that."

"And you arrived at a good time. The Grey Man has been seen again."

Holmes raised his eyebrows.

"Again? So soon? That is interesting. Previously he had let a day or two pass between attempts."

"Aye, but this time he wasn't spotted on the road," replied Morton. "It was Dr. Paul who saw him. He's waiting at the inn in Saxdale. Hop aboard. I will take you to him and let him tell you all."

We drove along the bare, undulating landscape. The trees had already lost most of their leaves, and the hillsides were brown and lifeless. Heavy rains had just ended, and all was wet and muddy under a dull grey sky. Holmes spent the journey asking Guy Morton about his own confrontation with the "Grey Man", but the farmer had little to add to Mrs. Hoftshot's version of the events.

We reached the inn, The Golden Plover, in the mid-afternoon. There we found Dr. Emmit Paul waiting for us alone in a sitting room, resting close to the fire. He was a squat man, a full head shorter than Mrs. Hoftshot. There was no hair atop his round head. His jaw would have been

175

undefined were it not outlined with a thin silver strip of beard. His thick glasses magnified his eyes, giving him a somewhat frog-like appearance. The man was clearly in a state of extreme agitation and seemed unable to stay still.

"I understand," said Holmes, after introductions were concluded, "that you have had a singular experience that may help us in our investigation."

"Singular it was, Mr. Holmes," said Dr. Paul in a thin, cracking voice, "and I should hope to never have an experience like it ever again."

"Tell us all, and leave no detail unsaid."

"I am a botanist, Mr. Holmes, spending most of my career at one of our smaller universities and having now retired. My love for the work hasn't dwindled, however, and I have recently been making a study of *Cornus suecica*, or dwarf cornel, which I discovered grows in abundance among the heather in many places across these moorlands. It is rare to see dwarf cornel in such amounts this far south, and I have been documenting where it can be found throughout Northmoor to determine what special conditions might cause it to thrive here.

"As the work has progressed, I've had to travel farther and farther from my home to document new areas. I have always been an extremely early riser, and I left the house at four this morning on foot with the plan to walk north five miles or so and begin my explorations in a new area.

"In order to avoid the climb up Raventree Hill, I turned off the road a little before it reaches Mrs. Hoftshot's property and cut across the moorlands headed northeast. To the north were the woodlands that cover the hill and circumference of Raventree Hall.

"My eyes are weak, and even with my glasses, I cannot see very far. I tend to keep my eyes focused on the ground just ahead of me. I reached the edge of the woodlands and began to walk around them, knowing it would be too dark under the cover of the trees to see my path. A gentle rain began to fall, and I had just started to consider turning back when I glanced up and saw a pale figure against the tree line. I stopped and waited as he made his way in my direction. Clouds were covering the small sliver of a moon, yet his ashen shape cut through the dark.

"Before I could make out his face, I could hear him shouting, crying out in a horrid wail. I couldn't make it out at first, but soon I understood he was repeating, 'Stay there! Come not near me! Stay there!'

"I remained rooted to the spot and raised my arms to communicate that I wouldn't move. He made his way closer, and as he came into focus, I held my breath to prevent myself from screaming in terror. His face was unlike any I had ever seen, a waxen cadaverous mask. But it was his arms that horrified me. They were bright red with blood and hung lifelessly as he walked. When he was ten yards away, he pivoted and walked around me in a wide circle. He breathed heavily, and his voice was now barely audible, but still he said, 'Stay there! Stay there!'

"As he passed me, I noticed the back of his right leg was red as well. He continued on, headed south. I stayed rooted to the spot until he was out of sight, and then for a few minutes more, frozen in horror of the vision that I had beheld.

"The rain grew heavier, which broke me from the spell this apparition had cast upon me. I headed for the road, back the way I had come. I made my way south toward the village. Within the hour, it was pouring rain."

"I found him," said Mr. Morton, "soaked to the bone and shivering on the road just north of the village. He told me of his encounter. I brought him here and told him not to tell another soul until I came back with you, Mr. Holmes."

Holmes had been looking up to the ceiling for most of Dr. Paul's account. Now he turned his gaze to the botanist.

"The blood," he said. "Was it his?"

"I cannot be sure, Mr. Holmes, my vision being what it is. But he did limp on the leg that was blood-soaked. The arms were both red below the elbow."

"I would say it was the dogs, more likely than not," said Morton.

"The dogs?" asked Holmes.

"Sir Willem's dogs. He's got nine of them. He keeps them in a paddock during the day, but they are free to wander all around his grounds at night. They leave the deer alone, but heaven help whoever else they come across, be they badger or human. They must have caught up with him, but he managed to escape."

"That would fit the facts," said Holmes. "He decided to cut through the woods instead of risking another incident on the road. Are there trails through those woods?"

"There are," replied Morton, "though I'm not familiar with them. Sir Willem is very protective of all his woodlands, as the dogs make clear, so folks don't tend to travel through them."

Holmes stared at the fire, his fingertips against his lips. We all sat in silence for a few moments until Morton broke it.

"So what's our plan of campaign, Mr. Holmes?"

"It doesn't change. I would consider travelling to the location of this latest encounter and tracking the man's movements from there, following the blood he would have invariably left in his wake, but the rain has made such a plan impossible. No, we continue as we'd intended before this newest development. Dr. Paul's account only adds a renewed urgency to what we have to do."

We briefly told Morton of our intentions to canvas all the houses between Lapwing house and the village. He agreed to accompany us.

"Not all the folks in this area are quick to trust strangers," he said, "especially London gentlemen like yourselves. But I know them all and may be able to put them at ease."

"Thank you, Mr. Morton," said Mrs. Hoftshot, "but you have already done so much to help that I cannot possibly ask you to do more."

"Nonsense, Mrs. Hoftshot," he replied, "I won't sleep easy either until I know that this 'Grey Man', be he man or phantom, is found and can no longer terrorize you or anyone else in this valley. Besides," he added with a grin, "you can make it up to me by feeding my animals while I'm with these gents."

Mrs. Hotshot let out a laugh.

"I would be happy to, Mr. Morton, happy to."

We all travelled together in the cart until we reached the first house on our list, Holbrook Farm. It was decided that at this point we should divide our party, Mrs. Hoftshot taking the cart to drive Dr. Paul and herself home, while Holmes, Morton, and I would proceed on foot.

"Be careful, and try to stay warm," said Mrs. Hoftshot before she departed. "We will be anxiously waiting for all three of you at Lapwing House and will have a warm meal prepared. Farewell!"

The three of us made our way to the farmhouse, where we met Mrs. Holbrook. Her husband was in the fields, she said, but she would be happy to help us in any way. Holmes asked her a few general questions, but the interview had only gone on for a few minutes before he announced he had all the information he needed and that we must move on.

As we walked along the road to the next house on our list, I struck up a conversation with our guide.

"You were a military man?" I ventured.

"Yes, Dr. Watson," he replied, "But how did you know?'

"As a former soldier myself, I recognized the bearing and manners of one who was in the service. And your use of the phrase 'plan of campaign' was suggestive as well."

"Well done, Watson!" remarked Holmes, "It seems the fogs of weariness have subsided, and you are in form again."

"Yes, I fought against the Zulus," Mr. Morton continued, "as part of the 60th regiment."

"The Royal Rifle Corps!" I cried, "That is an impressive regiment to be a part of. What caused you to leave the service?"

"I didn't care much for the military life once I started living it. And like so many who fought in that war, I often contemplated if it was one worth fighting. When I returned home, I sought a quieter, simpler life, one that was predictable and uneventful. That is just the life I have found here in Northmoor. There's nothing more I could desire."

"Except, perhaps, a lovely woman to share your simple life with? A woman much like our Mrs. Hoftshot?"

The farmer blushed.

"She is indeed a fine woman, sir, and I'd consider myself a lucky man to have her as a bride. I'm not so sure, however, she would feel the same way."

"As someone who often finds obvious that which others cannot," interjected Holmes, "there is no situation more vexatious than when two people have a clear mutual attraction and fail to recognize it, despite it being blatantly apparent. But here is our next stop – the home of Mr. Jack Peck, I believe."

We approached a small cottage that sat on overgrown grounds. Before we reached the door, it flung open, and out stepped a short, gruff-looking man of about fifty with thin black hair and a massive unkempt beard. He glared at us from beneath two thick eyebrows that almost met in the center of his forehead.

"You're Morton, are you not?" he asked with a deep, loud voice. "What right do you have bringing two outsiders onto my property?"

"Come now, Mr. Peck," replied Morton, "We don't mean any disrespect. There has been a stranger lurking about Mrs. Hoftshot's place, and these good men are helping us identify the scoundrel."

"If someone's been harassing Mrs. Hoftshot, that's her business, not mine. I haven't had any dealings with any strangers. I keep to myself."

"I quite understand, my good man. I think we all in these parts like to mind our own. That is what makes some outsider wandering about at night all the more upsetting. The bloke actually attacked me, decrepit though he was."

"Decrepit?" Jack Peck's eyes narrowed. "What do you mean, decrepit?"

Morton sketched out all that had occurred on the road past Lapwing House. As he did, the colour drained completely from the old gamekeeper's face.

"Well, that's quite the tale," he said when Morton was finished, "but as I said, I keep to myself and know nothing about it. Now, if you gentlemen would be so kind as to get off my property and leave me alone!"

Morton and I turned to go, but Holmes stood still.

"Just one question," he said. "How long ago did you depart Sir Willem's service?"

The man glared at Holmes.

179

"I didn't depart Sir Willem's service. I departed his father's – Sir Richard."

"And yet you still live on land belonging to the Darvish family?"

The man gave a snort of contempt.

"I have known Sir Willem since he was a tyke. He's a good man. I was renting rooms down in the village when his father died. He then offered this home to me as thanks for my years of service."

"Well, that is certainly in character with everything else we have heard of Sir Willem's generosity. Thank you, Mr. Peck. Our apologies for having disturbed you. Good day!"

"He isn't a bad fellow," said Morton as we walked away, "but he does have his moods. He reminds me of some of the men I served with, the ones who have seen things that no man should and are forever haunted by them."

"I had the same impression," I replied. "I know the symptoms well."

"I'm not so sure," said Holmes, thoughtfully. "I don't have anything definite to back my claim, but I get the distinct impression that we just spoke with a man who isn't haunted by something in his past, but something very much in his present."

We made our way up the road. The next house, that of the Widow Spiglett, wasn't more than a mile away. A little way before we reached her drive, however, Holmes stopped. There was a small footpath that diverted off the road. The entrance was so overgrown I wouldn't have noticed it if Holmes hadn't pointed it out. My eyes followed it and saw that it led toward a wooded area a half-mile away. Holmes took a few steps down the path.

"This wasn't on the map," he said, "Where does it lead?"

"I've never been down it myself," replied Mr. Morton, "but I know Sir Willem likes to hunt in those woods on occasion."

"Someone makes regular use of it on foot – someone who hand rolls his cigarettes." He bent down and lifted up a cigarette end. "Hmm. Well, let us visit the good lady in that house there."

The Widow Spiglett was very happy to have visitors. She offered us tea, which I thought Holmes would decline, as we had many more houses to visit. To my surprise, he accepted, and we made our way into the kind lady's parlour. Holmes sat opposite a large window that looked out over the road.

"How long have you lived in Northmoor, Mrs. Spiglett?" he asked.

"Oh, all my life. I was born in this very house."

"I daresay you know quite a bit about the goings-on up at Raventree Hall over the years?"

"Oh, I don't know about that. I did work there for a time when I was a young woman. And I have been invited up to tea with Sir Willem and Lady Clara on a small number of occasions. They are a fine couple."

"So you knew Sir Willem's father, Sir Richard?"

The elderly woman's sweet face turned into a sneer of contempt.

"I knew the brute. It is astonishing that so cold and vile a man could be the sire of so kind a man as Sir Willem. Northmoor is all the better now that he is gone."

"When did he pass away?"

"Some twelve years back."

"How did he die?"

"I cannot say. I am sure that I ever knew. All I can remember is that it happened quite suddenly. He had seemed to be in good health. But there are plenty of afflictions that can come on in an instant. My own poor Charlie was simply sitting before the fire when a stroke took hold of him, and like that, he was gone."

The widow began to tell stories of her departed husband. I expected Holmes to grow impatient listening to her banal reminiscences, but he sat listening with his full attention. Suddenly, his eyes grew wide as he looked past her and out the window. He jumped to his feet.

"Thank you for the tea, Mrs. Spiglett," he said with an excited tremor to his voice, "but I am afraid we must be going right away."

Our hostess was confused but gracious, inviting us to come back at any time.

"What is it?" I cried as he dashed out the door and toward the road.

"Look there!"

I followed his outstretched finger and saw in the distance a figure moving down the footpath toward the woods.

"Peck!" said Holmes. "The ground all around his front door was covered in hand-rolled cigarette ends, just like the one I found along the path. Let us follow him and see what business he has in Sir Willem's wood!"

Holmes turned swiftly off the road and down the footpath, Morton and I at his heels. We moved almost at a run at first but then slowed down to keep our distance. The sun began to set as we entered the woods, which were full of old-growth and new. Straight white birch trees stood in strange contrast to the dark green junipers and the twisted limbs of the ash trees, which the strong moor winds had bent into fantastic shapes. So dense was the vegetation that we had to pass single-file along the narrow trail.

For twenty minutes we walked in silence. As the sky dimmed, the cold, damp air began to cut through my coat. The trees started to thin. In the distance, I could hear the sound of a man shouting furiously. We came out into a small clearing where there stood a stone cabin, little more than a hut. Judging by the structure's shape and condition, it must have been built in the middle ages, though the ancient roof had been replaced with a modern one. The shouting came from inside. We were now close enough that I could tell the voice was that of Jack Peck, but I couldn't make out his words. Another voice joined, but it wasn't shouting. It was screaming in pain. Holmes indicated that we should take cover behind a large bush that stood only feet away from the door. Just as we did, the cabin door burst open, and there stood Jack Peck, his face red with fury, hot breath streaming from his nostrils and through the frigid air. He took a deep breath. We were so close that I could hear him whisper, "God help me!" to himself. He pulled on his cap and left, not down the path from where he came, but up another headed north.

Holmes held my arm until we could no longer hear the man's steps down the path. Then he let me go, and we all three rushed into the cabin. We were in a small room, barely large enough to fit all three of us. Inside was a wooden stool on an ancient fur rug and a small unlit stove. In the wall opposite the entrance was a thick door with heavy iron hinges. An oak bar went across it, held in place by a large padlock. From behind the door came the sound of a man whimpering.

"Hello in there!" cried Holmes, "Are you all right?"

"Go away!" the man behind the door shrieked, "Go! Go! If he finds out you are here, he will hurt me! He'll hurt me!"

"No one is going to hurt you, I give you my word," Holmes replied, "Just tell us how you escaped before. We will take you away from here, never to return."

"Go away!" the man cried, his voice cracking, "My son! My son will hurt me!"

"If you will not come out, we will find our way in!"

"But how will we, Holmes?" I asked, "It would take more than our three shoulders to break down so formidable a door."

"I think we can manage it, but we will have to wait – say twenty minutes."

"Why?"

"Because by then, Peck will be too far away to hear."

Holmes sat on the small stool and pulled out his watch.

Cries of "Go away!" and "Leave me!" continued to emanate from behind the door for a few minutes, but then they tapered off into silence. At last, Holmes put his watch back into his pocket and said, "Watson, your revolver, please."

I handed it to him and he stepped out of the cabin. Morton and I followed. Holmes pointed the gun in the air and fired. He then took the empty cartridge out of the revolver, along with one that hadn't been fired. He slipped the opening of the empty cartridge over the bullet of the unfired one. Holmes's strong hands used the empty cartridge to wiggle the bullet back and forth until it popped out of its casing. He handed me the now bullet-less but full cartridge. He pulled another from out of the gun and repeated the procedure. Once this was done, he handed back the revolver and took the two full cartridges inside the cabin. I watched through the doorway as he carefully poured the gunpowder out of the cartridges into the opening of the padlock. He then lit a match, stuck the unlit end into the lock, and hurried out of the building. A moment later, there was a loud crack of the powder exploding, followed by a thud of the lock dropping to the floor. The man behind the door was now screaming hysterically. Holmes, Morton, and I re-entered the cabin, lifted the bar, and flung open the door.

I was hit at once by a terrible stench. The room was no more extensive than the one in which we stood. Crouched in the corner opposite the door was a man such as I have never seen before or since. His transparent skin was stretched taut over a tall, thin skeleton. Every angle and nook of his skull could be seen beneath his face. His arms were still wet with blood. He continued to scream incoherently and thrust his hand under a straw mattress that lay on the floor. Out from under it, he drew a stick sharpened to a point. He jumped to his feet and began to charge, but suddenly collapsed to the floor. I ran to him and knelt beside him.

"He's alive," I said, "but the effort seemed too much for him. He's unconscious."

"Let us carry him out into the fresh air," said Holmes.

We carried the poor soul out into the clearing. I examined his arms and right leg.

"Dog bites, most definitely," I said. "They have already begun to show signs of infection."

"My God!" said Morton, looking down at the man, "I knew Jack Peck was no saint, but how could he, or anyone, do this to his own father?"

"Jack Peck isn't the son he referred to," said Holmes, his face stern.

"Then who is?"

"Peck took the path north, not south toward his home. He must be going to report to his employer, Sir Willem Darvish."

"No, not Sir Willem! I cannot believe it!"

"Look at the man's clothes," said Holmes. "Torn and soiled though they may be, it is clear that they were made of the finest fabrics, expertly tailored. Who else in Northmoor could afford such lavish vestments?"

"Twelve years, Holmes," I said, "Sir Richard Darvish hasn't been seen in twelve years."

"And look at him," he replied, "Doesn't it look as though he has been confined to this prison for that long?"

"It's a wonder he is still alive at all."

"Mr. Morton," said Holmes, turning to the farmer, "could you carry this unfortunate man back to the Widow Spiglett's house? Once there, restrain him. God knows what he might try once he awakens. Then send word to the village constabulary. Tell them to send as many men as they can here without delay."

"Yes, sir," Morton replied, suddenly the soldier once more. "But what will you do?"

"Dr. Watson and I will stay here. If my reading of the situation is correct, Jack Peck has gone to tell his master of Sir Richard's nighttime wanderings. No doubt they will both make their way back here to question and punish him. We will lie in wait and confront them."

I was conflicted. The feeble and injured man was obviously in need of medical attention, but I couldn't bring myself to leave Holmes alone to confront two dangerous men. I turned to Mr. Morton.

"Do you have knowledge of field medicine?"

"Enough deal with these wounds," replied Morton. "Don't you worry, Dr. Watson. I'll see what spirits Mrs. Spiglett has to clean them with, and then I'll dress them. I can even sew a stitch or two if need be. You will be all right, just the two of you?"

"We have found ourselves in more dangerous situations than this," said Holmes. "Besides, Watson still has a few rounds left in his revolver."

Morton lifted the unconscious man with minimum effort, for he weighed very little, and left.

Holmes and I made our way back into the cabin and the small chamber in which Sir Richard had been held captive. The room had no furniture, save the straw mattress I've mentioned that lay upon the stone floor. The noxious odor came from a waste bucket in the corner, filled almost to the brim. There was one small window, but it was shuttered with a bar welded into place.

"Holmes," said I, "if he was locked in here all the time, how did he escape to walk the road at night?"

"Look at the floor," he replied. "As you can see, it is very dusty, but the dust has been brushed away all around the mattress, showing it's regularly moved."

He kicked the mattress aside and leaned down to examine the stones. His fingertips curled under the edge of the largest of them, and with a great effort, he lifted and moved it to the side to reveal a hole dug into the earth below.

"He would have dug a little every day by hand," said Holmes, "deposing of the dirt by mixing it into his waste bucket."

"But where does it lead?"

"The fastest way to learn that is to travel through it," said my friend as he stripped down to his shirt, handing me his discarded garments. "I am quite thin myself, but not nearly so thin as the man who dug this tunnel. It will be a tight fit."

He climbed head-first down into the tunnel, and moments later, had disappeared entirely. I went back outside and walked all round the cabin. There was no opening in the ground anywhere I could see. Ten minutes passed, and I began to fear that Holmes might be trapped when I heard a "Halloa!" from behind me. I turned. Holmes was standing, covered in soil, behind a large rock on the edge of the clearing. I made my way to him.

"I almost became stuck a couple of times, but I managed," he said, breathless.

I reached him and saw a hole just at the base of the rock.

"Good Lord! The tunnel must be thirty yards long."

"Indeed. He would have to have been working on it for many years. My, this Northmoor air is brisk!"

I handed back his clothing articles as he dressed.

"But why," said I, "after years of such horrible conditions and agonizing labor, would he return to this place again and again? Why did he not simply escape and leave forever?"

"It would seem that the motivation behind Sir Richard's labor wasn't freedom, but revenge. Remember the sharpened stick and his nighttime attempts to reach Raventree Hall? He would wait until after sunset, then would crawl through this tunnel and walk four miles toward what was once his home. But strong as his will was, the labors took their toll on his starved and enfeebled body. The final mile up that steep slope always proved too much for him, and so he would turn back, take a few days to recover his strength, then try again another night. He tried a less-steep route through the woods, only to face Sir Willem's dogs, barely making his escape. If he didn't return to his cell, his captors would be on their guard, and he would never have a chance to get near them. But we must prepare. The baronet and his lackey will be here soon, and we best not be standing out in the open when they arrive."

We restored all in the cabin to appear as if no one had been there. Once again, we hid behind the bush near the cabin entrance. By now, the sun had fully set, and a waning moon shone in the sky. A breeze moved through the trees, and the shadows round us were in constant motion. For an hour we stood waiting, our feet slowly sinking into the damp ground. It was bitter cold, and frost began to form on our coats. Then I heard the

185

distinct sound of horses cantering, and a few moments later, two riders burst into the clearing. One was Jack Peck. The second could be none other than Sir Willem. He was tall and lithe, with a square jaw, high aristocratic cheekbones, and sharp grey eyes. He was impeccably dressed in black riding clothes. As he leapt from his horse, riding crop in hand, it struck me that although he presented himself as different from his father as possible, I could still see an unmistakable resemblance between them. He took a lantern from Peck and headed toward the cabin door. Holmes held his breath. I followed suit and held mine, knowing it would be seen by the baronet otherwise.

"Father!" Sir Willem cried and flung open the cabin door with enough force I thought he might knock it off its hinges. Jack Peck followed, and they both entered the building. Holmes and I ran round and blocked the doorway.

"He's flown again!" Peck cried, and the two turned to exit only to find themselves facing the end of my revolver.

"Sir Richard has indeed flown again," said Holmes calmly, "this time never to return."

"You!" cried Peck, "These are the two scoundrels that I told you of, Sir Willem – the ones that were with Guy Morton!"

"Who are you?" demanded Sir Willem. "And what have you done with my father?"

"My name is Sherlock Holmes, and this is my associate, Dr. Watson. Your father is far away from here by now, and the police are on their way. We will hold you in our custody until they arrive. You will be arrested for the crimes of torture and false imprisonment."

"It was mercy!" cried Sir Willem, "He deserved death for all his crimes."

"If you want to limit the charges levied against you, your best chance would be to make a full and complete confession," said Holmes with an authority few men could stand against. "Tell me now: What drove you to treat your own father is such a dreadful manner?"

The baronet sank down onto the stoop and put his head in his hands.

"My father," said he, "was always a hard man. He never provided me with the love or gentle guidance that a father owes his son. Yet he was, in his way, kinder to me than anyone else. To all others, he was a terror, but especially so for the women of the house. His lust was uncontrollable, and he forced himself upon every young woman who worked for him. Many would leave within months or even weeks of their hiring. Some would stay on, believing his molestations to be a bitter reality of their employment that they must endure. But the longer they stayed, the more my father would bore of them and so grow ever more violent in his attacks on them.

I remember a young chambermaid whose beautiful face he beat so furiously that she left our house permanently disfigured.

"The worst instance of all was that of Jack Peck's dear wife."

The old gamekeeper kept his eyes down as he muttered, "He came to my house almost every day, unknownst to me, and had his way with her. When she found out she was with child, she hanged herself, leaving a note confessing all."

"When Jack confronted my father," continued Sir Willem, "he fired him. The local constabulary did nothing. If they ever approached the villain, he would give them generous bribes before they even had a chance to open their mouths. On one occasion, he convinced the constables to arrest a woman who came to them for protection, claiming she was a thief.

"Twelve years ago, I married, and my Clara came to live with me at Raventree Hall. I was a fool to think that though my father would take advantage of the servants, he wouldn't dare do such a thing to his own daughter-in-law. Still, I made sure that the two were never alone together. One day, about three weeks after my marriage, he and I went out on a hunt. We became separated, and I searched for him for more than an hour, but eventually gave up and made my way back to the Hall. I could hear her screams before I even entered the house. I rushed up the stairs to my bedroom, and there he was, lying on top of her, pinning her arms down. I grabbed an iron from beside the fireplace and knocked him unconscious. I would have beaten him to death right there and then if Clara hadn't begged me to stop.

"What was I to do? I couldn't let my father continue to harm so many innocent women, yet I couldn't bring him to justice without his villainy being publicly known. The thought of the whole of England knowing what he did to my poor Clara was more than I could bear. I sent for Jack, who was living in the village, and the two of us devised a plan. We would imprison my father ourselves, and Jack would serve as his warden. Jack knew of an abandoned cabin that has stood on family property for over three-hundred years, and there we chose to keep him. Jack would stop in and give him food every morning.

"At the time, I was so full of hatred, I never considered the ramifications of keeping a man in such a state for so many years. I used to come down and see him on occasion, but began to do so less and less. He became so vile and pitiable in appearance that I couldn't bear to look on him, and it has been well over two years since I came here last. Oh, God! May no other son ever again have so cruel a father or a father so cruel a son!"

Sir Willem began to weep and grasped his hair tightly in his hands. Holmes stepped forward and put a hand on the man's shoulder.

"I can understand why you acted in the manner you have. I cannot, with certainty, say that I would have done otherwise."

He stepped back and addressed both men.

"But look at the cost. To protect your honor, you have put not only this man but yourselves through twelve years of torment. There was no justice done here. But now, there must be."

The police arrived shortly after, and though they were hesitant at first to believe Holmes's account of the day, the baronet proved willing to confirm all, and both he and Jack Peck were arrested. They were found Not Guilty in court, however, as their defense successfully argued that their actions had been in the public interest. The testimony of Mrs. Spiglett, in which she testified that she was herself once a victim of Sir Richard, did much to sway the jury. Sir Willem, in his shame, sold Raventree Hall, and he and his wife made for Canada, never to return to England. Of what happened to Jack Peck, I have no record.

Sir Richard developed a fever the night he was rescued. His determination to bring vengeance upon his son had allowed him to exert himself to an amazing extent, but with the hope of revenge gone, his will became as weak as his body, and he died eight days later.

I found in my notes of this case a letter I received from Mrs. Hoftshot some months after our trip to Northmoor, in which she thanked Holmes and me once again for coming to her aid. She then informed us that she and Mr. Guy Morton were to be married, and stated that it would be their honor if we were to attend. I remember asking Holmes if he was interested in taking the trip.

"Not in the slightest," was his reply.

I wrote back and declined while wishing the couple our best wishes. So far as I am aware, they have lived a happy and peaceful existence in Northmoor ever since.

The Hyde Park Mystery
by Mike Hogan

"I say, Holmes," I said as I eased open the door of the sitting room in Sherlock Holmes's Baker Street lodgings and edged through with my valise and rod case, "those cab rascals are on strike again and it's raining sheets. I'd like to – Oh!"

I paused in the doorway and blinked at Holmes and two gentlemen seated on the sofa and in my usual chair before the fireplace.

"Excuse me." I backed towards the hallway.

Holmes sprang from his armchair. "Come in, my dear fellow!" he said. "Come, take a seat. I was hoping you might be back in time to join us."

I laid my luggage on the rug and my gloves on the sideboard, slipped into a seat at the dining table, and regarded Holmes's visitors with interest. One was a youngish man who exhibited the manner and dress of a gentleman, while the other, an older, sallow-faced, bearded man, wore a cheap, wrinkled suit and had the cloth cap of a working man on his knees.

Holmes settled back in his chair with a mischievous smile. "Doctor Watson, let me introduce Mr. Renfrew of Addison, Chalmers, and Renfrew, Solicitors, and Mr. Salmon, Secretary of the Amalgamated Cab Drivers' Society," he said. "Mr. Salmon was just explaining the cabmen's grievances against the railway companies as a background to a case on which my opinion is requested."

I offered a frigid greeting. "I should be interested to know why it was that no cabs were available at Waterloo Station this morning," I said stiffly, "much to the inconvenience of myself and many other passengers burdened with luggage. I was obliged to cross the bridge to the Embankment before I could induce a cab to stop and pick me up."

"I'm afraid that old chestnut 'railway privilege' is to blame," Holmes said. "That is the iniquity the strikers aim to redress, is it not, Mr. Salmon?"

"The action is not a strike, if I may correct you, Mr. Holmes, sir," Mr. Salmon answered in a shrill tone. He turned to me. "I hope you will not blame the cabbies for your inconvenience, Doctor. Aggrieved street cabmen have temporarily and locally withdrawn their cabs from the vicinity of certain railway termini, as is their right under the relevant acts. Bluchers are voluntary, not contracted." He looked to Mr. Renfrew as if for confirmation of his statement, but that gentleman merely smiled and gave a slight shrug of his shoulders.

189

"If I may summarise the position," Holmes said. "The street cabbies object to the system under which certain cab proprietors pay the railway companies for their cabs' privilege of picking up passengers at the mainline stations. All other non-privileged cabs may drop passengers, but they are excluded from taking fares within the station."

"It is iniquitous," I conceded. "At busy times, cabs are scarce and long queues form at the stands. Station cabs, especially two-wheelers, are more knocked about than street cabs, and their horses are often inferior. Arriving passengers are anxious to get away, perhaps to catch a connecting train at another terminus, so they are obliged to be less particular than one would be on the street." I frowned. "'Bluchers'?"

"Non-privileged cabs," Mr. Salmon explained. "If the Boat Train, say, or a bunch of crowded excursion or race-day trains arrive together, the station staff have to call in street cabs to assist the station cabs – Bluchers, as we call them."

Holmes stood and reached along the mantelpiece for his briar pipe. "Doubtless named for General von Blucher's Prussians at the Battle of Waterloo who, according to partisan legend, reached the field of honour too late for combat and had to be content with merely mopping up stragglers from a French army thoroughly beaten by the English."

"And Scots," Mr. Renfrew said in a Highland accent.

"Quite." Holmes slumped back into his seat and began packing his pipe. "And with those general *desiderata* understood, we may return to the purpose of your visit, gentlemen."

Mr. Renfrew opened his briefcase, took out a brown file secured with silk tape, and passed it to Holmes. "Crown v. Thomas Long, Cabdriver, for the willful murder of cab company proprietor – or more accurately *erstwhile* cab company proprietor – James Ellerton Staines."

"The Hyde Park Murder," I said, leaning forward in my chair.

Mr. Renfrew winced. "So the case has been termed in the gutter press, Doctor Watson, but I think we might allow my client his statutory right of reasonable doubt and call it 'The Hyde Park Shooting'. My client maintains his innocence, and contends that the deceased committed the abominable sin of self-murder."

I bridled. "I read of the case in the *The Times* – hardly a gutter publication."

"A matter of perspective, my dear fellow," Holmes said with a smile. He stood. "Gentlemen, I shall examine the evidence and give you my opinion in due course." He confirmed an appointment at Mr. Renfrew's chambers the following day and ushered our visitors to the sitting room door.

190

I shifted to my usual chair and warmed my hands at the crackling fire. "At times there are fifty or sixty empty cabs milling about the entrance to Victoria Station, impeding traffic. If they were allowed inside to the cab stands, a lot of congestion could be avoided."

Holmes resumed his seat and lit his pipe from the fire with a spill. "Anything to do with London cabs, be it fares, licensing, privilege, or whatever, is bound to be contentious. Matters near to the hearts of the working and middle classes such as beer and cabs are best left alone, as Viscount Cross, our Home Secretary of some years ago, wisely observed."

He settled back in his chair and picked up the folder. He was instantly lost in its contents and soon wreathed in pipe smoke.

For an hour or so while Holmes pondered, I busied myself with thinking what I'd need to do when I went home: Unpacking my case, cleaning my fishing rods, and arranging with our housekeeper for my laundry to be seen to, before facing the onerous task of catching up with my correspondence. Finally Holmes yawned and tossed the folder to the floor at his feet. "Pass me a couple of telegram forms, will you? I am minded to do a little sleuthing before my appointment with Renfrew tomorrow. Are you game?"

"Certainly. Mary is away, and it will make a welcome change from squatting by the Thames at Chertsey in a steady drizzle as I did all day yesterday with a half-dozen minnows to show for my efforts." I passed Holmes a sheaf of telegram forms. "Suicides in cabs are, if not common, certainly not rare. I've often heard cabbies gripe about having to clean up their cabs after an incident. But from the facts as laid out in that notorious gutter publication, *The Times,* the case looks to be a fairly straightforward one of revenge murder."

Holmes stood. "There are singular elements to this matter that elevate it above the norm – if there a norm for homicide."

"Not suicide, as the solicitor proposed?"

"No, no. I suspect Mr. Renfrew's client has been economical with the truth."

Holmes filled in two telegram forms at his desk and called for the pageboy. "Inspector Tobias Gregson of Scotland Yard, whom we know to be competent despite his deductive limitations, is the agent assigned to the case. If the data presented in the file is correct, Gregson will see the cabbie hanged."

I sent Billy to fetch a hansom from the stand, and we set off for Scotland Yard.

Inspector Gregson sat erect at his desk in his office in the recently opened New Scotland Yard building on the Victoria Embankment, in the full glory of his befrogged uniform.

191

A mahogany ink stand, a silver-framed photograph of a white-haired gentleman – presumably a relative – a green-shaded Argon lamp, a telephone apparatus, and a single, slim folder were placed in exactly symmetrical juxtaposition on the gold-stamped leather before him.

Empty shelves lined one wall of the room, which smelled strongly of new wood and furniture polish, with files and books in tea chests ranged below them. An as-yet uncurtained, narrow window offered a view of the Thames, slightly obstructed by a bare-branched tree. A large map of London pinned to one wall was the only decoration.

A young, uniformed constable, fair-haired like the inspector, sat in one corner at a desk piled high with folders, evidence boxes, and untidy stacks of folded newspapers. He jumped up as Holmes and I entered, and he ushered us to a pair of upright chairs in front of the inspector's desk.

Holmes acknowledged the constable's attentions with a languid wave of his hand, and he and I sat. "How are you finding your new accommodation, Inspector?" he asked.

"Well enough," Inspector Gregson answered. "Your telegram requested a briefing on the Long case, Mr. Holmes." He opened the folder in front of him. "I have the cabbie's statement."

"Perhaps you would be good enough to summarise?"

Inspector Gregson slid the file across his desk to his assistant.

"Long picked up a gentleman at eleven-fifteen or thereabouts on Monday night from the night cabstand in Holborn Circus, his usual billet," the young constable began. "He says the gentleman appeared to be slightly the worse for drink, slurring his words, but not drunk. He gave Paddington as his destination, specifically the Great Western Hotel. He requested Long pass through Piccadilly, without giving a reason.

"The ride was unremarkable until they reached Hyde Park Corner, where Long turned his nag north towards his destination. His passenger banged on the roof and required him to take the Ring Road through Hyde Park instead."

"A straighter route," I suggested. "I've taken it myself. It's the only route through the Park open to cabs."

"You travelled in the daytime, I'll wager, Doctor," Inspector Gregson said. "The Ring Road is rarely used at night. It's pitch dark in the Park, save for the odd lamppost here and there, and the road isn't more than a narrow bridle path. One or two cabs have missed a turn and ended up awash in the lake."

"Was Long suspicious?" I asked.

Inspector Gregson nodded to his assistant.

"He says he thought his fare was befuddled," the constable answered, "and like you, Doctor, wanted to take his usual route. The Queen's Gate

192

was open, though the constable on the gate called to Long as they passed to remind him that the Park closed at midnight."

Holmes nodded. "Go on."

"They followed the edge of the lake to a point between the Receiving House of the Royal Humane Society and the Magazine, when the passenger again banged on the roof and ordered Long to pull up. The Ring Road was pot-holed, and Long thought the fellow had been made unwell by the bumps.

"He stopped and instantly both he and the horse were startled by a loud report. It took a moment to bring the horse under control. When he opened his hatch, a strong smell of gunpowder greeted Long, and he was shocked to see his passenger slumped across the seat.

"After vainly checking the man for a pulse, he drove on to the Victoria Gate where he alerted the constable on duty at eleven fifty-seven."

Holmes frowned.

Inspector Gregson leaned forward in his chair. "Yes, Mr. Holmes. Forty-two minutes for a journey that would take in daylight and with moderate traffic no more than twenty-two. At that hour of the evening, with no traffic to speak of, I would expect to do the journey in less time, not more. He contends he has a slow nag, but I have examined his horse and found it to be above average for a cabber. In fact, Constable Boland here did the trip at the same time of night, in a police carriage mind, not a nimble cab, with Long's so-called slow nag hitched in front." He leaned back. "In how long, Boland?"

"Nineteen minutes flat, sir."

The inspector smiled. "So what happened in the missing twenty-odd minutes?"

"An interesting question, Inspector."

On a nod from his master, the constable flipped a page of his report and continued. "The deceased carried no identification, just a wallet with a fiver in it, and some coins. His overcoat and suit are not Saville Row, but are good quality. His hat is Lock's of St James's, his gloves Dents." He smiled. "His bespoke boots have seen better days, but are very fine, crafted by Lobb – "

"An excellent company with records going back years," Inspector Gregson interrupted. "They recognised the boots, and we were able to identify the deceased as Thomas Ellerton Staines, owner of the Staines Cab Company, with nine cabs on the streets of the metropolis – well, that many until a month ago, when one cabbie had words with Mr. Staines, pulled out the twenty-three quid saved with his hire-purchase scheme, and stormed off in high dudgeon, vowing revenge for various wrongs."

I frowned. "Long?"

Inspector Gregson gestured for the file, set it squarely before him and put on a pair of gold-rimmed spectacles. "According to the cabbie, Mr. Staines fired one single round into his own neck. It was done with his Galand and Sommerville .44 calibre pistol. And indeed, his pistol was found to have one chamber expended and the remaining four loaded with unfired cartridges. Two more Webley centre-fire live cartridges were in his overcoat pocket."

Inspector Gregson looked up. "We live in a remarkable age for innovation, gentlemen, and Scotland Yard isn't behind in applying new methods in our investigations. Scientific evidence holds great sway with juries. The unfired cartridges in the victim's gun and coat were minutely examined by our experts at Woolwich Arsenal. One bullet in the gun and the two in the coat were clean and pristine. Three of the unused bullets in the gun were found to have traces of gunpowder – "

"That would be the case in any recently fired pistol," I said.

" – attached to the casing by smears of blood." The inspector sniffed. "Long's clothing and hands were also examined. Blood deposits and gunpowder residue were present on his right hand and sleeve – consistent, as you will agree, Doctor, with recently firing a pistol."

"May I see the weapon?" Holmes asked.

Inspector Gregson took a silvered revolver from his desk drawer. "The pistol is engraved with the victim's initials, and has been confirmed by Mrs. Staines to have been habitually carried by her husband."

Holmes closely examined the pistol, a rather old-fashioned-looking gun with a long extraction lever acting as a trigger guard. He returned the gun to the inspector, who replaced it in the drawer and stood.

"If you would care to follow me, gentlemen?"

The inspector led Holmes, the constable, and me down a dusty staircase smelling strongly of fresh paint to an enclosed stable yard at the back of the police building, where an unharnessed hansom cab stood.

"According to Long, Mr. Staines shot himself in the confines of the cab interior," the inspector said. "Not a roomy place, as you will agree. Suicides almost invariably press the gun barrel to their temple or put it in their mouths, but Mr. Staines chose to shoot himself in the neck from in front, so."

He mimed pointing a gun at his throat. "Awkward, no? The bullet passed through his neck. Where did it go? The cab has been closely examined and nothing found but this." The inspector pointed to a bright mark on the metal rim of one of the wheels. "No gunpowder residue was found on the victim, suggesting the gun was fired at a distance."

Inspector Gregson held out his hand. "Long's story is a tissue of invention, Mr. Holmes. How he lured his ex-employer into his cab, I don't yet know, but I will stake my reputation on this being a murder."

Holmes and I shook his hand, made our farewells, and boarded the waiting cab at the gates of Scotland Yard. Holmes tapped on the cab roof with his cane and the cabbie opened the hatch. "Dufours Place, Soho, if you please."

The cab turned out of the gates and into heavy traffic on the Embankment. "Fifteen-thousand cab drivers infest London," Holmes said. "I am surprised we experience so little cab crime."

I coughed and pointed to the hatch above our heads.

"The London cabbie is the most anonymous of men," Holmes continued. "Unlike the bus driver, who plies a regular route, the cab driver may roam anywhere in the city. His relationship with his passenger is a fleeting one, encouraging brusqueness of manner, or even downright fraud, or worse."

"The same may be true for passengers," I suggested. "I have heard respectable men brag of bilking cabbies of their fare by darting into the Burlington Arcade or Swan and Edgar's, or of treating them with contempt – even men of consequence at my club who in all other matters are worthy of respect."

"It is an interesting collision of the working and middle classes."

We drove in silence as the cab followed the line of the River, turned north, and crossed Trafalgar Square.

"Inspector Gregson seemed a little – how shall I say – aloof, or even cold towards us compared with our previous encounters," I suggested.

"Really? I didn't notice."

"He didn't offer tea."

Holmes and I got down outside St. James' Poorhouse, and we were directed by a common loafer to a modern extension of the main building where a porter in his cubicle enquired our business. He conducted us along a tiled corridor to the coroner's office.

We were ushered into a pleasant room warmed by a merry fire, and with its walls covered with maps and photographs. A trim, neatly dressed gentleman sat behind a heavy, cluttered desk. He stood, introduced himself as the coroner, Doctor Weaver, and waved us to seats set before his desk without offering his hand. "I received your telegram, Mr. Holmes. May I ask with what authority you are making your enquiries?"

"We act for Long, the defendant in the Hyde Park case."

"I see." Doctor Weaver adjusted a pair of *pince-nez* on his nose and peered down at a sheet of paper on his desk. "I am afraid I can find no provision in the parliamentary statutes regulating the conduct of my office that allows me to share information with private agents, however well-intentioned."

"I am retained by Chalmers, Addison, and Renfrew on behalf of their client," Holmes answered in a stiff tone.

"All well and good, sir." Doctor Weaver pursed his lips. "But as coroner, my duty is to report my findings in this matter to the relevant agencies and to them alone. If you can provide me with an authorisation certificate from the police, the Home Office, or another supervising body as listed in the decretum under which I operate," he tapped the paper on his desk, "then I would be pleased to cooperate with you gentlemen."

Holmes glared at the coroner and seemed about to make a possibly unhelpful remark, so I quickly interjected. "Coroner Doctor Ivor Purchase of the Middlesex Mortuary at St. Laurence, Pountney Hill, has condescended to work with Mr. Holmes on several occasions, to their mutual benefit."

Doctor Weaver smiled a cold smile. "Again, that is all very well. Purchase is free to make whatever decisions he may in his district, but this is my little domain, Doctor, and I require my '*T*'s to be dotted and my '*T*'s crossed."

"A man's life is at stake," Holmes said. "This is hardly a time for quibbles."

We sat in strained silence for a long moment.

I stood and went to the fireplace. "I couldn't help noticing this photograph above the mantel, Doctor. Netley Hospital, if I am not mistaken? I trained at Netley in '79, and went on to serve with the Berkshires in Afghanistan."

Doctor Weaver's stern demeanour softened. "Maiwand?"

I nodded.

"You would have known Surgeon-Major Preston."

"Very well. Like me, he was wounded during the battle, but recovered. I saw him off at Tilbury a few years ago when he was taking up a position in Hong Kong."

"He graduated from Netley with me." Doctor Weaver said. "I was with the Buffs in Natal." He stood and shook my hand. "This way, gentlemen."

Holmes and I followed Doctor Weaver along a green-tiled corridor to the mortuary, a long, narrow room, brightly lit, in which a dozen or so porcelain-topped tables stood in rows. Naked or sheeted bodies lay on several, and the inevitable reek of corruption polluted the atmosphere.

Doctor Weaver pulled the sheet from one table disclosing an obese male, face up, with a bullet wound in his throat.

"The ball entered his neck, severing the carotid artery and causing catastrophic blood loss before exiting behind his ear," Doctor Weaver said. "The victim was instantly doomed."

"This man has been badly beaten quite recently," I said. "He has bruises on his body and arms and a cauliflower ear." I borrowed Holmes's magnifying glass, leaned over the corpse, and examined strange discolourations on the victim's chin and between his nose and upper lip. "What are these pock marks on his face? A skin disease?"

Doctor Weaver frowned. "They are odd. I've taken samples for analysis. You can see where blood remains attached to the skin of the chin and couldn't be easily washed off. And the marks on his philtrum and around his nasolabial creases are equally puzzling."

I shook my head, and Holmes, smiling, said nothing.

"Those strange marks . . ." I said we climbed back into our cab.

"Hmm?"

"I saw your eyes light up."

Holmes tapped on the cab roof. "Fetter Lane."

"The coroner was as unwelcoming as Inspector Gregson," I suggested. "Everyone seems to have been tipped out of bed on the wrong side this morning." I wiped the cab window with my sleeve. "Or perhaps this persistent rain is putting a damper on people's spirits." I grinned. "Lucky Doctor Weaver and I were alumni of the Army Medical School, eh?"

"Stop at the next telegraph office," Holmes called to the cabbie.

We got down by The White Swan public house and I followed Holmes into a narrow alley lined with decrepit fencing, picking my way among mounds of loose cobbles and sand, stinking puddles, and heaps of horse droppings. The din of traffic in Fleet Street receded, overtaken by the ring of a blacksmith's hammer. The metallic tang of a farrier's hot iron tainted the air.

An empty cab trundled up behind us, and the driver hooted us out of the way as he turned sharp between open gates into a wide, cobbled yard, spraying my trouser bottoms with mud from his wheels.

Holmes led me in behind the cab. A smithy was on one side of the yard amid a heap of broken cab parts and twisted ironwork. The other side was taken up with an extensive stable. A two-story house stood in the far corner of the property with a glazed box on the balcony from which the entire yard could be observed.

I peered through the stable doors and saw narrow stalls for perhaps a score of nags. The roof was low. No windows pierced the walls, but light

197

streamed through countless cracks and crevices in the walls and ceiling. The stench repelled me.

The smithy side of the yard was lined with sheds, their open doors revealing rows of harness, bags of feed, and the like. A tuneless whistle came from one, and the scent of frying onions wafted from another, which despite the competing stenches made my mouth water.

Five cabs stood in a row in the centre of the yard, including the one that had splashed past me. Holmes addressed the driver as he got down from the box. "Staines Cab Company?"

The driver, a muscular, middle-aged man with a walrus moustache and a knowing look about him, folded a leather jerkin across his arm. "Staines as was. Not sure whose yard it is now."

"You worked for Mr. Staines?" Holmes asked.

"Whose asking?"

"I am Sherlock Holmes, consulting detective. The solicitor for Mr. Long has requested my help in his current misfortune. My companion is Doctor Watson. You are?"

"Joe Maudsley. I drove a Staines' cab until two weeks ago, four years in all. I was the senior man."

"You knew Long?"

"I did."

"I'm here to enquire into the circumstances of the shooting in Hyde Park – particularly the relationship between Long and his employer."

The cabbie laughed. "That's easy. They hated each other's guts."

"Why?"

Maudsley looked about him. I noticed the hammering has stopped, and several men in cabbie's capes or leather aprons were clustered outside the sheds staring.

"Best come up." Maudsley led Holmes and me to a rickety staircase attached to the main house, up to the balcony, and into the glazed shed at one end.

"Mr. Staines' aerie, where he kept his eye on us and did his books," Maudsley said. He leaned against a rough-hewn table and indicated a pair of stools. "Mrs. Staines is gone to live with her mother, down Chippenham way. I'm looking after the place until things are sorted."

"What was the cause of the rift between Long and his employer?" Holmes asked as we perched on the stools.

Maudsley sighed. "Look, gents, runnin' a cab business or driving a cab – it ain't easy either way. With fodder at ten shillin' a week per nag, wear and tear on the cabs, and all the regulations on the boss's side, and on the driver's the daily cab hire of twelve bob in January, going up a bob

198

a week after the Boat Race to as much as eighteen bob in Derby Week. It ain't easy."

Maudsley shook his head. "At the regulated fare rates, a cabbie's to drive thirty-odd miles or more just to pay back the cab hire. That's before he makes a penny for himself. And add to that yard money for stablemen and carriage washers, and tips to buck riders, hotel doormen, and the like."

"Were all Staines' cabbies on daily hire?" Holmes asked.

Maudsley nodded. "Till a month ago. That's the story behind all the trouble." He wiped a windowpane with his sleeve and peered out. "Cabman's weather. A fine morning, so people go out without their umbrellas – and now a drizzly afternoon so they regret it."

"We won't keep you long," Holmes said coldly. "The trouble?"

"I don't like to speak ill of the dead," Maudsley took a clay pipe from his coat pocket and gently tapped it out on the table edge, "but it's well known Mr. Staines liked his liquor. I won't say he was a drunk, but I can say I've never seen him completely sober. He'd a bad temper on him, and he was an unlucky wight." Maudsley opened a drawer under the table and took out a cloth bag. "Last year he bought seven horses from the Gypos fair down Brighton way, but only two was what we call a 'cabber', a proper well-made-up cab horse. Then one of them was lost when the stable boy watered him at a public trough, though told not to, and he caught glanders and died."

He took a pinch of tobacco from the bag and filled his pipe. "A proper cab master must be sharp. The trade is overcrowded, sirs, what with trams and omnibuses and the underground railway. And the telephone. Time was, we'd get easy shilling fares in the City – gents passing to-and-fro from Throckmorton Street to Leadenhall, say, well within a mile. Now the toffs do the work by telephone or messenger."

"The trouble?" Holmes persisted.

"Like a lot of drivers, Long put some of his money aside each week with the Guv'nor towards buying his own cab. He'd no money to get one new, but bit by bit he was saving and dreaming of buying his cab second-hand and being an owner driver, the only way to survive in this game."

Maudsley tapped his pockets and peered into the drawer. I passed him my matches and he lit his pipe and nodded thanks. "One day, Mr. Staines turns up in the yard gloating on how he's made a deal with the London, Brighton, and South Coast Railway. We were to move the depot to Clapham and be privileged at Clapham Junction Station."

"Lane was to become a privileged driver," I said. "What had he to complain about?"

Maudsley blew a stream of pipe smoke across the room. "Aside from having to pick up sticks and move his wife and little 'un across London,

Long was dead against privilege – all street cabbies are. And privilege means a higher daily cab rent to the owner to compensate for the money he pays to the railway.

"Long gave Mr. Staines notice and demanded his savings from the Guv'nor's kitty. Mr. Staines tried to talk him 'round, but Tom's more stubborn than hammered iron, and he damned Mr. Staines' eyes and dragged his money out. He borrowed from his wife's brother, and they went in together on a second-hand rig as solo owner-drivers. He joined the Amalgamated Cab Drivers' Society and encouraged others to do the same. That put him right up against his ex-master. Words were spoken on both sides."

"That was all?" Holmes asked.

"It was enough, if you know Mr. Staines and Tom. The drivers met together down the pub. Long stirred them up, and there was talk of a strike against the move. I calmed the men and it fizzled out."

Maudsley took a long draw of his pipe. "But Tom had set us a-thinking. I run a street cab. I don't want my cab weighed down with trunks and cases at the railway station with the roof needing fixing every six months. Nor chips and scratches on the cabinet work from the horses shying when the locos let off steam or hoot their whistles. And there's the penny fee you pay to enter the station. No, I leave all that to the four-wheelers. The railway companies fleece us cabbies both ways and backwards."

He folded his arms. "And I didn't fancy moving to Clapham. So I joined the Amalgamated Cab Drivers' Society and took out a loan to set up a solo rig. As did three other Staines men. The Guv'nor was furious – he has a temper on him – and he blamed Tom Long. They were at hammer and tongs. Yes, they had a row right there in the yard, and it came to fisticuffs. Between you and me, Tom gave Mr. Staines a right drubbing. They parted on bad terms, both vowing to make the other pay for their wrongs."

Maudsley stood, brushing tobacco strands from his coat. "Things went downhill for the Guv'nor from then on. More men left, the bank pulled in loans, and he drank more. His missus told him she'd had enough, and she went to her mother."

Holmes stood. "Thank you, Mr. Maudsley, you have been very helpful. I assume the police are aware of the facts you have detailed?"

"The inspector asked a lot of questions."

"Mr. Holmes?" a shrill voice cried from the yard below.

I went to the window. "A telegraph boy calling for you."

We descended the stairs to the yard and the grim-faced boy handed Holmes a telegram slip and bent to wipe the mud and worse off his once-shiny boots with a piece of rag. I tipped him thruppence, but that didn't improve the boy's mood. He stalked across the muddy yard, muttering to himself as he picked a path between the pools of filth.

Holmes checked his watch. "We have an appointment at the location of the crime in forty-four minutes." He turned to Maudsley. "But I should like to get to the Park a little early."

We watched as a groom and boy changed Maudsley's horse for a fresh one, wiped down the cab, and filled and trimmed his lamps. Then we climbed aboard.

The trap was open and Maudsley leaned forward and looked down on us. "After the fight, Mr. Staines boasted as how he'd chair-marked Long's cab license before he gave it back to him. Tom learned of that in the pub that evening, and it was all his mates could do to hold him back from coming here and pummelling Mr. Staines again."

Maudsley pulled on his driving gloves. "Tom has a fiery temper on him and he can be main stubborn on top. I shouldn't like to be his employer, and that's a fact." His expression became grave. "But Tom's no killer – at least, I should be surprised if he was proved to be one." He closed the trap door, flicked his whip, and the horse took the strain and started off.

"Chair-mark?" I asked.

"A secret mark added to the cabbie's license by his previous employer warning other proprietors that the man is unreliable or a troublemaker." Holmes pulled his briar pipe from his coat pocket, his tobacco from another, and stuffed the bowl.

"That may have exacerbated the bad blood between the men to breaking point."

"Quite possibly."

"I received your message with surprise," Inspector Gregson said as he stepped down from his cab onto the Ring Road. A closed police carriage pulled up behind.

"Your continued interest in the case surprises me, Mr. Holmes. While I won't say the matter is open-and-shut – if I may wax metaphorical, the case required a certain amount of teasing out." The inspector twisted imaginary fibres in his hands. "But I can safely assert that the vital threads of the matter are in my hands."

"There are one or two small questions that might be of relevance, Inspector," Holmes said with a smile. "How did Long lure Staines into his cab for a journey across the city to Hyde Park? If he planned a murder, why did he not provide his own murder weapon, rather than relying on his victim bringing his pistol? And why did he handle the three unused cartridges in the cylinder?"

"And what are the strange marks on the victim's face?" I added.

Inspector Gregson pulled his watch from his waistcoat pocket and checked the time. "Yes, yes, a quibble or two may remain, I'll grant you." He put his watch away. "I have accepted your request to meet you here with the prisoner, against the advice of my superiors, but you'll forgive me if I answer your questions with another. If I can prove the cabbie lied about the vital circumstances of the incident, and if I can categorically exclude suicide, would you not agree that would leave Long in a very invidious position? The prosecuting counsel, Sir Vandissart Bullimore, QC, could make much of that. He is pitiless in cross-examination."

Holmes pursed his lips and said nothing.

"I contend that Long lured Mr. Staines to this out of the way place intending to do him harm in revenge for alleged wrongs," the inspector continued. "He stopped his cab and pounced on his unsuspecting victim. At some point in the struggle, he gained possession of the victim's pistol and shot Mr. Staines at close range – close but not close enough to corroborate his suicide story. There is no powder residue around the death wound." He smiled. "Scientific analysis, Doctor – as I said, that always impresses a jury."

Holmes indicated a set of wheel marks in the muddy road. "The cab stopped here. The marks are still evident, although the rains have washed away blood and tracks in the mud. Did you make a thorough search of the undergrowth, examining the trees in particular?"

"What for, Mr. Holmes? What of relevance is missing?"

Holmes shrugged, and we watched as Constable Boland and two detective-sergeants helped their handcuffed and leg-ironed prisoner from the police van and escorted him towards us.

"Do I detect a gleam in your assistant's eye, Inspector?" Holmes asked.

Gregson smiled a thin smile. "We have a witness, Mr. Holmes."

"Inspector, now you have surprised me," Holmes said, returning his smile. He waved an expansive hand across the verdant grass, bushes, and clumps of woodland that stretched for hundreds of yards around us. "This is one of very few places in this busy city where I had expected mayhem could be committed with reasonable confidence of privacy."

"My witness lives no more than fifty yards from here, gentlemen." Inspector Gregson leaned back on his heels and grasped his lapels. "He heard four shots fired."

Holmes nodded. "That makes sense."

Inspector Gregson blinked at Holmes.

"A witness in Hyde Park at near midnight?" I asked, looking about me. I could see no habitation within several hundred yards, and no building except the Royal Humane Society's Receiving House about a hundred yards farther along the road.

"Barnabas awaits us at the Receiving House," the inspector said curtly.

A hansom drew up and Long's solicitor, Mr. Renfrew, got down.

Holmes drew his watch and checked the time. "We are assembled. Before we meet the mysterious Mr. Barnabas, might we attempt to re-enact the crime?"

He faced the prisoner, a sullen-looking, sallow faced man in his thirties in broad-arrow prison dress with his caped overcoat across his shoulders. "Good afternoon, Long. I am Sherlock Holmes, the consulting detective, and your only hope of avoiding the rope. Unless you cooperate with me and tell us the whole truth without equivocation, I regret to inform you that you will be hanged for the willful murder of your ex-employer."

Long glared at Holmes. "I did not murder Mr. Staines."

Holmes returned the cabbie's glare. "I believe you did not, but you do yourself no good with this nonsense of suicide. The inspector has a witness. Will you not do yourself the favour of telling us how Mr. Staines' life ended here?"

"I've said my piece." Long spat on the grass and looked away.

"Watch it, you." One of the detectives guarding the prisoner jerked the chain binding his wrists and arms. "Answer the gentleman nice."

Holmes balled his fists. "The man is as stubborn – "

" – nor hammered iron," I said.

Long remained silent. His solicitor murmured in his ear and then addressed Holmes and Inspector Gregson. "My client reserves his defence."

"I have followed your tracks to Long Water," Holmes said in an exasperated tone, "where you disposed of the evidence."

Long looked up, startled, and Gregson regarded Holmes through narrowed eyes "Evidence, Mr. Holmes?"

"In good time, Inspector. If Long will not cooperate, let us meet your Mr. Barnabas."

We walked along the Ring Road in a huddle, stepping around puddles, and in silence but for the jingle of the prisoner's chains. The drizzle had abated, but the clouds were low, grey, and threatening.

"Is Barnabas a first or family name?" I asked as we followed Inspector Gregson into the Royal Humane Society Headquarters. There was no answer.

The director, a Mr. Wick, met us at the door and ushered us through the handsome main building with its elegant rooms furnished in the Regency style, out to the lake shore, and to a rather incongruous *faux* Elizabethan structure that I must have seen a dozen times on visits to the Park, but took no notice of. Inside the high-roofed chamber were several hospital beds, a bath equipped, as we were informed, with a hot water furnace for warming frozen limbs, a hook in the ceiling for hanging the semi-drowned by their feet, and a large bellows for blowing reviving cigar-smoke into their lungs.

Everything was modern and sparkled with cleanliness – everything except for a wizened old man in a tightly buttoned, patched grey suit with a threadbare blanket across his shoulders who sat in a chair by the door. He looked up as we entered the room and gave us a rheumy-eyed, gap-toothed smile.

He was introduced as Barnabas.

"Your witness is a tramp," I said. I frowned at the old man's downcast expression. "I mean, ah, a gentleman of the road."

"Mr. Barnabas worked for the Post Office for many years until he became sick and was obliged to give it up," Mr. Wick said. "He gave the *view halloa* when a small boy fell off the bridge and the child was saved. Since then, he has been allowed to make a nest under a tarpaulin against the wall of the equipment shed where we keep lifebelts and the like. During the day, he earns a few pennies by picking up litter. The park attendants and police turn a blind eye."

"Hyde Park is the only Royal Park patrolled by the Metropolitan Police, rather than the Parks Constabulary," Inspector Gregson explained. "We perhaps take a broader view of public order than the specialised force. We are plagued with slum-dwellers washing their grubby offspring and filthy laundry in the lake, but Barnabas does no harm, and we're used to him."

The inspector addressed Barnabas in a loud voice. "You heard shots on the night in question – two nights ago, on Monday. Is that right."

"Indeed, sir," the old man answered. "That's right. Shots. Bangs, they were."

"How many bangs?"

"Four – four bangs." He lifted his arm and waved a trembling hand in the air, his finger pointed at Gregson. "'*D.T.*', sir."

"Inspector," I exclaimed, "your star witness's mind is befuddled by drink and circumstance. You see his shaking, crabbed hand. He admits he suffers from '*D.T.*'. *Delirium tremens*. I don't think even the majestic Sir Vandissart Bullimore would care to offer a trembling alcoholic as a witness in a capital case."

Holmes pulled up a chair and sat knee to knee with Barnabas. They conversed in murmurs.

The inspector rounded on Long. "What have you to say? This witness contends there were four shots."

Holmes looked up. "But we know better, do we not, Long?"

Long looked down at his feet, Mr. Renfrew put a consoling hand on his client's shoulder, and Inspector Gregson glared at Holmes.

"How do you account for the single fired cartridge case in the pistol if four shots were fired?" I asked the inspector.

"You may think we at Scotland Yard are not scientifically minded, Doctor, but you would be wrong, sir." Inspector Gregson addressed Mr. Renfrew. "Under normal circumstances, the prosecution would spring this on your client during the trial, but I am being as open as I can be. I think we can save ourselves a deal of trouble and save the Queen some money by showing you how tight my web is about your client.

"Mr. Staines' pistol is a five-shot. If he decided to carry a reload, it would be logical would it not for him to carry five more bullets? I believe he did so. Long fired four shots at his victim. One chipped a wheel rim and only one hit home and answered his purpose. Thinking to outwit the police and mimic a suicide, he took three unfired bullets from Mr. Staines' pocket and replaced the fired cartridges with new ones, accidentally smearing them with blood in the process. His hands were bloody when he was examined at the station." The inspector turned to Holmes. "How is that, sir?"

"Yes, I believe that is exactly what happened."

Inspector Gregson frowned at Holmes. "You do? Then that's an end of the matter."

"Not quite." Holmes stood and shook Barnabas' hand.

"Mr. Holmes, you spoke of further evidence," Gregson said as we stepped back onto the Ring Road.

Holmes looked up. "The heavens threaten. It's only four-hundred yards or so, but we might save time and ride. Follow me."

"I spoke with Constable Boland, the inspector's assistant," I said as I sat with Holmes in our hansom, leading the convoy towards the northern gate of the Park. "It seems Inspector Gregson has been criticised by his superiors for attempting to introduce some of your deductive methods into his department. His detective sergeants went over his head with complaints of the inspector's apparently oppressive zeal in avoiding contamination of the scenes where crimes have occurred, his arduous systematic methods, and his insistence on detailed record-keeping. The inspector has been warned off too close a collaboration with you."

"Is that so?" Holmes smiled a reptilian smile.

He tapped on the roof and called to Maudsley to pull up, and he and I jumped down. "Come along," he called to the vehicles behind us.

Holmes marched past a "*Kindly Do Not Walk on the Grass*" sign towards the lake, whistling, his cane over his shoulder, and his hat at a jaunty angle. I grinned as I followed him. With Holmes in this mood, I thought, anything was possible.

"Please don't step on the wheel tracks," he called to the police, prisoner, and Mr. Renfrew straggling behind us.

"Marks of a loaded hansom, Mr. Holmes," Gregson returned. "I noted the tracks when I surveyed the scene yesterday."

"I expected that you had done so, Inspector. I know how systematic and thorough your methods are."

We followed the wheel tracks to where they stopped by the edge of the lake and turned back towards the road.

"As you know," Holmes said. "Long paused here. Let us consider why."

One of the detective sergeants with the prisoner answered. "He pulled off the road to be better concealed while he reloaded the victim's gun and prepared his story."

"Four shots, Mr. Holmes," the other detective said. "That amounts to cold-blooded murder in my book." He grinned at his companion, winked at Long, and mimed a jerking a noose above his head.

"We know that Mr. Staines habitually carried a revolver, and his foreman says he had a fiery temper," Holmes continued, unabashed.

"These cab fellows stick together, Mr. Holmes," the same detective said. "Look at that recent strike at Waterloo – "

"It was a temporary and localised withdrawal of service, Sergeant," I corrected him, "not a strike."

The detectives exchanged amused looks and sauntered to the lake edge, lighting cigarettes.

Holmes beckoned to Gregson. "If you thought you might be stalked by such a fellow as Staines," he murmured, "what would you do?"

"I'd carry a weapon to defend myself." The inspector narrowed his eyes.

"And if you were Staines attempting to wreak your revenge on Long, you wouldn't wish to – "

" – be recognised." A slow smile spread across the inspector's face. He turned away, calling his men together.

"The marks on the victim's chin," I said.

Holmes echoed the inspector's smile.

Inspector Gregson picked up a fallen tree branch about a foot long and heaved it into the water. "Search in an arc from at that radius," he ordered.

"In the water, sir?" One of the detectives murmured something, and the other laughed. "Looking for what, sir?

Gregson frowned. "For what? Haven't you been paying attention? For a pistol and disguise of course. How else do you suppose four – "

Holmes succumbed to a fit of coughing.

"How else do you suppose *six* shots were fired?" the inspector asked.

The detectives took off their boots and stockings with a great show of reluctance. Constable Boland tittered behind his hand.

"You too, Constable," Gregson ordered.

We joined the inspector and watched with amusement as the policemen rolled up their trousers and waded into Long Water, shivering and cursing. I turned to Holmes. "More than four shots?"

"My dear Watson, not only have you *looked* but not *seen*, you have *listened* but not *heard*," he answered. "Mr. Barnabas will make an excellent witness – for the defence. The hand that you described with some exactness as shaking and crabbed is the key to his testimony."

"I recognised the cramped fingers of the telegraph operator," I said with a sniff.

"Exactly. You were precisely correct."

I gave Holmes a suspicious glare and said nothing.

Holmes mimed tapping a Morse key. "Barnabas was hunched over a telegraph apparatus for twenty years, until, as you saw, his fingers became stiffened and fixed by arthritis into the crablike claw with which he is now burdened. He was obliged to give up his employment. Incapable of using a telegraph key, and having no other skill, he is as we now see him, a gentleman of the road – but not, as you so rashly diagnosed, a drunkard.

"Barnabas informed me that he is fiercely temperance. He eschews all alcoholic beverages. His befuddlement isn't due to drunkenness, but rather to shyness. He has had little commerce with people for many years, other than begging for his bread. We must make some allowance."

"But he clearly said he heard four shots, and he suffers from – wait, Morse!"

Holmes nodded. "As Inspector Gregson and I instantly apprehended, Barnabas was not admitting to bouts of *delirium tremens*, he was describing what he heard on that fateful night in the precise language of his erstwhile employment. *Dah di dit and dah*: The letters '*DT*' in Morse code. *BANG, bang, bang, BANG*."

207

Constable Boland cried out, stooped, and held up a mass of hair wrapped around a shining bright revolver. He waded back to shore, handed the gun to the inspector, and held up a sodden false beard.

"A Webley .44 with two shots fired," Gregson said as he snapped the cylinder closed. "Those, plus four from Mr. Staines' gun. Six shots in all."

He turned to the prisoner. "You have a reputation as a stubborn fellow, Mr. Long, and that will be the end of you if you persist. I have built a fine web of circumstantial evidence around you, but you have a glimmer of hope. Six shots were fired that night – two from your revolver – "

"Four shots or six," one of the detectives said as he struggled to put on his stockings. "Long still killed Staines and covered it up."

"That's willful murder in my book," said the other detective.

"No, gentleman," the inspector corrected him, "*Six* shots: *Four* from Mr. Staines' revolver, and *two* from Mr. Long's, but Barnabas heard four bangs. You must try to develop a more deductive approach to your work." He beamed at Holmes.

Holmes addressed Long. "Let me stimulate your memory. You carried a pistol for self-protection against your erstwhile employer. It was in your pocket when you picked up a fare in Throckmorton Street at eleven-fifteen, a bearded gentlemen well wrapped up in an overcoat and scarf and wearing a bowler. The journey went as you have described it. When the customer ordered you to stop in an out-of-the-way place, you opened the hatch to see what was up.

"The inspector and I cannot reconstruct the details without your help, but we know this. You and Mr. Staines exchanged shots. He fired four times, and you twice. Your first and last exchanges were simultaneous, and that final shot was the fatal one."

Long looked from Holmes to grim-faced Inspector Gregson, and he slowly nodded. "You have it down pat, sir," he answered in a throaty rasp. "I got a gun because I knew Mr. Staines of old. He knew not the meaning of Christian forgiveness, nor of bygones. He thirsted for revenge.

"I didn't recognise him in his false beard and heavy coat sir, in the black of night, and I drove him here all innocent, thinking nothing of it 'cept my passenger was in drink. We stopped right where you said, sir.

"I opened the hatch and he was staring up at me, his face twisted and a pistol in his hand. I knew instantly who he was, beard or no beard. I slammed down the hatch, jumped from the cab, and ran for my life towards a clump of trees by the roadside, pulling my pistol from my pocket as I ran. I turned to a shout. Staines was out of the cab pointing his gun. I did the same, and we fired. We both missed.

"The horse reared at the noise and slid into the ditch, taking the cab with it. I turned, ran again, and heard two more shots. One hit a tree just as I dived behind it.

"Staines was coming towards me, waving his gun and shouting as to how I'd ruined him and his family and I was going to pay the price. I tried to reason with him, but my fear mounted as he advanced. He aimed and I did the same. We both fired. His bullet again hit the tree I was sheltering behind, and mine struck him down.

"I left my hiding place and ventured to him. The bullet had passed through his neck and blood was spurting out. I could do nothing. I took his gun and pocketed it and my own before I calmed my nag and drew her and the carriage out of the ditch.

"I thought to leave him and ride on to the Victoria Gate and fetch help, but although I had little hope he could be saved and he was my sworn enemy, I felt it was my Christian duty to make the attempt. So I dragged the body to the cab, heaved him aboard, and set off.

"I had to pull up the horse after a short distance as the body had shifted and was in danger of falling out. I checked on Staines. There was no doubt at all he was dead. His red-soaked false beard was half off, his eyes were open and staring, and his chest was drenched in his life's blood. I sat by the side of the cab and tried to make sense of what had happened. I could see the lamps of the Gardens across the Bayswater Road, and I knew there was a police box there, but I was afeard to give myself up – I knew my hot temper and our row when I left Staines' employ would be black against me.

"I looked through his pockets and found Staines' wallet, with a fiver in it, a few coins, and a letter from his wife. In his other pocket were five cartridges. That gave me pause."

Long hung his head. "It was a mad thought, borne of fear I would be charged with his death, gentlemen, but I thought if he were not identified and no connection was made to me, the police might accept he was a suicide. I reloaded the gun, all save one chamber, leaving two bullets in his coat."

"Tut-tut," said Holmes. "A foolish move."

"I turned the cab and crossed the grass back to Long Water. I ripped up the letter, God forgive me, and threw the pieces, my pistol, and the false beard into the lake."

Holmes addressed the two sergeants. "Of the six shots, the first two were fired simultaneously, as attested by Barnabas and Long. Then two shots came from Mr. Staines' gun, and finally two more simultaneous shots, one of which killed the victim. Murder, manslaughter, or justifiable homicide, gentlemen?"

"We shall enter a plea of self-defence, Mr. Holmes," Mr. Renfrew said, rubbing his hands together, "with every prospect of acquittal. The disguise will prove premeditation on the part of the victim and help corroborate my client's account." He smiled. "Perhaps the police might review the facts and decline to prosecute."

Inspector Gregson returned his smile. "Not my decision." He offered his hand to Holmes, Renfrew, and me, turned away, and marched back towards the carriages. His assistant grinned and trotted after him, carrying his boots, leaving the bewildered detective sergeants with the handcuffed prisoner.

Holmes held out his hand. "Key?"

Holmes and I stepped down from our hansom outside his Baker Street lodgings and I paid our fare, adding a half-crown tip.

"Very decent of you, Doctor," Maudsley said. "Without tips I'd starve, and that's the honest truth of the matter. Women never tip. I look for a swell nob with his lady, or a City man who puts his fare down without a murmur and adds a tanner on top. They're the fellows for me." He raised his whip to his hat in salute and trotted away.

"*The Times* was right. It was a murder," I said as Holmes and I divested ourselves of our coats in the hall. "I wonder why people hire a cab to commit self-murder?"

"I imagine they don't want to cause their relatives any inconvenience. Or perhaps their landladies. I believe Mrs. Hudson would be quite vexed if you decided to shrug off your mortal coil in her second-best bedroom."

I considered that hopefully unlikely prospect as we made our way upstairs to the sitting room.

"I'm not sure I approve of trade unions," I admitted as we settled by the fire and Holmes poured us restorative brandies after our busy day.

"You needn't be concerned," Holmes answered as he passed my glass. "The great bulk of cab drivers are too underpaid, overworked, and isolated to combine, and as long as they are underpaid, overworked and isolated, so they will remain."

The Adventure of the
Troubled Wife
by Arthur Hall

During my long association with my friend, Mr. Sherlock Holmes, I often witnessed his acute evaluation of the circumstances surrounding a case before he brought it to a successful conclusion. Many of these investigations were of conventional crimes, but as time wore on he became increasingly inclined towards situations of a strange or unusual nature, such as I have received his permission to relate here.

It wasn't long after the capture of Colonel Sebastian Moran that we returned to our lodgings one morning after an exhilarating walk in Regent's Park. Holmes, having newly resumed his Baker Street activities, was in high spirits.

"I don't think it will be long before more clients present themselves here. Scotland Yard is aware of your return, and the newspapers will ensure that word spreads quickly."

Divesting himself of his hat and coat, he answered cheerfully. "More so than you apparently expect. Surely you cannot have missed the young woman on the far side of the street as we set out? Or if you did, her presence near the corner on our return didn't escape your notice?"

"I confess to being aware of her only just now. You believe, then, that she will bring you a new problem?"

"Her behaviour suggests it, but we shall see." He had been about to settle himself in his armchair, but instead he crossed the room to peer down from the window. "Ah, it seems my surmise was correct. She has made her decision and is approaching our front door."

The doorbell rang and was almost immediately answered by our landlady, who showed the woman into our sitting room.

"Mrs. Ellen Cooper to see Mr. Holmes."

"Thank you, Mrs. Hudson." As she withdrew, my friend gave our visitor a curious look but made no comment except to welcome her with rather less enthusiasm than was his usual practice.

Mrs. Cooper was an imposing figure. Quite tall and slim, she wore a costume of dark green with a matching hat. I would have said she was in her early thirties, and it seemed to me that her most prominent features were hair of a rich auburn and a wide, sensuous mouth.

When we were all seated and introductions had been made, I offered her refreshment which she politely refused, stating that she was anxious to confide in us.

"I see that you have experienced some anxiety of late," Holmes said. "Very well. Take a few moments to place your thoughts in order, and then relate your experience from the beginning. Include even the smallest details, for they are often significant. There is no need to hurry."

"Thank you," she began. "I hope you will not think that I have wasted your time, for the fear that blights my life haunts me in a dream."

I glanced at my friend, wondering if he would dismiss her at once or recommend that she should consult a priest, but he simply nodded, his expression unaltered.

"Nevertheless, pray continue."

She glanced at me, then back to Holmes, and attempted to quell her restless fingers.

"In my dream, it is midnight. I am taken to a place where I am surrounded by fearsome images, grim statues that I somehow know would wish me great harm were they alive. I am forced to lie upon a long table and I cannot see clearly, as great black birds swoop down on me from above. You see, gentlemen, I have had a morbid fear of birds since childhood, when my father enjoyed the sport of falconry. He took me to a display, probably to arouse my interest in such things, but one of the hawks attacked me for a reason that was never discovered."

"Forgive me," I interrupted, "but did the creature leave marks upon you?"

"Mercifully no. It plucked the hat from my head and pecked my skull until I bled. The wounds healed, and any remaining scars are hidden beneath my hair."

"Do the birds attack in silence?" Holmes asked then.

"Not at all. Their cries are deafening, screeches that chill my blood."

"Yet they haven't actually pierced you in any way, nor shed blood as in your childhood experience?"

"No. I awake in my bed convinced that my dream is reality even in the cold light of morning, but I have no wounds. This doesn't diminish the effect on me, however. The horror of it persists."

We sat without speaking for several moments, the only sounds reaching us through the half-open window. The cries of newspaper sellers, the voice of someone prophesying doom should we fail to repent, and that of a woman selling apples, floated up to us.

"Does this occur every night?" Holmes enquired.

She shook her head. "No, there is no pattern to it that I can see. Over the past three weeks I have dreamed of this on two nights together, then single nights spaced apart irregularly. On one occasion there were three together, I think."

"Does your husband not confirm that you have remained in the bed-chamber throughout the night?"

"He and I have been separated for almost three months now, sirs. He knows nothing of this."

"May I ask why you are apart?"

Her head went down, and her gaze fell to the floor. "I long for a child. He thinks only of his business."

"I am exceedingly sorry to learn of this. What, in fact, is his profession?"

"He sells houses, usually to foreigners who wish to live here."

"I see. Has it occurred to you that he might be responsible in some way for your difficulties? This has to be the work of someone who is familiar to your aversion to birds, you understand."

Mrs. Cooper nodded. "I have thought of this, of course, but I cannot see how."

"Tell us please," I said then, "of the method used to prevent you from rising from the table."

"I am strapped down by my arms."

"And are there no marks from this visible on awakening?"

"None. In the dream, a man with a white beard binds my arms with thick cloth before securing the straps."

"Thank you," I murmured thoughtfully. "That is quite clear."

"Have you sought medical assistance on this matter?" Holmes asked.

"It was my first thought to do so," she replied. "Doctor Pressingham dismissed the dream as nothing more than fanciful and prescribed a sleeping draught."

"I perceive that you aren't excessively rich, but are you expecting to receive a large sum of money in the near future? An inheritance or legacy, perhaps?"

Our client looked surprised at the question. "Nothing of the sort, as far as I am aware."

"Have you lived at your current residence for long?"

"About six months." She considered for a moment. "Yes, it was about three months before my husband left that we bought the house."

Holmes got to his feet. "That, I think, is all I need to know for now. Thank you, Mrs. Cooper, for presenting us with a most unusual case. One thing I must ask of you, and that is that you despatch a telegram to this address immediately or soon after rising, the next and all subsequent mornings after you experience the dream. Kindly give your address, and any other details that you believe may be necessary, to Doctor Watson. I have no doubt that you will hear from us before long."

With that he surprised me by turning abruptly and crossing the room to the window without a word of farewell. I thought this most discourteous and resisted the urge to apologise for him as I escorted the lady downstairs and procured for her a hansom.

He hadn't moved by the time I re-entered our sitting room.

"Holmes," I called, waiting until he had half-turned towards me before continuing, "it is most unlike you to treat a lady so." Then a sudden thought struck me. "Did you approach the window so hurriedly in order to determine whether our client had been followed here?"

He shook his head. "No, that isn't it at all. But you may take it that I am accepting this case for no other reason than to satisfy my curiosity as to its actual nature."

"I can see the mystery here. We are unsure if there is even any crime involved."

"Are we?" he replied, and would say no more on the subject.

We heard nothing the following day, but the morning after brought the message that told us that Mrs. Cooper had again been troubled by the nightmare. When the breakfast things had been cleared away, Holmes took to his armchair and remained there for some time in deep thought.

When I returned in the early afternoon, he was replacing some volumes of his index to the overburdened bookshelves.

"You have been adding to your scrapbooks, then?"

"No, consulting them. It was necessary, I felt."

"Have you made any progress?"

"Only in recognising the necessity of watching our client's house tonight," he said slowly. "The visitations, if we may call them that, occur randomly and not in accordance with a pattern. Now that there has been another, it is as likely as not that it will be repeated tonight. If that fails to happen, I will keep guard for the next few nights. You are looking tired, so I will not expect you to accompany me."

"If I can be of service, I will of course go with you," said I, slightly affronted. "I can sleep for a short while in my room until dinner-time. It will be sufficient."

He smiled faintly, as he reached for the tobacco in the Persian slipper, but there was something cold in his expression. "I thought I knew my Watson."

It was half-an-hour before midnight when our hansom halted beneath a great old oak further along the street in Clerkenwell, near the address that Mrs. Cooper had given us. Holmes had explained to the driver, who he had used previously, that waiting and the possible following of a

214

carriage would certainly be involved, and that the fare would be increased accordingly.

Nothing came of our vigil, and we returned to Baker Street after almost three hours. However, on repeating our observation at the same time the following evening, we were rewarded by the appearance, not long after midnight, of a one-horse carriage driven by a man wearing a broad-brimmed hat and a dark cloak. As it came to rest near Mrs. Cooper's door, a small man with a white beard wearing a tall top hat jumped to the pavement and promptly let himself into her home.

"Holmes!" I whispered. "Mrs. Cooper mentioned a man with a white beard."

"She did indeed. We may now be able to see to where she is taken."

"It was no dream, then?"

In the meagre light from a distant street-lamp, I saw him shake his head. "I never thought that it was."

Moments later the white-bearded man reappeared, guiding Mrs. Cooper as one would a blind person. She wore a coat over long night-clothes and moved mechanically, her gaze fixed and spellbound. They boarded the carriage and set off, and my friend waited until they were out of sight before rapping with his stick as a signal to our driver. We moved slowly, ever conscious that we might be noticed at this hour on these deserted roads. Our driver was clearly experienced in such stealth, waiting until the carriage was about to turn the corners ahead before proceeding along each street that we came upon.

Our surroundings deteriorated considerably within a short while. The terraced residences were replaced by decrepit shops, and then by warehouses in dimly lit thoroughfares. We found ourselves in a street that boasted two taverns, one on each side. Each was in darkness, but from one of the doorways a figure emerged, staggering uncertainly. It crossed the street at a ragged run, constantly fighting for balance and directly in our path. I heard our driver exclaim as the horse reared in fright, and it took some little time to calm it. The drunken figure had disappeared by the time we were able to continue, and as we turned the next corner I was surprised to see the carriage we were pursuing only then increasing its pace ahead.

Holmes made a satisfied sound, which told me he had learned something, and he shouted to our driver, "The carriage is slowing down. There is no need to disguise our presence now. You may overtake and return us to Baker Street."

Our driver shook the reins, and the horse broke into a trot. As we passed our quarry we could see that it was now empty. I looked at Holmes, who answered my question before it was asked.

"You saw that the carriage wasn't as far ahead as would have been expected, despite the slight delay in our progress caused by our drunken friend back there. That was because it also had come to a halt, though which of those warehouses Mrs. Cooper was taken into I cannot yet tell."

"Should we not make some attempt to rescue her?" I asked urgently.

"I'm not inclined to do so now. You will recall that, although she has suffered repeated frights, she has come to no physical harm. There is more to this, I think."

The following morning the expected telegram arrived, and Holmes announced that he intended to make use of the details previously supplied by Mrs. Cooper and visit her husband in Soho. I had anticipated my need for the time to accompany him, and had therefore arranged for Michaelson, who was new to the profession, to act as *locum* at the practice where I had been lending my assistance, and add to his experience. As soon as the breakfast things had been cleared away, Holmes reached for his coat and his ear-flapped travelling cap.

"A hansom has just delivered a fare just across the street," he said after a glance from the window. "If we hurry, we will catch it."

We were soon on our way. The streets were busier at this hour, slowing our progress, and causing Holmes to show signs of impatience.

"I would prefer to find Mr. Cooper at home, rather than to arrive at his premises after he has left to conduct his business," he said.

I consulted my pocket-watch. "We may still be in time."

Holmes nodded but said nothing more until the hansom deposited us in a street of two-storey terraced houses that looked as if they might once have been the work-places of doctors or solicitors before becoming residential.

"Number Seventeen," I pointed out. "The address that Mrs. Cooper gave us, is over there."

We crossed to the other side of the street and Holmes rapped upon the door with his stick. Presently it was answered by a hunched-up elderly man in butler's attire, with the eyes of a bloodhound.

My friend wished him good morning. "We are here to see Mr. Uriah Cooper," he announced. "My name is Sherlock Holmes, and this is my associate, Doctor John Watson."

"I regret that Mr. Cooper isn't at home, sir."

"Has he left then for his employment?"

The man hesitated, which was its own answer.

"Kindly tell him that the matter is urgent, and concerns his wife," Holmes insisted.

After staring fixedly at us for several seconds, the butler appeared to make up his mind.

"Very well, gentlemen. Please step inside."

We entered a hall that smelled of polish and was hung with a portrait of our Queen and one of a stern-looking looking man in old-fashioned dress – an ancestor, I presumed.

The butler disappeared awkwardly down a corridor.

After a while a young man with the air of one who is in a great hurry emerged from the passage. I saw that he was tall, but not of Holmes's height, and that he apparently regarded us as one would a servant.

"Jenkins tells me that you are here on my wife's behalf," he began at once. "You may tell her that the divorce will proceed regardless. I expect to receive documents to that effect soon, which I will sign and forward to her representatives. Is there anything else, gentlemen?"

"Because she wishes for a child?" I said with some exasperation.

"Child be d----d! I will not be associated with anyone of such kin. She should have been honest with me from the beginning."

His remarks confounded me, but before I could reply I was silenced by a warning glance from Holmes.

"That isn't the purpose of our visit," he told Mr. Cooper. "I am a consulting detective, and we are investigating your wife's repeated abductions and subsequent torment."

Our host raised his eyebrows. "What is this nonsense? Something she has invented to delay things, I'll be bound. If you seek to accuse me of anything, you should know that I returned from France only yesterday. Whatever she complains of, I had no part in it."

"I understand that you sell houses to foreign residents."

"I do indeed, and I am quite sure that Monsieur Etienne Broullade, a prominent Paris businessman, will be prepared to swear that I was in his company almost constantly during the past four days."

Holmes nodded and changed his approach. "Are you aware of your wife's excessive fear of birds?"

Mr. Cooper looked surprised at the question, but laughed harshly. "More of her foolishness. I have noticed her avoid sparrows and pigeons, during our walks in St. James Park. I found her actions embarrassing."

"You didn't think to enquire the reason?" I asked.

"Why would that be necessary? She has her habits, as has everyone else. I didn't concern myself with her strange little ways when we were together, and I certainly will not trouble to do so now." He pulled a pocket-watch from his waistcoat. "Although this has been somewhat entertaining, I must conclude it now. I have a client waiting, and a carriage will arrive for me very soon. Good day to you, gentlemen."

He turned abruptly and disappeared the way he had come. The butler was at once beside us to promptly show us out.

"Odious fellow," I remarked when we had walked away from the house.

"There doubtless seems to be some mystery to you as to Mr. Cooper's explanation of his estrangement from his wife. All will be clear to you eventually, but I can say with utmost conviction that they deserve each other."

His tone, with which I was familiar, told me that it would avail me nothing if I attempted to extract an explanation from him. Accordingly, I remained silent. Moments later, he surprised me by answering one of my unspoken questions.

"I am satisfied that he isn't concerned in our client's predicament."

"How then do we proceed?"

"Come, Watson, is it not obvious? Who else is likely to be aware of our client's aversion to birds?"

"A sibling, perhaps?"

"She has none."

Not thinking to ask how he knew, I considered briefly. He hailed a passing cab. "Ha! She consulted her doctor."

"Precisely. We shall see if Doctor Pressingham is willing to shed any light on this."

The physician, as it turned out, proved to be a small man who was at first very guarded.

"You will appreciate, gentlemen," he said from across his desk, "that I am not at liberty to discuss my patients' ailments."

"As I doctor myself, I understand of course," I replied. "But in general terms, surely."

As I spoke, I noticed that Holmes was unusually quiet, his eyes roving around the room. When they settled upon Doctor Pressingham, I could have sworn that a fleeting smile was on his lips.

"I believe that Mrs. Cooper is suffering from delusions," the physician said. He rubbed his unshaven face. "I prescribed a sleeping draught, in the hope that she would rest sufficiently deeply to overcome these fantasies, but I am sorry to learn that this treatment has been unsuccessful. Clearly, it will be necessary to further examine the lady and define her ailment more precisely. I must make a note of it."

He took up a pencil and scribbled something on a pad, and to my surprise I saw that Holmes stared at me, inclining his head. There was no mistaking the signal – It was time to leave.

We got to our feet and I thanked Doctor Pressingham. He gave a little bow in return and we left.

"He is about to begin his surgery," I concluded as we passed through the waiting room that was quickly filling with coughing and bandaged patients. "Rather late, I would have thought."

"But not surprising," Holmes said as we reached the street. "You must have observed how tired he appeared, and that he was unshaven. The man has been up most of the night."

"I'm not unfamiliar with his situation," I reflected. "One call after another, during the night, is exhausting. That is surely the cause of his weariness."

The smile returned to Holmes's face for an instant. "Perhaps. But now I think we will return to Baker Street for the late luncheon that I see you are anticipating."

A hansom waited further along the street, and we procured it at once. My friend didn't prove to be very communicative during the journey, but I felt disposed to interrupt his thoughts to satisfy myself on certain points.

"Your behaviour in the presence of Doctor Pressingham puzzled me."

He turned from the window. "How so?"

"You were unusually hesitant. I cannot think that this was simply because you thought it better that I converse with one of the same profession."

"Not for the first time, you underestimate yourself, Watson. However, on this occasion I knew that you would ask appropriate questions while I observed the doctor and the contents of his surgery."

"And did you learn anything from your inspection?"

"Exactly what, by now, I expected to learn. But look, we are almost at our door, and I recall that Mrs. Hudson has a fine roast chicken for us."

The meal was excellent indeed, and we ate mostly in companionable silence. When we had consumed dessert and our coffee cups were empty, I enquired as to our next excursion.

"I think the time has come for us to examine the warehouse from last night," he announced, "although I expect that there will be less for us to see than there would have been previously."

Again we boarded a hansom and my friend instructed the driver to follow the route of the night before. After we alighted and our conveyance had left us, I saw that there were in fact four warehouses in a row, each securely locked. Holmes paraded before them briefly and then stood before that which he had selected.

"Are you certain that this is the one?" I asked him. "Or are we to try each in turn until we succeed."

He gave me a disdainful look. "My dear fellow, you surely know my methods better than that." After a moment he stood back and pointed to the entrance doors that were set into the much larger gates. "Observe, the lock of the door on the extreme left is corroded to the extent that it would be impossible to release without forcing the mechanism, while the next door has grass and weeds that would prevent its movement. The lock of the third door is in similar condition to the first, and so we are left with the fourth entrance. A further indication is the smear of oil on the relatively new lock."

"As always, you make it appear so simple," I said, feeling rather foolish at my failure to notice.

We looked up and down the short street to ensure that it was deserted. A cat, sitting atop a dustbin, watched us with disapproving eyes, but we were otherwise unseen.

Holmes produced his pick-lock, and in minutes I was pulling the door open. We stepped into the half-light of the cavernous space before us, and were immediately halted by the odious smell and a cacophony of noise.

"What is this place?" I asked, confused.

"Exactly what I had surmised. You will recall that Mrs. Cooper related that she actually *heard* the birds that threatened to attack her. Before you is the explanation of that, and of the remainder of her description of the place of her torment."

My eyes had become adjusted to the poor light. The place appeared to be one of storage for fairground or circus accessories, long abandoned judging by the profusion of dust and cobwebs. Along one wall were several tall cages, one of them having toppled onto its side. Within them a number of large black crows were imprisoned. The noise from their cries for release, and probably for food, was an assault upon the ears, and the stench from their droppings tainted the air. Along the walls were the remains of statues with roguish and evil expressions, not of stone but of some sort of imitation material such as one would expect in a theatrical production. Many were smashed almost beyond recognition.

In the centre of the expanse was a full-sized billiard table, with straps affixed to the sides – Clearly the place of Mrs. Cooper's restraint.

"There, Watson!" Holmes pointed into the murk above us, and I followed his direction.

A number of pulleys hung from the ceiling, their chains swaying slightly. These were the method of lowering hideous likenesses of predatory birds, made more so by the addition of grotesque colouring, to within a few feet of the table beneath.

"That must have been a disturbing spectacle," I observed. "Horrifying, to say the least of it."

Holmes nodded. "Indeed. Imagine how they would appear if presented with the accompaniment of the cries of those poor caged creatures to a woman drugged and mesmerised."

"Is that what happened to Mrs. Cooper?"

"Undoubtedly. It also appears that our pursuit last night was detected, since some effort has been made to clear out this place. There was insufficient time, I imagine, to complete the task."

I looked around us at the scene of the lady's torment. "But why? What is the purpose of this? Who is behind it?"

He crossed the room and began to release the captive birds, after unfastening the single skylight to open for them a path to freedom. When the last one had flown, he restored it to its former position and answered me.

"As to who is behind this, I can name but one, though there is certainly another. Regarding why, I have as yet only a suspicion. But what we see here is only a partial explanation."

Before he began, we made our way back to the street. We were, I think, both glad to breathe clean air again, and to be out of that depressing place. Before my friend could continue, I presented my own deduction.

"So Doctor Pressingham is concerned here, either alone or with an accomplice."

"Excellent. Kindly explain your chain of reasoning."

"This place has been cleared overnight, no doubt with the intention of impeding our investigation. For one or two men, this would be a task of several hours, and rather wearying."

"Quite so."

"And we noticed Doctor Pressingham's tired condition."

"Indeed, and you are correct, although this could have been from one or more summons to his patients' bedsides through the night, as you suggested. But when coupled with my observations of the certificates on his surgery wall, and the fact that he supplied our client with 'a sleeping draught', his guilt appears more likely."

"What did you see there?"

"Along with his qualification of medical competence, there was a similar diploma indicating that he is proficient in mesmerism. You see how this explains the condition of Mrs. Cooper at the times she was abducted. The effects of the preparation taken before retiring would have been enhanced by hypnotic means to induce her dream-like state of unreality."

"That seems likely, but it isn't conclusive, surely?"

"Not at all, but it became so when I observed the tiny white hairs adhering to the sides of the doctor's face. Evidently, in his depleted state he hadn't taken sufficient care in removing his disguise."

"The white beard!" I shook my head. "But what can he hope to gain by this?"

"Not *he* but *they*. You will recall that there was a coachman assisting. I have my own suspicions regarding his identity – or at least of several probabilities."

Some time later, we retired to our usual chairs after an excellent dinner. I began to read one of the medical journals that had long awaited my attention, expecting to pass the evening quietly. Holmes, however, continually displayed signs of restlessness, until he finally lowered his newspaper while shaking his head.

"It's no use. I cannot settle."

"Something troubles you, then?"

"I have given some thought to how this case should proceed. There are several sources that could provide useful information, and I cannot sit here when I could be consulting them. Don't let me disturb you, for I don't require your company on this occasion. Most probably it will be late when I return, but I'll share with you what I've learned at breakfast."

With that he rose abruptly, took up his hat and coat, and was gone. Feeling somewhat disconcerted, I poured myself a glass of brandy and continued reading.

I retired later than was my usual practice and lay awake for some time, but I didn't hear Holmes return. I had almost finished a hearty breakfast the next morning by the time he appeared.

He waved away his own meal and requested that Mrs. Hudson bring a large pot of coffee. As I finally laid down my knife and fork, I thought him deep in his own thoughts and unforthcoming.

"Well, were your enquiries of last night successful?" I asked when I could bear his silence no longer. "Do we now know the reason for the doctor's actions?"

He met my gaze unsmiling. "I believe that I'm now conversant with much of what surrounds the situation. Certainly Doctor Pressingham, though not innocent, is as much a victim as our client."

I prepared myself to listen to a possibly long narrative, but Holmes had barely begun when I heard a carriage come to rest outside our door. Listening, we heard our landlady speak briefly before admitting someone, and then quick footsteps ascended the stairs.

"You have another client, I believe."

"I think not. The footfalls are familiar."

My doubts that he could have ascertained this were dispelled, immediately Mrs. Hudson entered our room.

"Mrs. Ellen Cooper to see Mr. Holmes," she announced as before.

"Pray come in, Mrs. Cooper," he called, at the same time surprising me by gesturing to our landlady to withdraw without offering our visitor refreshment. "I perceive from your anxious state that there has been a recent development in your situation."

She sat at my invitation and soon recovered herself.

"There has indeed," she said then. "No more than an hour ago, I was accosted – no, *attacked* – while walking along Clerkenwell High Street. An elderly, white-bearded man attempted to abduct me!"

Holmes and I exchanged glances. "Did you recognise your assailant?" he asked.

"I didn't," she answered thoughtfully, "but after a few moments I experienced the strangest feeling that I knew him from my past. I was, however, unable to remember, and quickly dismissed the notion."

"If this was an attempted abduction, as you surmised, I would expect that there was some method of conveyance at hand?"

"Why, yes. A carriage waited not far off. I found this to be odd though, since the white-bearded man seemed not to be in a hurry to force me into it. He seemed to have more interest in speaking to the small crowd that had gathered around us. I was appalled when he accused me of approaching him for immoral purposes, but before I could speak in my own defence, he fled to the waiting coach and was promptly driven away."

"Most curious," I commented.

Holmes didn't appear to experience the confusion that I felt.

"What occurred immediately after this man left?" he enquired.

"The crowd, about five men, I think, were unanimous in their condemnation of me. One would have thought that the man's accusations were the truth. Then a constable appeared and they rushed to him, with the result that I was taken to the local police station where I was charged! It was only with the intervention of Jordan, my brother and a well-known businessman, that I was released on bail."

Holmes looked up sharply. "Were the 'witnesses' gone by then? Pray think carefully before you answer, as it is of the first importance."

She shifted in her chair. "Yes, I am quite certain that I was alone except for Inspector Radcliffe when I requested him to summon my brother, who guaranteed that I would attend court when the trial takes place."

"Excellent. First I must tell you, Mrs. Cooper, that you need have no further fears of torments during the night such as you have experienced recently. Doctor Watson and I have ensured that your enemies are unlikely to continue with this. The outrage of this morning was another attempt to achieve the same result, and I believe, having identified this, that we can soon bring this affair to a satisfactory close."

"You have now deduced the reason for all this?" I said with some surprise.

He nodded. "Is it not obvious, when you have recognised the common factor of each event?"

"Obvious?" she repeated. "I confess to being confused. What is the purpose of these people? What have they against me?"

"Their purpose, unless I'm very much mistaken, is to remove you from your residence for some little time."

Mrs. Cooper and I stared at him without comprehension.

"Consider the likely outcome of each of their schemes," he continued. "After repeated ordeals over several nights, would not the effects upon you, together with your account of the experiences, cause you to be thought either insane or on the verge of such a condition? Sooner or later, it's almost certain that you would be committed to an asylum or a private clinic. As for the events of this morning, will you not be imprisoned if found guilty? In each case, your premises would be left empty."

Her expression became puzzled. "But I keep nothing valuable there. If their intention is to enter in my absence, then why not now? And for what purpose? I think, Mr. Holmes, that you may be in error."

"It may not be valuables that they seek." My friend showed no sign of offence. "That I intend to confirm shortly. You have stated that none of those speaking against you were present at your release so, since they were certainly hired to play the part of accusers, they will have reported that you were detained. Therefore your house will, according to their understanding, be empty tonight. I suggest that you pack enough clothes for, say, three days, and take up residence in a distant hotel, or stay with an obliging relative if that is possible."

"You intend that we should watch the house tonight," I concluded.

"I do, and several subsequent nights, should that prove necessary. I don't expect that it will be so, however, since today's events reveal that these people have become desperate, but it would be unwise to ignore the possibility."

"Yes, I see that," she agreed. "But who is the instigator of this, Mr. Holmes? Is it my husband? Is it anyone of my acquaintance?"

"You will know all very soon," he assured her. "But for now, I have certain arrangements to make."

Recognising her dismissal, our client rose at once.

"Thank you, gentlemen. Good day to you." She smiled faintly and turned away, but it wasn't until she had almost reached the door that Holmes replied.

"Good day, Mrs. Cooper" He answered before I could speak. "Incidentally, I found it not without interest to be investigating on behalf of the former Miss Ellen Braithwaite."

With her hand on the door-knob, she became very still. "You knew, then?"

"I did." He returned her gaze expressionlessly. "From the moment I first set eyes upon you."

"Yet you accepted the case I brought to you."

"Only because, as I remarked at the time, it appeared to be interesting."

She regarded us somewhat resignedly, nodded, and closed the door quietly after her.

"Holmes, will you be so kind as to explain this to me?" I asked with some irritation as we heard her descend to the street. "I feel you have kept me in the dark for far too long."

We had settled ourselves in our chairs before he replied. "I suppose I do owe you an explanation, but as you are aware, it is my custom not to share such information until the problem is solved. However, it hasn't escaped my notice that you have been less-than-pleased with my treatment of Mrs. Cooper. Perhaps the reason will become clear when I explain that she is a member of one of the most notorious criminal families ever to terrorise the East End of London.

"Doubtless she allowed herself to believe that I would be deceived by her married name. The files of Scotland Yard record her numerous arrests for pick-pocketing, and one of suspected murder. This was never proven, but I have long since satisfied myself that her guilt was the most likely explanation for the outcome of the situation at the time. You will see, then, that my fear was that her true intention was to involve myself, and possibly you also, in some sort of lawless enterprise, perhaps to provide an alibi. Fortunately, although I have guarded against this throughout our investigation, no suggestion of such a hidden intention has appeared."

"But she stated that her brother is a prominent businessman," I objected. "Surely he could never have obtained her release, were it otherwise."

"Jordan Braithwaite?" Holmes smiled, I suspected at my perceived innocence of the matter. "He isn't the first criminal to live beneath a veneer of respectability, and therefore to wield a degree of influence."

As I paused to consider this, vibration caused our half-open window to rattle. A brewer's dray, badly loaded and driven too fast, passed along Baker Street.

When all was quiet once more, I asked, "But what of Doctor Pressingham? I had assumed, from our previous enquiries, that he was responsible for this affair."

"Never assume anything," Holmes advised. "All deduction must be based on established fact. One of the informants that I consulted last night

225

referred me to a former confidante of the doctor who, after some inducement, revealed that Pressingham is being blackmailed. Apparently there was a scandal years ago when he worked as a surgeon in Leeds. He was accused of drunkenness while operating. The patient died, and the family caused considerable uproar in the press. The doctor's only chance to save his career was to change both his name and his residence. Therefore he moved his practice to the capital. His troubles didn't end there, however, for his secret was known to another. A certain Mr. Elihu Sanderson somehow came by this knowledge, and it was the doctor's ill-fortune that this man was part of a criminal enterprise that rivalled that of the Braithwaites."

"He, then, is the blackmailer?"

"Indeed." Holmes began to fill his clay pipe. "He has used his hold upon Doctor Pressingham to force his co-operation in the persecution of Mrs. Cooper. I'm quite certain that it is he who was the coachman who drove her to the place of her torment, as I'm that there is something in that house that he desperately wishes to acquire."

"Since this man also is connected to a family or organisation of wrong-doers, is he not known to Scotland Yard?"

"Lestrade had indicated many times how pleased he would be to get his hands on Elihu Sanderson. Two years ago, Sanderson was being sought for his part in the Tailors and Weavers Bank robbery, in which both a member of the staff and a constable were killed. He hasn't been seen since, and it's suspected that his family concealed him until it was thought safe to arrange a passage abroad."

"With such a risk, is it certain that he has returned?"

"One of my informants is prepared to swear that he has seen Sanderson visit Doctor Pressingham several times."

"It's the hangman, then, if he's caught?"

"Undoubtedly."

"Will you advise Scotland Yard of your conclusions?"

Holmes nodded his assent. "I have to leave briefly this morning, to ensure that certain arrangements have been made, and I will certainly telegraph Lestrade before I return. By all means spend the time reading or otherwise amusing yourself, but after luncheon we should both ensure that our revolvers are well-oiled and serviceable. As soon as darkness falls, we'll set out for Mrs. Cooper's residence, where we'll lie in wait. As our adversaries have no means of knowing the extent of her absence, I expect them to appear tonight or very soon after."

The remainder of the day passed surprisingly quickly. Holmes's absence from our lodgings was as brief as he had promised, and we spent time servicing our weapons as he had recommended.

Mrs. Hudson served roast pork for dinner, and I was continually aware of the darkening sky as we ate. By the time our coffee pot was empty, all light had gone, and my friend wasted no time in springing to his feet and retrieving his hat and coat.

"It will be advisable to be there early," he said, "since our adversaries could arrive at any time."

A carriage awaited us, doubtless one of the "arrangements" that Holmes had mentioned earlier. The driver was as before, a shrewd-faced man who was evidently no stranger to either the detective or his requirements.

There were few exchanges between us during the journey through the gas-lit streets. Holmes sat with his head upon his chest while I watched the dramas that played in and out of the shadows. Beggars, urchins, women shouting at their husbands as they left them for an evening in the taverns and, now and then, watchful constables, all appeared briefly. Then our conveyance came to a halt, for we had arrived. As my friend had instructed, the driver reigned in the horse some little distance away. With weapons drawn, we alighted and moved stealthily towards our destination. A light mist had appeared, and Holmes paused momentarily to listen for what we couldn't see.

"There is another carriage, or at least a horse, at the other end of the street," he whispered. "I could hear the beast stamping its hooves. Take care, for they may already be here."

As we neared Mrs. Cooper's house, I saw a light shine briefly.

"Did you see that? You were right – our adversaries are already at work."

As we approached the door, he held up a hand as a sign that he had heard. Very slowly he turned the knob and we stepped into a hall that was dark, save for the faint light from the sitting room. We waited and watched shadows flitter across the ceiling as the lamp was moved from place to place, with no effort by the searchers to maintain a silence. I couldn't tell if there were one or more of them, but a wrenching groan of tortured wood suggested that floorboards were being removed.

Then – an exclamation told me that a discovery had been made. I turned to look at Holmes in the baleful illumination, and in doing so inadvertently stumbled against the door that confronted us. Immediately all activity and noise ceased, and I realised that my clumsiness may have betrayed our presence. Holmes clearly had no intention of waiting any longer regardless, for he threw open the sitting room door and entered with a flourish.

"Good evening, Doctor Pressingham!" he said lightly. "I trust you have found whatever it was that you were seeking. I am surprised to find you alone here, for I was certain that you would be accompanied by Mr. Elihu Sanderson."

"You were correct, Mr. Holmes," said a voice from the shadows. A tall clean-shaven man, extremely thin, stepped into view. "I am holding a twelve-bore shotgun with a most sensitive trigger. One tiny movement would discharge it, cutting both of you gentlemen down. Kindly drop your weapons to the floor, or I will be compelled to fire."

Holmes glanced at me and nodded, and we both complied.

"For what were you searching?" he asked.

"Something that will be of great benefit to my family and myself," was Sanderson's reply. "It will allow us to clear the Braithwaites from the East End, once and for all."

"Tell them no more!" pleaded Doctor Pressingham. "The less they know, the less will be the evidence against us."

Sanderson smiled grimly. "That doesn't concern me, Doctor. As Mr. Holmes can probably tell you, I have nothing to lose. Now, however, we are faced with an additional problem: Where do we conceal two bodies so that they will not be discovered until I am well clear of here?"

"No!" cried the physician. "Not murder!"

"But I am already wanted for murder," Sanderson shrugged. "They can hang a man but once."

He stopped suddenly and became very still. I could hear heavy footfalls outside, approaching the door. Two men, I estimated, constables from their angry commands to open the door in the name of the law. When there was no response, they began to beat on it with their fists.

"It seems that your difficulties have doubled," Holmes observed. "If you choose to begin shooting, the result will be four bodies in need of disposal."

Sanderson moved to the window, watching us every second. He displaced the curtain slightly and glanced out. It was done so quickly that neither Holmes nor I had the slightest chance to act. Indecision crept into Sanderson's face.

"If I croak these two, we might have a chance of getting away through the garden," he told the doctor. "Go and make sure that the back door is unlocked. If not, break it open with anything you can find."

Doctor Pressingham remained still – probably paralysed by fear, I thought.

Sanderson seemed surprised that his order hadn't been obeyed.

"Go!" he shouted with sufficient force for the cry to echo around the chamber.

Because of the poor light, I had managed no more than an approximation of the size of the room. The door near the rear window led to the back entrance, I presumed, and it was just possible to make out the narrow staircase that provided access to an upper floor. It was from this direction that a command rang out from a new but familiar voice.

"Stay exactly where you are, Doctor! As for you, Sanderson, I have a heavy-gauge pistol aimed at your head. I'm quite sure that I can fire before you can raise your weapon."

"Halloa, Lestrade!" cried Holmes. "I wondered how long it would be before you made an appearance."

The inspector raised his eyebrows. "You knew, Mr. Holmes? You were aware that I had concealed myself and was listening?"

"There were occasional creaks from the floor above. In an old house such as this, they are usually caused by movement. I therefore deduced that someone wished to remain undetected by Sanderson and Doctor Pressingham, and when the constables arrived unaccompanied by an inspector, no doubt to effect a distraction, I knew that you had responded to my message."

"I arrived early, since I had no way of knowing at what time either yourself or these two would put in an appearance."

Holmes nodded. "I trust that, prior to our arrival, their conversation was informative?"

"Indeed." A grim smile appeared briefly on Lestrade's bulldog-like face. "Sanderson is already for the hangman, but I was able to acquaint myself with the present situation also. It won't be long before we close this file at the Yard." He raised his pistol further. "No, Sanderson, don't attempt it. Place your shotgun on the floor slowly, before moving away from the door. Doctor Watson, I would be obliged if you would collect his weapon then lift the latch and allow my men to enter. We'll have these two in irons in no time, and I'll decide on Doctor Pressingham's part in this in my office."

I complied, and had hardly stepped back before the constables rushed past me. At Lestrade's direction the two prisoners were handcuffed and removed, by means of a police coach which appeared out of the mist.

"I must congratulate you, Inspector, said Holmes, "not only on your flawless arrangements, but also on saving Watson and myself from a possibly dangerous predicament."

Lestrade smiled broadly, an expression that appeared out of place on that normally serious face. "We do get it right sometimes you know, down at Scotland Yard. I don't understand though, what those two were searching for. Sanderson said that it was something that would benefit his family. That can only mean that it would assist their criminal activities."

"We shall see," my friend replied, as we approached the other end of the room where the floorboards had been removed. I reached into the void and felt nothing, until my hand touched a thick notebook. I extracted it and handed it to Holmes.

He opened it and began to turn the pages. After a moment he gave it to Lestrade, with the comment, "I think you will count this as a good night's work."

The inspector examined it briefly, before taking on the air of someone who has discovered something precious.

"Why, this is a record, possibly a complete one, of all the crimes organised by the Braithwaite family for at least the past five years. All those involved are listed, as are the amounts they were paid for their misdeeds." He lowered the book. "Gentlemen, we at the Yard have been after them for a long time, but have succeeded in prosecutions for only minor incidents."

"It therefore becomes clear," Holmes concluded, "as they wished the ruination of the Braithwaites and to take over their enterprises, why Sanderson and his family placed such importance on gaining possession of this document. Without knowing where it was hidden, or how long it would take to find it, and not wishing to alert the Braithwaites by way of alarming Mrs. Cooper, they came up with this plan – not simply to search with her removed nightly, but making sure that she was permanently gone."

"But why was it hidden here?" I asked.

"That we cannot tell with any certainty, as yet. I would speculate that Jordan Braithwaite concealed it within his sister's house for safekeeping without her knowledge, since she was genuinely puzzled as to what her tormentors sought there. Also, and I would remind you of your disapproval of my attitude towards her, the book reveals some recent instances of crimes carried out by Mrs. Cooper herself. That, together with Dr. Pressingham's fate, is for your consideration, Inspector."

The official detective nodded. "Thank you, Mister Holmes. I wonder how the Sandersons learned of this."

"Again, I can only speculate. Every now and then, each gang loses some of its men to the other. Usually the bodies are discovered floating in the Thames, after much ill-treatment. Might it not be that one of the Braithwaites, or a gang member in their confidence, disclosed such information during interrogation intended to reveal something different? This may or may not be true, but it is a possibility."

"And a likely one, I would say." Lestrade placed the notebook in his pocket. "But I must get this to the Yard. I can hardly wait to see Gregson's face when I tell him about it."

"Good evening to you then," said my friend, before turning to me. "But as for us, Watson, I think we will now return to Baker Street. I have a particularly fine bottle of porter which I think we will sample before retiring."

The Horror of Forrest Farm
by Tracy J. Revels

"**I** have blood on my hands, Mr. Holmes. Had I but listened to the maid, not dismissed her as a silly, superstitious woman, they would all still be alive. A man, two women, and – God forgive me! – a mere child!"

Inspector Edgar Wilkes spoke these words in a tortured moan. The policeman was yet another of Holmes's young admirers, a man in the first year of what became a long and distinguished career, where he received many commendations for solving cases originally given up as hopeless. On this morning, however, he was at his lowest ebb, and his handsome face, with its brisking ginger beard, was shadowed by guilt. Indeed, the first news of the shocking event had already reached the great metropolis, giving Holmes a chance to read of it in the papers, and to mutter darkly that Wilkes had badly handled the affair. Now, as we sat inside an express racing northward toward the little village of Eufurd, Holmes adopted a more conciliatory tone.

"Do not fault yourself for refusing to accept supernatural explanations, but let us hear it all from your perspective, and omit nothing."

The stalwart young man drew himself up, and I was reminded of a good-hearted schoolboy who confesses some moment of disciplinary weakness to his master.

"The maid's name is Florence Schnell, a very nervous woman of about thirty-five years, unmarried and somewhat simple, with an elderly mother in the village. She came to me in my office on Monday to report that her former employer's home, Forrest Farm, was haunted.

"As it happens, though I am a relative newcomer, I had heard much about Forrest Farm, a house so named for its location on the fringe of the great woods, exactly a mile-and-a-quarter from the village. It was all that remained of a formerly impressive manor that had been lost by a Regency wastrel. It was a tidy and well-run farm, with a sizeable barn and a cluster of pens and outbuildings. The current residents are – rather, *were* – Silas Brewster, sixty-five, his wife Marie, sixty-two, their widowed daughter Ruby Moore, thirty, and Ruby's son, Owen, ten. The family was not, I fear, a popular one."

"For what reason?" I asked.

"Silas Brewster had a reputation for being quarrelsome and tight-fisted, and more than once his wife and daughter were seen in the village

232

with black eyes and swollen lips. The boy told his teacher that his grandfather was harsh with him, free with the horsewhip if he shirked his chores. But that was only half the scandal." Wilkes shifted uncomfortably. "I do not enjoy repeating gossip."

"Yet it is often essential in our profession," Holmes reminded him. Wilkes nodded.

"Mrs. Moore's husband, Corporal Charles Moore, served in India. Five years ago, there was a fire in the barracks and a dozen men were killed, including Moore. Shortly after this sad news reached the family, Mrs. Moore behaved scandalously with Vincent Jones, the owner of Burrow Hill, the next closest farm, which can be reached via a short path through the woods. At the time, Jones was a married man, though his wife was an invalid. You can see how this set the neighbors against the young widow."

"Who, the papers said, was a striking woman."

"Indeed. There were times when I would see her walk past my window and think what a pity it was that such a lovely woman – tall, regal, brunette – couldn't find a decent chap to marry her. But here I must turn to my notes."

He removed a sheaf of papers from his pocket and placed a pair of spectacles on his nose.

"Six months ago, Jones's invalid wife died. There was no question of any foul play, as her end was expected, and both a doctor and a priest were in attendance at her deathbed. According to Miss Schnell, before the lady's body was cold in the ground, Jones came to Forrest Farm to ask Ruby to marry him. She readily agreed, but her father insisted they wait a proper period for mourning.

"One might have thought old Brewster would rejoice to see his daughter wed, but the housekeeper overheard him complaining that his daughter's marriage would deprive him of his grandson's labor, and that he was growing too old to manage the farm alone. Young Owen grew sullen, for he had a young boy's instinctive distrust of a stepfather and frequently made comments about how Jones was a sly and despicable man. This naturally caused friction between the mother and son. Mrs. Brewster was desolate at the thought of being left alone with her cruel husband. It was a miserable time at Forrest Farm, and Miss Schnell said she thought of giving notice and leaving, but stayed for the sake of the income. All of this might have been no more than sordid family drama, if not for a letter that arrived for Mrs. Moore exactly a month ago.

"Miss Schnell remembered the day well, for she was helping Ruby to sew upon her wedding gown. It was a very rare thing for anyone at the farm to receive a letter, as they had no relatives or friends. Ruby gave a cry, tore open the envelope, and read the contents rapidly. Then, with great purpose, she thrust the letter and the envelope in the stove."

"Did Miss Schnell note the postmark?"

"She did not. Owen brought the letter inside."

Holmes nodded for Wilkes to continue.

"From that moment, according to Miss Schnell, there was a great change in the bride. For a week, she wandered around as if in a daze, often falling into fits of uncontrollable weeping. It had become a custom for her fiancé to come over and sit in the parlor, just after twilight, but she sent him notes telling him she was unwell, and not to come. After two weeks of this, he came anyway, just after sundown, and there was something of a row. Miss Schnell said that she witnessed the couple talking in the yard, and that when Jones tried to kiss his beloved, she slapped him, and he stomped off shouting curses. The next day, there was the mournful tragedy of the dog."

"Mournful?" I asked.

Wilkes shook his head. "That was how Miss Schnell phrased it – she is quite the animal lover. The family had a stout old sheepdog. It was found that morning, dead next to its tin plate of food. The lad was quite bereft, and the old man annoyed because now he would have to buy another animal to protect his herd. Ruby mollified him by saying that her new husband, who was a noted breeder of dogs, would give him a puppy as a wedding gift, and the old man agreed to wait.

"Afterward, even stranger things began to happen. First, the old man's keys went missing. He kept them on an iron ring that he always hung in the kitchen. They stayed missing for three days – three days of hell, according to Miss Schnell, as the old man's temper was unbearable until the keys were at last located, dropped on a pile of hay.

"The next incident was stranger still. Miss Schnell had gone out to the barn and, as she entered, she smelled the strong aroma of pipe tobacco. Her employer forbade any use of tobacco on his property. She naturally assumed that Owen was being naughty, especially when she saw a curl of blue smoke arising from behind an unused horse stall. She said nothing, for she liked the boy and didn't want to get him in trouble. That night, just before he went to bed, she took him aside and warned him that he must be more careful, for there would have been a tremendous fuss had his grandfather caught him smoking a pipe. He vigorously denied that he had done such a thing, saying that he had never been out of his grandfather's sight the entire day, but she told herself that he was lying to save face.

"Another day or so passed before Brewster came into the house in a rage. He had found a London newspaper in the waste pile. He subscribed to no newspapers, and he wanted to know how such a thing could have come onto his property. Ruby said she had found it lying in the yard, assumed it had blown in from the road, and thrown it upon the trash heap. But Brewster wasn't satisfied with this explanation. He began to rave that he had seen tracks on the property, and that a ham had gone missing. Despite his daughter's efforts to calm him, he went over to Jones's property and asked his future son-in-law to lend him a gun. Jones refused. Brewster returned in an even worse temper, swearing that the wedding must never take place. Ruby, her mother, and Miss Schnell were working on the wedding gown when Brewster flew inside, in a rage. He snatched the dress from the women and threw it into the fireplace, where it burned."

Holmes held up a hand. "Did Miss Schnell comment on Mrs. Moore's reaction to having her frock burned before her eyes?"

Wilkes shuffled his papers. "Yes. These are her exact words: '*And Ruby stood there like a statue, just staring at the flames, never made a sound, even as her mama was wailing to heaven, "What have you done, you wicked, wicked, man?"*'"

"Does that not strike you as odd? What woman wouldn't react to any new dress being destroyed, much less her bridal attire?"

Wilkes shrugged. "Perhaps, after living so long with a brutal father, she had learned not to show emotion."

"Yet the mysterious letter produced a flood of tears. Let us file that away. But I sense the housekeeper's story draws to an end."

"It does sir, very dramatically. The next day was the Sabbath, and the entire family, with the exception of the housekeeper, went to church. She stayed behind, and after about an hour she went out to the barn. Once again, she smelled smoke, and heard a loan moaning sound, but saw nothing. She bolted from the property, coming to me the next day, saying, 'There is so much hatred there, so much trouble, that I fear an evil spirit has come upon them and taken up residence to carry away their souls. Please, sir, go and see what can be done, before it is too late!'"

"What did you do?" Holmes asked. Wilkes slumped in his seat.

"I acted a fool's part. I told the woman if she feared the devil, she should seek out a priest. Then, the more I mulled it about in my head, I wondered if Jones might be causing the mischief. He has a reputation almost as nasty as Brewster's, you see, and it occurred to me that if he believed his fiancée was about to throw him over, he might stage some pranks to make her believe she would be safer with him. So the next day I went to Burrow Hill and found him out with his sheepdogs and flock. I told him all the maid had said and put it straight to him that I would not take lightly to reports of trouble from Forrest Farm. He denied any part of it, of course, but swore that nothing should come between him and Ruby on their wedding morning.

"That was Tuesday afternoon. That morning, Mrs. Brewster was seen in the village, doing some shopping, including buying a bolt of blue cloth to make her daughter another wedding dress – or so she told the shopkeeper. It was the last time any member of the family was seen. The wedding was set for Saturday and was to be a small affair with just the family and the vicar in attendance at the chapel. The groom arrived, smartly dressed, at eight, and the wedding was to occur at nine. The gentlemen waited, expecting the bride and her family to arrive, but when it was eleven and no wedding had commenced, Jones became enraged. Leaving the vicar behind, he rounded up some loafers at the public house to help him go and fetch the bride to church. I saw them set upon their journey, and – fearing trouble – I hurried along with them."

My friend leaned forward. "Be very precise, Wilkes."

The young inspector took out his handkerchief and swiped his suddenly sweaty face. "That isn't difficult. The scene will forever be impressed in my mind. We walked along the road, and when we caught sight of the farm, nothing seemed amiss. I knocked on the door and received no answer, but the door wasn't locked, so we went inside. The front rooms of the house looked as if the occupants had just walked away from them, with all the normal debris of life – an open book, a beer stein, a dress upon a sewing machine – where one would expect them to lie. In the kitchen, we got our first hint that something was amiss, as there was a plate of ham that appeared spoiled and the dregs of coffee in a cup. The back door was left open, admitting flies.

"It was those flies, Mr. Holmes, that made my blood run cold. It turned my stomach just to see them, even before my nose caught the stench drifting from behind the house. At first, I thought some animals had died in the barn, but a quick inspection showed that the cows penned there, and the sheep in the corral, were healthy and undisturbed. At that moment, a cry went up from one of the men. He pointed to some marks in the soil that gave the impression something heavy had been dragged from the rear of the house toward another outbuilding. I told the men to stay back, and I examined the marks very carefully. They were exactly what one would expect if a body was being dragged along by its legs."

"Was there any impression of the individual who might have dragged the body?"

"Indeed, sir, one distinct print of a large, square toed boot."

"Only one?"

"That was clearly visible."

"And what did you find inside the outbuilding?"

"Hell, Mr. Holmes. It was a charnel house. The building itself was a storage shed for tools and harnesses, not very large. The moment I opened

236

the door, for it wasn't locked, a black wave of flies came out, and I was choked by the stench of decomposing flesh. Inside were bodies thrown together in a heap. Mr. and Mrs. Brewster had been savagely struck in the head and shoulders with an ax, the younger woman strangled, and the boy shot in the back."

"My God!" I gasped.

Holmes's eyes were closed – not from horror, I was certain, but to aid his concentration, as he was envisioning the scene. "How were they dressed?"

"They were all in their nightclothes, though the younger woman had a silken dressing gown over her nightdress, while her parents didn't. The boy's feet were bruised and filthy."

"Intriguing," Holmes said. "Clearly, the child witnessed some of the scene and tried to escape. I presume there was a trail of blood from the bedrooms to the door. Did you find any footprints within it?"

Wilkes blinked. I saw color rise in his face.

"No, Mr. Holmes. The blood was only in the bedroom where the parents were slain, and in the shed where their bodies were flung. I presume the murderer cleaned it up afterward, for he never left the farm."

This didn't surprise Holmes, but as I hadn't read the papers that morning, I was shocked by this twist.

"After we found the bodies of the family in the shed, I returned to the house and climbed the stairs. The Brewster's bedroom was an unholy scene, with dried blood on the ceiling, the walls, and the bed. In the next room, the boy's bed was disheveled, though his mother's bed was still tidy, as if she had never retired. The attic door was open and, drawing my weapon, I ascended the ladder. Once again, I was assailed by the smell of death, though not as strong as had come before. There, in a large oaken chair, sat a dead man. I had but to look at his distorted face, and the dried foam and blood on his lips, to know that he had swallowed poison. Indeed, a bottle containing arsenic was dropped near his feet. On the floor on his right side was a scrawled note, a confession. And the boots he wore were a perfect match for the print near the shed."

"Who was he?" I asked

"Corporal Charles Moore, late of the Indian army. I have the note here."

Holmes took the envelope that Wilkes offered him, and gently spread out the single sheet of paper. It read thusly:

God forgive me, I lost my mind. I came home to find my Ruby about to wed another man. I had words with her in the kitchen, at night, and when she swore that she loved him more than

237

me, I strangled her. Then I killed her parents. I was dragging them away when I saw the boy run out. I thought he was a servant, and so I shot him. My own dear lad, dead at my hand! I came back to the house, and here I have passed the days, but now I see it clear – better this than the rope. God forgive me! God forgive me!

"He did not sign his name," Holmes noted. "You are certain as to his identity?"

"There was an army pack in the attic – we took his papers from that. There was also an old wedding picture, framed in Ruby's room. It was clearly the same man. We believe he deserted the army on the night of the fire and had been working his way back to England."

Holmes frowned. "And what is your theory of the case, Inspector?'

"This is the way I see it – all was well until the letter arrived. It was from Charles Moore, and in it he told Ruby that he was alive and wanted to come for her. She was greatly upset, because she loved Vincent Jones and was on the cusp of marrying him after living in shame for having been his mistress. Moore arrived at Forrest Farm. He stole the keys to give himself access to all parts of the property, and went undetected by anyone except the maid, who came to believe these strange happenings were ghostly. Sometime on Tuesday night, he revealed himself to his wife, perhaps as she was sitting up to work on her wedding dress. She rejected him, and he strangled her. Then, in revenge, he took the lives of her parents and the lad – surely an accident, as he stated – and that drove him to despair. And so, at last, he killed himself. It all hangs together."

"By the slenderest of threads," Holmes said.

Wilkes seem poised to object, but the whistle of the train informed us that our station was approaching.

"You will want to see the bodies," Wilkes said. "We have turned the church cellar into a make-shift morgue in preparation for the inquest tonight."

"Dr. Watson will be of great assistance to us," my friend said. "Just give me a moment to find a fellow to carry a message, and I will be at your disposal."

Holmes fairly sprang from the carriage, instantly sighting a young urchin to do his bidding. Wilkes shook his head.

"He is disappointed in me, I can tell. I wish he would assure me that I have done right."

"At least you know that the murderer is dead, and there is nothing for the community to fear."

Wilkes shrugged. "That is true, and yet – I dread meeting Miss Schnell in the streets. She will have every reason to believe that I failed her."

A short time later, we walked into the dark cellar, where the bodies had been laid out on makeshift examining tables. The coroner, an elderly gentleman with enormous side-whiskers, was grateful to meet another medical man. I shall spare my readers the grisly details of what I saw beneath the sheets. Death is never pleasant – violent death, with bodies left untended, is even more gruesome. I was able to confirm the coroner's assertion that Mrs. Moore had died of strangulation, and that her parents had been killed with a sharp and heavy blade, most likely an ax, and that the child had been shot in the back. Though it was impossible to establish with any certainly the hour of their deaths, the condition of the bodies indicated that some time had passed before they were found, perhaps three to four days. Holmes gave these victims only a passing glance. Instead, he moved immediately to the corpse of the murderer.

I had imagined the killer, from Wilkes's tale on the train, to be a beast of a man. But the body before me reminded me, in an unsettling way, of my own physical condition when I was discharged from the army. The late Charles Moore had clearly been undernourished and living in rough conditions. His face and hands were weatherworn, his feet badly blistered. He was barely five-and-a-half feet in height, and one arm was withered and twisted from some past injury. The thinness of his chest made me wonder if he had been consumptive.

"Watson, Wilkes, look here." Holmes held up the dead man's left arm. "What do you see?"

"He is badly bruised on his wrists and forearms."

"You will find corresponding marks on his lower legs and ankles, and even here, in the corners of his mouth."

Wilkes shrugged. "He is clearly a man who has lived a sad and unfortunate life. His boots were held together with rough twine – that would explain the marks on his legs. As to his wrists, well – I have cleared many a tramp from beneath a bridge or a roadway, and I have been none too gentle about it."

Holmes started to speak, but then placed his fingers to his lips, as if realizing that words were unnecessary. He lowered the sheet over the man's corpse.

"Did you notice his fingers?"

"They were thin, his nails were ragged."

"Nothing else?"

"Should I have seen something?"

239

"Seeing an absence can be as important as seeing what is present. But let us move our inquiry to Forrest Farm."

A short time later, we found ourselves at the scene of the tragedy. Wilkes had preserved the property to the best of his ability, but Holmes said there was little to be learned from the room in which the bodies had been piled like cordwood. He asked if the murder weapon had been found, and Wilkes revealed that an ax had been located in the barn, and a service pistol had been found, along with some ammunition, in the man's pack. Both weapons had been vigorously cleaned, which of course the murderer had ample time to accomplish. In fact, he had also fed the animals, though surely that was to prevent their bleating and lowing, which might have raised some alarm, rather than out of any kindness.

Holmes focused his inquiry on the chambers of the house, a square, whitewashed, unattractive structure. The kitchen was neat and tidy, with the strange exception of the plate of spoiled meat and the dried coffee in the cup.

"This is the family's only table, I presume."

"Yes," Wilkes said.

"There were three adults and a servant, as well as a nearly-grown youth. Yet there are only three chairs here."

"The fourth is in the attic," Wilkes said grimly. "It was the chair in which Moore died."

Holmes's lips tightened. His eyes were gleaming, and I knew that he held a theory already, but wouldn't speak it. I wondered if he weren't giving Wilkes a chance to see some error in his own statement of the case, though I couldn't think of what it might be. The property certainly did appear large enough to conceal a determined man, especially one who might have spent years skulking from place to place.

"Here is what passes for a parlor," Wilkes said. "As you can see, nothing seems amiss."

Indeed, the room was a set-piece of rural domesticity: The fireplace with a wooden mantel, a few pictures taken from magazines, a good bit of knitting in baskets and, by the window where the light would have aided the work, a sewing machine with a dress upon it. Holmes picked up the fabric and turned it over in his hands.

"Watson will tell you, Wilkes, that I am no great admirer of the fair sex. However, there are moments when having a female assistant in my line of work would be a decided advantage."

I am certain that I must have gaped in shock. Wilkes sputtered through his beard.

"A lady! Preposterous, Mr. Holmes – a woman would have fainted at the sight of those bloody bodies."

240

"Perhaps, but she would hardly have a case of the vapors over this bit of evidence. I have no expertise in the manufacture of ladies' garments and can only assume that a wedding gown – even for a simple family event – requires some care in construction. If Mrs. Brewster purchased a bolt of cloth on Tuesday afternoon, in order to replace the incinerated dress, is it truly possible that the product could be at this level of competition by Tuesday at bedtime?"

Wilkes scowled. "It is possible that we have erred in our timetable."

"The bodies were placed in a very warm, enclosed room," I said. "That would certainly hasten their state of decay."

"But the coroner assured me that Moore hadn't been dead a full day when he was found." Wilkes shook his head. "It hardly matters. We still know he killed them, whether on Tuesday night or a day later."

Holmes turned and led the way up a narrow, dangerous staircase. There were three bedrooms on the upper floor. The room that had belonged to the recently departed maid was neat and tidy. The elderly parents' room a grim sight that I still see in my nightmares. Holmes, however, studied it calmly.

"Were their nightcaps found?" Holmes asked. "Elders of this generation rarely sleep with their heads uncovered."

Wilkes's face began to stain red. "No, none were found. If they had any caps, the murderer must have thrown them away, or burned them. In any case, we never found them."

We moved to the room that was shared by the mother and her son. The boy's bed had clearly been slept in, but the mother's bed was still made. I noted a wedding photograph in a silver frame – the bride had been little more than a child, and her first husband a dashing youth in his army uniform. Still, there was no question as to him being the same corpse who lay in the makeshift morgue.

"Now, let us see where the final tragedy occurred," Holmes said.

The attic was surprisingly large, and we were all three able to stand upright around the heavy oaken chair where the killer had been found, dead by his own hand. Wilkes pointed to the green bottle of arsenic on the floor.

"It must have come from the pantry – I have no idea if it was full or half empty, but if he swallowed even a small portion of it, he died in agony. And see, there is the pen and inkwell that he used to write the confession."

Holmes rose from inspecting the chair with his lens. "Yet there appears to be nothing in this room to write upon. No desk or table."

"I assume he used his knee."

Holmes chuckled. "I have witnessed Watson trying to take notes upon his knee. Illegibility is the usual result."

Wilkes reached into his pocket and pulled out the note. The swirls and loops of the letters, while written in haste, were truly formed.

"Mr. Holmes, this could only mean that – "

"Did you hear the knock? I believe we have company. Let us go and welcome him."

We descended into the kitchen, where a tall, robust man waited. He was deeply tanned, with curly black hair and small, hard eyes. He was dressed in rustic attire, with a checkered scarf tied around his bull-like neck.

"I had a note that you wanted me," he muttered, glaring at the inspector. "I've told you everything I know already, and I need to get back to work, so let us be quick about it."

"A small liberty," Holmes said, holding out his hand. "Mr. Vincent Jones, I knew my name would mean nothing to you, so I borrowed my friend's. Please, let us be seated here at the table – Watson, remove that horrible, stinking plate, thank you." Holmes pulled a pipe from his pocket. "There's no reason we can't be sociable as we conduct our business. Perhaps, Inspector, a glass of water would not go amiss? It is an unseasonably warm afternoon."

The man glared at my friend. "Who the devil are you?"

"His name is Sherlock Holmes," Wilkes said. "He is a detective from London."

This made no impression on Jones, who reluctantly took the opposite chair. "I don't see why anyone from London needs to meddle in our business. It's a sad state of affairs when a decent family can be murdered by a tramp."

"Ah, that is your theory?"

He nodded. "The inspector told me that they'd been hearing spooks over here – and why, even before he came to see me, old man Brewster was at my place, taking on about someone prowling on his land. He asked for my gun."

"What type of gun do you own?"

"No business of yours, since I didn't loan it to him. I always worried," he rapidly added, "about the old fellow's temper. I was afraid he might shoot his wife or Ruby when he was worked up like that."

Holmes nodded his understanding. "A sensible precaution. I am grieved for your loss."

The man stared hard, as if he didn't understand the words.

"The murder of your future bride – it must be painful to you."

Jones exhaled. "Yes, but it is best to not think on such things. A man might go mad if he brooded too much."

242

"Well said, sir. It is a very tragic affair, and I will be glad to put this sad scene behind me." Holmes gave his pipe a puff. "I only have one more question for you, Mr. Jones."

"Yes?"

"How long did it take you to clean up the blood?"

There was an instant where time seemed to stop. Jones's eyes were wide, the inspector gasped, I recoiled, and Holmes merely considered the murderer with the coolest expression possible. Then the man roared, lunging forward, a large knife suddenly appearing like magic in his hands, plucked in a heartbeat from his boot. Wilkes and I both threw ourselves at him, and all four of us went down in a pile. It was a miracle that none of us were harmed, but luckily Wilkes had seized Jones's left wrist, and forced the blade from his hand. There was quite a tussle on the kitchen floor before we finally subdued Jones, who swore the vilest oaths imaginable, frothing like a rabid dog. Finally, in frustration, Wilkes seized a pitcher and knocked him a blow on the head. He went limp, and the three of us gasped for air.

"Mr. Holmes!" Wilkes groaned. "I will thank you not to do that again!"

My friend worked at smoothing back his disheveled hair. "Watson will tell you that my flair for the dramatic often gets the best of me. I agree that was an unwise revelation. But your case will now come to a far more satisfying, and truthful, conclusion." Holmes glared at the unconscious man on the kitchen floor. "I have rarely met a fellow more deserving of the rope."

The morning of Vincent Jones's hanging was dark and grim. Holmes had been in a somber mood, and it was only reluctantly that he agreed to review the case, so that I could record his thoughts.

"It was clear to me from just the information in the papers and the details provided by the maid that Forrest Farm had been playing host to someone from the lady's past," he said. "The mysterious letter, the disappearance and reappearance of the keys, the smoking pipe in the barn, the newspaper and the killing of the dog – as we admit no ghosts to our consideration, the only possible culprit would be a human. I considered, very briefly, the possibility of an ingenious tramp, as the countryside has been plagued with them, but I returned always to the burned letter. The family had no correspondents, and what else could have so unnerved a bride on the threshold of her wedding other than the reappearance of a long-lost husband?"

"Did she know her husband was on the property?"

"I believe she did. Her assistance is the only thing that explains his ability to remain unseen, and she was quick with an explanation for all the clues that the family wasn't alone – certainly she took food to him, and she poisoned the family dog to keep him safe. She even feigned illness and thrust Jones away in the critical period before the wedding. As a deserter, her husband must have trusted her, for one word from her would have brought the law upon him. But clearly she felt couldn't confide in any member of her family. Perhaps she still entertained romantic feelings for Jones. She dithered on action and, ultimately, this sealed her fate."

"What made you so certain that Moore hadn't done as he claimed in the confession?"

"First – he couldn't have written the note when it was claimed he did, for there was no ink upon his fingers. Even if he had the remarkable ability to compose a strong hand on thin paper, while writing on his knee, there would have been some sign that he had used the pen. Second – there were the marks on his body that clearly told the tale. Just before he died, he had been badly bruised from being bound and gagged. Third – a gun was used to commit the lad's murder, and there was ammunition remaining. If you wished to do away with yourself – you, a former soldier – and could choose between the instant annihilation of a bullet to your brain or the agony of death from poison, which would it be? It was clear to me that he had been forced to drink the poison." Holmes shook his head and folded his arms. "But even more telling was the lack of blood in the house. It would have required a strong man to carry the bodies of two adults down the stairs. Once I saw Moore, I knew he couldn't have performed this task in his weakened condition. He could have dragged the bodies down, but then why clean the house? Remorse perhaps would have driven him to the action, but it seemed unlikely. There should have been blood, Watson – that was a further fact I couldn't dismiss. The real killer overplayed his hand, there were too many elements that were staged."

"But how were you certain it was Jones?"

"Who else would have had a motive? Jones was described as a man who, like his future father-in-law, was quarrelsome and unpleasant. Perhaps he learned the truth, that there could be no wedding, and flew into a murderous rage. Ironically, I hadn't one shred of evidence at that moment that would have held up in court. Thus, the nearly fatal baiting of Jones at the kitchen table. His attack on me was as good as a confession."

There was a knock upon our door, and a few moments later we were shaking hands with Inspector Wilkes.

"What brings you to Baker Street?" Holmes asked, pouring out coffee. "I had thought you would be at the prison, to see the end of Vincent Jones."

"I was there, yesterday. The prisoner, as you know, was silent throughout his trial. Your evidence, of course, is what condemned him, but at the end he decided to unburden himself and asked that I be brought in to record it. He also specifically requested that I read his confession to you."

The inspector pulled out his papers and his glasses, then coughed to clear his throat. He read directly from the document:

I loved Ruby Moore with a black passion. I wanted her and I swore I would have her, especially after she, in a weak moment, gave me every favor I asked. My wife's death freed me – you stare at me, Wilkes, but I tell you I shed not a tear for my invalid spouse, as she was useless to me. She was barely in her coffin before I had run through the woods to Forrest Farm and asked for Ruby's hand. I would have escorted her to the church that very morning, but the old man made a stink about it, and Ruby didn't have the heart to oppose him. I walked out after swearing to wait six months. As I did, I saw that brat, Owen, glaring at me. I made a note that as soon as he was my stepson, away to the navy with him, and good riddance if he died of scurvy.

A month before the wedding, Ruby suddenly turned queer. She sent the oddest notes, saying she was feeling low and uncertain if we should wed. I gave her two weeks to calm her nerves, then went over, just at dusk. She was coming out of the barn when I arrived. I had never seen her paler.

"What are you doing here? You must go away!" she cried.

"Is that any manner to treat the man you will marry?" I asked. I went to kiss her, but she slapped me and told me she had no wish to see me. My pride was wounded, and I stomped home. A few days later, the old man came and told me he believed there were thieves in the neighborhood, that he had lost his keys and a ham, and he believed his dog had been poisoned. He wanted my gun. I told him if there were thieves about, I had best keep my gun. He went off in a huff.

That night, I began to worry that Brewster might be correct about vile characters in the neighborhood. I had seen some tracks about in the dirt on the road, and one of my dogs had come home with a piece of cloth no doubt torn from a tramp's trousers. I dressed and went back to Forrest Farm. I can be as quiet and stealthy as a Red Indian when I choose.

245

There was a tree by the barn, and I climbed it, slipping into the hayloft. I stayed at the window for an hour, looking toward the house, before I saw movement in the shadows. It was my Ruby, in her nightdress, coming out of the house, bringing a plate of food to the barn. She came inside, and I looked down through a crack in the floorboards. I saw a ragged man emerge from hiding in a horse stall. They began to talk, and I listened. I soon understood that this man was her former husband, a dirty deserter from the army, and that he was urging her to gather their boy and run away with him. She held back – she spoke of her father and mother, the shame that would fall upon them. But never did she speak of me, of how I would suffer! At last, I heard him say that he knew she was engaged. He saw the ring on her finger and asked her who the man might be.

And then she said the words that damned her: "I do not love Vincent. I accepted him only because I wanted to leave this place, for I have never loved anyone the way I love you." He took her in his arms. What I saw next, I will not speak of. I can only say that I went mad at that moment, my brain filled up with fire, and I swore upon everything in heaven and earth that I would kill her and all her kin.

I could have murdered both of them in the barn – my gun was at my waist. But I knew a shot would draw all the residents of the farm, and before God I had nothing against the simple-minded servant. I would not have her blood on my conscience. It was only Ruby, whom I had worshipped, who must perish, and all her family as a sacrifice for her perfidy. I crept back down the tree and ran home, and from there I began to plan how I might murder them.

It was a short time later that you, Inspector, set the thing in motion. You came to me and told me that the servant had fled. I knew now the field was clear. On the Wednesday night before the wedding, all was ready. As soon as night fell, I went over to Forrest Farm and made my way into the barn. How shocked that filthy man looked when he realized I wasn't his wife, come to bring him food. You saw how thin and frail he was – overpowering him was no more difficult than catching a lamb. I heard a sound then. It was Ruby, arrived with his dinner. I had my hands around her throat before she could scream. You see how powerful my hands are? Do not fret, Inspector, she didn't suffer long.

246

I had worked it all in my head – how I would do it and lay the blame upon Moore. I took an ax from the barn, then I went into the house and climbed the stairs. The old folks slept soundly, and it was the work of an instant to bash both their skulls in. But when I finished and stood wiping my face, I heard a noise. I looked up and saw Owen standing in the doorway, staring at me. I had foolishly left the curtains back and he could see the scene clearly in the moonlight. He took off like a rabbit, and I gave chase. He almost made it into the woods. Just a few more paces and the game would have been given away. I shot him with no more feeling than I would have gunned down a dog after my sheep. Then I went back upstairs, dragged the old folks down, laid them all in the shed, and made an impression with Moore's boot.

I took him inside. His heart had gone out of him, for I showed him the dead, including his own son. I forced him to scrub away the blood that was in the hall, on the stairs, in the kitchen, lest some print of my boots be left behind. Then at gunpoint, I forced him to carry a heavy chair into the attic, and I bound him to it. For two days, I went back and forth to the house, feeding the livestock, tidying everything, so that no one passing along the road would think anything amiss. Then, at midnight before the morning of my wedding, I wrote out the false confession and put it on the floor beside Moore, along with the pen and inkwell. I forced him to swallow the arsenic and I watched him die. When he expired, I undid the ropes and removed them. I returned home, got into my wedding clothes, and went to the village to act the part of the forsaken groom, desperate to find his bride.

It would have worked. I had thought of everything. Moore was too broken to oppose me – I tell you he drank that poison down in great gulps – death was a mercy for him – but I know you will not believe me.

As for my body, I care nothing – perhaps one of the young doctors can cut open my brain after the execution and see what disease consumes it. Surely I must be insane, that I can speak so coolly of those I have killed, and feel no remorse, no sense of guilt or shame.

Wilkes took a breath, then folded the paper abruptly. My friend and I looked at each other, sensing something omitted.

"Was there more?" Holmes asked.

247

"Only one further line," Wilkes said, very softly. "He said: '*Tell Mr. Sherlock Holmes I will see him in hell.*'"

The Addleton Tragedy
by Terry Golledge

The months following Sherlock Holmes's miraculous reappearance after his supposed death at the hands of Professor Moriarty were busy enough to keep even his questing mind at full stretch. I have seldom seen him in better spirits than in that summer of 1894. I had lately disposed of my Kensington practice for a gratifying sum, once more taking up my old familiar quarters at 221b Baker Street. With an unusually healthy balance to my name with Cox and Company. I was free to fall in with whatever whims of fancy took my friend's attention, and I accompanied him on the majority of his cases where my presence was requested.

It was early June and we had lingered over the morning papers until Mrs. Hudson drove us from the breakfast table with clucks of disapproval at the sheets of newsprint scattered on the floor by Holmes's chair. I was as yet unshaven, but Holmes, unpredictable as ever, was fully dressed, having already been abroad on some errand of his own which he hadn't seen fit to confide to me. In fact, he hadn't uttered a word since his return, and I knew better than to intrude on his silence until I received the necessary encouragement. About to retire to my room, I was stayed by him addressing me sharply.

"What do you know of Wiltshire, Watson?"

The apparent irrelevance of the query took me unawares and I paused to arrange my thoughts.

"Come, my dear fellow," he said, a hint of amusement in his voice. "You must have heard of that pleasant county."

"Of course I have," I retorted impatiently. "All it means to me is Stonehenge, the Great Western Railway, and the great cathedral of Salisbury. Otherwise, it is somewhere to pass through on the way to the West Country. Is there a reason for your inquiry?"

He thrust a newspaper at me, jabbing a tobacco-stained finger at a column headed: "*Gruesome Find in Ancient Burial Chamber*".

"What do you make of that?"

I ran my eyes down the page to read that a party of archaeologists engaged in excavating a historical site near Devizes had come upon five skeletons, only four of which belonged to the period of the chamber. The fifth was of more recent origin, and among the bones was a rotting sack containing a quantity of gold plate, identified as the proceeds of a robbery which had occurred four years earlier at nearby Addleton Hall.

The report continued:

*Inspector Blane of the Wiltshire Constabulary is satisfied that
the remains are those of Edgar Barton, who vanished at the
time of the robbery and was suspected of being responsible
for the crime. He was the nephew of Mr. Willis Barton, the
owner of the Hall.*

I looked at my companion with eyebrows raised. "It seems plain
enough," I said. "I see nothing here to excite your interest."

"Do you not? Come, my dear fellow, you have seen sufficient
criminal activity to know when a matter feels right. Why should this man
commit a burglary, then hide himself to die with his booty hard by the
location of his crime? No, my good Doctor, it will not do."

I shrugged the matter aside and went to complete my toilet, and I had
forgotten it completely by lunch when Mrs. Hudson announced a visitor.

"Miss Elizabeth Barton," she said, standing aside to allow entry to a
young woman.

The name didn't at first register with me, but Holmes sprang to his
feet to greet her effusively.

"My dear Miss Barton. Come in and be seated, I pray you. I trust you
had a not too unpleasant journey from Wiltshire?"

She looked startled by his words, but lowered herself into the basket
chair and watched Holmes take his place facing her. She was tall and slim,
some twenty-five years of age, with warm brown eyes that held signs of
deep sorrow. When she spoke her voice was quiet, but with a firmness that
would hold the attention of those she addressed.

"I have heard of your powers of deduction, Mr. Holmes," she said.
"And this must be Dr. Watson, who acts so ably as your chronicler." I
bowed and she continued. "Yes, I have travelled from Wiltshire, but
whether the journey was pleasant or otherwise I didn't notice in my
agitated state of mind. I come to beg your help, sir, to clear my brother's
name of a foul calumny, yet I can offer no concrete facts for you to build
on, other than my own firm conviction of his innocence and integrity."

She paused and looked beseechingly from one to the other of us and
I, a widower of more than two years, felt a surge of compassion and
chivalry at her distress. Holmes, practical as always, leaned back with
hands clasped behind his head.

"Your brother being the late Edgar Barton, whose remains were
unearthed in the Bronze Age burial chamber?"

She nodded sadly, her eyes dry but holding a look of fierce pride.
"Then," said Holmes, "I will hear your story, and we shall see if logic and

reason can come to the aid of sisterly trust. Pray make me familiar with the events that have brought you so much distress."

"Edgar, who was four years my senior, and I lost both parents in a typhoid epidemic ten years ago, and our uncle, Mr. Willis Barton, gave us a home at Addleton Hall, some two miles from Devizes. I should add that Uncle Willis ls a very wealthy man who made his fortune in the African colonies before returning to England to enjoy the fruits of his labours. He bought the Hall on the death of the last Lord Addleton some two years before we went to live under his roof. He never married, and it was made clear to us that Edgar was to be his heir. Indeed, Uncle Willis treated us as his own flesh and blood, and in the six years that we lived there, he denied us nothing."

Here Holmes interposed a question. "You say six years. Am I to understand that you no longer reside there?"

"That is so, but I shall explain that shortly if you will bear with me. Due to our uncle's generosity, Edgar had no need to work, but he repaid that generosity by taking on the responsibility for the management of the estate, while from the age of sixteen, I was the virtual mistress of the Hall, taking complete charge of all domestic arrangements. It was a happy time, and the only cloud for me was the advent of an unwelcome suitor."

"Surely," said I, "there was no shortage of the young men of the district knocking at your door?"

"I accept the implied compliment, Doctor," she said modestly. "I fear there is a marked lack of eligible bachelors around Addleton and I had very little company of my own age of either sex. But to continue. The suitor of whom I spoke was a Mr. Elliot Langley. He was the son of my uncle's late partner during his Colonial days, and when he turned up at the Hall unannounced, he received a warm welcome. When he first showed an interest in me, I was flattered, despite he and Edgar having little liking one for the other.

"He had been with us for some two months when he showed himself in his true colours and – " Here Miss Barton averted her eyes and spoke in a barely audible voice. "He behaved towards me as no gentleman should."

"Did you tell your uncle or brother of his conduct?" asked Holmes.

"There was no need. Uncle came upon us as I struggled with him in a corridor and at once ordered him to leave the house. There was an angry scene of which I heard but part as I fled to my room, and I never set eyes on the wretch again."

My friend shot me a glance and, satisfied that my pencil was busy, he turned back to our client. "When did this disgraceful incident occur?"

"A month before Edgar's disappearance, four years ago this week, so Mr. Langley departed in the May. When my brother heard of it, he was for

251

going after him to chastise him, but he allowed my uncle to placate him – although Edgar vowed that if he ever set eyes on the man again, nothing would stop him."

"This Langley," asked Holmes. "What was his physical appearance??

"Tall, well-set up, and of a similar cast of countenance to my brother – so much so that on more than one occasion they had been taken for brothers or cousins, much to Edgar's chagrin."

"Thank you, Miss Barton. Now proceed to the night of the burglary."

"It was discovered by George, my uncle's personal servant, but neither I nor Uncle Willis heard anything unusual during the night. George had cause to go to the large drawing room to find the cabinet in which the plate was kept open and empty. He rushed to inform my uncle, who sent him to fetch Edgar, but my brother wasn't in his room. This gave no immediate concern, as he as often out and about the estate at the crack of dawn, but after the groom had fetched the police from Devizes and he was still absent, the inspector seized on the obvious and suggested that Edgar was the culprit."

Holmes frowned as the lady paused, and I ventured a query of my own. "You told us, Miss Barton, that your uncle had treated you both very generously, and your brother was his appointed heir. Did no one think it unlikely that he would sacrifice his future for a relatively small amount of gold plate?"

"Hardly a small amount, Doctor. The plate was worth more than three-thousand pounds and consists of five very fine pieces. However, I take your point. I think the police had it fixed firmly in their minds that such a sum would tempt anyone, and didn't see it in relative terms."

"And your uncle's view?" asked Holmes sharply.

"To give him his due, he resisted the idea most strongly until he was persuaded that with Edgar's sustained absence there was no other answer, and only then did he accept it with the deepest sorrow."

"But you did not." It was a statement rather than a question, and the lady at once concurred.

"No. At no time did I harbour the slightest doubt of my brother's innocence, and even this latest discovery does nothing to shake my belief. Let me say at once that I hold no animosity towards my uncle for his attitude, for there is no reason other than my stubbornness to think otherwise. "

Holmes got up and walked to the window where he stood looking down at the traffic below. Then he turned to face Miss Barton.

"Did Mr. Willis Barton ask you to leave Addleton Hall after this sad occurrence?"

"Indeed, he did not. He showed the utmost compassion for me, but with my feelings such as they were, I felt my position to be intolerable and was unable to be under any further obligation to him. I went to Marlborough and secured a post as companion to a widowed lady, hoping vainly to clear my brother's name. For four long years I have prayed for Edgar to return with a credible explanation, but the events of this week have plunged me into the depths of despair." Her eyes filled with tears, and she began to sob. "Am I foolish to still believe in him even after his death?"

I went to fetch her a glass of water while Holmes allowed her time to recover before going on.

"Pray forgive me if some of my questions are painful, but I am anxious to do what I can, and must have all the facts at my disposal. Who identified these bones as being your brother's? Was it you or your uncle?"

She looked at him blankly for several seconds.

"I don't understand, Mr. Holmes. Can a skeleton be recognized?"

"That is my point. Dr. Watson will tell you that without a precise medical and dental history, it is only possible to say that the remains are male or female and fall within approximate limits of height and age at the time of death. Again I ask: Who made the identification?"

"Are you saying that these remains aren't my brother's?"

My companion raised a cautionary hand. "I wouldn't have you delude yourself with false hopes, Madam. All I suggest is that those concerned have taken the obvious view that your brother vanished at the time of the robbery and now a skeleton has been found with the proceeds of the crime, so it follows therefore that the remains are those of Mr. Edgar Barton. That assumption would be tenable if there was one scrap of supporting evidence, but thus far I have heard nothing to point in that direction. I keep an open mind. Have the police spoken to you since the discovery?"

She shook her head. "There has scarcely been time. I saw the account in this morning's paper and knew it was my last chance to clear Edgar's name. I spoke to my employer, Mrs. Widgeon, and she readily gave me leave to come to London. Can you – will you help me, Mr. Holmes?"

"The matter intrigues me," he said. "Watson, the *Bradshaw*. We shall accompany Miss Barton back to Marlborough and then proceed to Devizes. I must warn you, young lady: I promise nothing, and it may well be that the truth will not be to your liking. Can you accept that?"

She lifted her chin bravely. "I am in your hands, sir, and will abide by your findings. You have my complete confidence."

During the journey Holmes remained deep in thought, often ignoring or not hearing words addressed to him. It was early evening when we alighted at Marlborough and, having sent the lady off in the station fly to her place of employment, we sought rooms at the Western Hotel.

"Nothing is to be gained by unseemly haste," my friend observed. "This is one case where a few hours makes little difference to our investigations, so I let us enjoy a good dinner and a night's sleep before proceeding further."

Eight o'clock next morning found us bowling along in trap with Holmes at the reins. Addleton Hall was located on the Marlborough side of Devizes beyond the village of Bishop Cannings. The house was approached through an impressive set of wrought-iron gates, with a broad drive curving expansively to the main entrance. It was evident that the owner of this magnificent pile had spared no expense in its upkeep. A tug on the bell-pull brought immediate response from a butler, who took the card presented by Holmes before standing aside to permit us entry.

"If you will be so good as to wait here, gentlemen," this august personage intoned, "I shall ascertain if Mr. Barton is free."

As we stood there, I gazed round the spacious entrance hall, noting the innumerable trophies of the chase adorning the walls, the most eye-catching of which was a mummified crocodile all of fourteen feet in length staring malevolently at us from a glass case. I was still looking askance at the fearsome memento when the sound of footsteps drew our attention to the man approaching us with a look of surprised welcome on his deeply tanned features.

"Mr. Holmes!" he cried. "This is indeed an unexpected pleasure, but I confess I am at a loss as to the reason for your visit. Nevertheless, you are welcome, and your reputation is well known to me."

Holmes introduced me, and soon we were sitting in deep leather chairs puffing appreciatively at the excellent cigars that our host pressed on us. Willis Barton was some sixty years of age, as tall as Holmes but of much heavier build, his muscular frame and shock of dark hair conceding nothing to his years. His eyes were bright and keen, giving the impression of gazing into far distances.

Dispensing with any small-talk, Holmes came straight to the point.

"My visit is occasioned as the direct result of an appeal made to me by your niece, Miss Elizabeth Barton, who is intent on removing the stigma attached to the name of her brother. I realize that the subject must be distasteful to you, sir, but the lady will not accept the general opinion that your nephew was the perpetrator of the theft that took place four years ago. To ease her mind, I have undertaken to review the matter while warning her that my findings may be disagreeable to her, but such is her faith in her brother that she discounts the risk."

A look of ineffable sadness came over Barton's bluff features and he drew deeply on his cigar.

"I will not pretend that I welcome further probing into this old wound, but recent events have made it inevitable. I admire Elizabeth for her loyalty, and it was with the greatest reluctance that I came to believe the Edgar had betrayed my trust. Even that reluctance worked against me, for had I thought from the start that he had stolen the property, I would never have made the matter public."

"You would have condoned the offence?"

"I would have pardoned him freely. Edgar was as a son to me, as Elizabeth was and still is a daughter, but there was never any need for him to steal from me. Had he been in any sort of trouble, I would have given him such help as he needed and asked no questions."

"Then you were persuaded of his guilt against your own instincts and your knowledge of his character?" Holmes asked keenly.

"I resisted the thought as long as possible, but the police presented an incontrovertible case, and at last I yielded to the evidence. Poor Elizabeth was distraught, and although she bore me no ill-will, she saw it as unfitting that she should remain under my roof." Willis Barton lowered his voice confidentially. "Between these four walls, I made an arrangement with the lady with whom she stays as a companion to pay her a more generous salary than is usual, but that isn't for her ears."

Holmes nodded absently. Then with an abrupt switch of direction asked, "I believe you spent much of your early life in Africa, Mr. Barton. Your entrance hall hold many trophies of your sojourn there."

"Thirty years I lived and worked there, from my eighteenth birthday until I returned to the Old Country in '82 following the death of my partner, Bob Langley. I made my pile and looked after it, but Bob died as broke as when he went out. Money ran through his hands like water, and every time we hit town after a few months in the bush, he threw his share around with both hands."

"What business were you in, Mr. Barton?"

The man chuckled reminiscently as he replied. "Nothing shameful by the standards out there, even if we did sail a bit close to the wind at times. Ivory, skins, and the odd bit of gold. Sometimes a diamond or two, but we always gave the Kaffirs a fair deal. A rusty rifle or an iron pot meant more to them than the occasional gold nugget they turned up with."

Once again Holmes changed tack. "Your late partner had a son who stayed with you for a while, I believe?"

Willis Barton nodded reluctantly. "That is so. Elliot called on me when he came to England and found himself down on his luck. Naturally I made him welcome, but we had a disagreement and he left."

255

"Due to his behaviour towards your niece," Holmes murmured, then went on without waiting for confirmation. "Had he no mother living?"

"She died at his birth, but I fail to see why that is pertinent."

"You haven't heard from him since his departure?" Holmes pressed.

"The last I heard of him he was in Chippenham, and that was a few weeks after he left here." Barton made it plain that the subject of Elliot Langley wasn't to his taste and Holmes appeared to drop it.

"What a magnificent set of fire-irons," he remarked, nodding towards the huge grate. "Such a pity the poker should be missing. That quite destroys its value. No doubt you are relieved to have your collection of plate restored to you at last."

The older man seemed bewildered by my friends' apparent inconsequential manner, but he managed a bitter laugh at the last sentence.

"I would give ten times its worth if that would restore my nephew and niece to my hearth, and without bragging that would still leave me a very wealthy man. I shall not keep those trinkets, Mr. Holmes, for they would serve as a constant reminder of what I have really lost."

There was a slight pause before Holmes spoke again. "This burial chamber – is it on your property?"

"Yes, two fields away towards Devizes. The excavations have been suspended while the police make their inquiries, but poor Edgar's remains have been removed to the mortuary at Trowbridge."

At that point a discreet tap on the door was followed by the butler entering to whisper a few words in his master's ear. The latter threw a hesitant glance at us and spoke apologetically.

"It seems that Inspector Blane is wanting a word with me. Would it embarrass you to be present, gentlemen?"

"Not in the slightest!" Holmes cried heartily. "I welcome the chance to meet the inspector and hear what he has to say. It will save us the time of seeking him out elsewhere."

Inspector Blane was young to be holding the rank that he did, but his eyes were alert beneath sandy eyebrows that matched his close-cropped hair. I put his age at a year or two either side of thirty-five, and he was plainly a man who knew his business and wasn't to be trifled with. He paused when he saw that Barton already had visitors, but was waved in to be introduced to us.

"Of course I know of you, Mr. Holmes, and Dr. Watson also, but what is there to interest you in this matter?"

Holmes gave a succinct account of our reason for being at Addleton Hall, and Blane spread his hands expressively.

"You're welcome to make any inquiries you wish, sir. It will be a great pleasure to see you at work, and you may call on me for anything you may wish to know. Alas, I fear your labours will be in vain, much as I would desire otherwise." He turned to the owner of the house. "I called on you, Mr. Barton, to let you know that the inquest on your nephew will be held tomorrow, and you will be required to attend to identify the remains. Eleven o'clock at the Golden Hind in Devizes. I would spare you, but the law must be observed."

Willis Barton's shoulders sagged despondently. Then his head jerked up as Holmes intervened.

"Can you state definitely that this collection of bones was once Edgar Barton, Inspector?"

"Who else can they belong to?" asked Blane. "All the evidence points that way."

"Then it doesn't need Mr. Barton to state the fact. You or I or Dr. Watson could say so with equal truth."

Blane stared incredulously. "Are you suggesting otherwise, sir?"

"Not at all. All I say is that the evidence is purely circumstantial, and these remains could be those of any male person of similar age and build to the young man in question."

"Then where is my nephew if that is not he?" Barton cried urgently. "Who else could have perished in that horrible tomb, and why has he not been seen these four years past?"

Holmes made no reply to this, addressing himself to Blane instead. "Is it possible to view this burial chamber, Inspector? I assume that your investigations there are complete."

"I'll take you there myself, but don't expect too much of it. It is very insignificant compared with the great barrow at West Kennet, and was only uncovered by chance. We can go at once if you're ready."

Accepting Willis Barton's fulsome invitation to return for luncheon, we followed Inspector Blane over the fields until we came to the site of the excavations. It was indeed insignificant by any standards, a low hump some three feet high, almost covered in bushy scrub, and with a raw scar where the explorers had entered by way of a low tunnel sloping down to the interior. Holmes halted some yards short, his keen eyes darting hither and thither before he began to circle the mound, scrutinising it intently until he arrived back at his starting point.

"Who was responsible for opening the chamber?" he asked Blane who had watched his every move.

"Members of the local Historical Society. They had been interested in it for years, and had tried to attract the attention of professional archaeologists without success. I heard they even went so far as to write to Professor Challenger and had a very dusty answer from him."

Holmes chuckled. "They would. Challenger wouldn't see enough fame or notoriety in this to tempt him. Unfortunately, these well-intentioned people were more enthusiastic than expert. However, one must not be too critical of them if they had tried to arouse interest and failed. May we go inside?"

"You will find candles just inside if you think it worthwhile. I've seen enough of the dismal place, so I shall await you here."

"Come then, Watson. You'll not refuse to bear me company, will you?"

Bent almost double, we ducked into the gloomy hole, our candles guttering. To my inexpert eye there was little to excite the interest, and apart from a jumble of old bones at which the rawest medical student would have turned up his nose and a few bronze artefacts, it was to me no more than a dank hole in the ground. My companion shuffled forward then squatted on his haunches, his neck twisted to inspect the roof, moving his candle in all directions. A muttered exclamation escaped his lips, but although my eyes followed his, I saw nothing to take my attention.

We retraced our steps and took in deep gulps of the sweet air without. Then Holmes shot off to scramble in the scrub growing on the mound, returning with twigs and grass stains on his trouser-knees and a look of smug satisfaction on his face.

He approached Blane and laid a hand on his arm. "Inspector, have you sufficient influence to have tomorrow's inquest adjourned for a week?"

"I shall need a reason," the inspector frowned. "Can you offer me one? I don't relish being kept in the dark."

"Well said!" cried Holmes, clapping him on the shoulder. "Let me speak to Mr. Barton over luncheon, then I promise to tell you what I propose. Can you be at the Hall at two o'clock?"

"I shall be there, Mr. Holmes, and if by throwing a different light on this sorry affair you can bring happiness to Miss Barton, I'm your man." He coloured to the roots of his sandy hair as he uttered these last words.

We ate a simple but satisfying meal, and as soon as the cloth had been drawn, Holmes got straight down to business.

"Mr. Barton," he began, "if I can clear your nephew of this shadow hanging over you all, how far are you prepared to go to help me?"

"I would go to Hades itself or perjure myself in any court in the land. Do that and I will meet any account that you see fit to render."

"The first two are quite unnecessary, and for the third my professional charges aren't such as to damage your credit. All I ask is that if I am to bring this matter to a successful conclusion, you will answer truthfully any questions I may put to you, with my word on absolute confidentiality."

"You have my hand on it, sir," said Barton.

"Then listen to what I have to say," and without more ado my friend proposed a plan so audacious that even I, used to his ways, was astounded.

Our client heard him in silence, consternation written all over his bluff features, but at the end he blew out his cheeks in hearty laughter.

"By George, sir! You ain't one for half-measures, are you? I'll go along with it gladly if it will clear Edgar's name and restore Elizabeth to my hearth."

"Then it only remains to secure Inspector Blane's agreement, and we may go ahead. Ah, I believe that is his hand on the bell now."

"Leave Blane to me," said Barton. "Nothing would suit him better than to have a hand in clearing my nephew's name. It would stand him in good stead with Elizabeth, if you take my meaning."

The policeman's first reaction to Holmes's extraordinary proposal was to mount a vigorous protest, but under pressure from the uncle of the two young people he at last capitulated, albeit with deep misgivings.

"If this goes awry," he said gloomily, "I can throw my career out of the window. The Chief Constable will demand my head on a plate."

"Then come, Watson!" cried Holmes clapping his hands. "The game's afoot!"

We made our best speed back to Marlborough, where I was set to packing our bags while Holmes busied himself by sending several telegrams to London and a note to Miss Barton which he had delivered by hand before hustling me willy-nilly to the railway station.

We caught the London Express by the skin of our teeth, and by half-past seven a hansom had deposited us at the door of our Baker Street rooms. I snatched an evening paper from a passing news-boy and trailed Holmes up to our sitting room where I thrust the paper at him. The black headlines shouted their message at us:

Arrest Likely in Wiltshire Skeleton Mystery

"It worked! They swallowed it!" I exclaimed gleefully.

He took the paper from me and began to read aloud:

It is learned by our correspondent that it is probable that Mr. Willis Barton of Addleton Hall in the county of Wiltshire will shortly be arrested in connection with the murder of his nephew, Edgar Barton, whose remains were discovered earlier this week.

259

He perused the remainder of the paragraph in silence before throwing himself into his chair, where he began stuffing tobacco into the bowl of an amber-stemmed briar.

"The morning papers will make more of it, you may be sure," he opined as the blue smoke wreathed around his head. "We must bestir ourselves early tomorrow. It would never do for us to be in disarray if we have a caller at the crack of dawn, as I hope we shall if my ploy bears fruit."

So it was that well before seven next morning our sitting room presented an unaccustomed aspect, our breakfast-table cleared, and even the newspapers folded neatly after we had read each in turn. They all carried similarly sensational stories as the one we had read the previous evening, although much amplified by speculation as to the course of events. Each one treated the matter in its own style, but all made a big play of the fact that the local police were acting on the advice of Mr. Sherlock Holmes, the renowned consulting detective of Baker Street.

For upwards of an hour we waited in silence, Holmes consuming pipe after pipe of tobacco and evincing signs of mounting impatience. I tried once to divert him, only to be quelled by a withering look. Then soon after eight o'clock a furious ringing of the doorbell brought him to his feet.

Heavy footsteps on the stairs preceded the violent bursting open of the door with the indignant protests of Mrs. Hudson pursuing the dishevelled figure that confronted us brandishing a copy of *The Daily News* in a shaking hand. Holmes strode across to placate our outraged landlady before turning to face the agitated intruder who was a young man of about thirty years, whose eyes blazed hotly in a face that in other circumstances could fairly have been described as good-humoured if not handsome.

"Sit dawn and compose yourself, Mr. Edgar Barton," commanded Holmes ere the man could recover his breath from his precipitate rush up the stairs. "I have been expecting you this past hour or more."

Our visitor appeared stunned by Holmes's words and the latter gently took his arm to propel him towards the basket chair and ease him dawn into it. "The brandy, Watson, if you will be so goad. Our guest seems to be somewhat confused. Here, my dear fellow, drink it down, then together we may unravel this four-year-old mystery. A cigarette, perhaps?"

With the brandy gone and a cigarette held in trembling fingers, the man had regained same measure of control. He thrust the newspaper forward, his eyes still wild and furious.

"Mr. Sherlock Holmes, for you must be he, what terrible thing is this that you have brought about? By what right do you scheme and connive with the police to place in jeopardy the life of a good and honourable man?" He half rose, and for a moment I thought he was about to launch himself in an assault on my friend.

Holmes fixed him with a compelling stare, and he subsided back into his chair, still white and shaking.

"Calm yourself, sir," Holmes admonished him. "Your uncle is in no peril from me or the police. Moreover, I suspect that your fears for your own liberty are quite unfounded, but until you tell me frankly of the sequence of events on that night four years ago, I shall reserve judgement."

"Then what is the source of these infamous stories in the newspapers?" demanded the man Holmes had addressed as Edgar Barton, and who hadn't denied the appellation.

"Merely a ruse on my part to bring you forward so that this whole sorry business may be resolved. Have you no care for the grief and heartbreak suffered by those who love you best? The uncle who was your benefactor was ever willing to accept you back into his house, while your faithful sister has never wavered in her belief of your innocence of any crime. Do you not owe it to them to stand forth and let the truth be known?"

Edgar Barton turned a haggard face towards us before dropping his head into his hands in a gesture of despair.

"Alas, Mr. Holmes," he groaned, "I fear I should give even greater sorrow to those of whom you speak, for although I am guilty of no great crime, the very course of events points an accusing finger. If you would spare them, let me return to the limbo from whence I came and say nothing of my continued existence."

"Pull yourself together, man," Holmes said sternly. "I already have a fair grasp of what happened on the night of the robbery. If my deductions aren't at fault, you may walk out of here to rejoin your family with a lighter heart than you have known these past years. Tell me your story, remembering that I am not a minion of the law but a seeker after truth and justice. There are no policemen lurking behind the curtains with handcuffs at the ready, so I implore you, trust me and all will be well. If you choose silence, I shall consider it my duty to tell the world of the facts and let things fall as they may."

The unhappy man looked at Holmes for a long minute, gnawing his lip in an agony of indecision. Then, with a resigned gesture, he nodded his head.

"So be it," he almost whispered, "I see I must needs trust you, but how did you arrive at the conclusion that I was still alive?"

"That I decided very early on. I became involved as the result of a plea by your sister, who has remained steadfast in her loyalty to you. Even before she approached me, I found it hard to believe that even had you been guilty of the theft as the newspapers suggested, it was against all reason to find your remains together with the booty so close to the scene of the crime. When Miss Barton told me her story, I asked myself who was likely to have been mistaken for you, and one name came to mind. Do I need to speak it?"

Edgar Barton shook his head and his cheeks flushed in anger. "No, you have the rights of it, but I am no felon, as you will see if you believe the story I tell."

"Then let us have some refreshment before we commence. Watson, pray ask Mrs. Hudson for coffee and some of her excellent plum cake."

A quarter-of-an-hour later the room was filled with the fragrant aroma of coffee, and we settled back to hear young Barton's narrative.

"You will have heard that on the death of our parents, Elizabeth and I were taken in by our uncle. He is a year or two my father's elder, and a finer man never set foot on earth. We were treated as his own, and we in turn did what we could to repay him, although that was little enough. The only discordant note came with the advent of Elliot Langley, the son of Uncle's late trading partner. He turned up with a story of being down on his luck, and our uncle's generous nature impelled him to offer the fellow a roof. It soon became obvious to me that he was no more than a parasite, his only goal being to extract as much as he could from Uncle Willis. He was selfish and lazy, and when I remonstrated with him about his conduct, he laughed in my face and told me to keep my nose out of his business, hinting that my uncle had swindled old Bob Langley out of his share of the partnership. I was patently untrue, and I was hard pressed to keep my hands off him."

Young Barton drained his cup, controlling his anger with an effort. "You gave no credit to the allegation?" Holmes interjected.

"None whatsoever. I knew my uncle well enough by this time to know that hard-headed business-man though he was, he was no swindler. After that, barely a civil word passed between Langley and me, but Elizabeth seemed to have a certain kindness towards him, despite my disapproval. However, a month or so after Easter, I returned one tea-time from a business trip to Trowbridge to find Langley gone, sent packing by my uncle. Both Uncle Willis and my sister were angry and distressed, but their wrath was nothing beside mine when I learned the reason for his dismissal."

"Miss Barton has apprised us of the incident," I said grimly.

"Well, gentlemen, you will also know that I was dissuaded from seeking him out with a horse-whip, but I vowed to exact retribution if he ever crossed my path again. After that, life settled down to what it had been before his arrival, but I detected a certain reserve in my uncle's demeanour. Reports reached me that Langley had been leading a life of debauchery in Chippenham before absconding with a trail of debts in his wake. I heard rumours that my uncle had made himself responsible for those debts, which was well in keeping with his generous nature.

"But to get on to the night of the burglary – that dreadful night forever stamped on my memory. I was working late in the library, preparing the accounts for the coming quarter-day, and finding myself drowsy, I thought to make myself ready for bed. It was my invariable habit to go round to ensure that all was secure for the night, and this I began to do. Imagine my surprise when I saw a moving light reflected on the terrace outside the large drawing room! I was still in the library and, seizing the poker from the grate, I stepped cautiously out on to the terrace in time to see a dark shape emerge from the drawing room. I must have been heard, for the figure turned to look in my direction. There was enough moonlight for me to recognize the features of Elliot Langley, and on seeing me, he at once took to his heels and with me in pursuit ran across the lawn and into the rough fields beyond."

"You made no outcry?" asked my colleague.

"I saved my breath. Besides," added the young man, "I wanted the satisfaction of dealing with him myself. He had a good start, but was hampered by a bulky sack slung over his shoulder, and I caught him as we crossed the second field. I grabbed his coattails and hurled him to the ground. I threw myself on him, expecting a desperate struggle, but to my total astonishment I met with no resistance. I sat astride him with my knees planted in his chest, but he made no move. Then it was I saw his face was suffused and his eyes wide open in a ghastly stare. I realised I was kneeling on a corpse, and I sprang to my feet in horror. Imagine if you can the scene there in the pale light of the moon, with me standing over a dead man on whom I had sworn vengeance for his insult to my sister and a poker in my hand. What interpretation would be put on it? For ten minutes I wrestled with my conscience before making a decision that I now know to be cowardly and foolish. I resolved to dispose of the body and vanish."

"Your reasoning was at fault," observed Holmes, stuffing tobacco into the bowl of his largest pipe. "Even if you were afraid of the truth not being accepted, you could have gone to your bed as if nothing had happened and be there when the burglary was discovered in the morning."

"That did occur to me, but I am no hand at dissembling, and most surely would have given myself away."

"Then you could have told your uncle the facts and relied on his trust."

"Oh, that's easy enough to say now," Edgar Barton retorted hotly. "Then I was in a state of terror and panic, and my thoughts weren't so logical."

"Logical enough to cast it into that hole," Holmes said severely. "Did you have any notion what it was?"

"No. It wasn't until I read of the discovery of the bones that I knew it to be an ancient burial chamber. The hole was covered by scrub, so I put a large flat stone over it, hoping it would never be found. The clothes I stuffed into a convenient rabbit-hole, together with the poker, and to the best of my knowledge they remain there still. Taking to my heels, I made my way by devious means to London, having enough money in my possession to maintain me until I obtained employment in a counting-house which paid sufficient to keep body and soul together. Oh, how often have I mourned my foolish and impulsive actions! I wanted to make a clean breast of it, but the more I procrastinated, the less likely it was that I would be believed. It was only this hare you started that brings me here now." He sat up and faced Holmes squarely. "Well, there you have it, Mr. Detective. What do you propose to do now?"

Holmes leaned back, his fingers stroking his long nose. "I believe your account, Mr. Barton, but you acted rashly and precipitately. As I see it, the only offences you have committed are failing to report a death and concealment of a body. Reprehensible as it is, I don't think the law will demand great retribution of you, but in my eyes the greater crime is the pain given to those who love you. Are you prepared to be guided by me in order to bring about a felicitous conclusion?"

"It seems that I am in your hands," said young Barton with a bitter laugh. "What have I to lose now? My own stupidity landed me in this muddle, and all I desire now is to have it over and done with. Have I your word that my uncle is in no danger and that the only purpose of the newspaper story was to induce me to reveal myself?"

"You have. Are you able to travel with us immediately to Wiltshire?"

"The sooner the better." He stood up. Now that a decision had been made it, was a different man now facing us from the wild figure that had burst into our chambers not an hour ago. His jaw was set in a firm line and his eyes were bright with a hope that had been lacking before. Holmes eyed him steadily, then gave him an encouraging nod.

"Good. Watson, do you run downstairs and secure a four-wheeler while I compose a couple of telegrams to prepare the ground ahead of us. I believe there is an excellent train at eleven o'clock"

So it was that we again found ourselves stepping from the train at Marlborough, making our way at once to the Western Hotel, where the manager greeted us warmly.

264

"The sitting room for which you wired is ready, Mr. Holmes," he said. "The young lady arrived not ten minutes since and awaits you there. Will you go straight up?"

"Not I," my friend replied. "Be so good as to conduct this gentleman to her at once. Is the dog-cart at hand? Good. Then the doctor and I will be on our way." He slapped the young man on the back. "Go on up, sir. I have one theory still to confirm, but we shall rejoin you later."

We never knew what took place between brother and sister, for five minutes later we were clip-clopping along the road to Addleton Hall. Holmes was in a blithe mood and refused to discuss the case, saying that if I hadn't grasped the situation yet, then I must wait upon events. We were met on the steps of the Hall by an excited Willis Barton, whose face fell when he saw but the two of us step down from the wagon.

"Where is Edgar, Mr. Holmes? Your telegram led me to look for him to be with you. Has something gone amiss?"

Holmes freed his arm from the other's importunate grip. "Curb your impatience, sir, I beg you. All is well, and your nephew is at this very moment with his sister. They are in Marlborough, but they will join you ere long. Before they do so, there is a matter that I would resolve between us – not only for my own edification, but to enable the good Watson to tie up the loose ends when he records the case in his chronicles."

"Ask what you will, and I shall answer if it is within my power to do so." He led us into the library, producing cigars and whisky before giving us his full attention. "Now, gentlemen, what would you know?"

"We have established that the skeleton in the barrow isn't that of your nephew," Holmes began blandly. "The question remains as to whose it is. Do you have any thoughts on that, sir?"

Willis Barton's eyes flickered, and he shifted uncomfortably in his chair. "Why, I assume it to be that of the burglar, but I can only surmise how it came to be there."

"I have the advantage of knowing that," said Holmes. "Let me tell you at once that the remains are those of Elliot Langley, buried in panic by your nephew."

Our host's face was ashen, and his big frame appeared to shrink before our very eyes. He took a huge gulp of whisky and immediately refilled his glass with a shaking hand.

"Tell me all, Mr. Holmes," he said when he had recovered somewhat. "Is Edgar still in peril?"

"I doubt it. He acted unthinkingly, but I think his offence will be looked on with compassion."

265

Holmes went on to relate the course of events as told by young Barton while the older man listened in silence. As the story drew to a close, he stared down at his hands with an expression between relief and sadness.

"So Elliot Langley is dead," he whispered. "God rest his soul, and God forgive me. I began to suspect as much when you displayed such confidence that it wasn't Edgar, but I feared to speak. What led you so quickly to the truth?"

My companion smiled. "The first hint came when Miss Barton told me that her brother and Langley were often mistaken for close relatives, and your tolerant attitude to his abuse of your hospitality confirmed my suspicion that he had Barton blood in his veins. Am I correct?"

Barton squared his shoulders and gave us a defiant look. "You are, Mr. Holmes. There is no point in denying it, as I am the only concerned party still living, but I would ask your discretion, Doctor, if you set this story down on paper."

"Be easy, sir," I replied. "I am adept at disguising places and people when preparing my stories for publication. I merely try to place before the public my colleague's unique powers, and I defy anyone to identify the players in these little dramas."

"Say on, Mr. Willis Barton," Holmes encouraged him. "Our discretion is absolute."

"Very well." Barton's eyes held a faraway look as he embarked on a tale that had its beginnings on the Dark Continent thirty years ago. "You will recall that I told you of my time in Africa and how my partner, Bob Langley, would go through his money as fast as he made it. We worked well together, but our temperaments were as chalk and cheese. I was ever a sober and prudent man, and it fell out that while we were in the Transvaal – Pretoria to be precise – disposing of our goods and laying in supplies for the next trek I met a lady with whom I fell deeply in love. My love was returned in full until I introduced her to Bob. You can imagine that I suffered by comparison with him – he with his zest for life and me so staid and careful. The upshot was that he couldn't tear himself away from her, and I couldn't bear to see them so happy together, so by mutual agreement between Bob and myself I went up-country alone. I returned four months later to find them married. You can picture my feelings, but I put the best face on it and wished them all the luck in the world."

Here he stopped to blow his nose on an outsize handkerchief.

"Worse was to follow," he resumed. "I hadn't been back in town many days when Mrs. Langley called on me at my hotel, and what she told me turned my world inside out. Marriage hadn't changed Bob in any respect, and he was out of funds and deeply in debt. He had approached me to get another safari under way, but I had no idea just how desperate he was for money until his wife told me. I wasn't reluctant to leave, as it wasn't the easiest situation for me to see the woman I still loved with my partner, although I bore them no grudge. As I mentally began to plan how I could stake Bob until we had made few sovereigns, and that without giving it the appearance of charity, she began to sob hysterically and upbraid me for going off on my own.

"I pointed out that as she and Bob were so wrapped up in each other, I felt my absence to be the wisest course, and the fact that I had returned to find them married confirmed it. 'You fool?' she cried. 'Why do you think I married him? Was I to wait indefinitely for you to come back and have my shame revealed to all?' At first, I didn't grasp her meaning, but eventually she made me understand that I was the father of the child she was expecting. I was stunned and ashamed, even though she convinced me that Bob had no inkling of the truth, and she wouldn't have come to me now if they weren't in desperate straits for money."

Holmes made no comment when the other paused, but I sensed disapproval in his somewhat Puritan nature.

Willis Barton began to speak again. "To cut a long story short, Bob and I went off, with me making him an advance on our expected profits and leaving his wife enough to support her. We were gone about six months and returned to find her dead and her baby son being cared for by a kindly old missionary and his wife. That was in '64, and four years later Bob got himself killed by a mad rogue tusker when his gun misfired. As you may guess, he left nothing and I made myself responsible for the boy's upbringing and education, but there was a fatal flaw in his character, and by the time he was seventeen, he had been in all kinds of trouble. I'll not go into any details, but he eventually went up-country on his own, and all I heard of him were a few discreditable stories that filtered down.

"I came back to the Old Country in '82 a disappointed man, for I had hoped that Elliot would become the son I had always wanted, but I had never had the courage to reveal the truth of our relationship."

"He must have learned it somehow," I hazarded. "His behaviour indicated that he had some hold over you."

"That is so. He came to England some four-and-a-half years ago and sought me out. By then my brother and his wife were dead and their children were living with me. When Elliot made himself known, I was unable to turn him away, and it wasn't long ere he saw Edgar's remarkable resemblance to him and put two and two together. When he confronted me with it, I couldn't in all conscience deny the truth, but surprisingly enough he wasn't interested in having the facts made known. Instead, as the price of his silence, he prevailed on me to make a larger allowance – much more than Edgar received. His conduct grew more and more intolerable until the incident with Elizabeth came as the final straw. I told him to leave my house and never show his face again, defying him to do what he would about our relationship." Willis Barton sighed. "Can you conceive of the pain and agony that decision caused me?"

Neither Holmes nor I replied, and the older man continued.

"Strangely enough, he went with nothing more than veiled threats, and for the next month I waited for his next move, but except for regular demands for money I was left in peace. Then came the burglary and my mind was on Edgar's apparent betrayal of my trust to the exclusion of all else. After that I heard no more of Elliot, other than he had left Chippenham with a trail of debts behind him which I felt honour-bound to settle."

Holmes rose to his feet, and I closed my notebook and followed suit.

"I don't think we need pry more," said my companion. "I think I hear the sound of wheels on the gravel, so we will leave you in peace with your loved ones. I believe you have sufficient influence in the county to have your nephew's impulsive actions dealt with sympathetically, but I see no reason for the distant past to be raked over. Is there an anteroom where Watson and I may wait until the two young people are safely in here with you and we can depart unobserved?"

We drove to Devizes, Holmes concerned that Blane's mind should be put at rest with a judicially edited story of events. We found the inspector at the police station, and between us we concocted the fiction that Holmes had been in the district on an entirely different matter and that the papers had wrongly made a connection with the four-year-old crime, leading to their false assumption that Willis Barton would soon be arrested.

"It's your case, Mr. Blane," my friend said. "Take what credit you can from it, but I would beseech you to spare the Bartons as much unpleasantness as you can.

"Rely on me, sir, and it has been an education to me to see your methods. One thing I would ask, though: What first put you on the track of the real truth?"

"Oh, that was the roof of the burial chamber," Holmes answered vaguely. "There was an obvious difference in the soil immediately over the skeleton indicating that it had been disturbed much later than the Bronze Age."

On our return journey to Paddington, Holmes sat huddled in a corner of the compartment, humming quietly to himself. It wasn't until we approached Newbury that I ventured a question.

"One small point: How will you account for the telegrams to the newspapers that hinted of Willis Barton's imminent arrest? Will not your reputation be damaged now that events have turned out differently?"

He turned a bland smile in my direction. "My dear Watson, those wires must have been sent by some malicious person using my name. They cannot be laid at *my* door. If newspaper editors are so gullible as to print that kind of thing without verifying the facts, it is their misfortune. I shall issue a firm denial and demand that they publish a retraction and apology immediately and prominently."

"Really, Holmes, you are incorrigible." I laughed. "Have you no shame?"

Thus, what started as a tragedy came to a happy conclusion, with Holmes opening a letter a week later to find a cheque enclosed, the amount of which caused me to whistle when he showed it to me. It was signed "*Willis Barton*".

Three months had elapsed when an item in *The Morning Chronicle* came to our attention. It announced the engagement of Chief Inspector Blane of the Wiltshire Constabulary to Miss Elizabeth Barton of Addleton Hall in that county, and in the next day's mail came invitations for Holmes and myself to be guests at the forthcoming nuptials.

"Blane has taken another step on the ladder of promotion," Holmes remarked. "A wife such as Miss Barton will be invaluable in his career."

However, events intervened which took us to Paris on the case of Huret, the Boulevard Assassin, in consequence of which we were forced to miss that joyful occasion, much to my regret.

The Adventure of the
Doss House Ramble
by Will Murray

I had neither seen nor heard from my good friend, Sherlock Holmes, for three days in that first week of October in 1894, but this didn't concern me, for I knew that in his work as London's only consulting detective, he was prone to disappear for weeks on end, hot on the trail of some crime or criminal yet to make the newspapers.

I found nothing in print to suggest which scent Holmes might be pursuing. No noteworthy crimes had been reported, but I gave this little thought. It was a common enough occurrence, this propensity for disappearing without warning or explanation.

Once the three days had stretched into five, my concern began to grow, but once again, this wasn't so unusual as to alarm me.

After a full week, Holmes's absence was another matter entirely. His bed hadn't been slept in. His clothing remained undisturbed. I decided to go round to Scotland Yard and make inquiries of Inspector Lestrade.

"Missing, you say?" he asked.

"One week as of today."

"I'm unaware of any case on which Mr. Holmes is working."

"Is there a significant matter unresolved by your force?

"There are many, of course – all manner of murders and robberies – but Mr. Holmes hasn't spoken to me about any of them. Whatever he's about, it's his own business, and not ours.

"Holmes's business is frequently the business of Scotland Yard," I observed. "As often as otherwise, they intersect."

"That I don't deny," admitted Lestrade. "Beyond that, I cannot imagine what scent he's pursuing. Or whether it's large or small matter."

"There, you are correct. I've known Holmes to spend as much time on a minor matter as on a capital crime. It's the mystery that acts as a lure. Yet once he has the solution, his interest dissipates, and he's on to the next mystery, if there is one.

"I cannot help you, Doctor – unless you have reason to believe that Mr. Holmes has come to harm.

"Given the man's professional habits, I can't say one way or the other," I admitted in exasperation.

Having learned nothing, I returned to Baker Street to await Holmes's eventual return. That he might not ever return didn't seriously cross my mind. Holmes was the most capable man I ever knew. His brain was sharper than a barber's straight razor, and his physical capabilities were surprising in a man so spare of form. Merlin himself would have envied his ingenuity.

Another night passed. I went to bed worried. Eventually, the oblivion of sleep overcame my troubled thoughts.

Upon wakening, I went downstairs to take my breakfast and was shocked to discover Holmes sitting at the table, calmly drinking coffee and perusing the morning *Times*

"My word, Holmes!" I cried. "Where on earth have you been?

"Good morning, Watson," he replied wearily. "I've been everywhere, yet nowhere at the same time."

"If that's a riddle, it's beyond my grasp. I haven't had my coffee as yet."

"Not a riddle. Merely a manner of expression. I've been drifting from doss house to doss house, attired as a crawler, subsisting on meager rations, while I pursued my man."

Sitting down, I poured my own coffee and asked, "Will you tell me about it?"

"I wish there was more to tell," stated Holmes. "He may be one of the lowest residents in greater London. I don't know his name. I don't know his face. Not the color of his hair, nor the shade of his eyes."

"Then how will you recognize him?"

"By the whistling of his broken nose – "

"That's an outstanding feature, but a deviated septum is hardly unique among a certain class of men."

"This fellow's nose was apparently broken during an altercation. I'm given to understand that it was all but flattened."

"What's your interest in this disfigured fellow?"

"That, Watson, I cannot say at the present time. I'm operating in confidence. I can only state that this man must be located, and I'm determined to find him, but after more than a week sleeping in doss houses and in coffins, my desire for a civilized existence, even if only as a respite, cannot be denied."

"Did you say *coffins*?"

"Sleeping in a coffin with a tarpaulin for a blanket was the most comfortable night I've spent since I last saw you. The two-penny doss houses, where one can hang over a stretched rope with one's fellows, weren't pleasant, but sleep could be had. Worse yet, I've sat on kneelers and benches for a penny, where if one dozes off, one is struck by a cane or a stick so that he cannot sleep. Awake those long hours, I listened in vain for my man's singular nasal breathing, but to no avail."

"Good heavens! I've read about the privations of the doss houses. You make them sound even worse than Fleet Street paints them."

"They are horrible, grotesque places where the difference between a penny enables a poor wretch to sleep after a fashion, or simply be sheltered and made to remain awake, for those are the rules of the establishment."

"Something should be done about such places."

"The Salvation Army is responsible for many of them, and they have established a strict hierarchy of poverty. But enough about such dismal things. I'll eat decently and sleep in my own bed tonight. Perhaps tomorrow night as well, but when I've restored my spirits and feel like a human being again, I must plunge back into this netherworld of iniquity, if I'm ever to find my man."

"And if you do?"

"*Once* I do," corrected Holmes.

"Very well, once you do, what will you do with him?"

"That I also cannot say."

"Well, it appears to me as if I won't be able to write an account of this particular case, queer as it sounds."

"What you do or do not doesn't concern me, friend Watson. I only wish to accomplish my goal and put the entire horrible experience behind me."

"That's understood," I said. "Should you disappear again, I'll not worry unnecessarily."

"Should I not return in another week," Holmes told me gravely, "I beg you to go to Lestrade and ask him to look for me in the doss houses of the East End, particularly about Whitechapel, for I intend to spend another week in my search, and then break off for another respite. I can only take so much of this sleeping in the rough."

"I'll not forget," said I.

That afternoon, young Wiggins turned up. He was the nominal leader of the Baker Steel Irregulars. I wasn't privy to their conversation, but I gathered that he had been relaying intelligence to Holmes as to the whereabouts of the missing man.

After he'd gone, I mentioned, "I see that your Irregulars have also been pressed into service."

"From the start. They've been scouring the rookeries of the East End, and while their reports have been helpful, by the time I reach the spot, my man has vanished once more."

"Pity."

"Oh, we'll find him. Never fear. We will find him."

Two days later, Holmes disappeared from our shared rooms, and while I retired to my comfortable bed each night, I couldn't help but imagine the horrid circumstances and conditions in which he sought sleep.

The ensuing days passed so swiftly that I almost didn't realize it had been a full week since I last laid eyes upon Holmes. Only my calendar reminded me that it was once again a Thursday.

Perhaps I had placed too much confidence in him and his uncanny powers, but I didn't worry the entire time. However, once I realized how much time had elapsed, my good friend's admonition to seek an audience with Lestrade returned forcibly to mind.

It was a day of perpetual drizzle, so I was reaching for my waterproof with the firm intention of going directly to Scotland Yard when Mrs. Hudson brought up a caller.

"This gentleman would like to see Mr. Holmes, and will not take no for an answer."

"I'll speak with him, Mrs. Hudson, thank you very much."

After she went downstairs, I shook off my waterproof and waved the man to a comfortable chair. I took the one facing him.

"I am Dr. John Watson, a friend of Mr. Holmes. He is away. What is it I can do for you, if anything?"

"When did you last see him?" the man shot out.

I let his excessively brusque demand go by without challenge. I was measured in my reply.

"I last saw Holmes one exactly week ago today. He is investigating a matter."

"What matter?" barked the other.

"I don't know, and if I did know, I'm afraid that I couldn't say. All matters with Sherlock Holmes are strictly confidential."

"Didn't you say you were his friend?"

"I did," I allowed calmly. "But Holmes doesn't take me into every confidence. He's quite careful in that regard. Do you wish to engage his services?"

"I *have* engaged them! And I haven't heard from the man in more than a week."

"That's distressing."

"Worse, it's infuriating. Holmes had kept me informed of his progress until recently."

"Was he making satisfactory progress?"

"No, confound it! He was making none whatsoever, and I had agreed to pay him fifty pounds a day. Fifty pounds a day, and for what?"

273

"I see. You must understand that Holmes's work is sometimes a plodding and painstaking affair, but he almost invariably achieves satisfactory results. I've seen him struggle with a problem for weeks on end, only to solve it virtually overnight."

The man wasn't placated. "How can one say a problem is solved overnight when it takes weeks and weeks by your accounting to reach a solution?"

"What I meant by that remark," I said carefully, "was that Holmes has been at an impasse for weeks and weeks and, through a terrific effort of might and mind, wrests his solution out of seemingly nothingness."

That seemed to mollify the man. At least, he had no immediate rejoinder.

I continued speaking. "Inasmuch as Holmes hasn't taken me into his confidence in the matter in which you have engaged him, I'll not question you further, but I'll inform you of the fact that my friend urged me to go to Scotland Yard if a week passed without his safe return. That entire time is now elapsed. I was on my way to engage a cab to the Yard to lay the matter before Inspector Lestrade."

The bluff fellow took in my words and his fiery eyes banked and then grew ruminative.

During this silence, I studied him carefully. Holmes had often upbraided me in no uncertain times regarding my failure to observe closely and carefully. I now endeavored to do so.

By his manner, he was obviously a fellow of means. His Chesterfield coat and polished buckram boots supported that assumption. His **moustache** was exceedingly well-groomed, and the John Bull hat that sat on his lap looked as if it had been purchased only in the last week, but I assumed it was simply extremely well cared for.

Slowly, the man took a cigarette out of a silver case which he removed from an inner pocket and lit it with a Lucifer. He did this methodically, blowing out the match and throwing it onto the hearth.

A careful man, I saw. One who was deliberate in word and in deed. That he was also hot-tempered, or at least upon this day exceedingly impatient, I had already observed.

No doubt Holmes would have already deduced his occupation, the approximate sum in his bank account, and his salient personal affairs by this time, but I saw no clues to anything beyond his personality.

I remembered hearing a carriage pull up before the fellow's arrival. Beyond the window overlooking Baker Street, I could hear the snorting and nickering of a brace of impatient horses. This told me that the fellow enjoyed a substantial living.

"My apologies," I said. "I neglected to ask you for your name."

"And I neglected to offer it," the unpleasant fellow returned shortly. Then he fell to smoking his cigarette.

I didn't care for his curt manner, but I kept my opinion to myself.

Instead, I said carefully, "Anything you have to offer that would lead to the current whereabouts of Mr. Holmes would be greatly appreciated by myself, and as well by Scotland Yard."

"I don't know that I care to involve myself to that degree," the man said, releasing a rushing cloud of greyish tobacco smoke.

Hearing these callous words, I took umbrage, but I kept my growing ire tempered.

"Once I lay the matter before Inspector Lestrade, I can hardly leave out this conversation. You didn't come to me in confidence, after all. It would be better for all concerned if you were more forthcoming."

"Oh no doubt, no doubt," he said distractedly. His eyes were moving all around the room, seemingly seeing everything, but I suspect noticing nothing in particular. What was going on in his brain I could only imagine. He was carefully weighing his alternatives, I thought.

It was clear to me that the fellow didn't want to volunteer his identity, or get into the particulars of his reasons for hiring Holmes, but I knew that I had to get at them somehow.

"I comprehend that this is a matter of some weight to you," I told him. "Permit me to give you some time to turn the matter over in your mind."

With that, I stood up, went to the window, and looked down upon Baker Street.

A brougham was directly beneath the spot where I stood. I had expected to see a mere coupe. I studied it carefully, making note of its handsome lines and committing to memory the colors of the two horses standing abreast in their traces. I could see little of the driver, but that didn't matter.

I remarked casually, "I assume that's your carriage?"

"I don't deny it."

"It wouldn't be difficult for Scotland Yard to trace it, if it came to that," I said pointedly, turning around to give the man the full force of my frank gaze.

The fellow took the cigarette out of his mouth and said, "Well played, my good Doctor. I admit that you give me no choice in the matter."

"Your cooperation would be greatly appreciated, I assure you," I said with more grace than I truly felt.

Standing up abruptly, the man offered, "Permit me to take you to Scotland Yard then. All the talking that I'm willing to do, I'll do there."

Rather pleased with myself, I reclaimed my waterproof and we went down into the drizzle to board the waiting carriage.

The run to Scotland Yard was chilly in all respects. The man continued to smoke and not a word did he offer, whether as pleasantry or information. Upon reaching our destination, we dashed for the entrance, for the rain had begun to pound, and we were soon shaking off our coats in Lestrade's office.

As we entered, he exclaimed, "Dr. Watson! What brings you here? And who is this gentleman?"

"I'll answer your second question first," I replied. "Although he was kind enough to bring me here in his brougham, my companion hasn't consented to reveal his name."

"Upon my word!"

The fellow spoke up. "Let me give it now. I'm Alford Grainger. Perhaps it's familiar to you, Inspector."

"Indeed it is."

"I confess that I don't know it," I admitted without prejudice.

"Mr. Grainger is the owner of several tanneries of some significance round the City."

"Hello," I said. "Pleased to make your acquaintance at last."

Grainger failed to see the humor in that remark and let it pass.

Addressing Lestrade, I continued. "As for the first reason I've come to see you, here it is: Holmes has been missing for another week. One week ago, he advised me to seek you out if he didn't return from his rounds."

"Missing again, you say?"

"I regret that it's true, and the affair seems to involve Mr. Grainger, who hired Holmes to undertake an investigation, the details of which I'm sure he can supply."

"Be seated, gentlemen," invited Lestrade.

After we were settled, Grainger finally explained himself.

"Over two weeks ago, I hired Sherlock Holmes on a confidential matter. I trust that this confidence will extend to Scotland Yard."

"If it doesn't conflict with our official duties," stated Lestrade.

"I must settle for that, I suppose," muttered Grainger. "Here's the crux of the matter: I hired Holmes to locate a man with a smashed-in nose, whom I believed to be without any means. I imagined that he passed his nights in various doss houses. Holmes agreed to conduct a search of those disreputable establishments in hopes of locating the man I sought."

"I see," murmured Lestrade. "What's this man's name?"

"Gunter Philbrick."

"Odd name."

"Quite. Philbrick is an odd fellow."

"What's your interest in him?"

"That," returned Grainger stiffly, "I would rather not divulge."

276

"Scotland Yard can hardly undertake an investigation without knowing all particulars," reminded Lestrade.

"I don't believe you need to know the particulars regarding Philbrick, in as much as Dr. Watson begs you to search for Mr. Holmes, who is well-known to you."

"Nevertheless," insisted Lestrade, "I must have your cooperation."

Here, Grainger's temper flared anew.

"And I've given it!" he exploded. "I've delivered Dr. Watson to you with all dispatch."

"After I threatened to report him to your office," I told Lestrade.

"I thought it expedient to present myself rather than putting Scotland Yard to any unnecessary efforts," mumbled Grainger defensively.

Lestrade asked, "You have reasons for seeking this man Philbrick? What are they?"

"They are quite personal, and I mean to keep them that way. I mean no offense to Scotland Yard, but the matter is private. I regret that Holmes may have run afoul of something risky during his investigation, and that's why I'm present now."

Lestrade could see that Grainger was a stubborn man. He was also canny enough to know that a man of his standing wasn't one to be trifled with. Grainger had a point. Having no official interest Philbrick, Scotland Yard's interest was confined to locating Holmes.

Grainger drove this point home when he stated, "To the best of my knowledge, Gunter Philbrick isn't wanted by the law."

"Yet you want him strongly enough to have hired Mr. Holmes," Lestrade pointed out.

"I do not deny it."

"I see," mused Lestrade. Turning to me, he asked, "What can you tell us about this latest disappearance, Doctor?"

"Only that he has spent several days sleeping in different doss houses without result. He returned to Baker Street for two days in order to refresh himself, and then set out once again, Thursday last. His parting words to me were to turn to Scotland Yard if he didn't return in a week's time."

"Apparently he feared for his safety."

"Who wouldn't – sleeping with the riffraff who habituate the doss houses of Whitechapel?"

"Was he in disguise?"

"I don't doubt it, but I cannot describe the nature of it. However, I've some familiarity with many of the more disreputable items in Holmes's wardrobe which would aid in identifying him, regardless of how he distorted or concealed his features."

"Very well then. Doctor. Are you willing to accompany me this evening as we scour these terrible places?"

"Of course I am."

Lestrade turned to my companion. "And you, Mr. Grainger – can you give us a better description of your broken-nosed man?"

"I'm willing to do that. He stands nearly six-feet high, and weighs twenty-stone. His hair is chestnut, but has been losing its color. He has a broad face, rough-textured skin, and his eyes are a dull brown, but you will know him best by his nose. It's so flat that when he breathes hard, the unobstructed nostril whistles like a kettle heard in another room."

"I daresay that will be enough," decided Lestrade. "If we find this broken-nosed man, what would you have us do with him?"

Here, Grainger hesitated again. "Unless you have a reason to arrest him, I can make no claim upon you."

"And if we do have cause to arrest him?"

"I would be grateful for the opportunity to speak with him in private."

I thought this last sentence was delivered in the mildest tone the man had so far uttered. I could see that it was an effort. Grainger was a man accustomed to being obeyed.

"I can promise nothing, but it's Mr. Holmes we must locate. Good day to you, Mr. Grainger."

"Good day, gentlemen."

With that gruff comment, Alford Grainger removed himself from our presence.

Left alone with Lestrade, I offered, "I'm ready to commence the hunt when you are."

"These are peculiar circumstances, Doctor. I'll have my officers made aware of the situation. Then we must go. There's no point in waiting for night to fall. The sort of people who gravitate to the doss houses can be found in certain neighborhoods at all times of the day. We'll begin by combing those spots."

"I'm most grateful to you, Lestrade, for I'm fearfully worried."

And so we went out into the miserable pouring rain, the good Inspector and me.

A hansom cab took us to the East End, where we reluctantly stepped out into the diminishing storm and commenced our search, beginning at the Whitechapel coal docks. Between the odor of heaped coal and the stink emanating from adjacent tanneries and breweries, I thought it best to close my mouth and breathe through nostrils only, but what good it might do me, I confess I didn't know.

It was too early for the doss houses to open for the night. For those unfamiliar with the term, *doss* is a corruption of the word *doze*. These unpleasant establishments permitted the indigent to pass the night in relative safety from such rough elements as we now faced, and from some of the dangers of the streets, but they were by no means safe refuges, for all manner of pickpockets and sharpers inhabited those warehouses for the unfortunate.

As I stood on the pavement of Whitechapel Street, turning my gaze this way or that and taking in the raucous profusion of dubious personalities, I despaired of ever picking out Holmes from the human tumult packed between the crowded-together beer-shops and sundry other disreputable establishments.

The characters who swirled around us were as varied as they were distasteful to behold. Here was a shawled older woman dozing in the shelter of a doorway, and there a beady-eyed dandy who looked as if picking pockets was his chief occupation. Other less-honorable individuals were idly lounging or looking furtively about, as if seeking some long-lost friend, or perhaps some imagined mortal savior.

Watermen and lumpers abounded, as did slatternly fallen women, the latter old before their time. On a distant corner, a street doctor was largely peddling his doubtful nostrums, claiming that his rare potion could cleanse the blood of all that befouled it. Urchins, some barely clothed, frolicked, adding to the mad cacophony.

Picking out a disguised Holmes from this human menagerie, it seemed to me, was all but hopeless.

Fortunately, Lestrade was of sterner mind. Without delay, he sought out the nearest policeman and began questioning him closely.

After first describing Holmes in a general way that permitted the possibility of identification, Lestrade asked, "Has such a man been carried off to the hospital in the last week?"

"Not that I'm aware, sir," the other responded.

"To the morgue, then?"

"Oh, many of those. I would say at least five."

"Give me the particulars."

The constable gave a rapid accounting of such indigents as were conveyed to the morgue and, after he was finished, the inspector thanked him tersely and then turned to me, saying, "I think only two of those unfortunates could possibly be Mr. Holmes."

"I trust not," I said fervently.

"As do I, but the possibility must not be excluded, no matter how much it offends our sense of decency and justice."

Moving on, Lestrade continued circulating through the crowd, which in turn percolated around us like white blood cells in the bloodstream. I locked gazes with all manner of characters, and many of those gazes were challenging. Others shied away. I kept clear of those I fancied to ply the pickpocket trade.

I thought I recognized one of the Baker Street Irregulars, but he took no notice of me. Before I could lift my arm to gain his attention, he had turned a corner and was out of my sight. Reaching that corner, I looked every which way, but I spied no sign of the scruffy fellow.

More and more, I felt the matter was worse than hopeless. It was useless. After an hour had passed, I began to believe that the morgue might be a reasonable alternative to this exercise in futility.

Lestrade would have none of it.

It was at this point that a thought struck me so hard that I hesitated to raise it, for I should have noticed this ere the moment it was brought to my attention.

"Holmes would no doubt upbraid me for missing this important point," I said suddenly.

Lestrade stopped in his determined tracks.

"What's that, Dr. Watson?"

"Alford Grainger named the man with the smashed nose, but Holmes told me that he didn't know the name, for Grainger hadn't divulged it."

"Peculiar point. Why wouldn't Grainger give his name to the one whom he hired to search for the fellow, but readily admit it to us?"

"In as much as you represent the law, he may have felt that he hadn't any choice in the matter."

"Reasoned soundly. Another possibility is that Grainger lied to us."

"Conceivably he lied to both parties," I pointed out, "Holmes and ourselves. The name may be a false one, calculated to throw us off."

"That's a possibility we must keep firmly in mind," asserted Lestrade. "The man isn't to be trusted. Let's continue our investigation."

Alas, our efforts were for naught. As the sun began to set, reddening the decaying buildings around us, Lestrade said, "We must remove ourselves to another part of the city, but before we do that, we should make a visit to the morgues."

Reluctantly, I agreed. I will not bore the reader with the details, except to say that we visited two morgues, examined several corpses, and came away satisfied that Holmes wasn't one of the recently deceased.

As much as this alleviated my immediate worries, I realize that not all bodies are given the courtesy of being conveyed to the morgue for proper burial – especially when stark murder is involved.

By dusk, we found ourselves in another part of town, interviewing still another constable but learning very little.

Late in the evening, Lestrade and I were forced to admit defeat. Having accomplished precisely nothing other than to wear out the bottoms of our shoes, we gave up our efforts as a bad job.

"Unless you're willing to look in all the doss houses," he said reluctantly, "I don't think we need to expend ourselves further tonight."

"As much as I worry about Holmes." I replied frankly, "I haven't the stomach to pass the night in such a wretched manner. Nor can I conceive of what we might accomplish, except by rare chance."

"My men will keep a keen eye out for him. Perhaps tomorrow's sunshine will shed a better light on this affair."

We parted rather morosely, Lestrade to return to Scotland Yard and I to make my way back to Baker Street.

I was startled upon alighting from my cab to see the front windows of our quarters illuminated. Entering, I mounted the stairs rapidly and stepped into our chambers.

Seated in his customary velvet-lined chair, smoking his habitual clay pipe, was Holmes, alone by the fireplace, looking frightfully drawn to the point of gauntness.

"Good God, where have you been? Lestrade and I've been wearing down the cobblestones of Whitechapel in search of you."

"Have you now?" replied Holmes, removing the pipe-stem from his mouth.

"Don't you remember exhorting me to seek the aid of Scotland Yard if you didn't return after a week?"

"I do, indeed. And today it has been a week. And here I'm. I imagine you rather jumped the gun."

"Jumped the gun! I've been beside myself with worry. Hasn't it been a full week?

"It has. I'm quite certain about that, but I've been here several hours, having returned, or so I believed, in the nick of time, as it were."

Shrugging off my coat, I took my own chair and availed myself of a cigarette.

"We were reduced to touring the morgues in search of you."

"I'm distressed to hear that. Perhaps I should be more precise in my speech in the future."

"I would appreciate that simple courtesy," I said without rancor.

Silently, we smoked for several minutes as I gathered my thoughts.

"While you were away," I offered, "a certain Mr. Grainger came calling for you. I'm sure the name is familiar."

"Yes, the client who sent me on what has so far proven to be a wild goose chase for the obscure fellow with the nasal whistle."

"Since you put it that way, perhaps you might explain the nature of the bird you have been pursuing."

"I believe I informed you that I wasn't given the fellow's name."

"According to Grainger, who told it to Lestrade and me, it's Gunter Philbrick."

"Hmm," mused Holmes, imbibing of his pipe. "Queer that he told you the name of the fellow when he claimed not to know it himself."

"Lestrade was wondering if the name given to us was, in fact, a truthful one."

"There is that," said Holmes thoughtfully.

Seated in his dressing gown, Holmes presented a placid enough figure, but I knew that behind that impressive brow, his brain was turning like a steady, remorseless grindstone. He was weighing this new fact that I'd presented, adding it to the accumulating store of grist, as it were. I expected the question of whether Gunter Philbrick was a true name or not to be the main bone of contention in his mind at present.

"This is a rather trivial problem," he said slowly. "I had largely solved it, once I heard Grainger's account of the central event, but I now suspect that there is more to the matter than I originally believed."

"Are you at liberty to divulge the details?"

"I am – especially as Grainger hasn't been entirely truthful with me. The salient facts are these: Mr. Grainger appealed to me over a matter of a missing piece of jewelry. A rather expensive diamond ring he hoped to give the woman he intended to marry. The circumstances of the purchase of this ring I thought rather ill-colored, but men of Grainger's station are prone to eccentricities. So I set that suspicion aside, without entirely dismissing it."

"Go on."

"Grainger purchased this ring from a private individual. He assured me that the ownership is undisputed, and I took him at his word, at least provisionally. As they say, men like Grainger can be more thrifty than the common fellow, despite their substantial means.

"The seller contrived to meet Grainger in a certain court in a part of London that's shabby perhaps, but not disreputable, and lies close to the man's tannery. The seller was accompanied by a rather preposterous individual, who was built along the lines of a human ape, with a nose so flat that one nostril whistled at times like a tea kettle just starting to boil. He was bundled up against the rain – hence his other features escaped Grainger's notice. This fellow was a bodyguard, according to Grainger. Not in a professional sense, mind you, but an indigent fellow that the seller

282

found in Whitechapel who was willing to stand with him in return for several shillings.

"During the exchange, the seller accepted the money, counted it carefully, and then tendered the ring, which was fumbled during the exchange. Whereupon, the ring somehow disappeared."

"The seller palmed it!" I suggested.

Holmes shook his head slowly. "Grainger was canny enough to suspect that. He made the accusation in his forceful way, whereupon the man removed his coat, rolled up his shirt sleeves, and showed very clearly that he hadn't done so. He also turned all of his pocket linings inside-out, and even went so far as to remove his shoes and shake them out over the cobblestones. This, despite the inconvenient fact that it was raining and the pavement quite wet.

"Convinced by this, Grainger returned to searching the ground around him, which he had previously done. In fact, all three men examined the ground. As it happened, they stood close by a storm drain. Suspicion perforce went in that direction.

"They made a valiant effort to see if the ring had dropped down the grate, but they couldn't see it. Time passed and Grainger became agitated at his loss. The seller, after donning his coat once more, allowed as how as he had completed the exchange and must be on his way.

"Grainger accused him of dropping the ring and therefore he must take full responsibility, and either produce it or return the sum paid. The seller refused, and an argument ensued. It produced nothing but noise and verbal accusations, with both men accusing the other of having fumbled the valuable ornament.

"Feeling insulted, the seller turned away, hailed a passing cab, and off he went. As for the man with the broken nose, according to Grainger he acted flustered and tarried long enough to continue searching for the errant ring, but he too eventually gave it up as a lost cause.

"Once that imposing fellow departed, Grainger was beside himself. He had lost a considerable sum of money and had nothing to show for it, and so came straight away to me and laid the entirety of the misadventure before me.

"I asked him if he had heard the ring splash into the storm drain, for it had been a rainy evening. He told me that he hadn't. Since his hearing appeared to be sound, I took him at his word. I next asked Grainger if he heard the ring clink on the cobblestones. He had not. He was certain of it. He said the ring fell from his fingers and when he looked down, it was nowhere to be seen."

"Remarkable!" I said.

"Inasmuch as the three men stood very closely to one another, Grainger and the seller as they made the exchange, and the bodyguard in order to watch over said transaction, all three men stepped back from one another to examine the pavement. They naturally lifted their shoes and looked under them. No sign of the ring came to light then, or during the subsequent frantic searching.

"It seems unlikely that the ring would have rolled into the storm drain without making a sound. It might have bounced, but that too would have produced an audible noise."

"Puzzling," I mused. "It seems as if the ring had vanished from this world."

"Incredulous persons might believe so," returned Holmes dryly. "But I understood that a falling object has to alight somewhere. The compass in which it might have landed was no greater than eight feet, even if it had bounced. It wasn't heard to have bounced, therefore the probable circumference of the circle of possibility was more likely to be four feet, or less. I was able to eliminate a great many possibilities, including palming and someone stepping on the ring, kicking it away, or contriving somehow for the ring to adhere to a shoe sole. The ring still must strike the ground audibly in order for one of the others to bring their foot into play."

"Could the ring have fallen upon the uppers of one of the men's shoes?"

"I considered that. Had the ring done so, it would have made a soft sound in bouncing, and as likely would have rolled off, striking the pavement audibly. Since this surreptitious meeting took place in a brick court, the object couldn't have been kicked in such a way as to land in soft soil, or a rubbish heap, for there was none. No, something else must have happened to the ring."

"But what could it have possibly been?"

"Something that takes place from time to time by accident, and happened to have occurred at this most inopportune time," said Holmes quietly.

"I cannot imagine what it would be."

"Of course not. Because it was such a whim of chance, no one would conclude it who didn't understand that this was a freak that transpires upon rare occasions."

Standing up, Holmes took a Lucifer from a matchbox and held it before him.

"Now, Watson, stand beside me. No, not facing me, beside me."

I took the proper stance. "For whom am I substituting?"

284

"Not the seller as you might imagine, but the broken-nosed bodyguard whose name might or might not be Philbrick."

Holmes snapped two fingers with his free hand so as to distract me as he dropped the match. Consequently, when I looked down, I didn't immediately see it. Nor had I heard the soft tick of it striking the floor.

Stepping back and looking about, I studied the floor carefully

"Upon my word! Where did it go?"

"It's in plain sight," drawled Holmes, returning to his seat and picking up his pipe once again. "You need only discern it."

"If it's in plain view, why can I not see it?"

"Because, my dear Watson, one end is protruding from the right cuff of your trousers."

Only then did I notice the slim thing.

Reclaiming my chair in order to pluck it free, I said, "You believe that the fumbled ring dropped into the trouser cuff of Gunter Philbrick!"

"I'm certain of it, and when I explained this theory to Grainger, he became convinced that this was the only explanation. Whereupon he hired me to find the bodyguard. His original intention had been for me to locate the ring, which he thought the seller had somehow retained through clever artifice, but I saw that as a blind end. There was no point in seeking him out, as far as recovering the ring was concerned."

"Could the item not have landed in the seller's cuff?"

"I discounted that possibility. According to Grainger, the seller was sharply attired, but Philbrick wore baggy work clothes. No doubt the bodyguard's trouser cuffs gaped like a fish's maw. In fumbling the ring, Grainger managed to cause it to leap toward Philbrick, as opposed to falling straight down. The natural instinct of all three men was to look for it in the cobbled space between seller and purchaser."

"An instinct that prevented them from glimpsing the ring as it sailed out of their sight in the poor light of the courtyard," I observed.

"Precisely. A sleight-of-hand conjuror couldn't have done a better job of fooling them. Given that Grainger professed shame for having leapt to the wrong conclusion, his avowed interest was threefold: To recover the ring, to reward the bodyguard, if the lost ornament was still in his possession, and to make appropriate apologies to the seller, who was entirely innocent."

"Alas, you haven't yet succeeded."

"No, but I haven't yet given up, either. Now that I have the name of Gunter Philbrick, perhaps this will open a new door in my laggardly efforts – if that's his true name."

"But why would Grainger lie about the name?"

"That isn't the question. The fundamental question is to whom did he lie – Scotland Yard or me?"

"For such a simple matter, this is a rather baffling case."

"I would call it unnecessarily tangled, but not necessarily baffling. Yet I fear that the longer it takes to find the fellow with the broken nose, the less likely it will be to locate the ring. If he were an honest sort, he would return it. That is, if he knew to whom to return it. As a man hired straight off the street, he might not have been provided sufficient information to affect a restitution."

"You have been to the pawnshops?" I inquired.

"Daily. The missing ring hasn't been pawned, but that doesn't mean that I dare abandon making my rounds of those establishments."

"Isn't it possible that this fellow pawned the ring outside of London and is now living off the proceeds?"

"I cannot rule it out. I would have had Lestrade wire the authorities in outlying towns and parishes to be on the lookout for it, but for the fact that Alford Grainger has requested the utmost privacy in this matter."

"There must be some explanation why Philbrick has deserted his Whitechapel haunts."

"Grainger said that the seller paid him decently enough. He may have gone to the country on those proceeds."

"If he did, the ring could very well have been dislodged by this time, with Philbrick being no wiser of the fact."

"I cannot dismiss that supposition, for it has occurred to me. The ring may well be lost, and Grainger out of luck, but until Philbrick is found, I'll consider the ring yet in play, and if in play, it may be recoverable."

"A notice in the agony columns, perhaps?"

Holmes blew out a gust of greyish tobacco smoke and his mouth sealed with disapproval. "Would that Grainger had permitted this, but he insisted that publication of a description of the ring might find the eyes of his would-be betrothed, which would be disastrous to his prospects for marriage. No, I'm for the moment stymied. Hence the need to sleep rough this last week and the one before. I'm weary of this case, but pride and determination, as well as the promised remuneration, demand that I follow it to its proper conclusion, whatever that may entail."

Laying aside his pipe, Holmes stood up and said, "I know it's a trifle early, but I intend to seek my bed. The wretched state of my back demands it. Good night."

"And good night to you. I'll see that Mrs. Hudson cooks a generous breakfast in the morning."

"That would be most welcome."

With that, Holmes retired for the night.

Over our meal the next morning, I saw that much of the color had returned to Holmes's complexion. As he drank his morning coffee and consumed his eggs, he seemed to fill out, as it were, with every bite he took.

"No doubt the last few weeks have been trying," I remarked.

"It would have degraded the constitution of a Samson," he admitted.

"And all for nothing, it would seem."

"If the fellow Philbrick has left his usual haunts, it can only be to seek fresh ones. I'll look for him in unaccustomed places, but I must first sort out what they might be."

"You have all of London to comb, as well as parts beyond."

"I should think I can narrow it down somewhat," allowed Holmes. "Especially with my Irregulars perpetually on the hunt in the places where I am not."

This was spoken as Mrs. Hudson bustled up with fresh toast and remarked, "It's good to see you back, Mr. Holmes."

"It's delightful to be home, and your cooking is, as always, excellent."

"Thank you. I should mention that during your absence a man came to speak with you, but I had to turn him away, for neither one of you was in residence. As a matter of fact, he called thrice."

"Did he leave a card?"

"He wasn't that sort, if you take my meaning."

"I see. Did he leave his name at least?"

"He didn't. He said only that he wished to speak with you on a private matter."

"That doesn't sound like our Mr. Grainger," I pointed out.

"Could you describe the fellow?" Holmes asked Mrs. Hudson.

"He wasn't so much tall as he was broad of beam and deep of chest, rather like a dray horse. He was thick with muscle from every direction you might look at him. His coat was greasy and rather slovenly. I took him for a dockworker, or some such tradesman."

Holmes became rather animated. "Mrs. Hudson, was his nose all but flattened?"

"Indeed, it was! How did you know that?"

"I leapt to a conclusion, as it were. Perhaps it was an overly optimistic conclusion, but it was a correct one. Did he say if he might return?"

"Alas, he didn't, but as he turned away, I rather imagined that he would, for disappointment was etched deeply upon his expression."

"Then he isn't necessarily lost to us. Very good. No doubt Philbrick is in possession of the ring and is confounded about what to do with it. Thank you, Mrs. Hudson that will be all."

After she had repaired to her kitchen below, I asked, "Do you think this man is intent upon returning the ring?"

"Unquestionably. Doubtless he found it in his trouser cuff and realized what had happened. He didn't know the name of Alford Grainger, never having been properly introduced, and he presumably doesn't know the true name of his employer, their association being so slight."

"Shouldn't he have gone to the police?"

"Given the furtive nature of the exchange, no doubt he had the wisdom to realize that was inadvisable. Apparently. this unfortunate fellow is an honest sort, and only wishes to find the ring's rightful owner."

"I suppose that there will be a reward."

"I imagine Philbrick has the same thought, but it doesn't detract from his motives any. Reward or no, he has the correct sentiment, and he turned to me while I was away seeking him. Peculiar luck, that."

"Then we only have to await his return."

"Unless he has gotten discouraged. A discouraged man might decide that fate had dealt him a straight flush and not a brace of deuces."

"Will you continue your search?"

Holmes considered this question at length.

"I don't wish to be out and should Philbrick return. Further disappointment might conceivably discourage him permanently. There is always the question of how safe is the ring in the hands of a man who may not have proper lodgings."

"Perhaps Lestrade would be willing to have a word with his men. You've assisted him many a time. Although Philbrick isn't wanted for any transgression, his officers would surely be willing to keep an eye out for him."

"I think that would be wise, and I would be grateful to you if you could convey my request to the good Inspector in person. Kindly add this morsel of data: The finding of this man may prove beneficial to Scotland Yard's interests, if I'm correct in a suspicion I harbor. I'll say no more. As for myself, I'll await whatever comes. I'm not pleased that my own efforts inadvertently thwarted the desired result, but so long as the ring ultimately returns to its proper owner, I cannot complain overmuch."

After breakfast, I went directly to Scotland Yard. Having hearing the story and agreeing that it merited official attention based upon Holmes's rather broad hint, Lestrade readily agreed to continue the search, this time for the broken-nosed man, and not for Mr. Sherlock Holmes. We now had the advantage of alerting the entire police force to keep watch for the fellow.

Alas, all of our efforts unfortunately were so much expelled air. Useless.

I returned to Baker Street with the deflating news.

"The man is either in hiding or has found distant shelter," suggested Holmes.

"We can only hope that he turns up as anticipated," I remarked. "And shouldn't Grainger be making another appearance soon?"

"He, too, I expect at any moment," allowed Holmes. "I would write him, but I would prefer to be in a position to offer tangible news."

That night, Holmes sat reading the newspapers after having consumed a substantial dinner of roast pork and boiled potatoes. Mrs. Hudson brought up the evening mail. Holmes took it and went through the envelopes. Nothing seemed to have interested him. As Mrs. Hudson prepared to descend to her own quarters, Holmes spoke up.

"Mrs. Hudson, upon which days did the man with the flat nose turn up?"

"Why, it was Thursday, Sunday, and Wednesday."

"Every fourth day. And the next fourth day is tomorrow. I wonder if he's a man of regular habits. If so, we might expect him tomorrow."

Reaching for a pen and paper, Holmes began scratching out a note. "It isn't too late for this to go out in the last mail. I'm inviting Mr. Grainger to visit me at his earliest convenience."

"Aren't you getting ahead of yourself?" I asked.

"I am, but I should like to put this distressing episode behind me as soon as humanly possible."

Holmes sealed the envelope and Mrs. Hudson took it downstairs and placed it in the letter box. He then went to the window overlooking Baker Street and stood there for some minutes, patiently watching the passing show. Before long, he made a cryptic sign with his fingers. Presently, young Wiggins was at the front door and soon came bounding up.

"Nothing new to report, Mr. Holmes," said Wiggins, holding his cloth cap in his grimy hands.

"I didn't expect otherwise," returned Holmes, "but I'm afraid that we have been expending a great deal of energy without result. I believe our Mr. Philbrick dwells outside of London and is prone to returning to the city on every fourth day. Post the Irregulars at all train stations early tomorrow morning, and I believe one of you will have good luck before the afternoon. When the man appears, conduct him promptly to Baker Street, saying that I have returned and am expecting him."

"As you wish, Mr. Holmes."

With that, Wiggins disappeared into the night.

"Where do you imagine Philbrick is holding forth?" I asked my friend.

"It's hardly important," replied Holmes wearily. "All that matters is that our chances of treating with him tomorrow seem secure."

After that, Holmes put the entire matter out of his mind. He seemed much more relaxed, and less like a clock mainspring that has been too tightly wound. I could see it in the slow relaxing of his facial muscles and the leisurely manner in which he puffed upon his pipe. This wasn't Holmes pushing his mental faculties to the upmost. This was a man unwinding after nearly completing a job to his satisfaction.

I sincerely hoped that this was the case. I didn't like to see the alterations that night after night of sleeping in the rough had wrought in the resilient fellow.

I was present when Gunter Philbrick came 'round the following afternoon. Mrs. Hudson brought him up, saying, "The gentleman I mentioned the other day has returned, Mr. Holmes. Young Wiggins has brought him."

"Very good, Mrs. Hudson. Send Wiggins on his way with my compliments. We shall see our visitor alone."

A broad bear of a man soon stood upon the threshold, holding a battered derby hat meekly in both hands. He boasted the roundest skull I've ever seen on a man and his nose was so far pushed to one side that I imagined his septum to have been crushed almost flat.

Rising from his chair, Holmes said, "Come in, come in, Mr. Philbrick."

The hat slipped from Philbrick's fingers. He grabbed it up before it touched the floor.

"What? Do you know my name?"

"Gunter Philbrick, is it not?"

"The very same, sir. I'm astonished. Blinkered, I am."

"No need to be, Philbrick. Kindly take a chair. You brought the ring, I presume?"

Hearing those words, the big fellow trembled like a tree that had been struck by lightning.

"Ring? How do you know about the ring? How *could* you know about the ring, for I've told no one. Not a soul. And how did that young man of yours know enough to pick me out of the hurly-burly of London and escort me here, and on the very day I was considering another visit?"

Holmes gave the dumbstruck man a reassuring smile. "All will be explained once you take your seat."

The fellow all but fell into the wicker chair and looked at Holmes and me by turns, his expression that of a loaf of bread that had failed to rise.

"I am at a loss for words, Mr. Holmes. Are you a natural man or, as some have it, supernatural by nature?"

"Allow me to put your confusion to rest. I've been hired by Mr. Alford Grainger to locate you. We had come to the conclusion that the ring so clumsily fumbled during the transaction you witnessed had fallen into your trouser cuff."

"Brilliant! That's a brilliant conclusion, sir, for it's exactly true. I found it that very night and couldn't believe my eyes. I was sleeping in a doss house and you may understand me when I say that sleep refused to come. I hung on the rope all night, my brain a-boil, until the valet cut us free. Then I went in search of the owner of the ring, but I didn't know his name. Nor did I know the full name of the man who hired me, except that it was Smith. That's what he asked me to call him, but he didn't look like any Smith I've ever laid eyes upon, for he was swarthy of complexion."

"I assume you wish to return the ring to its rightful owner?" asked Holmes.

"I do, sir, but only to the rightful owner. Not to an agent such as yourself. No offense. I'm certain you understand me."

"You are a very careful man, Mr. Philbrick, as well as a supremely honest one. As it happens, I'm expecting Grainger later today. Would you care for a cigarette while we wait?"

"I would be pleased to have one. I seldom smoke, but when I can, I'm reduced to making do with such curbside twists as I happen upon."

I had to think a minute before I understood the reference. Then I remembered the unfortunates who had sunken to Philbrick's position often picked up discarded cigar ends and finished them as best they could.

"Perhaps you would prefer a cigar," I suggested.

"Oh, that would be capital!"

From a pocket, I took out one of my best, unwrapped it, cut it for him, and handed over a Lucifer with which to light it.

Philbrick took his time doing so. When he inhaled his first draught, I could see the pleasure of its robust smoke suffusing his wind-burned features. It seemed to settle his nerves properly. I noticed how with each breath one of his nostrils – the left, I believe – whistled faintly.

"A bone-picker by trade, aren't you?" asked Holmes casually.

The man's dull brown eyes widened. "Now, however did you guess that?"

"You have the look, if you don't mind my saying so," returned Holmes. "Also, I see that your right shoulder is uncommonly greasy —the

291

result no doubt of carrying your bone sack over that shoulder, for I see that you are left-handed."

"I cannot deny it. It's a poor trade, but an honest one. This fine cigar is something an old bone grubber such as myself can never afford," added Philbrick with touching sincerity.

"I've been looking for you in the doss houses of the East End," Holmes remarked.

"Sorry to put you to any trouble. I've been moving around town, you see, seeking the two faces with which I was familiar. I imagined that if I found either one, it would lead me to the other, if I didn't find my man on the first try."

Philbrick continued smoking. All the tension had gone from his great frame. I had heard the fellow described as like an ape or a horse, but to my eyes he was more akin to a bear.

After a pause, he asked, "Do you suppose there's a reward?"

"I expect to be paid for the recovery of the ring," replied Holmes. "Beyond that, I cannot say."

"I've put in considerable effort to find the owner. Failing that, I turned to you, Mr. Holmes, knowing – as all of London does – of your excellent reputation."

"Not to the police, I take it."

"I didn't think that wise, sir, for a great many reasons."

"Say no more," murmured Holmes. "Do you have the ring upon your person?"

Without hesitation, Philbrick produced it from an inner pocket of his dilapidated coat and held it up to the light streaming in through the front windows.

Holmes studied it at length, but from the short distance. The marquis-cut diamond was quite impressive. This was no bauble.

"A handsome specimen of the jeweler's art," he said. "I fancy it's worth probably several thousand pounds."

"The man who sold it received three-hundred pounds."

"What! That's quite a bargain."

"I don't know the particulars beyond that. They may be shady, but they might not be. I don't fancy that the ring is a stolen one, but I don't know otherwise."

We passed the time talking of the weather. Before terribly long, Mrs. Hudson announced the arrival of Alford Grainger. It came as no surprise to Holmes or me, for we had heard his brougham pulling up to the curb and the sound of his horses was a familiar one to my ears.

"Come in, come in, Mr. Grainger," invited Holmes. "Take the empty chair. I've excellent news for you. I've found Philbrick – or rather he has found us – and he has the ring upon him. He has graciously offered to surrender it to you, and only to you."

Ignoring the empty chair, Grainger all but accosted the poor fellow.

"You have my ring! Where is it? Come, come, give it up this instant!"

Philbrick hesitated only slightly. He stood up slowly and with great ceremony produced the ring. Whereupon Grainger snatched it from his fingers without a by your leave.

From his pocket came a jeweler's loupe. This he screwed into one eye. Grainger studied the ring's setting intently.

"It's the very ring! And unscathed."

"I've been carrying it in my pocket with great care, Guv'nor," explained Philbrick in a quavering voice. "Lest I scratch the gold band."

"Commendable," said Grainger hastily. Turning to Holmes, he asked, "I must be off to make apologies to the man who sold this to me. Let me first write you a check to settle the account."

"That will be satisfactory," said Holmes without emotion.

Stepping over to the table, Philbrick removed his checkbook and the fountain pen, then scratched out a check with utmost haste.

Tendering it to Holmes, he said, "This concludes our business. I'm most satisfied with your efforts, Holmes. Should I need your services again, I'll be glad to call upon you."

"Before you go," Holmes stated, "a question remains unresolved in my mind: By what method did you happen to learn Mr. Philbrick's name at last?"

"By writing Mr. Smith, who reluctantly wrote back. I didn't communicate it to you simply because I couldn't. You were nowhere to be found."

"I see. Then Smith presently understands that he has been absolved of all blame, I take it?"

"I haven't tendered the fellow a formal apology as yet," stated Grainger. "As I said, that will be my next call."

Holmes fixed Alford Grainger with his frank gaze. "I hesitate to bring this up, but might some consideration be granted Mr. Philbrick for his admirable honesty?"

Grainger gave Gunter Philbrick a disdainful glance. Addressing Holmes, he said, "I've already paid twice for the privilege of owning this ring, and dearly. Am I expected to pay a third time? Besides, this fellow has already received his honest fee from Smith. It should suffice him. That isn't a cheap cigar in his hand."

Tipping his hat to all except Philbrick, Alford Grainger took his leave. It wasn't long before the sound of his brougham was heard departing Baker Street.

I broke the silence with a quiet observation. "Somehow, I don't think that man has any intention of making apologies to the other fellow, Smith."

Holmes didn't contradict me.

Gunter Philbrick stood in the center of the room looking crestfallen. I felt badly for the poor soul. He had expected some reward, no matter how modest, and he had extended himself considerably in order to do the correct thing. Now he stood as penniless and destitute as he had been before he discovered the wayward ring in an unlikely place.

"Well, I guess I had best be on my way," he muttered. "I thank you good gentlemen for your hospitality, and for the most excellent cigar."

Holmes spoke up. "Before you go, Philbrick, you might drop round to Scotland Yard. Ask for Inspector Lestrade. Tell him I sent you."

"And what would be my business at Scotland Yard?"

"The ring Alford Grainger purchased at such a steep discount is one I recognize. In fact, I had all along suspected that Grainer's unwillingness to describe the item pointed to this very possibility. A ring matching this one was reported stolen from Lady Ashfield's bedroom more than a year ago. There's a handsome reward, especially in as much as all hope of its recovery appeared to have evaporated. Since I've already been well paid for my services, I don't feel inclined to claim it. You, on the other hand, having found the ring and returned it to the person you believed to be the rightful owner, are now duty-bound to report the whereabouts of the stolen object to lawful authorities. Inspector Lestrade has already made the acquaintance of Mr. Grainger. He will know where to find him. And the inspector will, I'm quite certain, see to it that the reward for the ring's recovery goes directly to you. With it, you should be able to secure a room of your own and leave the frightful doss houses and their profound miseries behind you."

Gunter Philbrick's mouth twisted this way and that, and I saw a suspicion of tears start in the corners of his eyes. Manfully, he fought them back.

"If what you say is true, Mr. Holmes, this is wonderful news. I don't know how to thank you. This is most passing generous of you."

"You have earned it, Philbrick, just as you have earned my respect. And you are certainly entitled to this reward. Go now forth and claim it."

"Thank you, sir," said the man, crushing his derby between his thick hands.

The sound of his heavy feet going down the stairs eventually dwindled, and so Gunter Philbrick passed from our ken.

I turned to Holmes. "When did you first suspect that the lost ring belonged Lady Ashfield?"

"It was a possibility I kept in mind from the start,. That fact that Grainger wouldn't describe the ring, nor name the person from which he purchased it, aroused suspicion, but in the absence of concrete data, I was forced to pursue the matter on its face, as it were."

"Nonsense! You wouldn't have endured those dreadful nights in the doss houses if you didn't think the matter important."

"Don't forget that Grainger paid me well to do so, which is another suggestive point. Furthermore, I understood that all other factors were immaterial to my investigation. Locating the seller would do little good. I kept my attention where it belonged: On the prize itself."

"You had as much right to that reward as Philbrick," I pointed out. "Certainly to half of it."

"Unquestionably. I've earned my share, after spending day after day in the foul rookeries of the East End, sleeping under the most detestable conditions, but poor Philbrick has been doing so for far longer than I, and the money will lift him up far more than it will elevate me. That consideration aside, had I confiscated the ring on behalf of Scotland Yard, I would be out my fee, and the reward might have been offered to me at Philbrick's expense. I am satisfied with my decision. Let us speak no more of it."

True to his word, Holmes didn't mention it again – not even when the sordid matter landed in the newspapers. The ring was recovered and restored to Lady Ashfield's collection. The sum that Philbrick received was quite substantial.

As for Alford Grainger, he was soon arrested on a charge of knowingly receiving stolen property, and his testimony led to the arrest of the man who sold him the ring, whose name was Konstantin. Both men paid for their crimes.

Grainger never did find the opportunity to propose to the woman he intended to wed. I considered her to be almost as fortunate as Gunter Philbrick. But that is my opinion.

The Black Beast of
the Hurlers Stones
by Roger Riccard

Editor's Note: The Black Beast of Bodmin Moor *was the subject of several sightings in 1978. A government investigation in 1995 declared no evidence was found to support those sightings, but admitted finding no evidence against such a beast either. In 1998, video evidence proved a large black feline, or panther-like creature, did exist in the area. This led to speculation that such beasts do roam the moor and may have been doing so for centuries. – R.R.*

Chapter I

My friend, the celebrated consulting detective, Mr. Sherlock Holmes, has long made his feelings known regarding the supernatural. To paraphrase him: "There is evil enough amongst mankind. The supernatural is beyond my purview."

Thus, he had little interest in hauntings, spectral sightings, or legends – or in fools who would suffer to appeal to his talents to "prove" the existence of creatures or events which were beyond the realms of logic and science. In the years I have known him, he has refused such requests from numerous clients, including one to find the Loch Ness Monster. Even his celebrated exposure of the Hound of the Baskervilles had a reluctant beginning, until he became convinced there was a human agent involved.

Therefore, when I spotted a newspaper article one morning about *The Beast of Bodmin Moor*, a Cornish legend dating back several decades, I presumed it would be of no interest to him. Personally, I enjoy such stories – purely for their entertainment, of course, and out of curiosity at the lengths some legends will grow to.

My companion had already gone out on this particular autumn morning, and I had no patients nor hospital rounds to attend to. After consuming a hot and satisfying breakfast provided by our landlady, Mrs. Hudson, I was enjoying the leisurely warmth of reading by a cozy fire. Its yellow and orange flames dancing in frenzy, as if trying to escape the traces of blue which occasionally manifested themselves around the logs being consumed.

My perusal of this beastly story, regarding a large cat-like creature said to prowl the Bodmin Moor in Cornwall, was interrupted by the arrival

296

of the morning post. Mrs. Hudson had brought it up with a fresh pot of hot coffee. She set the pot on a trivet upon the table next to the sofa, replacing my now lukewarm breakfast tea with a fresh cup of steaming black coffee.

"The postman came by early, Doctor," she said, handing me a small stack of envelopes of various size and quality. "There's one there addressed to both you and Mr. Holmes."

I thanked her as she took away the breakfast dishes and I set my paper down. This particular delivery contained four items addressed to my companion. The fifth was inscribed to: *John Watson & Sherlock Holmes.*

My curiosity aroused and, not knowing when my flatmate might return, I attempted to apply his methods and studied the envelope carefully. It was thick and something of a cream colour. Carefully squeezing it with my thumb and middle finger, as I had seen Holmes do on many an occasion, I could just discern the presence of another envelope within. The handwriting was strong and a brilliant black ink. I believed I recognized it as that of a casual correspondent of mine.

There seeming to be no other distinguishing features, I took my penknife and slit carefully along the top. Inside, a pristine, white envelope, bearing the crest of the Baskervilles, greeted my eyes and brought a smile to my face. It was this same time of year when we first met Sir Henry Baskerville years earlier, heir to Baskerville Hall and the holdings thereof. After that case, wherein Holmes had stopped a rival heir from using a gigantic, ferocious hound to attempt the murder of the new baronet, Henry took a long trip to restore his shattered nerves. Upon his return, the young heir had upgraded the Baskerville estates even beyond their former glory, and was a generous and faithful benefactor to the surrounding community. We had kept in touch over the years. I had even visited him in Devonshire after the death of Mary, when I needed to get out of London and away from the memories of both my wife and my supposedly deceased friend, Sherlock Holmes.

Now, some six months after the reappearance of the famous detective, I was living back in Baker Street. I had written Henry with the good news of my friend's "resurrection" some months before. I presumed this letter to be an acknowledgement of that.

Knowing it was from an old friend, I no longer took the time to make a Holmes-like examination of the envelope and, instead, quickly slit it open and removed the sheet within.

In a strong hand with premium black ink, our former client had written the following:

Dear Friends,

It was happy news indeed to discover you are hale and hearty, Mr. Holmes. John has shared many a story of your adventures with me and, of course, I shall never forget the great service you provided upon my inheritance.

If convenient, I should like to invite both of you to join me for a visit. I must confess, I not only would relish your company, but I have a curious story to share with you on behalf of my neighbors across the river in Cornwall. You may have read of recent incidents regarding the Beast of Bodmin Moor. As your expertise was so instrumental in solving the case of my accursed hound, I believe I could lay more evidence than has been reported at your feet, so you might relieve the country folk of their fears regarding this feral creature.

Should the case be of no interest to you, due to its "supernatural", aspect, may I still entice you for the pleasure of your company by the fact the game birds are running thick this season and hunting has been delightfully successful?

I eagerly await your reply and look forward to renewing our acquaintance.

Sincerely yours,
Henry Baskerville

Baronet Sir Henry Baskerville was never particular about his title. Having been raised in the United States and Canada since his youth, peerage was nearly a foreign concept to him. The local folk always referred to him as *Sir Henry*, but our easy friendship, having developed from his first days in England, had led us to a first name basis. The signature was of no surprise to me. The thought of joining him, whether on a case with Holmes or the comradeship of a hunting trip, was a pleasant one. I confess, I was drawn to it and the pleasant environs of the Devonshire countryside as a welcome diversion from the crowds and choking London atmosphere in October.

It was during this reverie when Holmes came strolling through the door into our sitting room. He hung his coat and hat and dropped his cane into the stand. Greeting me with a "Good morning, Watson," he walked over to the mantel where he stuffed his pipe in preparation to sitting by the fire. I handed him his mail as he walked by and he glanced through it, briefly.

298

Having prepared his pipe and taken his seat in his favorite chair, he set the mail, unopened, upon the end table. Crossing his legs, he laid his left hand upon the arm of his chair and removed the pipe from his lips with his right. He gazed upon me and commented.

"I perceive your own mail to be much more interesting than any of these missives, Doctor. Is there something you wish to share from Sir Henry?"

"How the deuce did you know this letter was from Henry Baskerville?" I demanded, still getting used, once again, to this habit of his, which makes him appear to be a mind reader. "I'm not holding it in a manner where you could have read over my shoulder as you passed."

"Come, come, Watson! You know my methods. Look around you."

I glanced down at the gleaming white envelope on the cushion next to me. The Baskerville crest was on the side facing down, so it couldn't have given the sender away. The readable side said "*John Watson & Sherlock Holmes*" in Henry's handwriting. However, previous correspondence from Baskerville Hall had always been addressed to me at my home in Kensington. I wasn't aware of his ever having communicated directly with my companion. I asked him so.

"Has Henry written you before? Did you recognize his handwriting on the envelope?"

"I hardly have the inclination to memorize all my former client's handwriting, Doctor," he answered, taking a puff of his pipe, sending its blue smoke curling upward in a slow steady stream. "My only correspondence from the baronet was a heartfelt letter of gratitude at the time and a substantial cheque which, you recall, we shared equally. No, I haven't seen his handwriting for several years. Yet that is a significant clue as to the identity of the sender of the letter you hold in your hands."

Confused, I challenged him, "If you didn't recognize the handwriting, how could it be a clue?"

Holmes gazed upon me with a hint of self-satisfaction, which, I confess, occasionally irritates me until I am overcome by the logic of his reasoning. At last, he spoke, "Very well. Whereas Henry Baskerville was born in England, he spent the majority of his life living in North America. No doubt he received the proper instruction of handwriting as any English lad of his generation. However, as you well know, each of us develops our own style of cursive as we mature and assert our individuality. Baskerville has picked up several traits unique to the Canadian version of the English language. Certain letters, spellings, and even his ampersand, reveal no doubt that envelope was addressed by a North American."

"But how did you discern which North American it came from? We have both had several American clients in the past."

299

The detective merely tilted his head and continued. "I am aware you and he have remained in contact over the years and formed an informal friendship. You often refer to him merely as '*Henry*' rather than '*Sir Henry*' when his name comes up. Likewise, I would presume he doesn't often use your title of '*Doctor*' when addressing you. When I see an envelope written by a Canadian addressed merely to '*John Watson & Sherlock Holmes*' with neither '*Dr.*' nor '*Mr.*' as a prefix, it narrows the field considerably. Coupled with the fact it was enclosed in a larger envelope for mailing purposes, a habit preferred primarily by the wealthy, constrains it further. Finally, when I walked in, you were exhibiting a contemplative countenance and were looking toward where your shotgun and fishing pole reside. The moor provides excellent hunting for game birds so long as the Great Grimpen Mire is avoided, and the River Tamar isn't so distant that an excursion for a day of fishing would be any great exertion."

"Hmpf!" I snorted. "Well, since you have deduced the correct answer, I shall not object further. Yes, Henry has extended an invitation to both of us to join him for hunting. He has also implied that, should you wish to do so, we may stay with him while you investigate the latest incidents of *The Beast of Bodmin Moor*. I was just starting to read the newspaper account when the mail arrived. Apparently some new activity has stirred up the old legend."

The consulting detective raised his eyebrows and pursed his lips, "Interesting. Do be good enough to read it aloud. I've nothing pressing in London, and a trip to the country might do us both some good."

He wasn't fooling me for a bit. I knew he was concerned over my increased alcohol consumption since the death of my sweet Mary. One didn't need to be a doctor, or a detective, to know a turn in the country air might be just the thing to break my cycle of weekend benders.

I took up *The Daily Telegraph* and read as follows under the headline, *Bodmin Terror, Big Cat or Unholy Beast?*

> *Jamaica Inn, Launceston, Cornwall: For generations, local folklore in this sleepy Cornish hamlet has insisted a huge, cat-like creature inhabits the Bodmin Moor. It is an area of some eighty square miles of rough heather, punctuated by granite and peat deposits. The Cornish people who live here tend to lead sturdy, if ordinary, lives. They farm, raise cattle, continue to engage in tin mining, as has been done for centuries, and go about their business. There are a few local stories to recommend the place as special to history – one being the claim that Dozmary Pool, a scant*

300

mile from where this report is taking to paper, is where the Lady in the Lake granted the sword, Excalibur, to King Arthur.

Yet one legend persists to be still affecting this bucolic setting, even in our enlightened age. The Beast of Bodmin Moor is generally relegated to stories to frighten children to avoid the dangers of traversing out upon the wilderness alone. However, in recent weeks, there have been sightings of a cat-like creature roaming the moorland at dusk and occasionally being silhouetted against the moon, standing upon its hind legs clawing at the sky – seemingly more man than beast.

There has also been an influx of carcasses of weasels, foxes, and other small game, indicating the presence of a carnivorous predator. Recently a stray cow was found, its hide viciously torn and major chunks of meat ripped away. What has brought the story to a head, however, is the night of destruction at a camp of archaeologists, come down from London to study the ancient stone circles which abound in the area. On the southeast edge of the moor, near Minions Village, this group of scholars had left their camp set up while they stayed the night at the village inn. Next morning, the heavy canvas tents were slashed as if by a huge cat. Claw marks deeply scratched equipment and bite marks appeared to rip through thick canvas packs, apparently in search of food. The ferocity of the destruction has sent tremors through the local populace, and the paleologists have taken to arming themselves whenever they venture out.

It is confirmed they will call upon zoologists from the British Museum and the Zoological Society of London to assist in the expedition – not only for the scientific exploration, but their own safety as well. Locals are taking a more spiritual course and calling upon ministers, exorcists, and, it is rumoured, priests of cults who still practice their ancient rites it the area.

"That's all there is in this edition," I concluded. "Except for a map showing the locale." I handed over the paper so he could observe the engraving. He merely glanced upon it before setting it aside with a frown.

"A trifling matter, Watson. Still, it may provide some amusement, and Sir Henry is an excellent host. I am amenable to accompany you, if you care to telegraph him back."

301

Chapter II

Three days hence, we stepped onto the railway platform at Coombe Tracey and were met heartily by Henry Baskerville himself. The baronet, now thirty-five years of age, was already a sturdily built fellow when first we had met and, if anything, he appeared even more muscular today. He now wore his thick black hair a bit longer as it curled over the collar of his tweed jacket, and he had let his sideburns extend nearly to his jaw. His dark eyes lit with excitement as he spotted us and approached quickly.

"John, Mr. Holmes, it's good to see you again.

Middle-age hadn't dampened his youthful enthusiasm and his handshake was reminiscent of my boyhood, operating the water pump outside our kitchen. Several years in England had done nothing to affect his speech, and his Canadian accent was as strong as ever.

"I'm glad you could make it down. I hope you've brought your shotguns and fishing poles. The wildlife are teeming this season and the weather has been perfect."

Holmes smiled and I knew he had observed something. However, he merely nodded and replied, "We are looking forward to it, Sir Henry. A break from London will be most welcome."

The baronet turned and introduced us to a young lad of about twenty, "This is my new groom, Cadan."

We nodded to the youth and I asked, "Perkins has left you?"

"Retired and went off to the States to live with his son, a horse trainer in Kentucky. Cadan here is one of local lads who knows the country better than anyone – with the exception of Dr. Mortimer."

"How is Mortimer?" I asked. Though a simple surgeon, most folk referred to James Mortimer M.R.C.S., as "Doctor". He was a tall, thin man with bowed back and long nose sloping between two grey eyes. Not much older than Henry, he was something of a student of archeology, geology, and local history. It was he who brought the Baskerville case to Holmes's attention after the death of Henry's uncle, Sir Charles Baskerville.

"James is as talkative and curious as ever," replied Henry. "Doesn't walk about as much as before. His back has gotten worse and his cane is now a necessity. He's been confined to his trap to ride his rounds and visit his friends. Obviously, that limits his exploration of the moor, since some of the trails aren't wide enough. But he gets around considerably just the same."

Holmes spoke up, "What does Mortimer think of this *Beast* people seem so concerned about?"

Our host tilted his head, "I'll let you ask him yourself. He's going to join us for dinner this evening, and I'd rather not speak for him. Shall we go?"

Cadan assisted us with our luggage, loading it all into the rear of good-sized carriage, which was new since I'd last been down from London. A fine pair of sturdy Clydesdales trotted us away from the station and, once clear of village traffic, were encouraged to a steady canter by Cadan. This pace brought us to Baskerville Hall in under half-an-hour. As Henry had declared upon his first sight of the place, electric lights had been installed, and now stood sentry around the courtyard and above the entrance. As dusk was nearly upon us, we were pleasantly greeted when they came ablaze as we drove through the main gate.

"I see Crandall has kept watch for us," said Henry. "He and his wife have worked out quite well as replacements for the Barrymores." This last was addressed to Holmes, for I had met the middle-aged couple on a previous visit. The Barrymore's had received a significant bequest from Sir Charles Baskerville and left the hall to set up their own business after the conclusion of the case which brought Holmes down the first time.

Cadan brought the carriage to a halt under a newly constructed portico and Crandall came out to assist with the luggage. He was a well-built fellow about five-feet- nine, and muscular as a wrestler. His hair was light brown and short, and he wore a military-style moustache. Between the two servants, there was nothing left for Holmes or me to carry and so Henry showed us immediately to his drawing room where he offered us some libation after our long journey. We settled into some leather wingback chairs of deep brown with brass fittings which were arranged around the fireplace. We were enjoying a dry Madeira when Mrs. Crandall excused her interruption of our conversation and enquired about dinner. She was a charming woman of fine figure and pleasant face, and I felt a pang of envy toward Mr. Crandall, as I had been a widower now for some time.

Henry looked toward us and offered, "About forty-five minutes enough for you to unpack and clean up? I don't generally dress for dinner unless some of my more formal neighbors are joining me. But you and Mortimer are more like family and I prefer a relaxed atmosphere."

I nodded and Holmes replied, "That will be more than sufficient. Thank you, Sir Henry."

The baronet repeated his suggestion to the housekeeper and she left us with a curtsy to inform the cook. Holmes picked up the conversation. "Does anyone know we were coming down, other than Dr. Mortimer?"

Henry smiled. "I recalled your method of poking about in secret, Mr. Holmes. James and I have agreed to keep your visit quiet until you say so. The servants have likewise been instructed."

"Thank you," replied the detective. "I should like to get the lay of things before revealing my interest in this case to others. Since we have some little time, why don't you give me the particulars as to who you are acting for and their role in this situation?"

Henry actually blushed slightly, which surprised me but apparently not Holmes, who merely held out a palm in supplication for the baronet to answer truthfully. Our host cleared his throat and replied, "I have been courting a young lady, a nurse at Tavistock Hospital. She grew up in the area and her father is one of the archaeologists exploring the site known as the *Hurlers Stone Circle*. Are you familiar with it?"

Holmes tilted his head and declared, "I have heard the term, but haven't researched the particulars. Pray, continue."

Henry leaned forward. "Jenny's – that is, Guinevere's – father is Dr. Lionel Logan, a rather prominent archaeologist who has been involved with several digs and discoveries throughout Great Britain. He got up this small expedition to explore the site on Bodmin Moor. It is so named because local legend identifies the Hurlers as men who were turned to stone for playing the ancient game of hurling on a Sunday. Of course, the site requires excavation to verify the legends origins, as many of the stones are barely visible under centuries of dirt, grass, and heather.

"They had hardly started their work when the cat sightings began anew. Apparently, this beast seems to make an appearance every few years. This latest attack upon the campsite of the archaeologists is something quite new, however. Usually, legend has it, the Beast only attacks cattle and an odd creature here and there. It normally avoids humans, who have only had an occasional glimpse of it.

"Jenny knows my story of the Hound, of course, and your roles in it, gentlemen. She is the one who urged me to reach out to you. She fears for her father's safety, and I can't say I blame her, after hearing what that cat did to the campsite."

"I presume the campsite has been restored?" queried Holmes.

Our host nodded, "Yes. Oh, I know you would have preferred to see it in its disheveled state. I would have recommended they leave it that way, had I been notified sooner. Unfortunately, by the time it was brought to my attention and Jenny asked me to call upon you, Dr. Logan and his team had renewed their excavation."

"Pity" stated Holmes. "However, I require daylight to begin my examination. I suggest you take us there immediately after breakfast tomorrow."

Henry nodded, "I'll advise cook to prepare an early morning meal. It will take us a good five or six hours to get to Minions, the closest village to the site. We can wire ahead for rooms once we reach Tavistock. Hopefully there will be some vacancies. If not, we can try Upton Cross. It's only about a mile-and-a-half away."

With plans laid, we retired to prepare for dinner. When we later came down from our rooms, we found Dr. Mortimer had arrived and he greeted us with great enthusiasm. "Mr. Holmes! Dr. Watson! It is so good to see you again! Especially you, Mr. Holmes. Gave us all a bit of a turn when the doctor reported your death at Reichenbach Falls. I am happy to see you have cheated the Grim Reaper and remain among us."

Drily Holmes replied, "It has been a distinct pleasure to do so. My travels of the past three years have been educational and enlightening, yet there's nothing like returning to one's homeland. I see you have obtained a new dog since last we spoke. An Airedale, I believe, or at least some type of wire-coated terrier." Taking a second look, he corrected himself, "Actually *two* terriers. A black-and-tan, and a tricolor."

Mortimer started and asked, "How the deuce did you know that? Yes, I now have a pair of Airedales."

The detective gave a quick smile of gratification, "While it isn't common for Airedales to shed, this is one of the times of the year when they are most prone to do so and yours have. There are some few strands at different heights and different colors attached to the shins of your trousers."

Henry smiled and said, "Shall we go and continue this discussion over dinner, gentlemen?"

Dinner was a feast of meat and vegetables, fresh baked bread, and a bread-and-butter pudding. Naturally the topic of conversation was the Beast. Mortimer, being the longest resident of the area, was consulted for his knowledge of either facts or legends concerning such a creature.

"Ah, Mr. Holmes, there's very little facts to support the existence of the big cat. Eyewitness tales have been passed on from generation to generation. Certainly the occasional cow has been found, apparently mauled by something with large claws. However, there is one tale of old which says such an incident was the result of rustlers who wanted to make it seem like the animal was attacked, rather than actually being butchered by them for its meat."

Holmes nodded and commented, "There usually are logical explanations for such phenomena."

Mortimer took a sip of his wine and continued, his face now taking on a mysterious countenance, as one might do when about to embark upon a ghost story for children. "Then there are the ancient legends, gentlemen.

305

Some say the cats are descendants of a pair of black panthers brought to our shores by a Roman general. Others give the credit for the panther idea to a pirate named *An Dhiu Kath*, if you'll forgive my attempt at pronouncing a Cornish name. It translates roughly as *The Black Cat*, a ferocious marauder who supposedly smuggled some African panthers into the Jamaica Inn for auctioning to the highest bidder.

"Of course, we cannot forget the mysteries of Merlin, or the Lady of the Lake. Those ancient magical times may have resulted in descendants of such creatures."

Henry spoke up, "Tell them about the story going 'round now about the Hurlers."

Mortimer smiled, mischievously. I had never seen him give such a look. When he told us the story of the Baskerville Hound all those years before, he was more frightful than now. I supposed this was because he had actually seen the gigantic footprints of the hound which had literally scared poor Charles Baskerville to death. Now he was merely repeating legend. Normally, Holmes doesn't deal in legend. However, they may have some aspect of fact which led to their creation. It becomes data to be sifted through my friend's magnificent mind.

"Of course, there is the rumour there still exists a Druidic cult in Cornwall and its high priests call upon supernatural powers to defend their sacred places. The Hurlers Stone Circle, where the current archeological excavation is located, is said to be sanctified ground to the Druids. A local legend identifies the Hurlers as men who were turned to stone for playing the ancient game of hurling on a Sunday. To the Druids, this gives the area special significance and supernatural powers. A huge black cat is said to act as guardian of the site against interlopers."

Mortimer stopped at this declaration and took a sip of wine. Holmes seemed to absorb all the information imparted to him and I knew his brain was categorizing each tidbit for later recall.

"It is imperative I examine the scene as soon as possible," said Holmes, with determination. "Can we depart before dawn?" This last addressed to our host.

Henry started to reply, but Mortimer spoke first, "That would be highly inadvisable, Mr. Holmes. The road to Tavistock can be treacherous in the dark. I know Cadan knows the area well, but you should really wait for first light."

Holmes frowned, but Henry, with his natural bent toward practical problem-solving, offered a compromise, "I'll have cook prepare food for us to take with us in the morning. That will allow us to sleep until just before dawn and we can leave at first light.

With plans settled, we finished our meal and retreated to the drawing room for brandy and cigars where Henry was encouraged to recall meeting his lady fair, Nurse Guinevere Logan, and the resulting courtship.

"It was just after Christmas," he said, with a twinkle in his eye and a wistful smile. "I was in Tavistock, posting some mail and exchanging a gift I had received, which was the wrong size. I was on my way back to my carriage when a dog-cart came around the corner too fast for the icy road and careened toward me. In my haste to dive for cover, I severely injured my leg. I was unable to put any weight on it and had to be assisted to the hospital there, where I was admitted for examination. It turned out to be a severe knee sprain which kept me laid up for three days before they would allow me to leave with a pair of crutches. While I was confined, Jenny was my attending nurse. She's a real beauty with a heart of gold. She's quite a bit younger than me. Her fiancé died of consumption three years ago. She had resigned herself to a life alone, serving her patients instead of raising a family. Yet, somehow, we connected on a level neither of us understood but chose not to question. I gained her permission to call upon her and our courtship has progressed nicely."

He bowed his head, hesitated, cleared his throat and continued, "It is my intention to ask for her hand, and my sincerest hope we can be married by Christmas time."

I offered a hearty congratulations, which was graciously accepted. Mortimer was already aware of this news and merely smiled. Holmes also offered congratulations with a little less enthusiasm, but such was typical of him when he has a case on his mind. He then asked a question."

"How well do you know her father, Dr. Logan?"

Henry removed he cigar from his lips, rubbed his jaw in thought then, replied, "He's determined fellow. To a fault, according to Jenny. His stubbornness has resulted in some major discoveries over the years, but it has also, on occasion, led to very expensive failures when he refused to heed the facts which were piling up against him, in favor of his own beliefs. One particular expedition is apparently referred to in academic circles as 'Logan's Folly'. It was an attempt to find Avalon, the supposed burial place of King Arthur. Several hundred pounds were spent in the attempt and the results were merely some ancient burial grounds dating back to the Stone Age.

"He does have a loyal following of students who accompany him. I believe there are three of them on this latest dig."

"Interesting,' replied Holmes, gazing into the fire, seemingly lost in thought. I believed he was wishing he had this information prior to our coming down. I knew he would have consulted his indexes for more thorough information on this archaeologist. After several moments of reflection, he sat up straight and offered, "Thank you, gentlemen. You have been most enlightening. I believe I shall turn in and prepare for an early departure. If you will excuse me?"

Henry rose, tossed his cigar into the fire, and replied, "Good idea, Mr. Holmes. We should all turn in to get an early start. James," he added, turning to Mortimer, "if you don't care to drive back this late, you're welcome to spend the night."

"Thank you, Henry. I believe I shall. I just wish I could accompany you all tomorrow, but some of my patients require my services and I predict you will likely be gone for several days. Even if you solve the mystery immediately, Mr. Holmes," he smiled, "it's a full days' journey there and another back. I wish you God's speed, gentlemen."

Chapter III

Next morning, I was awakened by a knock upon the door. I threw on my dressing gown and opened it to find Crandall with a tray and a cup of steaming black coffee. "Good morning, Dr. Watson. I have been requested to inform you Sir Henry's carriage for Tavistock will be departing in half-an-hour.

I gratefully took the cup and thanked him. I sipped the welcome liquid as I surveyed the closet. Knowing we were leaving early, I hadn't bothered to unpack my clothes, save for my nightshirt and the outfit I chose for today's journey. I quickly changed, performed my morning toilet, and came down to the kitchen to return my coffee cup. There I found Henry giving instructions to the Crandalls regarding the household while we were gone. Soon Cadan came in and informed our host the carriage was ready to depart. Henry turned to me and said, "Well, we just need Mr. Holmes, then. Have you seen him yet, John?"

The lad spoke up, "Beggin' you pardon, Sir Henry. Mr. Holmes is already aboard."

Henry looked at me and I merely smiled, "When Holmes is on a scent, he is like a hound straining at the leash."

With Cadan's assistance, we loaded our traveling bags and joined Holmes in the carriage. Assuming that Holmes would wish to observe the terrain as we traveled, Henry chose the seat with his back toward the driver so Holmes and I could face forward and observe the countryside.

The faint light of dawn was just turning high clouds of the eastern sky a pale silver as we exited the gates of Baskerville Hall. We traveled west toward Tavistock, thankfully comforted by the thick traveling rugs. That leg of the journey took us roughly two hours thanks to the stamina of the Clydesdales and the ability of Cadan to know how to alternate their walking and trotting to best advantage. By eight-thirty, after Henry sent a telegraph off to Minions Village, we found ourselves being introduced to Jenny Logan at the hospital, while Cadan tended to the horses before the final twenty-mile trek to Minions.

Miss Logan was indeed a striking beauty. I judged her to be in her mid-twenties, putting her about a decade younger than the baronet. A pang of remembrance briefly crossed my mind, as their age difference was about the same as that of myself and my late wife, the former Mary Morstan.

Even in her nurses' uniform, a long white apron over a pale blue dress, her figure was lovely. For practical purposes, her reddish-brown hair was curled up and held in place by pins and a cap. Green eyes sparkled at the sight of Henry, but she demurely held her position and merely curtsied in the presence of strangers until our friend reached out to her. She took his hand and there was a brief flush to her cheeks as her round face reflected joy at his touch.

"Jenny," said Henry. "This is Sherlock Holmes and Dr. John Watson."

She reached out her free hand and I took it, bowing over it with an *Enchanté*. Holmes, on his best behavior, in spite of his anxiety to continue the journey, likewise took her hand and said "Pleased to meet you, Miss Logan. I confess, I believed Sir Henry's glowing description of you to be colored by his feelings. But I see now his words failed him and he is indeed a most fortunate fellow."

She blushed deeply and demurely lowered her head. While I wasn't well-versed in the new field of psychology, I believed she had shielded her emotions for so long since the death of her fiancé that she was now overwhelmed by the attention she was allowing herself to receive.

We excused ourselves to give Henry some time alone with her and strode across the street to a café where we took some hot tea to supplement the light fare Henry's cook had supplied to us, which we had enjoyed during the drive thus far.

Cadan was already there, eating his own breakfast, since he had been too busy driving to partake of the food we had at our disposal. Another half-hour passed by before Henry joined us and we all agreed the horses were rested enough to continue.

As we resumed our journey on Launceston Road, Henry informed us he had received a return telegram from the Cheesewring Hotel in Minions Village. They had no vacancies but did inform him that the Caradon Inn in Upton Cross had rooms available. A little before noon we crossed over the River Tamar and were officially in Cornwall.

The green rolling hills passed by our windows at a steady rate. Occasionally our road was like an emerald trench as hedges towered up on either side. The weather remained favorable – cool with high clouds but no precipitation, and only a light breeze. While in Tavistock, Holmes had procured a map of the Caradon District of Cornwall and followed our progress every so often, nodding in approval at the pace Cadan was maintaining. Less than two hours from our crossing of the River Tavar, Cadan was pulling the horses to a halt next to the Caradon Inn.

Henry, not one to stand on ceremony after his upbringing in Canada, engaged two rooms: One for Holmes and me, the other to share himself with Cadan. He enquired about the road to Minions, as to whether it was safe to travel at night. He was assured it was mostly straight and flat, though fairly narrow. It would be easy to navigate in decent weather. The moon was near full and set to rise shortly after six p.m. Our horses were in need of rest, so we arranged for a trap to make the final mile-and-a half journey to Minions.

"Goin' to see the Beast of Bodmin, Mr. – ?" He looked at the ledger and changed to a slightly more formal tone, "Excuse me, *Sir* Henry? You'll be in for lots of company."

The baronet, choosing to take on an attitude of formality befitting his title, replied, "Our business is with Dr. Logan, the archaeologist. I understood he is only leading a team of three besides himself."

"Aye, that be true enough," replied the innkeeper. "But ever since the news came out about their camp being destroyed by some creature, the curious have come out of the woodwork to have a look. Cheesewring Inn is filled to the brim, and now that you're here, I've only one more vacancy."

Henry looked at Holmes, who merely said, "Thank you, Innkeeper. We had better be on our way then while there is still light."

The distance passed quickly. Cadan remained behind so the three of us weren't an overload for the single horse trap. Shortly before we reached Minions, we passed East Acre, where three ancient towering granite structures rose up about two-hundred yards off the road. It was a testament to the ancient tin mining sites scattered throughout Cornwall which were responsible for the white cross on Cornwall's black flag, reminiscent of tin flowing from the native black granite when heated.

Finding the way to the campsite was no difficult task, as there was a well-worn path from the footprints of dozens of persons following what had become a trail out of the village to the dig site. We found a place to secure our vehicle and began the trek westward. Holmes was surveying the surrounding area with a practiced eye, but I knew he was disquieted by the passage of time and the destruction of so much evidence by the on-lookers.

As we approached the site, a small crowd of people were being addressed by a local constable and told to return to their homes. He and a fellow officer had pulled their truncheons to show they meant business and began waving the people away. The disgruntled crowd grumbled their way past us as we continued to approach. The senior officer saw us and pointed his truncheon directly at Henry, who was in the lead. "I said no one is allowed beyond this point. Now you just turn around and be on your way!"

Henry, with his typical bravado, walked right up to the man with the two of us at his heels. When we were face to face, Holmes and I took up positions on either side. Then he addressed the constable, "I am Sir Henry Baskerville. I am a friend of Dr. Logan's, and I've brought these men to assist him. If you would tell him I'm here, I'm sure he will allow you to let us pass."

The officer, a burly sort in his dark uniform and pickelhaub helmet, looked us up and down. Being about five-foot-eight-inches, he had to tilt his head up a bit to see past the lip of his helmet to get a view of Holmes at that short distance. "And who are these gentlemen?" he asked, suspiciously.

Henry looked to his right at me and said, "This is Dr. John Watson." Then he turned left and declared, "And this is Mr. Sherlock Holmes."

The constable took a second look at my companion and then stepped back, raising his truncheon into a defensive position causing his partner to join him. "Here, now. I don't know what you gents are trying to pull, but you just turn yourselves around and get out of here and don't come back!"

"What?" cried Henry indignantly.

"You English think we can't read down here in Cornwall? I know Sherlock Holmes is dead. Killed over in Europe years ago. Now you can leave, or you can be arrested. What will it be?"

Holmes crossed his arms, shook his head, and glanced over at me. Henry was dumbfounded. It hadn't occurred to him that the return of my friend to the land of the living hadn't received wide publication. This standoff had just about reached its limit of the constable's patience when finally my friend spoke softly, "May I know your name, Constable?"

Taken somewhat off guard by the request and the tone of Holmes voice, the constable automatically responded, "Truscott." Shaking his head in self-recrimination for answering, he demanded, "Now, who are you, really?"

Holmes replied, "Officer Truscott, I assure you that when Dr. Watson," he nodded toward me, "wrote his account of my demise, it was absolutely certain he had interpreted the evidence to its most logical conclusion. However, as a veteran policeman, especially one with a caring wife, a rambunctious son, and a loving daughter, you must be aware of how often the most obvious conclusion is proven to be the wrong one."

Truscott stared at Holmes with drawn eyebrows, "Here now – how do you about my family? Have you been spying on me?"

Holmes clasped his hands behind his back and proceeded to reply, "There is a trace of white powder, likely flour, on the back of your collar where your wife placed her hand when she kissed you goodbye this morning in your kitchen. Your son jumped on your back for a piggyback ride, leaving marks from his shoes on the sides of your coat down by the hem, and your daughter gave you a hug, leaving some curly hairs caught on your middle coat button.

"As to my still being alive: In order to round up the rest of Moriarty's gang, it was necessary for me to appear to have perished. I regret having put my friend through such an ordeal. However, it was necessary. The rest of Moriarty's gang have now been captured, allowing me to return to public life. If you will take the simple step of conferring with Dr. Logan, he will be able to confirm the identity of Baronet Baskerville and the fact that I was requested to look into this matter. I do wish you would proceed quickly, however, for we have little daylight remaining."

Looking upon Holmes now with more curiosity than suspicion, Truscott agreed and told his partner to go and fetch Dr. Logan. The well-known archaeologist came back quickly on the heels of the younger officer and immediately greeted Henry. "Thank you for coming! I presume this is Mr. Holmes and Dr. Watson?"

As he strode forward and took the baronet's hand, he addressed the constables. "It's all right, Truscott. Thank you for your diligence, but these men were invited and are most welcome."

Truscott give a two-finger salute with a nod and allowed us to pass in the company of Dr. Logan. As we walked, he spoke, "Thank you for coming, gentlemen. I am afraid there isn't much left to see. I wasn't aware you were alive and available, Mr. Holmes, until Henry mentioned it to me."

Holmes's eyes were continuing to observe the surrounding terrain. Low rolling slopes, covered mostly in heather and scattered in black-and-grey rock outcroppings, dominated the landscape. The area of the Hurlers Stone Circle was more level and punctuated by large upright stones and other mounds which were likely stones which had fallen over and been covered by centuries of wind-swept soil.

Dr. Logan demonstrated to Holmes how the camp had been scattered and the detective closely examined the claw marks and patched tears in the canvas tents and packs with his magnifying lens. He even took measurements with his pocket tape. Henry and I engaged the three other team members in discussion. Two of them were convinced there was some sort of wildcat or puma loose on the moor. The other, Gregory Culpepper, had a revolver holstered at his side. He was in his mid-thirties and solidly built. His deportment was that of a soldier, and I said, "I served in Afghanistan as an Army Surgeon at the Battle of Maiwand. I perceive you also are a veteran?"

Culpepper looked at me and nodded, "Yes, Doctor. I've read of your service in one of your tales of Mr. Holmes. I was a corporal under General Wolseley when we defeated the Egyptian Army in September of '82."

"A man of action, then," I replied, nodding toward his sidearm. "Have you determined some battle plan against this intruder, whether it be man or beast?"

He replied, the palm of his hand resting on the gun butt and tapping the hammer with his trigger finger. "Yes, Doctor. Whatever it is will be met by a .455 slug if it shows up again."

"Is it loaded with silver bullets?" [1] I asked, attempting to deflect the fellow's temper.

"What?" he asked, clearly confused by my remark.

"I've been hearing from local folklore the creature may be of supernatural origin," I continued. "It is generally accepted the only way to defeat such beings is through the use of silver."

"Surely you don't put stock in folklore and old legends, Dr. Watson?" said the former soldier.

At this point Holmes interrupted our conversation, "The doctor has a vivid imagination and is much more open-minded about myths and legends than I, Mr. Culpepper. However, I should like to request that, should you come across the perpetrator of this incident, please attempt to wound it rather than shoot to kill. Whatever or whomever it might be will be an interesting study if captured."

"'Whomever', Mr. Holmes?" replied the former soldier.

"A conjecture on my part," answered the detective. "I require more data to determine the facts. Gentlemen, if you will follow me?"

This last was addressed to Henry and me and we followed Holmes about one-hundred feet away from the camp. This brought us to a lump of ground marked by the expedition with a small white flag. It was then we noticed several similar flags in the area, interspersed among standing stones and forming a rough circle. By now the sun was low on the horizon and throwing long shadows from the stones and flags.

From here Holmes led us in a large arc out from the camp from south to north, giving us each a few of the white flags he had borrowed from Dr. Logan. He enjoined us to be on the lookout for anything resembling tracks, footprints, or other signs of trespass, and to mark them. He had Henry go about twenty feet further out and requested me to take up a position twenty feet closer to the camp. We proceeded to walk slowly in a clockwise direction. When our line reached a roughly northwesterly direction emanating from the camp, Henry called out, "Here's something!"

I looked in his direction and also saw Holmes was kneeling over a small bush and plucked something from it with a pair of tweezers. He called out, "One moment." He stuck a flag into the ground and he placed the object from the bush into an envelope, stuffing it in his pocket. Looking first toward Henry and then to me, he said, "Watson, stand where you are and let me come to you. Sir Henry, we shall be with you momentarily."

Holmes walked toward me very gingerly, examining the ground closely as he did so. At one point he stooped and measured something, making a note of it. After marking it with another flag, he then continued on to me, still examining the ground. Finding nothing else of note, he took my arm and pulled me a few feet back the way we had come.

"I don't wish to disturb the ground further along the line I have created by my two flags and Sir Henry's discovery. Still, please mind your step in case we missed something."

We carefully proceeded to where the baronet stood. He had placed one of his flags into the ground a few inches from what appeared to be the paw print of a large feline. Holmes knelt and measured the track. It was nearly five inches across and just over four inches from heel to toe, with one-inch claw marks.

"This matches the print I found near you, Watson," he said.

I nodded, "I've seen panthers in captivity during my brief stay in India before my orders took me to Afghanistan. I don't recall any with paws quite so large. Is that due to the cat's weight dispersing the earth around it?"

"All cats are stealthy by nature," replied the detective. "Still, their weight isn't insignificant, and the act of walking could do as you suggest and make the print appear larger. However, I believe – "

His statement was interrupted by a yowling sound carried across the moor on the light breeze coming from the west. Our heads all snapped around. On a ridge, perhaps three-hundred yards away, the silhouette of a large cat seated on its haunches next to a gorse bush appeared to be crying out to the sun as it settled on the horizon.

Chapter IV

Instinctively, I reached for my revolver, then thought better of it. If we chose to pursue the creature, I could run faster with it in my pocket until we were closer, then withdraw it when we slowed to prowl after it.

Holmes raised his hands to the side, signaling us to hold back as he observed, "It's much too far to reach before it retreats to its lair. With the sun falling fast, it will have the advantage in the dark. I've marked the location in my mind and am sure we can track it in the morning."

This statement was made to us, but not loud enough for Culpepper to hear back at the camp. He drew his weapon and took off at a dead run. "Culpepper!" shouted Holmes. "Wait, don't kill it!"

The war veteran ignored Holmes's plea and kept charging through the gorse and heather, steadily rising up the slope toward the ridgetop. Reluctantly Holmes realized we must follow. Since Henry wasn't armed, the detective advised him to return to the camp as he and I trotted off after Culpepper. We were joined by Constable Truscott, who had ordered his partner to remain and guard the camp. Like his English counterparts, he didn't appear to carry any sort of gun and I determined I would remain close enough to cover him, should we confront the creature.

With the sun half-covered by the horizon, the already-cool temperature was dropping rapidly and affecting my old war wound, so I couldn't match Holmes's speed. He was well over fifty feet ahead of me, and Truscott was about halfway between us. Culpepper was out of sight on the other side of the ridge when we heard a shot and a cry of pain. We all picked up our pace. When my companion reached the top of the ridge, he drew his own revolver, a five-shot Bulldog which fit easily into his coat pocket. I tramped up the incline as quickly as I could, drawing my weapon when I reached Holmes's side. The gorse bushes were thicker on this side of the hill and the dusk made it difficult to see. I kept looking for any sort of movement, assuming the big cat wouldn't have stood still after the gunshot. After a few seconds Truscott, more experienced at spotting things on the moor, pointed slightly off to our left about two-hundred feet away. The prone figure of former Corporal Culpepper lay prostrate against a thick gorse bush. "Keep an eye out, Watson," said Holmes, "but if you must shoot, try to wound rather than kill."

We approached the body quickly and found him still alive, but bleeding profusely from a wound to his femoral artery. It seemed apparent he had tripped and his gun discharged into his own leg. I applied a tourniquet, but he had already lost a significant amount of blood and was deathly pale. He looked up at Holmes, who had knelt at his side. Shaking from shock, he reached up to take my friend's lapel and pull him closer as

315

he tried to speak. I could barely make out the words, as I was busy trying to staunch the pulsing flow of blood.

"Holmes – No! – *ccc* . . . cat . . . hind legs . . . boo . . . ."

Femoral artery wounds can cause a person to bleed to death in under five minutes, and that had nearly expired by the time we had crested the hill, spotted the Corporal, and made our way to him. The words he had spoken to Holmes were to be his last.

It was getting darker by the minute now and too dangerous to continue pursuit. Holmes and Truscott took up the body and we made our way back to camp. I kept watch with my weapon at the ready, though it wasn't cocked and the hammer was sitting on an empty chamber, a lesson which the corporal seemingly had not learned. Thankfully, the moon had begun its rise and I had a pocket torch with me, so we were able to navigate the coarse landscape safely back to camp.

When the others saw their comrade being carried in, there was a ripple fear among them. At first, they thought he had been killed by the "Beast". When Truscott announced Culpepper had tripped and accidentally shot himself, their fear turned to remorse and anger.

A makeshift litter was put together and the body was wrapped in a tarpaulin for movement to town. The constable bargained with the local innkeeper for room in a storage place to lay it until morning, when he could arrange transport to the nearest morgue. Holmes and I had accompanied the constable and his partner to the village. When arrangements for the night had been made, Holmes suggested to Truscott he should like to more closely examine the scene of the incident in the morning and would welcome his company. "There are one or two points I should like to satisfy myself upon," he said. "I should also like to ensure that, once the news of Culpepper's death gets out, we don't have frenzied crowds traipsing all over and destroying evidence. Can you return at first light, with perhaps one or two more men, to keep the curiosity seekers under control?"

The fellow looked at Holmes thoughtfully, then replied, "You're probably right. Even if we announce it was an accident, there'll be some who will decide there's a conspiracy about the Beast going on. I've got two more constables I can probably pull in, if my superiors will allow it."

He started to turn to go and then looked back at us with another question, "There's a London reporter in town. Would it be helpful if I used him as a source to get the truth out there? He seemed to write a fair piece the other day."

"Reporters must be cultivated and fed carefully, Constable," replied the detective. "They are like a rose bush, usually presenting more thorns than flowers. Their care must balance precisely. Too much water and they will give out more information than the public needs or wants to know.

Too little and weeds of made up 'facts' will spring up around them, eventually choking out the truth. If you see him tomorrow, point him out to me discreetly and I will judge if and how he may prove useful."

Chapter V

The next morning, with Henry's horses now well-rested, we took the carriage back to Minions at dawn. Our arrival at the dig site coincided with Logan stoking the campfire to heat a large metal coffee pot. A low fog spread across the moor. The flags we had set out the evening before were barely visible, appearing as ghostly shades within the slow grey currents as the rising sun heated the air.

The events of the evening before had set a melancholy mood upon the archaeologists. The remaining two were much younger, being students from University College, London. One of them, about twenty years old with dark skin and features, was thin as a rail with a moustache to match. His name was Ryan Fogg and he always wore an old pith helmet, which was a bit large for his head. He claimed it was the same one worn by his father, Phileas, when he crossed India in his famous eighty-day trip around the world in 1872. His name, "Ryan", we were informed, meant "king" in the language of his mother, the Indian Princess Aouda.

The other was a year or two older with an athletic build and standing an inch or two over six feet. His background was Welsh and his name was Henry Jones. His black hair was long and flowed down over his collar, unlike the modern fashion of the day where most men were wearing their hair short. It gave him a rugged appearance and it somehow seemed fitting for an archaeologist – though more for one exploring ancient ruins in Egypt rather than in the rugged but civilized regions of Cornwall.

Holmes engaged Dr. Logan in conversation. "I don't wish to interfere with your work, Doctor. I expect my investigations shall take me out and about on the moor. I do implore you, however, to please keep me informed of any recent disturbances you may discover around your site which may indicate present-day activity by the locals or the creature."

That said, Holmes, Henry, myself, and Cadan walked out to where we had placed the flags the previous evening. He then instructed Henry and Cadan to continue to explore along the line formed by the three locations we had marked in a westerly direction, looking for any more signs such as tracks, footprints, or anything out of the ordinary. As they moved out to do so, he turned to me, "Watson, I'd like you to join me in examining the scene of Culpepper's incident. Along the way, I wish to observe the ground near where we saw the Beast on the ridge."

317

We made our way across the heather-spotted landscape and up the shallow rise. My companion knelt near where we had seen the cat on its haunches, appearing to yowl at the sunset. Again, he measured the paw prints we found there and also the distance between them, though few were visible. He suddenly spotted something on the ground and carefully moved around behind the bush. He again knelt and made some measurements, though this time they were about a foot-and-a-half apart. "See here, Watson – what do make of this?"

I knelt beside him, heavily leaning on my cane, for the morning again was chilly and damp. Peering to where he pointed, I saw what appeared to be two oblong indentations. "I see them, but what are they?"

"If my suspicions are correct . . . ." he said, leaning forward and pulling back at some of the lower branches of the bush. "A-ha!" He took more measurements between the markings and whatever it was he had found under the bush, making note of them. Standing, he brushed off his knees and slowly began walking down the backside of the hill. Carefully examining the ground as he went, he noted things in his book which I couldn't see, but meant something to him. At last, we arrived at the scene of Culpepper's demise.

Stopping several feet short of where the archaeologist's body had fallen against the gorse bush, Holmes again knelt and began a closer examination of the ground. He shook his head slowly as his gaze meandered from side to side. "It won't do, Watson."

I was about to ask what wouldn't do when we were interrupted by a shout from behind us on the ridge. "You, there! Stop what you're doing!"

We both turned at the sound. Constable Truscott was standing there next to another man. This second fellow was dressed in tweed trousers with high brown boots and a Norfolk jacket. It was obviously he who had delivered this command, his voice being much deeper than the constable's. He led the way down to us, bulling his way along with no regard for any evidence he might be trampling. His agility in navigating the slope was uncommonly keen and sure-footed. He was a wiry fellow with dark, leathery skin which had obviously received much exposure to the sun of these southern climes. He was clean-shaven with dark brown eyes burning in accusation as he addressed us. His Cornish accent was broad as he said, "I understand you claim to be Sherlock Holmes and Dr. Watson. I am Inspector Teague of the Bodmin District Police. I order you to cease and desist. I'll not have a pair of Englishmen mucking up my investigation merely to add to their inflated reputations. You have no jurisdiction here, and I'll thank you to leave. This situation is my responsibility, and I'll brook no interference!"

Perhaps it was his accent, but I couldn't help but think back to my Scottish youth and how often my brother would call someone who did something he perceived to be stupid, as "thick as mince". I noted Constable Truscott stayed behind Teague's back shaking his head and shrugging his shoulders, as if in apology for his superior's behavior. Holmes, having run into this attitude often in his career as a consulting detective, voiced his reply in more diplomatic terms than where my mind had gone.

"Pleased to meet you, Inspector," he said, surprising the man with his cordial attitude. "I assure you, we are who we say we are. However, despite what you may have heard, I have no intention of interfering with your investigation. My primary concern is the safety of Dr. Logan's expedition. I shall leave the rest to you. As far as this scene of the unfortunate Mr. Culpepper's death, I merely suggest you examine the ground for a few feet uphill from where the body came to rest."

With that statement, he gave me a nod and we hiked up to the top of the ridge and back across the moor to the archaeologists' camp. Henry and Cadan were there with the other three men, drinking coffee. The baronet was pacing and clearly upset when we walked back into camp.

"Mr. Holmes," he said with anger tinging his words, "I don't pretend to know all the ins-and-outs of British government or exactly how the peerage system works, but over the last five years I have been under the impression my title meant something, and that law enforcement was obligated to listen when I made a request. At least that's how it has worked over in Dartmoor. That damn fool," he cried, pointing off in the direction from which we'd come, "shows no respect at all. He ordered us back to camp and forbade us from following any further along the track you had requested."

He then pointed out toward the line of flags and I noted there were two more, farther out than before. "We found two more paw prints, so we appeared to have formed a general direction of the cat's retreat."

Holmes and I accepted cups of coffee from Logan, and my companion explained the delicate political situation between England and Cornwall.

"As with Scotland, Ireland, and Wales, the Cornish people consider themselves unique from the rest of England. While the titular head is the Duke of Cornwall, who is traditionally the eldest son of the reigning British Monarch, most Englishmen consider Cornwall to be just another English county. However, Cornwall is legally a territorial and constitutional Duchy with the right to veto Westminster legislation. It has never been formally incorporated into England through an Act of Union. Therefore, every so often, a movement arises to declare their independence

319

as a separate country. Apparently, Inspector Teague is sympathetic to that position. Were you to travel much in the area, you would likely see many more Cornish flags than you would a Union Jack."

Henry had been standing with his arms crossed tightly as he seethed in anger. When Holmes finished his comments, the baronet slid his hands into his pockets. His face softened somewhat, and he remarked, "I wasn't aware that was the situation. Having spent several years in Canada, I can understand how such feelings can stir up a people. But where does that leave us?"

"It severely hampers any further investigation of the moor itself," answered the detective. "However, I believe I have sufficient information on that score as it stands. Did the new tracks you find look like the previous ones we found? Roughly the same size with four toes and claw marks?"

Henry looked to his groom for confirmation and nodded. "Yes, Mr. Holmes. I'd say they were done by the same animal at the same time."

Holmes finished his coffee with a satisfying swallow, licked his lips, set down the cup, and took out his pipe. Addressing the whole group of us, he remarked, "I have some research to conduct, but I can assure you, gentlemen, the Black Beast isn't what it purports to be, and it's certainly *not* supernatural. Should it be necessary to defend yourselves, do try to aim for its back half in order to wound it. Captured alive, it will prove most illuminating."

By now a few onlookers had gathered at the ropes set up by the police to keep the crowds back. There were two officers manning this blockade and Holmes casually strode over toward them. Seeing his approach, one of them walked over to meet him before he got too close.

"Would you be Sherlock Holmes, sir?" he asked.

"Yes, Constable."

The fellow nodded back over his shoulder without turning. "Truscott said you were looking for a reporter. He's the gent in the grey suit and black hat. Been a pesky sort for days now. Always wantin' to get a closer look and bother them archaeologists. Would you care to speak with him now, sir? If not, I can keep him at bay."

Holmes surreptitiously shifted his gaze toward the handful of on-lookers. Easily spotting the Londoner, he flashed a brief smile as he re-positioned his pipe. "Thank you for your consideration, Constable. I shall be happy to speak with him, but not here. Please quietly advise him that Dr. Watson and I shall meet him for lunch at the Cheesewring Restaurant at noon. I would appreciate you not let the other gawkers overhear this invitation, for I would prefer not to have our conversation intruded upon."

"As you wish, sir."

The constable returned to his post, calling out the reporter for a quiet conversation off to the side. Holmes returned to us and reported his plan to Henry and me. To the baronet he said, "Sir Henry, I would prefer not to subject you to the speculations of the London press. May I suggest you have Cadan drive you and your prospective father-in-law back to Upton Cross for lunch while Watson and I deal with this persistent newsman?"

Henry looked over his shoulder, as if afraid someone might have heard the detective's comment. With a lowered voice he leaned forward. "I haven't yet spoken to Guinevere of any commitment to marriage, nor have I asked his permission to propose to her."

Holmes looked askance at the young gentleman and replied quietly, "I am no expert in the matters of women. I leave such things to the good Doctor here. But I believe I don't steer you wrong in stating there is no time like the present to seek out Dr. Logan's permission to request his daughter's hand. A quiet lunch at the Caradon Inn should provide an adequate setting."

Henry straightened up, looking first to Holmes then to me. I nodded and replied softly to his unspoken question. "Your feelings, as well as hers, were quite transparent when you introduced us. In your shoes, I shouldn't lose a moment in making such a declaration." I placed a hand upon his shoulder, "Life is too short, my friend."

While always possessed of a youthful appearance, the boyish grin which broke out upon Henry's face seemed to transform him into a callow youth. "By thunder, I will!" he declared. "Thank you, gentleman."

Chapter VI

I'm sure the rest of the morning hours dragged by interminably slow for the baronet as he seemed ready to burst with the decision he had made. Holmes and I busied ourselves with restricting our examination of the area to the Hurlers Stone Circle, which seemed to be the only place Inspector Teague would allow Dr. Logan to explore. I chose to let the detective examine the grounds for more footprints or other signs of the feline. For myself, I decided to delve more into the personalities of Fogg and Jones.

The half-caste Fogg was highly excitable and constantly on the move back and forth between various mounds and comparing them, his oversized pith helmet rocking on his head with his movements. Jones, in spite of his size and athletic countenance, was quite studious. He moved with deliberateness and took careful measurements, all the while sketching and making notes in a brown, leather-bound, octodecimo-sized journal. As his note-taking habit was a kindred spirit to my own, I struck up a conversation with him.

"Tell me, Master Jones, your name is obviously Welsh, yet you have a distinct Scottish accent. Did you spend some of your youth in Scotland?"

"Aye, Dr. Watson. I was born near here, but my father took up a post at the University of Edinburgh and I was raised there. When I came of age, I thought it best to get some education where I would not be thought of as a professor's son with the supposed privileges thereof. Thus I took up my education at the University of London."

I nodded, then asked, "Do you intend to make archaeology your career? Exploring the world's ancient ruins and civilizations?"

He kept looking at the ground where one of the Hurler Stones was almost completely covered in dirt and growth, still making notes as he replied in a pleasant baritone voice tinged by his Scottish accent. "I do indeed, Dr. Watson. I am moving to the States in the spring, where I have been accepted into the doctorate program at Princeton University in New Jersey. My intention is to alternate expeditions with teaching assignments."

"A wise choice," I replied. "A steady teaching income will stand you well should you ever be a member of an expedition which fails its backers' expectations. Is there any particular aspect of archaeology which interests you most?"

This time he looked at me with his deep brown eyes as he answered, "I've a particular affinity for the world's religions," he commented, pointing his pencil at the stone he was standing above, "which is why this site interests me. I should like to understand what drove people to believe as they did and to see if we can separate fact from legend. Confidentially, Doctor, being born a Welshman, I've also a keen interest in the stories of King Arthur and the Holy Grail. If my work feeds my passion, so much the better!"

"Wisely said, sir," I replied. "As they say, 'the man who enjoys his job never has to work a day in his life'. I wish you success, Master Jones."

I assisted him with measuring distances between the mounds and stones. Even taking meticulous measurements of their current locations wasn't going to reveal the exact historical distances, however. Cattle using them for scratching posts and centuries of invasive plant growth, likely had moved them by up to several inches. It was hoped, however, a close approximation might lend a mathematical aspect to their layout and help determine their original purpose.

These tasks occupied me until it was time for us to repair to the Cheesewring Hotel, which boasted the finest restaurant in the area. We arrived a few minutes early so that Holmes might choose the most optimal seating. As we awaited the reporter, I read over the back of the menu which included a bit of history behind the famous name. The moniker derives from the resemblance of the piled slabs to a "cheesewring", a press-like device which was once used to make cheese.

The Cheesewring Formation on Bodmin Moor

Wilkie Collins described the Cheesewring in 1861 in his book *Rambles Beyond Railways*:

If a man dreams of a great pile of stones in a nightmare, he would dream of such a pile as the Cheesewring. All the heaviest and largest of the seven thick slabs of which it is composed are at the top; all the lightest and smallest at the bottom. It rises perpendicularly to a height of thirty-two feet, without lateral support of any kind. The fifth and sixth rocks are of immense size and thickness, and overhang fearfully all round the four lower rocks which support them. All are perfectly irregular; the projections of one do not fit into the interstices of another; they are heaped up loosely in their

323

extraordinary top-heavy form on slanting ground, half way down a steep hill.

I had also picked up a pamphlet in the hotel lobby describing the local area and its features. Interestingly, it contained the legend of the Cheesewring. The story goes it was created by a competition between the giant, Uther, and Saint Tue.

> *When Christianity first came to Cornwall, the giants who inhabited the high, rocky places became angry when the saints began to invade their land and Christianise their wells and springs.*
>
> *Uther was given the task of removing the saints. He confronted Saint Tue, who suggested they have a rock throwing contest to resolve the dispute. They agreed that if Uther won, the saints would leave Cornwall, but if Saint Tue won, the giants would convert to Christianity.*
>
> *Uther was first to throw and his rock landed on Stowe's Hill. Saint Tue prayed and picked up a larger rock which he threw with ease. It landed on top of Uther's rock.*
>
> *Taking turns, they threw their rocks, stacking the stones in perfect piles. After twelve stones each, Uther threw a thirteenth stone but it missed its target and rolled down the hill, landing near the feet of Saint Tue. He picked up the stone and an angel appeared. It carried the stone back up the hill, placing it on top of the pile of rocks.*
>
> *Uther accepted defeat and agreed that he and his fellow giants would follow Christianity.*

Since the archaeologists were staying at this hotel, I presumed Master Jones had picked up one of these pamphlets already, and I resolved to discuss this information with him to obtain his thoughts on the subject.

As I finished my reading, the newsman arrived. It took him but a moment to spot us in the far corner of the dining room and he approached rapidly. Seeing him up closer now, I noted he was tall and lean, much like my companion. He walked with a singleness of purpose, never taking his eyes off us as he weaved through several tables, servers, and diners being shown to their seats.

He removed his hat upon his arrival and I noted his hair was already beginning to recede, though I put his age only in his mid-twenties. Yet, his youthful enthusiasm was quite evident, though tempered by a mature and deliberate voice when he spoke.

324

"Mr. Holmes, Dr. Watson, thank you for seeing me gentlemen. My name is Trent Osborne. I work for *The Strand Magazine*."

Holmes nodded in reply, and with an invitation. "Mr. Osborne, pray, take a seat." I gestured for him to sit next to me, as I knew most of his questions would be directed to the detective. As he lowered himself into his chair, I commented, "I've read some of your work, Mr. Osborne. You have a talent for your craft, sir."

He modestly tilted his head, "Thank you, Doctor. Certainly not in your class. Your stories were the jewel in the crown of the magazine. Now that Mr. Holmes has rejoined the living, will you continue?"

Before I could reply, Holmes spoke up, "I believe we have more important matters to discuss than the romanticizing of my life's work, Mr. Osborne. If you have questions of me, ask them. If not, I have questions for you."

This statement seemed to intrigue Osborne. For a moment, I thought I saw in his eyes a moment of indecision. I'm sure the thought of answering questions for Sherlock Holmes was fighting for priority over the inquiries he had of my friend. Finally he made up his mind. He pulled out a small notebook and pencil and began his probe into Holmes's current investigation. Like all good reporters, he began with the "*W*" questions regarding Holmes's involvement: *Who, What, When, Where.* All of which received short, clipped answers until the *Why.* Here Holmes was discreet in stating Sir Henry Baskerville was a former client and had sought Holmes's intercession into the case for his friend, Dr. Logan. He made no mention of Logan's daughter or exactly how the gentlemen knew each other. He put more emphasis on the fact that Sir Henry Baskerville, being a highly influential man in the neighboring county, was merely expressing concern for his district, should the so-called "Beast" be real and wander across the River Tamar into his jurisdiction.

When asked the nature of Henry's case, Holmes merely stated it was a trifling matter of inheritance and succession which he was able to sort out. Questions regarding the current case were met with more stonewalling.

"I need more data, Mr. Osborne, and this is where I have questions for you. I have competing theories in mind, but I cannot form a viable hypothesis without additional facts. You aren't a recent arrival to this scene. You have been here since the story first came about, I believe."

"Why, yes, Mr. Holmes. How did you know?"

My companion waved his hand and merely referred to the tanning of Osborne's skin, the condition of his suit and boots, and depth of pages into his notebook wherein he was now making entries.

Holmes then went on with questions of his own. He asked if the reporter had done background on any current Druidic practices in the area. What did he know about the local police – especially Inspector Teague? Were there any recent sightings or evidence of the Beast before Dr. Logan's expedition arrived? Who were the most influential men in the district?

The young newsman answered as best he could. His greatest contribution, to my mind, was the ideal place to track local gossip was the Jamaica Inn. It was six miles' walk across the heath, though he advised it was safer to go by carriage on a round-about drive to the north and circle back on the western side of the moor.

In some of the other areas where he lacked in-depth information, Osborne volunteered to do some more digging on Holmes's behalf. My friend usually prefers to do his own research, and I was a bit surprised when he readily agreed to this. We parted ways with the reporter after a light repast, agreeing upon a signal as to when to meet again.

Holmes explained afterward, "Teague is already resentful and suspicious of us, Watson. If we were to go poking about, he would react with even greater vehemence – possibly even banishing us from the district. If our young friend is confronted as to why he is seeking such information, he has the quite natural explanation – that it's to provide background for his story."

I nodded in understanding, and then asked, "You seem particularly interested in this Teague fellow. You have suspicions?"

"I always have suspicions, Doctor. Everyone is suspect until I eliminate them – just some more than others. At this point, I have yet to eliminate even the possibility that Dr. Logan has created this situation to gain more publicity. Though that is far down on my list.

"Teague, on the other hand, is in a position to know things and even to cover up evidence, should it be necessary. He may be complicit or merely incompetent. It's one of the facts I need to determine."

We returned to the excavation site to find Jones, on duty so to speak, while Fogg was off to lunch. There was also another gentleman. He was a tall, lean sort, nearly six feet but very thin. He wore a long black Inverness coat with a slouch hat to match, which he doffed at our approach. This revealed medium-length black hair, parted on the right. (Holmes had observed to me long ago this often indicated a left-handed person). The state of his moustache and beard indicated he hadn't shaved for several days, but they weren't yet full, as they should be if they were a constant affectation. His voice was a natural tenor as he extended his hand and introduced himself to us.

"Professor Sylvester Bowman of the Zoological Society and the University of London. It is a pleasure to meet you Mr. Holmes, Dr. Watson."

We each shook his hand in turn and proceeded to sit in the camp chairs around the fire to which Jones had attended. Apparently not one for small talk, Bowman jumped right in with the pressing question, "So Mr. Holmes, what say you? Is there a 'Beast of Bodmin Moor', or are these rumours just the tales of a superstitious population?"

Holmes had continued to observe the fellow with a scrutiny which only I, as his close friend of many years, would have recognized. He has an uncanny ability at being surreptitious. After a moment's hesitation, he replied, "I suppose it would depend upon your definition of 'Beast', Professor. If you are referring to something supernatural, I assure you that isn't the case. Appearances lean toward the existence of a large feline – certainly not native to these parts – but then appearances can be deceiving. We were only able to observe it from a great distance and heard what seemed to be a large cat's yowl. Presently available physical evidence supports this, based upon the claw marks made to the expedition's equipment and the tracks found. We have been banned from further exploration of the creature by the local constabulary. However, I believe the short walk to the first track found wouldn't be considered going too far afield, if you care to see it?"

"I would indeed, Mr. Holmes!" replied the zoologist, with enthusiasm.

Jones chose to remain in camp while Holmes and I escorted our guest to where he had found the closest track. Bowman crouched and peered at the wide paw print, nodding his head this way and that to see it from several angles.

At last he stood. "It appears to be a fairly large feline from the width and depth of this track. I presume the moor has been getting damp at night. Panthers can grow to one-hundred-fifty-pounds or more. Was the creature you saw black in colour?"

Holmes replied, "It was in silhouette against that far rise next to the gorse bush and it was dusk. It appeared dark, but its actual colour was indiscernible."

"You couldn't get a closer look?"

I spoke up at that remark, "The one who tried died in the attempt."

"The creature attacked him?" ejaculated Bowman, appearing surprised.

Before I could expound further, Holmes interrupted, "The gentleman who chased after it first was quick, but foolhardy. With the restrictions placed upon us, what will be your plan, Professor?"

Bowman scratched at his beard along the jawline as he looked off toward the rise where we had seen the creature. His gaze seemed to linger with longing to explore the area. "What is the objection raised by the police? This is but a scientific investigation, after all."

Holmes thrust his hands deep into his pockets, his cold grey eyes narrowed at the frustration he must have felt and he pursed his lips prior to answering. Then, in a tone and manner I had never heard him use before, he spat out, "It's damned political prejudice! These Cornish coppers refuse us merely because we are English. The only reason the expedition was allowed in the first place was due to Professor Logan being a former instructor of Prince Albert. As Duke of Cornwall, the Prince extended the courtesy of exploration, apparently without consulting the locals. So they are observing the strictest letter of the allowance and confining the expedition to the Hurlers Stone Circle and no further. It's a foolish waste of time and resources!"

The zoologist hesitated at the vehemence of the detective's remark, and then queried, "Why stay then? It appears the constables have at least posted guards for the expedition's protection. What more can you do?"

Holmes straightened to his full height and a calmness came over his face, as if he had made a decision which lifted a weight from his shoulders. "By George, you are correct, Professor! There is no longer a reason for us to stay here another moment. Come along, Watson. We shall leave these country bumpkins to their fate!"

He turned on his heel and quickly strode back to the campsite. I was flabbergasted at both his outburst and his manner. I stole a glance at Professor Bowman, who was looking after my friend with surprise and a tilt of his head. I shrugged my shoulders, excused myself, and walked quickly after my companion.

Chapter VII

Our departure crossed paths with the return of Henry Baskerville and Lionel Logan, both of whom were in good spirits. Congratulations were in order as the Professor had consented to Henry's proposal of marriage to his daughter, if Jenny was so inclined. We adjourned to the Professor's tent, Holmes standing by the flap to ensure we weren't overheard. He then laid out his plan and obtained agreement from all of us to do our part.

Holmes and Henry then chose to leave and prepare a return to Tavistock, where Henry would propose formally to Miss Logan and Holmes could move on to Coombe Tracey to catch a train back to London. I was to stay with the archaeologists a few more days and telegraph any significant developments to Holmes which might justify his return.

328

Throughout this great show of leaving the encampment, Holmes made no effort to hide his disgust at the political manipulation and incompetence of the Bodmin Constabulary.

Upon their departure, I introduced Professor Bowman to Professor Logan, then returned to the circle to offer what assistance I might to Jones and Fogg. Our exploration was cut short as a late afternoon storm rolled up from the southwest and sent us scurrying back to our hotel rooms. As Henry had taken his carriage, I was planning to see about hiring a horse or driver in the village to take me back to Upton Cross, but Professor Bowman saved me the trouble by offering to drop me off on his way back to the Jamaica Inn, where he had set up his own lodgings.

Fortunately, he had an enclosed little one-horse buggy, just big enough for the two of us. We spoke of Holmes's departure, and he enquired, "Is Mr. Holmes always so infuriated by bureaucracy? I don't recall reading that in any of your published works."

I replied, "It is an aspect of his personality which I prefer not to expose to the public. It could have a deleterious effect upon his reputation and the sales of my tales."

He looked at me with a smirk. "So the public image of Sherlock Holmes is a fiction then? What about his powers?"

"Oh, his powers are quite real, and his breadth of knowledge is beyond the ken of most men. But like many geniuses, his patience can run short at the inability of others to see or act upon what is so clearly the obvious and logical choice in his mind. At such times his exasperation can get the better of him, and he will leave the bureaucrats to suffer from their ignorance."

Bowman merely nodded and drove on. The light sprinkle, which had sent us all packing, had turned into a heavy rain by the time he dropped me off at the Caradon Inn and continued on his way to the Jamaica. I stepped into the pub for a brandy to warm my inner man and read over my notes as I sat at the bar. After about twenty minutes, I took up my umbrella and ventured out during an easing of the rainstorm to walk the three-hundred yards to the local post office. Here I sent off a wire to Sir Henry Baskerville in Tavistock: "*Excavation arrowheads in prime condition. Weather stormy.*"

In Tavistock, where the weather was cool but dry, my telegram found Henry and Holmes at the Bedford Hotel. The baronet had stopped by the hospital just long enough to arrange for a dinner with Miss Logan that evening. Now our friend and host was inpatient for the approaching hour. Holmes would spend the night in Tavistock, awaiting the right time for his next move. When my telegram arrived, with my substitution of "*arrowhead*" for "*Bowman*", the detective was surprised but pleased I had accomplished my task so quickly. This meant he could move forward with his plan on the morrow, if he received an appropriate answer to a telegram he had sent off to London.

The following morning, I returned to the excavation site. The rain had passed, but it was cold with a light mist, and the fields and paths had turned to mud. There was no crowd on hand, likely due to the threatening weather and the police presence. Constable Truscott greeted me cordially and waved me on by, asking, "No Mr. Holmes today, Doctor?"

I replied, "Holmes has returned to London. He has more pressing cases than chasing down wild animals. I am merely curious as to the excavation itself and its archaeological implications, so I thought I would stay a few more days."

The constable nodded. "As you wish, sir. I am sorry for Inspector Teague's temper toward you gentlemen. He has always held an anti-English opinion."

"The British Isles are made up of a variety of peoples, Constable," I replied. "Descended from ancient tribes within the various geographic regions, their differences run deep and long. However, as the world grows smaller, it is imperative the United Kingdom remains united."

"Agreed, Doctor," answered Truscott. "So long as the cultures are allowed to remain intact and not everyone is forced into the English ways of thinking and acting."

"As a good Scotsman, I couldn't agree more," I smiled, then nodded toward the camp. "I should go join the others. Have a pleasant day, Mr. Truscott."

Professor Logan and his students, Fogg and Jones, had completed the last of the measurements they needed prior to actual excavation. Fogg was now in the process of taking photographs of the various stones and mounds where it was believed stones had fallen and were buried. The stones still standing for the most part were roughly four to six feet high. They were somewhat rectangular in shape, each standing on end, much like ancient monoliths or headstones. Many had sharp corners, as if hewn into shape, while others presented more natural, rounded edges. There appeared to be three circles, a large central one about one-hundred-forty-feet across with one stone in the middle but off center. Slightly to the northeast was another circle of around one-hundred-fifteen feet. To the southwest, the final circle of perhaps one-hundred-five feet.

I noticed there was no sign of Professor Bowman and mentioned his absence to Logan. "I suspect the weather will keep him at bay, Doctor. The tracks are probably washed away, and a feline beast would certainly not come out in the rain, so there would be little for him to do."

Meanwhile, at the Jamaica Inn, an elderly gentleman approached Professor Bowman. He was slightly stooped and walked with a cane. His red hair and full beard were shot through with grey and age spots were making an appearance on the backs of his hands, which shook slightly. He walked with a shuffling gait as he approached the London zoologist, seated at a table in the restaurant. Bowman was talking with Police Inspector Teague. Teague noted the old man's approach and motioned his companion to silence.

In a heavy Scot's brogue, the visitor introduced himself. "Excuse me, gentleman," he said, "I am Dr. Thane Shaw from the Royal Zoological Society of Scotland. I understand ye to be Professor Bowman?"

Bowman looked up at the fellow and replied tersely, "Yes, what do you want?"

Teague, with at least some semblance of courtesy, stood and introduced himself. "Dr. Shaw, welcome to Cornwall. I am Inspector Teague of the Bodmin Constabulary. Won't you have a seat?"

"Thank you, Inspector," replied the new arrival. "The journey has been long and the last leg especially jostling to these old bones."

He sank heavily into a chair with a sigh and a grimace and Teague signaled for a waiter to bring another cup of coffee, much to Bowman's confusion. A sidelong glance from the inspector kept him silent, however, and he let the official take the lead in the conversation.

"I presume you've come down regarding the reported sightings of the Beast on Bodmin Moor?"

"Aye, Inspector. We've had similar sightings and signs of such big cats in the Highlands, but have yet to capture any such beast. I hoped to see if evidence here was more conclusive."

Teague smiled and replied, "Professor Bowman is here for the same reason. There *have* been some recent sightings. Tracks and the destruction of an archaeologists' campsite clearly indicate something is out there."

The coffee arrived. Shaw took a heavy gulp, leaned back, closed his eyes briefly, and commented, "Ah, much better. Thank ye kindly, Inspector."

Leaning forward again and setting the cup on its saucer, Shaw continued the conversation, "Have ye come close to catching the Beastie?"

Teague shook his head, "As I was just telling the professor, the Beast's actions seemed to have had the opposite effect to its likely desire. Our opinion is, it attacked the camp to drive the invaders away. Instead, the publicity created has drawn even more people down to the moor. I have had to put officers on duty to keep people away before someone else gets hurt."

"It attacked someone?" the Scotsman asked in surprise.

Bowman finally spoke up. "Actually someone tried to attack it. One of the archaeology students went after it with a gun. He slipped, fell, and accidentally shot himself. The wound proved fatal."

"How terrible!" cried Shaw. "You're not trying to kill it, are ye?"

Bowman said, "My only interest is to ascertain its existence and verify what it is. Its fate is of no concern to me."

Teague shook his head. "I'd just as soon let it alone as well, but it has killed some cattle and the farmers want it captured or killed."

Shaw cried, "Ye mustn't kill it!" Then, realizing the commanding tone of his outburst, continued in a softer tone. "Forgive me. It's just that it would be much more valuable if captured alive for study. Our zoo would pay handsomely for such a creature to exhibit."

Teague seemed intrigued by such a possibility and replied, "I could make the attempt, Doctor, but it isn't likely anything will happen so long as it's been driven into hiding by all the tourists."

"My society would be most grateful, Inspector. If there is anything I can do, please don't hesitate to ask. I'll be staying here for a few days. Would I find the archaeologists at their encampment today?"

"So long as the weather holds," Teague answered, "I should think they will be there daily."

"Thank ye, sir. I shall bid ye good day then." The elderly scholar shuffled away, leaving the professor and the inspector to resume their discussion."

Chapter VIII

That same afternoon, I met with Trent Osborne for lunch. He was shocked when I informed him of Holmes's withdrawal from the case. I assured him, however, the detective was still interested in any information he could dig up during his background investigations. I would be his conduit to pass it along.

That seemed to mollify him to some extent and he reached into his inner breast pocket. He handed over three sheets of paper. "There's too much there to send via telegram, Doctor. I was hoping to hand them over to Mr. Holmes himself."

I looked over the papers and was surprised at some of the material Osborne had uncovered. "This explains a lot," I said. "How did you come by these facts? Surely they were meant to stay secret."

He looked at me with a sly grin, "Doctor, you know a good reporter doesn't reveal his sources. I can't hide behind fiction and name changes the way you do when you write up Mr. Holmes's cases."

I nodded, "Understood, Mr. Osborne. I'll see Holmes receives this information as quickly as possible."

"And I still get the exclusive story when he's ready, right?"

"I'll see to it."

When I returned to the campsite, I found a new visitor in discussion with Professor Logan. As I entered the main tent, this elderly, red-haired fellow turned toward me and spoke with a Scot's brogue. "Ah, this must be me fellow jock [2], John Watson."

I smiled and replied, "And you, sir, are obviously a Sassenach." [3]

The familiar grin of Sherlock Holmes appeared between the moustache and beard. He continued in his own voice. "Really, Watson! There's no need to be insulting."

"How did things go at the Jamaica Inn? Bowman never showed up here today."

"I didn't expect him to," replied Holmes. "He's no more a zoologist than I am."

I tilted my head quizzically as I sat on one of the empty camp stools, "So what was the point of his coming here?"

"He was here to spy on us. The people he's working with wanted to gather information to plan their next move. My departure hastened his. He may still drop by to keep up appearances, but he daren't allow himself to be questioned thoroughly for risk of exposure for the fraud he is."

"You checked with London to see if he was legitimate?" asked Professor Logan.

Holmes shook his head, "I didn't have to. The moment he looked at the cat's supposed paw print without identifying it as an imitation made it obvious his claims to his credentials were phony."

"Imitation paw prints, Mr. Holmes?" enquired the professor.

"Besides the obvious lack of a proper pattern of tracks left by a cat on the prowl or on the run, the tracks themselves had a fatal flaw. Unless a cat is using its claws for a specific purpose; such as an attack, or to climb a tree, it keeps them retracted. The paw prints we observed clearly showed the claws extended. A true zoologist would know that."

"But we saw the Beast up on the hillside. We heard it."

Holmes shook his head, "We saw a silhouette at dusk. The sound we heard was likely caused by a mechanical device hidden behind the bush next to it at the time. The marks left behind in the dirt were obviously from some man-made object. Unfortunately the police banned us from investigating further, or I am sure we would have seen evidence of where it had been set up, as well at tracks which would have proved the Beast walked like a human, perhaps wearing specially made boots to leave paw prints."

"But the attack on the camp – the claw marks left behind."

"Far too uniform to be left by a natural creature," replied the detective. "There should have been differences in the spacing of the claws, depending upon which paw was being used."

"So what is the end game, Mr. Holmes? What are they after?"

"I believe I can answer that," I said, reaching into my pocket, retrieving the papers given me by the reporter and handing them to Holmes.

He began to go through them, as I had already done. Stopping at one paragraph in particular he nodded. "This confirms what I found in Bowman's room."

"You searched his room?" asked Logan. "Wasn't that dangerous? You could have been caught. Maybe arrested."

"Bowman happened to be eating lunch with Inspector Teague at the moment," replied Holmes. "I knew I had plenty of time. What I discovered corroborates what Osborne found. Bowman is member of the same group as Teague, and he has been much more involved in the mystery of this Beast than he has let on."

"What group is that?" queried the archaeologist.

Holmes stood, slipping the papers into his own pocket, "One which wishes to stop your exploration of this ancient site. Tell me, Professor, was there any specific resistance to your excavation when you first arrived?"

"Not for a day or two. Then Inspector Teague showed up with a couple of his coppers and demanded to know my authority for excavating on government land. Fortunately, I had written authorization from the Duke. That seemed to settle the issue. As you are aware, of course, he is confining us very strictly to the letter of that decree and kept us from going beyond the general area of the stone circles."

Holmes nodded, then pulled his pipe from his pocket. "I need to smoke a pipe or two on the matter, gentlemen. I think I shall take a stroll upon the moor for a bit."

As he did so, I joined Logan and his students at the Hurlers Stones and assisted wherever I could. Occasionally I would glance in my companion's direction. His actions alternated between pacing about and sitting upon a boulder, staring off in the direction the false cat tracks had gone.

After about a half-an-hour, he wandered back in our direction. I saw him approach the professor and I strode over to join the discussion in time to overhear the professor answer a query. "Yes, Mr. Holmes. When we first arrived, one of the tasks we undertook was to take to the high ground – that same rise you crested the other night. From there we made notes of landmarks in all directions for future reference, should they prove

334

pertinent to our research. There are a few small depressions and other stone formations about. Siblyback Lake is off to the west. There is a mine about three quarters of a mile to the northwest near Stowe's Hill. Daniel Gumb's Cave [4] is about the same distance due north, but it's closed to the public due to the partial collapse of the interior. You can also see the top of the Cheesewring stones above the hill beyond."

Holmes turned to me, "Watson, are you up for a little nocturnal exploring tonight?"

"Certainly," I replied.

Logan expressed concern, "Won't that be dangerous, Mr. Holmes? I know you've shown me the paw prints around here are counterfeit, but there are still many unexplained sightings and evidence of a large cat somewhere on the moor."

Holmes tamped out his pipe and restored it to his pocket. "I appreciate your concern, Professor. Be assured, Watson and I shall be armed, for there is a more dangerous predator to be concerned about than a stealthy feline."

At the archaeologist's questioning look, he clarified, "I'm referring to the human being who made the false tracks, and who may possibly be the murderer of Mr. Culpepper."

That evening, after the two constables on duty had left as our expedition closed up for the evening, Henry Jones remained to guard the camp while the rest of us returned to town. I shared "Dr. Shaw's" cart, as he could drop me at Upton Cross on his way back to the Jamaica Inn. At least, that's what the constables saw and overheard. In reality, Holmes turned off the main road and followed a cart path which took us in the direction of Gumb's Cave. When we came to a certain fork in the path, we veered to the right instead of taking the way which would have deposited us within one-hundred feet of the cave itself. As he made this deviation, he explained to me, "Gumb's Cave lies off to the left here. However, we cannot discount the possibility our night prowler may show up, and we cannot let him see our cart. Off this way we shall have some rocky mounds between us and can hide our vehicle in a small copse of trees, where it will not be observed."

Fortunately, the weather was cooperating. It was decidedly cold, but there was no wind nor rain to obstruct our mission, and the moon provided adequate light on this cloudless evening. We traversed the landscape for about a quarter-mile and approached the cave quietly. There were no carts nearby. However, Holmes had calculated the cave was a mere four miles across the moorland from the Jamaica Inn, should someone choose to cut across on a more direct route by horseback.

335

We approached the cave entrance quietly. Holmes, himself, moved with an almost cat-like stealth. Stopping about twenty feet out he knelt and studied the ground, still damp from the previous days' storm. He motioned to me and pointed to a track on the ground. The rain had washed most of it away. The depression left behind could certainly not be identified as any particular animal, though its size was roughly that of what we had seen around the camp. What didn't completely wash away were the deeper impressions left by the claw marks. We were able to follow the marks into the cave with our eyes. The pattern mimicked a biped's step rather than any four footed creature.

Holmes motioned me to follow him off to the side where there was more wild grass than mud upon the ground. This allowed us to enter the cave without leaving obvious tracks of our own.

Once inside, beyond the entrance, we both lit our pocket torches and began a systematic sweep of the interior. At one point he motioned to a particular portion of the rock wall and said, "Note the scratches, Watson. Something metal was scraped along here recently."

We used their direction to pursue our way farther into the cave. We must have been a good thirty feet inside and around a corner from sight of the entrance – thus, totally dependent upon the light of our torches. Not an ideal condition, but Holmes's sharp eyes caught what he was seeking: A thin flat rock was laid across the top of three others which formed a rectangular stone box against one wall. It was about the size and height of a small settee and probably was designed by Mr. Gumb. Holmes pointed to a line of scratches along the wall above it and then handed me his torch. Obtaining a good lifting posture, he heaved the thin slab up and leaned it against the cave wall, exactly upon the marks he had indicated.

Within the confines of this hidden compartment there were several items of interest. A pair of boots, two hiking poles, a mace, and a mechanical device of some sort. Holmes reached in and measured the device's bottom legs, nodding in satisfaction. "Here's the match to the indentation we found on the hill." He pulled another item out for closer examination. At first, it appeared to be some sort of bathing cap, but when Holmes spread it apart, we could note that there were two large appendages on either side, resembling feline ears.

"A mask of a cat's head!" I cried. "

Yes," replied my companion. "From a distance in the dusk, a man crouching properly with this on his head could indeed mimic the silhouette of a large cat." Suddenly, we heard the whinny of a horse outside. Quickly he pulled the lid back down upon the box and we took up separate positions farther back in the cave, extinguishing our torches as we crouched out of sight.

I saw the glow of a lantern light up the cave walls and rubble. It brightened as this unexpected visitor came closer. When he rounded the corner, the lamp was dangling at arms-length near his left knee, keeping his face in shadow. Yet I could see he was a tall thin man in a long black ulster and slouch hat. Bowman's name leapt immediately to my mind. When he knelt by the stone box we had just found, his face came into the light and my deduction was verified. He lifted the lid and removed the boots and the mace. It was then I was able to observe the medieval weapon in the brighter light of his lantern. It had about a two-foot handle with a cylindrical metal end and evil-looking, curved iron spikes protruding at the top.

He lowered the lid, took up the items, and left. In the total blackness, I waited for my companion before I dared to move. At last, when the sound of the horse's hooves had faded into the distance, Holmes re-lit his pocket torch and came out from his hiding spot.

"Hurry, Watson! There's no time to lose!" he cried. We scrambled over the rock-strewn ground of the cave, extinguishing our torches as we neared the moonlit entrance. At the cave mouth, Holmes stopped momentarily to ensure Bowman was no longer in sight. In that moment I asked, "What does he intend to do? Another attack on the campsite?"

"I'm afraid so. Only this time there is murder afoot. He cannot attack the camp without attacking Jones! We must hurry. On horseback he only has half the distance to go than our cart path!"

As Holmes drove furiously back to the encampment, I observed, "Surely he cannot approach the camp on horseback. He'll have to dismount out of sight and sneak up on foot."

"Yes," agreed the detective, whipping the horse to full gallop. "It's our only chance of arriving in time to prevent another tragedy."

Arriving at Minions, we drove out onto the moor, keeping a small copse of trees between us and the campsite. Unbeknownst to us, Constable Truscott had stopped by the pub for a drink after duty and was just mounting up to return to his home in Liskeard when he spotted us. Curious at our activity, he followed slowly behind.

We dismounted our cart and stealthily approached the camp. A lantern burned in the main tent and Jones' shadow could be seen against the canvas. A shallow gully ran alongside the campsite about thirty feet away and we had stopped there upon our approach. Holmes advised me to wait and keep an eye out, but not to act until he called for me. He crawled along the ground, approaching the tent from the east. When he arrived there, he lifted the side of the tent slightly and whispered Jones' name. While I couldn't hear the conversation, I saw Jones stand quickly in surprise.

My observation was interrupted by a sound behind me and I turned quickly, aiming my gun at a figure approaching at a crouching trot. Fortunately the moonlight gleamed off the silver buttons upon Truscott's uniform and he dropped to a low stoop. I held a finger to my lips and waved him forward.

He whispered to me when he arrived at my side, "Dr. Watson, what's going on? Who was that who went to the tent?"

Not deigning to take the constable into my full confidence, I merely replied, "We believe there is going to be another attack on the camp tonight. You may be just in time to make an arrest."

"Arrest? How can I arrest a panther, or whatever the Beast is?"

Before answering, I saw a dark shape approaching from the direction of the rear of the tent. I noted Jones had sat back down, but there was no shadow of Holmes to be seen. I motioned for Truscott to be quiet and pointed toward the skulking figure. His eyes widened at the sight of a man, walking in an odd manner, and carrying a club of some sort. As we had arranged, I maneuvered into a position where the tent was between me and the culprit and tossed a pebble against the side of the canvas. Truscott wisely chose to say back and observe.

The person had come around to the tent's entrance, where both flaps were closed against the night air. In a clear voice he called out, "Dr. Logan, It's Bowman. Can you come out? I believe I've made a discovery about your Beast."

Truscott had come up beside me again and started to stand when he saw Bowman raise the mace. I quickly pulled him down again and shushed him, whispering "Holmes has a plan. Don't interfere yet."

We saw the shadow stand and heard Jones' voice call out, "Just a moment, Professor." Jones' shadow went to the table and took up the lantern. While he was still apparently a good eight feet from the entrance, the flaps suddenly exploded outward and Bowman found himself on the receiving end of one of the better rugby tackles I had ever seen. Truscott ran forward and I was on his heels, gun in hand should it prove necessary. Jones came rushing out of the tent as well and added his considerable muscle to subdue the intruder, kicking away the mace to leave him unarmed.

With Bowman flat on his back from having the wind knocked out of him, Holmes, still in his Dr. Shaw guise, stood and pointed his revolver at the prostrate predator and ordered him not to move. Already dazed, hearing Holmes voice from this red-bearded zoologist confused Bowman even further. "What? Holmes? Is that you? What are you doing here?

"Stopping you from committing another murder in your quest to halt this excavation," answered the detective.

Truscott spoke up, "*Another* murder, Mr. Holmes? Are you saying he killed Culpepper?"

"That will be for a jury to decide," answered the detective. "The footprints, which your inspector so carelessly trampled over and ignored, indicated a struggle between Culpepper and someone wearing these unusual boots."

He pointed toward Bowman's footwear, and we could all now see the boots he wore were made up to leave the paw prints of a large feline wherever he walked. The mace was shaped in such a way as to leave the claw marks found in the previous attack on the camp, and would certainly have been deadly on any human being.

"If you will search the inner chambers of Daniel Gumb's cave, Constable, you will find a rock-covered storage trunk with further evidence of the conspiracy to perpetuate this legend of the Beast of Bodmin Moor – although, in this case, a more appropriate moniker would be the Beast of the Hurlers Stones, for that was its only purpose."

The constable scratched his jaw and replied, "I don't understand. You're saying there is a group of people behind this beast, trying to scare off the archaeologists? Why?"

"That would lead us into more speculation than I care to indulge in at this time," answered the detective as he knelt and placed handcuffs upon Bowman. "Once I take him in for questioning," he pointed his pistol more aggressively at his prisoner, "I believe I can confirm one of the hypotheses I have formed."

Truscott looked at Holmes askance, "Here now, Mr. Holmes! What do you mean, *you'll* take him in for questioning? I'm the only one here who can arrest him. He'll have to go back to Bodmin Jail with me. Inspector Teague will have my badge if I let you take him."

Holmes holstered his pistol and looked upon the young man, "I am afraid I cannot let you do that, Mr. Truscott. Whichever of my theories proves correct, I am afraid your Inspector Teague is a member of this conspiracy. It's more likely you will be required to take his badge than he yours."

Holmes handed the young man a telegram which the constable tilted toward the lantern to read. Truscott then tilted his helmet back from his forehead and let out a sigh, "But Teague is the inspector in charge of this District, Mr. Holmes. He'll have every officer on the force to back him up, whether they like him or not. I can't possibly do this by myself."

"You will not have to, Constable. If you follow my instructions."

Chapter IX

Having obtained a larger vehicle, we led Constable Truscott back to the cave house and retrieved the rest of the items stored there. The two hiking staffs were likewise fitted with devices to make the large paw prints, so, together with the boots, Bowman could appear to leave four tracks. The mechanical device was a unique mechanism which could create the sounds of a large cat's yowl.

With this evidence we proceeded south – Holmes driving the wagon, while I stayed in the back with our prisoner. Truscott rode alongside on his own horse. We traveled through the night and the dawn found us at the Royal William Navy Yard at Plymouth, named for Queen Victoria's uncle, King William IV.

At the Devonport Dockyard, we reported to Marine Major Nigel Pennington aboard the *HMS Conqueror*. After turning our prisoner over to be held in the brig, Holmes, Truscott, and I sat in Pennington's office, where he handed an envelope to the detective.

Holmes didn't perform his usual routine of examining the stationery, handwriting, postmark, or any of the other clues he seeks when receiving mail in Baker Street. From my seat next to him, I observed a Royal Seal atop the letterhead of the paper. He read through the single page quickly, then handed it to me, saying, "Please share this with Constable Truscott, Watson."

I read as follows as I leaned over so the constable could also view the document:

Mr. Sherlock Holmes,

> *Your information corroborates reports of which we have been made aware regarding the Bodmin Constabulary and the situation in Bodmin Moor. Due to your many past services on behalf of the Monarchy, for the purpose of your investigation we are granting you special powers in this instance. You will work with Major Pennington and his marines to arrest or detain such person or persons implicated in the crimes being committed in relation to the Hurlers Stone Circle expedition or the Beast of Bodmin Moor. Pennington has received orders to lend the appropriate assistance to you. The use of force is to be avoided unless absolutely necessary to self-defence of yourself or any troops assisting you. The situation in Cornwall is tenuous and military incursion is always suspect by those who favor Cornish independence.*

Any prisoners or detainees are to be transported to London for dispensation. Pennington has his orders regarding the establishment of martial law in the Bodmin District only as a last resort. It is our desire that you and the Major shall find suitable local personnel to take charge of civil order and be able to withdraw with your prisoners in a peaceful fashion.

Upon completion of your mission, you are to report to us at your earliest opportunity.

By Royal decree this 13 October, 1894
H.R.H. Edward Albert
Duke of Cornwall

While Truscott and I were reading this extraordinary document, Holmes was speaking with the Major, outlining a plan which should result in the least amount of casualties or disruption to the civil order.

The next day, the expedition at the Hurlers Stone Circle was proceeding as normal. Truscott and one other constable were on duty per their usual routine, but there were no crowds on that day – just an occasional passerby who would wander out, take a look, and move on. The skies were clear with just a few wisps of clouds and the warming temperature was drying the fields from the previous rainstorm. A large covered wagon had driven out onto the moor and was next to the archaeologists tents.

Logan and his two students were out among the stones in the circle just before noon when Inspector Teague arrived on horseback. He dismounted and tied his bay to a small tree. He marched up to Truscott with a scowl on his face and pointed at the wagon as he demanded, "What the hell is that? What are those damn English up to now?"

Truscott nodded to his superior and said, "That's why I telegraphed you, sir. Come take a look."

He led the way to the back of the wagon. With Teague at his side, he pulled on a rope which lifted the canvas flap up to reveal what was inside.

Teague staggered back, "What is this?"

A voice behind him spoke, "The end of your reign of fear, Inspector."

Teague whipped around, reaching for his pocket, but froze when he found himself facing Sherlock Holmes's pistol, cocked and pointing between his eyes. "Constable Truscott," said Holmes. "Please be so kind as to relieve Mr. Teague of his illegal weapons."

Truscott pulled a small revolver from Teague's pocket and a large knife from his boot. The inspector growled at his man, "Your career is

341

over, Truscott! This English dog can prove nothing, and your name will go down as a traitor to Cornwall!"

Truscott pulled the inspector's hands behind his back and handcuffed him, "It is you who have been exposed as a traitor, Teague. Possibly complicit in murder as well, according to Bowman."

When Teague heard Bowman's name he grew hesitant. In the ensuing silence, Truscott continued, "You are under arrest. Mr. Holmes has been given authority by the Duke of Cornwall to escort you to the Royal Navy Yard at Plymouth where you and Bowman will be transported to London for trial. These marines," he tilted his head toward the back of the wagon where six armed marines sat with rifles and side arms, "will be returning with me to the police station to ensure a new chain of command is peacefully put into place, while we await your replacement from Truro" [5]

Teague and Bowman's transport to London came off without incident. Truscott, with the marines to back him up, was able to organize the Bodmin police force in good order and a suitable replacement was appointed within the week. The investigation and trial of Bowman and Teague revealed a much deeper issue involving not only agitators for Cornish independence, but also a secret Druidic society, of which Bowman was apparently a priest, who were especially upset over what they considered the desecration of sacred grounds by the archaeologists. The joining of these two forces created the idea of resurrecting the legend of the Beast. Teague insisted Bowman said the Beast was only meant to scare people away, and they were both surprised it drew larger crowds than ever.

Teague was adamant the shooting of Culpepper was the result of the man's tripping. However, Holmes's testimony to the dying man's words indicating that Culpepper could testify the Beast was really a man in special boots, and the positioning of the tracks indicated that Bowman, realizing he couldn't outrun the athletic veteran, had lain in wait until he could attack him. During the struggle, he saw his only chance to get away would be to shoot Culpepper so the other pursuers would stop to assist him. When confronted by this, Bowman insisted he only meant to wound, not kill the man.

This explanation broke down when confronted by the fact he planned a murderous attack with the mace upon someone at the camp. Teague insisted he knew none of this. He believed Bowman's account of the Culpepper incident and was unaware of the plan against Logan.

Eventually, Bowman was found guilty of murder and attempted murder. Teague was convicted as an accessory after the fact on Culpepper. Both were sentenced to long prison terms.

The unfortunate aspect of this adventure was in regards to the excavation of the Hurlers Stone Circles. The incident had drawn attention to the fact Druidic practices still existed, and that their ancient sites should be as protected as any sacred site of the Church of England. The fact Royal Marines had been involved in the change of the police authority in Bodmin also didn't sit well with many of the locals. Put together, all this "interference" by Englishmen had roused some of the old feelings of Cornish independence.

To placate the populace, Prince Edward Albert felt a responsibility to act in his capacity as Duke of Cornwall to ensure the peace. He put a temporary halt to Dr. Logan's excavation at the Hurlers Stones Circles [6]. To compensate the archaeologists, he personally sponsored a new expedition in conjunction with the Society of Antiquaries of Scotland to investigate the Ardoch Roman Fort in Perthshire. Dr. Logan would be one of its leaders and Ryan Fogg would be on the team. Henry Jones passed on this opportunity and went off to Princeton University after the New Year. I kept in touch with him over the years. He eventually became a professor at Princeton and had a son, Henry Jones, Jr., born in July 1899. I understand that he has also become a successful archeologist.

With the changes in Dr. Logan's plans, his daughter, Guinevere, and Henry Baskerville chose to schedule their wedding on St. Valentine's Day 1895. I was fortunate enough to be in attendance. Holmes was engaged by one of the Royal Families of Europe at the time, on a case which I am restricted from publishing.

In Cornwall, there were no more sightings of the big cat for quite a while, though as years wore on, the legend continued to rear its head from time to time, and even to this day, the local folk still tell tales of *The Black Beast of Bodmin Moor and the Hurlers Stones.*

NOTES

1. While the use of a silver bullet to destroy supernatural creatures became popular with the *Werewolf* movie of 1941, it was proposed as early as 1812 to kill a witch by The Brothers Grimm in their tale *The Two Brothers.* Silver has been associated with the ability to ward off evil for centuries.
2. *Jock*: Slang for one Scotsman referring to another.
3. *Sassenach*: Slang for a Scotsman referring disparagingly to an Englishman.
4. A man-made cave-house built by the mathematician Daniel Gumb around 1735.
5. Truro is the county town for Cornwall, where all government administrative functions are headquartered.
6. The Hurlers Stones Circles would remain undisturbed until the 1930's. The Ardoch Fort Excavation began in 1896.

The Torso at Highgate Cemetery
by Tim Symonds

Part I – Inspector Lestrade Comes
Hurrying to 221b Baker Street

My notes are dated April 1895. The nation would soon be wilting under a heat wave. It isn't the blistering heat or the fetid smells on the streets outside the lodgings I shared with Sherlock Holmes I remember most. It is the utter horror I was shortly to experience in a London cemetery.

I had sold my medical practice and settled back at 221b Baker Street, a London boulevard of brick houses of great respectability and convenience, being close to rail and omnibus routes. When I could get Holmes to sit down, I had an open notebook ever at the ready, checking details of past cases in hopes of some future publication in *The Strand*. In particular, I wanted to commit to paper the more obscure features of Holmes's epic struggle four years earlier with the late Professor Moriarty, "The Napoleon of Crime", the most dangerous of the many malefactors Holmes had ever encountered.

Moriarty's vast criminal enterprise had been so badly affected by Holmes's "predations" that in 1891 he pursued Holmes and me to the tiny hamlet of Meiringen in the Swiss Alps, where I had reason to believe both had plummeted into the nearby Reichenbach Falls, locked in a violent death-struggle. Unbeknownst to me, Holmes had used his knowledge of *baritsu* to free himself and hurl Moriarty off the cliff edge to his doom. It was almost three years before Holmes felt safe enough to return to these shores and take his chances with the bitter remnants of the evil Professor's gang, not least his former chief-of-staff Colonel Sebastian Moran. The Colonel was the only person who knew Holmes had survived the struggle at the Falls. Where he himself was hiding out was the subject of much conjecture.

Now, nearly four years after Holmes's supposed death, he stood up from the breakfast table and said, "Don't wait up for me tonight, Watson. I shall probably not be back before the witching hour. Your questions have inspired me to make a nostalgic visit to the scene of several of our cases, starting at the barge-building yards of Limehouse and the dark waste of water beyond. Once again I shall breathe in the fumes of the rum, the stink of stale fish, and rub shoulders with firemen and boatswains from Canton, cooks from Hainan Island, stevedores and winchmen, yardmasters and boilersmiths."

On the morrow I found a copy of the halfpenny newspaper *The Echo* on the breakfast table. It contained an article titled *Daring Robbery: Burglars Break into Scotland Yard's Black Museum*. Our landlady Mrs. Hudson came up the stairs, bringing me a fine breakfast of scrambled eggs, toast, kedgeree, kidneys, and broiled kippers, and the familiar well-polished, silver-plated coffee pot. I unrolled the napkin and turned to look through the window. The sun had risen to produce a cyan sky dotted with cotton-like cumulus clouds. Inspired by a gift of Henry Seebohm's *A History of British Birds*, I would take my customary morning stroll to the nearby Regent's Park to observe the antics of our spring visitors, especially the garganey, shoveler, wigeon, and pintail.

I poured myself a cup of coffee and picked up *The Echo*. The article titled *Daring Robbery* continued with:

> *Only now revealed by Inspector Lestrade of Scotland Yard, a fortnight ago one or more area-sneaks made a daring entry into the Black Museum, the home of criminal memorabilia kept at the headquarters of the Metropolitan Police Service. The Police are still assessing which objects have been stolen. The collection includes letters ascribed to Jack the Ripper and a substantial collection of mêlée weapons, some overt, some concealed, including shotguns disguised as umbrellas, and numerous walking-stick swords, all of which have been used in murders or serious assaults in London.*

I was well-acquainted with the Black Museum. The collection had come into existence over twenty years before as an aid to the police in the study of crime and criminals, a teaching collection for police recruits, and only ever accessible by those involved in legal matters, Royals, and other important persons.

At the very end of the article came an unwelcome surprise:

> *Despite a blanket of secrecy on the matter,* The Echo *believes one important display may have been a principal target of the thieves, the powerful air-gun, noiseless and of tremendous power, employed by the assassin Colonel Sebastian Moran in an attempt to kill the famous consulting detective Mr. Sherlock Holmes in revenge for his role in the death of criminal genius Professor James Moriarty at the Reichenbach Falls.*

346

I remembered the extraordinary weapon well. It was an air-gun, yes, but unique, ingeniously adapted to take real bullets. The firearm had been custom-made by Von Herder, a blind German mechanic, to the order of the late Professor Moriarty. More to the point, it brought Moran himself to mind. Outwardly respectable, with an address in Conduit Street, Mayfair, and a member of the Anglo-Indian Club, the Tankerville, and The Bagatelle Card Club, he had acquired an evil reputation in London's underworld which led to his recruitment by Professor Moriarty.

I put the newspaper open at the page on Holmes's chair and turned to an article in *The British Medical Journal* titled *Cholera and The Meccan Pilgrimage*. Outbreaks of the deadly disease were occurring at Kamaran and Djeddah in the Red Sea, and at Mecca itself, blamed on the large number of Mohammedans arriving from Hyderabad. In my time as an Army Assistant Surgeon on the North-West Frontier, I learned no more likely way exists for spreading the deadly bacterium *Vibrio cholerae* to all four corners of the Earth than to have tens of thousands of human-beings setting off for Mecca on the mandatory Haj pilgrimage, sharing make-shift latrines and washing facilities en route.

The clink of horses' hoofs closing in on the pavement came through the open window, followed by the sound of carriage wheels grating heavily against the kerb. I went to the window to observe Scotland Yard Inspector Lestrade leaping from a brougham and striding to our front door. His familiar voice was raised to a high pitch, shouting ahead to our landlady.

I raised the window and called down.

"Inspector, if it's Holmes you want, I'm sorry to disappoint you – either he's still asleep or he didn't return last night from a visit to the Docks."

"No matter, Dr. Watson," Lestrade called up, "it's you I've come for! I must ask you to come down at once and accompany me. A body has been found at Highgate Cemetery. The first thing we'll want is your estimate of how long he's been dead and how he died."

"A body?" I repeated, smiling quizzically. "Is it so surprising, given it's a cemetery?"

He waved a hand around him at the inquisitive gaggle of passers-by already drawing a circle around him.

"I'll tell you more when we're on our way," he replied. "At least what little I know at the moment."

I seized my coat and bowler and went down the stairs two at a time. Lestrade said, "Get in the cab, Doctor, and we shall be on our way."

I informed Mrs. Hudson where I was going. Then, the moment I was settled at his side, Lestrade shouted out, "Constable! Highgate Cemetery,

347

if you will! Right. Now, Doctor," he continued, "I can only tell you what I know. A man walking his dog through the graveyard only an hour ago says he came across the still-bleeding corpse of a man seated upright on a grave. A ghastly sight, he said. He had to restrain his dog from attacking it. Who has done this – and why – is up to us to determine. The local police have ringed the spot off and forbidden anyone to approach the body."

Lestrade had no other information to provide – simply that my presence had been requested. Twenty minutes of pensive silence ensued until my companion leaned out of the window and shouted, "Constable, can't you go any faster!"

Back came the words, "Only if you and the other gentleman get out and walk, sir. The hill that the horses are pulling us up is one of the steepest in the whole of London."

The horses' breath became harsher and excessively rapid. I recalled similar signs of respiratory stress from a fine cavalry horse I saved hard to buy during my time on India's boiling North-West Frontier. In the middle of a small but brutal skirmish against the Pathans, I was unable either to stop to rest him or to throw water over him. The blood supply to the animal's intestines and kidneys shut down. He dropped dead from under me. I threw open the window and shouted to the driver to bring the brougham to an immediate halt. Lestrade and I clambered out.

Part II – Lestrade and I Arrive at Highgate Cemetery

The driver called down, "The entrance is a hundred yards ahead, on your right, sir. You'll be met by Constable Choat. He'll tell you where to go."

The cemetery was a fashionable place to enter the Afterlife. Over the years I had attended burials of a number of my more well-to-do patients. A romantic attitude to death and its presentation led to the creation there of a labyrinth of Egyptian sepulchres, Gothic tombs, and a litany of silent stone angels, safe from the pitting and weathering of cemeteries lower down, brought about by the Capital's acute atmospheric pollution.

Constable Choat was blocking off the path to visitors. He saluted, giving me a nod of recognition. We had first met on a case concerning a bizarre matter that was one of the few cases where Holmes failed to bring the villains to justice.

"You're wanted in the northwestern area, Doctor," Choat advised, "the heavily-overgrown part. A roundabout route via the Circle of Lebanon is the easiest way to get there."

348

We soon came upon the Circle. At its heart was a massive cedar tree which must have long predated the cemetery. It towered over the landscape like a huge bonsai, its base surrounded by a circle of tombs.

On spotting our approach, another policeman emerged from the shadow cast by the Circle. Lestrade introduced me. This time, other than a hasty salute the man paid me no attention. He pointed Lestrade towards a patchwork of toppled gravestones and decaying mausolea.

"Over there, Inspector," he instructed. "Best is if you . . . ."

On saying this, his words came to an abrupt halt. He turned to look at me and then back at Lestrade.

"Inspector," he began, "you said this is Dr. Watson. Do you mean Dr. John H. Watson, the biog – ?"

"The biographer of Sherlock Holmes," I interrupted, smiling.

The smile was not reciprocated. A look of concern passed across the constable's face. He continued to address Lestrade, saying, "Can we speak over here, sir?"

He moved a short distance away, followed by the Scotland Yard Inspector. I watched as the policeman took out a notebook and read from an open page. He spoke in a whisper. Lestrade's face turned ashen. He turned towards me, looking grim.

"Dr. Watson," he began, "there's something the constable has just told me. It's about the corpse we've come to inspect."

"What about it?" I asked.

"I wonder if the constable gives you a description, you might recognise the dead soul."

The constable looked down at the notebook.

"Age about forty, with an angular face – " he commenced.

"That could refer to any of fifty of my patients, Constable." I replied.

" – with a thin hawk-like nose and pointed chin."

"Now, gentlemen, we're down to about twenty-five," I responded, nodding. "Lips?"

"Thin."

"Hairline?"

"Receding."

An icy hand began to clutch at my heart.

"Colour of eyes?"

"Grey."

"My God!" I cried. "Lestrade, those features seem to be narrowing down to Holmes! Given your grim expression, I fear you agree?"

"I do, Doctor," Lestrade responded. "Especially when the constable tells me the remains are clad in the particular sort of coat Mr. Holmes likes to wear. I can see no alternative but to believe he has been murdered."

The wild and disused northwestern part of the cemetery was full of mature trees, shrubbery, and wildflowers, providing a haven for birds and small animals. Without further word, rather than follow the length of the path, the constable forced a way for us through the undergrowth. With whispered apologies we stumbled over the mounds of long-abandoned graves until at last we came to our destination. It revealed the most terrible sight imaginable. Next to me, Lestrade turned swiftly to the side and was violently sick.

Perched on a grave was the upper body of a man placed as though standing, except the head and torso had been severed from the legs at the waist. As though anticipating we would push our way through the thicket, the piercing grey eyes were turned towards us. The torso was buttoned into a Prince Albert, a double-breasted frock coat with a flat velvet collar which Holmes would wear on formal occasions. It was a grisly touch. The coat's skirt extended down only to where the knees would have been, had the legs been left attached. Pinned to a lapel was a Chevalier degree of the *Légion d'Honneur* like the one awarded to Holmes by the President of France for his part in the arrest of Huret, the Boulevard Assassin. I couldn't bear to look at my old friend, imagining the agony of losing his legs to saw or axe. In my fevered brain I half expected to hear the familiar stirring words, "Watson – the game's afoot!" – sending us clattering off across Tower Bridge in yet another hansom cab to new adventures.

I switched my gaze to the incisions on the polished black granite headstone, plain to see in the bright spring sun. The numerals and lettering were divided into four freshly-cut clusters – a top row over three columns. The row read *District of Birth Yorkshire*. The left column read *Born – 6 January, 1854. Assassin. Died – Meiringen May 4 in the 58ᵗʰ Year Of The Reign Of Victoria Regina Imperatrix*. The right-hand column read *Place of Birth – Unknown*. The name of the individual being memorialised was displayed in larger lettering on the middle column. Strikingly, the surname *HOLMES* came first, and below it *SHERLOCK*.

My immediate thought was a mistake had been made over the date of death. Clearly Holmes was already dead, yet the date on the stone still had over three weeks to run. My attention turned to a bullet entry through the cadaver's left temple. There was something remarkably indicative about it, the placement above the ear, the precise shape of a soft-nosed bullet entering the skull at a slight upward angle. I began to move forward for a more forensic examination when a voice from behind me said, "Well, Watson, what do you make of it?"

Lestrade and I turned as one. Before us, with only his torso and head visible in the thicket, dressed in a Prince Albert coat exactly like the Holmes on the slab, stood Holmes himself.

Smiling at our incredulity, he pushed out into the open.

"Don't worry, gentlemen," he assured us, chuckling at our expressions, "the real Holmes stands before you, fully bipedal. Mrs. Hudson told me where to find you."

He pointed at the grave.

"Did you know Ancient Egyptians believed wax images retained the personality of the dead?"

I turned swiftly to the inspector at my side.

"Lestrade," I exclaimed, "tell us precisely what was stolen from the Black Museum. You gave no account to the newspapers."

"I can, yes," Lestrade said, as relieved as I at the sight of my comrade-in-arms. "There are some hundreds of objects on display, many valuable, but the picklocks selected only two – the air-gun ingeniously adapted by the blind German mechanic to fire soft-nosed bullets which Colonel Sebastian Moran employed that time in trying to kill Mr. Holmes . . . ."

". . . and clearly the second, gentlemen," Holmes broke in, "was the bust of me which sits upright upon its torso on the grave before us, my alter ego which Moran shot through the head with the air-gun. As you'll recall, Watson, we gifted both the weapon and the bust to the Black Museum after Moran's arrest."

Lestrade nodded.

"Yes, Doctor, just those two objects were taken. This dummy and the Von Herder air-gun. They must have been stolen to order, just like Gainsborough's oil of the Duchess of Devonshire nearly twenty years ago and not yet recovered."

"Just the dummy and the weapon?" I repeated. I looked across at Lestrade. "Do you have any suspects?"

"Not a one."

"What does this all mean?" I asked no one in particular. "What are we being told?"

"Do you think there's a clue over here, Watson?" I heard Holmes asking in a wry tone. He had moved across to a parallel grave only a few feet away. In the same beautifully formed inscriptions, the headstone spelt out the following: On the top row, *West Cork, Ireland*. On the left column, *Died 4 May, 1891, in the 54th Year Of The Reign Of Victoria Regina Imperatrix*. On the right column, *Eyeries*, presumably the precise village of the deceased's birth. On the middle column, again in larger lettering than the columns to either side, it read *MORIARTY* with directly below it *JAMES*.

I knew Eyeries from childhood visits to Ireland, the last village at the end of the beautiful Beara Peninsula.

Was this grave truly the final resting-place of Holmes's arch-enemy, a man Holmes had once described as the spider at the centre of a criminal web with a thousand threads? It would explain why the Swiss authorities had never pulled his body from the creaming, boiling pit of incalculable depth. Accompanied by the remaining members of Moriarty's gang, Moran could have waited for the body to reappear, even dug a make-shift resting place for it in the sustaining cold of a nearby glacier. The date of death was right. He was thrown into the raging Falls on that day and month four years ago. The day and month inscribed for Holmes's death on the neighbouring headstone would be the exact anniversary in three weeks' time.

By no means was it good news. The evil Moriarty's equally malevolent former Chief-of-Staff could be on the hunt in the herbage around us right now, obsessively seeking revenge on Holmes for the death of the Professor – for what else could all this mean? Even famous hunters like Colonel Julius Barras, devoted to the *shikar* in India and the Nepalese *terai*, acknowledged Moran as the finest Big Game shot in the Far East. These years later, Moran's "bag of tigers" was still the record in India. No single British hunter had taken more. Nor was he supreme as a Big Game shot only in the Orient. He had gone on safari in East Africa, leaving the camp one morning with a black powder breech-loading .461 No 1 Gibbs

Metford Farquharson single shot rifle and just five cartridges. He returned to Meru Township with the eight-foot tusks of a bull elephant, the horns of a rhinoceros, the skins of a leopard and a large male lion, and the massive dense horns of a Cape Buffalo, an animal so dangerous to hunters it was known as "black death".

I looked back at the grisly bust with the realistic crimson patch below the torso. To entrap Moran, Holmes had placed a startlingly lifelike wax dummy by a window at Baker Street, luring the would-be assassin into firing a bullet through its head in the misbelief it was my flesh-and-blood comrade. We had lain in wait in an empty house opposite our lodgings and grabbed Moran the moment he fired. He put up a fight but we subdued him. My notes recorded:

> His eyes had fixed upon Holmes's face with an expression in which hatred and amazement were equally blended. "
>
> "You fiend!" he kept on muttering. "You clever, clever fiend!"
>
> "Ah, Colonel!" said Holmes cheerfully, arranging his rumpled collar, "journeys end in lovers' meetings', as the old play says. I don't think I have had the pleasure of seeing you since you favoured me with those attentions as I lay on the ledge above the Reichenbach Falls."

The remarkable air-gun secured, Moran was carted off to a holding cell near Marble Arch, ready for a first hearing before Magistrate Plowden the next morning. The case would have moved on to the Central Criminal Court with Moran quickly found guilty of numerous murders. With his bad character, there would be no successful appeal for commutation – not only would the Home Secretary have been opposed it, but Queen Victoria herself would have stood in the way. Considered cruel to prolong the wait, he would have been executed within the fortnight.

This quickly became notional. To Lestrade's deep embarrassment, a faked-up mêlée by remnants of Moriarty's gang at the Magistrates Court enabled Moran to escape even before the hearing could take place. The Yard's East End informants tracked him to the docks, by which time he had slipped unnoticed aboard one of any of thirty ships with steam up, all about to leave for far-flung foreign parts.

At the cemetery Holmes broke the brooding silence.

"Does anyone note some oddities about the graves?" he asked. "For example, the headstones?"

"What about them?" I responded.

He pointed towards a nearby cluster of overgrown graves.

"Observe the ones over there. Which direction do they face?"

"Why, east of course, Holmes," I replied, smiling at his apparent lack of knowledge of such matters. "When the Christians' Day of Resurrection comes, the person buried there returns to life and sits bolt upright, directly facing the risen Redeemer coming from the east, as expected."

"And these two headstones? Which direction are they facing?"

"That *is* odd," I replied, staring at them. "They face south."

"Why so, do you suppose? Both Moriarty and I were born in Christian countries. This is a Christian burial-ground, not Buddhist or Muslim. There's sufficient space around them for the graves to be dug following the custom of facing east."

"They must have been dug in haste," I suggested, "and in the dark, not realising the direction the headstones should face to match the others."

"Perhaps," Holmes murmured dubiously. "And yet why the lack of an epitaph on the headstones? '*In Loving Memory of*' or '*Devoted Father of* . . . .' Look at the other stones over there. They include fine verses – '*Time Passes, Love Remains*' – and that one, Shakespeare's '*To unpathed waters, undreamed shores*'. Mine does not. Moriarty's does not. The Professor was endowed with a phenomenal mathematical faculty. At the age of twenty-one he wrote a treatise upon the Binomial Theorem which had a European vogue, on the strength of which he won the Mathematical Chair at one of our smaller universities – Marischal College, I believe, where he had studied under James Clerk Maxwell. Why not record such an exceptional gift?"

"I'm afraid I make nothing out of any of this," I replied, adding, "However, the calligraphic-style carving is wonderful!"

"Indeed it is," Holmes returned. "Each letter is quite beautifully formed."

He turned to the silent but watchful Lestrade.

"Inspector, presumably you made every effort to discover who broke into the Black Museum that night. Did you come across anything unusual?"

"Every effort *was* made, Mr. Holmes, I can assure you," Lestrade replied earnestly. "Not a stone left unturned. Alas, we came up with nothing. Not even how the raiders got away. They disappeared into thin air."

The inspector paused.

"There *was* one curious matter, a sighting by a passer-by in the early hours of the morning. A rickshaw was standing by some stables in an unlit side-street nearby. Rickshaws and pedicabs can legally ply-for-hire on any

354

street, though while they may be a common form of transport with the Chinamen in Poplar, you don't often see 'em along our stretch of the Thames."

Holmes turned back quickly to me. With Lestrade's words, an urgency had suddenly appeared in his demeanour.

"We are in great danger," he informed us. "Until we identify the source, I shall go nowhere without my .450 short-barrelled Webley. Equally, Watson, you must go nowhere without a revolver in a pocket, cocked and ready."

"In great danger!" I parroted incredulously. "From what? A break-in at the Black Museum? A rickshaw standing in the shadows? So what if the graves face south? If you're implying our great enemy Colonel Moran is at the heart of this, surely we've heard the last of him? The newspapers agreed to keep his escape quiet, but Lestrade here kept us abreast of Moran's movements. Sightings came in over the next few months – admittedly wrong in the case of Sark, but more surely at a Continental port, then Leipzig, then after a gap of several weeks a Scottish archaeologist reported meeting him aboard a shallow-draft steamer on the River Irtish. By now he must be two- or three-thousand miles from here. All we know is at Imeni Bakhty in Kazakhstan, the trail went cold. I hazard such a circuitous route must mean he has returned to his old haunts in the Punjab while deliberately trying to mislead anyone determined to follow him to his destination."

Holmes looked back and forth at the two graves.

"I'm as baffled as you are," he responded. "As you say, Moran himself cannot be the immediate danger to us right now, but in terrible danger we are."

He paused for a moment. "If Moran isn't hiding in these thickets with Von Herder's gun, nothing makes sense. The break-in at the Black Museum, the headstone for Professor Moriarty, the clear threat to my life 'in the 58th Year of Her Majesty's reign' – all point to the one man."

He put his two forefingers between his teeth and whistled shrilly, a signal which was answered by a similar whistle from a waiting horse trap. Without offering any further development of his thinking, Holmes set off apace towards the great cedar tree and the exit beyond. Lestrade and I followed in his wake, like dinghies bobbing in the wash of a great ocean liner.

Sotto voce, Lestrade asked me, "Doctor, exactly when *is* the Queen-Empress's fifty-eighty year?"

"We're in it right now," I murmured back. "The would-be assassin must strike very soon if the gravestone is to be an augury."

Part III – We Encounter Mr. Tsang

I was in my chair in the sitting room the next morning when Holmes came bounding up the stairs. He was clad in clothing bought from an old clothes shop in Stepney for his more inconspicuous visits to "Darkest London". It was from there he was returning, in the frayed jacket with one remaining button, the well-worn but stout trousers, and the pair of brogans which had plainly seen service where coal was shovelled. On his head was a very dirty cloth cap which he threw expertly onto the hat-stand. He was positively wriggling with excitement.

"Success!" he cried out. "Watson, we find ourselves in the midst of a very remarkable inquiry. The chappie we're looking for is Mr. Tsang Wing Ma. Tsang is the family name. He's a community scribe of high standing, famed for his exceptional skill in the centuries-old practice of Chinese calligraphy. We must pay him a visit at Toynbee Hall, unannounced.

"I spent the night," he continued, "in Ah Sing's on Upper Swandam Lane. That opium den is the vilest murder-trap on the whole riverside, but as a source of information it's nonpareil. Once inside the building, I had to tread carefully. An electric bell under the floor acts as a warning system, and progress through the house is obstructed by a set of stout oak panels, ropes and pulleys, levers, and a trapdoor at the top of the stairs. Even then, the opium-smoking room has to be accessed by clambering out on to a sloping roof and climbing back into the property through a skylight. We should be rich men if we had a thousand pounds for every poor devil who's been done to death in that sordid, squalid place. Had I been recognised at any stage of my passage through the house, my life wouldn't have been worth an hour's purchase."

I waited expectantly as he threw himself into his chair, warming his hands in front of the coal fire.

"I suppose," he continued, smiling, "you imagine I've added opium-smoking to my seven-per-cent solutions of cocaine and all the other little weaknesses on which you favour me with your medical views."

"More to the point, Holmes, why a Chinese scribe?" I asked. "What's that to do with the headstones? Why should Chinese calligraphy be of any concern to us?"

I pointed at the calendar over the mantel.

"Must I remind you" I continued, "that you may only have twenty-one days to live?"

"It has very little to do with Chinese calligraphy *per se*," came the cryptic answer, "though a very great deal to do with the inscriptions on the two headstones."

356

Holmes reached into the frayed jacket and pulled out a slim volume.

"Last night I took the chance to visit several bookshops in Limehouse and Poplar. This is a book on Chinese gravestones, especially those from the region north of the Yangtze and south of the River Huai. The Chinese community in London likes to keep to their ancient traditions surrounding death, you see."

"Holmes!" I burst out, snorting with laughter. "Why on Earth would you want to learn about – " At which Holmes passed the book to me.

"Page eight, please," he ordered. "Note the pictures of gravestones. Does anything about them strike you as interesting?"

I studied each of several pictures and looked up.

"I'm sorry. All I can see are headstones covered with Chinese characters. What connection could there possibly be between the nature of headstones found between the Yangtze and the – (I looked back at the page.) – Huai, and the headstones at the cemetery?"

In a decidedly mocking tone, Holmes replied, "Gentlemen of the jury, yet again we have an example of my amanuensis *seeing* but proving he is not *observing*! Watson, look at the *pattern* of the logograms on the Chinese headstones. Both you and our Scotland Yard friend Lestrade failed to notice that while the wording on the two headstones at Highgate Cemetery was in English – like all the other gravestones – the lay-out on Moriarty's and mine was classical Chinese. The row across the top, the three columns under it, the middle column in larger characters. Even the family name first, the given name beneath. As to why Mr. Tsang: He is a Chinese scribe, and you yourself admired the sheer beauty of the lettering. The stones must have been inscribed by a mason under the tutelage of a scribe of the highest reputation. Then when Lestrade told us about the rickshaw waiting in the dark near the Black Museum – "

Holmes got to his feet.

"I admit this is one of the most mystifying cases in which we have ever become entangled. Unless we can forestall violent forces set against us, it's a case which may truly end with my death on the fourth of May. In fact, I urge you to compose an authentic epitaph for me, just in case – perhaps including some reference to my life's work."

"How about something like '*Universally Considered the Most Famous Consulting Detective of His Day*'? I asked impishly, testing the extent of his modesty.

He looked back from the door to his quarters. "Yes, that might do. Have it inscribed over the Shakespearean elegy we saw at the Cemetery – '*To unpathed waters, undreamed shores*'. I tell you, Watson, while your *métier* is action and not thought, your questioning has caused a most unexpected idea to form in my mind, a scenario which includes the elusive

Moran, but partnered by a malignance far in excess of our usual East End river pirates and scuffle-hunters. Truly my life may depend on what we can learn from Mr. Tsang."

As he left the room he called back, "I don't wish to be interrupted. To work this out I shall need five pillows and at least an ounce of shag."

Over the next several days our minds were occupied in a case I was eventually to publish under the title "The Solitary Cyclist". Holmes brought the matter to a satisfactory conclusion and we were able to return to the threat to his life, as so clearly carved into the headstone at Highgate Cemetery. Thus we found ourselves rattling towards the East End, squeezed together in a hansom, a Webley Mark-IV Top-Breaker six-shot revolver in .476 calibre in my inner pocket. Holmes was looking pensive. As always, he was continuing his infuriating penchant of springing surprises rather than taking me into his confidence.

With an impressive "Whoa!" the cabbie brought us to a halt outside Toynbee Hall. The building's resemblance to a manorial residence in Elizabethan style stood out in a neighbourhood full of cramped slum housing. Once inside, Holmes asked where we could locate the eminent Chinese community scribe Tsang Wing Ma. He was, we were informed, to be found in the drawing room, an elaborate chamber decorated with eastern rugs and Oriental-style wall hangings. Mr. Tsang stood up and bowed as we entered. He was formally attired in a one-piece dress worn by scholar-officials as far back as the Song Dynasty. On noting my interest, he explained the four panels of fabric making up the upper part represented the four seasons, the lower twelve panels the number of months in the year. He gave a sweep of his arm, inviting us to a black lacquer mother-of-pearl sofa.

"How may I help you, gentlemen?" he asked.

"We are here to consult you in your professional capacity," Holmes began portentously. "My friend here is an eminent doctor. Among his patients is an Englishman who is dying, a man of standing who made his considerable fortune in the Orient – in China. The poor fellow has no living relatives. He has little time left. He has begged us to order his headstone. He wants the inscriptions to be laid out in the Chinese style, the top row over three columns and so on. Hence our presence here."

Holmes paused, his hands held forward in a disarming manner.

"Is that something you are able to design – your work fully remunerated of course?"

"That is part of my service to the Chinese community," the Chinaman responded. "Tell me, do you want the inscriptions drafted in traditional Chinese – Cantonese or Mandarin perhaps?"

Holmes's hands rose.

"No," he said solemnly, "our dying friend merely wishes the *format* to remind people of his years in China. The wording itself he wants in English."

I had been looking back and forth between my companion and the man before us, nodding in agreement as Holmes laid out the cock-and-bull story. My eyes were on the scribe at the moment Holmes ended his explanation. Had the Chinaman's eyes narrowed suddenly? Had his earlier relaxed posture stiffened? He had been attentive in a friendly way until Holmes explained "our dying friend" wanted the lettering laid out in the Chinese style but "the wording itself he wants in English". Certainly the scribe's eyes were now locked unwaveringly on Holmes's. The brush dropped from his fingers. He got quickly to his feet and sped across to the window. He gave a quick glance into the open roadway.

He turned back to face us.

"Gentlemen," he said, "I am sorry I cannot be of help. If I understand truly why you are here, I must ask you to leave at once, please – never to return."

Without further ado, he crossed swiftly to the door and left the chamber.

Holmes said, "As you saw, Watson, my suspicions are correct. He fled fearing for his life."

The fourth was fast approaching. As far as I could see, Holmes was making no further advances in the case of the two headstones. Then, on a morning Mrs. Hudson brought a tray with another fine breakfast – ham and eggs, followed by curried mutton and her family heirloom, the magnificent silver-plated coffee pot – Holmes again disappeared. I was taking the meal alone. The dishes were accompanied by a further copy of *The Echo*. A small piece on a back page announced: *From our Woolwich Correspondent: Chinaman Found Drowned. Possible Suicide.* I put down my knife and fork.

> *In the early hours of this morning, the corpse of a Chinaman was dragged from the Thames at Woolwich by the ferryboat* Hutton, *a side-loading paddle-steamer. Identification will be difficult as it is not known where the man entered the water. The tidal flow may have brought him down-river from the St. Katherine Docks or Limehouse Wharf area. The deceased was dressed in a "shenyi", a traditional if outmoded Chinese men's outfit made from bleached linen. Both wrists had been slashed, severing the tendons, though death appears to have been from drowning, weighed down by his garment, rather than exsanguination. No investigation into the tragedy will take place. The river police at Wapping have taken it to be a clear case of suicide.*

I put the newspaper down. I felt that this was almost certainly Tsang, and it was too much of a coincidence for his death to have been anything but an outcome of our visit. Why had we so heedlessly barged in on the scribe, and in broad daylight? What foul agency had sliced through the *flexor carpi* of both wrists, rendering useless a heaven-sent prowess without which the scribe's *raison d'être* was destroyed? As Assistant Surgeon at the terrible battle of Maiwand in 1880, I had seen the effect of a sword slash across a wrist raised defensively. The hand becomes functionally inoperable. Did the fiends slash the tendons and leave it to Tsang himself to decide he could no longer face life, unable ever again to perform the brushstrokes for his beautiful logograms? Was his drowning a suicide – or *murder*?

I was deep in meditation over the now ever-more credible threat to Holmes's life when I heard Mrs. Hudson calling up the stairway. With the

360

passing years, she was less inclined to take on the steps except to bring us our meals. I opened the door to the landing and called down, "Yes, I'm still here. If you're bringing up today's post, may I ask for a further pot of your excellent Java coffee, please?"

Ten minutes later, she came through the door with the coffee and a letter on a salver. It was addressed to me. Even before I looked at the signature, I knew from the Xuan paper and the several sublime logograms in lampblack ink it was from Mr. Tsang.

Dear Dr. Watson, [he began]

> *As I feared, the secret society was keeping watch over my visitors to Toynbee Hall. They recognised you and Mr. Holmes. Therefore this will be the last letter I shall be able to write. I have only a short time left before outriders of the Green Gang (青幫) will come for me. To themselves, they are known as* "Friends Of The Way of Tranquillity and Purity" *(or 安清道友) but violence is their major trait. Their rituals include ancestral worship, astral worship, Taoism, Buddhism, and Confucianism. Their common aim is to avenge the Five Ancestors by bringing about the overthrow of the Qing Dynasty and the restoration of the Ming.*
>
> *They assumed I invited you to meet to reveal that the plot written into the headstones which – I assume you have already calculated – involves Professor Moriarty's former Chief of Staff, Colonel Moran. I have now been informed of the fate awaiting me, the same punishment they threatened if I refused to design the headstones. They will sever the wrist-joint tendons with a cutlass so I can never move a brush across the paper ever again. Second, they will lock me standing in an iron cage known as a water dungeon, to be lowered into a tank until the water level reaches my neck. Very quickly I shall become cold. Unable to sit or sleep, I shall become unconscious and drown.*
>
> *However, it can be said that before a man embarks on a journey of revenge, he should dig two graves, in this case the one for me but the other for the Green Gang. Hence this letter to you.*
>
> *The westerly of the two gravestones speaks for itself. It is an affirmation Professor Moriarty who died at the Reichenbach Falls (i.e. at the hands of Mr. Sherlock Holmes) on that date – nothing more, though it implies retribution is*

required. The easterly stone reveals much more. By being placed next to the Professor's grave, it threatens Mr. Holmes with revenge – namely a similar fate for toppling Professor Moriarty to his death, which in Chinese we depict as:

报应，天谴；应得的惩罚；不可避免的失败

This is "a cause of punishment or defeat that is deserved and cannot be avoided", *to be effected on the anniversary of the same day and month that Professor Moriarty died.*
I now come to how the plot to kill Mr. Holmes will play out through an agreement between the Green Gang and Colonel Moran. By now, the Colonel will be –

Suddenly the clear writing turned into scribble:

They are here. Three rickshaws have arrived together. My life is about to return to the Yellow Springs.

寿比南山 *(May you live as long as Southern mountain).*

Tsang Wing Ma

I went across to the window and looked down at the rows of cabs. The letter confirmed a murderous secret society was involved, one reported to rely on magical charms to ward off bullets. As wretched bad luck would have it, just five more minutes and Tsang would have given us the details of the plot.

Again and again I went over our encounter with the scribe and the way it had ended so abruptly. The death could only have been our fault, Holmes's and mine. As we had departed that day, I looked back and saw him, watching us. Again and again the expression on his face came back to me as he stood looking at us from a window. If ever a man wore an expression of abject resignation, it was Tsang's at that moment. Surely we should have foretold he had been pressed by a merciless element into devising the headstones. There would therefore be consequences in our visit. It wasn't long after Holmes began offering a cock-and-bull reason for our being there that Tsang himself realised it was Holmes settled on the sofa couch, with me at his side. By then for Tsang it was too late.

Holmes returned early that evening. First I showed him the cutting from *The Echo*. He read it carefully. Then I handed him Tsang's letter, saying "It is you and I who dug his grave." He read the letter and looked up with an expression of excitement, waving it in the air.

"They made a blunder of the first water!" he exclaimed. "The realisation they would murder him provoked Tsang's letter to us. They may have dug a grave for him, but he has dug a second grave – for them!"

Confounded, I asked, "How has he done that? He was interrupted right when he was going to reveal the plot against you. The letter tells us nothing. Worse, he wasted precious minutes writing about an oath the Gang imposed on initiates, the one swearing to avenge the Five Ancestors and bring about the overthrow of the Qing Dynasty and the restoration of the Ming. What has that to do with anything?"

"You say Tsang wasted precious minutes," Holmes replied. "I say he did not. That oath is the very clue we needed to solve the puzzle – it answers the question as to how can I be murdered on the fourth if Moran is thousands of miles away."

He led me quickly to the terrestrial globe next to the grandfather clock.

"Show me, Watson, where Moran was last spotted before the trail went cold."

I spun the globe to the vast stretches of Central Asia.

"Here," I said. "Imeni Bakhty in Kazakhstan."

I ran my finger down the globe.

"Probably pretending to be an archaeologist," I resumed, "he will have turned south and taken this route, through Bishkek and Dyushambe, and onward to his old stamping-grounds in The Punjab."

"He may have assumed the profession of archaeology," Holmes replied, "but it wasn't south to The Punjab he is going."

Nonplussed, I asked, "Then where? Are you suggesting he turned around completely and will soon be back among us?"

"I am not," Holmes replied.

His finger replaced mine on the globe.

"This way. This is the way he's going."

His bony finger ran directly eastward.

"By now he'll have reached Sinkiang," he added.

"Sinkiang!" I echoed. "But that's in China!"

"My old friend,' Holmes replied, smiling at my puzzlement, "remember what Tsang has just told us of the 'Friends of the Way of Tranquillity and Purity'? To overthrow the ruling Qing Dynasty, sometimes called the Manchu Dynasty, and the reinstatement of the Ming regime. The secret books of the Green Gang would reveal they continue

363

with that goal unabated by time. Moran's destination isn't The Punjab. It's the Forbidden City."

"The Forbidden City!" I cried. "So what exactly *is* Moran's part? Why is he in China? He can hardly kill you from there!"

"He can, through an ineffably cunning *quid pro quo*," Holmes replied. "Nothing less than a plot for Moran to assassinate the Manchu Dowager Empress Cixi herself, sparking a Han uprising against the Qing and a restoration of the Ming. The moment news comes that he has succeeded in murdering her, the Green Gang will kidnap me, transport me back to Meiringen and the Reichenbach Falls in time for the fourth of May. Moran will have drawn them a map. Four years ago, from high in the cliffs above, he observed the struggle. At the exact hour I pitched Moriarty into the roiling waters, they'll hurl me from the same ledge into the depths, fulfilling the fate ascribed to me on my headstone at Highgate Cemetery."

Part IV – We Meet the Foreign Secretary

After a restless night, I awoke to the sound of voices from our sitting room on the floor below. I dressed and hurried down. Holmes was in his customary chair at the fireside. He was talking to Inspector Lestrade and a well-dressed man of middle age. The latter's face was familiar.

"Watson," Holmes said, "Lestrade you know well. You may recognise our other guest. He is John Wodehouse, 1st Earl of Kimberley."

"I do recognise him," I replied, stepping forward to shake hands. "England's Secretary of State for Foreign Affairs."

"At least for a few more weeks, Dr. Watson," the Earl replied. "After June, I shall be out of office."

"June is long enough," Holmes intervened. He waved a hand at Mrs. Hudson's silver-plated coffee pot, placed precariously over a spirit-lamp on the chemical bench. "Help yourself, Watson, and bring a chair and join us. We've finished discussing the weather and are now deciding what to do about Moran's imminent arrival in Peking. As Foreign Secretary, the Earl has his own hand of cards to play."

"Mr. Holmes is right," the Foreign Secretary agreed. "There's a very considerable wish among Her Britannic Majesty's Cabinet to rebuild the promising relations we had with the Empress Dowager Cixi some years ago when she appeared open to diplomatic incursions, until her attitude towards foreigners changed. Last year, China was heavily defeated in the war with Japan. China's entire fleet of battleships was wiped out, and Cixi humiliated. She needs powerful friends. We believe the present time is opportune. Our trade, such as it remains, is concentrated at the treaty ports. Interior China is still *terra incognita* to our traders. By no means does the

British Government wish for a return of the Ming. Colonel Moran could be a very timely pawn. We could start the process of ingratiation by warning Cixi of Colonel Moran's advance on the Forbidden City and the likely weapon he'll be carrying."

The Foreign Secretary gave a shudder.

"Heaven knows what they'll do to him. They may drive sharp bamboo sticks underneath the fingernails with a hammer. While they start off with one finger at the least, sometimes all fingers are "treated". He would never be able to pull a trigger again. They might then pass him to the *Daozi jiang*, the knifer responsible for castrations. I'm told the local anaesthetic they use is hot chilli sauce. Or he might suffer the appalling death they call *Lingchi*, 'Death by a Thousand Cuts'. Fortunately we don't need to be told."

An hour later a decision was reached: I myself would supply a physical description of our old enemy to be collected the same evening by special envoy and sent to the Dowager Empress via "our man" in Peking. The *entente* included an unusual but firm stipulation made by Holmes over Moran's fate, to which the Earl agreed. We toasted Her Imperial Majesty, England's Great Queen, with a cobwebby Margaux 1890 retrieved by Mrs. Hudson from the cellar.

I looked back at a description I made a year earlier when we captured Moran and his remarkable air-gun. "*It was a tremendously virile and yet sinister face which was turned towards us . . . one could not look upon his cruel blue eyes, with their drooping, cynical lids, or upon the fierce, aggressive nose and the threatening, deep-lined brow, without reading Nature's plainest danger-signals.*"

I would accompany the description with a sketch of the air-gun.

The following day Holmes volunteered to accompany me on my after-lunch walk to the Regent's Park to observe the heron which had recently taken up residence on the lake. We settled ourselves on a favourite bench.

"Holmes," I began, "before we go any further in our conversation, I want an explanation from you. At yesterday's discussion with the Earl of Kimberley, you called for a particular proviso: That Her Majesty's government should insist on a promise from the Empress Dowager *not* to execute Moran, but instead imprison him under close guard and only for a period of ten years. The Foreign Secretary went along with that. I ask, why not simply have done with it – have Moran executed. The Green Gang will not pursue you if Moran fails to live up to his side of the *quid pro quo*, but he might escape and try again, no matter how he's locked up and no matter how many eunuchs are assigned to guard him. Your life would again be at terrible risk. Call in on the Earl tomorrow. Say that on reflection you've changed your mind, that given you yourself once called Moran the second-most dangerous person in London, after Moriarty, you would have no qualms if he's executed within days of being captured. It doesn't have to be *Lingchi* – it could be a simple beheading. Surely that would be best for the world?"

"My comrade-in-arms," came the reply, "my life as a consulting detective has become singularly uninteresting since Moriarty's abrupt departure. Ten years from now I may be on the point of retiring to write my magnum opus, *The Whole Art Of Detection*. Already I have in mind a bee-farm on the Sussex Downs. And then Moran returns. I have no doubt he will have spent his time in the Forbidden City hatching a most diabolical plot to avenge his master. Think what a fresh great game would be afoot!"

"Then I hope you'll invite me to join in!" I exclaimed.

"My old friend," came the welcome reply, "you have my word

NOTE

Colonel Sebastian Moran does eventually return to England to seek revenge on Holmes in another of Tim Symonds's short stories titled "A Most Diabolical Plot", found in *The MX Book of New Sherlock Holmes Stories – Part III: 1896-1929*.

ACKNOWLEDGEMENTS

- Professor Judith Rowbotham, for her extraordinary knowledge of Ancient China, in addition to her specialism in Victorian crime and punishment.
- Dr. Ian Dungavell, Friends of Highgate Cemetery Trust.
- Paul Bickley, Curator, Crime Museum (formerly Black Museum), New Scotland Yard.
- Research material:
    o *The Evolution of The Luo Teaching And The Formation Of The Green Gang*. Abstract by Ma Xisha.
    o *East End Chronicles*, by Ed Glinnert. Allen Lane.

The Adventure of the
Highgate Flowers
by Tracy J. Revels

It was a dour, damp afternoon in early May, and I felt myself encumbered by the sense of an unfinished obligation. An old acquaintance from my university days, Doctor Fulton Winston, had been killed in a carriage accident and buried in Highgate Cemetery a month before. I could claim no special intimacy or ties of friendship with Winston, but he had kept abreast of my literary as well as my medical career and had, from time to time, sent me notes of congratulations and expressed a keen interest in the adventures that I shared with Sherlock Holmes. I had been shocked to learn of his passing, which had occurred while I was away from London on a case with Holmes. I missed Winston's funeral, and though I had written the expected condolences to his widow, I was nagged by the feeling that I had not honored a good man as he deserved. Holmes – whose patience for any outward expression of mourning was limited – was busily engaged in some chemical research. I donned my hat and coat and was putting my hand to the doorknob, engaged in drawing the breath to inform him of my intentions, when his voice rose sharply from behind his philosophical instruments.

"For what it is worth, Watson, you may give the late Dr. Winston my regards as well. It is always gratifying to know that one has admirers, and rather disheartening to learn that they have passed on."

I would be prepared to swear that I had given no indications of my plans for the day, nor spoken a word of Winston's demise. Muttering yet again that Holmes would have been burned alive had he lived in an earlier century, I departed.

A short time later, having paused only long enough to purchase a spray of lilies, I found myself navigating the great avenues of the dead at Highgate Cemetery. It was truly a Valhalla of the age, filled with majestic markers, stone testimonies to lives of heroism, service, and piety. A sexton directed me to my friend's grave, which had just been marked with a small marble column topped with an urn. The ground was still overturned, black rather than green, and bore the sad remnants of a few faded flowers. I cleared these away and left my offering in their place. Winston had been my own age, and there is something about the death of a contemporary that perhaps causes one to pause and reflect at greater length. Many memories rose from that reverie, not only of Winston, but of other friends, relatives, and one most dear who awaited me in some better land. It was difficult to think of them, yet as I did something of the weight that had oppressed me seemed lifted, even as the sun dared to peek around the gray clouds.

I turned to go back and was halfway to the gate when I heard the distinct sound of a woman crying. Such a noise would not, of course, be uncommon or unexpected at this hallowed place, but there was a quality to the wailing that gave me pause. It was not mere grief. I felt I heard something within, something more to the quality of terror. I paused and oriented myself towards the weeping. I made my way through the labyrinth of tombstones until, at last, I located the source of the sorrow.

A woman was kneeling beside an ornate stone monument, her face sunk into gloveless hands. She was clad in full mourning garb, though her bonnet had fallen away, revealing a long plait of nearly white hair wound tightly around her head. She gave a start at my approach, and I quickly doffed my hat and begged her pardon.

"Forgive give me, Miss," I said. "I did not mean to intrude. I only feared – from the sound – that you might have been injured."

She wiped roughly at her face. She had been beautiful once, but grief had scarred her. Her eyes were so sunken they appeared bruised, and her cheekbones seemed ready to protrude through gray-tinged skin. I guessed her age to be almost forty, though I later learned she had not attained thirty years.

"No, sir, I am not hurt. Only sad – and perhaps angered. I do not understand this strange persecution, and there is no one I can appeal to for help, no one who can aid me."

"Persecution?"

"Yes. Tell me, sir, why would anyone leave flowers on a stranger's grave – flowers bearing notes that seem, by turn, to plead and threaten?"

I looked to the stone she knelt before. It bore the name of Azreal Pooler and a death date of only eight months past. "Your father's grave?" I asked.

"Yes, he who had not a friend in the world. And yet, almost every day for a month, I have found *this*."

She pointed to a strange, almost gaudy arrangement of flowers, all held together with a white satin bow. They looked more appropriate for a bridal bouquet, or perhaps a centerpiece for a lady's luncheon, than as a tribute to the dead. The woman began to weep again.

"Oh, if only someone could help me! If only someone could make it clear!"

"Dear lady," I said, "I know someone who can."

369

"My name is Zora Eaton," the young woman said. I had returned to Baker Street with her in time for tea and was grateful that Mrs. Hudson had taken it upon herself to send up a generous selection of sandwiches, for upon closer inspect, Miss Eaton was not only suffering from grief, but also from malnourishment. "Thank you for agreeing to hear my story, Mr. Holmes. I hope I'm not intruding upon your work. As I said to Dr. Watson, what seems to me a terrible torment may be nothing more than a mistake, but if so I cannot account for its bizarre regularity."

My friend had been examining the bouquet with great interest, murmuring the names of the flowers it contained. He dropped it carelessly back onto his desk.

"Do begin at the beginning, Miss Eaton. Your father's name was Pooler?"

A tiny hint of color came into her cheeks. "It was, sir. Twenty-five years ago, Azreal Pooler was a young architect hired to supervise some repairs on Elmwood Manor where my mother was in service as a chamber maid. The two of them were taken with each other – my father promised her marriage – and then, most cruelly, he abandoned her when the work at the manor was completed. Alas, by then my mother was carrying me. She was dismissed from service when her condition was known. She wrote most piteous letters to my father, who at first insisted that I must be given away. My mother bravely refused. At last, through the good offices of the village vicar, my father conceded to settle some money on my mother and myself, but not to marry her or give me his name. And so I was born into a kind of village infamy, and grew up being tortured by my schoolmates. Father provided just enough for us to rent a small cottage, but never enough for all the things we needed. Mother worked herself into an early grave, doing sewing and nursing and whatever job the local women would send her way. She died and was buried there in the village churchyard when I was fifteen.

"I had thought I would be sent to a workhouse or an orphanage, but on the day of my mother's funeral, my father appeared, nicely dressed and riding in a fine carriage. He took me to my old home and looked me over, the way one might inspect a hound or a horse.

"'You're my girl, all right – there is no mistaking the Pooler hair, so fair as to be white, even in youth. I will admit I've been no father to you, but now that your mother has died you must live with me. I'll not have it said that I was cruel and put you in the streets. There now, dry your tears and pack your things. You will not be coming here again.'

"And so, before my mother's grave was even covered, he took me away to his home in London. At first, it seemed like a fairy tale, for everything in the house was beautiful and there was plenty to eat and new clothes for me to wear. But Father's kindness lasted less than a month. Once he saw that I could clean and cook, he dismissed his servants. He went out to his office every day, and each morning I would find a list of things he expected to be accomplished. I barely had time to swallow a cup of tea, for woe be it if a domestic task was neglected.

He was a difficult man, and he did not hesitate to strike me, with his hand or with a stick, for even the smallest infraction. Once, when he caught me laughing with a handsome young lad who had come to collect a tradesman's bill, he kicked the poor boy across the yard and then beat me so badly that a doctor had to be called, and for almost a week my life was despaired of. After that day, I swore that as soon as I was twenty-one, I would leave him and make my own way in the world."

"You must have hated him," I said softly.

"I tried not to, sir – for my mother always taught me that hatred was the pathway to darkness and Hell. I struggled to forgive Father – to tell myself that he had been made hard and mean by the dogged pursuit of wealth. I saw that he had no friends, no one who visited or called upon him, or sent good wishes upon his birthday or compliments of any season. Even the men who were employed in his firm avoided him as much as possible. He drank, but never immoderately, and he did not deny me adequate food or clothing, though he would not spend so much as a farthing for a book or a matinee performance at the theater. He did not allow me to attend church, or to venture out alone beyond a walk in our small garden, so that I made no friends and certainly cultivated no gentleman callers. I merely marked out the time until my twenty-first birthday.

"When it came, I informed Father that I was leaving him. He was furious, and told me that he would disinherit me, that I was throwing away a fortune. I told him I did not care – that I could no longer bear being worked to death inside my own tomb. I ventured out with no more than a carpetbag and my ambition. I found a place in a boarding house only a short distance from Highgate Cemetery. The landlady had a small business in making ornaments for mourning – fixing hair into broaches, engraving names into brass lockets, and such. She took me on as a helper, and in this simple way I lived.

"After a year, Father came to see me, and we made amends. He sent me miniscule monetary gifts from time to time, and I visited him occasionally, but I never stayed for long. It was clear to me that Father was a man without the capacity for love, and that nothing I could do would change his nature. He continued to live alone in his fine house until he suddenly sickened, some eight months ago. The doctor called me in, and I

371

had just time to ask Father's blessing – which he gave only grudgingly – before he died."

"Yet surely he made you his heir," Holmes said. "His name was not unknown to me when you stated it, and he was among the most successful of his occupation in the city."

The lady's answering smile lacked humor. "Father left very precise instructions, and quite a good deal of money, to see that he was put away in style, though all of his wealth could not purchase an excess of mourners for his funeral. His house was not his own but rented. Everything he owned was sold and the money put into a trust for me, from which I am not allowed a shilling until I reach the age of thirty, and I have just turned twenty-four. Until I attain thirty years, nothing but my own labor and the kindness of my elderly landlady stands between me and complete impoverishment. Perhaps that is why the notes and the flowers on Father's grave seem so cruel."

"Tell us how it began," Holmes said.

"I live only a stone's throw from the cemetery, and I make a point of walking over to visit Father's resting place every day if the weather is not too harsh. I realize this will seem strange to you, but for all his sins, Father was the only family I had left in the world. There is comfort in that cold and lonely place, and I have grown so familiar with every stone and epitaph that I could name the entirely of Highgate's residents. It was a month ago that I first noticed the bouquet on Father's grave. I was certain that it had been placed there by mistake, for Father had no friends or living family besides myself. I picked it up and took it to the sexton, inquiring if he had not erred in its placement, and he told me that no one had given him flowers to deliver. Not knowing where they belonged, I decided to bring them to my rooms, for they were very bright and gay, and looked lovely in a vase. It was while I was arranging them that a folded note fell out. For an instant I thought the mystery solved until I read the paper.

"The sentence was: *'If you love me, you must not bear it'*."

Holmes and I exchanged a puzzled glance. "What did you make of it?" I asked.

"I made nothing of it. I thought about returning the flowers to Father's tomb but decided that since they were clearly left there in error, it would do me no good to return them. Two days passed, and on the third, I was shocked to find another bouquet left on the soil, its white ribbon flapping in the breeze. Once again, I pondered whether Father might have had some admirer from his profession who was grieved at his death. But surely, such an individual would have placed roses or lilies on the soil, not this bright spray, so alive with color. I plucked it up, searched it, and found yet another folded bit of paper. This time, the message read – *The sacrifice is for the best.* Once again, I went to the sexton, who was rather vexed with me, and asked why I even thought someone would be so ignorant as to place flowers upon the wrong grave. Again, not wishing to return them to the grave, I took them home."

Holmes leaned forward. "How many more times has this strange event occurred?"

The lady began using her fingers to count upon. I noticed how red and chafed her hands were – in places they looked raw and bloody. I imagined that in her line of work, using needles, wire, and pins to create cheap mourning jewelry, it was inevitable that her hands would be tortured.

"At least eight more times, counting today – so ten messages in all."

"Do you visit your father's grave at the same time every day?"

"Perhaps not at the same minute, but always between one and two in the afternoon."

"And the flowers are fresh?"

"As if just picked from a garden." The lady shook her head. "After the fourth occasion, I began to look closely for anything that would give a clue as to my Father's visitor. I have seen boot prints, and lady's shoeprints, but there are such marks everywhere when the ground is wet."

"Indeed, in a public venue, such marking would not be instructive," Holmes mused, leaning back in his chair. "You have never seen anyone near the grave?"

"No, sir."

Holmes waggled a finger. "You said you were very familiar with the tombs in the vicinity. If I gave you a paper, could you write down the names?"

"I will try sir."

Holmes handed her some foolscap. Deliberately, she marked an "*X*" for her father's resting place, then began to draw other marks and names around it.

"Imagine yourself facing Father's tombstone," she said. "There is a large cedar tree to the left, which Father is buried beneath. To the immediate right is the Hoyle family mausoleum, with its great brass door. Behind Father are three members of the Neville family – Edward, Allan, and Abigail – a father, son, and mother. Before Father, behind any visitor, are the tombs of Manuel Jose, the South American general, and his wife, then another large stone in honor of Mr. James Seymour, the philanthropist."

"Nothing that honors maidens, I suppose?" Holmes asked.

"Hardly, sir – though about twenty yards beyond, past the Hoyle mausoleum, is a large and very beautiful statue of an angel, which I have seen many people stop and admire."

Holmes nodded. "Have you disposed of the notes?"

"No sir, I have kept them, though I threw them into a drawer, and I cannot swear to their order."

"Allow my friend to escort you home, retrieve the messages, and send them back to me by him. There is nothing more that can be done today, but perhaps if I can see the notes – "

"You could make some sense of them. I will do so immediately. Thank you, sir – I feel much better already."

"Do let me know if more of these strange bouquets are found." Holmes caught me by the sleeve as the lady stopped at the door, exchanging a kind word with Mrs. Hudson. "Your professional opinion, as a physician?"

I understood why he was asking, and why he was insisting that I accompany Miss Eaton rather than merely hailing her a cab. She had grown paler as we talked and had pushed her tea away with a single sip, flinching as if the beverage pained her when swallowed.

"Perhaps some cancer," I said. "I fear she will never live to claim her inheritance."

I returned to Baker Street feeling even more mystified than before. Miss Eaton had been so weary and ill that we had made little in the way of conversation on the journey to her lodging house. Her landlady was a very motherly sort, and immediately took charge, assuming that I was a doctor her boarder had gone to consult.

"She's been ill, on and off, for almost a month now, she who was never strong to start with. Her hands shake too badly to work some days, poor girl," the lady said, as our client climbed up to retrieve the notes. I recommended some hearty broths, and plenty of rest, then bid Miss Eaton goodbye. I will never forget her gentle smile and sincere thanks.

I resisted the temptation to open the notes. Each was folded twice and written on sturdy paper that felt expensive. I had no doubt that Holmes would immediately know where it was made, what it cost, and where it might have been purchased. As I entered our rooms, I found my friend brooding over a large book.

"Hello, Watson. Tell me, when you were a romantic young swain, did you know that flowers spoke a language? Or that this study is called *floriography*?"

I chuckled. "I have heard of such, but never felt the need to investigate further. A simple rose or carnation was usually enough to charm a pretty girl when I was a lad. But what messages are contained in that bouquet? You seem intent upon deciphering it," I noted, as Holmes had taken the arrangement apart and laid the flowers out across his table.

"Indeed, I have, and I find myself none the wiser. This bouquet bears quite the mixture of sentiments. In it, we see the morning glory which, according to this *Ladies' Almanac*, signifies affection, as well as tulips, which indicate passion."

"A strange code to place on an old villain's grave."

"Indeed. The hydrangea is more fitting, as it speaks to heartlessness, as well as the wolfsbane for misanthropy, the foxglove for insincerity, and the marigold for jealously. Yet entwined with them is the yarrow for everlasting love."

I considered the colorful blooms. "Surely not all of these are native plants, or bloom in the same season."

"A wise observation, Watson. These are not flowers readily acquired in city gardens, yet they were fresh in the middle of the day"

"They must have been grown in a greenhouse!"

Holmes settled in with his pipe. "Elementary. You have the notes in your pocket? Will you read them aloud to me?"

I cleared my throat. Each card was brief.

If you love me, you must not bear it
The sacrifice is for the best
For God's sake it must be soon.
If you tell her, you will kill me.
Will you do it or not?
I will not break my vow.
She will cast me out if she learns.
You will not suffer.
I love you more than life.
M is the problem.

Holmes frowned. "No wonder the poor young woman is terrified. Whatever is afoot, it sounds like a bad business. Now, Watson, would you be so kind as to take down my index books? Let us see what, if anything, we may learn about Mr. Pooler's eternal neighbors."

"You think there is an error in the placement of the flowers?"

"No – I think the placement is purposeful, but for what purpose I have yet to surmise. An error might have been committed once, but surely not a further nine times."

"Clearly," I said, as we divided up the relevant volumes, "the message was meant for someone other than Miss Eaton. Do you think that person received the messages?"

"I cannot theorize without data," Holmes reminded me. "Let us see what we can learn from these pages."

We spend the remainder of the evening pouring over the books. We learned a great deal about the distinguished career of General Manuel Jose, who had battled guerillas in the Andes before retiring, covered with honors, to his wife's homeland. We also learned of the many hospitals, orphanages, and museums which had benefitted from the benevolence of Mr. James Seymour, the owner of a dozen factories in the north of England, a man who had buried three wives, five sons, and all his grandchildren before passing away at the age of ninety-nine. The Neville family proved singularly uninteresting, though Holmes made a note to do further research, as he believed a Neville cousin had been associated with certain unpopular Parliamentary reform measures in the 1870's. It was only when we turned to the volume containing his collection of *H*'s that Holmes became animated.

"Ah, at last – a thread of hope, even if a very thin and fragile one. See here, Watson. The mausoleum holds the mortal remains of Bradley Hoyle and his wife, as well as two sons. There is a widowed daughter-in-law and one grandson still in the land of the living."

"Why is this hopeful?"

"Because Bradley Hoyle was a noted botanist," Holmes said, his eyes gleaming with triumph. "His home in St. John's Wood contains one of the largest greenhouses in England."

"But surely his descendants would have a key to the mausoleum, and if they wished to leave floral tributes, such would be placed within its chamber," I challenged. "And anyone wishing to somehow salute the family's achievements could hardly miss such an imposing structure and lay the flowers on Pooler's grave instead."

"As you say, it seems unlikely that the grandson – he would be twenty-eight years of age – or his mother would leave a bouquet propped against a brass door, for the wind to blow away. And yet . . . ."

Holmes collected the notes that had been tucked inside the bouquets. He mumbled, "Written by a man, on paper that is at least five shillings a packet . . ." and then wandered off to the window. Great swirls of smoke emerged from his pipe, making the atmosphere of the room so oppressive that I wished him a good evening and took myself off to bed. I had barely managed to tug my nightshirt over my head when the door was unceremoniously banged open.

"Watson, into your clothes again! Make haste, man – our client's life depends on it!"

It was early morning before we returned to Baker Street. Many was the time we had raced through London, but rarely had the stakes felt so high. It was difficult to hear Holmes's words over the wild snap of the whip, the swearing of other drivers, and the great clatter of hooves on pavement.

"Poison!" Holmes shouted in my ear. "Every one of those flowers is poisonous. There are even a few I have not yet identified, but I would wager my soul that they also leak dangerous sap or grow toxic leaves."

"Many flowers are deadly if eaten."

"Yes, but these, if merely touched by a person with delicate or broken skin, can do harm. In a hale and hearty person, a mild rash might be produced. Taken together, on the skin of a woman already malnourished and sickly . . . ."

I found myself shouting at the driver to go faster. At last, we reached the boarding house. Our frantic knocks were met by the worried countenance of the landlady, who had been on the threshold of sending for me. Holmes raced up the stairs. The poor girl was gray-faced and clearly in great peril. I did what I could, and a few hours later, as her breathing grew less labored, Holmes carried her down the stairs and together we saw that she was made comfortable in a private hospital operated by a friend from my days at Barts.

"I will never forgive myself if she dies," Holmes growled over coffee. "I am a damned fool, not to have realized it from the start."

"Who could bear her such a grudge? Do you suppose someone could have hated the father enough to take revenge upon the daughter?"

"If so, it is indeed the coldest of dishes," Holmes whispered. He turned again to the notes and began to rearrange them.

"It is only a suspicion, but if we now place the messages in this order . . . ."

If you love me, you must not bear it
The sacrifice is for the best
I love you more than life.
I will not break my vow.
You will not suffer.
M is the problem.
She will cast me out if she learns.
If you tell her, you will kill me.
For God's sake it must be soon.

377

Will you do it or not?

"It is clear that something is building. A crisis is about to come to a head."

"What should we do?"

Holmes gulped down the last of his coffee. "I must return to Highgate and place myself where I can watch the Pooler grave. If the flowers are fresh, they must be placed there in the morning."

"We will both go," I insisted. "I feel equally responsible for Miss Eaton's fate."

Holmes nodded wearily. "Then let us try and solve this mystery, for if we cannot save the lady, we may perhaps avenge her."

And so we departed our rooms to make the journey to the great City of the Dead. As ill luck would have it, an omnibus was broken down, and the streets jammed with carriages, cabs, wagons, and their assorted irate drivers. Because of this, we did not reach Highgate until nearly ten that morning. The Pooler grave was easily found, thanks to the markers of the tree and the massive monument to the general and the public benefactor. Holmes froze as we stepped into the narrow pathway that faced Pooler's tomb.

"On the Hoyle mausoleum steps. Look!"

A bright bouquet, almost an exact mate to the one that Miss Eaton had received, was resting against the brass doors. It looked new, freshly cut. Holmes scowled.

"There appears to be more than one step in this dance. Very well – Watson, I think if you take a position behind the general's tombstone, I shall loiter behind the tree."

It made for a quiet morning, and more than once the effects of the evening nearly lulled me into sleep. But then, just before noon, I heard the rustle of a lady's dress. Cautiously, I peered out from behind my post.

A striking young woman was standing before the Hoyle mausoleum. She was wearing a gay, pink-checkered dress that clashed with the solemnity all around her, and a straw hat with an absurd festooning of yellow silk flowers. Her face was round and sprinkled with freckles, and her wiry hair, the color of a prize pumpkin, hung long and untamed down her back. She seemed to consider the brass doors for a moment, then glanced around and picked up the bouquet with purple-gloved hands. She plucked out the note, read it, and gave an angry growl. Returning the note to the blooms, she purposefully bent down and jammed the stems of the arrangement into the soil by Pooler's tombstone.

She looked up to find Sherlock Holmes standing over her.

"Good morning, Miss – ?"

"It's no business of yours!" she snapped and turned to march away. Holmes, however, had her fast by the elbow. "Let me go, you masher! I'll scream!"

"You will do no such thing – not unless you wish to be arrested for the theft of the Hoyle family's flowers."

"What? Theft? No – no sir. What are you, some kind of a constable? I've done nothing wrong!"

"I believe that Dr. Watson can verify your perfidy. He was also a witness," Holmes said, signaling for me to step forward. The young woman's reaction was immediate.

"Watson? Not . . . not *the* Dr. Watson? What writes the stories?" At my nod, she whirled back, her thick jaw bobbing open. "Then you're Sherlock Holmes."

"I am indeed. And you are a murderess."

"What! No! No!" The girl began to weep. "All I've done is move Billy's flowers. Billy was the one who set it up. I haven't hurt anyone. I would never hurt anyone, especially not now."

My doctor's eyes told me the truth, just as I suspect her unconscious communication, the way she suddenly clutched at the front of her oddly gathered skirt, made everything clear to Holmes.

It was perhaps the strangest luncheon Mrs. Hudson had ever served. The young woman – whose name was Nellie Morgan – ate like a ravenous wolf. Holmes, I, and our other guest watched in bemusement.

"I worked in a music hall," Miss Morgan said, between bites of her chicken. "Billy used to come there all the time. His mother didn't like it – she's a snob, all for the opera and such fancy things – but Billy likes to drink beer and sing. He fancied me right from the start. I know there were much prettier girls there, but somehow, I caught his eye and stole his heart. He promised me he would marry me. See, he even gave me this ring." She held out a chubby hand, exhibiting a cheap silver circle with a piece of blue glass atop it. "At first, we didn't even think we needed a priest to make it right. We stayed in my rooms over the hall, except of course Billy had to go home at night. Then his mother went to someplace in Germany, to take a water cure, and Billy had the whole house to himself. Ta, didn't we have fun, making merry everywhere, even in the greenhouse. Truth be told, I think our little stranger was sent down from heaven right there, amid all those beautiful flowers."

"Miss Morgan – "

"No, let me finish, Mr. Holmes. You said you wanted to hear it all and, quite frankly, I'm sick and tired of this sneaking around. Billy loves me. Maybe we didn't do everything prim and proper, but he's going to marry me and together we're going to raise our little one with more love than that sour old lady called his mother could ever provide. As soon as I knew for certain that the stork was paying us a visit, I told Billy. And that's when he turned queer. He stopped coming to the music hall. He stopped sending letters and gifts. It made me so mad I went to his house in St. John's Wood one day – something he said I must never do, on account of the old lady – and he took me out back and told me how he couldn't come to the music hall no more, but he would make up bouquets and put them on his family's tomb in Highgate and put letters in them. I said that was all right, for a time, but with the baby on the way he would have to stand by me. That's when . . . well, I shouldn't say any more."

Holmes took the messages from his pocket and laid them on the table. Miss Morgan's breath caught in a hitch.

"But how did you get them?" Her eyes were wild. "Billy told me to make sure I threw them away."

"You placed them back in the bouquet, and put the bouquet on Mr. Pooler's grave. Why did you do that?"

The girl shrugged. "It looked lonesome, that's all. And I didn't want to get caught with the flowers. They always made my gloves sticky. I prefer roses – I never understood why he didn't give me roses when he knows I fancy them!"

I thought of Miss Eaton's poor, gloveless hands, already covered in sores and wounds from her work making jewelry.

"Did you reply to the messages?" Holmes asked.

"I did. I used to write notes back to him and put them in the lion's paw. You know that lion on Mr. George Wombwell's grave?"

Holmes nodded. "Billy asked you to rid yourself of your baby. You told Billy you intended to be a mother."

"Yes. It would be a sin to kill our baby!"

"And you threatened him."

"You make it sound wicked, sir. I told him to be ashamed of himself. And then, a few days ago, I told him if he didn't meet me at the Registry Office next Monday, I would go straight to his house and tell his mother everything. He knew he couldn't stop me."

Holmes slipped open the final note, the one he had removed from the most recent bouquet. "'*I cannot come, you must be patient. Smell the flowers deeply, know my love is true.*'"

The girl sighed. "I do love him but – I meant what I said. If I'm not a bride on Monday, then his old battle ax of a mother had better be ready to buy a mourning dress." Miss Morgan cocked her head at the individual across the table from her. "Are you a constable?"

The motherly-looking woman who had also joined us shook her head. "I am only a matron at Scotland Yard, though I hope one day to be on the force. It seems strange that they will not let women help, when we could do so much good."

"But does this mean I'm under arrest?"

"No, dearie, but it might be necessary for you to come in and tell your story to the inspectors. We will discuss it more, in the cab."

Miss Morgan stuffed a large spoonful of pudding into her mouth. "Very well and – oh, this pudding is so good. Might I run down and ask for the recipe?"

The moment she vanished through the doorway, our guest, whose name was Mrs. Galt, turned to Holmes. "You were right to send for me, I think."

Holmes nodded. "As the girl lacks a mother or even a close female relative, I felt it would be better for her to learn the news from a sympathetic individual. Be sure to impress upon her the danger she and her child were in from young Master Hoyle's actions. In this last note, he instructs her to smell the flowers deeply. Angel's Trumpet, which featured prominently in the bouquet, can sicken from inhalation."

"Miss Morgan will either break down herself or . . . let us just say that I understand why you wish her to be informed in a room with no fragile objects in it." Mrs. Galt said, indicating Holmes's chemical apparatus and his violin with a swoop of her hand. "If she refuses to swear out a warrant on the lout, however, there is nothing we can do."

"Unless Miss Eaton dies," Holmes agreed. "Let us hope it will not come to that."

Later, after the women had departed, Holmes began to pace. He talked through the case so briskly, so absorbed in his own thoughts, it was as if he had forgotten I was in the room.

"I should be kicked from here to Charing Cross – no, from here to Canterbury or Coventry – for such a blunder. I assumed the flowers were a code, when the flowers were a weapon. Thus, the dangers of theorizing before all the data could be collected. By shifting my mind to think of some type of message in the flowers, I neglected to see the intensity of the written messages. I dismissed them as trivial love letters, when in fact, they were merely a blind to the dangers inherent in the bouquets."

"So, the boy wished to kill his girl? It seems a rather inefficient way to commit a murder."

Holmes scowled. "No, Hoyle never intended to murder Miss Morgan. His goal was to make her sick enough that she would lose the unborn child, and thus he could deny the evidence of any liaison with her. Note that he

381

was careful to tell her to dispose of the notes, but not the flowers. It was her own simple and genuine goodness, her sadness that a tomb looked neglected, that spared her from suffering."

"Holmes," I said, as gently as I could, "this sad situation is not your fault. It is a terrible misfortune, caused by the selfish nature of a spoiled young man. And besides, Miss Eaton had already become ill before you met her." I nodded toward the now withered remains of the flowers. "Had you not retained those for study, she surely would have died. You have saved her."

"Have I?" my friend muttered. "I fear I have not, for if I had recognized her peril immediately, you could have treated her in these rooms, or taken her to the hospital immediately. Surely, Watson, you cannot write this case as one of my successes."

Fortunately, my friend was in error. The next morning, we received a message from the hospital that Miss Eaton had rallied and would make a full recovery. A short time later, we received another message that Miss Morgan, upon learning of her beloved's perfidy and intentions towards their unborn child, had indeed sworn out a complaint against him. The boy confessed all, but a sympathetic magistrate, unmoved by Miss Morgan's delicate condition, freed him. The events caused such a scandal in the newspapers that Mrs. Hoyle sent the boy off to Australia, supposedly to collect specimens for the family gardens, and while in the hinterlands of that wild country, he met his death. Luckily for Miss Morgan, a young barrister who had been assigned to the case was quite smitten with her. I learned, sometime later, that they were married and happily raising her little daughter as his own.

Miss Eaton lived to come into her paternal inheritance. In time, she founded a number of institutions that cared for mistreated children. When she died, just before the Great War, her funeral was one of the largest the city had ever witnessed for a private citizen, and her grave, marked by a simple stone, never lacks for flowers.

The Adventure of the
New York Professor
by Wayne Anderson

The fact that I've freely published the address of the rooms I shared with Sherlock Holmes at 221b Baker Street undoubtedly brought numerous clients to our door. Sometimes that was a boon. Other times it did not turn out so well.

One of our more memorable – albeit brief – cases began on an afternoon in early June of 1895. Holmes and I were engaged in some of our usual activities: I was organizing and sorting my notes on previous cases, and he smoking a pipe of his favorite shag tobacco while perusing the agony columns of several of London's finest newspapers. Without looking up from *The Times*, he surprised me by saying, "Prepare yourself, Watson. We have a visitor coming."

"And how did you know it this time?" Still, trusting to his perceptions and his word, I started bundling my slightly-more-organized sheaves of papers into the tin dispatch box that served as their repository.

"First, the barking of distant dogs, shortly followed by nearer dogs, and then nearer still. This followed by heavy footsteps at a running pace. This is not some child at play – that is a man running, and I put it to you that the most likely destination of a man running on Baker Street would be our front door."

As if on cue, the bell rang, and we heard Mrs. Hudson downstairs, moving to answer. Voices followed, her familiar tones alternating with the deeper timbre of a man – somewhat agitated from the tone, though I couldn't make out the words.

This was followed by steps coming up the staircase, then a tap on our sitting room door, and Mrs. Hudson announced, "A gentleman to see you, Mr. Holmes."

The man who entered was tall, somewhat over six feet, and lean, narrow of shoulder in a way similar to that of my friend. On his nose he wore a pair of wire-rimmed spectacles. His suit was disheveled, his bowler hat was in his right hand, and he mopped perspiration from his brow with a handkerchief in his left. He appeared to be in his late forties, with grey making itself seen at his neatly-trimmed temples.

"Come in, please, sir," said Holmes, folding *The Times* on his knee. "What brings a man of your distinction in such haste all the way from

America?"

Our visitor gaped for a moment, then closed his mouth. "Clearly I've come to the right place," he said, and his accent was undeniably American. "I need your help, Mr. Holmes. I've read of your abilities, and – " He glanced at me, with a little nod. " – and you are the man who can save my life."

"Your life! Tut, that sounds serious," Holmes responded. "Mrs. Hudson, can you please get our guest some refreshment – some tea, perhaps?"

Mrs. Hudson nodded and stepped out, closing the door quietly behind her.

"Please take a seat, sir," Holmes gestured to the basket chair, "and tell us how we may help." The stranger settled into the chair, and as he did, it seemed to me that I caught a momentary flicker of surprise in Holmes's expression.

The stranger looked at me. "You'll be Dr. Watson," he said, knowingly. I nodded. "I know that I can count on both of you."

"We shall do our best to assist you, sir," I put in.

Holmes leaned back and steepled his fingers. "And now, please tell us who you are, and how we can save your life."

"My name is Professor Samuel Meyer," he said, and then paused. He turned his head a little sideways. "How did you know I came from America? Even before I spoke."

"Quite obvious, Professor – your suit is of an American cut, and at least three years old. While an American may very well wear a suit of English cut – as English tailors are counted to be the best in the world – an Englishman would never – willingly – wear a suit of American cut."

The professor gave a little barking laugh and again mopped his forehead with his handkerchief. "So obvious, as you say," he said. "Where was I?"

Holmes watched in quiet bemusement as the professor took off his spectacles and wiped them with his handkerchief, succeeding only in smearing them with sweat. "You were about to tell us about yourself and your troubles."

"Yes, sir, yes, I was. I am a professor of Medieval Literature at Cornell, a university of some repute in Ithaca, New York."

"We have heard of it," I said. "It's said to be quite good – for an American institution."

For a moment the Professor looked nonplussed, like he didn't know whether to be complimented or insulted at this. Then he chose to ignore it and pressed on. "In the most recent school year, I have had one particularly troublesome student, a certain Luther Harris. He's the only son of a very

384

rich man, and is clearly accustomed to having his own way in everything. He would rarely attend my lectures and, when he did, he was quite obviously not attentive. I took him aside one day and warned him that such behaviour would eventually result in his failing the class.

"'I think not, Professor,' he replied. 'I think, if you know what's in your interest, you'll pass me with top marks.'

"I was quite upset at this, for it seemed both a threat against my person and an affront to my academic integrity. You will agree, Mr. Holmes, that a professor at a good university cannot allow students to dictate to him what their scores must be."

"Quite so," nodded Holmes. "Pray continue."

"After this exchange I made some discreet enquiries. It seems this young man had said similar things to other instructors, and two of them – having refused his veiled threats – had met with suspicious accidents that could not be proven to be connected to the lad."

"Maybe not proven," I said, "but that certainly sounds suspicious."

"Indeed," Holmes concurred. "Were these 'accidents' fatal, by any chance?"

"One was a riding accident that was not fatal, but resulted in serious injury to the professor in question. The other occurred when a two-horse carriage lost control – the horses spooked – and the professor was run down and fatally trampled."

At this point we were interrupted by the reappearance of Mrs. Hudson, bringing in a tray of tea and scones, along with butter and marmalade. She poured teacups for our guest, Holmes, and myself, and again withdrew quietly.

Holmes lifted his cup and saucer. "Besides the circumstantial evidence of the veiled threats – which could be dismissed as coincidence – what makes you believe the young man was responsible?" He sipped at the tea while I buttered a scone.

"His father's profession, sir." Here our guest's hands began playing nervously with his hat in his lap, but his voice was steady. "On the surface his father made his wealth in iron smelting in Pennsylvania. But he is also reputed to have connections to criminal enterprises, including certain gambling and moneylending rings." He seemed oblivious to the refreshments on offer.

"So you believe young Mr. Harris would be able to arrange such 'accidents', and has people in his employ willing to kill for very little cause?"

"I have every reason to believe it so, sir. If not in the son's employ, then at least in the father's, which is tantamount to the same thing. When I found out about the death of my colleague, I don't mind telling you that

385

my blood ran cold." The gentleman's spectacles flashed for a moment as he looked at the window, fearfully.

"And you did not give him top marks in your class, despite his threat?"

At this, he sat up a little straighter. "Sir, when he turned in his thesis, it was clearly not written by him. It was not handwritten, but done on a typewriter, so I could not identify the hand. There was nothing of his writing style in it, and besides, I had seen exactly the same thesis – almost verbatim – three years before. I looked up the original one to confirm this."

"What did you do?" I asked.

"What could I do? I dismissed him from my class. Further, I reported to the dean both his cheating and his threat, as well as my suspicions of other misdeeds – especially the 'accidents'. He was summarily expelled from the university, and of course he blames me for it."

"And now you are an ocean away from your university, and still you fear him?"

"This trip was long in the planning, and all my students knew of it. I have come to England to study rare manuscripts at the Bodleian Library, as I do every summer."

"Indeed?" Holmes put in. "Have you had occasion in your studies to utilise the Radcliffe Camera?"

"No, sir," said the Professor. "My studies do not extend to photography."

Holmes smiled and nodded, and gestured for our guest to proceed. "In any event, I believe he has followed me, accompanied by his father's henchmen. They have evil intent toward me, sir, and they doubtless feel they can act upon it here, beyond the reach of American justice."

"Yet they are within the reach of British justice," said I. "I assure you, sir, that British justice is no small thing. Indeed, its reach goes round the world."

He nodded, looking at me. "That may be so, Doctor," he said, "but your British constables do not, as a matter of course, carry guns."

"And why do you believe him to be here?"

Professor Meyer again fumbled nervously with his hat. "I have seen him here, Mr. Holmes. I have seen him on a train, watching me. I have seen him with two confederates, whom I believe to be his father's men – in fact, at least one of them followed me to your very door. That's why I ran, hoping to lose him."

"Can you describe these men?" Holmes set his teacup aside and leaned forward, his eyes alert.

"One is a short man, whom I believe has been a professional prize-fighter. When he watched me on the train he took off his hat, and I noticed his ears – they have the deformity that ears of such fighters often show."

"It's caused by a breakdown of the cartilage that gives the ear its natural shape, due to continual and repeated impacts," I said.

"Yes yes, Doctor," he nodded quickly. "This man wears a brown suit and moves very quickly. He is small but seems quite ruthless.

"The second man is taller – taller than I am, but strongly built, broad of shoulder and chest. He wears a dark suit, and can be identified by a knife scar on his left cheek, almost a parabola from his eye downwards to his jawbone. He is the one who followed me here." Again the Professor's spectacles flashed as he looked nervously at our windows overlooking Baker Street.

"And young Mr. Harris himself?" Holmes asked.

"He is rather short, but taller than the one in the brown suit. He has reddish hair and keeps his beard trimmed in a neat goatee. He seems to think himself rather a rakish dandy with the ladies. Both the other men are clean-shaven."

Holmes stood and walked to the window, gazing out casually with his hands clasped behind his back. "Professor," he said, "would you be able to identify any of them from across the street?"

"Any and all of them, Mr. Holmes. Their faces are burned into my memory."

"Please approach the window, then, and have a look in the shadow of the doorway of J. Crawford's, the bookseller's shop across the street. There is a tall man waiting there, of military bearing. But keep yourself in the shadows, well back from the window."

The professor did as Holmes bade, peering nervously from behind the curtain on one side. "That's him, Mr. Holmes," he said. "That's the man with the knife scar. He followed me here, and he's waiting for me to leave."

Taking his elbow, Holmes led him back toward the chairs in front of the fireplace. After they were seated, he took and carefully buttered a scone from Mrs. Hudson's tray. "Your dilemma does have certain features of interest, Professor," he began, spreading some marmalade, "but . . . ." Holmes let his voice trail off.

"But what? Is it your price? I can pay you well, sir!" Bringing out his wallet, the Professor placed several large-denomination banknotes on the table. "There's more if it'll cost more."

"The money isn't the issue, Professor," Holmes said. "Money is quite irrelevant in this matter. What you need is a bodyguard, sir, and I am a detective. My job is to see and understand things that others might miss, and to draw conclusions from subtle clues. This is a straightforward issue of protection."

The professor looked stricken. "But – you are the only one who can help me!" He pulled out several more banknotes and added them to the table.

"Put your money away, sir," Holmes said, gathering the notes and handing them back. "As I said, I am a detective, not a bodyguard. This is not what I do, no matter the price."

The professor appeared numb as he folded the banknotes back into his wallet. "Where am I to go? They mean to harm me, I tell you!"

"Do you have a hotel?"

"Yes, sir. I have reservations at Claridge's, in Brook Street."

"Then," Holmes said, "I should hate to see you suffer harm upon leaving our premises. Watson, would you be willing to join me in escorting the professor to his lodgings?"

"Indeed I would," I responded. "I believe the two of us can keep him safe from one man." Speaking these words, I rose and ascended the stairs toward my room.

Behind me, I heard Holmes say, "We shall escort you as far as the hotel door, sir. From there you must make your own arrangements."

"Where is he going?" I heard the Professor ask Holmes.

He chuckled. "Doubtless to get his revolver. If you would be so kind, sir, please await us at the bottom of the stairs, while Watson and I gather what we need."

When I returned with my coat, my hat, and my Webley service revolver in my right pocket, Holmes said to me in a soft voice, "Something is amiss, Watson. He tells a good story, but some parts do not precisely add up. Still, let us see where this leads."

When the three of us stepped out onto the pavement, the lurker across the street was not immediately visible. Holmes looked up and down Baker Street, letting several hansom cabs pass us by. "I want a growler," he said to the professor. "A four-wheeler, so that all of us can ride together until we get you to your lodgings."

At that moment it happened that there were no four-wheelers to be had. "Let us begin walking," Holmes said cheerily. "It's a lovely day, and walking will at least draw out any pursuers to where we can see them." He took a position on one side of Professor Meyer, and I took the other, and together we moved south in the direction of Oxford Street, occasionally changing to single file to allow other pedestrians to pass.

"Don't look back," Holmes said in a low voice after a short while. "Your friend from the doorway has fallen in behind us, about a hundred feet back. Let him think we are unaware of his presence. It may make him careless."

"How do you know he's following us?"

"I am watching his reflection in shop windows. He seems content to follow for now – he isn't getting any closer." The pedestrian traffic was light, and it would be easy for the man to keep our client in view, but similarly easy for Holmes to observe him.

"He is probably unwilling to approach the three of us by himself," I said in a low voice.

"Doubtless you are correct." Holmes nodded, glancing across the way. "However, the situation has just changed. Another man has begun following us, across the street and a short distance back."

"Are you certain?" I asked, risking a quick glance sideways.

"I am," replied Holmes. "A red-bearded fellow whom I take to be Luther Harris himself. I have been watching him for some time to make certain."

"What do we do now?" asked Meyer nervously.

"We complicate the trail," Holmes answered. "Watson, at the upcoming intersection, the professor and I shall turn right on New Street. Do you please stay behind and feign interest in the shop window. Your presence will help to mask our movement at the corner of Dorset Square. Let the man behind us pass you. Then you follow him, and give him something new to think about. Meanwhile his partner must perforce cross the street, and will be considerably further back."

As we approached the corner I slowed, looking into the shop window. It was a millinery, and I pretended interest in the hats displayed therein. Holmes and Meyer rounded the corner, and through the glass I saw Holmes quickly snatch his top hat from his head and exchange it with the Professor's bowler. A moment later he had removed his jacket and turned out the sleeves, pulling it back on with the blue silk lining exposed, while at the same time he stepped to the other side of our client.

I shifted my attentions to our followers. From the opposite corner of my eye I saw the man who had been behind us slowing, seeming unwilling to approach me too closely. At this closer distance I could see the scar upon his left cheek, faded but unmistakable, as if from a long-ago knife wound.

Reflected in the window I observed that his partner suffered no such misgivings, and was crossing the street to continue behind Holmes and our client. This man was shorter, with reddish hair and a goatee – this would be Mr. Harris, the chief malefactor!

More alarmingly, I spotted a third man in a brown suit approaching briskly from down the street, where he had apparently awaited us. He was short but stoutly built, and his eyes darted back and forth between myself and Holmes.

389

As the first follower steeled himself and approached, I spoke in a low voice when he was but a few feet away. "Beware! Do not make an attempt on the Professor. I have a gun in my pocket, and I am quite skilled with it."

He stopped, astonishment written clearly on his face. "Professor? What professor?" His was the second American accent I had heard in so many hours.

"Professor Meyer, our client." I turned to face him directly. "We know you are seeking to harm him, and we will not allow that to happen."

He was indeed a formidable-looking fellow – a few inches taller than me, and built like a Viking, but his eyes were alert and intelligent. When he smiled, he looked dangerous – especially with that scar – but there was that about him that seemed honest. "You've been gulled, buddy," he said. "That man is a professor of fraud, if anything. He's a fugitive, wanted in America for kidnapping, fraud, and extortion."

"Can you prove that? And who are you?" I asked, my hand on the revolver in my pocket. I knew I was quite capable, at that close range, of shooting directly through my pocket and hitting him without drawing the gun.

He held out his hands so that I could see them. "I'm going to reach into my jacket, and show you something. I give you my word that I'm not drawing my gun."

I noticed that he didn't say that he didn't have a gun. I kept my eyes and my gun on him. Uncomfortably, I observed that at least the man built like a prize-fighter had stopped – behind me – and was watching this encounter closely.

The tall man reached slowly into his breast pocket, pulling out a badge. "Adam North," he said. "Pinkertons. These men with me are Michael Thompson and Jack McNab. We have followed this 'Professor' of yours for weeks now. He is armed and very dangerous. Does your friend know that?" He cocked his head in the direction that Holmes and our client had gone.

"There is very little that my friend doesn't know," I said, but I felt my heart sink inside me.

Mr. North pulled out a folded paper and opened it. It had a portrayal of "Professor Meyer" – quite a good likeness, though without the spectacles – but it said *his* name was Luther Harris, and he was indeed wanted for kidnapping, fraud, and extortion. Further, it offered a reward of five-thousand American dollars for his capture alive, or half that if taken dead.

"You see?" he said. "Now, let's not let him get away! But you will want to keep your gun at the ready."

390

He and his partner proceeded round the corner, and I followed – but Holmes and the false Professor were nowhere to be seen.

The third Pinkerton man – whom I had taken to be the fictional college villain – was stopped halfway down the block, near the mouth of an alley that I knew led to a mews. He looked back and saw us, waved to his two partners, and pointed in toward the mews. Then he peered around the corner. The two Pinkerton men broke into a trot, and I followed suit.

The bearded man approached us, laying a finger across his lips to indicate silence. He looked at me, but the other two nodded. "They went into the mews," he said quietly. "The alley doesn't go through, but they have gone to ground and seem to be waiting for us to pass by and miss them."

Mr. North, who seemed to be their leader, gave a low chuckle. "Well, then, don't let's disappoint them. That's what we'll do." He looked at me. "What's your name, sir?"

"My name is Watson. I'm a doctor."

"Well, Doctor Watson – " He paused. "Did you say 'Doctor Watson?'" His eyes grew wide.

I couldn't help smiling. "I did, sir."

"Then your tall friend is – Sherlock Holmes?"

"The same, yes."

The three men all exchanged glances. "I would have never thought it . . . ." said the bearded one.

Mr. North quickly recovered from his surprise. "I'm pleased to make your acquaintance, Doctor," he said, "but this is not the time for pleasantries."

"Indeed not," I said. "What is your plan, then?"

"We will proceed across the mouth of the alley, making comments as if we believe they have gone further. Then we conceal ourselves and wait for them to emerge."

"No doubt that would work in many cases," said I. "But you won't gull Holmes that way. He is like no quarry you have ever followed." I smiled. "Knowing him, he might come out disguised as a horse."

"Do you have a better plan, Doctor?" This was the smaller man, with the red hair and beard.

"No matter how this ends," I said, "we must perforce confront your criminal – and convince Holmes of the truth. So anything else is a waste of time. I suggest we simply enter the alley."

This is what we did. I took the lead. "Holmes," I cried, "it's me – Watson! New facts have come to light. Please bring the Professor out!"

Holmes stepped out from a doorway, and I noticed he had again reversed his coat, so that it was now worn correctly. "What are you saying,

Watson? What have you learned?"

"The professor – our client," I said. "He's not who he claims. In fact – "

Suddenly the "Professor" emerged close behind Holmes and wrapped his left arm tightly round Holmes's neck, elbow close under his chin. From underneath his long grey coat he produced a long-barreled pistol in his right hand. This he cocked with his thumb and clapped to Holmes's right temple.

"Get back!" he shouted, and started twisting left and right, oscillating to keep changing his position behind Holmes.

The Pinkerton men and I all froze in our tracks. I had my own Webley service revolver in my hand, and I'm a fair shot at such close range, but there was no way I could shoot him due to the grave risk of striking my friend instead.

But I could avenge him. "If you shoot him," I cried, "as God is my witness, you'll never draw breath again!"

He looked me in the eyes. "If you want him to live," said he, "you'll listen to what I say."

Glancing round, I saw that the Pinkertons had all drawn weapons of their own, trained on him as well, but none dared fire.

"All of you!" he shouted, clearly forming a plan, "gather together, against that wall." He gestured momentarily with his pistol, indicating a brick wall to his left, our right. "And drop your guns!"

Fearful for my friend's life, I moved quickly toward the indicated wall. I looked at Holmes, but his eyes gave nothing away. Once in position near the wall, I crouched and, without taking my eyes from the false Professor, set my revolver on the cobblestones at my feet.

The two nearer Pinkerton men did the same. I noticed they were all thinking as I was: Neither of them relinquished their guns until they had stopped moving. Thus we all appeared to comply with his demands, yet stayed near to our weapons.

The third Pinkerton man was apparently moving too slowly, for, without further warning, the gunman turned his pistol away from Holmes's head and fired. With a cry, the bearded Pinkerton man spun round, dropping his own gun as he went down.

"Let me attend him!" I cried. "I am a doctor!"

The false professor pressed his pistol against Holmes's temple again. "Nobody move!" he snarled.

As if that were a signal, Holmes moved. With the speed of a striking serpent, his right hand shot upward and seized the pistol in an iron grip. There were a few seconds of struggle, a contest of wills and strength, during which I feared I would see Holmes slain before my eyes. But the seconds went by, seeming like forever, and still the man's pistol remained silent. Instead, Holmes slowly forced the muzzle away from his head, twisting it outward and down, until a shot would hit nothing but the paving-stones beneath him. Then he lurched forward, bent down, and somehow contrived to throw the fellow over his shoulders, slamming him onto his back on the cobbles.

While this was happening, the Pinkertons and I all retrieved our guns. When it ended, Holmes was holding the man's pistol, trained on him. "Watson!" he barked. "See to the injured man, please."

I was already making my way to the bearded man's side, as was Mr. North, the scarred Pinkerton agent. The other joined Holmes in apprehending the false professor, applying handcuffs to his wrists and hoisting him rather roughly to his feet.

"I'm a doctor," I told the bearded Pinkerton man. "Let me examine you."

All the colour had drained from his face, but he seemed quite a robust fellow. He gritted his teeth against the pain. "How bad is it, Doc?" he asked in his broad American accent.

To my relief, opening his coat and shirt, I was able to quickly ascertain that his injury, while obviously painful, was only a flesh wound, and posed no threat to his life. The bullet had passed cleanly through the deltoid muscle of his left shoulder, striking neither bone nor major artery.

"You are considerably luckier in your shoulder injury than I once was," I commented. "Keep it clean, get to hospital, have a surgeon stitch it up, and I expect you'll make a full recovery." So saying, I tore his white shirt to bandage the entry and exit wounds, and sacrificed the rest of it to improvise a sling for his arm. "I'd sew it up for you, but this isn't the place for it, and I haven't my kit with me."

"Thanks, Doc," he grinned through gritted teeth. "Send the bill to Pinkertons!"

"So the Pinkertons had been closing in on him in New York, and he took ship to London in hopes of losing them?" I asked later that evening, as Holmes and I sipped brandy in 221b Baker Street.

"To Liverpool," Holmes responded. "He might have done better to sail direct to London."

"Did they actually have a man onboard, following him through the entire voyage?"

"No, but they noted the ship on which he sailed. Their New York office telegraphed ahead to their London office, and they had six days' time to prepare a welcome in Liverpool. Their man had no trouble spotting him as he disembarked, and, unbeknownst to him, followed him to the train station and stood in the queue immediately behind him as he bought his ticket. As it was known that Mr. Harris went armed, they felt it better to keep a close eye on him and let him transport himself to London, where their man could call on assistance to apprehend him."

"So he took the train to London," I said. "And at some point on the train he realized that he was still being followed. So when he arrived here he decided to disembark at Paddington and come here, in hopes of hiring your help to evade his pursuers."

"Quite so," Holmes replied, lighting his pipe. "He concocted his false story at some point along the journey, and it might have convinced many people. But it would have been wiser for him to slip off on the platform of one of the towns between here and Liverpool. He could have left his pursuer on the train, and caught a later one to travel unobserved. But he's new at this game, and doesn't know all the tricks. He had read your accounts, Watson, and knew our address here, so he hurried here and tried to enlist our aid. It almost worked, too, though there were some things about him that didn't ring true."

"Did you know he was armed?"

"Oh, definitely," he replied. "I observed the gun under his jacket when he sat down. Its position also confirmed my supposition that he was right-handed."

"Yet you said nothing?" I took another sip of my brandy.

"It's not unreasonable," said Holmes, "for a man who feels threatened – as he told us – to carry a gun for his own protection."

I was forced to concede the point. "But you mentioned, even before we left, that something was amiss with his story."

"As well it was. There were a few clues that gave me reason to doubt him. First, his spectacles – did you notice how the light from the windows reflected from them?"

"I did, but I paid it no mind."

"When an entire piece of glass reflects the same light, evenly across its surface, that means the glass is flat – not curved like regular lenses. Curved lenses reflect a bright spot. Those spectacles were a theatrical prop, intended to create an illusion, not to correct deficient vision." He smiled. "Also, a man accustomed to wearing spectacles would know better than to wipe them with a sweat-soaked handkerchief."

At this I admit I responded with an amused snort.

"And when I asked him about the Radcliffe Camera, that was no mere casual trivia. A scholar who utilises 'the Bod', as they call it – as I have done when researching some of my monographs – would know that the Radcliffe Camera is a building housing a part of the Bodleian Library's collection, based on the Latin word for a room or chamber. As I expected, our guest took it to mean some sort of photographic apparatus – thereby confirming my suspicion that he was not the harmless scholar that he claimed."

"I must confess," I said, "that for a time I was quite frightened that he would indeed shoot you!"

My friend smiled. "And I did appreciate your ferocious defence of me. I assure you, I am quite as fond of my own life as you are. But once the first shot was fired, there was almost no chance of his shooting me, my dear fellow."

"And how did you prevent that?"

"First, as he saw me as his ticket to freedom, it was unlikely that he would throw that ticket away. If I were dead, there would be nothing to stop the Pinkertons, or you, Watson, from gunning him down. Indeed, it would almost be guaranteed – I know well that what you said was no idle threat. He was therefore more likely to shoot anyone else than myself – as he did. But I'm the last man to gamble his life upon something merely unlikely.

"The gun he had was a revolver, the model they call a 'Peacemaker', made in America by Colt. I have encountered them on occasion in my travels. Quite an ironic name for a weapon, wouldn't you say?"

"Very droll. I can only assume it's the American sense of humour."

"No doubt," said he, sipping his brandy. "But he did shoot that other Pinkerton chap – which did my hearing no favours – and that is doubtless why I am still alive."

My expression at this must have been one of puzzlement, for Holmes chuckled. "Simplicity itself. You are obviously familiar with the workings of a revolver. He had initially cocked the weapon, but after he shot that Pinkerton chap, it was, of course, discharged. In order to shoot again, the action of the trigger must revolve the cylinder, bringing a new round to the barrel."

"Of course – I know that quite well."

Sherlock Holmes smiled. "And how many times have I emphasised that knowledge means nothing without its application? I knew that the weapon could not be fired again without the cylinder revolving, and there was probably only the briefest of moments before he would think to cock it again. So I seized the chance when it presented itself – I gripped the gun tightly at the cylinder, holding it with the full strength of my right hand. The strength of his trigger finger, working against mechanical advantage to rotate the cylinder into the next firing position, was quite unequal to the strength of my entire hand holding it locked in place. I knew that as long as I gripped that cylinder tightly he could not fire the gun."

"Brilliant!" I raised my brandy snifter in salute. "And you somehow managed to throw him over your back, while retaining your grip on the weapon."

"Ah – a little trick I learned in my studies of *baritsu*. First I bent forward, pulling him forward with me, such that the weight of his arms and upper torso were supported upon my back. Bending further, I actually caused his feet to leave the ground, as he refused to release the hold of his arm round my neck. So I took another step forward, imparting to him more forward momentum, then suddenly dropped lower and reversed my own movement. This carried his centre of gravity over and beyond my support, and he took a flying somersault that ended on his back upon the cobbles."

"And as I had retained my death-grip on his pistol, when he flew over my back it wrenched the weapon from his grasp. The rest you know."

"Splendid!" I rose to take a cigar from the humidor on the sideboard. "Quick thinking literally saved your life this time."

"All in a day's work, my dear fellow. I only wish more people would apply it to their own lives."

"And this," I said, reaching into my coat pocket, "is yours. You have undoubtedly earned it." It was a cheque, written by the Pinkerton agent, Mr. North, for the sum of five-thousand American dollars, the reward for the capture.

"Sometimes," Holmes chuckled, taking it from my hand and reading it, "modesty prevents my accepting payment for my services. But in this case, as you say, I do agree that I've earned it." He looked at me with a twinkle in his eye. "Do you know," he said, "the Pinkertons actually offered me employment?"

"It's a compliment," I replied. "Take it as such. Professional respect, and all that."

The Adventure of the
Remarkable Worm
by Alan Dimes

Readers of Dr. Watson's story "The Problem of Thor Bridge" will recall that he left a cache of unpublished accounts in a locked dispatch box in the vaults of Cox and Company, Charing Cross Road. The building containing Cox's was totally obliterated in the Blitz in 1940, and for many years it was believed that these final records of Sherlock Holmes had been permanently lost. It transpired, however, as recent discoveries have confirmed, that the box had been removed from the vaults, only a few days prior to the bombardment, by my grandfather Colonel Henry Watson, the late doctor's great-nephew and closest remaining relative.

The reader might reasonably ask why Colonel Watson did not have the manuscripts immediately prepared for publication, since the greatest public interest would have been aroused, resulting in no small profit for their copyright holder. In Holmes's own words, the world was not yet prepared for the content of the stories – at least, not the world of the 1940's. We live in more enlightened times - or, at any rate, so we imagine. But I shall now hand you straight over to Dr. John H. Watson, who can explain and introduce the stories in a far pithier and more entertaining fashion than I.

– Simon J. Watson

I feel it is incumbent upon me, as chronicler of the cases of Mr. Sherlock Holmes, to explain why I have left explicit instructions that these, the last remaining narratives of his long career, must not be published until seventy-five years after my death. Throughout my adventurous life, both as an army surgeon and as a general practitioner, and also as the companion and amanuensis of my distinguished friend, I have seen and experienced a great many things which I would hesitate to lay before the general public.

Holmes and I were men of science. As such, it was our duty to observe and record events, however distasteful, from a detached and clinical viewpoint. In selecting which of our adventures I would commit to print, however, I was guided by strict principles, and even when reporting unsavoury characters and deeds, I strove to stay within the bounds of what was generally considered good taste. The stories the reader will find collected here go beyond – indeed, in several cases far beyond – those limits set by the society of our time. They cannot be told in a manner in keeping with our current sense of propriety, and yet, I

397

have set them down as they happened, both because they are interesting as narratives and because they provide further confirmation of the great heights of intellect and ratiocination of which my late friend was capable.

It may be, as I hope it shall, that by the time you come to read these words, the subjects dealt with in these tales will be topics for open and dispassionate conversation and study. I begin with the case I have entitled: "The Adventure of the Remarkable Worm".

– John H. Watson

It was a beautiful, balmy evening, and I had thrown wide the windows of our sitting room at No. 221b Baker Street to let in the cooling breeze. I was content to do nothing more than sit back quietly and relax, but my fellow lodger was of a rather different humour. He'd had no cases for a full five days, and this idleness rendered him a difficult companion. The previous fortnight had been filled – indeed, crammed – with activity, which made his present lack of work the more frustrating. There had been the singular experience of M. Aristide Dubois, a merchant banker who had gone to bed in Paris and woken up two days later on the floor of the British Museum, and the case of the Thornton Heath Horror – to say nothing of the affair of Carew, the blind cracksman, which had so nearly cost us both our lives.

To do him justice, my friend had tried to fill the time constructively. He had spent a day on some malodorous chemical experiments, and then, perhaps sensing that the noxious fumes were making me uncomfortable, put his test tubes and Bunsen burner to one side and turned to the production of a first draft of a monograph he had long intended to write upon the specialised argots of various professions. For a few hours he made preliminary notes and consulted his scrapbooks, but then he stood up with a gesture of frustration and paced back and forth across the room, threw himself into his armchair, sat there for a short while, stood up again, and went over to the window.

He gazed down upon the street below for a minute or so, then turned and gave me a searching look, as if hoping to deduce something from my appearance and facial expression. As I hadn't left our rooms for some time, and felt relaxed and contented, I fear there was little for his genius to work upon.

He then went to the corner where he kept his violin, pulled the instrument from its case, and ran his bow across it, producing a gentle melody which I didn't recognise and presumed to be one of his own compositions. He continued in this vein for one or two minutes, and then concluded with a discordant cadenza. He threw the violin and bow down on a chair with an exclamation of disgust.

"A whisky?" I said, reaching across to the tantalus.

"No, thank you."

"A case will come, my friend. Depend upon it."

"I wish I shared your optimism, Watson. If I don't have work soon, then I shall be forced to seek stimulation elsewhere."

I confess I went a little cold at these words, for I had been struggling to help him rid himself of his addiction to cocaine, and knew that the little morocco case containing his hypodermic needle lay within easy reach in the drawer of his desk. My relief, then, when I heard the ringing of our doorbell may be readily imagined. Mrs. Hudson opened the door to our rooms to admit a little ferret-faced fellow in a grey lightweight cotton suit.

"Good evening, Mr. Holmes. Doctor."

It was Inspector Lestrade, the tenacious Scotland Yarder whom the consulting detective had assisted on many occasions.

Holmes smiled broadly.

"Lestrade, my dear fellow! Please, take a seat. Watson, perhaps the inspector would like a glass of whisky."

"Thank you very much," said the wiry little professional. "Don't mind if I do."

"And one for me, if you'd be so good. Now then, my friend," said Holmes when we were all seated with a drink in hand, "what brings you to our humble abode on this fine evening?"

"Well, Mr. Holmes, it's like this: Have you heard of Isidore Persano?"

"The journalist? I've read one or two of his articles. I can't say they were especially to my taste. What has he done?"

"Well, we've had our eye on him for some time at Scotland Yard. He lived in Paris for a while, and got himself quite a reputation there as a duelist."

"Ah, yes," said Holmes. "There was some contretemps in Pere Lachaise, I seem to recall."

"Yes. I don't know if that's why he left Paris, but since he's been in London, he's had a couple of very public altercations with men who later appeared to have sustained bullet wounds: Thomas Marlowe, another journalist, and Arnold Campbell, a hotelier. We couldn't pin anything on him on either occasion, but it seems highly probable that he had shot them in duels. Since dueling is illegal, neither man could press charges without incriminating himself."

"But what was the nature of these disagreements? They must have been serious to provoke such a reaction."

"Well, by all accounts, he's a bit of a strange chap. Spanish, I take it, by his name, with a proud and passionate nature. Claims to be thirty, but looks a good deal younger. Short, slim, a bit swarthy."

"Essential as these details are, you haven't answered my question: Why should he challenge these men to duels?"

Lestrade cleared his throat and looked somewhat uncomfortable.

"Persano has a very close relationship with the noted chemist, Dr. Thomas Poulteney, of 17 Margrave Villas, Stoke Newington. Dr. Poulteney is a bachelor of forty-five, and . . . well . . . ."

"And these two men suggested that the relationship between them is . . . *unnatural*?"

"You've hit on it, Mr. Holmes. Persano is also unmarried and lives by himself."

"Was there any indication of blackmail? You are aware, I'm sure, that homosexuality is at the root of the majority of such cases?" The whole subject was clearly a source of embarrassment to the Scotland Yarder.

"Thankfully I've had little to do with that sort of thing. There was no evidence of blackmail."

"So, Lestrade, what is there for me to do? Have there been fresh clues to these mysteries? Perplexing threads that you would wish me to untangle?"

"No, sir. It is the strange disappearance of Mr. Isidore Persano that we need your help to solve."

"Disappearance? Pray continue."

I offered Lestrade another whisky, and he accepted it gladly, taking a short sip of it before resuming his account.

"Persano was residing at 24 Monckton Street, just off the Strand. He came home two evenings ago at about six and asked the maid to bring him a cup of coffee before dinner. When she came into his study a few minutes later, she found him in a state of raving madness, hysterical and incoherent, and pointing at a matchbox that lay in front of him."

"A matchbox? Was there anything in it?

"I have it here, Mr. Holmes. See for yourself."

Holmes took the proffered Vestas box and pulled out the little cardboard drawer. I leaned over eagerly to see what it might contain. Inside lay a dead worm, but such a worm as I had never before seen in my life. It had a distinct head of a slate-blue colour, while its fat body was a darker blue mottled with red-and-yellow dots. "No one at the Yard had ever seen anything like it. I sent a man to Westminster Library and he looked it up, but it wasn't there. The Inspector brought in the curator of the Kensington Museum, and he didn't recognise it either. It seems to be completely unknown to science."

"Fascinating. But the disappearance?"

"The girl went to the door and called a boy to fetch the nearest doctor. The man was just a general practitioner and didn't feel confident diagnosing a mental illness, so he just gave Persano a sedative and despatched a message to Colney Hatch to come and get him. They sent a carriage with an attendant. When they arrived at the asylum he was still asleep, so they locked him in a room and waited till he woke up so they could make a proper diagnosis. When they opened the door some time later, there was no one there. The room was completely empty. They contacted the Yard, so I took a couple of constables with me to search the building and grounds while I questioned the staff. My men did a very thorough job and found nothing."

"How often did the nurses check on him?"

"Once every quarter-of-an-hour."

"Any signs that the lock or hinges had been tampered with?"

"None at all. The windows were barred and the room was on the fourth floor."

Holmes pressed the tips of his long bony fingers together. "Did Persano's maid accompany him to the asylum?"

"No, Mr. Holmes. It was all she could do to get a lad to the nearest doctor. I spoke to her the next day and she was still shaken up, poor girl. She was relieved when I took that thing out of the house."

"How long has she been in Persano's employ?"

"Ever since he's been in London, apparently."

"Has he any other servants?"

"Not that I saw. She appears to be the only one that lives in, at any rate."

"What measures have you taken?"

"Well, the whole area's being combed for him, naturally, but I thought – "

"I am much obliged to you, Lestrade," said Holmes, standing up. "If you care to leave this with me, I will give it my fullest attention. Oh, by the way," he added as the inspector turned to the door, "would you mind if I take possession of that singular worm?"

"Certainly not," said Lestrade, handing over the matchbox. "As I said, we can make nothing of it down at the Yard. Well, good night, Mr. Holmes. Dr. Watson." When the street door had closed behind Lestrade, Holmes reached for his clay pipe and filled it with tobacco from the toe of his Persian slipper. "Well, Doctor, what do you make of it?" he asked through preliminary puffs of smoke.

I took a moment to think. "It seems to me that what we have here are two mysteries, and both are equally perplexing. What can be the connection between the two, other than that the same person is involved in both instances?"

"That is for us to discover. We must make a thorough investigation of both ends of the case, and as we progress they will doubtless throw light on each other. But give me your first impressions."

"The worm certainly seems to be of an exceptional character, but that is surely not enough to drive one insane at the mere sight of it. Fear of snakes is common enough. It even has a scientific name, *ophidiophobia*. But fear of worms – "

"*Vermiphobia*?" asked Holmes with a smile.

"Perhaps. It may exist, but it would be the first I have ever heard of it. That particular species of worm must have some special significance for Persano. But if it is unknown to science, how could he have seen one before?"

"How indeed? And what of his disappearance?"

"Supposing Lestrade's men didn't search as fully as they thought? From what I recall of Colney Hatch, it has a high wall and very secure gates. What if Persano is hiding somewhere in the building. Or the grounds?"

"If that's the case, then he'll be discovered very soon. I think, however, that you are being a little unfair to Lestrade and his men. They may be lacking in imagination, but we shouldn't cast aspersions on their diligence."

"Perhaps not. But then we have another mystery: The gates aren't only locked – they are guarded. How could he get through them? As for the locked door, I believe I have a solution to that." Holmes smiled again and sent a plume of smoke upwards.

"Pray tell."

"The windows were barred. Lestrade described Persano as small and slim, but even if he had been slender enough to get through the bars, the room was on the fourth floor. The walls are sheer."

"Ergo?"

"The door must have been unlocked, Persano freed, and the door locked again."

"Bravo, my dear Doctor! In this instance, the simplest and most obvious solution is the only one that will serve. But by whom was the door unlocked? Persano was asleep, so there was no opportunity for him to get a key. You will recall that I asked Lestrade if the maid had accompanied him. She hadn't, so who was there at the mental hospital who had any motive for being his rescuer? I shall think a little more on this matter and then have an early night – as should you, for I expect we shall have a busy day tomorrow."

The sun rose early the following morning, and after a light breakfast we set out by cab for Monckton Street. The traffic was fairly heavy, but our destination was no great distance from our lodgings, and we were there within twenty minutes. 24 Monckton Street was a narrow, elegant, terraced house with three floors. Holmes rang the bell, and a few moments later, it was answered by a pale-faced, petite young woman in a neatly pressed maid's uniform.

"Good morning. I am Sherlock Holmes, and this is my friend and colleague, Dr. John Watson. We have been engaged by the police to aid them in their investigation into the disappearance of your employer. I should like to come in and ask you some questions."

"Please do, sir," the maid said eagerly. "I shall do anything if it helps Mr. Persano." She showed us into a spacious drawing room. We seated ourselves in two of the four chairs.

"Please sit down, Miss – ?"

"Maisie Tiverton, sir."

"You are from Devon, I think, Maisie."

"Yes, sir, but how on earth did you know that?"

"Despite your years in London, you still retain slight traces of your original accent, and Tiverton is a very common name in the west of England."

I have mentioned before in these memoirs that while my friend had no great respect for the female sex in general, he was capable, when the occasion demanded, of treating individual women with care and consideration. I sat silently listening while he gently coaxed information from this girl, who was clearly still upset by the event which had overtaken her employer.

"Is Mr. Persano a kind master?"

"Oh yes, sir, one couldn't hope for a kinder. Very considerate, he is, sir. Very understanding and very generous."

"On the day of Mr. Persano's . . . *illness*, did anything come through the post for him? A package, perhaps, or a letter?"

"Oh no, sir. I was in all day and there was nothing."

"Were there any callers?"

"No, sir, not one."

"Thank you, Maisie. And now, could you show us to Mr. Persano's study?"

The maid's already pale face blanched still further. "Oh, please don't make me go in there again, sir!"

Holmes reached out and patted her little hand.

"You needn't come in with us. Just show us where it is."

She took us up two flights of stairs to a small door, and then reached into the capacious pocket at the front of her starched white apron and produced a small key, which she pressed into Holmes's hand. Then she turned and hurried back down to the ground floor. Holmes turned the key in the lock and we entered Persano's private room. It was small and square, with one window looking down on a backyard, and sparsely furnished. There was a leather-topped desk with a plain chair in front of it, where Persano presumably produced his journalistic efforts, and on the opposite side of the room was a comfortable armchair with a little round table next to it. This was doubtless where he took occasional refreshment and rest from his labours.

The walls were painted a uniform cream and had no pictures on them. The floor was covered only by bare wooden boards, save for a thick round rug which lay under the leg space of the desk. I stood in the doorway and watched as Holmes carried out a very thorough examination. He pulled out his glass and ran it along the sill, the edges, and catches of the window. After covering the floor, he went to the desk and pulled out its three drawers. The second and third contained some sheaves of paper, which he gave only a cursory glance, but a small revolver lay in the first. Holmes opened it up and looked at the chambers, then sniffed the barrel and put it back.

"Well, Watson, I think the study has provided us with all the information it can. Let us return downstairs." On the ground floor once more, Holmes asked Maisie to let us see the backyard. It was a small square space covered in concrete with three walls, about six-and-a-half-feet in height, which separated it from the yards of the houses on either side and of that of the corresponding house in the next street. The back wall of Persano's house was plain, save for a drainpipe about a foot-and-a-half from the window of the study.

"Thank you for your help, Maisie," Holmes said to the maid as she showed us to the door. Once we were back in the street, he turned to me, and, before I could ask what he had learned from the house, said, "You may as well return to Baker Street. I have several more visits to make, and some laborious tasks to perform. But have no fear. I assure you that as my friend and chronicler you will be present at the denouement of this little drama."

He waved his long thin hand in farewell and was gone. It being a warm, sunny morning, I decided to walk back to our lodgings and arrived there to see that the morning papers had been delivered. I sat down to read them, but found the problem of Isidore Persano preying on my mind, so that I had to lay *The Daily Telegraph* aside and give my thought over to it entirely – but I could come up with no solution to the mystery that didn't either rely on some untenable coincidence, or failed to address all the aspects of the case. In the end, I gave up the enterprise and concentrated on the splendid lunch Mrs. Hudson served me at two o'clock. Two hours later, Holmes returned in an excellent mood.

"Well, Watson, I have managed to carry out all my researches successfully."

"And?"

"I will apprise you of the results on our journey to Stoke Newington."

"Where have you been?" I asked.

"Oh, to the shipping office, the Registrar of Births, Marriages and Deaths, the files of *The Daily Star*, Colney Hatch, and West Kensington. But come, I have a hansom waiting for us."

Once in the cab, I was eager to hear what progress Holmes had made in the case.

"Were you able to find out anything about the worm?" I asked as the hansom moved off.

"While the flora and fauna of Africa have yet to be fully categorised, those of South America are even less so. I considered that the balance of probability was that any hitherto unknown species was likely to originate there, and my supposition turned out to be correct. I took the liberty of having the worm examined by Professor George Edward Challenger, who has recently returned to London from one of his expeditions to the Matto Grosso. He recognised it instantly. The creature is indigenous to a very confined region on the banks of the Amazon River. It is the totem animal of the Sigoro Indians. The Professor himself had intended to bring a sample of it to the Royal Society, but it was lost, along with several other interesting specimens, when a pack mule missed its footing and plunged to its death while the expedition was negotiating a narrow cliffside pass."

"Interesting, but how one did come to be in a matchbox on Isidore Persano's desk?"

"Clearly it was placed there by someone who wished Persano no good, since they must have known what kind of reaction it would produce. You will recall that Maisie assured us that no packages had been delivered that day. So either Persano had brought it in himself, which was unlikely, or another person broke in and left it there. When I examined the window, I found signs that it had, indeed, been forced. Persano's study looks out onto the yard and the study is on the third floor. But a young, fit man might have climbed over the walls and up the drainpipe, and done the deed without being observed."

"But why his extreme reaction?"

"I have formulated three possible answers to that question, but I have as yet insufficient data to form a definite conclusion."

"You said you went to the shipping office."

"Yes, to ascertain the most recent arrival times of ships from Rio de Janeiro. Brazil figures largely in this case, and I shall be surprised if we don't discover that Isidore Persano's native language isn't Spanish but Portuguese. It has to be said that the English aren't a race noted for our ability with foreign languages, and the two are easily confused."

"So someone has come from Brazil with the intent of harming Persano."

"So I read it."

My features, which Holmes has often told me are a true mirror of my thoughts, must at that moment have displayed the bafflement I was feeling.

"Why didn't they simply kill him? If they were able to get into his study, why didn't they just wait until he arrived home and went in there, do the deed, and then escape by the way they came?"

"Clearly his immediate death wasn't part of their plan. My apologies, my dear Watson. Again, I have suppositions, but I will not share them with you until they have some substance. Anyway, from the shipping office I went to the Registrar of Births, Marriages, and Deaths, where I made an interesting discovery concerning Dr. Thomas Poulteney: Far from being a bachelor, he has been married for the last seventeen years to one Alice Poulteney, *née* Dawson, of Selsey in the county of West Sussex."

To my mind, Holmes's endeavours seemed to have produced more questions than answers.

"Then why does he represent himself as single, particularly when people are interpreting his friendship with Persano as meaning, well . . . that he is of the 'other persuasion'? And if he really is that way, wouldn't marriage be a way of silencing that sort of gossip?"

"I have no experience of the married state, Watson, as you well know, but I imagine that sort of arrangement wouldn't make for a happy union, whether the spouse knew the truth or not. It would explain his estrangement from his wife, but I'm reasonably sure that Thomas Poulteney isn't, as you so quaintly put it, 'of the other persuasion'. From the Registrar, I went to the offices of *The Daily Star*, where I spent rather longer sifting through the back issues in search of details of his career. It turned out that while he is now most famous as a chemist, he began as an alienist. While researching the composition of certain drugs used in the repression and control of undesirable mental states, he discovered that chemistry was more congenial to him, took a second degree in that subject, and has flourished ever since."

"Are you saying that Persano has always been mad? That his friendship with Poulteney is rather a relationship between a doctor and his patient?"

"No, Watson, that is not what I am saying, though Poulteney's former career certainly has a bearing on the case. But if you have any more questions about Dr. Poulteney, you may ask the man himself, for unless I am mistaken, we have arrived at 17 Margrave Villas, Stoke Newington." The hansom had indeed drawn to a stop even as he spoke.

The house was old and large without being ostentatious, and was surrounded by a small border of greenery with a sturdy iron fence. While I paid the cabbie, Holmes jumped out, opened the gate, bounded along the concrete path, and pulled at the bell. I managed to draw alongside just as the door was opened by a tall and imposing butler with muttonchop whiskers and an air of command.

"Yes?" he said, raising his bushy eyebrows. Holmes produced one of his cards and handed it to the man. "Sherlock Holmes and Dr. John Watson to see Dr. Poulteney."

The butler took the card into his master and returned after a few seconds. "The doctor will see you, gentlemen," he said, and ushered us into Poulteney's receiving room. The man sitting behind the desk was in his mid-forties, his thick wavy black hair and beard streaked with grey, but still remarkably trim and handsome. As he rose to greet us, it could be seen that he was a little under the average height, but this slight lack of stature did nothing to diminish the aura of power and intelligence that hung around him like a cloak.

"That will be all, Hanson. You may go."

"Hanson," said Holmes as the servant turned to the door, "you were a sergeant-major."

"Yes, sir."

"In the infantry."

"Yes sir, 13th Regiment."

"Hanson?"

"Begging your pardon, sir. Good day, gentlemen."

"Clearly a non-commissioned officer, but too heavy to be a sapper or a lancer," said Holmes after the butler had closed the door behind him.

"Mr. Holmes," Poulteney began, "I have heard a little of your reputation. I take it you haven't come to my house merely to demonstrate your ability at parlour tricks."

Holmes gave a little smile. "I do apologise, Dr. Poulteney. The exercise of the faculty of logical deduction can become a little addictive. No, we are here to ask you some questions about the disappearance of your friend, Mr. Isidore Persano."

"I gave all the information I have to the police yesterday, but I have no objection to giving it again if you think it will be of value."

"I think that it will, Dr. Poulteney, but let me first say that, unlike the detectives of the official force, I am a free agent, and therefore not restrained by professional delicacy. I trust you understand me."

"Completely. Ask me whatever you like. I have nothing to hide."

"Very well," said Holmes, leaning back slightly in his chair and crossing his ankles. "Firstly, can you tell us exactly where and when you first met Mr. Persano?"

"It was something like three years ago. I was invited to a literary dinner by a mutual friend and Mr. Persano was also present."

"And did you hit it off straight away? How did you become friends?"

"Well, he certainly struck me as a charming and erudite individual, but as to when I began to truly consider him a friend, who can say? How does someone cease to be merely an acquaintance and become a friend?"

"Would you say that Mr. Persano is your best friend?"

"Yes, yes I would."

"Then I must say I am rather surprised at the lack of concern you appear to be showing at his disappearance."

"I am not the kind of person who puts his emotions on display, but I assure you, I am deeply disturbed by this event, or I wouldn't have agreed to answer your questions. Though I must say, I doubt the relevance of what you have asked me so far. And now, if you don't mind, I generally have a cup of tea at this time. Will you join me?"

"Why not?" said Holmes. Poulteney tugged at the bell pull, and a minute later the door behind us opened and a maid brought in a tray. I caught no more than a glimpse of her slim back and a loose black braid of hair surmounted by a little white cap, and then she was gone. "And now," resumed Holmes after a sip of tea, "I must ask you a question which will seem the height of impertinence to you, but which must be asked if I am to penetrate to the heart of this case."

"Then ask, sir," said Poulteney calmly.

"Were the relations between you and *Señor* Isidore Persano . . . *abnormal* in any way?"

"I can promise you," Poulteney said with a steady voice, "that our 'relations', as you call them, were in no manner what could be termed unnatural. Nor has there been any impropriety, of any kind, between us."

"Such was my belief," said Holmes, "but I was bound to ask. Do you know anything of Mr. Persano's life before he came to London?"

"I was aware that he had lived in Paris, but I know nothing of his life before that."

"And do you have any inkling of his present whereabouts?"

"None whatever. If I had, I would of course have informed the police."

"Dear me, Dr. Poulteney," said Holmes, shaking his head in mock sorrow, "for the most part, you have, with some difficulty, stayed broadly within the bounds of truth, but your last two statements were outright lies."

Dr. Poulteney rose to his feet, his face white with anger. "How dare you, sir! I must ask you and your colleague to leave my house this instant!"

"Sit down, Doctor," said Holmes imperturbably. "Allow me to assure you that my sympathies in this matter are entirely on your side, and that the best possible outcome will be achieved by your complete cooperation." The chemist resumed his seat, but his expression was tense and wary. "I shall reconstruct the situation as I understand it, and you may correct me whenever my deductions diverge from the strict truth," continued Holmes.

Dr. Poulteney nodded. "Very well."

"On the evening in question, you received an urgent message from *Señor* Persano's maidservant, informing you that her master had been taken to the asylum at Colney Hatch. You immediately put a set of women's clothing and a long wig in a valise and hurried by carriage to the asylum. There you had no difficulty obtaining entry, for this was the place where you had been a resident immediately before your change in profession, and your face was still well known. You had either retained a set of keys, or knew where in the building a set could be easily obtained. You also knew the location of the holding cells where a new patient was likely to be brought. You waited until an orderly had checked on *Señor* Persano and, being aware of the asylum's routine, you knew how long it would be before he or she returned.

"You opened the cell door, stripped Persano of his male attire, and dressed him in the woman's outfit. Doubtless you put his clothing in the valise, since it wasn't found in the room when his disappearance was discovered. I don't know if Persano was conscious or not by this time, but in any event, it would have been easy to take him to another cell until he awoke. Then you waited until a new security shift came on, and you and Persano were allowed through the gates. The new guards recognised you but didn't know that you had entered the asylum on your own. They had no reason to assume that the woman accompanying you was an inmate. And so you and Persano made your escape."

"I had kept my keys from the time of my residency," said Poulteney. "I found Isidore asleep, and yes, I carried him to another cell. But after he awoke, I allowed him to change his clothes himself while I kept my back turned. Otherwise, your deductions are correct. However, for all your cleverness, sir, there is one crucial aspect you haven't uncovered."

"Oh, I have uncovered it, Dr. Poulteney, I merely haven't mentioned it yet. Watson here can tell you that I have a lamentable predilection for the dramatic." So saying, he leaned forward and gave the bell pull a sharp jerk. Moments later the maid reappeared, her head modestly bowed, and moved to take the tray. As she bent to do so, Holmes seized her cap and hair and pulled them off, revealing a closely cropped head. "Watson, allow me to introduce Isidore – I beg her pardon – I should say, *Miss Isadora* Persano." For while her face might have passed for that of a handsome young man, her form, though slim, was unmistakably female.

Dr. Thomas Poulteney instantly stood and enfolded her in a protective embrace. "It began as friendship," he said in a gentle tone, "but it blossomed into something deeper. Then one day Isadora revealed her secret to me, and I realised we were in love. But there was a reason why I couldn't ask her to be my wife."

"You were already married – to Alice Dawson."

"Yes, and I rue the day that ever I stood beside her at the altar. She had deceived me into completely misreading her character, and no sooner was the ring on her finger than she embarked on a series of adulterous affairs. She drank, and experimented with stimulants of various kinds. It became obvious to me that while there had as yet been no public scandal, it was only a matter of time. Finally, I reached an agreement with her that she should move out of my house. I provided her with a monthly allowance on the condition that she lived under another name and made no further demands on me. My existing friends knew of this arrangement and kept my secret, so that when I made new acquaintances, I was thus able to represent myself as a bachelor. Although in the course of my social life I met many women, I had hardened my heart against the emotion of love. And then I met Isadora." As he said this, he took the young woman's hand in his own. Both smiled, and they gazed into each other's eyes with such clear affection that I felt a wave of warmth and sympathy towards them.

"And now, Miss Persano," said Holmes, "I believe the time has come for you to give us an explanation of those points which we haven't already resolved."

"Very well, Mr. Holmes," she began in a low, melodious voice. She lowered her eyes, and when she raised them a few seconds later they were full of frankness and resolution.

"I was born on the banks of the Imara, a river which runs into the Amazon some five hundred miles from its source. My father was a Portuguese missionary named Dr. Jorge Persano, and my mother was a member of the Sigoro Indian tribe which inhabits that region. My father converted many of the tribesmen and women to Christianity – including of course my mother – but the majority of them continued to adhere to the cult of Tumaq, a god whom they worshipped in the form of the worm that appeared in my study. For some years this was of no matter. My father also ran a school, and all were encouraged to make use of it, whatever their

410

religious persuasion. But the time came when the followers of Christ began to outnumber those of Tumaq, and the priests began to mutter that my father should be expelled, and those he had converted forcibly returned to their original creed.

"Sensing the danger, my father formulated plans to send me to Manaus to ensure my safety, but before this could be done, there was an uprising. My parents were killed, and the worship of Tumaq restored. I was then nine years old. It was decided that when I attained womanhood, I was to be a 'Bride of Tumaq', which meant that I would be sacrificed to the god at the summer solstice following my first menstruation. Until that day arrived I would be a prisoner, although I would be clothed in the finest fabrics and given the choicest foods. I lived in dread of the day when I would first experience my monthly courses, but before that evil hour arrived, I was spirited away by a small group who still secretly adhered to Christ, and taken to Manaus as my father had originally planned. There I sought out the Archbishop, who was an old friend of my father and grieved much to hear of his fate. He raised me in his house and saw that I was educated.

"I turned sixteen, and thought that my previous unhappy experiences were well behind me, but I discovered, to my sorrow, that I was wrong. I mentioned that my father had run a school in the Sigoro village. He had unwittingly nurtured a group of young men who could speak Spanish, Portuguese, and English, but remained fanatical devotees of the Worm God. When they heard of my escape, they swore that, if it meant going to the ends of the earth, they would capture me and take me back to become a Bride of Tumaq, for if one who had been promised to him didn't meet her fate at the designated time, the whole tribe would suffer for it until the situation was rectified. An attempt was made to kidnap me in Manaus, but it was thwarted, and one of the offenders captured by the police, and it was he who warned me that, go where I would, the followers of Tumaq would track me down.

"I determined that I would go to Europe, and the good Archbishop readily gave me the wherewithal. I arrived in Paris, where I first cut off my long hair and assumed men's clothing. As further protection, I carried a gun and learned how to use it well. My education enabled me to obtain work as a journalist, but I was young, and unwise enough to write an article criticising an eminent businessman and accusing him of corrupt practices. He challenged me to a duel in the cemetery at Pere Lachaise, and I killed him. Both his sons then challenged me, and met the same fate as their father. I thus acquired a reputation as a duellist, though I had challenged no one. I was unhappy with this, so I quit Paris and came to London. It was here, as you have heard, that I first met Thomas, and when an intimate friendship began to turn into love, I revealed my true sex to him.

"Because of the English divorce laws, we couldn't marry, but we spent as much time together as possible. A fellow journalist named Marlowe made sly accusations. I lost my temper and challenged him to a duel. Later, we took adjoining rooms at a hotel run by Arnold Campbell when we holidayed in Brighton together. He also accused my darling of having a perverted passion. For myself I didn't care, but these men were impugning the honour of the best man who ever drew breath. I couldn't let such insults pass. I challenged Campbell too, and in both cases I was careful to merely wound them. Honour was satisfied. As to the Sigoro totem, I confess that when I came home that evening and found that despicable worm on my desk. I succumbed to hysteria.

"Do you wonder at that, Mr. Holmes? Dr. Watson? Since the age of nine this thing had been a symbol of horror in my life, and now at the age of thirty, when I believed that I was more or less safe, and felt secure in the love of the best of men, this abomination was back to haunt me. I understood only too clearly the message its presence sent: That the followers of Tumaq had managed to pursue me to London, that they would capture me and take me back to the banks of the Imara to die at the next summer solstice. I suppose that by taunting me thus, they hoped to frighten me so badly that I would be rendered incapable of clear thought or action. The rest I think you know."

At Holmes's instructions, the police made a thorough and painstaking list of all those who had come into London from Brazil in the last two months, and by a process of elimination and identification, assisted by Miss Persano, they were able to arrest the handful of men from the Sigoro tribe who had threatened her life. All suffered permanent deportation. For the first time in her life, Isadora felt completely free.

We were back in Baker Street a few days later, enjoying a pipe after our evening meal, when I turned to Holmes and said, "There's one thing I don't understand. I almost got the feeling that Poulteney wanted us to find out the truth. Why else did he ring for Isadora to bring the tea?"

"Well, Dr. Poulteney isn't a criminal, but in this respect he shares one of their characteristics: That when an imposture has been carried off successfully, the perpetrator has an unspoken desire for it to be discovered, so that everyone may see and admire his cleverness."

"That is surely rather fanciful."

"Is it? Well, if that doesn't serve your turn, consider this: Here we have two people who for almost three years have been forced to conceal their true relationship and unable to openly express the deep love they feel

412

for each other. Imagine how great a relief it must be to finally be able to openly acknowledge those feelings, even if there is still an element of danger in the revelation."

"That, I suspect, is closer to the truth."

"And is, no doubt, the version you will give your readers."

"No, Holmes. I may make a record of this case, but I hardly think it can be published in our lifetimes. It contains certain themes, certain references . . . ."

"Ah, to what Lord Alfred Douglas called 'the love that dare not speak its name'. But there was no true instance of such a love here. It was all in the minds of a few individuals."

"Even so, I suspect that the public wouldn't wish to hear of it. Perhaps one day . . . ."

"Yes, let us hope so."

Little more remains to be said. Thomas Poulteney and Isadora continued to remain in their celibate state for another year or so, when they received news that Poulteney's estranged wife, Alice, had been killed in a boating accident, freeing them to marry. Thomas received a knighthood for his services to science in 1905. He and Lady Poulteney became well-known members of high society, to say nothing of producing three beautiful, olive-skinned children. "Isidore Persano" was never heard of again.

The Stone of Ill Omen
by Mike Chinn

Sherlock Holmes and I had returned to Baker Street after what I considered to be the coldest night I have ever endured. My friend had chosen it as the one wherein he would challenge his latest hypothesis, and afterwards, I was ready for a hearty breakfast and some rest.

Mrs. Hudson laid on a meal of kippers and scrambled eggs, accompanied by a large pot of coffee which blunted the edge of my fatigue only slightly. Holmes did the repast justice, piling his plate high, which I took as a sign that last night hadn't been a waste, and his theory settled to his satisfaction. We had been eating for only a minute or two, however, when Mrs. Hudson announced a visitor.

"Inspector Lestrade," she said, conveying in those two words her exact thoughts on those who disturbed her tenants' meals.

Holmes glanced up from his kippers, his thick eyebrows drawing down in the briefest of frowns. "So early?" he said. "It must be urgent indeed. Show the inspector in, Mrs. Hudson."

The good lady ushered Lestrade into our rooms. He was dressed for the weather in heavy overcoat and woollen scarf, and his thin face was quite waxen with the chill. Holmes spared him a glance before gesturing at a chair.

"Have you eaten?" he asked.

Lestrade looked at our meal with a certain longing, but he shook his head. "Thank you, Mr. Holmes – but I would appreciate a coffee, if you can spare it."

"Mrs. Hudson – !" began Holmes, but she had already produced a third cup. I poured and Lestrade took it gratefully, settling himself in the chair which Holmes had indicated.

"So, Inspector," said my friend. "What is so urgent? Your collar stud is unfastened and you have yet to shave. Such a cavalier approach to your toilet is unusual – even for Scotland Yard. You are in haste."

Lestrade gave a thin smile and sipped at his coffee. Its warmth put a little colour in his pallid cheeks. "You will have your little joke, Mr. Holmes – but yes, there is an urgency. I had to act before the newspapers were able to summon their troops, you see."

Holmes glanced towards me. "You intrigue me, Lestrade. What can be so precipitous that the city's journalists must be pre-empted?"

414

The inspector took another warming sip. "Are either of you familiar with the term *doppelgänger*?"

It was an odd response, quite a *non-sequitur*. I shook my head. "I don't believe I've heard the word before."

Holmes's thin lips quirked in a smile of his own. His eyes closed as he quoted from memory: "*Ere Babylon was dust, the Magus Zoroaster, my dead child, met his own image walking in the garden . . . .*"

"A little early for Byron," I commented.

"Shelley, in fact." His eyes opened once more, twinkling with private amusement. "It appears that Lestrade has risen early to amuse us with Germanic fairy tales, Watson. *Doppelgänger*: A spiritual double or exact twin. Similar to the old English notion of a *fetch*. In the more unenlightened corners of Europe, where such fanciful notions are still entertained, I believe witnessing your *doppelgänger* is considered bad luck. A harbinger of death, to some."

"Certainly bad luck in this case, Mr. Holmes. You know the name Dalton Stopwell, of course?"

"Indeed," said I. "A rising star of the House of Commons, well regarded by both sides. He has been tipped as a future Prime Minister."

"That's as might be, Doctor – but his future is a little less assured at present."

"How so?" asked Holmes.

"Because late yesterday evening, at the Guildhall, in full view of half-a-dozen witnesses, he shot a man dead."

Holmes pushed his plate aside. "Reliable witnesses?"

"Four parliamentary colleagues, a cousin, and an old school fellow."

"Then you must have your man. I fail to see why you have hurried along to see me – nor why Germanic spooks need be invoked."

Lestrade drained his coffee. "Because, Mr. Holmes, at the same time as the murder, just as many people – all as equally well acquainted with Mr. Stopwell, and including the Speaker of the House – were listening to him address a gathering of the party faithful at a dinner in Mayfair."

"Then clearly one was an impostor," said I.

"So reason tells us," agreed Lestrade. "However, I have interviewed everyone who saw the murder, and everyone who was at the dinner, and all are willing to swear that, in both cases, it was Stopwell."

"I take it the assassin wasn't apprehended?" said Holmes.

"He made his escape in the confusion."

"But you have Mr. Stopwell?"

"Under house arrest at his home on Wilton Crescent. Safe from intrusion from the press – for now. You understand the reason for my haste."

415

Holmes nodded slowly.

"There is no doubt about the time?" I asked. "Mr. Stopwell couldn't have left the dinner and travelled to the Guildhall?"

"We have checked the times, Doctor. Stopwell left Mayfair and returned to his house quite late."

"Did you also check the clocks at both scenes?" Even as I spoke, I was aware of how absurd my question sounded.

Lestrade ponderously shook his head. "There was nothing out of the ordinary in either place. Only that a man was witnessed to be in both at the same time."

"Who was the victim?" asked Holmes. He took cigarettes from his coat, lighting one with a match. He didn't offer either myself or Lestrade a smoke. His breakfast seemed quite forgotten, and I leaned back in my chair with a silent sigh, recognising the symptoms.

"An Australian gentleman by the name of Burgess MacNamara. Two years ago, he established an opal mining company in Queensland, becoming quite rich. There was a recent discovery of a large black opal – the MacNamara Raven – "

"I recall it well," said Holmes. "It was meant as a gift for Queen Victoria, but disappeared in transit. The ship upon which is was being transported was searched thoroughly, although nothing was ever found. The packet company tried to explain it away as a bungled robbery, resulting in the gem being lost overboard." He drew thoughtfully on his cigarette.

"Why was this MacNamara in London?" I wondered.

"Probably to establish closer trade links for his opals with Britain." Lestrade rubbed at his face. "Although more than one guest at the Guildhall was of the opinion he was attempting to recover his black opal."

"Stolen from the ship, then sold in London?" Holmes shook his head. "The gem would be too distinctive. No trafficker in stolen items would risk the inevitable discovery when attempting to sell something as memorable as the Raven opal – except the most foolhardy ones."

"London has more than its fair share of fences whose greed outstrips their brains, Mr. Holmes. But clearly you think the murder and vanished opal are connected."

"I think nothing of the kind, Lestrade. You know I never theorise before I'm satisfied I have all the data."

"Yet you will concede the coincidence is intriguing," I said.

"What is coincidence but the preferential selection of two or more unconnected incidents? Their importance exaggerated by a quirk of the human brain." He stubbed out his cigarette in a half-eaten breakfast. "Although I will admit this case of yours does have elements of interest,

416

Lestrade. Do you propose we go straight to Wilton Crescent, or is there anything to be gained by interviewing the various witnesses first?"

The inspector smiled. "As you see fit, Mr. Holmes."

My friend stood. "You are transparent, Lestrade. I trust you are more inscrutable when interrogating suspects. Then it is Dalton Stopwell. Come, gentlemen."

Stopwell's Belgravia residence stood within a pristine terrace, rendered frontage and window frames all of a clean white. Only the front door stood out differently, gleaming under a coat of what looked like recently applied gloss-black paint. There was little to mark it out as different from its neighbours, and a casual by-passer would likely have no idea as to the identity of the owner.

There was no police presence near the door, and so far Lestrade's efforts to keep Stopwell's possible connection to the tragic events of the previous evening away from the gentlemen of the press seemed to be bearing fruit. There wasn't a reporter to be seen. Indeed, Wilton Crescent was generally quiet, with only two delivery carts visible along its length. If anyone should recognise Holmes though, I wondered how long that peace would last.

We stepped down from Lestrade's cab. Quickly he ushered us both up to and through the front entrance – the door opening as we approached, and closing silently once all three of us were in the reception hall. Liveried staff took our hats and overcoats, and a solemn gentleman whom I took to be Stopwell's butler led us through an open double door.

We stood in a light, elegant reception room, sparsely decorated, with an assortment of matching chairs and sofas arranged about a carpeted floor. There was the air of a club room about it – cosy and welcoming, at the same time strangely aloof. More of a meeting place than family room.

As we seated ourselves in comfortable chairs, the butler enquired as to whether we would like refreshments. Holmes waved away the offer with a curt gesture, keen as ever to dispense with the pleasantries and proceed to business with all despatch. Lestrade and I also declined. The gentlemen left, and moments later Dalton Stopwell himself entered the room, accompanied by another, sober-suited personage – not quite so tall as the Minister, and younger – although a thick ginger moustache added a gravitas beyond his years.

Stopwell's was a daunting presence. Several inches over six feet in height, his broad frame hung from wide, muscular shoulders which even the finest tailoring could scarce contain. Fierce black eyes burned from a chiselled face, the lowered half of which was covered in a long, thick brown beard – the minister's most recognisable feature. His hair, a shade

417

or two darker than his magnificent whiskers, was brushed back, falling past his collar in untamed curls.

A broad smile split his dark beard at sight of us all and he stepped forward, shaking us each by the hand even as he bade us stay seated. Then he threw himself into a *chaise-longue* which protested softly at such treatment. The other fellow remained standing, his be-whiskered features carefully neutral – although his pale grey eyes were watchful.

"The inspector will have briefed you all, I trust?" the Minister began without preamble. His black eyes were fixed directly on Holmes, and even though he included the three of us in that sentence, there could be no doubt as to whom he addressed himself.

"As much as I can, sir," said Lestrade.

"Indeed," said Holmes. "There are few enough facts in this case, but I believe Lestrade has conveyed them succinctly."

"Yet you will have questions of your own, I'm sure." Stopwell reached across to a plain wooden box and opened it. "Would you care to smoke, gentlemen?"

We each took a cigarette – all except for the one standing behind the chaise-long. Once they were lit, Holmes continued.

"There were a number of reliable witnesses to the Guildhall shooting, I believe – all of whom were quite certain it was you who shot MacNamara."

Stopwell frowned. "Indeed. Four members of my party – all of whom I have worked with closely over the past three years. My cousin Randolph Inverson here – " He indicated the one standing behind him. "– and an old school chum, Wilson Stirling."

Inverson nodded as he was introduced, I studied him again, and thought I could detect a faint familial resemblance.

"All of whom know you well," continued Holmes.

"Exceptionally well. Cousin Randolph is perhaps the least intimate of that band, for we are a large family and we tend to see him mostly at Christmases and funerals."

The shadow of a smile ghosted across Inverson's lips. "You make me sound like the family black sheep, old fellow." He raised his hands in a faintly alarmed gesture. "I'm a writer, do you see – like you, Dr. Watson – or have ambitions to be one, and I travel extensively, chasing the muse."

"And Stirling?" asked Holmes.

"My oldest and dearest friend," said Stopwell. "We have been together since my first days at Rugby school."

"Do any bear resentment towards you?"

Stopwell laughed. "We are politicians, Mr. Holmes! I have often considered Parliament to be little more than a child's playground, but with better tailors. I am successful. Therefore, resentment must always follow."

"Enough for someone to swear they saw you commit a crime where you did not?" I asked.

Stopwell's broad smile faded a little, to be replaced by a wry, sad expression. "There are some who would," he admitted quietly. "I have no doubt there are those who would wish to see me disgraced and fallen. But unjustly accused of murder – ?" He crushed out his cigarette. "That I think would be a step too far."

"Besides, Watson," added Holmes, "among the witnesses are a relative and old school friend. Unless we include both of them as co-conspirators – " He glanced towards Inverson.

The young man slowly shook his head, expression grave – although he seemed to be suppressing a smile, and his eyes twinkled, as though amused by the suggestion. "It's a fair plot for a slice of fiction, though – possible ne'er-do-well cousin implicates respected family member in murder plot. Would *The Strand* take it, do you think, Doctor?"

It was my turn to shake my head.

Holmes templed his long fingers, resting them against his chin. "What of the victim, Mr. Stopwell – Burgess MacNamara? Were you acquainted with him?"

"I knew of him, of course, but we had never previously met."

"Then you will not be conversant with his reasons for being in England."

The minister shrugged. "Presently not my purview, Mr. Holmes. Business of some kind, certainly. Ferguson – who was also at the Guildhall last night – would be the man to tell you. He is an Undersecretary for Trade."

"You don't think his visit concerned the missing black opal?"

Stopwell laughed. "The legendary MacNamara Raven? That stone is either stolen or lost, surely."

"Perhaps." Holmes looked up to the young man standing beyond the chaise-long. "And you, Mr. Inverson – did you know MacNamara?"

"Afraid not. Never been as far as the Antipodes yet. But like Dalton, I knew of him. Who doesn't?"

Holmes pursed his lips. "Then why were you at the Guildhall?"

"Wanted to see the rich Australian, I suppose. Dalton managed to wangle me an invite, since he wasn't expected to attend himself. Probably though I'd report back anything the other snollygosters said about him."

Stopwell laughed at that. "And now you see why Randolph is rarely allowed in civilised society."

"And what did you witness last night?" asked Holmes. "In as exact detail as you may recall. Be precise."

Inverson frowned. "I'd arrived something like fifteen minutes beforehand. MacNamara and Ferguson were in deep conversation, when in pops Dalton. Or whom we all thought was Dalton. I remember being a little baffled, since – as I said – he wasn't expected to be there."

"And what did the one you thought was your cousin do?"

Inverson blinked. "Marched straight up to MacNamara, drew the largest revolver I have ever seen from his overcoat, and shot him."

"Did he speak?"

"Not a word. Just – " He raised his right hand, forefinger extended.

"Before he was shot, did MacNamara react in any way?"

He looked thoughtful for a moment. "No. Only once the pistol was drawn. He bridled at that – but so would I."

Holmes nodded. "And after the shot was fired?"

Inverson huffed a short laugh. "Damned chaos. MacNamara went down. He fell forward I think, or tried to grab his assassin, as for a moment the one with the pistol grappled with him. No one seemed to know what to do apart from shout contradictory orders. When order was restored, the killer had vanished."

Holmes sprang to his feet. "Thank you, Mr. Inverson, you have been invaluable. Mr. Stopwell, I will not keep you a moment longer."

The Minister also stood, extending his hand. "If you need me for anything more – anything at all – please do not hesitate to notify me. This is a bad business, and must be resolved as quickly and discreetly as possible."

Holmes shook his hand. "Agreed, sir. However, once the press learn that they have been deprived of a particularly tasty story, they will not be kind."

"That, Mr. Holmes, may well be quite the understatement. However, I have broad shoulders, and thick skin." He gave an exaggerated shrug as though to illustrate his point. "I shall weather the storm when it breaks."

He shook hands with Lestrade and myself before we left. His grip was firm and steady. If he was concerned over the murder and his apparent involvement in it, he disguised it well. Inverson saw us to the door, apologising for not being more help.

When we stood once more in Wilton Crescent, Lestrade turned to us. "I must stay here for a while longer. You may take my cab back to Baker Street, gentlemen. If you should receive any inspiration about the case, Mr. Holmes, you may notify me via the Yard."

"Of course. In the meantime, may I recommend you set some men to search the more hidden corners of the streets surrounding the Guildhall."

The inspector frowned. "Looking for what, exactly?"

"It is a long shot, but a large horse-hair beard, perhaps. And a wig. Less likely will be material that might be used as padding."

Lestrade winked. "I'll see to it."

We climbed into the waiting cab and settled ourselves. As it pulled away, I commented, "So we have a man shot by a person unknown and with no obvious motive, who is clearly impersonating a member of the British Government. An obtuse one, even by your standards."

"On the contrary, my dear Watson, this is perfectly straightforward case. There remain a few points which require further investigation, but I'm confident I will have my answer before nightfall. We have more pressing business after all – or have you forgotten last night's vigil?"

I had not. "But why such an impersonation? Stopwell is such a singular person: Well-known, with a unique physical presence. It would be a difficult impression to carry off."

"Stopwell's very fame and appearance makes him an easy target for imitation. He is very meat to music hall impressionists: Affix a huge beard, stand tall, and utter any phrases for which he is known. Instantly your audience will know to whom you refer. People see only the familiar – what they expect."

"Even so," I agreed, "a performer on the stage is a far cry from someone standing close by those who know a man intimately, and yet fooling them."

"Quite so. They would have to be of a similar height – the physique would easily be attained by the type of padding for which I suggested Lestrade's men search. If young Inverson hadn't been a witness, he would be an obvious suspect. But again we have the simple matter of an audience seeing only what they expect."

"But Stopwell was not expected at the Guildhall."

"Indeed – yet his presence could easily be explained." Holmes's thin lips twitched in a faint smile. "The MacNamara Raven is at the core of this mystery, friend Watson. I am sure of it – but I lack any proof." He rubbed his hands together vigorously. "This is what adds spice to an otherwise mundane case! MacNamara was shot by someone performing an exceptional impersonation of Stopwell, but we don't know why, or by whom."

"And how do you propose to find out?"

"How indeed. Now here is Baker Street . . . ." As the cab drew to a stop Holmes leapt out and hurried towards our simple door. As I stepped down at a more sedate pace, I heard my friend calling out for Mrs. Hudson, telling her to summon Billy, the page, with all haste. When I reached our rooms he was sorting impatiently through a jumble of newspapers – some dating back several days – strewn haphazardly in a corner. I hung my overcoat and hat and settled myself by the fire, thankful for its heat.

After five minutes or so, Holmes stepped back with a harsh cry of frustration. "Nothing! I had hoped to – Ah, Billy!"

The young lad had opened the door, his face keen with expectation. Holmes strode towards him, a strip which I imagine he had torn from a newspaper pinched between thumb and forefinger. He scratched a few hurried lines upon it and handed it to the boy, along with a few coins. Billy squinted at the words, no doubt trying to decipher my friend's sometimes appalling hand.

"Are the instructions clear?" asked Holmes.

After a moment's longer concentration, Billy nodded. "Indeed, sir."

"Then quickly! I fear time may be against us."

Billy grinned, once more disappearing beyond the door.

Holmes threw himself into his chair, reaching for his noxious pipe. Until Billy returned, I realised, with an answer to whatever my friend had scrawled in his note, conversation was at an end.

It was a little short of three hours before Billy came back. In that time Holmes grew increasingly restive, consulting his watch more and more frequently. Each time he found it wanting, responding with a soft yet harsh sound of displeasure. Several times I asked him what was so pressing, but he merely waved my enquiry away. I found it curious that my friend – who could wait for an entire evening with the patience of the ages – now fretted over the return of a boy and whatever information he had been despatched to retrieve.

Shortly before Billy returned, Holmes received a telegram, brought up to us by Mrs. Hudson. He snatched it from her with a curt "Ha!" and then paced across the room, scanning the lines with an intense eye.

"Important news?" I asked as she retreated. Holmes simply grunted an ambivalent monosyllable, thrust the message into a coat pocket, and went back to his fretting.

At length Billy returned, in his fist the scrap of newsprint replaced by two quarto sheets of paper. Holmes took them from him and glanced at both, the tension in his frame dissolving as he did so. A smile of relief briefly lightened his features.

"Ah – capital! Capital! We have time after all. Our quarry is still at hand!" He presented Billy with another note and more coins. "One last errand: A telegram to Lestrade. See that the wording is exactly as I have written it."

Billy grinned, enjoying the excitement, and left once more.

I extinguished the cigarette I was smoking. "Then may I now expect some sort of explanation of the past hours? Or will you simply growl at me again?"

"My dear Watson – apologies. My impatience has made me boorish."

"No more than usual."

"A palpable hit! However, you have tolerance enough for us both, combined with a fortitude which I too often take for granted."

"And am I also susceptible to flattery?"

Holmes's lips twitched. "I initially sent Billy forth with instructions to enquire at the appropriate shipping offices with regard to the most recent passenger arrivals from Australia, as well as any imminent departures."

I glanced towards the far corner. "You found nothing of help in those rumpled newspapers, I take it."

"Alas, no mention of either an Australian-bound packet or arrival of such. And the relevance of that rested upon the first telegram I asked Billy to send." He pulled the now crumpled telegraph message from his coat and flourished it with his free hand. "I enquired of the Agent-General for Queensland whether or not Burgess MacNamara ever had a partner, requesting they respond post haste. That was my lynch-pin. That simple nugget of information would reveal if my thoughts ever since Lestrade walked in this morning were baseless speculation, or had a solid foundation. The data must fit the hypothesis, and if it doesn't, then the hypothesis shall be rejected and we must start again."

"I take it that the data did fit?"

Holmes offered me the creased telegram. I took it but didn't bother to read, since I knew he would convey its meaning soon enough.

"When MacNamara first landed in Australia twenty-three years ago, he set up business with a Cyrus Wyborough. Yet there is no record of the man. History has all but erased him. Burgess MacNamara would appear to be sole owner and beneficiary of his Queensland opal mine."

"Or he was."

"Your humour has a definite morbid twist today. Indeed, with MacNamara gone, Wyborough – if he still lives – may well still have a claim upon the business."

"You think it was he who shot MacNamara?"

"I will not speculate at this juncture."

"The Agent-General gave you no clue as to Wyborough's appearance, I suppose."

"The barest details only, I'm afraid. He is but a name."

"Even so, from your interest in the next sailing to Australia, I'm guessing you suspect whoever it was killed MacNamara to be on the earliest ship to depart."

"You excel yourself. And Billy will be telegraphing Lestrade with that very information presently."

"And the name of this ship?"

"The *Australis Borealis* – a freight and passenger auxiliary due to begin embarkation in – " He glanced at his watch. " – three hours and seventeen minutes."

"Then had we better not begin to make our way?" I enquired, surprised Holmes wasn't already donning hat and coat and calling for a cab.

"The embarkation point is less than an hour's journey from here. I don't imagine our man will wish to turn up early and risk being spotted while he cools his heels at the dockside. His plan to impersonate Stopwell and shoot MacNamara bears all the hallmarks of careful planning and a logical brain. He will have allowed for the possibility of someone deducing the Minister isn't the perpetrator of the crime. He will be caught between the desire to urgently leave the country, or to lay low for an indefinite period while the trail cools – and any number of ships bound for Australia are searched fruitlessly before being allowed to sail."

"Or he may take an indirect route. From London he could flee to any port in the world."

"Capital, Watson! Your reasoning does you credit. However, I also believe a certain impatience underscores our prey. He is a man of action who, once decided upon a course, will strike out swiftly and with determination. The last ship to arrive from Australia was three days ago. The previous one was over a week before that. It is my belief he timed his arrival in the capital to coincide with MacNamara's appearance at the Guildhall, giving him opportunity to perfect his disguise, execute his plan, and vanish into the night – no longer impersonating Stopwell. He will have discarded the beard and anything else necessary to carry out the deceit as he fled – to be seen as the Minister, walking the streets unaccompanied rather than in a carriage, would complicate matters further. Passers-by may wish to greet him, or pester him with questions.

"No. This is a plan dependant on speed. He strikes, and while the capital's police are still grappling with the notion of a prominent Member of Parliament committing murder in the most blatant manner, he makes his escape."

"Yet if his disguise is gone – "

"He must still cut a remarkable figure. Padding will add bulk, and a beard and wig provide the facial similarity – but even tall-heeled boots with raised insoles can only add a few inches. The killer must himself be of unusual height – certainly tall enough to be obvious, even in a crowd."

424

I found myself smiling. "Was there perhaps such a person on the most recent ship to arrive from Australia?"

"Am I that obvious?" My friend raised the quarto sheets. "Indeed there was. Remarkable enough for the clerk to whom Billy spoke to offer the information with barely any prompting."

"Then we just need to be at the *Australis Borealis* shortly before embarkation, arrest our man – with Lestrade's help – and the case in done."

"Almost – there is still the matter of the MacNamara Raven, and its particular role in the events."

"Which is – ?"

"A hypothesis I'm still constructing. I'm hoping our murderer, when we have him, will confirm my suspicions. It's a small thing, but I should like all the facts to be assembled neatly – even if only for my own satisfaction."

The day had turned dank and drear. A persistent drizzle hung over the city, bringing a premature twilight which, for all its wretchedness, worked somewhat in our favour. Holmes and I took a cab to within a few hundred yards of the *Australis Borealis'* berth, proceeding the rest of the way on foot, keeping to the many shadows and blessing the poor light for providing a degree of anonymity. We were within a few yards of the ship's lowering silhouette when a muted challenge came from a nearby hut. My hand fell upon my service revolver, safe within a coat pocket – our prey had already shot dead one man, and I didn't deceive myself he wouldn't attempt to do so again. But it was just Lestrade, sheltered in the tiny, two-windowed building with one of his men. Swiftly we joined them, I for one glad to be out of the chilling rain.

"Nothing to report," murmured the inspector, "although – " He held up two slightly damp objects and smiled: A long fake beard and curly wig. "As predicted, Mr. Holmes." Then he nodded at the ship. "So far no one has stepped off or onto that boat."

"Most likely getting themselves ready to welcome the passengers," I observed. "No one will want to be queueing up any longer than necessary in this weather."

Holmes nodded silently, his keen gaze upon the ship. From what I could make out in the dimness, she was a large but ageing liner, with four masts for the auxiliary sails to complement her boiler. Likely it would be a comparatively slow voyage to Australia, but I imagine Wyborough – if he was indeed our man – might consider himself removed from danger once the ship had sailed. The only lights presently burning were in what I guessed was the wheelhouse, just above and forward of the low superstructure. None lit the deck, or shone from any of the hull's portholes.

425

If the crew were busy preparing for embarkation, the damp air muffled any sounds. It would be easy to imagine the vessel deserted.

Lestrade consulted his watch. "Several minutes to go before boarding starts," said he. "Will they be punctual, do you think?" He looked through the hut's second window, face pressed close to the glass as he tried to see up and down the dock's length. "I can't see anyone who looks like a passenger. No one at all, in fact."

"Keeping out of the weather in the steam packet offices, most likely," I said.

"Hullo," murmured Lestrade. "Something's happening – "

Fresh lights flared into life across the *Australis Borealis'* length. Against the grey dismal sky it now took on quite a cheery mien. Various members of the crew appeared on deck and began to lower an awning-covered gangway. Once it was resting on the dockside two crewmen – in long dark coats, as far as I could ascertain in the poor light – descended, affixing two lamps to the awning supports.

Holmes was out of the hut in a second. Lestrade and I followed closely. The rain had worsened, and I pulled up the collar of my overcoat, adjusting my hat. We formed a line, hoping to appear to be no more than voyagers eager to be out of the cold and wet.

I glanced around. More overcoated figures were appearing out of the dankness – Lestrade's men, I had no doubt. They too joined the short queue, casting about surreptitiously – if with little subtlety – watching the dockside for anyone of unusual height.

More lights blazed aboard the *Australis Borealis*. The ship let loose a deafening howl from its horn. Embarkation time had begun.

Passengers began to appear, huddling against the rain as they moved quickly towards the awaiting ship. Lestrade and his men boarded, ascending the gangway and spreading themselves across the open deck. Holmes and I stepped aside, positioning ourselves behind the gangway, the better to see without being seen. Or such was our hope.

I would estimate that most, if not all, of those lining up to board the *Australis Borealis* were assisted passage immigrants, all hoping to make a better life for themselves than the ones they endured in England. Many were wretched individuals, small bundles containing all they valued in their lives. Others had battered portmanteaux or faded carpet bags that spoke of precious little in the way of worldly goods. Some had children, frightened shivering creatures who clung to their mothers' coats, more apprehensive of the life awaiting them than the one they were abandoning. I heartily wished every one well and prayed they might take full advantage of their new world.

426

Holmes watched the tide of drab humanity pass slowly, his chin resting on the handle of his raised stick. His features were impassive, although I fancied there was a flicker of some emotion deep within his eyes. At length he lowered the stick and straightened himself.

"This will not do!" he muttered. "I have been a clumsy lackwit!"

Pushing through the assembled passengers, oblivious to the angry remonstrances at his behaviour, he approached one of the crewmen checking through the embarkees' passage documents.

"When does this ship load its freight?" he demanded.

The crewman glanced at Holmes for a moment. "For the last day-and-a-half, thereabouts. We finish an hour or so before the passengers are allowed on board, as a rule."

Holmes spun about. "He has preceded us, Watson! Our man is already on board!"

Without another word he sprinted up the gangway, calling for Lestrade. Apologising to the waiting passengers I made my way past them and followed my friend up onto the liner.

A seaman, most likely alarmed by the commotion, came onto the deck – to be waylaid by Holmes.

"Where is the cargo hold?" demanded my friend.

The seaman pointed past Holmes's shoulder. "Aft, sir. The forward hold has been converted for steerage passengers."

Holmes spun about without hesitation, crying out for me to follow, along with Lestrade and some of his men who were coming along the deck, skirting the ship's superstructure.

"Have the steerage compartments searched!" cried Holmes. "In case he has made his way out of the hold. Watson – !" He hurried towards the liner's rear, I following in his wake, a moment later caught up by the inspector after he had issued his orders.

The hold was covered by three sets of huge twin hatches, dominating the portion of the deck aft of the superstructure. At a word from Lestrade, two of the hatches were swung laboriously upward, Holmes fidgeting impatiently as they were secured and a ladder run down into the dim interior. The moment the ladder was fixed, Holmes sprang onto it, descending rapidly. Lestrade passed me a burning oil lamp, and I followed as smartly as I could – for holding onto both rungs and the lamp simultaneously wasn't a task I found myself best suited to.

I reached the floor of the hold and raised my lantern. Everywhere were tall crates lashed in place and bundled sacks the size of a man secured under hempen webbing. In one dark corner I could just make out the upright boiler of a stationary steam engine.

427

I pulled my revolver from its pocket. "Holmes!" I hissed, for there was no sign of him. His head peeked around a large crate, yellow in the lamplight, a finger to his lips. Then he vanished. Behind me, Lestrade reached the floor, shortly joined by two more policemen and three crewmen. All bore oil lamps.

At a gesture from the inspector they spread out silently, spanning the width of the hold, and began to move carefully forward. I joined the line, and we crept around the lashed crates and sacks, alert for any attempt at ambush from the shadows or hidden corners, allowing the lamplight to fall into every nook. Of Holmes there was no sign. If he was ahead of us he would have needed the eyes of a cat to piece the unlit gloom. I consoled myself with the thought that Wyborough would also be similarly disadvantaged.

There was a short, sharp noise from ahead. I paused, extending lamp and revolver. The men to either side of me also went on the alert, their eyes narrowing. After several seconds, during which time there was nothing but the distant sound of voices up on deck, we continued forward. My heart had begun to pound uncomfortably, my breath to hitch. My hands were steady, though, my revolver unwavering.

I moved between two towering crates, the channel between them too narrow for more than one man. I slowed as I approached their far sides, only too aware of possible ambush by someone awaiting around a corner, out of sight.

I stepped through. There was no one beyond – only more crates. To my left and right my companions appeared, smiling their own relief as we acknowledged each other.

There was a noise behind me. I turned, and there stood a towering figure in a dusty black suit – so similar to the formal wear in which I had seen Dalton Stopwell attired earlier. An enormous revolver was clutched in one hand – Randolph Inverson hadn't exaggerated when he described it – aimed directly at me. In the other was a length of taut rope, leading up towards the darkness at the top of the crate

"That's quite far enough, mate." His voice was deep and clear, containing hints of an Australian accent. Even in the uncertain light of the oil lamp I could tell he was easily the same height as Stopwell, although his shoulders were narrower, his face lean and gaunt. Only a generous beard and judicious padding would disguise the obvious differences.

"You will be Cyrus Wyborough," I said, keeping my own revolver aimed at him.

"I would be indeed." He raised his voice. "I'd advise anyone imagining they can jump me to forget it. I have this fellow right in my

428

sights, and this gun could probably put a hole in this tub's hull at close enough range. You know what it can do to a man."

"What do you imagine you're going to achieve?" came Lestrade's voice. "My men are everywhere – and there is also the ship's crew."

"Why, the two of us are going to climb out of here and disappear off the ship, copper. Try to stop me and I will shoot to kill. I have little to lose after all, unless you have a way to hang a man more than once over here."

"You're bluffing."

"Then call me on it, if you dare. You have me cornered – and a cornered man is twice as dangerous – "

I caught a flicker in the darkness behind Wyborough – something flashing in the lamplight. A moment later Wyborough staggered, grunting. He recovered and raised his pistol. A black walking stick cracked down across his wrist, and the revolver tumbled to the floor. There was a shot, and I realised the large revolver had gone off as it struck the floor. Wyborough fell to one knee, cursing.

Sherlock Holmes stepped out of the darkness, his stick held like a rapier. He levelled it under the Australian's jaw, forcing back the man's head, even as he kicked Wyborough's revolver out of the way.

"Are you well, Watson?"

"I will live – if my heart ever slows." I glanced down at Wyborough – and the dark pool spreading across the floor under his right knee. He had been hit by the wayward gunshot. I leapt forward, placing the lamp on the floor. "Quickly – lay him down!"

In a second Holmes grasped the situation. He took Wyborough's shoulders and lowered him flat as I stretched out both legs. Around his right thigh his trouser leg was drenched in blood.

"The femoral artery!" I said, feeling for a bullet hole. The shot had torn through fabric and flesh, catching the blood vessel on the way. If I didn't halt the bleeding, Wyborough would be dead in a minute. I tore away the ripped trouser leg, tearing it into crude strips which I twisted into a tourniquet. As I did my best to tighten the crude ligature above the wound, Lestrade bent over me.

"We need to get him out of here," I said. There was a seaman standing just inside the lamplight. "Does this ship have a sickbay?"

"Not much of one – "

Wyborough was laughing softly. "Don't waste your time, mate. Looks like I'm going to cheat the hangman after all."

"Not if can stop the bleeding."

He shook his head. "Not much of a choice, eh?" He saw my friend standing above him and smiled. "If he's Watson, you must be the lauded

429

Sherlock Holmes. Gave you a dance there for a while, eh? Not many as can say that."

"Your anonymity certainly stalled my deductions – for a while." Holmes crouched, as well as he could in the cramped space. "Am I correct in thinking you and MacNamara had a falling out some years back? Severe enough for you to hold a grudge?"

Wyborough hissed. "He got greedy. Seen it many times. Had some hired toughs beat me ragged and then left out in the wilderness during the monsoon. Thought that or the crocodiles would finish me. Took my name off the company list, like I'd never existed."

"All over the MacNamara Raven?"

"The Wyborough Raven!" A pale fire kindled momentarily in eyes that were almost as black as Stopwell's. "I dug it up. It was mine! But he took it – never let it out of his sight."

"He was to present it to Her Majesty," I commented even as I checked his wound, the blood had slowed, but still flowed far too readily for my liking.

Wyborough shook his head again. "It never left the country."

"The loss on board the ship was a feint," said Holmes. "An accomplice on board, discarding the fake presentation box before raising the alarm."

"If the world thought it stolen, or lost, he could keep it forever. But I – " He shivered. " – I knew better. Burgess could always find men to do his work for him. Paid toughs. That's why I couldn't take him in Queensland. Never get close."

"Until you discovered he would be in London, lacking that protection."

The Australian sighed. "And imagine my thoughts when followed him here and I realised how easy it would be for me to impersonate one of your Ministers at the Guildhall. He would have an alibi, and I would gain immediate access and an escape route."

"Even so, MacNamara recognised you the moment before he was shot. Or your pistol, anyway."

"Old Bessie . . . ." His voice was growing fainter with each heartbeat. "That big old smokebox has served me true for over twenty years. I knew Burgess would be sure to recognise it – know who had killed him"

"Yet catching MacNamara after you shot him so that you might take the opal," said Holmes. "Grappling, as a witness described it. An unnecessary risk, and likely to kindle a spark of curiosity in anyone observing you closely enough."

Wyborough's pale lips twitched in a feeble smile. "I couldn't let him take it – not even into death. It couldn't be found on his body . . . ." His voice tailed off.

I leaned in close. He was gone. I glanced around at Lestrade and shook my head.

The inspector straightened. "Saved us the cost of a trial, anyway. Justice is served."

"Of a sort," said Holmes. There was a hint of regret in his tone. "I would have preferred it if the law had been allowed to take its course. I acted precipitously."

"The doctor's life was at risk," said Lestrade. "I doubt any of us would have acted differently."

Holmes grunted something, then slipped a hand inside Wyborough's coat, withdrawing it almost instantly. Pinched between his thumb and forefinger was what looked like a pebble. One black as jet, but shot through with veins of dark fire that burned deep within it. He came to his feet. "The Raven, gentlemen – whichever of the late opal miners would care to lay claim to it."

I stood. "It's certainly a remarkable gem."

"'For the love of money is the root of all evil, which, while some coveted after, they have erred from the faith, and pierced themselves through with many sorrows.' Opals were once considered good luck. Now, thanks in part to Sir Walter Scott, the opposite is often true. *Doppelgängers* and opals, gentlemen – harbingers of ill to some. And it's certain MacNamara and Wyborough have both suffered their own degree of sorrow." He stared at the black gem a moment longer before tossing it carelessly to Lestrade. "Perhaps, Inspector, it's better if that stone remains lost after all."

The Commotion at the Diogenes Club
by Paul Hiscock

I have witnessed many disturbing scenes during my adventures at the side of Sherlock Holmes. However, by far the most disquieting experience was to hear a man shouting in the staid setting of the Diogenes Club.

We had arrived at the club in the late morning to meet with Mycroft Holmes, who was eager to learn the truth behind the baffling case of the Home Secretary's spectacles. It took some time to explain every aspect of the case to Mycroft's satisfaction, and by the time we stood to leave, I was eagerly considering where we might adjourn for lunch. However, all thoughts of food evaporated when, upon opening the heavy, padded door to the Stranger's Room, I heard the sound of shouting coming from further inside the building.

I turned to the Holmes brothers and was about to ask if they had also heard this unexpected noise. However, before I could utter a single syllable, Mycroft raised his finger to his lips and indicated that I should stop. With the door open wide, even the Stranger's Room was subject to the Diogenes Club's interdiction against speech.

With a nod of his head, Holmes confirmed that he had also heard the sound, and together we stepped out into the hall to investigate. We had barely left the room when the door to the Reading Room was flung open and a man ran out. He was muttering to himself, over and over, "I'm sorry. I'm sorry. I'm sorry."

He paused for a moment in the hall and looked around. However, his gaze passed over us as though we weren't there. Then he turned and ran towards the front door and out into the street beyond. The door slammed shut behind him, and with his departure, the habitual silence of the club was restored.

I wondered if we should give chase, although I didn't yet know what he had done wrong, other than breaking the club's cardinal rule. However, Holmes was already striding towards the Reading Room, and I elected to follow him instead.

At first glance as I stepped into the room, everything seemed the same as normal. The members were seated in their nooks, like always, reading their newspapers. Usually they ignored anyone who entered, choosing to remain oblivious to the world around them. However, that day, some of them actually looked up to see who was there.

Holmes beckoned me forward to stand beside him, and it was only then that I noticed that not all the members were sitting in their chairs. One man was lying on the floor in the middle of the room, next to an upturned table. I ran to his aid, dropping to my knees next to him, but now I was closer, I could see that it was too late. The pallor of death on his face contrasted starkly with the dark red blood seeping into the carpet from the back of his head.

I dutifully checked for a pulse anyway, before reaching up and closing his eyelids. Then I looked up at Holmes. Just like his brother had earlier, he raised a finger to his lips to remind me to remain silent. This time I baulked at the interdiction. Surely the death of a man was more important than obeying an arbitrary rule. However, I reluctantly allowed him to lead me back across the hall and back into the Stranger's Room, and waited for the door to close before I said anything.

"You both saw the dead man in the middle of the Reading Room?" I asked.

"Of course," replied Mycroft. "Lord Browning had been a member for many years. He will be missed."

"Then why are your fellow members acting as though he isn't there? They should have been trying to help, not continuing with their reading as though nothing had happened."

"You confirmed for yourself that he was dead. Could they have done any more than you?"

"Probably not," I conceded. "It looked like he bled to death quickly."

"Very well then, we can put the matter behind us. I will make the necessary arrangements."

"Yes, the police should be called at once."

"That will not be necessary," replied Mycroft. "We have people to handle this type of incident."

"You have people to handle deaths?" I asked him, incredulously.

"Many of our members are quite elderly, and sadly, more than one has passed away on the premises. The members expect such matters to be dealt with discreetly. There is a local undertaker who will remove the body and clean up any mess."

"This isn't a case of a man drifting away in his favourite chair. That man was violently murdered. The police must be called to investigate."

I turned to Holmes, who had sat down in an armchair and was observing us both silently.

"Surely you agree with me. One cannot simply tidy up a man's death as though it is a minor inconvenience."

"Watson has a point, Brother," he replied. "I believe that in this case an investigation is in order."

"Very well," said Mycroft. "I will have the body sent for examination by the police."

"Surely they will arrange that for themselves once they arrive," I said.

"The police will not be coming here. Can you imagine constables stomping around the Diogenes Club? It would be intolerable."

"But the Reading Room is the location of a crime," I said.

"The Reading Room is a safe haven in this stormy world," replied Mycroft. "If I were to allow it to be desecrated by the police, it would undermine the very principles upon which this club was founded."

"The police will want to come here," said Holmes.

"Whatever for?" replied Mycroft. "There will be plenty of evidence on the body, and while the members of the detective branch might not be capable of discerning the story it tells, I am certain you could explain it to them."

"A detective, such as Lestrade, will not be deflected so easily," said Holmes. "He is not observant, but he is stubborn and persistent. He will insist upon seeing all the evidence, and speaking to everyone who was there. However, he might, perhaps, be persuaded to accept my findings, if I am allowed to carry out a thorough investigation."

Mycroft stared at us, assessing our resolve. Then he sighed deeply.

"Very well, you will be allowed to investigate, if that is what it takes to satisfy you and the police and resolve this unfortunate incident. However, you will still be expected to conduct yourself in accordance with all the rules of this establishment. If you fail to do so, even my support will not be enough to prevent your immediate and permanent expulsion from the premises."

Holmes stepped forward and held out his hand. Mycroft took it, and the two brothers shook in the manner of two men agreeing upon a wager.

"First," asked Holmes, "did either of you recognise the man who caused the disturbance?"

"I don't think so," I replied. "Although I didn't get a good look at him."

"Likewise," said Mycroft. "I have never seen him before, and I didn't have time to observe much about him. Only that he was young, in his early twenties, I would guess. He'd tried to dress smartly, presumably in an attempt not to look out of place here, but his suit was obviously secondhand and not tailored for him. The jacket was tight around him, which might have indicated that he had gained weight, except that the sleeves were also too long. It clearly never fitted him properly."

"That much was obvious," replied Holmes, "and you will have noted the dirt and grease on his hands, suggesting he is employed in some form of manual labour."

"Yes," said Mycroft. "That grease was dark, almost certainly from a large piece of machinery."

"Even if he isn't a member of the Diogenes Club," I said, "someone must know who he is. He cannot have just walked in and entered the Reading Room without an invitation."

"On the contrary," said Holmes, "I suspect that is exactly what happened. Did you not see how wet his jacket was? He had obviously been outside in the rain for some time before coming inside."

"That is hardly surprising," I replied. "It is a foul day, and I got quite wet just running between the cab and the front door when we arrived."

"However, did you not see that his left shoulder was much wetter? I would surmise that he sought shelter, probably in a spot where he could observe the entrance to the building, where he found himself standing beneath a steady drip."

"There is a broken gutter on the building opposite," said Mycroft. "I imagine that is where he waited until he saw an opportunity to sneak in. I suppose you will want to speak with Rogers."

Without waiting for a reply, he walked over to a bell-pull near the door and tugged on it. A few moments later, the doorman entered the room and went straight over to Mycroft.

"Do you require a cab?" he asked in a low voice, which was barely audible from across the room.

"No, Rogers," said Mycroft. "I need you to tell me about the young man who was here earlier. Who was he, and who invited him in?"

"I'm afraid I do not know. I did not admit him. He must have sneaked past when I was procuring a cab for Mr. Baker. I am most dreadfully sorry that my inattentiveness led to such an uproar. I promise he will not be allowed to enter again."

"That is fine, Rogers," said Mycroft. "We had surmised as much. You may return to your duties."

"Wait one moment," said Holmes. "I wish to speak to the gentlemen who were in the Reading Room at the time of the incident. Please, will you fetch them for me, one at a time, working around the room clockwise from the door?"

Rogers didn't answer Holmes. Instead, he turned to Mycroft for permission.

"You may convey my brother's request to the members."

"Very good, sir," Rogers replied and quietly left the room.

"Why do you suppose this man wanted to get into the Diogenes Club, of all places?" I asked Holmes while we waited.

"It is a serious matter," replied Mycroft. "It isn't just newspapers which are perused in the Reading Room of the Diogenes Club. On any given day, you will find more confidential documents there than you would find in the case of any Minister of State."

"While that is true," said Holmes, "I don't think this man's motive was espionage. I suspect this business is a more personal matter."

"You think he had some connection to Lord Browning?"

"It is possible."

Before Holmes could elaborate further, the door opened, and Rogers stepped inside again. He looked unhappy.

"I am sorry, Mr. Holmes, but I am afraid they refused to speak to you."

"That's fine, Rogers. I suspected some members might resist being questioned. We can leave him for now and you may send in the next man."

"No, Mr. Holmes, you don't understand. It isn't just one gentleman who refused your invitation. They all did."

A cloud of anger crossed my friend's face, but out of the corner of my eye I spotted that Mycroft was smiling. Clearly Holmes saw it too.

"Do you find this amusing? Have you forgotten there is a dead man in your Reading Room?"

"I have forgotten nothing, but it appears that you have forgotten where you are. Did you expect these men to submit to your questions like common criminals? They are among the most influential and powerful men in the country, and they come here for peace and privacy, not to be interrogated."

"Nevertheless, I need answers from them. Rogers, please return to the Reading Room with the message that Mr. Holmes insists that they come."

Once again, Rogers turned to Mycroft for permission, but this time it wasn't forthcoming.

"That will not be necessary. You may leave us now."

Rogers nodded and left quickly before Holmes could object any further.

Mycroft turned to his brother. "When I allowed this foolish exercise to take place, you agreed to follow the rules of the Diogenes Club. This institution insists not only upon silence, but privacy. As I expected, you will get no information from them, just as you would get none from me if I were in their position. Each member's business is their own, and if they don't wish to speak to you, that is their prerogative. They will certainly not speak of any other member's affairs which they might have inadvertently witnessed."

436

Holmes scowled as Mycroft said this, but then he smiled. "Very well. If I cannot learn anything by talking in here, I will observe the scene instead. Come, Watson."

He didn't wait for a response, but jumped to his feet and headed for the door. I followed, slightly more slowly, and saw Mycroft exerting himself to lift his heavyset form out of his chair to join us.

By the time I reached the Reading Room, Holmes was already kneeling down next to the body of Lord Browning. I stepped forward to join him, but felt Mycroft place his hand on my shoulder and hold me back. Acquiescing to his request, I stood next to him, near the door, and watched as Holmes carried out his investigation.

As we all watched, Holmes studied the body on the floor. Unsurprisingly, he started with the bloody wound, carefully lifting Lord Browning's head so that he could see it clearly. Once he was satisfied, he started working his way down the man's body. I didn't know what he hoped to find, since the cause of death seemed quite obvious, but he took his time examining every inch of the corpse.

When he finished studying Lord Browning's shoes, I expected him to stand up. However, he seemed to notice something of interest on the floor and started to examine the carpet.

After what felt like an age, Holmes finally stood up and I readied myself to leave, eager to return to the Stranger's Room and hear what he had deduced. Yet it transpired that he wasn't done in the Reading Room. Having finished with the dead man, he turned his attention to the members who were still living.

Holmes walked over to the first of the occupied nooks positioned around the room and stared down at the man seated there. He was an elderly gentleman with a pointed white beard. I recognised him, although I couldn't remember his name at that moment. I vaguely recalled that he had something to do with the railways.

The man lowered his newspaper, and stared back at Holmes, as though challenging him to say something and give them an excuse to eject us from the club. However, Holmes didn't say a word. He didn't dazzle the assembled company with his customarily astounding deductions about the man's occupation, the state of his marriage, or what he ate for breakfast. Instead, he just stood there for two or three minutes, silently taking in every detail, before moving on to the next man and repeating the process.

I noticed that Holmes seemed to be spending far longer on his observations than in most cases. Usually, he would take in a scene with just a glance, and be able to tell the entire story of what had taken place.

437

However, today he lingered, getting close to each person in turn. He didn't touch them, or ask them to move, yet I had the sense that his observations were more thorough than any medical examination I had ever performed.

I looked across at Mycroft. There was a scowl on his face, and his hands were clenched into fists. If he had been able to speak, I felt certain that he would have told his brother to step back and cease his intrusive examinations.

For their part, the members seemed horrified, yet transfixed by his attention. Only one man baulked at Holmes's examination, pushing the detective aside in order to stand up and storm out of the room. Holmes didn't appear concerned or try to stop him. He simply moved on to the next nook and the member who sat there.

Eventually, Holmes made his way around the room to where we waited by the door. I saw Mycroft relax slightly, thinking that his brother had finished. However, Holmes didn't open the door. Instead, he beckoned for me to follow him and led me back to the body of Lord Browning. He lifted up the man's head, as he had done before, so that I could see the wound, and the heavy glass ashtray that had caused it.

It was immediately clear that, while there had clearly been a fight, Lord Browning's death had been an accident. If the intruder had used the ashtray as a weapon, it would have been tossed to one side, not lined up perfectly with the fatal wound. It must have fallen to the floor when the table was knocked over, before Lord Browning fell and hit his head on it. No wonder the young man had been distraught when he ran out of the club.

I thought that was all Holmes wanted to show me, but he hadn't finished. Next, he directed me to look at the man's jacket and shirt. However, I could see nothing out of the ordinary. I almost asked him to explain what I was meant to be looking at, but remembered at the last second to hold my tongue. Instead, I let him show me the patch of carpet that had attracted his attention earlier. I could see that the fibres had been flattened, as though something had been dragged along the floor, but without an explanation I couldn't understand its significance.

Holmes stood up, and finally I thought we had finished. However, then I saw Mycroft shaking his head, and I realised, with horror, that the body was just the start. Holmes intended to reprise his entire examination of the Reading Room and its occupants for my benefit.

Sure enough, he led me over to the gentleman from the railway. He pointed to the man, but I didn't know what I was meant to be looking for. Since there was no way to ask Holmes to explain, I just nodded, hoping it might end this ordeal more quickly. Holmes seemed satisfied by this response, and we moved on to the next gentleman.

We repeated this little pantomime all around the room, with Holmes pointing and me nodding, despite seeing nothing of interest.

Finally, we reached Mycroft again. For a moment I wondered if Holmes planned to undertake yet another circuit of the room, and its increasingly disgruntled occupants, with his brother. However, he clearly didn't think that was necessary, as he opened the door and led us out into the hall and back towards the Stranger's Room.

The door had barely closed before Mycroft turned angrily to confront his brother.

"That was entirely unnecessary! There is nothing you can have learned with your boorish tactics that you didn't observe within moments of entering the room. All that you have achieved is to antagonise some of the most powerful men in England."

I had seen the brothers disagree before, but it had always had an undertone of gentle rivalry. However, in that moment, Mycroft seemed genuinely enraged. For a moment I felt guilty that I had insisted upon this investigation, until I reminded myself that a man was dead, and that discovering the truth about that was more important than the internal politics of a gentleman's club, even this one.

Holmes didn't immediately respond to his brother, but turned to me instead.

"Watson, would you agree that I carried out a full and thorough examination of the Reading Room?"

"I have never seen you pay such attention to a room. I don't believe you could have missed anything."

"And you would tell the police that and be willing to swear to it under oath in a court of law."

"Of course."

"Then, Mycroft, I achieved my objective. My reputation will ensure there is no doubt in anyone's mind that this death was thoroughly investigated, without the police needing to set one foot within the hallowed halls of your club. I am sure your fellow members will quickly see that, rather than betraying them by allowing me to investigate, you have saved them from a far more substantial intrusion and embarrassment."

Mycroft nodded. "Your reasoning is sound, but I think you could have achieved the same result far less intrusively."

"Maybe," said Holmes, "but it was better to be certain."

"The police may be content to accept your assertion that this wasn't a crime," I said, "but I would like to know who the intruder was, and why he sneaked into the Diogenes Club to confront Lord Browning. He may not have intended to commit murder, but he is responsible for this tragic accident."

"My dear Watson, I am sorry," said Holmes. "I thought I had highlighted all the pertinent evidence quite clearly back in the Reading Room."

"I am afraid it wasn't clear at all. What do you think they were fighting about?"

"The intruder's quarrel wasn't with Lord Browning," replied Holmes.

"Then why were they fighting?"

"Browning was a military man," said Mycroft. "Unlike most of the members of the Diogenes Club, he considered himself a man of action. I believe he stepped in to try and remove the intruder."

"The evidence of their struggle is quite clear," said Holmes. "Lord Browning came up behind the intruder and tried to pull him away, causing the drag marks in the carpet that I pointed out to you. In the process, he knocked over the table. Then he lost his grip and fell backwards. He was just unlucky to land where he did."

"How can you be certain he wasn't pushed?" I asked.

"The evidence was on his clothes – or rather, it wasn't. Do you remember the intruder's hands? They were covered with dirt and grease. Some of that would have rubbed off on Lord Browning's shirt or jacket if he had been pushed, but as you saw, they were clean. The intruder never laid a hand on him."

I nodded. "That makes sense, but it still doesn't explain why that man came here."

"It was a private matter," replied Mycroft, "and none of our business."

"It is hardly private when every man in that room witnessed the altercation and will have heard the truth," said Holmes.

"As far as they are concerned, they heard nothing," said Mycroft. "Any member who so much as mentions what they heard, let alone tries to exploit that knowledge for personal gain, will find themselves expelled from the Diogenes Club immediately."

"I suppose that is why they all refused to be interviewed," I said. "I guess we will never know what really took place in there."

"It isn't just the threat of expulsion that keeps them in line," said Holmes. "The silence of the Diogenes Club helps maintain the illusion that all their transgressions remain secret. However, the truth is that, whether they speak or not, everyone knows each other's business. Today it was Henry Clarke's past that caught up with him, but it could have happened to any of them."

"Henry Clarke?" I asked. "Is that who the intruder was looking for? I vaguely recognise the name. Isn't he a shipping magnate?"

"That is right."

"I suppose he is the man who fled the room when you tried to examine him."

"No, that man is a junior minister. Politicians are always the most terrified that their secrets will be exposed. Mind you, if he wants his affairs to stay hidden, he would be well advised to check his shirt collar for traces of his mistress's make-up before he leaves her boudoir."

"Which man was Henry Clarke then?" I asked, "and what did the intruder want with him?"

Holmes didn't answer my question, but instead he turned to Mycroft.

"Do you think Mr. Clarke is ready to talk with us yet?" he asked.

Mycroft sighed. "I doubt he will be happy about it, but maybe it is for the best."

He stood up and used the bell-pull to summon a servant. We only had to wait a few moments before Rogers stepped into the room.

"Is Mr. Clarke still in the Reading Room?" Mycroft asked.

"I believe he is, sir."

"Please ask him to come and speak with us."

"He was quite clear that he didn't intend to speak to Mr. Sherlock Holmes, sir."

"Yet I am certain he will speak to me."

"Very good, sir."

It took longer than expected for Rogers to return, and when he entered the Stranger's Room, he was alone.

"I am sorry for the delay, gentlemen. I was incorrect and Mr. Clarke wasn't to be found in the Reading Room."

"Has he run away to avoid our questions?" I asked.

"Why no, sir," replied Rogers. "He had retired to the dining room. He will be here momentarily."

Sure enough, at that moment the door opened and Mr. Henry Clarke stepped inside. He was a weasel-faced man who I remembered looking up at us with contempt when we were in the Reading Room.

"What is it, Mycroft? I was just sitting down to my lunch," he said as soon as he entered. They he looked around the room and saw that we were also there. "I thought I was clear. I will not be talking to your brother."

He turned to leave.

"A man has died today, because of your indiscretions," said Holmes. "I think the least you could do is spare a few moments to speak with us."

441

"Browning was a d--n fool. Tackling intruders is a job for the servants."

"But the intruder was here to speak to you."

"Nonsense. You cannot possibly know that."

"Mr. Clarke, I make it my business to know everything," said Holmes, then he turned to me. "Do you see now, Watson? Remember how there were no marks on Lord Browning's jacket? You can see here how it would have looked if the intruder had grabbed him."

I looked closely at Mr. Clarke's jacket and saw there was a grimy hand print on each of his lapels.

"Why did the intruder go after you?" I asked.

"How am I meant to know? He burst into the Reading Room shouting at the top of his voice. I have never seen such a thing in all my years at the Diogenes Club. It isn't good enough, Mycroft. He should never have been allowed through the doors. I will complain to the committee about it, and about the behaviour of your brother."

"Please stop, Henry," said Mycroft. "We all saw the boy. His resemblance to you is quite obvious."

"The intruder was your son?" I asked.

"My son is in Liverpool, overseeing our business interests there. I have never seen the ruffian that assaulted me today before in my life."

"Did he want you to give him money?" asked Holmes.

"He kept going on about his mother, and how on her deathbed she had made up some absurd story that I was his father. I have no doubt that he would have demanded money, if he hadn't got into that fight with Browning. They always do. Not that I would have given him anything. I already paid his mother handsomely to keep quiet, and we saw how that turned out. If you acknowledge these bastards, they become a millstone around your neck for the rest of your life."

Mr. Clarke seemed not to notice the contradictions in what he had just said. I wondered how many other illegitimate children he had sired. It sounded like this wasn't the first time one had sought him out.

I felt a pang of sympathy for the boy I had briefly seen that morning in the hall. He had lost his mother, and now had to live with the guilt of his involvement in a man's death. Still, I suspected he would be better off if he had nothing to do with his father.

"I think you have said enough, Henry" said Mycroft. "Your indiscretions are none of our business, as long as they remain outside this club."

"Shouldn't we be telling the police about this, when we report Lord Browning's death?" I asked.

"My brother carried out a full investigation, which concluded that his death was an accident," said Mycroft. "Anything else is just rumours and conjecture. We will not bring the Diogenes Club into disrepute by spreading such gossip."

Mr. Clarke smiled smugly as he listened to this, and I had to resist the urge to punch him.

"However," Mycroft continued, "as chairman of the committee, I will recommend that you are censured for allowing your personal business to disturb the peace. I suggest you get your affairs in order, all of them, as any future incident will certainly result in your expulsion."

For a moment it looked like Mr. Clarke might be going to deny any responsibility once again, but a final glare from Mycroft was enough to change his mind, and he just nodded meekly before fleeing the room as fast as he could.

The Case of the
Reappearing *Wineskin*
by Ian Ableson

There is a geographic peculiarity of England that I think we – which is to say Holmes and I – sometimes take for granted. If we were based somewhere in America – particularly in the southwestern deserts, or somewhere in one of the country's various vast mountain ranges – we might have to deal with a criminal element spread across thousands of miles, rather than our relatively compact organizations in England. In the end, despite our country's technological prowess and vast cultural impact, when one looks at a globe we are still ultimately nothing more than an insignificant island out at sea.

And yet, despite its handful of advantages, our proximity to the ocean also lends itself to some very unusual cases, the likes of which our landlocked colleagues could never dream. I think it's fair to say that we are proud of our seas in England – they have fed us, transported us, and defended us throughout our history. Nevertheless, there is a certain degree of mystery associated with those deep and roiling waters which we may never truly comprehend. As much as we may have a fondness for it, the ocean is also a prime place for a man's imagination to drift away with the wind and land in some foul and unsettling place.

This particular case came to us on a rather lazy autumn day. The weather had taken a turn for the grim around late afternoon, dousing London in harsh sheets of rain that occasionally drifted into sleet. The miserable conditions had prevented Holmes and me from pursuing any outdoor activity for the remainder of the afternoon and evening. Holmes had lit his long cherry-wood pipe – a sure sign that his ever-shifting mind had settled on a desire for conversation rather than meditation – and we were deep into a discussion that crossed the line between politics and philosophy when there was a frantic knock on the door.

The man who entered may have been in his fifties or sixties, although his facial details were somewhat difficult to discern underneath a massive, roughly-shorn salt-and-pepper beard. He wore a long and ragged black coat to shield him from the rain, evidence of hard use apparent in its many worn patches. The bucket hat atop his head may have once been olive green, but time had left it as a patchy sort of muddy beige. What little skin

444

could be seen between the beard and the hat had the wrinkled and sun-reddened appearance of a man who had spent several decades of life exposed to the outdoors. When his right hand emerged from his coat pocket to shake both of ours, I noticed that the tips were missing from his middle and ring fingers.

"Beggin' your pardon, Mister Holmes," he said in a thick, gravelly voice. He hesitated. His eyes, dark and beady beneath the brim of his hat, darted uncertainly between the pair of us. "Erm . . . Before I go on, might I know which one of you I'm apologizing to?"

"Certainly," said my friend. "My name is Sherlock Holmes, and this is my colleague, Dr. Watson. You may speak as freely in front of him as you would in front of myself, for anything that you tell me will be known to him soon enough anyway. Would you care for a glass of brandy, or perhaps wine? I find both to be effective antidotes against days such as these."

"Brandy and wine are both a touch beyond my tastes, to tell you true, but if you've any whisky lyin' around, I'd be hard pressed to say no to it." Holmes poured three glasses of a scotch whisky that he'd once been given as part of a payment from a case in Edinburgh. The bearded man made a movement when he received his glass as though to swig it down with a single swallow, but he apparently decided against it and sipped instead.

"Can't go to the police, not with this," he murmured. "To them, I'll just look like some crazy old hagfish who's been soaked with seawater a few years too long. Can't say I blame them either, not with what I got to say, but I trust my own eyes, least until I'm at the pub. But we folk of the sea have a reputation for superstition, and I'm afraid that might work against me. One of the dockhand lads, though, he told me that you'd believe me, even if the police won't." He gave us an appraising look. "I'm here to see if he might be right."

"A dockhand lad?" said Holmes thoughtfully. "Would his name be Willie McGlen, by chance?"

"Aye, it would," the man answered. Holmes gave me a significant look, which I took to mean that Willie McGlen was a member of his ever-growing group of Baker Street Irregulars. "He's a good lad, so I didn't think it likely he'd be pulling my leg."

"Well, seeing as you've braved both the weather and your own self-doubt to get yourself here," said Holmes lightly. "Why don't you tell us what's brought you?"

"Very well, Mr. Holmes, very well," the man murmured. He took another sip as though to strengthen himself before he spoke. "My name is Reuben Stolens, and it would likely come as no surprise to you gentlemen to learn that I am a fisherman. My boat's moored at Southend-on-Sea, a few dozen miles outside of London. It isn't a large stock there – got nothing on the pilchard fishery in Cornwall – so most of the large schooners left the area a few years back, looking for more productive seas. The fishing's all done with small dories now, crewed by one man at least and three at most. It's difficult work, but those of us locals that are willing to make the effort and put in the work do well enough to get through the year with a little extra.

"Now, last year a younger lad started fishin' the waters – unfamiliar to all, hardly out of his teenage years, and goin' by the name of Alec Slack. I'll be the first to admit that we anglers can be a touch protective of our waters – only so many productive lots of sea to go around, I'm sure you understand – so we weren't the kindest to him at the outset. But he was a pleasant lad, and he respected everyone's territories well enough, so gradually we each warmed up to him. I've no sons of my own, nor any living family to speak of, and I took a particular fondness to him. All last year I helped him to learn the fisherman's ways – keeping watch for storms, avoiding the shipping routes, tracking what time o' day to fish the water for each given species, and all that. I even taught him the business side of things, which is much harder than the fishing side for any man with a shred of decency. Taught him that old Leonard Clarke down on the southside of town will give you the best price for your catch by far, so long as you're willing to make the long walk down the road and deliver them straight to the old codger's doorstep.

"I took a bit of a shine to the lad, make no mistake, to the point that one day I noticed that my own catch was sufferin' a bit for time lost to tutelage. But that was fine, as I had enough to get by on, an' I am not a man for luxury anyway. But young Mr. Slack noticed my dwindling fortunes, and eventually he started insisting that I return to my own trade. I thought he had a handle on his business well enough, so eventually I acquiesced. We still saw each other plenty – like I said, there aren't too many lots on the sea anyway – but suffice to say I knew much less of his affairs afterwards.

"About two weeks ago there was a vicious storm swept by Southend-on-Sea. Blasted thing lasted nearly two days, wind shaking the trees like they were late to pay the landlord. Not much to do as a fisherman during the storms, 'cept fix your nets in the morning and stop by the pub in the evening, so that's exactly what I did. During that time, I saw no sign of young Mr. Slack, neither at the pub nor at the docks, but it didn't concern me much. The room he was renting was a bit of a walk from town, far enough that I figured he was just hunkering down till the skies were fair again.

"On the third day the skies were clear and, wishing to make up for lost time, I made my way down to the dock an hour or so before sunrise. I rent a space at the dock to tie up my dory, you see, as I am not blessed enough to live on the sea myself. As I was casting off, I glanced around at the other boats tied at the same dock and noticed that Mr. Slack's boat was missing. I thought nothing of it at the time – he wasn't the only man to beat me to the docks, despite my own early start – and I went out for the day. Took in a decent day's catch, but I didn't see hide nor hair of young Slack or his boat, which I thought odd. That evening, on my way home from the pub, I passed by the dock and saw his boat still missing. Now that I found a good deal more concerning – night fishing's not unheard of, o' course, but to go all day and night on a one-man dory is like shaking hands with the devil. Might be fine, might be a disaster. Man gets tired, makes mistakes, and the sea isn't known for being a forgiving mistress. I decided to go check on the lad at his rented room.

"To my relief, young Slack was there, though more downcast than I'd ever known him to be. His boat, as it turns out, had been lost to sea in the storm. He failed to tie it down properly – said he watched helplessly from the dock as the winds took it out to sea. He apologized to me for not listening better to my teachings, else his dory surely would have stayed where it was moored. He admitted to avoiding the docks and the pub for the day out of shame, not wanting to face the rest of the anglers (myself included). And last of all, he told me that he'd taken this as a divine sign that he wasn't meant for the fishing life, and he intended to leave Southend-on-Sea the following morning.

"Now I argued against him on that last point – even offered to loan him what I could for a new dory – but he wouldn't hear it. He thanked me profusely for all my teachings and promised that he would visit if life ever again brought him to that part o' the country. I left the house that evening with a heavy heart. In the morning I went to see him off, but the landlord told me he'd already left.

"Well, an angler can't afford to be glum for long, and it was early that I was back out on the sea. But here's the problem, gentlemen, and I hope you won't laugh me out of London for what I have to say.

"The lad's been gone for nearly two weeks now, of that I'm certain. No one in town's seen him for all that time. And I believe his story about the boat – a few pieces of it have washed ashore, and there's damage to the dock as well. And yet – and I hope you'll hear me out, gentlemen – for the past three days I promise you that I've seen his boat on the horizon, but it's at such a distance that I can't see the man who steers it. Fishermen are a superstitious lot, I'll be the first to admit it, at least as far as the sea's concerned. Had I not spoken to him myself, I might think that I was seeing

447

Slack's ghost out on the sea, doing his best to bring in his catch. But all doubts aside, I'll swear on my mother's grave that the boat looks the exact same as Slack's. Most of the time I see it, the boat's out in the afternoon, at times that no proper angler would bother to be fishing. On a few occasions I've cast off myself to go check the boat, but I can never quite seem to get there before the boat gets away from me."

"Hmm," said Holmes. "And what has you convinced of the boat's identity?"

"Ah, it's a touch difficult to explain, Mr. Holmes, but each boat treats the seas differently. One dips a little far at the bow, one rocks more against gentle waves . . . But even without those details, his boat's got a funny color to it that none of the others have – a sort of deep maroon. He named it the *Wineskin*."

Holmes didn't immediately react to the end of Mr. Stolens' story, instead simply gazing at nothing in particular, a habit that, in this case, I took to mean that he was considering every possibility. Seeing as Holmes's unflinching stare could be rather unnerving to those who were unfamiliar with it, I engaged Mr. Stolen in small talk to keep him distracted. Sensing him to be a somewhat single-minded fellow, I primarily suggested a variety of nautical topics, which kept him relatively calm as Holmes pondered.

"I don't suppose," Holmes said suddenly, "you happen to know where Slack first acquired his vessel?"

"He wouldn't say. It was a fairly ordinary sort of dory, apart from the color. Must've transported it from somewhere though – certainly wasn't built or sold in Southend-on-Sea."

"And he gave no indication as to his life prior to joining your fishery? No mention of other family or close companions?"

"Afraid not. We mostly discussed the here and now. Actually, we mostly discussed the sea, to be honest, but it was the here and now otherwise."

"Well," said Holmes with a lazy, cat-like smile, "I'm sure I could use one more visit to the sea before the gloom of winter sets upon us. What do you say, Watson? Care for a trip eastward?"

"Of course."

"Excellent. Mr. Stolens, if you wouldn't mind providing us directions to your mooring, we will arrive there in the morning tomorrow. There are a few supplies I wish to gather that I believe will prove valuable for our investigation."

Stolens' shoulders sagged in relief. "You have my thanks, Mr. Holmes, for believing me, and for taking my concerns seriously. Until tomorrow then."

I didn't expect Holmes to be at all forthcoming with the details regarding the mysterious supplies that he wished to acquire for the case, so I didn't bother to ask what he carried in the travel sack that he brought along with him the next morning. I guessed that my curiosity would likely be sated very soon.

Southend-on-Sea was much closer to 221b Baker Street than most of the cases that took us out of London, and so our time spent traveling proved to be relatively short. Soon we were beset by the all-too-familiar sights and sounds of a seaside English village. Cries of men and seagulls intermingled in the air as we made our way to the pier in question. It was a long pier, of a length to have dozens of dories moored to it at a time and still let each one coexist without bumping into the others. I don't have the exact length recorded in my notes, but suffice to say that it stretched a fair distance into the sea. Stolens was already waiting for us, smoking a well-used clay pipe and gazing contemplatively into the horizon.

"Gentlemen!" he cried when we first approached. "Thank you for coming."

"Is this where the *Wineskin* was tied?" asked Holmes.

"It is, it is. Slack used to tie it to the right-hand mooring post, second from the end of the pier, just over there. Blamed his own complacence for its loss – said he didn't use the proper knots, just something more slapdash. With the wind and the rain coming down like it was, it's hard to blame the lad for wanting to get out of the weather."

"Hmm," said Holmes noncommittally. He took a moment to peer at the post itself, but he seemed to be more interested in the area around it, kneeling on the wooden pier that he might inspect it more closely. "How deep is the water here?"

"Oh, not deep. Four feet or so?"

"And according to Slack, the boat was completely destroyed in the storm?"

"Blown out to sea, more like. Said that he last saw it in the distance, near quarter-of-a-mile away, being pushed out by the wind. Still, must have been at least some damage before it sank – I found and kept a piece of the boat that washed in."

Holmes rounded sharply on Stolens. "You kept a piece of the wreckage?"

Stolens shrugged. "Well, sure. Didn't turn up until Slack was long gone. Otherwise, I'd have given it to him as a memento."

"Do you still have it?"

"I do. Couldn't tell you what possessed me to hang onto it, waterlogged and sea-worn as it was, but it's back in my room."

Holmes's eyes lit up, as they occasionally did at an unexpected windfall in a case. "Would you be willing to go retrieve it? Examining it could prove to be most helpful."

Stolens shrugged. "Certainly, Mr. Holmes, though I fail to see what insight you'll glean from it. Can't be more than a foot or so of wood shorn off the starboard cap rail."

After Stolens had left, Holmes opened the travel bag and pulled from it a handful of very simple, yet nonetheless rather peculiar, items. The first was a flat disk, perhaps a foot or so in diameter. It was divided into four quarters by black-and-white paint, such that each half of the disk included one white quarter and one black quarter. A length of string, similar to fishing line, attached to it at the center. The other objects appeared at first to be brightly colored baubles, similar to Christmas ornaments. They were small red and blue balls, each about the size of a man's fist.

"I paid a visit to our friend Ferdinand Brandt at the Natural History Museum yesterday. His knowledge proved so useful in the recent Gila monster case, it occurred to me that he may have some guidance in a few questions of oceanography as well. He proved most helpful, and directed me to a colleague of his who is something of an expert on the matter and was willing to lend me the items you see before you."

I laughed. "I am glad to hear that I was able to make such a productive introduction. * But what is all of this for?"

Holmes lifted the black-and-white disk first. "This is known as a *secchi disk*, a simple but ingenious device for measuring visibility in water. We lower the disk into the water, and once it's no longer visible we will use the markings on the line to determine the depth at which it vanished from our view. Given Stolens' estimate of the water depth, then I would say we should hope for a visibility of at least a yard or so of visibility if we're to have any hope of seeing pieces of the *Wineskin*."

We did as Holmes described, with me slowly lowering the disk into the water by the attached line, him squinting at it until he asked me to stop. I then pulled the disk from the water and we counted the marks. Holmes laughed ruefully.

"Barely two feet of visibility. Given the storms of late and the outflow of the nearby Thames, perhaps that is to be expected. I'd hoped we might have a chance of seeing extruding pieces of the boat from the seabed, but it seems that will not be possible. We shall have to rely on the piece that Stolens retrieved."

"And the rest?" I asked, pointing to the unfamiliar brightly-colored balls.

"An even simpler technology," he said wryly. He took one of the balls and lightly tossed it into the sea, at exactly the point where Slack's boat

450

would have been moored. "It's a primitive but undeniably effective way to test sea current. If the storm knocked Slack's boat around in this area, we can expect that much of the wooden debris would have floated somewhere inland right by now. With luck, these small floatation devices – Brandt's colleague referred to them as 'drifters' – will lead us to the spot where the currents would naturally have deposited them. Of course, the wind from the storm would have complicated matters, but if we can determine the wind's direction on the day the incident took place that we may be able to guess at a rough location of any other wreckage. Here, Watson, toss the next one."

Feeling slightly childish, I picked up the next drifter and tossed it lightly into the water. The bright red coloration made it distinctly visible against the murky blue-grey water. It bobbed beside its cousin, appearing as no more than a piece of miscellaneous debris in the water. Together, Holmes and I watched them float unhurriedly for a minute or so. Holmes chuckled quietly.

"Undeniably effective it may be, but perhaps not the most riveting piece of deduction, eh Watson? Come, let us continue our search of the pier and see if it will reveal any further clues to us. We'll find where our drifters washed to shore later."

A few minutes later, Stolens had returned. Apart from the coloration, the piece of debris in his hand was as unremarkable as he had warned. It appeared to be a small piece of railing, between six inches and a foot in length, longer than it was wide. The railing appeared to have taken very little of the rest of the boat with it. Apart from the gray-brown color of the interior wood, the entire piece was the deep, soft red of a dying sunset.

Holmes took the piece of wood and examined it for some time, running his fingers lightly along the edges and the interior. Finally he finished his examination and looked up at our client, his expression unreadable.

"And tell me, where did you find this piece of the *Wineskin*?"

"Why, just outside of the pub. It's called The Cornucopia, you can see just a touch of it on the outcropping of land over yonder."

"Thank you, Mr. Stolens. Now, I think that we have taken more than enough of your time. We can continue our investigation from here."

Stolens looked anxious, but he nodded nevertheless. "Yes, yes, of course, Mr. Holmes. Wouldn't want to get in your way. But let me know if you find the lad, will you?"

"Likewise, I hope you will let me know if you see the *Wineskin* on the water today. We'll doubtless be somewhere in town." Stolens nodded his acquiescence, and with a tip of his cap to both Holmes and myself he left the same way he'd come.

451

"It has become clear to me," said Holmes after Stolens was out of earshot, "that the facts of this case aren't as they were initially presented to us. The unmistakable taint of deception has filtered in, but unfortunately I'm not yet sure who is being deceived. It's possible that Reuben Stolens has told us the truth of the matter as far as he is aware of it, and it's equally possible that he hasn't. Either way, I felt it best not to have him join us for the remainder of the investigation."

It wasn't an unprecedented fear. It would be neither the first nor the last time that a client presented Holmes with a set of facts that was either totally false, or at least incomplete – whether due to malevolence, embarrassment, or some other complicating factor that depended entirely on the circumstance.

"Deception?" I asked curiously. "What makes you so sure?"

"I invite you to examine this piece of debris. Does anything seem unusual about it?"

I took the wood in my hands, curiously running my fingers along the smooth wood grain, much as Holmes had done earlier. "Nothing comes to mind."

"Look at the edges in particular. The break with the main body of the boat isn't jagged and erratic as could be expected from a storm-induced breakage. A collision with a rock, a pier, a buoy, or another boat wouldn't tear off a piece that smooth. Look at how the breakage follows the natural grain of the wood – it looks almost more like it was peeled off of the boat, and indeed I believe it was, in a way."

"Peeled? How?"

"Run a finger now along the sides of the railing. Do you feel the two small indentations? They are visible as well, if one looks carefully. I believe those to be the marks of a crowbar. Someone appears to have taken some tools to the *Wineskin*."

"A crowbar! Then Stolens' story of the boat's destruction by storm seems unlikely indeed. How should we proceed?"

"First, I would like to determine if there are any more pieces of the boat to be found, and for that we'll unfortunately need to watch the drifters. This could also help us assess Stolens' reliability – if the location that he said he found this piece seems a plausible location based on our assessment of the drifters and the wind of the storm, that will be a point in favor of his truthfulness. The wind is a sticky issue – I intended to ask Stolens for a guess at its direction that night, but seeing as his trustworthiness is now in questions we must use alternative methods. Come, let us return to shore."

452

"What of the drifters?" I asked. They hadn't yet made much progress from where we had tossed them into the water, and they seemed content to bob along at their own serene pace.

"I think they can be trusted to do their part."

We walked together to the shoreline, where Holmes cast his gaze upwards, towards the sky. Following his line of sight, I eventually realized that it wasn't the sky, but the trees that had apparently captured his imagination.

What followed is best summarized thusly: For the next half-hour or so, Holmes spent his time darting back-and-forth between the trees and the pier. At first he simply walked back and forth along the treeline, his eyes always glued to the canopy, and eventually he picked several trees seemingly at random and walked around their entire circumference. He darted back to the pier once more.

I must confess that I had slept poorly the previous evening, and was lightly dozing while seated on a nearby bench when he finished this particular piece of analysis.

"I have good news, Doctor," he said cheerfully. "I believe the chances that our fishing friend is telling us the truth are fairly high."

"Do you?" I said, attempting to appear wakeful. "And what has brought you to this conclusion?"

"By observing the movement of the drifters and the pattern of snapped branches in the canopy. We are somewhat in luck in that regard – many of the trees in the treeline here appear to be somewhat sickly, and thereby prone to losing branches in high winds. By observing which branches appear to have snapped off relatively recently, I was able to get a general idea of wind direction on the night of the storm. Given the weight of this piece of debris and the sea's natural currents according to the drifters, I do believe it to be plausible that this piece could have arrived at The Cornucopia, where Stolens said he found it."

"Wonderful! Although it doesn't seem to be a complete assurance of the man's innocence."

"Indeed it isn't. There is every chance that he could have found the debris after whatever nastiness occurred and chose to keep it. In that case, his reason for coming to us is harder to discern, but it's still a possibility which we must not dismiss. But as I said, it is a point in his favor."

"Where does that leave the case, then?"

"At a crossroads, I'm afraid. We've proven very little definitively, save only that the few facts we thought to be certain are anything but." Holmes thought for several long minutes. "If we're left with no other options, we may need to try and catch the *Wineskin* ourselves. However, another option presents itself to me, which may or may not bear fruit. If it

453

does, however, it will confirm a few particular points of this case without taking quite so much time. In his discussion with us, Mr. Stolens casually revealed that there is one more person, one that lives outside of town, who may be able to provide us with a little more insight. I believe we need to locate and pay a visit to a Mr. Leonard Clarke."

Locating Mr. Clarke turned out to be a relatively simple endeavor, but reaching the man took some time. His home was nearly two miles beyond the furthest outskirts of the town, with no convenient alternate transportation, and so Holmes and I could do nothing but walk. Blessedly, the majority of the road adhered to the seaside, and so we were able to enjoy the sights and sounds of the waters. Gulls cried overhead, and the waves lapped serenely at the sand. A cormorant spread its wings wide as it sunned on a rock not far from the coast, drying its saturated plumage.

The house, when we reached it, was modest but well-kept. It was small, but it appeared to be diligently maintained and in fairly good condition. It sported a relatively fresh coat of paint, and there was even an extensive and varied vegetable garden, which showed signs of a recent and productive harvest. We knocked on the door.

The man who appeared was short in stature, with the very top of his head only just reaching Holmes's shoulder. I guessed him to be older than Stolens by a decade or so. He was clean-shaven and bald, although the bushiness of his eyebrows appeared to be trying to compensate for the lack of hair elsewhere on his face. The eyes below his eyebrows were quick and darting. The bushy eyebrows knitted together in confusion when he saw Holmes and myself.

"Eh? And who might you be?" he asked, his voice as lively as his eyes.

"Good afternoon, sir," said Holmes pleasantly. "My companion and I have been taking a stroll across the countryside, and I couldn't help but notice the vitality of your garden there. I have never seen its like! I understand if you, like any magician, choose not to reveal your secrets, but I must at least inquire as to your methods!"

Many people have painted my friend Sherlock Holmes as a man of pure, cold rationality. I myself have perhaps occasionally been guilty of placing too much emphasis on the machine-like precision of his analytical mind rather than exploring his humanity. And yet, sometimes even I was astonished at my friend's charm, when he chose to present it. Here he stood, wearing no disguise, knowing nothing about the little old man who chose to live alone in such an isolated location, and yet after perhaps five minutes of conversation about gardens he had the man laughing as though they were old schoolmates. I have noted before that Holmes's knowledge of practical gardening was limited, yet between his knowledge of general botany – useful, for example, for analyzing poisons – and his talent at steering conversation, it didn't matter in the slightest. Soon Mr. Clarke had invited us in for tea, and about ten minutes from knocking on the door Holmes and I were seated at his neat kitchen table.

"Your home is very fastidiously kept, Mr. Clarke," Holmes observed.

Clarke laughed as he poured the tea. "Oh, yes, I can't stand letting the house go. I've a tidy pension from London that keeps me comfortable these days, so I've plenty of time to keep the place in order.

"But surely it's difficult to get the supplies you need, being as far from town as you are."

Clarke nodded contemplatively as he sat with his own mug of tea. "Aye, difficult it can be, but I wouldn't have it any other way. I lived too much of my life in London, gentlemen, a city where a moment's peace is even more difficult to come by than a breath of fresh air. No, I am content with my choice. I am perfectly capable of walking into town when it suits me, and for a little money I can usually convince someone to cart whatever I need back with me."

"Indeed," murmured Holmes. "And the vegetable garden raises your self-sufficiency by a wide margin, I'd imagine. I can see in your kitchen there that you have a few fish bones left on the counter. If you fish for yourself as well, a man in your position would need acquire only specialized foods and luxuries from town."

"A fair assessment, and mostly an accurate one. Although truth be told, I'm an awful fisherman. To my regret, it seems that my skills with a rod and reel are the exact inverse of my abilities as a gardener. Any morning I spend fishing may as well be spent staring at the sun for all the nourishment it gets me."

"Ah!" said Holmes, and he laughed. "Well, I suppose some things can't be helped."

"Not a man amongst us can argue with our natural proclivities, I'm afraid," Clarke agreed. "Thankfully, the fishermen know me well, and they're willing to bring some portion of their catches straight to me. I'll even pay an extra delivery fee for the strain that it saves my legs. In truth, I have rather more fish than I need at the moment."

Holmes arched an eyebrow. "Oh? Has the supply so outpaced your demand?"

"In a sense, gentlemen, in a sense. There's a new lad, young, that makes the hike a touch more easily than the older fellows. He's a kind-hearted young fellow, and I haven't the heart to turn him away without buying anything, not when he seems so desperate to sell. Used to be he only made the hike out here once a week or so, but it's near every day now."

"A true entrepreneur, it would seem," said Holmes. "Has he already come by today?"

"That he has. He typically stops by in the morning. I bought a few off of him today, but I made it clear that I'd be purchasing fewer from here on out. Say," said Clarke, his eyes glinting. "You gentlemen wouldn't happen to be interested in a few fish to go, would you? I've some salting right now that I'd be downright eager to part with."

"I think we would rather not take them on the train back to London, so I'm afraid we must decline."

"More's the shame."

"This case is quickly coming to a close," said Holmes cheerfully as we left Clarke's house. "Our gambit has paid off."

"So Slack is still fishing in the *Wineskin*? And selling his fish to Mr. Clarke?"

"Indeed. This has become a question not as to why a ghost ship is appearing on the horizon, but rather a question of why a man has apparently fled town and cut himself off from contact with his colleagues. And there is still a matter of deception to resolve."

"Whose deception?"

"As I see it, the presence of the crowbar marks on the piece of the *Wineskin* presents two possible options. Either Slack lied to Stolens about the circumstances of his boat's destruction, or else Stolens lied to us about what he knew, and perhaps Slack is avoiding him specifically. Either is plausible." Holmes paused for a moment, considering. "We could simply return in the morning and try and catch Slack at his delivery, but all things considered, I think perhaps we can finish this case before the day is out. We know that Slack is avoiding town but still selling fish to Mr. Clarke. I think we can presume that after his flight, he would choose to camp somewhere relatively near the man's house, to make the walk at least somewhat easier. If we follow the coastline for a while, perhaps we can find where the *Wineskin* is moored."

In truth, the walk was shorter than either Holmes or I could have dared to hope. We hadn't gone half-a-mile before we found the evidence for which we were searching, albeit in a very different fashion than we had expected. Holmes threw a sudden arm out to stop me and pointed silently. Although it took me several moments of observation to find what he indicated, I too soon spotted the signs. The foliage before us, between the road and the coast, hid at least two men, of whom only a few details could be easily identified. The back of a shoe, the top of a hat, the crook of the elbow on a worn and patched coat. They hadn't yet noticed us, as their backs were to the road as they watched the sea. One of them shifted slightly to ease sore muscles, and a knife glinted in the sunlight.

Through a series of hand signals, Holmes indicated to me that he wished for us to hide as well, and quietly wait behind some nearby shrubs to see what these men might do. It took us a few tense moments to situate ourselves such that we were properly hidden, and there was one instance where I thought they might have heard us, but soon we were also concealed by the foliage.

Blessedly, we didn't have to wait long. No more than a quarter-of-an-hour had passed before the men tensed and grew agitated. The moment that they'd awaited had come. Although I couldn't see the coast from my vantage point, I heard a loud scraping and splashing from the direction of the sea.

The two men straightened and burst from the foliage, disappearing from my view. "Surprise, Slack!" one of them growled. The statement was followed by a chittering, hyena-like cackle. "You're out of time, boy. On'y a little damage at first, if you don't struggle, and then you get another few months to get the mon – " He stopped mid-sentence, interrupting his own threat with a yelp of pain. "Now you're in for it, boy! Your head for the boss!"

At this moment Holmes and I, by unspoken agreement, followed after the would-be assailants. A strange tableau was arrayed before us: The two men who had been hiding were large, rough, and of an intimidating stature. They were the sort of men that can be found as the reliable core of any one of a dozen criminal elements scattered throughout London – and, indeed, the world. Both wore patched coats and identical brown bowler hats.

The third man was undoubtedly Alec Slack. He was a thin, gangly, scarecrow of a lad, pale but noticeably sunburnt. He had a wild mop of curly blond hair, with a thin, scraggly beard to match. Both appeared to be unkempt. He stood in his maroon dory, the *Wineskin,* which he had apparently already dragged ashore. One of the dory's oars lay on the ground near one of the rough men, who clutched his leg in pain, and Slack had already grabbed the second and held it like a javelin.

Holmes lunged immediately for the uninjured man, leaving the other for Slack and myself. I didn't fear for Holmes – I have previously described his prowess in various martial disciplines before, and I don't feel the need to reiterate here – but I did fear for young Slack should his assailants reach him. I scooped up the oar before the injured man could react to our presence and swung it bodily at him. He scurried out of the way, hissing curses. He crouched into a fighting stance, knife at the ready, his attention now on me rather than young Slack. The man lunged with the knife, aiming at my midsection, but thankfully my military training took over and I easily twisted out of the way. I swung again with the oar and swept the brown bowler hat from his head.

A cry of pain erupted from my left, and I caught sight of Holmes's opponent, bleeding heavily from the nose and backing away warily. I nearly paid dearly for this moment of distraction, and I was just barely able to twist away from the knife yet again. I swung once more with the oar, and this time I managed to connect with the rough man's shoulder, and he howled in pain. The howl doubled as Slack slammed into the man's back with the second oar.

Between a bleeding nose and two oar-induced injuries, the cutthroats had had enough. They fled down the road, caution and stealth abandoned. We stood together and watched them go, wary of any trickery, and didn't relax until they had disappeared from view. Slack cleared his throat.

"Friends, I cannot fathom what grace of God led you to me at just such a time, but I thank you both deeply, from the bottom of my heart. I beg you, allow me to repay you in some way. I've little to my name but fish and an old, battered dory, but if you've a desire for either they are yours."

Holmes chuckled lightly. "You may keep both, Mr. Slack, and pay us with a story instead. Your story, specifically. And you should know that in this particular case, the grace of God of which you speak is an old fisherman named Reuben Stolens."

The three of us sat, half-an-hour later, with Reuben Stolens in the latter's house, each nursing mugs of tea. Stolens was clearly shocked and overjoyed to see Slack again, although the younger man was for his part much quieter at the reunion. He had, however, smiled broadly when Stolens shook his hand upon opening the door.

"It's my brother's debt," Slack said without preamble, once we were all seated. "That's what they'd come to collect. I don't know who they are – not exactly, anyway, though I suppose I understand the generalities well enough. My brother . . . fell in with a bad sort. He seemed to survive only by trading his debt around – borrowing piles of money from one group of people in order to pay the debt he owed to another group. Then he died, in mysterious and fairly unpleasant circumstances, and the last group that he owed money to decided that I, his only living relative, would be responsible for paying it off. My brother and I hadn't spoken for nearly a year at that point, so I'm sure you understand that this came as quite a shock to me, and I didn't have the means to pay them. I fled London and came here, hoping that I was far enough removed from London to escape their clutches. The dory belongs to a friend of mine who lives along the

Thames. He was willing to let me borrow it as a means to make a living while I hid. But my brother's creditors found me, somehow, on the night of the storm."

"They attacked your boat," Holmes murmured. "A threat?"

"Yes. They told me to watch carefully to what happened to the boat, for I myself would be next. I begged them to leave it be, told them that without it I had no way of making enough money to pay them back. They tore some pieces from it, but they left it intact enough to be usable." He looked at Reuben Stolens, guilt in his eyes. "I'm sorry I didn't tell you the truth. You were so kind to me, so patient, I couldn't bear to admit to you the trouble that I'd brought with me. So instead I ran, though I didn't make it far. I couldn't think of any way to live in such solitude apart from fishing, but I couldn't stand to show my face in town anymore, so I set up camp and moored my boat three miles outside of town and sold fish only to Mr. Clarke, and disguising my face and voice when I buy goods in town. I've lived there ever since, praying to God that the debt collectors wouldn't find me. But somehow they have, and I am lost again."

"Ah, lad . . ." said Stolens sadly, "life's dealt you a difficult hand. But it's nothing that can't be overcome. Not," he said, the smallest hint of a smile creeping into his somber expression, "if you're willing to take this old fisherman's advice once more. And perhaps our guests may have their own suggestions as well."

This is where I must end the story of Alec Slack, captain of the *Wineskin*. While it has been many years since this particular case, I learned that the criminal elements of London tend to have very long institutional memories, and I wouldn't wish my recounting of this particular tale to put Slack's life at risk. Suffice to say that between the four of us in that room, we were able to devise a plan that allowed Slack to evade his brother's debt collectors. As far as I'm aware, he is still alive and well. Sometimes, at the end of a case, that is all we can wish for.

NOTE

* See "The Adventure of the Transatlantic Gila" in *The MX Book of New Sherlock Holmes Stories – Part XXII: Some More Untold Cases (1877-1887)*

459

About the Contributors

The following contributors appear in this volume:
The MX Book of New Sherlock Holmes Stories
Part XXXII – 2022 Annual (1888-1895)

Ian Ableson is an ecologist by training and a writer by choice. When not reading or writing, he can reliably be found scowling at a clipboard while ankle-deep in a marsh somewhere in Michigan. His love for the stories of Arthur Conan Doyle started when his grandfather gave him a copy of *The Original Illustrated Sherlock Holmes* when he was in high school, and he's proud to have been able to contribute to the continuation of the tales of Sherlock Holmes and Dr. Watson.

Wayne Anderson was born and raised in the beautiful Pacific Northwest, growing up in Alaska and Washington State. He discovered Sherlock Holmes around age ten and promptly devoured the Canon. When it was all gone, he tried to sate the addiction by writing his own Sherlock Holmes stories, which are mercifully lost forever. Sadly, he moved to California in his twenties and has lived there since. He has two grown sons who are both writers as well. He spends his time writing or working on the TV pilots and patents which will someday make him fabulously wealthy. When he's not doing these things, he is either reading to his young daughter from The Canon or trying to find space in his house for more bookshelves.

Brian Belanger, PSI, is a publisher, illustrator, graphic designer, editor, and author. In 2015, he co-founded Belanger Books publishing company along with his brother, author Derrick Belanger. His illustrations have appeared in *The Essential Sherlock Holmes* and *Sherlock Holmes: A Three-Pipe Christmas*, and in children's books such as *The MacDougall Twins with Sherlock Holmes* series, *Dragonella*, and *Scones and Bones on Baker Street*. Brian has published a number of Sherlock Holmes anthologies and novels through Belanger Books, as well as new editions of August Derleth's classic Solar Pons mysteries. Brian continues to design all of the covers for Belanger Books, and since 2016 he has designed the majority of book covers for MX Publishing. In 2019, Brian received his investiture in the PSI as "Sir Ronald Duveen." More recently, he illustrated a comic book featuring the band The Moonlight Initiative, created the logo for the Arthur Conan Doyle Society and designed *The Great Game of Sherlock Holmes* card game. Find him online at:
www.belangerbooks.com and
www.redbubble.com/people/zhahadun and
zhahadun.wixsite.com/221b.

Mike Chinn's first-ever Sherlock Holmes fiction was a steampunk mashup of *The Valley of Fear*, entitled *Vallis Timoris* (Fringeworks 2015). Since then he has written about Holmes's archenemy in *The Mammoth Book of the Adventures of Moriarty* (Robinson 2015), appeared in three volumes of *The MX Book of New Sherlock Holmes Stories*, and faced the retired detective with cross-dimensional magic in the second volume of *Sherlock Holmes and the Occult Detectives* (Belanger Books 2020).

Alan Dimes was born in North-West London and graduated from Sussex University with a BA in English Literature. He has spent most of his working life teaching English. Living in the Czech Republic since 2003, he is now semi-retired and divides his time between Prague and his country cottage. He has also written some fifty stories of horror and fantasy and thirty stories about his husband-and-wife detectives, Peter and Deirdre Creighton, set in the 1930's.

Sir Arthur Conan Doyle (1859-1930) *Holmes Chronicler Emeritus*. If not for him, this anthology would not exist. Author, physician, patriot, sportsman, spiritualist, husband and father, and advocate for the oppressed. He is remembered and honored for the purposes of this collection by being the man who introduced Sherlock Holmes to the world. Through fifty-six Holmes short stories, four novels, and additional Apocryphal entries, Doyle revolutionized mystery stories and also greatly influenced and improved police forensic methods and techniques for the betterment of all. *Steel True Blade Straight.*

Steve Emecz's main field is technology, in which he has been working for about twenty-five years. Steve is a regular speaker at trade shows and his tech career has taken him to more than fifty countries – so he's no stranger to planes and airports. In 2008, MX published its first Sherlock Holmes book, and MX has gone on to become the largest specialist Holmes publisher in the world with over 500 books. MX is a social enterprise and supports three main causes. The first is Happy Life, a children's rescue project in Nairobi, Kenya, where he and his wife, Sharon, spend every Christmas at the rescue centre in Kasarani. They have written two editions of a short book about the project, *The Happy Life Story*. The second is Undershaw, Sir Arthur Conan Doyle's former home, which is a school for children with learning disabilities for which Steve is a patron. Steve has been a mentor for the World Food Programme for several years, and was part of the Nobel Peace Prize winning team in 2020.

Arianna Fox is a triple-published and bestselling author, keynote speaker, actress, professional voiceover talent, award winner, and public figure whose passion is to inspire, educate, and entertain others through her work. From modern stories that connect with a teenage audience to classical-style works of literature, one of Arianna's foremost passions has always been writing. An avid Sherlockian and lover of all things Victorian, Arianna disliked reading for years until she read the first few paragraphs of *The Return of Sherlock Holmes* in a bookstore and immediately fell in love with classic literature and the intricate themes woven into its messages. As a whole, Arianna's ultimate goal is to empower others to achieve maximum success and rock their lives. Arianna can be found at *www.ariannafox.com*, Facebook: *@afoxauthor*, Twitter: *@afoxauthor*; LinkedIn: *Arianna Fox*; and Instagram: *@afoxauthor*

Mike Fox is a CEO, entrepreneur, multi award-winning filmmaker, director, producer, writer, designer, creative professional, actor, voiceover talent, and illustrator. His professional work is known across the U.S. and has received numerous accolades and awards. In addition, Mike has been named "Top Pioneer & Entrepreneur" by *K.I.S.H. Magazine*, and named "Local Business Person of the Year" by Alignable. Mike and his films and creative designs have been featured numerous times in many media channels. Mike can be found at *www.splashdw.com* and *www.crystalfoxfilms.com*; Facebook: *@splashdw*; Twitter: *@splashdw*; LinkedIn: *Mike Fox*; and Instagram: *@officialmikefox*

Mark A. Gagen BSI is co-founder of Wessex Press, sponsor of the popular *From Gillette to Brett* conferences, and publisher of *The Sherlock Holmes Reference Library* and many other fine Sherlockian titles. A life-long Holmes enthusiast, he is a member of *The Baker*

Street Irregulars and *The Illustrious Clients of Indianapolis*. A graphic artist by profession, his work is often seen on the covers of *The Baker Street Journal* and various BSI books.

James Gelter is a director and playwright living in Brattleboro, VT. His produced written works for the stage include adaptations of *Frankenstein* and *A Christmas Carol*, several children's plays for the New England Youth Theatre, as well as seven outdoor plays co-written with his wife, Jessica, in their *Forest of Mystery* series. In 2018, he founded The Baker Street Readers, a group of performers that present dramatic readings of Arthur Conan Doyle's original Canon of Sherlock Holmes stories, featuring Gelter as Holmes, his longtime collaborator Tony Grobe as Dr. Watson, and a rotating list of guests. When the COVID-19 pandemic stopped their live performances, Gelter transformed the show into The Baker Street Readers Podcast. Some episodes are available for free on Apple Podcasts and Stitcher, with many more available to patrons at *patreon.com/bakerstreetreaders*.

Hal Glatzer is the author of the Katy Green mystery series set in musical milieux just before World War II. He has written and produced audio/radio mystery plays, including the all-alliterative adventures of Mark Markheim, the Hollywood hawkshaw. He scripted and produced the Charlie Chan mystery *The House Without a Key* on stage; and he adapted "The Adventure of the Devil's Foot" into a stage and video play called *Sherlock Holmes and the Volcano Horror*. In 2022, after many years on the Big Island of Hawaii, he returned to live on his native island – Manhattan. See more at: *www.halglatzer.com*

Terry Golledge (according to his son Niel Golledge, who provided these stories to this collection) had a life-long love of all things Conan Doyle and in particular Sherlock Holmes. He was born in 1920 in the East End of London. He left school at fourteen, like so many back then. In 1939, he joined the army in the fight against the Germans in World War II. He left the Army in 1945 at the war's end, residing in Hastings. There he met his wife, and his life was a mish-mash of careers, including mining and bus and lorry driving. He owned a couple of book shops, selling them in the 1960's. He then worked for the Post Office, (later to become British Telecom, equivalent to AT&T), ending his working life there as a training instructor for his retirement in 1980. His love of Sherlock Holmes was obviously inspired by the fact that his mother worked as a governess to Sir Arthur Conan Doyle when he lived in Windlesham, Crowborough in Sussex. She married Terry's father after leaving Sir Arthur's employment around 1918. Beginning in the mid-1980's, Terry Golledge wrote a number of Holmes stories, and they have never been previously published. A full collection of his Holmes works will be published in the near future. He passed away in 1996.

Niel Golledge was born in 1951 in Winchester, England. He retired some years ago and currently resides in Kent, UK. His last employment for over twenty years was with a large newsprint paper mill, located near his home. He is married to Trisha, a retired nurse, and they have a son and daughter who have carved out careers in mental health and physiotherapy. He is an avid football fan of West Ham and loves to play golf. He is also a keen reader – but that goes without saying.

John Atkinson Grimshaw (1836-1893) was born in Leeds, England. His amazing paintings, usually featuring twilight or night scenes illuminated by gas-lamps or moonlight, are easily recognizable, and are often used on the covers of books about The Great Detective to set the mood, as shadowy figures move in the distance through misty mysterious settings and over rain-slicked streets.

Arthur Hall was born in Aston, Birmingham, UK, in 1944. He discovered his interest in writing during his schooldays, along with a love of fictional adventure and suspense. His first novel, *Sole Contact*, was an espionage story about an ultra-secret government department known as "Sector Three", and was followed, to date, by three sequels. Other works include seven Sherlock Holmes novels, *The Demon of the Dusk*, *The One Hundred Percent Society*, *The Secret Assassin*, *The Phantom Killer*, *In Pursuit of the Dead*, *The Justice Master*, and *The Experience Club* as well as three collections of Holmes *Further Little-Known Cases of Sherlock* Holmes, *Tales from the Annals of Sherlock* Holmes, and *The Additional Investigations of Sherlock Holmes*. He has also written other short stories and a modern detective novel. He lives in the West Midlands, United Kingdom.

Jeffrey Hatcher is a playwright and screenwriter. His plays have been produced on Broadway, Off-Broadway, and in theaters throughout the U.S. and around the world. They include *Three Viewings*, *Scotland Road*, *The Turn of the Screw*, *Compleat Female Stage Beauty*, *Mrs. Mannerly*, *Murderers*, *Smash*, *Korczak's Children*, *The Government Inspector*, *A Picasso*, *The Alchemist*, *Key Largo*, *Dr. Jekyll and Mr. Hyde*, and his Sherlock Holmes plays *Sherlock Holmes and the Adventure of the Suicide Club*, *Sherlock Holmes and the Ice Palace Murders*, and *Holmes and Watson*. His film work includes the screenplays for *Stage Beauty*, *Casanova*, *The Duchess*, *Mr. Holmes*, and *The Good Liar*. For television, he has written episodes of *Columbo* and *The Mentalist* and the TV movie *Murder at the Cannes Film Festival*. He has received grants and awards from the NEA, TCG, Lila Wallace Fund, Rosenthal New Play Prize, Frankel Award, Charles MacArthur Fellowship Award, McKnight Foundation, Jerome Foundation, and a Barrymore Award for Best New Play. He has been twice nominated for an Edgar Award. He is a member and/or alumnus of The Playwrights Center, the Dramatists Guild, the Writers Guild, and New Dramatists.

Paul Hiscock is an author of crime, fantasy, horror, and science fiction tales. His short stories have appeared in a variety of anthologies, and include a seventeenth-century whodunnit, a science fiction western, a clockpunk fairytale, and numerous Sherlock Holmes pastiches. He lives with his family in Kent (England) and spends his days taking care of his two children. He mainly does his writing in coffee shops with members of the local NaNoWriMo group, or in the middle of the night when his family has gone to sleep. Consequently, his stories tend to be fuelled by large amounts of black coffee. You can find out more about Paul's writing at *www.detectivesanddragons.uk*.

Mike Hogan's early interest in all things Victorian led to a university degree in English and research on nineteenth century literature. He taught English and creative writing at colleges in Japan, the Philippines, Libya and Thailand. He is settled now for much of the year on the island of Mersea in Essex, UK, where he writes novels, plays, and short stories, many set in Victorian London and featuring Sherlock Holmes.

In the year 1998 **Craig Janacek** took his degree of Doctor of Medicine at Vanderbilt University, and proceeded to Stanford to go through the training prescribed for pediatricians in practice. Having completed his studies there, he was duly attached to the University of California, San Francisco as Associate Professor. The author of over seventy medical monographs upon a variety of obscure lesions, his travel-worn and battered tin dispatch-box is crammed with papers, nearly all of which are records of his fictional works. To date, these have been published solely in electronic format, including two non-Holmes novels (*The Oxford Deception* and *The Anger of Achilles Peterson*), the trio of holiday adventures collected as *The Midwinter Mysteries of Sherlock Holmes*, the Holmes story collections *The First of Criminals, The Assassination of Sherlock Holmes, The Treasury of Sherlock Holmes, Light in the Darkness, The Gathering Gloom, The Travels of Sherlock Holmes*, and the Watsonian novels *The Isle of Devils* and *The Gate of Gold*. Craig Janacek is a *nom de plume*.

Roger Johnson BSI, ASH is a retired librarian, now working as a volunteer assistant at the Essex Police Museum. In his spare time, he is commissioning editor of *The Sherlock Holmes Journal*, an occasional lecturer, and a frequent contributor to *The Writings about the Writings*. His sole work of Holmesian pastiche was published in 1997 in Mike Ashley's anthology *The Mammoth Book of New Sherlock Holmes Adventures*, and he has the greatest respect for the many authors who have contributed new tales to the present mighty trilogy. Like his wife, Jean Upton, he is a member of both *The Baker Street Irregulars* and *The Adventuresses of Sherlock Holmes*.

David Marcum plays *The Game* with deadly seriousness. He first discovered Sherlock Holmes in 1975 at the age of ten, and since that time, he has collected, read, and chronologicized literally thousands of traditional Holmes pastiches in the form of novels, short stories, radio and television episodes, movies and scripts, comics, fan-fiction, and unpublished manuscripts. He is the author of over ninety Sherlockian pastiches, some published in anthologies and magazines such as *The Strand*, and others collected in his own books, *The Papers of Sherlock Holmes, Sherlock Holmes and A Quantity of Debt, Sherlock Holmes – Tangled Skeins, Sherlock Holmes and The Eye of Heka*, and *The Complete Papers of Sherlock Holmes*. He has edited over sixty books, including several dozen traditional Sherlockian anthologies, such as the ongoing series *The MX Book of New Sherlock Holmes Stories*, which he created in 2015. This collection is now over thirty volumes, with more in preparation. He was responsible for bringing back August Derleth's Solar Pons for a new generation, first with his collection of authorized Pons stories, *The Papers of Solar Pons*, and then by editing the reissued authorized versions of the original Pons books, and then several volumes of new Pons adventures. He has done the same for the adventures of Dr. Thorndyke, and has plans for similar projects in the future. He has contributed numerous essays to various publications, and is a member of a number of Sherlockian groups and Scions. His irregular Sherlockian blog, *A Seventeen Step Program*, addresses various topics related to his favorite book friends (as his son used to call them when he was small), and can be found at *http://17stepprogram.blogspot.com/* He is a licensed Civil Engineer, living in Tennessee with his wife and son. Since the age of nineteen, he has worn a deerstalker as his regular-and-only hat. In 2013, he and his deerstalker were finally able make his first trip-of-a-lifetime Holmes Pilgrimage to England, with return Pilgrimages in 2015 and 2016, where you may have spotted him. If you ever run into him and his deerstalker out and about, feel free to say hello!

Kevin Patrick McCann has published eight collections of poems for adults, one for children (*Diary of a Shapeshifter*, Beul Aithris), a book of ghost stories (*It's Gone Dark*, The Otherside Books), *Teach Yourself Self-Publishing* (Hodder) co-written with the playwright Tom Green, and *Ov* (Beul Aithris Publications) a fantasy novel for children.

Will Murray has built a career on writing classic pulp characters, ranging from Tarzan of the Apes to Doc Savage. He has penned several milestone crossover novels in his acclaimed Wild Adventures series. *Skull Island* pitted Doc Savage against King Kong, which was followed by *King Kong Vs. Tarzan. Tarzan, Conqueror of Mars* costarred John Carter of Mars. His 2015 Doc Savage novel, *The Sinister Shadow*, revived the famous radio and pulp mystery man. Murray reunited them for *Empire of Doom*. His first Spider novel,

The Doom Legion, revived that infamous crime buster, as well as James Christopher, AKA Operator 5, and the renowned G-8. His second *Spider, Fury in Steel*, guest-stars the FBI's Suicide Squad. Ten of his Sherlock Holmes short stories have been collected as *The Wild Adventures of Sherlock Holmes*. He is the author of the non-fiction book, *Master of Mystery: The Rise of The Shadow*. For Marvel Comics, Murray created the Unbeatable Squirrel Girl. Website: *www.adventuresinbronze.com*

Sidney Paget (1860-1908), a few of whose illustrations are used within this anthology, was born in London, and like his two older brothers, became a famed illustrator and painter. He completed over three-hundred-and-fifty drawings for the Sherlock Holmes stories that were first published in *The Strand* magazine, defining Holmes's image forever after in the public mind.

Tracy J. Revels, a Sherlockian from the age of eleven, is a professor of history at Wofford College in Spartanburg, South Carolina. She is a member of *The Survivors of the Gloria Scott* and *The Studious Scarlets Society*, and is a past recipient of the Beacon Society Award. Almost every semester, she teaches a class that covers The Canon, either to college students or to senior citizens. She is also the author of three supernatural Sherlockian pastiches with MX (*Shadowfall*, *Shadowblood*, and *Shadowwraith*), and a regular contributor to her scion's newsletter. She also has some notoriety as an author of very silly skits: For proof, see "The Adventure of the Adversarial Adventuress" and "Occupy Baker Street" on YouTube. When not studying Sherlock, she can be found researching the history of her native state, and has written books on Florida in the Civil War and on the development of Florida's tourism industry.

Roger Riccard's family history has Scottish roots, which trace his lineage back to Highland Scotland. This British Isles ancestry encouraged his interest in the writings of Sir Arthur Conan Doyle at an early age. He has authored the novels, *Sherlock Holmes & The Case of the Poisoned Lilly*, and *Sherlock Holmes & The Case of the Twain Papers*. In addition he has produced several short stories in *Sherlock Holmes Adventures for the Twelve Days of Christmas* and the series *A Sherlock Holmes Alphabet of Cases*. A new series will begin publishing in the Autumn of 2022, and his has another novel in the works. All of his books have been published by Baker Street Studios. His Bachelor of Arts Degrees in both Journalism and History from California State University, Northridge, have proven valuable to his writing historical fiction, as well as the encouragement of his wife/editor/inspiration and Sherlock Holmes fan, Rosilyn. She passed in 2021, and it is in her memory that he continues to contribute to the legacy of the "*man who never lived and will never die*".

Tim Symonds was born in London. He grew up in the rural English counties of Somerset and Dorset, and the British Crown Dependency of Guernsey. After several years travelling widely, including farming on the slopes of Mt. Kenya in East Africa and working on the Zambezi River in Central Africa, he emigrated to Canada and the United States. He studied at the Georg-August University (Göttingen) in Germany, and the University of California, Los Angeles, graduating *cum laude* and Phi Beta Kappa. He is a Fellow of the Royal Geographical Society and a Member of The Society of Authors. His detective novels include *Sherlock Holmes And The Dead Boer At Scotney Castle, Sherlock Holmes And The Mystery Of Einstein's Daughter, Sherlock Holmes And The Case Of The Bulgarian Codex, Sherlock Holmes And The Sword Of Osman, Sherlock Holmes And The Nine-Dragon Sigil*, six Holmes and Watson short stories under the title *A Most Diabolical Plot*, and his novella *Sherlock Holmes and the Strange Death of Brigadier-General Delves*.

Emma West joined Undershaw in April 2021 as the Director of Education with a brief to ensure that qualifications formed the bedrock of our provision, whilst facilitating a positive balance between academia, pastoral care, and well-being. She quickly took on the role of Acting Headteacher from early summer 2021. Under her leadership, Undershaw has embraced its new name, new vision, and consequently we have seen an exponential increase in demand for places. There is a buzz in the air as we invite prospective students and families through the doors. Emma has overseen a strategic review, re-cemented relationships with Local Authorities, and positioned Undershaw at the helm of SEND education in Surrey and beyond. Undershaw has a wide appeal: Our students present to us with mild to moderate learning needs and therefore may have some very recent memories of poor experiences in their previous schools. Emma's background as a senior leader within the independent school sector has meant she is well-versed in brokering relationships between the key stakeholders, our many interdependences, local businesses, families, and staff, and all this whilst ensuring Undershaw remains relentlessly child-centric in its approach. Emma's energetic smile and boundless enthusiasm for Undershaw is inspiring.

The following contributors appear
in the companion volumes:
The MX Book of New Sherlock Holmes Stories
Part XXXI – 2022 Annual (1875-1887)
Part XXXIII – 2022 Annual (1896-1919)

Hugh Ashton was born in the U.K., and moved to Japan in 1988, where he remained until 2016, living with his wife Yoshiko in the historic city of Kamakura, a little to the south of Yokohama. He and Yoshiko have now moved to Lichfield, a small cathedral city in the Midlands of the U.K., the birthplace of Samuel Johnson, and one-time home of Erasmus Darwin. In the past, he has worked in the technology and financial services industries, which have provided him with material for some of his books set in the 21st century. He currently works as a writer: Novelist, freelance editor, and copywriter, (his work for large Japanese corporations has appeared in international business journals), and journalist, as well as producing industry reports on various aspects of the financial services industry. However, his lifelong interest in Sherlock Holmes has developed into an acclaimed series of adventures featuring the world's most famous detective, written in the style of the originals. In addition to these, he has also published historical and alternate historical novels, short stories, and thrillers. Together with artist Andy Boerger, he has produced the *Sherlock Ferret* series of stories for children, featuring the world's cutest detective.

Andrew Bryant was born in Bridgend, Wales, and now lives in Burlington, Ontario. His previous publications include *Poetry Toronto*, *Prism International*, *Existere*, *On Spec*, *The Dalhousie Review*, and *The Toronto Star*. Andrew's interest in Holmes stems from watching the Basil Rathbone and Nigel Bruce films as a child, followed by collecting The Canon, and a fascinating visit to 221b Baker Street in London.

Thomas A. Burns Jr. writes *The Natalie McMasters Mysteries* from the small town of Wendell, North Carolina, where he lives with his wife and son, four cats, and a Cardigan Welsh Corgi. He was born and grew up in New Jersey, attended Xavier High School in Manhattan, earned B.S degrees in Zoology and Microbiology at Michigan State University, and a M.S. in Microbiology at North Carolina State University. As a kid, Tom started reading mysteries with The Hardy Boys, Ken Holt, and Rick Brant, then graduated to the classic stories by authors such as A. Conan Doyle, Dorothy Sayers, John Dickson Carr, Erle Stanley Gardner, and Rex Stout, to name a few. Tom has written fiction as a hobby all of his life, starting with *The Man from U.N.C.L.E.* stories in marble-backed copybooks in grade school. He built a career as technical, science, and medical writer and editor for nearly thirty years in industry and government. Now that he's a full-time novelist, he's excited to publish his own mystery series, as well as to write stories about his second most favorite detective, Sherlock Holmes. His Holmes story, "The Camberwell Poisoner", appeared in the March-June 2021 issue of *The Strand Magazine.* Tom has also written a Lovecraftian horror novel, *The Legacy of the Unborn*, under the pen name of Silas K. Henderson – a sequel to H.P. Lovecraft's masterpiece *At the Mountains of Madness.*

Josh Cerefice has followed the exploits of a certain pipe-smoking sleuth ever since his grandmother bought him *The Complete Sherlock Holmes* collection for his twenty-first birthday, and he has devotedly accompanied the Great Detective on his adventures ever since. When he's not reading about spectral hellhounds haunting the Devonshire moors, or the Machiavellian machinations of Professor Moriarty, you can find him putting pen to paper and challenging Holmes with new mysteries to solve in his own stories.

Craig Stephen Copland confesses that he discovered Sherlock Holmes when, sometime in the muddled early 1960's, he pinched his older brother's copy of the immortal stories and was forever afterward thoroughly hooked. He is very grateful to his high school English teachers in Toronto who inculcated in him a love of literature and writing, and even inspired him to be an English major at the University of Toronto. There he was blessed to sit at the feet of both Northrup Frye and Marshall McLuhan, and other great literary professors, who led him to believe that he was called to be a high school English teacher. It was his good fortune to come to his pecuniary senses, abandon that goal, and pursue a varied professional career that took him to over one-hundred countries and endless adventures. He considers himself to have been and to continue to be one of the luckiest men on God's good earth. A few years back he took a step in the direction of Sherlockian studies and joined the *Sherlock Holmes Society of Canada* – also known as *The Toronto Bootmakers*. In May of 2014, this esteemed group of scholars announced a contest for the writing of a new Sherlock Holmes mystery. Although he had never tried his hand at fiction before, Craig entered and was pleasantly surprised to be selected as one of the winners. Having enjoyed the experience, he decided to write more of the same, and is now on a mission to write a new Sherlock Holmes mystery that is related to and inspired by each of the sixty stories in the original Canon. He currently lives and writes in Toronto and Dubai, and looks forward to finally settling down when he turns ninety.

Martin Daley was born in Carlisle, Cumbria in 1964. He cites Doyle's Holmes and Watson as his favourite literary characters, who continue to inspire his own detective writing. His fiction and non-fiction books include a Holmes pastiche set predominantly in his home city in 1903. In the adventure, he introduced his own detective, Inspector Cornelius Armstrong, who has subsequently had some of his own cases published by MX Publishing. For more information visit *www.martindaley.co.uk*

Hal Glatzer *also has a story in Part XXXI*

Terry Golledge *also has stories in Parts XXXI and XXXIII*

Arthur Hall *also has a stories in Parts XXXI and XXXIII*

Stephen Herczeg is an IT Geek, writer, actor, and film-maker based in Canberra Australia. He has been writing for over twenty years and has completed a couple of dodgy novels, sixteen feature-length screenplays, and numerous short stories and scripts. Stephen was very successful in 2017's International Horror Hotel screenplay competition, with his scripts *TITAN* winning the Sci-Fi category and *Dark are the Woods* placing second in the horror category. His two-volume short story collection, *The Curious Cases of Sherlock Holmes*, was published in 2021. His work has featured in *Sproutlings – A Compendium of Little Fictions* from Hunter Anthologies, the *Hells Bells* Christmas horror anthology published by the Australasian Horror Writers Association, and the *Below the Stairs, Trickster's Treats, Shades of Santa, Behind the Mask*, and *Beyond the Infinite* anthologies from *OzHorror.Con, The Body Horror Book, Anemone Enemy*, and *Petrified Punks* from Oscillate Wildly Press, and *Sherlock Holmes In the Realms of H.G. Wells* and *Sherlock Holmes: Adventures Beyond the Canon* from Belanger Books.

Kelvin I. Jones is the author of six books about Sherlock Holmes and the definitive biography of Conan Doyle as a spiritualist, *Conan Doyle and The Spirits*. A member of *The Sherlock Holmes Society of London*, he has published numerous short occult and ghost stories in British anthologies over the last thirty years. His work has appeared on BBC Radio, and in 1984 he won the Mason Hall Literary Award for his poem cycle about the survivors of Hiroshima and Nagasaki, recently reprinted as "Omega". (Oakmagic Publications) A one-time teacher of creative writing at the University of East Anglia, he is also the author of four crime novels featuring his ex-met sleuth John Bottrell, who first appeared in *Stone Dead*. He has over fifty titles on Kindle, and is also the author of several novellas and short story collections featuring a Norwich based detective, DCI Ketch, an intrepid sleuth who investigates East Anglian murder cases. He also published a series of short stories about an Edwardian psychic detective, Dr. John Carter (*Carter's Occult Casebook*). Ramsey Campbell, the British horror writer, and Francis King, the renowned novelist, have both compared his supernatural stories to those of M. R. James. He has also published children's fiction, namely *Odin's Eye*, and, in collaboration with his wife Debbie, *The Dark Entry*. Since 1995, he has been the proprietor of Oakmagic Publications, publishers of British folklore and of his fiction titles. He lives in Norfolk. (See www.oakmagicpublications.co.uk)

Naching T. Kassa is a wife, mother, and writer. She's created short stories, novellas, poems, and co-created three children. She resides in Eastern Washington State with her husband, Dan Kassa. Naching is a member of *The Horror Writers Association, Mystery Writers of America, The Sound of the Baskervilles, The ACD Society*, and *The Sherlock Holmes Society of London*. She's also an assistant and staff writer for Still Water Bay at Crystal Lake Publishing. You can find her work on Amazon. *https://www.amazon.com/Naching-T-Kassa/e/B005ZGHTI0*

Susan Knight's newest novel, Mrs. Hudson goes to Paris, from MX publishing, is the latest in a series which began with her collection of stories, *Mrs. Hudson Investigates* of 2019 and the novel Mrs. Hudson goes to Ireland (2020). She has contributed to several of the MX anthologies of new Sherlock Holmes short stories, and enjoys writing as Dr. Watson as much as she does Mrs. Hudson. Susan is the author of two other non-Sherlockian, story collections, as well as three novels, a book of non-fiction, and several plays, and has won several prizes for her writing. She lives in Dublin, Ireland. Her next Mrs. Hudson novel is already a gleam in her eye.

John Lawrence served for thirty-eight years on personal, committee, and leadership staffs in the U.S. House of Representatives. A visiting professor at the University of California's Washington Center since 2013, he is the author of *The Class of '74: Congress After Watergate and the Roots of Partisanship* (Johns-Hopkins, 2018) and *Arc of Power: Inside the Pelosi Speakership 2005-2010* (Kansas, 2022). His collected "history mystery" Sherlock Holmes pastiches have been published in *The Undiscovered Archives of Sherlock Holmes* (MX Publishing, 2022), in numerous volumes of *The MX Book of New Sherlock Holmes Stories*, and in Belanger Books' *After the East Wind Blows*. He blogs at *DOMEocracy* (johnalawrence.wordpress.com). He is a graduate of Oberlin College and has a Ph.D. in history from the University of California (Berkeley).

Gordon Linzner is founder and former editor of *Space and Time Magazine*, and author of three published novels and dozens of short stories in *F&SF*, *Twilight Zone*, *Sherlock Holmes Mystery Magazine*, and numerous other magazines and anthologies, including *Baker Street Irregulars II*, *Across the Universe*, and *Strange Lands*. He is a member of *HWA* and a lifetime member of *SFWA*.

Jeffrey Lockwood spent youthful afternoons darkly enchanted by feeding grasshoppers to black widows in his New Mexican backyard, which accounts for his scientific and literary affinities. He earned a doctorate in entomology and worked as an ecologist at the University of Wyoming before metamorphosing into a Professor of Natural Sciences & Humanities in the departments of philosophy and creative writing – hence, insect-infested nonfiction and mysteries. He considers Sherlock Holmes a model of scientific prowess, integrating exquisite observational skills with incisive abductive (not deductive) reasoning.

David MacGregor is a playwright, screenwriter, novelist, and nonfiction writer. He is a resident artist at The Purple Rose Theatre in Michigan, where a number of his plays have been produced. His plays have been performed from New York to Tasmania, and his work has been published by Dramatic Publishing, Playscripts, Smith & Kraus, Applause, Heuer Publishing, and Theatrical Rights Worldwide (TRW). He adapted his dark comedy, *Vino Veritas*, for the silver screen, and it stars Carrie Preston (Emmy-winner for *The Good Wife*). Several of his short plays have also been adapted into films. He is the author of three Sherlock Holmes plays: *Sherlock Holmes and the Adventure of the Elusive Ear*, *Sherlock Holmes and the Adventure of the Fallen Soufflé*, and *Sherlock Holmes and the Adventure of the Ghost Machine*. He adapted all three plays into novels for Orange Pip Books, and also wrote the two-volume nonfiction *Sherlock Holmes: The Hero with a Thousand Faces* for MX Publishing. He teaches writing at Wayne State University in Detroit and is inordinately fond of cheese and terriers.

David Marcum *also has stories in Parts XXXI and XXXIII*

Kevin Patrick McCann *also has a story in Part XXXI*

Tracy J. Revels *also has stories in Parts XXXI and XXXIII*

Dan Rowley practiced law for over forty years in private practice and with a large international corporation. He is retired and lives in Erie, Pennsylvania, with his wife Judy, who puts her artistic eye to his transcription of Watson's manuscripts. He inherited his writing ability and creativity from his children, Jim and Katy, and his love of mysteries from his parents, Jim and Ruth.

Geri Schear is a novelist and short story writer. Her work has been published in literary journals in the U.S. and Ireland. Her first novel, *A Biased Judgement: The Diaries of Sherlock Holmes 1897* was released to critical acclaim in 2014. The sequel, *Sherlock Holmes and the Other Woman* was published in 2015, and *Return to Reichenbach* in 2016. She lives in Kells, Ireland.

Alisha Shea has resided near Saint Louis, Missouri for over thirty years. The eldest of six children, she found reading to be a genuine escape from the chaotic drudgery of life. She grew to love not only Sherlock Holmes, but the time period from which he emerged. This will be her first published work, but probably not her last. In her spare time, she indulges in creating music via piano, violin, and Native American flute. Sometimes she thinks she might even be getting good at it. She also produces a wide variety of fiber arts which are typically given away or auctioned off for various fundraisers.

Robert V. Stapleton was born in Leeds, England, and served as a full-time Anglican clergyman for forty years, specialising in Rural Ministry. He is now retired, and lives with his wife in North Yorkshire. This is the area of the country made famous by the writings of James Herriot, and television's *The Yorkshire Vet*, to name just a few. Amongst other things, he is a member of the local creative writing group, Thirsk Write Now (TWN), and regularly produces material for them. He has had more than fifty stories published, of various lengths and in a number of different places. He has also written a number of stories for *The MX Book of New Sherlock Holmes Stories*, and several published by Belanger Books. Several of these Sherlock Holmes pastiches have now been brought together and published in a single volume by MX Publishing, under the title of *Sherlock Holmes: A Yorkshireman in Baker Street*. Many of these stories have been set during the Edwardian period, or more broadly between the years 1880 and 1920. His interest in this period of history began at school in the 1960's when he met people who had lived during those years and heard their stories. He also found echoes of those times in literature, architecture, music, and even the coins in his pocket. The Edwardian period was a time of exploration, invention. and high adventure – rich material for thriller writers.

Tim Symonds *also has stories in Parts XXXI and XXXIII*

Kevin Thornton was shortlisted six times for the Crime Writers of Canada best unpublished novel. He never won – they are all still unpublished, and now he writes short stories. He lives in Canada, north enough that ringing Santa Claus is a local call and winter is a way of life. This is his twelfth short story in *The MX Book of New Sherlock Holmes Stories*. By the time you next hear from him, he hopes to have written his thirteenth.

Thomas A. (Tom) Turley has been "hooked on Holmes" since finishing *The Hound of the Baskervilles* at about the age of twelve. However, his interest in Sherlockian pastiches didn't take off until he wrote one. *Sherlock Holmes and the Adventure of the Tainted Canister* (2014) is available as an e-book and an audiobook from MX Publishing. It also appeared in *The Art of Sherlock Holmes – USA Edition 1*. In 2017, two of Tom's stories, "A Scandal in Serbia" and "A Ghost from Christmas Past" were published in Parts VI and VII of this anthology. "Ghost" was also included in *The Art of Sherlock Holmes – West Palm Beach Edition*. Meanwhile, Tom is finishing a collection of historical pastiches entitled *Sherlock Holmes and the Crowned Heads of Europe*, to be published in 2021 The first story, "Sherlock Holmes and the Case of the Dying Emperor" (2018) is available from MX Publishing as a separate e-book. Set in the brief reign of Emperor Frederick III (1888), it inaugurates Sherlock Holmes's espionage campaign against the German Empire, which

473

ended only in August 1914 with "His Last Bow". When completed, *Sherlock Holmes and the Crowned Heads of Europe* will also include "A Scandal in Serbia" and two additional historical tales. Although he has a Ph.D. in British history, Tom spent most of his professional career as an archivist with the State of Alabama. He and his wife Paula (an aspiring science fiction novelist) live in Montgomery, Alabama. Interested readers may contact Tom through MX Publishing or his Goodreads author's page.

DJ Tyrer dwells on the northern shore of the Thames estuary, close to the world's longest pleasure pier in the decaying seaside resort of Southend-on-Sea, and is the person behind Atlantean Publishing. They studied history at the University of Wales at Aberystwyth and have worked in the fields of education and public relations. Their fiction featuring Sherlock Holmes has appeared in volumes from MX Publishing and Belanger Books, and in an issue of *Awesome Tales*, and they have a forthcoming story in *Sherlock Holmes Mystery Magazine*. DJ's non-Sherlockian mysteries have appeared in anthologies such as *Mardi Gras Mysteries* (Mystery and Horror LLC) and *The Trench Coat Chronicles* (Celestial Echo Press).
DJ Tyrer's website is at *https://djtyrer.blogspot.co.uk/*
DJ's Facebook page is at *https://www.facebook.com/DJTyrerwriter/*
The Atlantean Publishing website is at *https://atlanteanpublishing.wordpress.com/*

Mark Wardecker is an instructional technologist at Colby College, and has contributed Sherlockian pastiches to *Sherlock Holmes Mystery Magazine* and *The MX Book of New Sherlock Holmes Stories – Part XIII*, as well as an article to *The Baker Street Journal*. He is also the editor and annotator of *The Dragnet Solar Pons et al.* (Battered Silicon Dispatch Box, 2011), and has contributed Solar Pons pastiches to *The New Adventures of Solar Pons*.

I.A. Watson, great-grand-nephew of Dr. John H. Watson, has been intrigued by the notorious "black sheep" of the family since childhood, and was fascinated to inherit from his grandmother a number of unedited manuscripts removed circa 1956 from a rather larger collection reposing at Lloyds Bank Ltd (which acquired Cox & Co Bank in 1923). Upon discovering the published corpus of accounts regarding the detective Sherlock Holmes from which a censorious upbringing had shielded him, he felt obliged to allow an interested public access to these additional memoranda, and is gradually undertaking the task of transcribing them for admirers of Mr. Holmes and Dr. Watson's works. In the meantime, I.A. Watson continues to pen other books, the latest of which is *The Incunabulum of Sherlock Holmes*. A full list of his seventy or so published works are available at: *http://www.chillwater.org.uk/writing/iawatsonhome.htm*

Marcia Wilson is a freelance researcher and illustrator who likes to work in a style compatible for the color blind and visually impaired. She is Canon-centric, and her first MX offering, *You Buy Bones*, uses the point-of-view of Scotland Yard to show the unique talents of Dr. Watson. This continued with the publication of *Test of the Professionals: The Adventure of the Flying Blue Pidgeon* and *The Peaceful Night Poisonings*. She can be contacted at: *gravelgirty.deviantart.com*

Sean Wright makes his home in Santa Clarita, a charming city at the entrance of the high desert in Southern California. For sixteen years, features and articles under his byline appeared in *The Tidings* – now *The Angelus News*, publications of the Roman Catholic Archdiocese of Los Angeles. Continuing his education in 2007, Mr. Wright graduated from Grand Canyon University, attaining a Bachelor of Arts degree in Christian Studies with a *summa cum laude*. He then attained a Master of Arts degree, also in Christian Studies.

Once active in the entertainment industry, and in an abortive attempt to revive dramatic radio in 1976 with his beloved mentor, the late Daws Butler, directing, Mr. Wright co-produced and wrote the syndicated *New Radio Adventures of Sherlock Holmes*, starring the late Edward Mulhare as the Great Detective. Mr. Wright has written for several television quiz shows and remains proud of his work for *The Quiz Kid's Challenge* and the popular TV quiz show *Jeopardy!* for which the Academy of Television Arts and Sciences honored him in 1985 with an Emmy nomination in the field of writing. Honored with membership in The Baker Street Irregulars as "The Manor House Case" after founding The Non-Canonical Calabashes, the Sherlock Holmes Society of Los Angeles in 1970, Mr. Wright has written for *The Baker Street Journal* and *Mystery Magazine*. Since 1971, he has conducted lectures on Sherlock Holmes's influence on literature and cinema for libraries, colleges, and private organizations, including MENSA. Mr. Wright's whimsical *Sherlock Holmes Cookbook* (Drake), created with John Farrell, BSI, was published in 1976, and a mystery novel, *Enter the Lion: a Posthumous Memoir of Mycroft Holmes* (Hawthorne), "edited" with Michael Hodel, BSI, followed in 1979. As director general of The Plot Thickens Mystery Company, Mr .Wright originated hosting "mystery parties" in homes, restaurants, and offices, as well as producing and directing the very first "Mystery Train" tours on Amtrak beginning in 1982.

The MX Book of New Sherlock Holmes Stories
Edited by David Marcum
(MX Publishing, 2015-   )

"This is the finest volume of Sherlockian fiction I have ever read, and I have read, literally, thousands." – Philip K. Jones

"Beyond Impressive . . . This is a splendid venture for a great cause!
– Roger Johnson, Editor, *The Sherlock Holmes Journal*,
The Sherlock Holmes Society of London

Part I: 1881-1889
Part II: 1890-1895
Part III: 1896-1929
Part IV: 2016 Annual
Part V: Christmas Adventures
Part VI: 2017 Annual
Part VII: Eliminate the Impossible (1880-1891)
Part VIII – Eliminate the Impossible (1892-1905)
Part IX – 2018 Annual (1879-1895)
Part X – 2018 Annual (1896-1916)
Part XI – Some Untold Cases (1880-1891)
Part XII – Some Untold Cases (1894-1902)
Part XIII – 2019 Annual (1881-1890)
Part XIV – 2019 Annual (1891-1897)
Part XV – 2019 Annual (1898-1917)
Part XVI – Whatever Remains . . . Must be the Truth (1881-1890)
Part XVII – Whatever Remains . . . Must be the Truth (1891-1898)
Part XVIII – Whatever Remains . . . Must be the Truth (1898-1925)
Part XIX – 2020 Annual (1882-1890)
Part XX – 2020 Annual (1891-1897)
Part XXI – 2020 Annual (1898-1923)
Part XXII – Some More Untold Cases (1877-1887)
Part XXIII – Some More Untold Cases (1888-1894)
Part XXIV – Some More Untold Cases (1895-1903)
Part XXV – 2021 Annual (1881-1888)
Part XXVI – 2021 Annual (1889-1897)
Part XXVII – 2021 Annual (1898-1928)
Part XXVIII – More Christmas Adventures (1869-1888)
Part XXIX – More Christmas Adventures (1889-1896)
Part XXX – More Christmas Adventures (1897-1928)

In Preparation

Part XXXI (and XXXII and XXXIII???) – However Improbable . . . .

. . . and more to come!

The MX Book of New Sherlock Holmes Stories
Edited by David Marcum
(MX Publishing, 2015-   )

Part VI: *The traditional pastiche is alive and well . . . .*

Part VII: *Sherlockians eager for faithful-to-the-canon plots and characters will be delighted.*

Part VIII: *The imagination of the contributors in coming up with variations on the volume's theme is matched by their ingenious resolutions.*

Part IX: *The 18 stories . . . will satisfy fans of Conan Doyle's originals. Sherlockians will rejoice that more volumes are on the way.*

Part X: *. . . new Sherlock Holmes adventures of consistently high quality.*

Part XI: *. . . an essential volume for Sherlock Holmes fans.*

Part XII: *. . . continues to amaze with the number of high-quality pastiches.*

Part XIII: *. . . Amazingly, Marcum has found 22 superb pastiches . . . This is more catnip for fans of stories faithful to Conan Doyle's original*

Part XIV: *. . . this standout anthology of 21 short stories written in the spirit of Conan Doyle's originals.*

Part XV: *Stories pitting Sherlock Holmes against seemingly supernatural phenomena highlight Marcum's 15th anthology of superior short pastiches.*

Part XVI: *Marcum has once again done fans of Conan Doyle's originals a service.*

Part XVII: *This is yet another impressive array of new but traditional Holmes stories.*

Part XVIII: *Sherlockians will again be grateful to Marcum and MX for high-quality new Holmes tales.*

Part XIX: *Inventive plots and intriguing explorations of aspects of Dr. Watson's life and beliefs lift the 24 pastiches in Marcum's impressive 19th Sherlock Holmes anthology*

Part XX: *Marcum's reserve of high-quality new Holmes exploits seems endless.*

Part XXI: *This is another must-have for Sherlockians.*

Part XXII: *Marcum's superlative 22nd Sherlock Holmes pastiche anthology features 21 short stories that successfully emulate the spirit of Conan Doyle's originals while expanding on the canon's tantalizing references to mysteries Dr. Watson never got around to chronicling.*

Part XXIII: *Marcum's well of talented authors able to mimic the feel of The Canon seems bottomless.*

Part XXIV: *Marcum's expertise at selecting high-quality pastiches remains impressive.*

Part XXVIII: *All entries adhere to the spirit, language, and characterizations of Conan Doyle's originals, evincing the deep pool of talent Marcum has access to. Against the odds, this series remains strong, hundreds of stories in.*

The MX Book of New Sherlock Holmes Stories

Edited by David Marcum

(MX Publishing, 2015-   )

MX Publishing

MX Publishing is the world's largest specialist Sherlock Holmes publisher, with over five-hundred titles and over two-hundred authors creating the latest in Sherlock Holmes fiction and non-fiction

The catalogue includes several award winning books, and over two-hundred-and-fifty have been converted into audio.

MX Publishing also has one of the largest communities of Holmes fans on Facebook, with regular contributions from dozens of authors.

www.mxpublishing.com

@mxpublishing on Facebook, Twitter and Instagram

CPSIA information can be obtained
at www.ICGtesting.com
Printed in the USA
BVHW040916130622
638549BV00015B/122/J.

9 781804 240090